EMPRESS CROWNED IN RED

Also by Ciannon Smart

Witches Steeped in Gold

EMPRESS CROWNED IN RED

CIANNON SMART

HARPER TEEN
An Imprint of HarperCollinsPublishers

HarperTeen is an imprint of HarperCollins Publishers.

Library of Congress Cataloging-in-Publication Data
Names: Smart, Ciannon, author.
Title: Empress crowned in red / Ciannon Smart.
Description: First edition. | New York, NY : HarperTeen, [2022] | Audience:
    Ages 14 up. | Audience: Grades 10–12. | Summary: "Witches Iraya and
    Jazmyne must once again work together as a new enemy threatens Aiyca,
    even as betrayal lurks around every corner"— Provided by publisher.
Identifiers: LCCN 2021063009 | ISBN 978-0-06-294601-0 (hardcover)
Subjects: CYAC: Witches—Fiction. | Fantasy. | LCGFT: Fantasy fiction.
Classification: LCC PZ7.1.S59443 Em 2022 | DDC [Fic]—dc23
LC record available at https://lccn.loc.gov/2021063009

Typography by Chris Kwon
22 23 24 25 26 PC/LSCH 10 9 8 7 6 5 4 3 2 1
❖
First Edition

To those of you who have been here since the beginning

The Orders of Xaymaca

ORDER OF ALUMBRAR

JUDAIR CARIOT

Witches Council Doyenne

Métier: Stealth

JAZMYNE CARIOT

Witches Council Emissary

Judair's last living daughter

Métier: Healer

MADISYN CARIOT

Judair's late daughter

Métier: Healer

ORDER OF OBEAH

CORDELIA ADAIR

Former Empress of the Xaymaca Empire

Iraya's late mama

VINCENT ADAIR

Former Aiycan Navy Admiral

Iraya's late dada

Métier: Squaller

IRAYA ADAIR

Sole daughter and heir of Cordelia and Vincent Adair

Métier: Warrior

PART I

EVERY
UNFAIR
GAME
IS
PLAYED
TWICE

JAZMYNE

Knowing how heavy the crown would feel still doesn't prepare me for its weight.

"On tonight's coronation eve, we bestow this cradle of riches upon your head," the Alumbrar Seer before me intones, setting the gold circlet atop my curls, "to represent Aiyca's greatest treasure you will serve and protect: its people." Her movements are unsteady, bafan; withdrawing clawed hands, the witch steps aside as she says her next words. "Never forget that they, and they alone, are between you and the Supreme Being."

Beyond the Seer, on the dais steps below the throne, stand her fellow witches, the cabinet of fourteen who have served the crown for a decade. The wall of windows in the throne room behind them showcases cold teal light from a steepening dawn. As it bleeds through the vestiges of the rising sun, it stains the Alumbrar faces in the crowd gathered to witness my ascension, casting their wariness, their fear, in a lattice of shadows. Not even twenty-four hours earlier, their last doyenne fell—was *felled* by an axe that may swing at my neck too, yet.

Swallowing, I focus on the Seer, who steps back into my line of sight.

"All decisions henceforth must respect your people them, you understand?"

An internal war is fought. Fear versus fervor. The former cannot have an inch.

"I understand."

If the warning of the Seer's words isn't enough of a reminder about how my past decisions have impacted my order's present, or the tried prescience of her métier reflected in her milky eyes as the spirits of the long dead commune through her, the scarlet kaftan she wears is more than sufficient. Last night, before the events of the Sole, that color mirrored fire; my plans were set to purify an inflicted isle. Now it slinks down the dais steps like blood—in addition to mine, my order's is in danger of being spilled if I make the mistake of faltering for even a second.

"We place this scepter in your hands," the Seer goes on to cantillate, her salt-and-pepper twists quivering with her intensity, "to remind you that your reach alone is limited; seek out additional hands in your plight to keep Aiyca, its people them, hale and protected." She places the baton of gold into my waiting palm. "Never forget to pursue those hands should you need them."

A shadow catches my eye beneath the east mezzanine. Anya, dressed for Stealth in obsidian silk, is ever stalwart, like the pillars to her left and right. Her silver ponytail bobs in a proud flag of victory; light catches the unspent tears in her eyes as the intention we set for me to take the throne, so long ago now, comes true.

"Upon this night," the Seer continues, the rhythmic cadence of her voice a lullaby to soothe the roiling unease in my belly, "we pronounce you, Jazmyne Amancia Cariot, former emissary to the crown and second-born pickney of the late Doyenne Judair Cariot, Regent of Aiyca and all its territories."

A bolt of shock electrifies my insides—disbelief.

Regent?

Stunned, I look up into the white eyes of the witch leading the coronation. In the polished mahogany of her face, they are consuming. *Doyenne.* My frown castigates where my words cannot. Not before an audience of Alumbrar, including what remains of the Witches Council, who stand vigil close to Anya. *I told you to crown me* doyenne, *not a glorified babysitter.*

"Until such a time as when you inherit your magic," the witch continues, "meeting the eligibility to become doyenne of this great and noble land." She pauses as though in explanation, in a face-slapping reminder that I am still not enough. "Do you accept?"

Even as my cheeks burn at the slight, how public it is, my world narrows down to those three words in the Seer's question. With Iraya out there somewhere, allied with Kirdan, the rebels, pride would be a fool's error.

"Yes." A gelid determination replaces the hot flare of my embarrassment. I draw myself up taller in the throne. "I accept."

"And do you promise to protect this island, its territories, and its people to the best of your ability, even if it means giving your life to do so?"

That determination morphs from ice to steel around my bones, and something more intrinsic—my will.

"I do."

The witch retreats down the dais steps to join her sistren; they stand in a line, arms aloft before them. "*And so it is promised,*" the cabinet says in unison, "*so things do. Long live Aiyca's regent, Jazmyne Amancia Cariot, Favored by the Supreme Being, Healing Hands of Aiyca, Watchful Eye of Carne Sea, first of her name, and sole living heir of Doyenne Cariot.*"

Though the Sibyls and I crafted them together, with Anya's aid, hearing them called by my order transcends me from myself, from emissary to the crown.

"*Long live Aiyca's regent*" is returned by a crowd that isn't as sure as I need them to be, yet; my titles follow.

Standing, I allow myself one shallow breath, one moment to mentally savor the bittersweet paean of a title I never wanted, knowing it's the final hurdle before the one I've fought for and sacrificed in the name of. As my order will soon learn. A declaration of gold, my kaftan glows in the growing dark. More of the conduit metal graces my feet, neck, fingers, and finally crowns my head in an obscene finale of power and wealth. Word will spread, and my enemies won't remember that I cannot summon, that as regent I have yet to inherit my ancestors' magic, this morning.

"Wahan, Alumbrar," I call. "From light we are born."

"And to light we cleave."

"Yesterday eve was one of loss," I begin, aware of the mount I need to overcome. "But we are no strangers to dark skies. It is the time our naysayers see how incandescent our shine truly is." Dawn blooms outside, a flare of a triumphing sun. My chin rises in acknowledgment of the Supreme Being's blessing, Their support as I attempt to shift the winds in this throne room from hesitant to confident. "While this morning we usher in a new era for Aiyca, it does not negate who we have been in the past: leaders, healers, protectors." Some in the crowd nod. Others only stare with hard expressions, doubt. "We walk into a future shadowed by our past. To that end, it is incumbent on us to be a shining light, to expose our enemies who would rather rely on that darkness, hide in it. Can I place my faith in you, Alumbrar? Can I, in doing all that I can, trust you to do the same? Not only for your families, for our rule, but for Aiyca?" The angle, the threat, is a gamble, one Anya didn't wish for me to make when I scrambled to formulate something inspiring for this moment. *There will be no reward*, I told Anya, *without showing them they are at risk too*. There is no time to earn my order's admiration, and hereafter, the island's. I must incite their fear instead. I'll show them that while I am their sole option, standing alone does not lessen my suitability for this position. "Will you stand with me, for our home?"

I'm met with silence. One so deep that, for a moment, I wonder if I might drown in it.

Was Anya right? My titles, my clothing, everything crafted to cast a greater shadow than I can at this time, after being swallowed by the late doyenne's, aren't enough to intimidate them into taking the knee. They won't follow me. They don't—

"In your words, Regent" is called from the crowd. "We do not fear dark skies!"

One. Thank the gods.

"It's true that we own the night, Alumbrar." There are more cries of affirmation, but they're hollow. I need *more*. "However much our enemies may think themselves comfortable there. Which is why we will defeat them! We will defeat them as we have done for the past decade. As we will do for decades more!" The cries of the crowd finally reach a pitch that makes me feel shot as high as the stars I can no longer see, thanks to the dawn. Is this how the late doyenne felt? Despite the pounds of gold around her neck, her wrists?

The thought of her, Mama, encases my ankles, drags me back down to earth in a breath-stealing jerk. She had the jéges. Magic. None of which saved her, in the end. Six phases stand between me and my inheritance. Compared to eternity, it is but a blink. This I tell myself as the crowd continues to holler and bellow. A time Aiyca will survive, with the aid of Roje, standing guard in the palace grounds with the rest of the pirates.

But we cannot grow complacent.

I cannot.

My left hand is held aloft; the crowd cows before it, row by row. "Victory, Alumbrar, may not look to you as it always has done, but while I sit on this throne, in Aiyca's Golden Seat, I assure you death's shroud will not find its resting place here again. Tonight, we mourn the late doyenne, as we will for the next nine. Thereafter, we live, Alumbrar." I look to Anya, still crying silent tears. "We do more than survive. We triumph. We thrive."

My sistren sinks into a curtsy first, and though the movement brings her forward, the action travels back. Warmth spreads from my chest and through my limbs as, row by row, Alumbrar in the throne room sink into a sign of estimation, with the exception of the Sibyls, who are too old to lower more than their chins, which they do. The three remaining Witches Council presiders also remain standing, their faces tight. We four will need to talk, later. For now, I open my arms to my kneeling order. The line has been cast, the bait taken.

"Rise, Alumbrar. Rise and honor me by honoring the late doyenne."

To their riotous applause, I pick my way down the steps with care, kaftan in hand. Anya meets me at the dais base.

"Regent," she says with a bow.

For all my earlier bravado, the title rips through my belly like a hot knife.

Catching my reaction, of course, Anya edges closer, lowers her voice. "I'm sorry, Jaz. I didn't know."

"Not now," I murmur. Alumbrar edge close, waiting to address their new leader. "Sister Grenich, how lovely to see you." Anya falls to my side as I approach the Alumbrar Healer I remember well from my time training at Sanar, Aiyca's Alumbrar medical alcázar, the frontrunner in our order's healing. In fact, many Healers approach to bid me good fortune, to take my hand and bow their heads. They are a welcome salve to the late doyenne's court, one filled with vipers whose tongues birth poisonous comments about my succession and lack of magic.

"Will you wed?" an uncle asks. I've never warmed to him, the surviving husband of one of the late doyenne's first cousins. Or the slight daughter standing in his shadow; both watch me with narrowed eyes. "I'm sure you think I'm too old," Ivan goes on to say. "Even though we aren't bound by blood." He rubs bejeweled fingers across a rotund belly. "But my daughter is close to your age, you know."

Demar *is* my blood, though, and strange enough that not even Anya has invited her to bed. I used to see her in the gardens, unsmiling and all but mute, burning ants with glass.

"If it is attraction that concerns you," Ivan says when I am silent for fear of shouting *no* in his face, "or the bearing of pickney, there are matters we can discuss."

"Um. I will take what you've said into consideration, Uncle."

"About both of us?" He makes to step closer, but then Anya is there.

It is but a casual shoulder she angles Ivan's way, but with a wary look in her direction, he keeps his distance.

"It was good of you to come" is my verbal dismissal.

And as if that harrowing conversation set the tone, the next are just as unpleasant when Alumbrar begin to inquire about the next Yielding. Mention of the sacrifice, their willingness to send their firstborns to slaughter, severs through my already-thin patience. I turn to find Filmore; always close, he's become the right hand to my left, in Anya. With a nod that has him brushing his twists out of his face, he imparts a murmured order, magical, by the faint illumination of the conduit beneath his tunic. The remaining six Stealths in my private vanguard disperse; trained wraiths, they intercept the stingers the doyenne populated her court with before their tips can sink into all the places I am soft.

Taking up a glass from a passing tray between well-wishers, I turn to the wall of windows to seek out another sign from the Supreme Being. Peace rests two hands on my shoulders as the teal light brightens outside, like the opening of eyelids, its color strengthening into something luminous. Something . . .

Something *jade*.

Witchfire.

My throat constricts around the drink at the familiarity, as if its murderous flames have drawn away all moisture from my mouth. For there, a faint growth across the horizon, nascent flames flicker their way to a dangerous maturation.

"Did the drink go down the wrong way?" Anya queries as guests turn to ascertain what's wrong. "Or does your throat burn? Tell me quick. We have an audience."

"Not poisoned," I force out, spluttering. "*Window*." The green light begins to seep across the sky, like poison oozing from a gash; it will touch those around me first, however distracted they may be by my choking. Though the light will be without the heat of the Witchfire it no doubt belongs to, it will burn away any hard-won belief in my capabilities as a leader. "Anya," I say, my voice barely louder than a whisper for my Stealth-trained sistren. *Aiyca's insurgents*, I cannot say. *They're mounting an attack outside.* "I need the curtains closed. *Now*."

Turning to the glass, her face blanches as her magical will makes the fabric swing closed with a muffled thump.

"Send one of the Stealths after the council," I say, my voice low. "They're to extract the witches clandestinely, and fast."

My sistren imparts the order in a low murmur, conduit alight, so she doesn't need to leave my side. The Xanthippe keep those gathered at bay as we cross the throne room. I share polite nods, comments that I'll return soon; all the while sweat runs down my neck, and my hands, which hold my kaftan, shake.

"I need four of the Stealths to remain inside," I tell Filmore once we're in the quiet emptiness of the cavernous marble vestibule, with only the statuaries and gilt-framed art to overhear. "They're not to let the guests near any windows. All curtains must be kept closed."

"Why?" Ionie Lewis snaps upon approach, her infamous Squaller temper blustering already. A gray cloud that accompanies her everywhere and takes up residence above my head too, since I can only blink at her, at Mariama and Ormine as they join us in their finery. Bangles and chunky necklaces clink like the shackles we might soon find ourselves bearing. I am without the words until I know—and that knowledge is sought from a vantage point north of the throne room. I head there without further delay.

So rarely was this observatory used by the late doyenne, it's garlanded with cobwebs thick enough that the accompanying Xanthippe must use magic to clear them away. She didn't need this outlook, not when with the one eye she possessed she saw everything. Well, almost everything.

Once the golden hands extending from all seven Stealths' conduits have rescinded back into their coins, wind gusts through the ragged tendrils of dust, and my stomach lurches. Spherical, with teeth of stone connecting roof to floor, Cwenburg's Eye provides a panoramic measure of Aiyca—and where magically impotent sight fails, there are several telescopes infused with guzzu to see the distance.

I don't require the latter to discern the bowls of jade flame on undulating rooftops across the parish. The bright flame is alive and growing more audacious by the minute. My hand goes to my neck, where the locket—the Amplifier I haven't the magic to use—lies.

The Jade Guild are here. Obeah. Insurgents. Drawn arrows aimed at this Golden Seat, at me, which can only mean one thing. *She* is here too.

2

IRAYA

By dawn's light, a crimson wound that takes its time bleeding through the enormity of dusk, the Deleterious Doll takes its form between my fingers.

Half my focus is on the grass I weave, strands of hair hastily plucked from my head dispersed throughout. The remainder is on Delyse, the slow pull and give of her breaths. It isn't our earlier trek of the peninsula alone that tired her. Slumped against a felled tree in our camp, hers is a plant-induced slumber.

If I were a gods-fearing witch, I might have believed the dogwood I came across earlier, endemic to coastal zones such as this craggy peninsula, was put before me by Sofea, the Mudda's Face of Pathways. Either way it was a stroke of fate that enlightened me as to how I should step: as we set our guzzu to protect our camp for the second and final night, I fumbled enough that Delyse added poor dexterity to the list of grievances she has with me, leaving her to work alone and thus inhale the sedative flower I concealed in the grass. It didn't take long for her to fall prey to its debilitating, but otherwise harmless, spores. Ones, I find, with a shake of my head and widening of heavy eyes, I'm fighting the effects of myself. A small price to pay when, should I step quick, most of the Impediment Glyphs Doyenne Cariot incised deep behind my ears can be burned away before Delyse wakes and Shamar returns from his watch to find me missing. As for Kirdan . . . though I cannot see him, I turn to where he's spent almost two straight days resting above this verdant declivity, atop the rocky ledge overlooking the sea where I dashed whatever we might have been to the mercy of the rocks and waves below. With the strength in his hair reduced after Jazmyne had it hacked away, he should sleep awhile yet.

I haven't.

Each time my eyes close, I'm plagued by one thought: *They know how this will end.*

Them. The shadows in my periphery. Always there, but never discerned. Not even now, no matter how closely I scour my memory. For Them. The nebulous clouds that hid themselves in skies they were aware I've only ever known to be stormy. Obeah, once. Ilk, once. . . . No more. If the insurgents wanted to tussle for Aiyca, they needn't have twisted my arm with a force of monsters from the other side of the veil. Aligning themselves with the Alumbrar to kill my family was more than enough to coax me into the ring—where I won't simply bring them war. I will introduce them to Death.

Slipping away from the camp, I fold myself into the shadows within the knot of dense vegetation. At once my skin becomes damp beneath the weight of the oppressive heat below the canopy. In the dark, I will my conduit to light. After several tries, returning to Delyse's fundamental of imagining my magic as Aiyca's Great River, golden light spills across the ground, only just illuminating my path. A further push of will, of want, incites a tendril of cool breeze to brush across my temple. Busy weighing the time I have left until Shamar returns from his watch, where I might find a beast to bleed to summon the ancestors, and my distance from the camp, it takes a moment to realize something is amiss. The hairs on the back of my neck rise as my survival instincts tell me I am no longer alone. That, perhaps, I never was.

"You'd make a lousy Stealth," I say.

Made, Shamar steps out of the shadow of a trunk to my left. My relief that it's him, not Delyse, is extinguished by the tautness in his body; he stands tall, ready for battle.

"That depends on what I was keeping an eye on."

Who.

The smile I flash Shamar is more a show of teeth. "I wasn't going to run, back at the palace." It's the first time I've been able to explain myself to any of them since arriving here, against my will, in Kirdan's arms. I tried with Delyse, but she's ignored me since I told her of my plan to head to the Skylands two nights ago. Not even my intention to recruit their extensive aerial army to fight the Unlit has unthawed her. "You didn't figure that out when the army of the dead came? You know, the skeletons I raised from an ancestor's tomb that saved our lives and enabled our escape from the palace?"

Shamar's face doesn't budge. "And now?" he asks.

"Now I was—I was trying to free my magic." The truth is light in a way I've never known it to be before. But then, what use are lies when we face the possibility of war? And Shamar has always appreciated the need for soldiers.

Folding his long arms across the dark tunic on his chest, he nods for me to continue.

"I can see why you'd doubt my intentions when I've done nothing these past few months but fight to avenge my family. A personal vendetta? Yeh mon. A selfish one?" I swallow as the truth finally weighs what I always thought it would. "Maybe. But I'm not myopic by nature. You know that. My plans for after the doyenne's death would have helped Aiyca."

Curiosity softens in Shamar's expression, maybe some guilt too. "What were they?"

"I would have searched for my coven, rejoined them. If they still lived."

"And if they didn't?"

Guileless, a rare occasion, I shrug again. "I still would have helped my order, *our* order, regardless. You see my scarification; you saw me fight the pirates back at the palace."

"You'll fight for us, I understand, but what about leading us?"

Grateful for the darkness, I turn from him, from a truth unlike the others; if I buckle beneath it, Shamar would break. "You don't need an empress now. *We* don't. For one thing, there's no throne to keep warm." At that, Shamar huffs a small laugh. Progress. "Doyenne Cariot had Aiyca, ruled Aiyca, and the Unlit still came." The enemy she allied with to kill my family, before betraying them and setting us all on this bloody course. "Politics can do little against a sword when it's already falling." I take a step closer to Sham, allowing the glow from his conduit to illuminate my sincerity, rather than knocking it into him. "Though it looks different to what you want, helping our home has always been in my plans. I overcame the Vow of Protection to kill the doyenne. If you won't trust my words, trust that action. We need a Genna. We need to raise a sword and parry, or face losing Aiyca to the Unlit." Being stripped of their magic doesn't mitigate their threat. They're Obeah. There is no greater threat to my parents' legacy.

Surveying me, Shamar rubs his chin, fingers dragging back and forth across the horizontal row of scars there. Is he trained to identify poison in words too? Can he tell my intentions, this time, are pure? Mostly.

"You're not wrong," he eventually says. Dropping his hand, he sighs. "I'll help with your magic."

My brows shoot upward.

"But we won't tell Delyse. Or Kirdan. She was . . . hurt that you hid who you were from us at Cwenburg, your plan to kill Doyenne Cariot. So was I." His eyes darken with something that makes my stomach clench. "And the Zesian I'm not sure we should entirely trust."

Smart.

"I'm not sure about trusting you either."

Smarter.

"So if I put my faith in you, Iraya—"

"I would be putting mine in you also."

And though neither of us mention our use of *if* and *would be*, Shamar tracks down a beast while I arrange the Bidding Circle.

16

We're unsuccessful in burning the Impediment Glyphs away in full.

It's understandable since the doyenne incised the symbols down to my bone. Still, I'd hoped to last longer than several minutes before passing out.

"Enough." Shamar is supporting my head in his lap when I wake the second time. "The day is long. When we move on from here, we can find a Bush Healer to treat you properly. If you die on my watch, no one will forgive me. Least of all myself."

Sticky with sweat and fever, I couldn't fight him even if I was sure I wanted to. What I have access to will need to be enough.

Once I've recovered enough to stand, we return to camp. Me with a pocket full of allspice leaves to chew whenever the burned skin behind my ears pulsates with pain. Shamar with serious doubts in his eyes whenever he looks my way. Kirdan crests the hill along with the sun. Prince Divsylar. General of his island's military of lauded bastards. As he raises his cloak, we lock eyes; the skin beneath them is smudged with purple bruising and yesterday's smoky kohl. The two of us haven't been alone since he confessed the truth about the Unlit, their plans for war, and the feelings he had. For me.

"We move out in five." Rough from sleep, Kirdan's voice is all edge. His focus is acute too; those eyes like shards of emerald cut a path down the baggy pants and tunic I swapped my shield uniform with, for clothing he provided last night.

Shamar clears his throat. "Sounds good to me."

Turning from Kirdan, I head over to the fire and refuse to look up while I fix a breakfast of cold fish. This is sure to be a long day, journeying with him and his long stares to the Skylands. Gods give me strength.

Once Delyse has been shaken awake—hard enough that Shamar sends a suspicious eyebrow lift my way—we four leave the verdant peaks of the peninsula, sifting somewhere I'm not privy to. A necessity, Kirdan explained when he took my hand, since the secrecy tricks the Shook Bargain around my wrist into believing I'm being moved against my will, preventing the magical agreement from activating its seven-day countdown for me to leave Aiyca for good. As to whether it will work when I tell them we're going to the Skylands remains to be seen.

Once we're spat out of the breathless cyclone of magic, rather than the invisible band around my wrist, it is the prince my attention turns to. That sift was rougher than others I've had with him. Unsteady after the magical expenditure of the travel, he relinquishes my hand and braces against a wall in the cramped ginnel with a wince; his ruined locks scissor past wan cheeks in jagged black blades. Before he catches me in the beam of that unrelenting focus, I turn away, pretend I don't see what I suspected before we left: that the days he slept have done little to restore his strength. Good for me, now we're in the Skylands. Shamar and Delyse have just as little gold as I do, with none of my training. If need be, escape is all but guaranteed. Seeking a higher vantage, I throw my focus to the mercy of a sky now heavy with the burden of a triumphant dawn—a familiar sky at that.

These bandulu have brought me home.

"Why in the gods' names have we returned to *Aiyca*," I say, my voice low with a deadly calm, "when we all agreed that there's an army to recruit in the Skylands? *The* army we need to save this island, in case I wasn't clear two nights ago."

"Is there internal change with the Shook Bargain?" Shamar, who I thought was my partner in deceit, scans me from head to toe. "I've heard the pain starts in the mind."

"None." *Not to the partially burned glyphs behind my ears, or the Shook Bargain.* "No pain anywhere." *The Deleterious Doll was a success.* "Now—"

"We can all hear she's fine," Delyse cuts in. "Concealing where we travel is still tricking the bargain into believing movement is against her will."

My eyebrows hike up. *Her?*

"Bringing me back to Aiyca certainly is that."

Delyse doesn't even look my way. "We have a plan."

"*We* would imply *all*."

"You're going to have to trust us." Her voice is heavy with sarcasm. "Or, we can knock you out each time we move and wake you when we arrive." *Try me*, the pinched expression on her face begs. *Please.*

"What about once we've reached our destination," I push, swatting at a buzzing blood eater rather than Delyse. "As we have now. You can tell me the next steps, surely?"

"We'll share what we can, when we can," Shamar evades.

My mouth twitches, fighting words that would scorch the earth between us beyond revival. Here it is, the dictating, the control. Autonomy and ruling are not synonymous, as many believe. As I knew. In Aiyca, a crown doesn't give you a voice. It takes it away.

"You'll know soon enough, Iraya." The authority in Kirdan's tone succeeds in making Shamar and Delyse stand down. "There is conviction to be gained on all sides."

Indeed.

I won't tell them, for instance, that while the late Doyenne Cariot is dead, her usurper is *still* Doyenne Cariot, and, last I heard two nights ago, very much alive, nullifying my part of the agreement to leave Aiyca in seven days and stay away for good. Not when all Delyse, Kirdan, and even Shamar continue to show me is that they're adept at deception—one they tie off with a bow, dressing it up as something *for my own good*. Or worse still, *for the greater good*.

If subterfuge is currency around here, I can pay my way with the richest.

"We'll discuss matters more later," Kirdan, who seems to have assigned himself the role of de facto leader—*irritating*—goes on to say. "For now, we have somewhere to be."

For now, I listen.

Nana Clarke would say to bend the tree while it's young; before day gives way to night, I might have to cut the Taciturn Trio loose and move on to the Skylands, alone.

Just-Ira.

They wanted me to fight; that is the danger of backing me into a corner. Everyone becomes an enemy.

3

JAZMYNE

From the palace observatory, I watch the bowls blink out one by one across the parish.

Time passes with a fraught lethargy, a battle of opposites, as Xanthippe extinguish the Witchfire with caution, anticipating attack. But there's been no bangarang from Jade Guild insurgents, only the feeling that the entire island, beyond the ignorant guests in the palace, is holding its breath—I know I am. What are the Jade Guild doing? More to the point, what is *Iraya* doing? Up until now the fires have been destructive. The Obeah rebels have always been more intent on ruination than the flair of this stunt, but she has proven herself to be a witch who loves to pop style. To what end can it be other than mine? If she uses the guild to kill me, she'll override the Shook Bargain we agreed to. While we can't hurt one another, we can command others to. Iraya's intention all along. I should have known.

"Jaz," Anya murmurs beside me. "You need to start

communicating with the presiders."

Distracted, I glance across the observatory to where the witches are clustered together. After putting off their questions in favor of intercepting quarterly reports from Filmore—and whispered castigations from Anya to learn the other Stealths' names—it's time to cross the first bridge toward the truth before Iraya Adair arrives and blows it to smithereens. My eyes fall on the late doyenne's chair at the head of the strategy table. How many times did I watch her sit, command, ensorcell the masses and the minorities without magic, regardless of the surplus at her disposal?

That is ruling, Emissary, she told me once. *Baring your teeth like a predator even if at times you feel more like prey.* For better or worse—I hope for better—I am her daughter.

I must show Aiyca I am the predator she never reared me to be.

The smoke-hued wind blown up from the parish below urges me to the table, like a nudging hand that impels me to put a stop to any further fires. I draw out a chair and sit. Anya stands at my left shoulder. Drifting, as though a duppy along with the son she believes dead, Ormine follows. After Presider Phelony comes Presider Ionie Lewis, and Presider Mariama Antwi. The latter's skin is as gray as the kaftan she sports for her métier. I forget that she lost a daughter in the Yielding too. Amoi. Grief is another companion at our table, manifesting differently for the three of us who carry the spirits of our dead like additional limbs.

"I assume you're finally going to enlighten us as to whaap'm?" Ionie cuts a stark look my way, her sightless eyes reinforced with the twist to her mouth. Without the silver nimbus of her afro, drawn back beneath a tight head tie, her face is severe, as bracing as the chilled wind Squallers like her are trained to control. "If you know, that is. After watching you this past hour, I have many, many doubts."

With the Obeah insurgents at large, her insults roll off my back. "I can assure you I know what's happening. Before the doyenne's death you were alerted about an Obeah-witch she added to the Shield Initiative."

I'm met with furrowed brows, shakes of the head.

"She spoke to you of the shield days before her death," I clarify. "Following the Obeahs' bruckout in their Cuartel here, on the palace grounds?" I heard the conversation myself, with Anya, the night we eavesdropped in the Corridor of Power.

"We knew of the trouble Judair was having, but it wasn't with an Obeah-witch." Mariama bites her bottom lip. "I suppose there's little harm in sharing the truth now she is gone. . . . It was the Unlit giving her difficulty."

For a moment I'm thrown, cast out, adrift in a sea of confusion where the waves knock me to and fro.

"The former Obeah castouts?" I shake my head, look out to the fewer flames in the parish once again. "No one has heard anything from them in years."

"Judair had history with the Unlit."

True, but I haven't heard about the magically exiled Obeah since Madisyn told me the story of what they did to Nana Cariot and the late doyenne, whose dada took her eye in recompense for being unclean. Not when the Jade Guild have been a great enough enemy. The proof of their influence still burns in the parish.

They've come to reclaim something I took, the late doyenne said before handing me the Grimoire during the Sole. She meant Aiyca. She meant that she took the island, the Golden Seat, from the Obeah. Why would she fear the magicless Unlit now, years after her trauma?

"I don't believe it was them she spoke of."

Presider Lewis scoffs.

"How could she," I continue, steeling my nerves. "When the Jade Guild's leader, Iraya Adair, lives and breathes."

Her name commands a silence that leeches the air from the room.

"I'm sorry," Ormine says, visibly emerging from herself. "Did you say Iraya Adair? The Lost Empress?"

I cast a look around the table. The three presiders wear various states of distress, disbelief—bafflement. The sensation of something very cold trickles down the back of my neck.

"She's the one the Jade Guild have been fighting harder for, these past several months." *Right?* I almost add. "She killed the late doyenne."

"*She* killed the doyenne?" Mariama crosses herself in the Mudda's sign of seven.

My stomach plummets.

"Why wouldn't Judair tell us about her?"

"Because you *would* have sentenced her to death," I exhale.

"And the rest!"

"Then you weren't speaking of Iraya the night the shields revolted." It isn't a question, and though it's said mainly to myself, Mariama answers.

"She wouldn't have been worth the additional risk when the

doyenne was already facing challenge from the Unlit. Their missive all but announced war."

"Which missive?"

"They sent one. I—"

"Where is it?"

"Last we saw, her office." Mariama stands as if she means to go for it.

"Anya."

Without a word, my sistren slips out the door.

"When did Iraya arrive?" Ionie asks.

I lean forward in my seat, keeping my damp back away from its wood. The others mirror my body language as I tell the story, as though I am a griot. But this isn't a work of fiction. It's a waking nightmare I'm still recounting when Anya comes back. We all turn at the opening of the door. My sistren's face is inscrutable, even to me, as she passes the missive my way. It is but a scrap.

"There was more," Mariama says, fingers twitching as though she means to try to take it from me. "It was lengthy. Did you not find the rest?"

Anya's response fades as I unfold the note and read the three words written there.

I AM COMING.

The shift is sudden and seismic, as if the very fabric of my reality has been snatched from around me, pulled away by the writer of the words I just read—by their unnoticed hand that has fisted itself around Aiyca, because, gods above, there's someone *else* to contend with.

25

It's a shock to find that my voice remains steady. "And you have no idea who wrote this?"

All three presiders shake their heads.

"Judair shared very little," Presider Antwi proffers, tucking a lock of her silver bob behind an ear with a quivering hand. "And we think in part because her shock was so great. The missive arrived in a meeting not unlike this one. She seemed to retreat, mentally. To go somewhere else, I remember."

It's a reaction I've seen from her before, when she spoke of the bruckout in Carne Prison months ago now. Then I thought it was Iraya she feared, which was why I could never understand why she kept her alive. At least, until I learned about the jéges. But now . . .

The jéges.

Mudda have mercy.

With a chilling injection of clarity, I know why the late doyenne kept Iraya alive. She did need the might of the Adair magic, that omnipotent naevus. But not because she required another defensive shield in her cadre of Obeah, no.

She needed a *weapon*.

The longer the presiders and I debate, Anya too, the greater my certainty grows about the late doyenne's actions: she *did* unite herself with the castouts in some scheme to take Aiyca from the Obeah a decade ago, though it's an act I've yet to fully unfold. Then she betrayed them, a move of hers I have little trouble digesting, one that, yet again, leaves me exposed, a nerve vulnerable to nature's will. Most daughters inherit jewels from mamas. I have the enemies of mine.

The only part we've yet to settle on is who wrote the missive. Who is coming?

Or, worse still after the Witchfire, who may already be here?

"Again," Ionie snaps when I voice the question. "Does it matter?"

"Again." Anya rolls her eyes. "Yeh mon. It does. You of all witches should understand the impending danger, Squaller. They're trying to take Aiyca."

Too. Take my island *too.*

And if they're here in St. Mary, where is Iraya?

"Tell me." Presider Antwi reaches for the steaming pot of coffee delivered by attendants moments ago. "Why do we need to fear them when we have the Adair witch?"

"And my boy's blood." Presider Phelony's eyes turn glassy; a solitary tear runs a course down one cheek, the rich brown dull without any joy to illuminate it from within. "He died to protect us against this storm you speak of."

Anya and I exchange the briefest of glances.

How could I forget Javel, still alive and imprisoned in the palace holding cells while an imposter decomposes in the Temple of the Supreme Being?

"True," Ionie says, adding a log to the pyre by which Anya and I will burn if our deception is learned of. "Where is the Adair witch, in the holding cells with the other shields?"

The three presiders' heads swivel my way; this time, I cannot lie.

"She's gone," I have to admit. "She fled after killing the doyenne. With Kir—with Emissary Divsylar."

"Your *pet*?"

"Prince, actually." My throat is filled with the sharp consonants in his title. But better this than discussing Javel. "He's the Zesian doyenne's firstborn son. She sent him here to steal magical artifacts from our late doyenne. I understand that information puts Aiyca in a precarious situation, but—"

The door flies open, smacking against the stone wall at its back.

"Forgive me, Regent," Filmore breathes. "Additional fires have been started in St. Jayne and St. Catherine."

Mudda have mercy.

"Has anyone been attacked?"

He shakes his head. "The Xanthippe who sifted reported no injuries, only fires. The coven is putting them out, and the battalion soldiers have been instructed to go door to door to ensure parishioners remain inside."

"What is the Unlit *doing*?" Anya utters a curse.

"Triple patrols in every parish," I tell Filmore, just as nescient about their movements. "And come to me with anything else."

With a sharp bow, he leaves.

"As I was about to say . . ." My words come slowly, thickly. "I have a plan."

"I hope it begins and ends with you stepping down."

Presider Lewis's words are a slap of cold water to the face, as sobering.

"Stepping . . . down?"

"You haven't the experience, the magic, or the wherewithal to lead this island," the witch continues, her words a maelstrom of malice. "You, closer to the Zesian emissary than anyone else, and you missed his true allegiances? You will do no more damage here." Ionie stabs a finger at me; I recoil from its tip. "You will step down from the throne, renounce your claim to your mama's legacy, and *we three* will prepare Aiyca for what comes."

Without words, I can only gape at them. Through the haze of outrage, one matter rings clear: no leader in their right mind would sit here and take mutiny from their subordinates. Mama wouldn't have. And as much as I hate to think it, Iraya wouldn't either.

To the presiders I have not yet graduated from making foolish decisions. They are not entirely wrong. The question of when my youth will fall out, an infantile tooth pushed aside by its stronger superior, has long haunted me—but it cannot any longer.

My chair grinds against tile as I stand, forced back with the velocity of my action. "There will be no *standing down* on my part. I am the late doyenne's heir, in a custom entrenched in this island's history by the Seven-Faced Mudda, and I know none here would dare challenge the authority of our Supreme Being, despite being presumptuous enough to think yourselves a part of my council." My pause is perfunctory. An inhale between sentences I use to ensure they listen. They do. "I had no wish to discard the wisdom you carry after your tenure serving the late doyenne, but should you disrespect my authority as regent even one more time, you will be cast out—properly," I find myself promising.

Though they are stiff with reluctance, their nods come. My legs tremble, and my palms are damp, but I lift my chin.

"Now—"

The door opens with a startling abruptness for a second time.

"*Now*," Roje repeats, devastating grin, axe, and entirely unwelcome attitude in tow, "seemed as good a time as any to come in and introduce myself. Wahan, Alumbrar."

"Sea snake!" Ormine hisses first, flying out of her seat; her conduit's light pulses on her chest in an angry strobe. The two others are quick to follow. "Emissary?" She turns to me as I sink back into my chair, her red-laced eyes wild. "Do you know this bandulu?"

"*Regent* Cariot is no longer your emissary," Roje all but purrs, with an insouciant toss of his dreadlocks. "She is your leader—and soon to be the Queen of Carne Sea too."

Mudda have mercy.

"Blasphemy," Ionie whispers, stunned. "That title was never legitimized."

"There are thousands of pirates who dwell on the Iron Shore who will think differently, when she bears the Coral Crown. And I have to say—" With a practiced grace, Roje rests one booted foot atop a chair and leans on his knee. "Unlike you Alumbrar, my ilk are liberal with our weapons and who we use them on." At odds with his relaxed posture, the tide changes in his voice, eddying from amiable to dangerous. "Disrespect Aiyca's regent, the Pirate Queen, in my presence or outside these walls again, and you will feel the weight of my blade on your neck."

"Roje is helping to *protect* Aiyca—the goal here," I hurry to tell the presiders, to remind him since he seems to have lost his mind. It's like he's deliberately trying to antagonize them.

"I spoke of a plan. He and his crew are helping me to enact it."

"And what of the Unlit?" Ionie's bottom lip juts out. "What will be done about them and their fires?"

"I have that under control," I lie. What else can I do at this point but say what they need to hear and then shunt them out? "Your only task, at present, is to arrange the Nine Night celebrations for the late doyenne. Send me the written itineraries." It feels like a foolish request, but what else are they good for, recalcitrant as they are? I take my seat and wave for Roje and Anya to do the same. Taking the cue, the presiders bow their heads in deference—though not very low—and vacate the observatory.

Breathe.

"What were you thinking?" I ask Roje the moment the door closes.

Anya snorts. "*Were* you thinking?"

"It was a classic posturing move, mon." He shrugs those shoulders, their line strong beneath his leather vest and billowing white shirt. "Vea and I had something of a double act, though she was typically the bitter and I the chaser that followed. I rather enjoyed taking up the opposite mantle just now." Golden eyes slide my way and wink. "Forgive me, my queen. When I heard how they questioned you, I couldn't not act."

"In the future I expect more control, Roje."

Not sobered in the slightest, he nods.

"Since you're here, there have been some updates you need to know about."

"Like the fact that you're regent, not doyenne? I know."

"It's a temporary measure." I sniff. "And not what I meant." I make short work of filling him in about the new Unlit enemy.

"Will you use the shields to help?"

Caught off guard, it takes me a moment to gather my sensibilities. "No. In fact, I should—I should send them to Carne." I glance askance at Anya in question.

She frowns. "We shouldn't launch any ships until we know more about the Unlit's plans beyond the fires."

"The crew can take to the streets."

"Are you not listening, or just stupid?" Anya turns to Roje. "We can't go marching through Aiyca without a *plan*."

"Marching is the plan."

"Don't bat those lashes at me, pirate. I am immune."

I rub the Shook Bargain that connects Ira, Kirdan, and me still. Might they know the truth about the rebels?

"Has anything changed?" Anya asks, catching my movement.

"No."

"I've been wondering if she stays because she knows about the Unlit."

Roje rocks back in his seat. "Who?"

"Iraya."

"Would she care?"

"Yes," Anya and I say in unison.

"Would she work with them?"

"I don't think so." My lower lip stings between my teeth. "Unlit are not Obeah, and for that very reason the former's consternation will be directed toward the latter as much as it will be toward Alumbrar."

"Maybe more so," Anya muses.

Roje rests his weight on the back of his chair. "What do you think they want?"

"What everyone wants from Aiyca. Its gold. Its power."

"Then Iraya and the Zesian might help to keep them at bay, no?"

I don't know. With my failure to see and hear Kirdan's deceit, I am down two senses and rapidly numbing my way out of a third. *Does* animosity fester in the scar of Zesia's and Aiyca's damaged relationship, or was that another ruse? And as for Iraya . . .

Someone has made us enemies, she said. *Perhaps they feared the damage we could do together would be far greater than what we could ever do apart.*

It was a lie then, but could it come true?

I wasn't able to kill Javel last night. I don't have the Grimoire; the map was secreted somewhere I know not by the late doyenne, and like her I need a weapon too—one forged by an amalgam of life's cruelty and necessity, a blade whose potential to destroy the world is as great as her potential to destroy herself. Unless . . . she saves it.

Unless *we* save it.

"I'm not sure if she'll help us, me, after our last," I begin, hating myself for being here, in a position where I need her. Again. "But the only way to know is to find her." Before her seven days to leave expire. At least that part of the bargain is foolproof.

Roje's eyebrows shoot upward. "You'll ask her?"

I nod, unable to bring myself to say that I *need* her. "There's a great chance they're still here. Pirates are to be stationed at every port; Kirdan can't sift any great distance with his hair, and the others haven't the gold. Summon an Artisan. We'll have them create renderings of Iraya and Kirdan that can be distributed to all Alumbrar. I want word sent to the Sea Defense too. All vessels leaving and entering these shores will require inspection for stowaways." Exhaling, I mentally commend myself.

"Consider it done," Anya says, with an impressed look my way. "I can send missives to request that the Nameless Gennas in the parishes raise guzzu too, like an alarm, to go off whenever anyone sifts. The moratorium is still in place, but it will work in our favor since Kirdan is one of the few who had permission from the late doyenne to magically travel."

"The council's guzzu will stand?" I check.

"You haven't sworn in new members, and three of its witches still live."

The door opens; Filmore enters again.

"Another fire?"

"No, Regent. The Xanthippe patrol in St. Deirdre Parish have picked up an increased number of Aiycans. They're unsworn to either order and congregating in public places. Given what's happening—"

"You were right to tell me."

Anya crosses the room to the observatory's vast map. Crinkled with use and jaundice-colored with age, it's pinned vertically to one of the inner walls.

"What is it?" I follow her.

"Strategy." Wind whips her hair away from a face tight with worry. "Stealths are taught the art of distraction, and I wondered— Yeh mon." She taps the map. "Coral Garden."

"A port city," I whisper. They're lighting fires to keep us occupied while they go after the ships, like they did in Black River, when Anya and I first met Roje. And last saw Vea. "I need Coral Garden locked down now!" I command Filmore. "Queenstown and Port Royale too. Anyone proceeding toward them is to be captured for interrogation. As for any hostiles—"

"They should be killed." Roje joins us. "I'll go personally to make sure that happens."

"I have to be there too." My stomach clenches. "St. Deirdre has no presider."

"They have a mayor," Anya argues.

"An Aiycan mayor." Secular, with no magic at all. "I have to support him. He has no cock in this Alumbrar-Obeah-Unlit fight. And I have the Stealths, more Xanthippe, and Nameless. I'm going. But the guests—"

"Illusion Glyphs can replicate people too," Anya concedes, waving Filmore over, and instructs him to imprint my face on one of the cadre to fool those who dine beneath us.

"Wouldn't it be easier if I slay the boy in the cell?" Roje suggests. "You could have the blood you need instead of seeking the aid of your enemy."

Killing Javel would be simpler, but I shan't begin my rule in the chill of the late doyenne's shadow.

"It isn't blood we need." It's to fight fire with fire. Something Iraya will help with, once I've found her—if I find her, a problem to contend with after securing my island. *Breathe*. But first, "Notify St. Deirdre's mayor, as well as the Nameless in the city, that I'm on my way."

4

IRAYA

Pursued by the brume curling in from the Xaymaca trench like a great serpentine cousin of the Unlit's amorphous monsters, we beat a stealthy path across the city.

Rainy season has given way to a dry air as weighty as it is suffocating. Sweat is immediate and uncomfortable. Delyse leads our descent down cobbled back alleys, narrowed by parked oyster carts in the built-up settlements; they're stacked atop one another like building blocks. It's my first time witnessing her Stealth prowess, and it is singular. Bound in the colors exclusive to shadows, dark browns, grays, her body doesn't just become the magically trained shadow her métier demands she be, it manipulates them; far from embracing *her*, she seems to command *them*, drawing their darkness out in a silent lullaby to conceal us as the city wakes—Coral Garden, I don't need anyone to tell me.

Faint shouts carry on a briny breeze, as the smallest of the island's five port locales stirs with divers preparing to retrieve the coral that gives this town its name. There'll be Squallers among them, ready to manipulate the winds to fill the sails of sloops, calm storms that toss waves. Can they know, I think, back pressed against the damp stone of an innocuous building as an Obeah street sweep makes his way past, tiny golden conduit coin ablaze to implement his will on the brushes, what occurred in the palace last night? It's a question I don't ask the others when we group before great steel doors of an abandoned warehouse, its face turned toward the sea.

"Adriel." Shamar clasps the proffered hand of the solitary Obeah-man standing guard. "This is—"

"Iraya," I interrupt, stepping forward to shake the magi's hand myself.

Adriel is both tall and wide enough that Kirdan no longer takes up all the space. But as his hand turns limp in my own and his gaze widens, I'm under the impression that for all his appearance of might, Adriel is as lovely as the cadence of his name. All the better for me. I bet this sweet Obeah won't mind telling me a few things.

He bows his head. "E-empress."

"Is everyone here?" Delyse asks.

"Who?"

Adriel sends an apologetic look my way before turning to Delyse. "Yeh mon. You're late. They were worried something happened."

"Something did," I cut in. "Our usurper is dead, her daughter occupies the Golden Seat, and we face a monstrous threat. Now, who are we meeting?"

With a helpless grimace, Adriel opens the door and exchanges quick words with someone inside, exposing the scarification on the back of his neck. "All will be revealed, Empress." Turning back with a wide, even-toothed smile, he offers me his arm.

"Wonderful," I lie. Dodging Kirdan's attempt to sidle between the two of us, and stepping neatly over Delyse's foot, I wrap both hands around Adriel's arm. "A Transmuter?" I ask, calling attention to the alchemical scar at the base of his hairline. "Impressive. Were you close to Mastery?"

Shamar's snort is only significant to me, and Delyse perhaps, as she was there when he and I first met, and I asked a similar question to distract. It works even better with Adriel, who regales me with stories about his time in one of two energy plants on the island where conduit metal is transmuted into fuel—enough to weaponize Aiyca's Obeah. He doesn't say this, but I wonder if that's the plan. Obeah would know better now, than when Mama ruled, that if we want peace, we must prepare for war.

"Let's not ruin every surprise for the empress, Adriel," Delyse interrupts. She walks close to my left shoulder. I suspect she wants nothing more than to pinch me silent.

"Of course not. You'll find clothing through these sets of doors." Adriel slows in the innocuous warehouse corridor; like its surroundings, it's bleak in the way forgotten things are. "There's a room for each of you." He detangles himself from my snare. "I'll return once the guild is ready to see you."

"Any room in particular?" Delyse asks.

"You all seem to be standing where you should be." With a

tip of his head, Adriel continues down the hall.

Before Delyse can reprimand me again, or Kirdan can say whatever his little side glances are about, I step into the room across from where I'm standing triumphant, somehow, despite my overwhelming desire to learn what the hell is going on.

"Iraya Adair, it's good to see you're still alive."

The familiarity of the voice is the only reason I don't free Kirdan's blade from where I secreted it in the waistband of my trousers at my back. The Bonemantis from Cwenburg Palace's Cuartel, the Master who welcomed me, my first day on the estate, rises from a seat in a dim corner.

"Master Omnyra." My surprise fills the empty space. "You escaped?"

"Long before the shields' revolt during the Sole. But that's a story for another day. We have limited time together this morning." She speaks in a voice that feels reinforced by many of her ancestors; while her eyes are their typical brown, the third-eye scarification on her brow is an alabaster flame in the gloom of our surroundings.

"We're not alone, then."

Her smile is another shadow. "The dead are always with us, Iraya. It's with thanks to them I can see that your path will take you far from here, for a time rapidly approaching, so let us all make this fast. Do you recall what I said on your first day at the Cuartel?"

A shiver unfurls down my spine. How could I forget the words that enabled me to kill the doyenne?

"To believe in the vow I took," I tell her.

"Then you know that there are different degrees of

leadership, Iraya. The entire reason you surmounted Doyenne Cariot's vow was because you became a leader in your own right. Far from being limited to sitting on a throne, it's about the people you serve; it's about your intentions." She clasps her hands before her like she's in prayer; the room modulates to something weighted with significance even before she speaks her next words. "You can aid Aiyca, or you can be its destruction if you refuse to acknowledge it."

"Its destruction? I'm leaving to save this island. And actually," I start as an idea pushes to the fore, "I need a favor—"

"To keep the island safe in your stead?" She shakes her head.

"No?"

She shakes her head again.

"Are you telling me I need to stay?"

"The stone already rolls," Master Omnyra intones, in those many voices that seem to crawl up from the pit of her belly to slither out from between her lips. "But before you go forward, it might be wise to look back."

I take a step toward her. "You reference my magic, don't you? Do you know of a way for me to fully remove the Impediment Glyphs?"

"Sift through the sands for the answer you seek. The vanguard you chose will be on hand to offer you aid," she continues, her voice flat; her eyes fog over until they are entirely white. "Use them wisely. When fires start, there's less likelihood that they will spread if the one sounding the alarm isn't also trying to stamp the blaze out, you understand?"

"Not in the slightest."

"You will." Her scarification dulls to its typical white-gold, and her eyes clear, but it's the thinning of the air that truly signifies that we are now alone. "Seven blessings to you, Iraya Adair. You shall need them all."

"Wait—why can't you keep an eye on matters here for me? You haven't told me anything concrete."

"The future is only concrete once in the past." And with a final parting nod, Master Omnyra slips out of a second door in the shadowed recesses of the room.

Bonemantises, always so damned confusing. So dramatic.

But that doesn't mean their scrying is something to be sneered at.

The dead are always with us, the Master said. She meant Mama, I know it. I can all but feel her elegant hand rest on my shoulder, smell the sweet coconut oil in her afro as she leans down to whisper, *Diplomacy. The mind must be sharper than the blade.*

Ticking with thoughts, theories, I peel away the mismatched pants, then tunic, and finally slide into the sleek silk of the Stealth-black garments left for me. Aiyca's relations with the empire are worse now than they were the last time the Unlit rose against my family. This island does require a leader in place to hold the Unlit at bay—but it had an Adair at the helm last time, two: Mama and Dada couldn't stand against monstrous creatures from beyond the veil. Knowing more than they did, the fact of the matter is simple, to me at least: Aiyca cannot win this war without aid. The history has been told; we lost. It didn't matter that we had all our Masters, lived and trained freely, as opposed to existing in a decade of magical dormancy.

I cannot remain here. I cannot send someone else on in my place. While noble of cause, the Jade Guild haven't the notoriety to rally the numbers we need, not like the Adair name—which they wanted to stoke fires in the bellies of Aiyca's Obeah when I was a shield. My order will benefit when I join forces with the Skylands, the empire's most secretive nation, known only for the aerial army they command, the creatures they haven't flown into battle since Xaymaca's inception, when monsters, brigands, from far and wide set their sights on ruling the golden isles. That time has come again, and I will be the one to lead the legends home. If the others let me, I can—my hand falters on the leather bandolier I strap across my chest.

Let me?

My snort cuts through the silence, the fetid heat.

Cha mon. This is where holding my tongue, avoiding conflict with the others to keep some semblance of peace, gets me. *Me.* Iraya Cordelia Boatema Adair. Avenging Warrior, Heir of Aiyca's First Protector, Envoy of Death Herself. Conflict is the altar before which I was created to worship.

For my own good.

For the greater good.

For Aiyca.

And the island will do better with Shamar and Delyse here—*I* will do better knowing they're here, overseeing a resistance that has only succeeded in making itself a front for the Unlit. Trust them in my absence? Please. Trust them to make additional errors, more like. . . . But Delyse and Sham won't stay. They won't want to leave me.

I'll have to leave them.

A hollow knock sounds against the door to my room. Arranging my features to look irritated, curious, though the latter isn't entirely fabricated, I egress outside where the others already wait. Like me, they are all draped in slips of silken night. Delyse takes Adriel by the arm before I can attach myself to his side and strikes ahead. With a grimace, Shamar follows, leaving Kirdan and me to bring up the rear.

Magi are noticeably absent as we stride through dirty halls. Witchlights, those that aren't shattered, flicker with a foreboding dimness. Either the Jade Guild's numbers are few here, or they're concealing how many are on guard. No doubt to make my escape difficult.

They think they know me. How . . . charming.

"You've been quiet," Kirdan says, his voice still rough with exhaustion. Despite this, he matches my stride with too much ease. "I've learned to be concerned when you aren't being inappropriate and relishing in the discomfort of others."

He is a complication I haven't decided to keep or ditch. His haircut weakens him, but he has skills I could use in the Skylands.

"Perhaps I've turned over a new leaf."

"Unlikely." Kirdan snorts. "How much farther?" he calls ahead to the Transmuter. "You can't lead us in circles forever."

"It's just through here." Adriel, not looking the least bit guilty about trying to conceal the warehouse floor plan, nods at a set of double doors.

Delyse pokes her face in one of the glass windows and draws back so fast she almost knocks Shamar in the face. "*All* of them?"

Adriel shrugs apologetically. "The council forbade me from speaking."

"Council?" I crane my neck to catch a look. "As in Witches Council?"

"*Obeah* Witches Council," Shamar corrects, tall enough to see over Delyse.

Sheepish, Adriel shrugs again. And here I thought we were becoming bredren.

Delyse draws a rattling breath. "Ira, mon, now really isn't the time to be smart, you understand?"

"You say that as if I've ever been anything but."

"Ira—"

"You're needed inside." With one final apologetic look at Delyse and me, Adriel flings open both doors and ducks beneath the frame to enter. "Announcing Delyse Powell, Shamar Barnes, Prince Kirdan Divsylar, and Iraya Cordelia Boatema Adair, Blessed of Aurore, First Face of the Supreme Being; Arrow of Clotille and Duilio, Battle Faces of the Supreme Being; Defender of Carne Sea; Heir of the Xaymaca Empire, her territories, and the Monster's Gulf; first of her name; and the only living heir of Empress Cordelia and Admiral Vincent Adair."

The gathering behind the doors is more civilized than I thought it could be, given our locality. Balance, Mama would say, kept the scales of leadership from tipping. I see her Masters have applied this aphorism as, rather than the late Alumbrar doyenne's council of six, with Judair's seat making the seventh, there are seven Obeah seated side by side beneath the fractured remains of a ceiling, one witch from each of my order's most valued métiers: a Bush Healer, an Artisan of Metal, a Recondite, a Squaller, a Poisoner, a Transmuter, and a Warrior. Master Omnyra is not among them. A frown draws the corners of my mouth down. If she meant for me to entreat the council to keep watch in my stead, why isn't she here?

"Empress Adair," the Recondite states, with her métier's typical superiority carried on a face curtained by two sheets of long, thin braids.

"Call me Iraya, please."

Something flashes in her eyes. Displeasure.

A fisherman will never say his own produce stinks, but perhaps Master Omnyra is doing just that, with her absence. Something . . . something doesn't feel right here.

"As you wish. Though we are making history this morning. For the first time in a decade, an Obeah Witches Council sits before the empire's heir. You've been called to this panel to answer a number of questions about where you have been and what you have been doing these past three months since your release from Carne Prison."

Beside me, Kirdan tenses.

Forcing my own tight limbs to unspool into their typical nonchalance, I tip my chin up. "Since we're answering questions, how about you tell me on whose authority both you as a council and this *judgment panel* have been called."

Someone chokes down the line. I think it's Delyse.

"I'd also like a seat," I add, popping the final *t*. "If it isn't too much to ask."

Kirdan clears his throat, masking something that sounds a lot like a chuckle.

"I'm rather weary after killing the doyenne, and I'm sure the others are too, given the fight with the Cariot heir's pirate allies we had to win in order to make it here."

A gloved contraption of rings and chains adorning the clasped fingers of the Artisan of Metal brightens in her lap. Fallen metal beams rise from the ground as though picked up by invisible hands. Four chairs, sturdy, steel, are twisted into being with no more effort than a pickney making a chain from flowers.

"Blessings." I nod at her and drop onto one of the hard lids of metal.

"Then you have killed her." The Recondite leans forward and studies me as though trying to glean my every thought. "Why is it you do not occupy the throne?"

"Esteemed one," Delyse begins. She is silenced with a look from the formidable Squaller.

"Sometimes victory is won." I shrug, mentally rearranging how I thought this conversation would unfold, what my role would be. "Other times it is conceded."

"You speak in riddles, girl." The Poisoner frowns.

"Our questions must be answered plainly," the Bush Healer adds.

But not mine.

"Why aren't you in the palace?" the Recondite repeats.

"Because we need an army."

The Warrior laughs. "And *you* mean to raise one? Cha mon."

Beside me, Kirdan flexes the hand resting on his left thigh.

"Do you have any other suggestions, Genna?" I ask, my voice light.

"Of course." She shifts in her seat, chest puffing beneath its armored chest-plate. "You take your rightful seat here on this council, and I will recruit your army. What's proper."

"It's proper for a soldier to sit back and do nothing?"

"Are you a Warrior or an empress, Iraya?" the Recondite asks, shrewd as ever. "There have been rumors surrounding you that leadership is not your primary concern. We have heard that you are plagued by the beast of revenge, shackled to its saddle and dragged wherever it roams."

Lounging in my seat, I weigh my options, aware that while I have been toeing the line, challenging an elder to her face will mean crossing it, and Shamar and Delyse will need these witches when I'm away. Some of them, anyway.

"We are speaking plainly?"

The council members nod; my companions to my right peer down the line at me. Delyse's eyes are wide as she wills me not to be honest, Shamar's wary as he wonders if tying me up as the former suggested might have been the wiser choice, and Kirdan's curious, always curious.

Time to shake the tree and see what falls out. "Then I wish to know about the Unlit among you."

The Warrior shakes her head. "You believe this council has been infiltrated? No." She's vehement; it turns the sweetness of her Aiycan accent into something bitter, sharp. "I have served with these sistren for five years, from the time we managed to gather the scattered to unite for our shared purpose. What do you know?" She sneers at my scarification. "A Warrior pup and a spoiled heir."

"I know the Unlit helped the Alumbrar kill my family."

47

Amplified by the height of the room, my voice rings with the clarity of a death knell. "I know that they've been working to take back that which they believe Judair Cariot stole from them—after Mama banished them to this island's fringes for their crimes. And I know that they must be here, in this Babylon gathering you dare call a council. Whether it's one or all of you." I rise, slow, menacing. Delyse, Shamar, and Kirdan are quick to follow. "Since I know without a shadow of doubt that no allies of the Adairs would call themselves a council without being sworn in by a member of my family—wouldn't dare to evade any question asked by a member of my family. One or more of you have made the others believe this is acceptable, no doubt for your own nefarious ends. Which, I'm happy to report, I'm about to be." I meet every face, my mouth twisted in something no one would call a smile. "So show yourselves, bandulu."

"Criminals? How *dare* you?" The Squaller blusters to her feet, teeth and metal gnashing.

"Oh, Genna, my scarification should tell you that I will always dare, unlike the Unlit who have been hiding behind the banner of jade to capture the golden flag." I throw my arms wide. "Here I am! Why don't you come and get it?"

"*Empress!*" the Recondite says, outraged. "This is not to be borne!"

The Bush Healer stands, her hands shoved deeply up the opposite sleeves twisting beneath the reams of fabric. "Perhaps Carne, her time with the shields, has unhinged her."

"Ira." Delyse starts for me. "I told you not to do this!"

As I glance at her, prepare to ward her off, something silver glints in my peripherals, and the world slows. There's no time to run for Delyse, to shout a warning; there is only my will, and with it my magic. It swells and courses toward my conduit in a haphazard deluge, still tempered by the partially burned Impediment Glyphs incised behind my ears. A thunderclap booms as my naevus breaks its banks, rocking the ruin around us; Delyse and I are shunted apart as though we collided, forced back by my intent and sent skidding across the floor and out of the path of the silver—a thrown blade. Delyse holds a hand over her arm and looks incredulously at the Obeah-witch who threw it, but the dark gaze of the Bush Healer is already waiting for me; there's a dearth of anything kind in her face as she removes her second hand from the depths of her sleeves. It's fisted around something I cannot see.

"It is not us who have been hiding," she calls. "But *you*."

The rest of the council are on their feet in a clash of weapons and wood.

"Don't kill her!" I shout, rocketing up off the floor.

The Bush Healer cocks her head to the side. "Do you think you'll get the chance to end my life?"

"Do you plan on attempting to end mine first?"

Beside me, Kirdan frees both the length of his saber and the shorter, brutal hunting knife.

The Healer doesn't look his way. "Your card has been called by another," she says to me.

"Who?"

She only sneers.

I return it in kind. "Your master will see themself that Aiyca won't bend."

"And you speak for Aiyca? The empress once lost, now found," she mocks. "Well, they would tell you that you're mistaken. My master does not mean to bend Aiyca, or indeed Xaymaca." Her brows lower in twin scythes. "They will break it." She launches her second arm into the air. Darkness, thick and immediate, falls like two hands have pressed over my eyes, and quietness descends with the foreboding promise of a quick death.

5

JAZMYNE

The sift puts us high on a hill thick with bush before a solitary Nameless outpost villa.

Displacement vibrates through my bones, making my ears ring with the typical abruptness of the magical travel—only it's louder than it's ever been, and it isn't just my body that's quivering. It's the earth.

"Something's happening down in the garden." Roje frees his axe as soon as he gets his bearings. He's ventured to the edge of the verge. "Other than the fact that there's no garden I can see, I mean."

"The Coral Garden is in the water," I breathe, clinging to the only certainties I know ahead of my meeting with the city's mayor.

"I know, Genna. I was jesting."

"How about you don't, mon," Anya snaps.

"There are Alumbrar in the crowd gathered down there

now." Filmore's Stealth-honed sight is fixed on the parish beneath us. "Perhaps they're curious about the number of Xanthippe, and what precipitated the near-tripling of guards?"

"What about the unsworn?" I ask, never craving magic more.

"Their numbers have dissipated."

That's something, at least. "Then we should head to the town hall now. You said the mayor would meet us in the square, Pasha?"

Filmore's second nods.

The door to the villa opens behind us. I glance at Anya, exchange a wordless request.

"On it," she murmurs.

"Ask for prowlers," I call up after her. "As many as they can spare, since we didn't have time to retrieve our own."

"What about the Unlit?" Roje asks.

"They're still not attacking." Though I shrug, my heart thumps with a volume to rival the crowd in the town beneath us. "Xanthippe will keep the port protected." And the first and second battalion soldiers are on the lookout for Iraya and Kirdan.

"Wahan, Doyenne Cariot."

A witch, draped in the soft blue of her Squaller métier, comes around the back of the villa leading a pack of jungle-prowlers. "I'm Jannah. These belong to some of the Genna inside."

"What do you mean?"

"When I received the missive that you were coming here to meet with the mayor, I notified the other outposts across the parish. Do you need us to come with you?"

"No." This is from Anya, who jogs back down the steps. "We need the outposts in the city to be ready to offer support, while the mayor makes his address. Will you send word? We can't linger." She mounts a dark jungle-prowler with a solitary horn on its tamarind-colored brow and velveteen paws the size of my head.

"My objective is to support the mayor in lieu of a presider," I expound to Jannah; taking the hand Anya offers, I slip into the saddle ahead of her. My plainer kaftan, acquired from the late doyenne's suite before leaving, ripples down its powerful flank as the subtle conduit gold thread catches the morning light. It's the most protection I've ever worn.

I hope I won't need it.

"Will you return here afterward?"

"Council," Anya whispers against my neck.

They're expecting me to discuss who will serve beside me *now*?

Helpless, I look to my party. The cadre sit two to a prowler; axe returned to the strap across his back, Roje sits astride a golden-haired jungle-prowler with a mane that fans around its cruel, beautiful muzzle. They're expecting one thing; the crowd growing like a rising tide below is expecting another. And the Nameless? Beyond ensuring this villa was open and ready for us, they weren't meant to factor in today at all.

"When I return," I tell Jannah, "I'll address you all."

She nods and retreats back up the steps into the villa.

Breathe.

"Should the enemy arrive while the mayor is addressing the city and attempt to use force," I begin, sure to meet the eyes of the Stealths and Roje, "we do not engage in combat. We leave them to the Xanthippe and return here." Brooking no further discussion, I tug the reins of the prowler around and dig my heels into its sides; with a toss of its shaggy mane, the horned beast breaks into a canter. I lean low against its neck; the island is reduced to brown and green streaks by wind and tears, until, with a bounding leap, we break through a border of bush and burst out into the bright square—landing with a scream of claws against stone right in the midst of the crowd heard from atop the hill. "Alumbrar!" I call, drawing on the reins. "Please, do not fear!"

Our prowler growls, juts its horn in a minatory bid for them to step back, but, undeterred, the crowd closes in. The air turns. As if under control by the same set of invisible strings, the crowd raises their right hands and press against the side of their necks. Glyphs flare crimson, and their hair melts from silver and black to black alone; their clothing fades from color to gray.

The marker of Unlit.

My face plummets, along with my courage.

One of the crowd darts in and jabs something at our prowler. It rears up on its hind legs with a tormented wail. Screaming, I fall back against Anya, sending us both tumbling to the ground. Dazed from the fall, deafened by the cyclonic roar of the crowd, I squint up at the sky. It burns with green flame.

Hands tug me to my feet. Anya's. Roje's too. Blood trails from a gash down the former's brow; she encases the two of us and Roje in a golden sphere of protection. The crowd is gone—they've been replaced by the Witchfire. Smokeless, but hot enough that Aiyca's damp air is already beginning to dry; it has cut us off from our Stealths. Roje thrusts a dagger through Anya's shield at its wall; when he draws it back, the metal is dripping, melted.

"Don't let the fire—" She breaks off in a coughing fit; her shield flickers, dims, flashing in and out of existence as her concentration wanes.

I clutch at my own chest, mouth dry and lungs ablaze. What will kill us faster: suffocation or burning? The latter seems to be the stronger contender as, heat mounting, we're forced closer together. The prowlers toss their heads, mewl with a heartbreaking melancholy. When Anya looks at me, red-eyed, with streaks of tears or sweat—I can't tell—running down her cheeks, her face is bleak. It says, *there is no way out of this.* Clutching his axe, Roje looks between the two of us, and resignation seems to settle on his brow too.

No. We cannot die. Not here at the beginning. This cannot be the end!

Was it the mayor? Did he betray us to the Unlit?

Or was it *Iraya* somehow? My hand curls around the bargain on the opposite wrist. She could be here, managing these flames as they burn away my claim to the throne. As if in confirmation, the fire flares, sparking as it grows in ferocity. Within its depths, something seems to stir. Something seems to . . . No.

That isn't a pair of *eyes* looking back at me from the flames.

"Jazmyne, someone's coming!"

I turn, squint at where Anya levels a finger. A sizzling gateway bisects the flames, through which a familiar witch swaggers. Mudda have mercy.

Roje steps forward, draws his axe back, but Iraya Adair doesn't even look at him. Arrogant, always so arrogant, she sends a half smile my way before glancing around at the cyclone of flames, whistling. "If you wanted my attention, all you had to do was say so."

"I didn't even know you were *here*." But I suspected.

"Since I am, why don't I do what we both know you need me to?" She proffers her left hand; the right I notice now holds on to Kirdan's wrist.

"This isn't your fire?"

"No. This is a rescue, Cariot. But by all means, take your time. It's not like this is a life-or-death situation or anything." She glances over my shoulder, into the flames; the levity in her expression hardens. "Well?" she snaps, suddenly fierce and impatient.

Though it pains me, I take her hand.

"If you want to live, pirate, Stealth," she says, "I suggest you hold on too."

Anya's hand slides into my own; before I can check that Roje is with us, we're sifting away from the fire, tunneling through time and space to where the heat no longer touches us—and then I'm being hauled onto my feet, choking and spluttering, yanked mercifully away from Iraya and Kirdan.

IRAYA

One Hour Earlier

More than being impenetrable, whatever concoction of instant night the Healer threw is *cold*. Gelid air scrapes against my skin like a thing with claws of ice. A shiver rakes down my neck, spikes through each finger; every part unprotected by the Stealth apparel burns beneath a frigid flame. A conduit flares before me; the lambent light blinks in the hilt of Kirdan's shadowcat pommel, illuminating the violent purple beneath eyes that are, even now, fierce with wrath. In response to his silent call, one by one, golden lights respond in the gloom, revealing the remaining five council members, as well as Delyse and Shamar.

"Where's the Bush Healer?" Kirdan demands.

"Gone." The Warrior shakes her head. "And so is the Squaller. We thought we knew our allies. They served with us for five years. They know *everything*."

"And we know something too now. They have a Master.

They march to the drumbeat of a conductor. But really, from here on out, you have to be smarter." My breath swirls in an angry, chilled cloud. "None of us can assume. You shouldn't have before, and you can't when we know the Unlit and Jade Guild are entangled." I look into every shocked, wary face. Only Kirdan is alert, unsurprised. "Now isn't the time to talk particulars." Not when I don't know who among them I can trust. "But if you're against me when the time comes, I will find and deal with you. If you are with me, you already know what needs to be done."

Rally the Obeah, spread the word: a battle will be fought on these shores imminently.

The council, shaken, nods. Still, who among them will run back to the Unlit? Any? All? This is why I need Shamar and Delyse to remain here and keep Aiyca out of the Unlit's hands—out of *everyone's* hands except our own.

"It may not mean much," the Recondite says; her fear makes her look decidedly less haughty. "But we will do what we can to keep Aiyca safe." She glances over her shoulder, into the gloom. "Did you hear—" With a scream so pained it spears through me, the witch is tugged back into the darkness by something I cannot see. I *feel* the malignance of its presence beneath the choking chill though—a spiky wrongness that curls around my heart and clenches, slowing its beat. It's unlike anything that's befallen me before.

"They're here." The Warrior raises her conduit, a beautiful golden broadsword. "The beasts are *here*. Take the empress and leave. Now."

"No."

"No?" Shamar, Delyse, and the witches return in unison.

Kirdan sighs.

"No," I repeat, anger burning away the chill of the darkness.

Like responds to like, the Unlit seem to have forgotten; I'm all too happy to show them that in killing my family, they didn't create the monster I will set upon them.

They freed her.

"Give me some light."

Kirdan's conduit alone brightens; Shamar's is weak beside it. Delyse, and what remains of the council, looks from me to the Warrior. For the gods' sakes.

"Light *and* heat," she finally relents.

The conduits each witch carries, swords, gauntlets, jewelry, batons, swell in a golden chorus of power and warmth—true warmth. The kind derived from love, from their ancestors, a white-gold shield of it that pushes and pushes at the surrounding darkness until there is a crack—a splintered fragment, and the evernight begins to peel away.

"Keep going," I urge, eyes scanning the place where the Recondite disappeared.

Shamar curses. "There!"

A thick obsidian tail slinks across the witch's face and draws back into the shrinking dark. I start for it; Kirdan whips an arm out to block me.

"I wouldn't," he warns. "You don't know this enemy well enough to get close."

He's not wrong. Leaning around him, my next words are for the council. "Is that all you've got?" I shout. "We need to blind that bastard!"

I do.

Beneath the cowl of the hood, Kirdan's eyes, luminous as Witchfire, narrow as if he heard my thought.

"This is the time to stop looking at me," I warn him, and then, "Cover your eyes!" I shout to the others.

"Whaap'm?" someone calls.

"I'm about to."

For the second time, my naevus builds. It's a controlled crescendo now, building toward an epic chorus in my bones, my blood, my flesh—and then it explodes, spreading out in a flare of white-gold light. Peeling my eyes open beneath its glare is like looking through the sun, but it becomes easier with every passing second, like I am that glowing ball of ancient flame. I scan the space. There, by the door, something vast yet indeterminate in shape smashes through to evade my power. Maybe if I push more, I can catch it. My body burns with will, like I could remake myself if I so choose.

A chilled hand slips into my left. Another sweeps my braids back. "Enough," Kirdan breathes into my ear. "Enough, Iraya."

You haven't the gold, I tell myself. Even with the cool bite against my palm—more than Kirdan's hand, another of his conduit weapons to help me channel. Holding on to his voice, repeating *Enough* in my ear, I blink back the light until it fades, rescinds.

"My gods." The Warrior gapes at me; Delyse and Shamar do too.

Kirdan's hand falls from my neck. "I knew it." He relinquishes my hand too. "When did you find the time to get into trouble with the ancestors on the peninsula?"

"Never mind that now," Shamar says. "Your coin."

Charred and smoking, it's closer to black than gold now. I'm not without dismay as I clasp its smoking remains. However tiny, it was my first conduit.

Sobs echo through the heights of this wreck, distracting me from my ruined coin. The remaining council members surround the fallen Recondite.

"She's dead," Delyse doesn't need to clarify. "And the beast escaped."

Someone needs to ensure no one else dies today.

You?

"We should leave." Shamar watches the council, his brow laden with grief. "It isn't safe."

"No," I say again. *Me.*

Kirdan shakes his head. "You've become fond of that word."

What reason have I to leave if there's nothing to return to?

"Shamar, I need you and Delyse to go and warn the Obeah in the building that there is a monster on the loose."

"What about you?" he asks.

"We all saw that I can defend myself." I force myself to hold his gaze, lest he realizes that the moment he leaves with Delyse, I plan to run. "I used a Deleterious Doll on the peninsula." For a moment like this. "My naevus will come with more ease, more impact, than those in the building who have only a coin."

"But your conduit is dead," Delyse argues. "The dagger you have is borrowed."

"She can keep them," Kirdan says, settling. "I'll stay with her too."

Delyse takes one look at the exhaustion in his face, unavoidable since his hood was blown back by my magic, and sets her jaw like she means to argue.

"No more Obeah can die today," I cut in before she can voice her objections. "Go find Adriel, any others, and watch Shamar's back." I look at him too. "And you watch hers."

"Stick to the plan and we'll meet again," Kirdan adds.

He's not entirely wrong. There is a plan. Mine.

Step one is dismantling the group, which happens as Delyse and Shamar run for the hall; next is to convince Kirdan that, if he wishes for me to help with pest control in Zesia, he needs to sift me to the Skylands first. We two go—he doesn't need to linger after we've arrived—I win them round, and then we fly back to Aiyca on the backs of their lionized creatures to extinguish the Unlit's pets.

"You and I should talk," Kirdan says.

"I agree. A promising start."

But before any more is said, screams rend the air, coming from the city outside. We jerk toward their direction. A visceral pitch of terror, it sets my teeth on edge.

"They're attacking the parish," the Warrior clarifies, her voice hoarse. "The Unlit." She rises, leaving her fallen sistren to approach Kirdan and me. "It was our intention, the guild's, to commandeer the ports." An almighty crash, like two boulders being thrown against one another, booms with deafening efficacy. "We wanted them under Obeah control before using your presence here, Empress, to rally the Obeah into rising against the Alumbrar." The foreknowledge doesn't lessen the sting of her words. "Now the Unlit are using the strategy against us! It's why they sought to kill us today."

"They didn't mean to kill you."

The other witches join her in looking at me like I'm stakki.

Stalwart beside me, Kirdan nods his agreement. "To do so out here suggests amateurism, and we know the Unlit to be calculated. Patient. They've waited ten years to move against Aiyca."

"Killing off any symbol of resistance where no one can bear witness?" I add. "Come now." Chaos rises in volume; the thud of fleeing footsteps, the cries of the terrified. "Hope isn't something to be quietly snuffed out. It's a blaze to be smothered before an audience." By those wreaking havoc outside. A frown bows my forehead. "And if they knew I'd be here, then they're expecting that show . . . from me." Less than a person of flesh and bone, a symbol.

"Iraya," Kirdan cautions, somehow knowing me too well. "It's a trap."

"If what you say is true, then yeh mon, it is. And you cannot give them what they want," the Poisoner adds; her sistren nod their agreement, emphatic. "For our order to have a chance, you must be a cure, a salve, not the weapon running others through."

Above, the ceiling releases the groan of something dying. We all turn our faces up to a sky that's suddenly more visible as the metal roof, the sharp severing edge of it, angles downward like a guillotine and falls—for one second at least. In the next, my hand is in Kirdan's and we have sifted through the magical spaces to the council; in the third, with the five witches in tow, we sift once more and slip back into existence outside the building in a heap on the ground. Kirdan rolls away, but not before I notice the blood streaming from his nose. We all turn to the warehouse; part of its roof burns with green flame, Witchfire.

"Unlit. We need to get to the port," I say, lowering a hand to help the Warrior to her feet. "That's what they're going after, and the Unlit cannot triumph here."

"I agree," she puffs. "But not with your aid."

"Do you think this is the time for tradition?"

"Who are we when we abandon the principles we have relied on for so long?"

Different.

New.

Necessary.

"They can see me as they have never seen an Adair ruler before." I can be the symbol the Jade Guild want. For this morning, *I can be that.* An emblem to rally Aiyca's Obeah. Dawn after the choking darkness of night.

A Lost Empress who has indeed been found.

The Warrior shakes her head. "Changing strategy means our ruler needs to be somewhere our enemy does not expect. So bring us back that army, Empress." Haunted, her eyes flit between my own. "Or there might not be an island for you to rule when all is said and done."

"Respectfully—" Or its opposite, I don't care. "I'm not going anywhere yet." Not while babel continues to sing its bitter refrain across the city. "Coral Garden cannot fall."

"You can't either." Kirdan's eyes narrow at the city. "You know we should leave."

"I know they wanted a show." And my order *needs* a show. After all this time, they need to see Empress Adair, to know the family they followed is fighting for them, to keep the hope alive while I'm away. "Far be it from me to disappoint them. Now, are you with me?" I ask Kirdan, challenge him and his lingering stare as he rises back onto his feet.

"*I* am certainly not with you," the Warrior blusters, unsheathing the mighty broadsword. "We are not," she amends, as her sistren fan out on either side of her. "If you won't leave, we'll send you somewhere safe."

A shield balloons out of my ruined conduit coin; the size of my upper torso, head, and shoulders, it's hardly impressive, a fact confirmed by a scoff from the Master before me—until a second shield condenses around my own, particle by shimmering particle, magnifying it into a coruscating wall between the Warrior and Kirdan and me. Beside me, the prince glowers.

"Kidnapping doesn't become you, Obeah," he growls. And I can forgive his hypocrisy, for though he holds both weapons, there's no mistaking that he doesn't require either of them to take this witch on—that he is willing to. For me. "I don't want to hurt any of you, but I will."

"Either you can listen to my plans," I call across to the witches, "give me orders of your own to help, or I'm going to the port to stand between it and the Unlit."

"You are doing no such thing!" The Artisan of Metal takes a menacing step forward.

So it will be like this.

"I'm going to ensure the city's residents closest to the port remain indoors. Any Jade Guild I see will be incapacitated for you to take in for questioning. You should do so too. Stand between the port and the Unlit, magically. Shielding is a good idea." Holding out my hand, I glance up at Kirdan, willing him not to let me down. "See you there." He's obedient, for once, and his hand engulfs mine before we sift away once more.

We land in the cramped confines of the city, on a sidewalk thick with running residents. Anticipating Kirdan's weakness, I grab his arm to keep him afoot. A stampede of frightened people rush toward us. We're forced to slip between two stone town homes.

"Why are you helping me?" I demand, now we're alone. However interesting it was that he stood by me, while Delyse and Shamar did not, Kirdan never does what I want.

With a wince, he tightens the vambrace strapped to his left wrist. "You're determined to fling yourself into the path of danger at every opportunity, without the full range of your magic, and I know you have another idea than the one you told the council." He tugs at the right vambrace. "You always have ideas you don't share. So what is it? Confessing will be easier than guessing how you need help."

He's not wrong. Coral Garden's residents don't need me to tell them to seek cover. They're doing that on their own.

"But why do you want to help me?"

The clamor quiets as his eyes meet mine. "Do you need me to say it again?"

No.

"I want to lure out the Unlit master the Healer spoke of. Or let slip," I proffer, answering his first question. "Knowing that someone is controlling them makes this all easier. To go after the one is to go after them all. And the easiest way to do that is to start a fire of my own." Word about my presence in the city needs to spread, fast. There is no conflagration like the Adair name.

"And the Unlit?"

"Once I've seen the face of whoever is leading them, I leave." I can't fight and win today. I can't do either without an army, the full extent of my magic, and a conduit of my own. "*We* leave."

No surprise passes across Kirdan's features. "Without Delyse and Shamar?"

They'll be done with the warehouse by now and moving on to the next step in the plan they haven't shared with me.

"Aiyca needs them here, and me in the Skylands." I'll send a message before they can attempt to join me.

"Why not Zesia?"

"What?"

"Why didn't you consider traveling to Zesia?"

Stumped by the question, I answer honestly. "Um, history?"

Straightening, Kirdan hits me with the full intensity of his stare. "I asked you once if you considered being more, doing better. Did you think I was omitting the dissolution of the relationship between our islands?"

A tumultuous crash rocks the city.

"I don't have the time or patience to stand here and argue common sense with you. I'm going to the Skylands one way or another," I tell Kirdan, scanning the alley walls for purchase. "Either come, or get out of my way." Identifying a ladder, I stride toward it and begin to climb, hand over hand, until I reach the rooftop and hoist myself up.

Kirdan's already there, swine.

"You could have offered me a . . ." My words trail off at the sight of the skyline, the undulating rooftops of the city punctuated by small jade fires that are candles in comparison with the blaze to the north, a great cyclone of flame that curls upward to the sky. That looks like something this mysterious master would create—one with a god complex, for it looks as though it had been wrought by some great celestial hand.

"Say we leave," Kirdan begins, turning my focus from the burning skyline to him. "You and me. Are we chasing a better world, or running from this one?"

"If you're asking whether I'm afraid to walk into the fire—" I pace back several steps. "Come and find out." Breaking into a run, I clear the rooftop and leap onto the next. Footfalls sound behind me, gain, and match my speed; together, Kirdan and I sprint across the city to the beacon, the signal, that can only be for me.

A war won't be won today, but I'm not averse to landing the first blow.

7

JAZMYNE

Iraya stands across the stretch of cracked concrete with Kirdan, between two rusty ships in this graveyard teeming with dead vessels. It's ripe with the stink of rot, and if we're killed, the carrion crows will find us before people do. And Kirdan looks like an emissary of Death, concealed beneath the wide lip of his cloak's hood. As for the Obeah-witch, dressed in Stealth black, she carries her smirk like she is of their métier too. All bite, a thing of shadows and venom.

"You're with the Unlit now?" I call across the distance.

"As I can trust you to make an ass out of you and me," Iraya returns without missing a beat. "So can you trust that my brain hasn't hemorrhaged. If you're struggling to keep up, that's a no. I haven't sided with the true enemy." Her head tilt reduces the range between us; her face, her *smug* face, becomes all too clear. "One of them, anyway."

"Then what do you want?" Anya calls across the distance.

"That's an interesting way of offering your blessings, mon." All rhythm and song, Iraya sounds unperturbed. Relaxed. She isn't . . . she isn't surprised about what is happening here. "You can think about how you'll make things up to me while I have a talk with your leader. Alone."

"No."

"It's all right," I tell Anya, though I wouldn't put it past the Obeah-witch to rescue me only so she can kill me herself. "I'll be fine."

Iraya yawns. "Can you be fine over here, then?"

"If that's the case, then we keep the prince." In his grip, the handle of Roje's axe groans.

Iraya glances at Kirdan as though she'd forgotten he was by her side—close, by her side. Enough that I cannot see where they meet, only that they are connected in a way he and I never were, for all her next words try to convey.

"Have at him." She steps away; Kirdan sways as if they truly are joined by some invisible thread. "This way, Doyenne—or is it Queen?" She turns with a look of mock bemusement. "Difficult to tell."

I bite back the reality of a magicless *regent*.

"Jazmyne." Anya taps her head, reminding me about the combs she installed in my afro before we left the palace, conduit gold infused with a fragment of her will.

My curls fall around my face when I catch up to Iraya. She leans against a wall with an insouciance so potent, she could bottle it.

"I'd say don't try anything funny, mon," she says, straightening like the snap of a whip. "But you've attempted to kill me twice now, so do." That indolent air modulates into something tighter, more predatory.

I edge forward a step. "I still taste your magic, Obeah."

"And I your hatred, Alumbrar." She mirrors my movement. "Tell me, descendant of stars." Her voice is a caress. "Is it true you burn brightest when you start to collapse? Because the Jade Guild are not who you think they are—many are Unlit, and they have plans to douse all light in Aiyca."

"I know."

An elegant brow arches on Iraya's forehead.

"I was going to tell you that."

"To *take* me, you mean," she corrects, dares. "If you managed to find me."

I could.

I could draw on the intentions simmering in those fire-touched eyes and force her to come with me—take Kirdan too, to keep him from causing further strife.

"But I found you."

"How?"

"I was looking for someone else. The Unlit's leader has made a declaration for Aiyca. Did you know that too?"

"I did. You mean to stop them too, this leader."

Ira scuffs her sandal against a fragment of metal. "This feels familiar."

"Indeed. So what if I didn't take you?" I pose. "Where would that leave us, with our backs *to* one another again?"

"I suppose that would make it easier for you to put another knife in mine."

"I mean it, Iraya." My tongue traces across my bottom

lip. It's as dry as my mouth. As acrid tasting. "Can we shelve what's between us until this threat has abated? An amnesty, if you will. I can't—I need—" I shake my head; perhaps it will loosen the words that won't come. "I've won the fealty of a ship, its crew, to enter the race for Pirate Queen."

Her eyes burn all the way across the shipyard. "How?"

"I need the map for the Conduit Falls," I say, ignoring her question. "You said you were unaware of its whereabouts, but *do* you know where it is?"

"No. And I wouldn't hand over its whereabouts if I did. You can't give away the location to the falls. If the pirates get hold of its—"

"You think me that stakki?"

"You asked the question, didn't you, mon? Not to mention the fact that you're going to leave the island. While it's under siege. What sort of doyenne does that?"

Leaving is what's best, I don't bother justifying. Frustrated, always frustrated in her presence, I scrub a hand across my forehead. "What do you plan on doing to help? *Will* you help?"

She takes a long look at me. Her face is now unreadable with a calculated blankness, and just as I'm ready to give up and demand Anya sift us out of here—

"There's a door in the doyenne's study," Iraya says, "to the right of the rear side of the desk. It leads down into a trove." She exhales. This is costing her something, to give me this information. "There's gold in there. Some of it conduit. As you say, you have my blood. You'll need it to get in, along with saying my surname—murmuring it over and over, as you would a lover's."

"I *despise* you."

Her laughter rings like the mocking cry of the gulls over-head.

When they come, my next words are halted. "What will I do with the gold?"

"Every story is a lie until someone breathes truth into it." Iraya shrugs a single shoulder. "Including Anansi's tale about the jéges. It doesn't have to be a perennial cataract of golden coins. You don't have to embark on a voyage that will take you away from Aiyca for a great length of time. And you shouldn't."

"You mean for me to deceive my allies?"

"A tone of surprise, and yet you have already shown your-self to be a liar to your supposed allies." She points at herself. "Do you think your footing will be any steadier at sea than it is on land? Give them a semblance of what they need, if you must, and then return to what matters, protecting Aiyca. It isn't magi alone you have to fear." She goes on to explain why the enemy have been using Witchfire, and the ground that *was* solid beneath my feet seems to buckle and withdraw, along with my nerve.

"Monsters?" I whisper.

"From beyond the veil."

In the flames . . . Mudda have mercy. I *did* see eyes.

"Who's bringing them here?"

"I don't know. I was hoping you'd have some idea of how long they've been operating?"

"I—I do!" The missive. Blessings to the Supreme Being. "I don't have a name, but I do know they've been active since around the time you arrived from Carne."

Iraya frowns. "Almost months and they're still setting fires. That suggests they're not ready to do whatever they're planning. And I won't be here to learn what that is. . . ."

"You're leaving?"

"Did you kill the shields?"

"You can't leave." *You can't leave* me.

"Stay with me, will you?" She clicks. "The shields! Did you kill them?"

"No. We—we've retained only two thirds of those you kill—" Her eyes darken. "Of those that remained after what occurred in the vestibule. The rest fled."

"Whoever is commanding the Unlit tried to kill us both, this morning. It won't be the final attempt on our lives. While I can defend myself, you, on the other hand, require all the aid you can muster. So if there's a *Ford* in your custody, ask for him. Or Nel. They can rally those who fled too. Tell Ford it's time to put those fingers to good use."

"I'm not saying that. It's foul."

"This is war." Her mouth tightens. "Or it will be unless we cut it out at the root. Things will become far fouler if you're gallivanting at sea, and Aiyca is left exposed. Arguably, it's exposed now as you haven't inherited your magic."

I flinch, her words a physical slap.

Regent.

Who with monsters on reins will fear me, Aiyca's magically impotent leader?

"Stay," I find myself whispering.

Something torn crests the surface of her face for a moment.

"I can't. We need a skilled army. But I will return. In the interim, I need to trust that you won't let the Unlit control this island. That you'll fight them as hard as you fought me these past few months. Only, don't lose this time." Before I can tell her that *she* lost, she plows ahead. "They've tried to box the island in by burning ships and ruining trade from our ports. They haven't succeeded with Coral Garden; the real Jade Guild are finalizing that as we speak, and they can help with the last two ports. Once you've freed the shields, send Ford to liaise with them. They have a thing with rulers getting involved in matters of war." She waves a hand, rolls her eyes. "But no matter how much they try to push you out of the decision process, don't let the Unlit establish a center of gravity, you understand?"

"I don't."

"Do not let them pick where we meet in battle."

That's no small feat, especially when I'll be sailing for queen.

"What if the war starts before you return?"

She tips her head to the side and looks at me with something like pity. "We lose."

You wanted this, I remind myself, choking back the sick feeling in my belly.

"So you *will* free the shields, and they *will* connect you with the real Jade Guild. Together you *will* find whatever it is the Unlit want, and you *will* prevent them from taking it. If not forever, then at least long enough for me to return with an army. Can I count on you to do that, or do I need to—"

"You can." They might be the first words spoken without guile between us.

"Good. I won't let anyone who doesn't deserve Aiyca claim it."

Threat noted. We are not allying, only sharing an enemy. But then . . . which of us will rule in the end? Iraya issues a secretive smile as if she heard my unspoken question and has no doubts about which of us, which witch, will emerge the victor.

"Keep the Mirror of Two Faces at hand," she says. "Should you need anything that doesn't involve your feelings or emotions—if Aiyca is about to be sundered and the palace under siege—you can communicate with me through it."

"There are two mirrors?"

Her smile is saccharine enough to hurt my teeth.

Of course there are two. . . .

My sigh cuts through her silence. "What about the bargain?"

"It's still in play." The fingers on her left hand flex. "But while none of us can kill one another, others can." She glances across the city where chaos still rings, however diminished. "Before, I didn't mean it when I said we could be stronger together. Unlike you, who's clearly been thinking about it, I can't remember the exact words I used then, but I won't forget these next ones—we may have been born enemies, and once this war has been fought, no doubt we'll find ourselves on opposite sides of the line once more."

"The words you used before were better."

She issues a soft laugh, a genuine one. "No doubt, but these next ones will at least hold truth: I have looked upon your true face, Jazmyne Cariot." She sobers in her quick way, always moving from emotion to emotion before she has time to feel any too deeply, for there is pain in depth. This we both know. "And I know that it isn't your allies who will flee from it, but *our* enemies."

"Cariot and Adair." A double-edged blade angled at the heart of this world's darkness.

"Adair and Cariot," she corrects. "You'd better walk good, Alumbrar. If you fall and Aiyca is lost—"

I'll kill you myself, she doesn't need to say.

"Hold the line." She gives me an appraising look; I might think a faint glimmer of respect lurks in those fire-touched depths. If I didn't know better. "Until I return."

And the gauntlet for Aiyca is thrown.

"I'll be ready."

8

IRAYA

The bargain around my wrist seems to tighten as Jazmyne, her pirate, and her Stealth sift away.

Remember the last time you trusted that witch?

"What happened?" Kirdan asks; the question's timing is one I almost laugh at.

"I didn't kill her."

Not when the dead are watching.

Master Omnyra said someone needs to be here, in my stead. It's been confirmed more than I needed it to be that the Jade Guild don't know the length of the claws the Unlit have sunk into their side. Gods, they didn't even know they were bleeding until earlier. Greater than a flesh wound, it could exsanguinate their numbers. Where will Aiyca be then? Not to mention the fact that they're no closer to the palace now than they were when I was in Carne, training with Kaleisha, who would always defend their slow pace. Which could be a blessing, all things considered.

Jazmyne, though, she's without any green blemishes. The witch raised to inherit her mama's stolen seat. The witch who signed her death warrant for it. She will fight at every turn. Better with me than against me—a successful war cannot be fought on two fronts. This way, Obeah versus Unlit becomes Aiyca versus Unlit. Shamar and Delyse can keep an eye on Jazmyne too, feeding me missives about her movements so I can better deal with her when I return. Whatever her . . . *successes* during the Sole, Aiyca deserves a leader who incites fear, respect.

As for who that will be in the end, I don't know yet.

Exhaling, I roll my shoulders, my neck. "We should head back into the city." My order needs to see Empress Adair before we leave.

"Iraya—"

There's a muted thump, and the friction of cloth against stone. I twist around to find Kirdan slumped against a wall, his eyes closed. No. *No.* Running to him, I drop to my knees and touch his forehead. Slick with fever, it's too hot.

"Why didn't you say something!"

But he did. He said my name—called it.

Shit. *Shit.*

I scan our bleak surroundings—concrete and brick and weeds. There's nothing to roll him onto, and I can't carry him, this great lump of a man. We'll never make it back into the heart of the city like this, let alone the Skylands. *Gods-damnit.* Kirdan groans; pinched in discomfort, his forehead tightens beneath my hand. As bad as I feel, how this weakness must gut him when the scope of his body has so often borne the brunt of his pride as well as his strength—the only skill Simbarabo are valued for. The very skill I need from him to get me to the Skylands. Unless . . . unless I find a way to leave this chaos behind, travel to Queenstown, where I can catch a ship to the Skylands alone.

"You're considering leaving me, aren't you?" Kirdan's voice cracks.

Could I leave him here knowing no one will find him until the Jade Guild have finished securing Coral Garden? What if he dies? The answer is born from a quickening heart, a twisting in my belly. My hand drifts down to his cheek. I can't. For whatever reason, I can't. But what do we have besides the mirror, the Grimoire I don't have the magical acuity to use, and my scarification, that can get us out of here? Us. Him and me.

Wait. My *scars*.

Taking Kirdan's left forearm, I wrench up his sleeve and find the twin to my Glyph of Connection there. Anansi said magi would use these glyphs in battle, sharing blood with one another to combine their magic, each becoming the pillar the other needed when their foundations splintered. That seems to be about now.

"New plan." Coral Garden is out. Returning with the Skylands' aerial army is more of a dramatic *hello, remember me* anyway. My order will still see me, an Adair, only later. "I have an idea. As usual, it's brilliant." Kirdan doesn't move when I lean across his body and unsheathe his hunting knife. "Nod if you can hear me."

After a moment, his chin dips.

"We're going to exchange blood, and I'll give you the energy you need to sift us to Queenstown." As for how we'll find Shamar and Delyse, a ship out of here, I'll figure that out once we're there. "Are you with me?"

After too many seconds, and right before I'm about to slap him alert, he nods.

Kirdan's skin parts with ease beneath the blade. I draw in a breath, another, and then run my tongue across the back of his hand. Potent with dirt and sweat, his blood is even less palatable than it would be otherwise, and yet . . . the hairs on the back of my neck stand as something inexplicable washes over me. This, the sharing of blood, is intimate, beyond that of skin-to-skin contact. After this, the two of us will be more than linked. We'll be one. Bonded in a bid against death.

Once a neat tourniquet has been tied around Kirdan's wound, I slice the palm of my own hand and offer it to him. He doesn't move.

"Come on." Cupping the back of his neck, I guide him to my hand, shivering as his tongue stutters across it. "What's the guzzu?"

"There are no words," he murmurs. "Only will. You have to . . ." He runs his tongue across his bottom lip; it's still stained with my blood. "Want it. Want life. Want . . . me. As I want you." He doesn't hold my eyes for long, but his words . . . they are enough.

Enough to undo me.

I wish there were more resistance, but the door I shut on the peninsula swings open without difficulty. The union of two glyphs would have meant enough if I linked with Delyse, or Shamar. But for two founding family members, two heirs, even reduced as we are, I know it's going to be significant before Kirdan clasps my hand, opens his eyes to meet mine, and awakens the power slumbering inside each of us.

Life sparks between our palms and then plumes outward. Detritus rattles and slams into the walls. Kirdan's mangled hair blows back from his face as color filters into his cheekbones, softening their angles and hollows; it rises up into his eyes, which brighten as they become less hooded—as the Adair might raises its primogenial head in acknowledgment to a twin power and purrs as they twine together. Far from feeling depleted, I am replenished, filled with an effervescence I did not expect. It's like being bathed in supernal light.

"I didn't think it would be like this." My voice comes out as a whisper. "I feel stronger too. Why?"

"The glyph recycles energy, filters it through both magi." Kirdan stands, in fine fettle once more, and pulls me up with him. "And not every magi has a will as strong as yours."

One my order need to see before we leave; I say so to Kirdan.

"We can't go back into the city."

"Yeh mon," I murmur, taking another look at our surroundings, the high mast of a disused chimney, the neighboring buildings that share its height, its unignorable presence. "I caught on to that fact, but I have an idea."

With Kirdan's aid, we don't have to climb up the building to sketch my message with magic, to emblazon a burning sigil of my own in white-gold flame.

"Steady." Chin tipped toward the sky, Kirdan follows the

words I will into being. "Just like writing a message in a mental journal."

"Not quite," I grind out, sweating at the effort it takes to render each letter on the buildings above. It's more than keeping them alight, it's making them legible, attractive, and believing I can do it with the glyphs behind my ears, my borrowed weapon. The last element of channeling magic I thought I'd have difficulty with is self-belief.

"Almost there." Kirdan's hand tightens around mine; the flow of magic between us, a circling current, a wind tunnel, strengthens as the last letters come to life in a sizzling manifestation of will, and my message is at last complete.

THE ADAIRS REMEMBER
THE LOST EMPRESS LIVES

"Any more detail and my order will take it as an invitation to fight, I think."

"I agree. And we need to go anyway. Delyse and Shamar know what to do if we separate. As do I."

"And what's that?"

"Apologize now." Kirdan's eyes dip, and time seems to slow, to slide and slither like something insidious. "You'll need your anger where we're going. Forgive me, Iraya. Again. And don't forget to hold your breath."

Before I have time to process his words, we blink out of sight; the world percolates around us in a blurred vacuum before we tear into existence somewhere bright, indiscernible—*high*, I realize as my stomach shoots to my mouth, and we fall. Down. Down.

A hand clenches around mine. "Remember to hold your breath!" Kirdan shouts before obsidian waters swallow us both in one fell gulp.

Warm, it's not unlike being submerged in a bath. Willing my chest to calm, to wait until I can draw breath, I kick out once, twice, my eyes squinting to find daylight to guide me out. But my movements are slowed by the thick sludge of liquid, and there is no light to be seen. The black depths fail to react like the water I was accustomed to as a pickney. Rather than washing over me, the salt eventually buffering me to the surface, watery *fingers* latch on to my pants with an otherworldly strength; they lace through my hair until bony knuckles grind into my scalp, cutting and slicing with their too many joints. My chest tightens against a scream.

These fine fingers do not belong to Kirdan.

Did this bag-o-wire miss the Skylands and sift us into the *Monster's Gulf* instead? That tightness in my chest expands in a band of fire, one that urges me to open my mouth and give it release. I don't. But I won't be able to fight for much longer.

Will it be the water or the creatures that dwell within it that kills me?

No. That honor is Kirdan's. He'll likely present my bloated corpse to the Obeah Witches Council, might even shed a few false tears about how I fought to save both our lives. They'll no doubt honor him in my death—for, enthralled by the grip of a living sea, I am dying.

Knowing Kirdan, I was likely dead before I hit the water.

9

JAZMYNE

I always believed chaos was fast, like a break.

While my coronation dissolved into anarchy in less than half a day, in the wake of the Unlit's latest attack, I understand that it's more akin to erosion. Their subtle deterioration of the late doyenne's rule, now mine, has left the strongest parts of this island, the ports from which we trade, where the magic-less majority travel from, weakened. It's a problem that only portends further issues, both with the strain it will place on the use of conduits for magical travel, something I'll need to limit to preserve gold stores for the impending war, and whatever they mean to do next.

Chaos isn't about speed. It's about perseverance.

Once the attack has ebbed and the too few bag-o-wires who didn't flee when faced with Iraya's council have been rounded up and transported back to the palace holding cells, Anya and I return to Jannah's villa. But my sistren's focus, like mine, remains down in the parish. Roje lingered to oversee the Jade Guild Squallers extinguishing the Witchfire that devoured diving and trade ships. From a distance. As Iraya said, her order wasn't in the mood to talk with me; whether that's due to the fact that I am Alumbrar, or the leader they didn't choose to stand behind, I do not know, but working together as she suggested is not an option.

The Nameless stepped up to commission Artisans of Metal, non magical stone-masons, and Wood to begin repairs in the city; they also supplied provisions and places to rest come nightfall for those whose vessels lay like confetti in the harbor.

"If this is victory," I murmur, "I don't ever want to witness loss."

Leveling a look of caution my way, Anya casts a silencing sphere around us. Still recovering from the effects of the Witchfire, her protection is only large enough to go around our heads.

"They had no presider," she says, now that we're safe from being overheard by the Nameless waiting in Jannah's villa. "Neither do two additional parishes. The Jade Guild helped us today, but at Iraya's behest. The sooner we fortify the island with a new council, the harder the Obeah and the Unlit will find pulling it apart. Is it four seats for Nameless and two to Roje?"

"Yeh mon." More than managing their parishes, whoever I select will need to keep the island safe from threat while I am at sea. I'll need cunning custos, but not too cunning that they'll join forces with Ionie, Ormine, and Mariama to overthrow me. "Two councils. Or one main council and then a second group, a Witches Council and seven presiders."

"But that's never been done."

"We have experienced many firsts, sistren. I could ask the Nameless to choose," I muse. "They know each other better than I."

"That's not a bad idea."

"It won't make me look weak?"

"Meting out responsibility is part of being a leader, Jaz. The worst part, in my opinion."

"Indeed. We'd better make haste."

With a tense nod, Anya rescinds her silencing sphere and we dismount.

"There is one good thing to come from all of this, you know," she murmurs as we climb the steps, her voice as soft as the cicada and cricket in the encroaching bush. "At least Roje didn't come; you won't have to tell the Nameless about him, the pirates, and risk a repeat of what happened with the presiders."

As quick as he is, he might have offered to stay behind to avoid this meeting—something I envy him for when, the moment we cross the threshold, Anya and I are bombarded with a volley of questions, demands really, not unlike the earlier meeting with the presiders.

Shields spring from the cadres to force the Gennas back.

"Say the word, Regent," the closest cadre member to me murmurs—Pasha, I think the shaven-haired Stealth's name is. "I have guzzu to silence every tongue in here."

"Your gold," I return. "It should be preserved, the cadres' too. Put out your shields." Pasha's head turn is the only indication he heard me. The shields fall one by one.

"You forget yourselves," I say to the Nameless, keeping myself from shouting. The late doyenne had little difficulty quieting a room with her softest voice. "You, the vanguard meant to stand between this island and panic, who now shriek like calves in the face of a butcher's knife." I make myself meet every face, even those that are filled with scorn—the naysayers; without Light Keeper as my shield, I suspect those doubters will be eager to land their silver-tipped barbs.

But I will take no further hits today.

"To the astute among you, you will know by now that we are under siege. To the less wise, perhaps your disdain overwhelms your logic—and that is all it will overwhelm." No matter my fear, I must be brave. "Firstly, in addition to the traditional council the late doyenne instated, I require four of you to make up numbers on a war council of seven—" I decide, now I'm forced to think about it. Two councils means more opinions, yes, but also more magical protection. Roje's pirates won't care about the parishes. This way, there is space for all. "Mastery or close to, with examination certificates to verify," I continue. "I'm also instating six Gennas to sit on the traditional council, and watch over a parish each. To do what I deem best for Aiyca as our sun retreats under the shadow of war."

"Against who?" someone calls. "Obeah?"

"Unlit."

There are murmurs of shock, expressions of disbelief.

"The fringe outcasts have been rallying against this island for quite some time. All instances of Witchfire, the attacks on the ports—them. Our enemy for the first time is not the Obeah. They have their own grievances with the Unlit." I hesitate. To mention uniting with Iraya's order now might alienate the Nameless and prompt another overthrow. Ruling is more than being a predator, it is being a secret keeper too, a lone force to bear the weight of a world that will shatter should it fall. "We must prioritize, Alumbrar, if we are to survive to fight any greater battles down the line. Tell me." I turn to Anya, standing close behind my right shoulder. The place of a first. "How many Nameless are there approximately?"

"Tens of thousands."

"Tens of thousands," I muse. "Consider your first challenge mathematical," I say to the crowd. "I need only eleven to stand by my side before the island when I tell them that our decade of peace may reach a dark end."

"Regent." Jannah steps forward. "How will we choose?"

I wet my lips with my tongue. "The challenge is yours." But the mistake will be all mine if the Unlit continue to triumph in their crusade. "And I expect your answer no later than the night following the Ninth."

An evening storm rides into Cwenburg on the heels of the jungle-prowler Anya and I share.

Forks of lightning illuminate St. Mary in harsh intervals; the parish is otherwise overwhelmed by the battalion of clouds gathering overhead. Sonorous peals of thunder follow, drowning out the collision of paw against earth as we gallop up the palace drive; the combined din is worsened by the crack of death banners hanging from villa windows in the parish below, audible even from our vantage atop this palm of rock.

It's as if St. Mary Parish is breaking. No, the entire island, splintering around us—a reality we've raced against as the afternoon darkened and the sun retreated. Low against Anya's back, my coiled muscles loosen as the palace gates open like an embrace ahead. Rather than go to the stables we dismount right here, hand the reins over to Xanthippe, and run up the north stairs as the sky opens its tempestuous eye and the estate is doused in rain.

A sense of unease creeps around my body like a snare as we hurry beneath arcade and between pillar, eager to see the Adair gold Iraya spoke of. Across the palace from the throne room—where the guests, attendants, are still concentrated, ignorant to all that happened across the island several hours ago—Anya and I do not encounter a soul.

Not any of the living, at least.

The dead tend to linger where they were last living, clinging to the most recent memories of what they knew. The late doyenne's echo would have been beneath this floor, but hours have passed since then. A shiver shudders across the back of my neck.

It's likely her duppy has made its way up here now.

I place a hand over Anya's before she opens the late doyenne's study door. "Do you feel that?"

"Yeh mon." Her throat bobs as she swallows. "Since we entered. But it's too early for her duppy to have any real power."

We both pretend we don't hear the question in her voice, the quiver of doubt.

Though the late doyenne's study door doesn't creak upon

opening, there's little comfort to be found as a streak of lightning flashes outside the windows; the attendants charged to clean up the mess left after the Sole unleash a unified, startled shriek.

"Leave," I order, hiding how shaken I too am. "Now."

Another charge of lightning nips at their heels.

"Iraya said she and Kirdan fought something in the trove, when they came on All Souls' Night."

Anya's face blanches. "You know I don't carry any weapons."

But I do. Slipping her combs from my afro, I pass her one, and use the second to cut my fingertips. When blood wells, I press it onto the space on the wall behind the desk and speak Iraya's surname with clear diction. Again and again the Adair name falls from my lips, is spat out, *not* murmured like a lover, but only the sky outside the windows changes, darkening while the parish flails beneath the weather's sinister salvo.

"This isn't working!" Anya snatches at my hand too long later. It's sticky with blood and stinging with the pressure of touch. "Why believe Iraya? We know she's a liar."

"Not about this."

"You say that like you know her."

"I know she means to fight for Aiyca." I take my hand back and continue smearing my blood on the walls. "Even if it's only for her to try and take it from me when she returns."

"Will you release the shields as she said?"

Xanthippe and battalion soldiers now flood Aiyca's streets in a steady stream rather than the trickle of before, which means fewer coven members here at Cwenburg, a weakness the shields in the holding cells could fortify—but what's to stop Iraya giving the order that they rise against me once we've defeated the Unlit?

"It doesn't seem wise," Anya says, with caution.

"I agree. Iraya will return with an army." The Simbarabo, at the very least, I suspect. "I don't think it wise to install more of her allies on Cwenburg's estate, not when there's the high chance of a second war before the Unlit's beasts are cold in the ground." My fingers catch a groove in the wall, finally, and a doorway separates from the wall. "Help me!"

With Anya's aid, the door yawns open; the foul stink of something rotting lands like a punch. We both retreat behind our hands.

"Gods. At least we know it's still down there and hasn't been eaten by something else."

I turn to Anya sharply. She shrugs in apology.

An unavoidable pulse from her conduit breathes life into the sconces on the walls behind the secret door. The witchlights on the walls flare white, and for a second time I am struck; in this moment, it's by the memory of the shields coming to Iraya's rescue draped in alabaster on All Souls' Night. . . . To Obeah, these sconces would be a comfort, not a blazing caution of the last time our two orders clashed.

With another look, one conveying that under no circumstances will we talk until we reach the bottom of the ancient stone steps, Anya and I enter the narrow corridor; the stench grows in strength with every descending step. I'm treated to a promise of what I can expect at Iraya's hands when Anya and I come upon the decomposing beast in the cavern at the foot of the stairs. We grimace at one another across its large body—though we soon forget the horror of its slack jaw and stiff, rotting limbs when we enter the Adair trove. Conduit gold spills from baskets and chests, hangs from hooks on the walls, and flows across the floor in a river of wealth not entirely unlike the mythical falls from Anansi's story.

"I'm not sensing any more creatures," Anya says, her conduit dulled amidst all the finery. "And thank all seven faces for that, mon." She sinks her hand into a circular pot of coins, letting them glide over her fingers in a cataract of power. "Your mama had no idea this was beneath the study all this while?"

"It's difficult to say." How well did I know her, really. "Do you think the map is in here?"

"I thought Iraya said it wasn't?" Anya cocks a challenging brow at me.

"Fine. She does lie about some things."

"Most."

"Whatever. Do you know any guzzu to summon the map?"

"I can try a few things." Anya takes an assiduous turn around the cavern, pausing to kneel in coves to ensure the guzzu she whispers penetrate every crack, all the while her conduit beams golden light across the riches.

Every story is a lie until someone breathes truth into it.

We might not find the map; indeed, wasting this energy on something only the late doyenne knew the whereabouts of might be foolish of me when I could expend my time on something else: securing a Transmuter to melt this gold down and turn it into coins. Conduit coins I might fill a waterfall somewhere in the bush with, somewhere close, enough to convince the pirates of its existence. Enough that they make me queen without having to be away for however long it would take to find the real falls.

"Lying to the entire fleet of pirates?" Anya questions when I tell her of my scheme. "Are you sure that's wise?" Arms folded across her chest, she shakes her head, silver ponytail snaking behind her. "What am I saying, of course it's unwise."

"I can't sail for an unspecified amount of time—there *isn't* any time."

"In that I agree. The Unlit did this while you were in the palace. Who can say what they'll do when they catch word that you're at sea. But why must you go at all?"

"We need—"

"To keep them compliant, yeh mon, but why does that have to be with you beneath their Coral Crown?"

"They had another candidate. Roje said as much, back at the drinking house. Even if she didn't win, none of the other nominees would work with Alumbrar, but they would ally with Obeah. It had to be me. It *has* to be." Iraya wasn't wrong, but that doesn't mean I have to remain in Aiyca. If I can settle the conflict, right the scales, my leaving doesn't have to affect matters. "So, is the ruse doable?"

Twin lines etch between Anya's eyebrows as she retreats deep in thought. I know what she'll be thinking. No Alumbrar worked with conduit gold before, and though there have been many trained in the past decade, their acuity isn't as unparalleled as one from the Order of Obeah. It'll be another risk, to ask one of their Transmuters, which means another Shook Bargain to guarantee silence. And then there's the Xanthippe who will need to come down here and carry this gold upstairs. What Iraya didn't contemplate, would never, considering how conceited she is, is that the bigger the lie, the weaker it becomes, and the likelier it is to snap.

"So long as you won't mind deceiving your pirate," Anya finally says. "It's doable."

"Roje isn't *my pirate*. He isn't even my bredren." I intend for the words to be hollow, but they sink in my belly with a foreboding weight; anchors cast down to the seabed below—is that where I'll be pitched if my deception is found out?

This isn't the Yielding; I'm not killing pickney to further my rule. But be that as it may, the decision to deceive makes me feel a lot less like the soon-to-be-crowned Doyenne Jazmyne Cariot and worryingly more like the last. And I won't ever forget how she met her end—Iraya Adair, yes, but also me. The person closest to her in the world.

"Jazmyne?"

But I can't lose Aiyca, and I cannot lose to that Obeah-witch.

"Let's see it done."

10

IRAYA

"Was she trying to swallow half the Obsidian Trench?" The question slams into my head with the weight of an axe. "Almighty!"

"Get out the way, mon! Her lungs need clearing." A second speaker, their lilt familiar, accompanies a physical blow to my chest, and then another.

Stop, I long to shout, but a barbed pain splinters through me. The water.

That sentient black sludge. Ancient and conniving, it was determined to choke me out of life, I remember, as another blow swings into my chest—a pendulum, one ticking ever closer to a permanent darkness. Because Kirdan killed me, didn't he? Or he tried to.

No shadow will be greater than the golden reach of my will.

It is but a small pith at first, but I feel its growing intensity, that slumbering power uncurl and hold on. Not *for* dear life, but *to* it. With the next swing of the pendulum, I emerge retching and spluttering up what feels like every single one of my organs.

"She's breathing!"

Slim arms limned with muscle tighten at my back, hold me while my belly empties until nothing but air and spit come out. That second voice, Delyse's, mutters words to salve while rubbing circles on my back.

"That was disgusting" is muttered by the first speaker.

My eyelids peel open beneath a bleach of light. Black slime is pooled in the sand between my hands. A grimace twists my mouth. It *is* disgusting. When I squint up, the soldier who proclaimed it first watches me the way one would a feral prowler. He stands in a rich umber uniform, like the first flare of a rising sun; a sheet of long silver hair ripples along with the alabaster cloak across his shoulders in the breeze cast from waters I cannot see but know are famous for running rivulets through this sand-dominated nation.

Not the Skylands—Zesia.

"Bag-o-wire." The word rasps through my ravaged throat.

The soldier blinks. The movement is doll-like in the flawless dark marble of his face. "It's Lieutenant General Garaycía, actually."

"Not you," Shamar says from beside him. "The prince."

"You call General Divsylar traitor?" Caution is replaced by umbrage. "You call the prince traitor?"

"Where. Is. He?"

Lip curling, the lieutenant angles his head across the way.

Stiff, it's an effort to turn my neck across the headland jutting out into obsidian waters. It's edged with bush and palm for privacy and crawls with umber-clad soldiers. Simbarabo. A phalanx of them, more with silver hair, huddle around a bundle of washed-up rags across the sand. Kirdan.

"Alive?" I croak. Though, if he didn't survive the journey here, I'll cross the veil to bring him back.

"His body needs rest to recover."

In that case, how much effort would it take to drag him back to the waters lapping at the sand? He betrayed me, *again*.

"We used our Glyphs of Connection."

Lieutenant General Garaycía's eyes widen. "Right. Well, the connection is best used for short bursts of magic. The medics are assessing him, as they have done you."

"You'll be fine after some rest too, Iraya," Delyse murmurs.

Not prison?

As a member of his doyenne's military, it's the lieutenant's job to arrest me, us—this Alumbrar lieutenant—to take us before this island's judicial system as illegal arrivals, insurgents, outlaws, not to have a Healer check me out. Despite matters clearly being different here.

Every muscle in my body screams at me to lie back down, but, eschewing help from Delyse and Shamar, I plant my feet in the sand and push. My legs quiver, my body, but it takes more mental than physical will until, with about as much grace as one can have with sick rimming their mouth, I stand to look upon who I assume to be Kirdan's right-hand man. He regards me with a cool look.

"You knew we'd come here."

"I can't say I did."

"Wrong answer, and one that, months from now"—my voice is a sinister croak—"when I am but an amusing anecdote you tell to the audiences of Zesia's drinking houses, means that I will find you when you are walking home, or perhaps already in bed with a lover between your thighs, and I will split your neck open from ear to ear." I pause, blink back tears of pain at forcing out so many words. "Slowly. Now, how about we try that again. You knew we'd come here."

His jaw clenches and then releases. "The Genna has spoken of you before."

Not a lie, but not the response he and I both know I'm looking for.

"You have a security measure, protecting this isle—the black waters we fell into." The sun is higher than it was in Aiyca, and, freed from behind the barrier of storm plaguing my home, blinding when I stare out across the surf dancing to the shore and back again. But I'm sure the black waters eventually return to blue far out at sea. "I assume it catches whoever doesn't have an invitation to visit these shores?"

Lieutenant Garaycía yields a nod.

"Why didn't Kirdan make it through?"

"It didn't recognize him. Likely for your blood in his veins. He was meant to be awake to go toe-to-toe with you. It's something he would enjoy far more than I currently am."

"Then he *was* always going to bring me here, regardless of what I said."

"Oh good," another soldier says, joining us. Obeah, judging

by his dark twin braids. "The Genna told her."

"No, mengkeh!" The lieutenant scowls at his kinsman. "He didn't."

The confirmation of their plan knocks the hard-won wind right out of my stomach.

They weren't going to keep me in Aiyca, but they never planned on accompanying me to the Skylands either. This was the destination all along.

"Iraya." Delyse's voice is small. "The Skylands wouldn't have helped us."

Damn her Stealth prowess. It takes a single thought to clear my face, to conceal the tempest eddying between my brows. Kirdan's betrayal I understand. He can't help but engage in this dance with me. Two steps forward and ten back. But Delyse and Shamar?

Am I so terrible that they chose him over me?

"We don't even know if they still have the winged army. It's been centuries since they were seen," she continues.

Like the Lost Empress?

That's beside the fact. Does she think I would hinge the plan to rescue Aiyca on a hunch? That I wouldn't gather intel, interrogate Carne's many prisoners, including runaways who were caught in the Skylands and glimpsed enough, before being transported to the prison island? Had Delyse bothered asking me, I would have told her about the prisoner who saw the creatures the Skylanders rear from foals, ushering them through the secretive Wing Ceremony once they reach maturation and are ready to join their riders in the skies. But they didn't ask. And I won't tell them now.

"I need to dry, change," I say, rather than hit them with more questions, accusations. "Before I'm taken to the palace." *Before I can find a way to escape and move on.*

Delyse, Shamar, Lieutenant Garaycía, and the unknown soldier all balk at my change in attitude.

"Actually," the lieutenant says, "the general only wanted to get you here, to show you what you already know hunts across our island." He exchanges a guarded look with his kinsman. "After that, everything was up to you. Things have to change since he's not himself, but there's somewhere we can take you—the place he would have taken you first. It isn't the palace." He holds out a cape.

With a smile that's all teeth, I snatch it.

Accompanied by Esai, as the loose-lipped soldier informs us he's called—after which the lieutenant begrudgingly reveals his name is Zander—Delyse, Shamar, and I are led to a narrow kanoa, the plainer cousin of an Aiycan sloop built for navigating the narrow deltas that twist and coil through this land of slumbering vipers. To avoid the questions in Delyse's face, Shamar's, I glance over at where Kirdan still lies, immobile, on the sand.

"His arm was near torn off months back, only hanging on by a sliver of muscle and bone, and he faints after his hair is cut." Zander snorts, catching my point of focus. "We'll never let him live this down."

Is that jesting between compatriots, or typical Obeah/Alumbrar relations I might exploit?

"You mean *we* won't live this down," Esai adds dryly. "There'll be drills from dusk through dawn while he shows us how tough he really is."

"Still wet," I drawl, unwilling to be drawn into their humor.

"Far be it from me to keep you that way for long." Zander's conduit gold begins to brighten. Rather than count the quantity on his person, it would be easier to note where he isn't armed. Fugitive, their name means—that scarification curling down the side of his face must mean, twin to the pattern that curls around Kirdan's neck, though Zander's is one that wasn't visible before he called forth his will, each spiked angle wrought with the disdain held against him and his for what this island believes they stole, and yet the fabled warrior doesn't look the accidental recusant; he looks, I hate to admit, gods touched. Like a beam of sunlight given flesh.

"All that to unmoor the kanoa?" Esai rolls his eyes as the boat begins to drift along between banks of sand that turn into silt, no sails or paddles required. "Wonder if the general will let me out of drills if I tell him you were popping style before the empress."

Zander's expression turns sheepish. "We need to get along."

"Yeh mon." Esai snorts. "Sure."

Their bickering becomes as constant as the gentle motion of the kanoa atop the endless green of the waters. Arid in a way Aiyca is not, sand banks rise like half-set suns on either side of the delta; the gentle slopes soften the monolithic red stone wall at their backs, from which sharp golden minarets spear upward toward a sky latticed with delicate cloud.

"Have you been to Zesia before, Empress?"

Esai, rounder of face than Zander, Kirdan, and almost puplike with his large brown eyes and long lashes, raises his brows with an eagerness that would have entertained me, had my own Aiycan ilk not tossed me aside in favor of Kirdan. But, the looser-lipped of the two soldiers, perhaps he'll let something slip.

"Never."

"These are private waters," he offers. "They belong to the royal family, who in turn permits certain merchants to travel here. Officially it's the Delta Province, though, to confuse matters, the few fortunate enough to own homes here actually call it the Merchant's Paradise."

Zander snorts. "The few fortunate enough?"

"The wealthy," Esai clarifies. "The farther east you travel, the busier the island becomes and the less water you'll find. The Simbarabo, for instance, live in the northeast, where the delta turns so narrow it cannot be traveled upon."

"And buguyaga piss in it plenty," Zander adds.

"Water is a luxury here?" Delyse questions. "But it's a necessity."

Neither soldier answers her. I suppose they know first-hand what it means to be punished by a doyenne and what she deems *necessary*. All the more reason to leave this dictatorship and migrate onward, to the Skylands. Their supposed lack of an aerial army is a convenient reason to force me to stay here. The prisoner could have been lying, though I didn't discern deceit when she told me, only awe. I will see that army for myself. Delyse won't deter me with absolutes of something she knows nothing about.

Perhaps it's the cooling wind atop the delta, the iridescent shimmer of dragonflies skimming across its surface, or the ripples created by fish as they nose the moss-colored water beneath us, but a couple of hours into our journey my fury at Delyse, Shamar, and Kirdan's betrayal cools to hurt. The beauty of our surroundings only darkens the cloud we bring with us, the mountain that grows to cast its shadow over us, one vast enough that we may never escape its reach. For all I did at Cwenburg, I never stole choice, free will. In hunting monsters, they've lost sight of what it means to be human—a problem I once would have solved with the pointy end of whatever I could get my hands on, with my enemies. My allies?

You don't have any here, a small voice whispers, warns.

The first lavish villas materialize between the dunes in a haze of white rounded stone just visible behind bordering walls, with private docks that stretch out onto the delta; larger and more elaborate kanoas than the one we travel in are docked alongside. Ones with jewel-toned awnings, others garlanded with shimmering bells. None are plain enough to be missed. Except the one we're currently in.

"Is it Obeah alone who live here?" Shamar queries.

"No." This is from Zander. "Doyenne Divsylar permits her favored Alumbrar and secular Zesians to own homes here too. There's more integration between orders, from the top to the very bottom with the Simbarabo, to avoid, you know . . ." His words fade.

"To avoid what happened in Aiyca," I'm only too happy to finish for him. Silence follows my words, one that turns the caw of the delta herons slightly sinister the rest of the way to one of the more modest docks.

The villa overlooking the edge of the bank is concealed

behind walls bleached into brighter whiteness by the sun. Once we're through the metal gate—conduit gold of course, and likely reinforced with protection guzzu—it takes a while for my sight to soften to the warm coziness of a fruitful courtyard and the witch standing in it.

"Wahan." Tall, with almond-colored skin softened by age, she extends a hand to me. After a protracted moment in which I consider snubbing her, I take it. Let them all think me pliant. "Welcome to Zesia, Empress Adair." She bows her head.

"Iraya is fine."

"As you wish." Straightening, she brushes her long braid, threaded bronze with age, over one elegant shoulder and turns to the Simbarabo. "Where is the prince?"

"He took ill, Miss Lucia," Esai supplies.

"That explains why you are late." She turns on a bare heel. "This way."

A pair of glass doors lead into a tiled space crowded with objects and decorations. We could be in one of the bazaars Zesia is famous for. I've never been, but Dada would bring me back various trinkets whenever he sailed here to converse with General Divsylar, senior. Perhaps this witch, Lucia, works a stall. She bears no scarification I can see as she leads the way through her cramped home, alighting in a room draped with richly dyed fabrics in an array of patterns everywhere but the floor, which is covered with sand.

"Close the door, Iraya."

In doing so I notice for the first time that we're alone.

Escape may come far sooner than I thought.

"I was Prince Divsylar's nursemaid, when he was a pickney."

Back to me, Lucia kneels before a low circular table and tinkers with items I cannot see; their scent is pungent, though, medicinal. "Firstborn sons of the nobility are often given to the care of another in Zesia." She waves a dismissive hand at the quotidian nature of it, but this woman might be more of Kirdan's mama than the doyenne lying on her sickbed in the palace.

In between her next intake for breath, my fingers curl around Kirdan's dagger in my bandolier; it's edged out, inch by inch.

"A second-born daughter," she goes on to say, "I had no métier but my wits and a love of stories. I told the prince many when he was a pickney, and continued to do so long after he grew out of my care."

And he purchased her this home? With no métier, no trade, and charged to look after the son the Zesian doyenne never wanted, Lucia wouldn't have been honored with this house any other way. My second realization takes longer to come.

"You told him the story about the Witch of Bone and Briar."

"I did."

"Why?"

"If you've heard it then I'm sure you know."

"It's but a tale."

"Every story is a lie until someone breathes truth into it."

My breath shallows.

Those are the very words I said to Jazmyne. But this griot could never—

"You're no storyteller. What are you really?" I demand.

"I am Obeah." She rises, turns around; in her hands she cups a crude bowl.

My eyes bounce between her own. While darker than Kirdan's, they hold just as many secrets. To say she is Obeah, even without magic, doesn't nullify the potency of her will.

"I see Kirdan didn't heed my advice to be entirely honest with you."

"You scry."

"I tell stories," she corrects. "As I said."

Like the Griot-Bonemantis from the Cuartel? The witch who straddled the line between fact and fiction. Obeah don't need gold to communicate with the ancestors, but I've heard its absence can turn scryers mad.

"Life has made you mistrustful; being betrayed by those closest to you has made you distrustful, but I assume that before you decide whether you will leave for the Skylands or remain here, you'd like some autonomy?" Lucia raises sparse eyebrows, along with the bowl, proffering it.

Her words, her prescience, may have caught me by surprise, but I don't budge, don't release the blade I'll run her through with if she stands in my way. Kirdan could have found a way to tell her about my plans, no matter how weak he is.

She tips her head. "You know better than that."

I startle for a second time.

"It's not your thoughts I'm reading, but rather your emotions."

Her words sink in.

"You're a *Tempera*. But that's incredibly rare, and only ever the case with—"

"Twins. Yeh mon. I was one of the blessed to escape my home in my youth before my sister realized that my capacity to understand the emotions of those around me was draining her own abilities. Many of my kind are not so lucky."

Many are killed to prevent just that, and by their own siblings. It's not even illegal; doing so wouldn't earn a magi Unlit status, in Aiyca. I knew a girl in the Virago who fled from home when her parents killed her twin to prevent her magic being siphoned away. They saw it as mercy.

"At least you know you can believe me when I say I know how you feel." Lucia's eyes twinkle. "A beaten prowler won't see a loving hand as anything other than a violent fist for a long while. You have been beaten by life, Iraya, it's true. You can either continue to snap and bite, or you can make the decision to see my hand for what it is. This poultice needs to steep for seven nights, during which time you'll be packed into sand that will absorb the impurities Aiyca's late doyenne placed in your neck. You will sleep for the duration of the guzzu, and no harm will come to you. Your magic will be yours when you wake."

I glance down at the floor for a second time. What was it Master Omnyra said? *Sift through the sands for the answer you seek. The vanguard you chose will be on hand to offer you aid.* Did she know—did she see that my path would be forsaken?

Or was this my path all along?

Irritated, exhausted, I utter a curse. Lucia raises her brows once more. I turn from her but keep her in my line of sight. A decision needs to be made. Fast. And I don't need her mapping my choice using my face. The dogwood I found on the peninsula was one thing, and the job it did was incomplete. But this? Divine intervention or otherwise, I'd like to know why so many others believe they have any right to dictate what my journey will look like. But what I'd really like to know?

Why am I letting them?

"What you do after will be entirely up to you."

"Stay out of my head," I croon, but Lucia's words snag on the conflict she no doubt read on my body. Losing the Impediment Glyphs means it'll be me, Just-Ira, as it's never truly been. Not when I was bound to the shields by magic, to my order by guilt, and to Aiyca by honor. With my magic unfettered, no one will be able to deny my suggestions on the basis that I'm fragile. Not the council, Shamar, or Delyse. Nor will they be able to spirit me away again, to make decisions for me—and the choice is mine.

I decide whose helping hands I accept.

I decide what my path looks like.

"So?" Lucia checks, though her small secretive smile tells me she already knows my answer.

JAZMYNE

"You need to rest."

Anya's warning echoes across the circular observatory, where she finds me on the Fifth Night, my eye pressed to a telescope, as it has been since the Unlit's attempt to wrest Coral Garden from me. Across the island, calmed by the triumph in St. Deirdre and ignorance about the true enemy in the Unlit, for now, street parties close roads, and neighbors offer Jákīsa in the hopes that the late doyenne won't return to haunt them. Sightings of her duppy in the palace have been flooding in as we approach the Ninth Night, and her spirit strengthens; the demoted presiders visit me several times a day with reports. I've yet to see the late doyenne around the palace. May the gods permit my wish-bags to deter her forever.

"Jazmyne!"

"I heard you, Anya. I'm trying—"

"To discover what the Unlit want, yeh mon, I know. But you can't keep allowing these obsessions to overwhelm your better judgment."

I *have* to keep looking. In the days since their last attack, the Unlit have become the Unseen too, and we all know noise doesn't always forewarn attack. The bag-o-wires we brought back from St. Deirdre told us nothing and now rot in St. Jayne's jail, two parishes away from this one, since we can't risk any transfers to or from Carne. Not when the Unlit might attempt to free prisoners to join their crusade. I was of the mind to turn them over to the Obeah who helped save Coral Garden, but I have no means of contacting them, and they certainly haven't tried to reach out to me.

"Look at me, Jazmyne, and tell me what you see."

With a sigh, I step away from the telescope. It isn't Anya's scowl that gives me pause, or even the alterations to her Stealth blacks—a leather vest with complex gold straps. It's her hair, which is drawn back from her face in two *braids*.

"What have you done?" It isn't the Alumbrar way to wear our hair for combat.

"I've been wearing it like this for days." Irritated, she paces away. "You haven't noticed anything other than the island, and you're getting too close to see it clearly. The defunct council challenged your inheritance once already. Have you checked in on their activities? Idle hands will always find something to do, and I don't think you'll like how they keep themselves busy if you neglect to stay on top of them!"

There was a missive from the presiders, actually, about

dinner plans for the Eighth and Ninth Nights I cannot miss, as I have the first four. Before I can relay this information, Anya has moved on.

"And then there's your earthstrong. It's less than six phases away. About the same length of time until the Yielder guzzu falls. What if you're with the pirates? Speaking of the race, the faux falls—" She breaks off at the expression on my face. "What is it?"

"You stay on top of them."

"What?"

"The advisors. You've already handled the transfer of the gold from Iraya's family trove to the Transmuters' workshop." An Obeah by the name of Adriel, a prodigy in this métier apparently, struck a Shook Bargain with Anya. Something I was furious about when she returned and told me I wasn't needed. "I see I must state it again: if I am Light Seeker, it is only because you have been my guide. Be my first, sistren. You are in all but official title—something I won't take from you either. When the new council is sworn in, you will be too. Walk beside me, Anya. Become my official family, take root."

"Jaz." Her hands fall to her sides. "I don't know what to say."

Her own family are wastrels—magi happier to drink and laze about while she sends them provisions. Both of us were dealt an unfair hand, and yet we have triumphed against the odds.

"Say yes." I'm halfway to where she stands, blinking back tears, when a series of words echo through my thoughts— *earthstrong, be my family, take root.*

Pivoting away from Anya, I charge toward the map of the island.

"I thought we were having a moment!"

"I think I know where the Unlit will strike next."

She joins me in an instant.

I point out its location on the map. "Carling Hill."

"What do the family trees matter to them when theirs have been chopped down and used for firewood long—"

"The Witchfire helps them bring in their beasts, but Iraya didn't realize it's also a *symbol* of their ire. Their magic was taken from them, their ancestral families, their roots, and so—"

"They mean to take ours," Anya whispers, the words not meant to be spoken any louder.

It is an unmentionable horror to burn a family tree, one that risks angering generations of ancestors. Not even the late doyenne dared do it to the Adair family's. But what do the Unlit, stripped of every aspect of their past, have to lose?

"Their actions have shown them to be adept at distraction," Anya muses. "They might go for Queenstown and Port Royale at the same time, use them to keep us busy while they infiltrate Carling Hill." The aforementioned ports are the final gateways to our trade and escape, forcing us to rely on magic. Something we now know they'll never allow. "They could even hold trees ransom to win fealty from families."

Mudda have mercy.

"We need numbers there."

"We don't have them to protect Carling Hill and both ports equally, not now you've spread brigades of coven witches across the island to defend places weakened by Unlit attacks."

And to locate their center of gravity, as Iraya suggested.

Anya swallows. "A choice will need to be made."

By me.

The breath I take feels too short a time to make a decision, and yet, my next could be my last if Carling Hill falls. "We cannot lose Queenstown. Not when it's so close to the palace." And the Unlit are already in this parish. "Port Royale is far enough away not to be a nuisance. Take whatever additional numbers you need from there."

"It's the decision I would have made too, Jazmyne."

For now, maybe. But what will I have to sacrifice next?

"Will you tell Iraya?"

"And have her berate me for not thinking of Carling Hill sooner? No. I'd rather go there and make sure it isn't taken."

"You have to stay, Jazmyne. Especially when there's the race to contend with soon. I'll go to Carling Hill with the Xanthippe in your stead." Anya lands a look that brokers no discussion. It says, *if I am your first you will not object*—and though it pains me, I don't. I can't. She's right.

"Three days," I tell her. "And then I want you back regardless."

Silent, Anya moves toward the door. Her braids say the words she is without: I mustn't wait for her. But even she doesn't object when, in the palace vestibule, I enclose her in a fierce hug that leaves the two of us bereft of air.

"Take two of the cadre, at least?" I murmur.

"Filmore stays with you. Pasha too. I'll use some of the others."

A throat clears across the entrance. Anya and I break apart to find Roje standing there.

"You're back," I say. After St. Deirdre, he sent a missive explaining a quick trip to the Iron Shore. "Is all well with the crew?"

"Yeh mon." He gives me an odd look. "I saw the sign too."

"What sign?"

"'The Lost Empress message Iraya left?'"

Anya sighs. "We saw that days ago, in Coral Garden."

"You haven't seen it." Roje's strange expression bleeds into concern. "Someone left a similar message to the one in Coral Garden in Morant Bay. 'The Lost Empress Remembers.' It was written in a message of Witchfire across as many Alumbrar homes as there are letters in the statement."

"But Iraya is—"

"Gone," Roje finishes. "Yeh mon. I thought there was a chance you knew about whoever is using her name to send messages."

To the Obeah.

"But you don't know," he confirms. "What was going on here?" he asks.

"I was meant to be leaving for a few days, but—" Anya looks my way, her face tight with worry. "I'm staying."

"No," I say. "You have to go and oversee the Xanthippe. The Unlit are using Iraya's name to turn the Obeah against me. We can't let them prevail at Carling Hill." Even when she's not here Iraya causes me nothing but trouble. "Go, now. Please, sistren. I will increase patrols in St. Elizabeth." If the Unlit's army is there, they will be found.

Anya lances Roje with a fierce stare. "Behave yourself while I'm gone. My body might not be here, but I have eyes everywhere."

He crosses his heart.

"Be safe." My words are choked.

"You too. And don't forget—" She taps her head in the place where I still wear her magic-infused combs. With a final cautionary look at Roje, Anya strides across the entrance to the west doors that will take her to the kitchens for supplies.

"Chin up, Genna." Roje knocks my shoulder with his arm. "I'll be here, and as your first mate, your battles are mine, your enemies mine. Your wants, mine." Though his breath is free of rum I still taste dark, wicked things. "No task is too wrong, too shameful, too impossible."

How quickly he would redact those words if I told him I don't possess the map to the Conduit Falls that not only secured his patronage but also holds the location of the gold it's looking like this island will need in the end—that I might never.

Unless I *ask* for something shameful rather than *share* it.

Something I never could have gotten away with if Anya was still here.

"Do you know guzzu to speak with the dead?"

Roje blinks, taken aback by the divergence in conversation, my tone. "Not personally, but I can ask around."

"Do. Before the Ninth Night. And tell me when you have it."

"Should I know why?"

Because there is only one witch who knows the map's location, and I cannot reach her without help.

116

"I need to speak with Mama."

His eyebrows raise. "I didn't think that was something Alumbrar did."

We don't. How the late doyenne managed the switch from pious Alumbrar to bloodletting victor so seamlessly, I don't know. All I heard as a pickney was that Obeah dwelled among the shadows, and my order followed the blazing path of righteousness. But perhaps life isn't so much about keeping to the light as it is about understanding which parts of the dark you will walk in.

IRAYA

On the seventh night, I am reborn.

The packed sand Lucia piled on top of me crumbles away as I sit up with a groan, brush it off my cheeks, away from the now healed burns behind my ears. She sleeps where I saw her last, on a cot by the door, her thick braid curled around her fist.

By the Tempera's forethought, provisions wait nearby atop a round stool to sate the gnawing teeth of my hunger. I shovel the fried dumplings with ackee and saltfish in so fast I barely taste them, washing everything down with sweet lemon water before leaving. None of the others wait to accost me in the villa—it's my second reason to be grateful for the later hour. My first is the absence of the sun. The soft glow of witchlight lamps irritates my eyes enough after so long in the dark. There were no dreams in the place Lucia sent me. I think that was me. My mind didn't have the energy to conjure doorways for me to escape through, fantasies for me to live while the sand eked out the last of the late doyenne's malignant will.

She once said I'd never know the feeling of freedom. I hope that wherever she is in Coyaba, the dank nadirs of its most unforgiving places, she's aware that she was wrong, and it kills her over and over again with a neck-snapping abruptness.

Beyond Lucia's tiled courtyard, moonlight stretches across the dusk-cloaked dunes of the Merchant's Paradise. Docked kanoas sit still as any stagnant breeze. In this moment it's just me and the endless night sky, each star a wish I might spend.

My snort startles a delta heron.

Alumbrar might cling on to the whimsy in that thought, but options are another burden, in a different way to the absence of choice. I've only ever known fight or fight harder. In Aiyca, I could hide, fighting alone. But what if this time victory hinges on the ability to put my sword down, to reach for something else—a crown? It would place a monster-sized target on my back, for every single one of the Unlit leader's beasts will know where I am, that Aiyca is without my protection. That I'm alone.

But not powerless.

Behind my ears, the poultice Lucia painted over my Impediment Glyphs is long dried. My fingers chip it away as I summon my will. A beast on four fast legs, its golden eye, the knife strapped to my thigh, brightens into a glare that welcomes challenge. Embraces it with teeth and claws until anyone looking out of their window might mistake me for the white-hot heart of the sun—however fleeting my light show must be with Kirdan's borrowed conduit. The general. Will he take me shopping for a new weapon, a treat for staying, or will I move on to the Skylands and find one there alone?

The Alumbrar Mourning Bell rings in a delicate melody of chimes that echo from the city's minarets, dull in the dark; they remind me not that I've woken on a holy day, but that Doyenne Divsylar will have allies within the Alumbrar Order as well as the Obeah. She is a different animal to Doyenne Cariot, but the latter did teach me something invaluable: better the enemy you know than to swap a black dog for a monkey. I know the Zesian doyenne is the exposed edge of a blade, with an appetite for power in place of the late Doyenne Cariot's blood. What if the Skylands doyenne is worse? I've been so focused on the might of their winged creatures, I haven't considered the barriers between us. Their riders, soldiers. Their commander. And, of course, the witch who oversees them all. Seven days have already passed since I was taken from Aiyca. It will take me at least that to cross the Monster's Gulf. *If* I can find a ship to smuggle myself on with plans to cross the treacherous waters.

But I'm already in Zesia.

The Simbarabo are trained to fight the beasts, according to Kirdan's intel. They don't have their own to go toe-to-toe with the Unlit's monsters, but their magic, their skill—could it be enough? The Unlit's leader means to break my home, that Healer said. I need a greater force. Not an equal one.

"Iraya?"

The soft tread of Shamar's sandals atop the wood of the dock are almost upon me when I notice them. There's a fainter shuffling too. Delyse. She stays back. In the time I've been recuperating, they've adapted physically to our change of locale: Shamar wears the longer-sleeved tunics more popular in Zesia, and Delyse's pants are diaphanous and loose; both fabrics are brightly jewel toned, with diametric patterns. Their new wardrobe only serves as a reminder. These clothes were waiting for them here. Because they knew everything. They worked with Kirdan. Against me.

"How do you feel?" he asks, soft concern bowing his forehead.

The silence between us falls markedly, beads of sand in some sort of countdown.

"Do I still want to rip your heads off, you mean?"

His swallow is audible. "If that's more accurate."

Smoke curls upward from chimneys of the villas along the delta as households begin their days. Alumbrar might emerge to sail to their temples within the city for evening prayer. Will I accompany them? Walk into the storm I know awaits behind the facade of clear skies—let it know I can bring the bigger disaster?

"Why didn't you trust my choice to go to the Skylands?"

"I—"

"It was too big a gamble." This is from Delyse.

For the first time since she held me on the beach, I look into her face.

"They might not have helped." She shrugs. "We would have wasted time going there and appealing to their better nature when they have never shown one."

"Come now." My head tips to the side. "That can't be all."

Let us have this talk now, when we did not back on the island.

"It's not."

"Delyse."

"No, Shamar. We three have been deceiving one another for too long. You want the truth, Iraya?" Her voice is as cutting as the spires of the minarets from which bells begin to ring again. "There wasn't time to allow you to make another mistake before you realized that coming to Zesia was the best course of action."

"Is that so?" I murmur.

"There's been no word from the Skylands, and the Jade Guild *have* reached out."

I blink, too startled to conceal my surprise.

"Yeh mon," she says, noticing. "Scouts return having been refused entry into the island. I sent fire messages myself. Zesia *is* our best bet considering that we have their prince, their general, on our side. So now we're here, what will you do while Aiyca is belted by the monsters that helped the Alumbrar doyenne? Sneak around as you did at Cwenburg? Run and leave us? Or will you do more, for once? Will you step into the role of our empress and lead?"

Tug, tug. There go the marionette strings jerking me to and fro.

"We wanted to bring you here to show you how we might work with Zesia," Shamar hastens to add. "We hoped you'd come to accept that this is the right place to be. To help the Zesians would guarantee—"

"Nothing," I interrupt, having heard enough to surmise the rest. "It would guarantee *nothing* for Aiyca. You thought that in coming here, helping, we would garner a debt to be repaid, but the Simbarabo army serve Zesia's doyenne. No one over-rules her authority."

Except, I think, *an empress.*

"And certainly not Kirdan," I continue, my thoughts cir-cling back to the general, his health. If he's brought me here and died before anything can be leveraged—his soldiers' fealty, for instance—I might have to kill him a second time. "So what you have done in bringing us here is put us at the mercy of a forgot-ten son, and an isle that hates Aiycans almost as much as they wanted to *be* Aiycans, once." Again Delyse tries to interrupt, and I cut her off by turning and addressing her directly. "If it is your wish for me to lead, to step up, how do you propose I do that from beneath your thumb? I am not, and have never aspired to be, a figurehead." There it is, the words I haven't been able to say aloud. "Opinions I welcome, sometimes, but choices made *for* me? No. Never. You and I will both be hap-pier, and if not happy then at least satisfied, if you let up your hand before I fling it away." Delyse recoils at this. "Stop work-ing against me. Stop viewing my choices as weapon strikes you must parry. If Aiyca matters to you as you say it does, then why are you fighting me and not the villain determined to sunder it?" When I next speak my voice is tight, corseted against a rising anger. "I will stop anyone whose decisions will negatively impact my home." The warning is there, unmistakable as any-thing other than a line etched in the sand between us. And yet I don't want this to be the way. Master Omnyra said I chose those who help me; I cannot do what must be done here alone.

Wind gusts across the desert, a sweeping hand of calm amidst the heat between us.

"Your passion does you a great service, both of you." Exhaling, I look at Shamar, Delyse. "Don't mistake the difference in our way of emoting for apathy on my part. I . . . I don't blame you for confusing my actions with indifference, and I'm . . . I'm sorry. For how long it's taken me to speak frankly about this, and all that happened as a result." The dead Obeah in the palace, the imprisonment of the shields. I could go on, tell them every time I close my eyes I see their bodies, the vacant eyes, all the blood. But we all played our part, and it would be cruel to use the deaths of the shields against them. "I have said this before, but neither of you are tacticians. To remain here and succeed will rely on you trusting me." I shrug one tired shoulder. "No more scheming behind my back, no more private parleys with Kirdan. If Aiyca stands a chance of defeating the Unlit, then we three must stop lying to one another, as you said, Delyse."

The Mourning Bell rings on and on in the quiet; it isn't for me to break first, or Shamar.

Delyse pushes from the gate to join us. "Forgive me too. Just . . . forgive me, sistren." She lays a tentative hand on my forearm.

And though I am programmed to resist her touch, her words, I nod.

She exhales. "In the spirit of honesty, Zander and Esai are expecting to smuggle us into the Simbarabo Cuartel at first light to wait for Kirdan to recover."

My grimace tugs my mouth corners way, way down.

"Do you have another plan?"

"Since we're doing so well with the honesty, no." Not yet, anyway. "However . . . I do accept that we need to stay here."

Better the enemy you know. "But I don't think it wise to skulk into Zesia and hide from Doyenne Divsylar. Or operate on Kirdan's terms. We should go to the palace properly, demand an audience before the doyenne and her council."

"She'll only see you if—"

If I claim my title.

"I know." Even if I can't accept who it needs me to be—docile, obedient. Won't ever. A problem I can't see a way around, as yet. "Did either of you go through my pack?" They shake their heads. "I reclaimed some gold from Mama's trove back at the palace." Stuffed it down my waistband when Kirdan's back was turned All Souls' Night and buried it along with the mirror. "Take it and buy whatever we need to make Doyenne Divsylar sit up and take notice. Including something for me to wear."

"I can help with that last one."

We three turn to Lucia, standing in the courtyard with a steaming cup of tea cradled between her hands.

"Take the kanoa and the Simbarabo," she tells Delyse and Shamar. "They'll help you into the city and take you to the few sellers who will do business on this holy day. And you." Her focus shifts to me. "Come inside. I have garments for you to wear."

"Be safe," I tell Delyse and Shamar. "And don't let yourselves be seen."

Inside the cluttered villa, Esai and Zander break from a conversation to ask after my health.

"Better than ever," I tell them. "How fares the general?"

Esai blinks at me, surprised. "He'll be well and active, in several days."

"We'll mention you asked after him," Zander says, his expression blank.

"Tell him to stay armed."

In pursuit of Lucia, who disappears around a corner, I take my leave knowing that Delyse and Shamar will tell them what they need to know about my next steps, and stalk after the Tempera to the items she means for me to wear. Fitted to a mannequin, the ensemble stands amidst more of the same accoutrements that crowd all the other rooms, but it fades them into insignificance, silences the loud shout of their colors and textures with a single, regal whisper. Magically sewn, for no one but an Artisan of Cloth could make their stitches so fine, so delicate, the alabaster creation is a work of art. The fitted pants, the train attached to a split-fronted tunic, its sleeves loose enough to conceal the accompanying vambraces beneath, but tight enough not to get in the way during a fight. It's a marriage of audacity and practicality. A juxtaposition of duty and indulgence. I've never been one for sumptuous apparel, but this . . . this embodies both the Harbinger of Justice I would have been as a Virago, and a Returned Empress. If the two could ever exist in the same world.

"There's a breastplate too," Lucia says, reminding me that I'm not alone. "Kirdan had everything created for you." With a knowing look, the witch pushes a basket along with her foot.

Inside, beneath a beautiful head tie, is an even better breastplate. Feathered with soft shards of gold that rise higher on the shoulders, it's malleable with soft peaks for my breasts and belts at the back to cinch in my waist—but the best part is its shine. Proud and glossy, each one of its feathers, the frame of it, is crafted entirely from conduit gold, which makes it impossible for me to see it for anything other than what it is.

"He meant to bribe me into staying." And that, despite my decision, makes me want to leave. Yesterday.

Lucia sips from her cup. "Or apologize. If you note the feathers."

Lifting the breastplate is easy, it's so light. I wrap it around the front of the mannequin, step back. Its design could be wings enfolded around my ribs. The wings from the tale of the Witch of Bone and Briar that he believes will cast out the empire's evil.

My exhale is loud, long.

What would wearing this mean, to him, when he sees me? What would it mean to me?

Believe in the oath. Be a leader.

Master Omnyra's final words echo in my thoughts as though she calls them all the way from Aiyca, her wisdom able to surmount water, to defeat distance. Jazmyne can't rule Aiyca indefinitely, and the Unlit trying to steal my parents' legacy won't plant a single cheek on the golden throne in my lifetime. But not because mine will already be there.

But whose will? Who will rule Aiyca?

"There's water behind the screen for you to wash with, and more clothing at the bottom of the basket, should you decide Kirdan's taste is not your own." Lucia leaves me alone.

I take my time washing with a verbena-and-ginger soap bar, squeezing the sponge and letting the freed water run over my body in cooling rivulets. Each deluge sweeps away more sand and my own inhibitions, until, dried, fresh, and tingling ever so slightly—the ginger—I stand before a looking glass in the clothes Kirdan chose for me.

My chest is tight, though not due to any ill fit. It's as if every time he looked at me, he mapped the lines of my body, the places it dipped and curved. If I was the sentimental sort, I might call this ensemble a letter of adoration, of promise. For a second, I tighten beneath the ghost of his touch, and then I shake it away, banish it from my thoughts.

That bag-o-wire doesn't matter.

What does is ensuring that his mama recognizes that she is no longer the authority here, because as far as I'm concerned, the moment I killed Doyenne Cariot, everything that Alumbrar viper agreed to with Zesia and the Skylands became null and void.

This island—and Shamar, Delyse, Kirdan—will see me as Empress Adair, and I will work to secure Aiyca's safety, for whoever I deign to let occupy the Golden Seat. But my scarification should tell them I am, always and forever, first and foremost, who I swore to be before the molten conduit metal was poured into the bisected skin on my forehead: Virago. Witch. Warrior. Weapon.

13

JAZMYNE

By the Seventh Night, Anya's second away from the palace, I've yet to receive any updates.

Go with her, Benito, I beseech the Mudda's Face of Fortune. *And go with me tonight.*

As a last resort, Filmore and Pasha left to sift in and out with an update. A risk, to have my closest Stealths leave my side, but with the canopy of trees in the concentric glade obstructing even the observatory's magically charged telescopes, it's easy for my thoughts to suffocate beneath the weight of every eldritch, terrible image of what my sistren, my soldiers, might face. More messages have been appearing across the island. *The Lost Empress Remembers.* Word has reached me that Obeah are beginning to congregate. If they rise against the Alumbrar, I'm not sure I'll be able to hold them off.

As low as I already am, it isn't too much farther a drop onto my knees in my bathing chamber, where I pull back the panel beneath the sink and extract the Mirror of Two Faces.

A waning moon casts sharp shadows across the floor in my bedroom; they scissor across my feet as I sit on the edge of my bed. I'd like nothing more than to crawl beneath the covers and forget about being regent, forget about the island. But I cannot forget about Anya.

Iraya will have strong-armed allies into accompanying her back to Aiyca by now, surely. Perhaps even in time to thwart whatever is happening to my forces guarding the family trees.

"Why am I staring at your chin?"

Jolting at the voice, I fumble the mirror.

"Oh yes, drop and shatter one of the most important magical weapons we have."

"Sorry," I breathe, instantly regretting it when I get my first look at Iraya, dazzling like a fabled messiah in an audacious ensemble of gold and white.

"What is it, Jazmyne? What have you done?"

"Me? Why haven't you returned yet? It's been an entire phase. I see you've had time to shop."

"This was a gift."

I bet it was.

"I don't want to argue with you, even though your stupidity has left Aiyca in an even greater position of weakness. 'The Lost Empress Remembers'? The Unlit have stolen your calling card and are currently leaving it across the island."

"That's . . . troubling."

"When will you return?"

She glances off at something I cannot see. "That's why I called; plans are in flux at the moment. I might be away for longer than initially planned."

"Zesia is treating you that well?"

Her focus shifts back, quick and sharp. "I didn't tell you where I was going."

"As if you needed to."

"If you have something to say, say it." She pops the *t* so hard I flinch back.

Only that I've been a fool, trusting you to keep me abreast of your plans.

"Why do I need to speak when your ensemble says enough."

This talk was a terrible idea.

"It takes time to recruit an army, Cariot. And you have a cabal of skilled Obeah there who can help with the Unlit stealing my identity. Tell me you're utilizing the shields properly."

How do I end this talk? Perhaps the mirror is reliant upon touch to function. I drop it into my lap.

"Your chin again, wonderful."

Not touch.

"I want to see Ford."

Perhaps if I flip it over.

"Jazmyne! I swear to the gods, if you don't—"

Her voice cuts out, and I exhale, shoulders lowering from my ears. Needing to move, to get away from the conversation, I return the mirror to its hiding place and venture out into the palace. The shields are the last thing I need. Perhaps I can try to find Anya in the telescopes again. Perhaps—

"My queen!" The shout echoes across the landing. Roje jogs toward me. Emthera waves from her watch post to remind me I'm not alone. "I have something for you."

Though cautious of dark, wicked things, I force myself to stand firm before him. "What is it?"

"The guzzu you asked for."

My wariness evaporates. "You have it?"

"Yeh mon." He raises a sack. "It's more of a summoning than an enchantment. The Obeah who gave it to me said it's best worked tonight, the Seventh, to coincide with the Supreme Being or something. What do you say?"

I don't. Instead I hesitate, poised between safety and the point of no return—only aren't I caught between the two already? Haven't I been since my sister was killed and I vowed to work with the Nameless to remove the late doyenne from the throne?

"If you've changed your mind, I'd understand. You might not be ready."

Fear had drawn my skin taut against bone, but at the delicacy of Roje's tone, like I am fragile, it pimples with a painful indignation. "Would you tell an Obeah-witch that?"

"That's not what you are," he says; all I hear is, *That's not who you are.*

"No." My eyes dip to the sack he carries, one weighed down with the bulk of the taboo instruments required for this fell task. "But I am soon to be your queen, Roje. Aiyca's doyenne. As it would be foolish to ask an Obeah, so it is to ask me."

"Not any more foolish than those words."

Startled, I gape up at him.

"Honesty doesn't make cowards of men."

I recover quickly. "I am not a man. We're doing the summoning. Tonight."

Across the palace in the late doyenne's wing, lamps are

draped with cloth to suffocate bright lights and choke havens of safety clean off. This hallway is no place for the living. Every shadow drawn across the marble floor makes Roje and me pause, listen. Every sigh of breath from the restless winds still gusting through the parish sends a cold panic through my blood. A coward keeps sound bones, Alumbrar say. There is no peace for the valorous.

One touch and the suite door yawns open beneath my hand, which doesn't shake, I'm pleased to note. Yet. But every step through the columned suite, rich and fussy in a way I would have thought the late doyenne despised, and that indomitable metal lining my bones retracts a little more. When the late doyenne lived, I had little desire, and few invitations, to enter these rooms. They were a place she retreated to with none other than the Xanthippe, or her first and second. I don't know if it's colder now with her dead, or as it was when she lived.

"I didn't mean to offend," Roje says behind me. "Only—you're not letting me in. I see how you are with your sistren, the Stealth, and while I understand that the two of you have been closer for longer, matters are different at sea than they are on land." The sack hits the floor with a discordant jingle. "There is no purchase like that from your crew. Is it . . ." He hesitates. "Does your distance have anything to do with—to do with—"

Please don't mention the drinking house. Please don't mention the drinking house.

"The Divsylar prince?"

Thank the gods.

"The two of you were close. In a way, you could say that he was as much your first mate as Anya."

"And then he betrayed me, you mean?" I don't know what makes me take the words from Roje. Ownership, perhaps. That claiming what was done to me would be better than hearing it from another. "Reminding me of his betrayal isn't the way to secure my confidence in you." I'm aware that I'm pushing Roje even further away, but . . . I don't know how to stop. "Now, how is this bedroom for the ritual?"

"Good," he says, thankfully not raising his own weapon to parry with my sharp tone.

"How can I help?"

He fishes inside the sack and excavates a fistful of candles. "Make a circle with these, lighting them as you go."

If Anya was here, or we were six and a half moon phases in the future and I had my own magic, the task could be completed in seconds. There are my combs but I don't want to waste them.

"Keep the Hearkening Circle big enough for you to sit inside," Roje advises. "You'll need something of your mama's. Anything will do."

There are countless possessions of hers about, and yet the only object that feels remotely right is the diadem I crowned my afro with earlier tonight. Careful not to dislodge Anya's hair combs, I remove the delicate circlet of gold. Roje is busy pulling a clear container out of the bag. It's filled with blood.

My stomach twists.

"Rest easy," he says, catching my expression. "It's from the kitchens. I thought we'd stick to beast rather than boy. You can put that crown in the circle, across from where you'll be sitting."

"And where will you be?" I pose the question lightly.

"I need to paint the deep patwah with this blood while it's still warm, in the circle and on you, I'm afraid." He grimaces. "And then there's the summons; after that, I'll be on hand in case anything goes wrong."

"And if it does?"

"Extinguishing the candles should put it to rights. Do not, under any circumstances, remove the diadem from the circle."

"If that's all, then I can do it alone."

The silence lasts a little too long before Roje answers.

"As you wish."

He spends the next half an hour painting words I cannot read onto the floor inside the circle with his fingers. When it comes to the time to add the deep patwah to the skin around my mouth, to promote the late doyenne's ability to listen to me, the chicken blood has cooled; I'm not sure what's worse, the smell of death or its slime-like texture on my face.

"I'm going to say something. Don't anger." Roje's eyes bounce between my own; a shadow of stubble falls across his cheeks, his neck, and there's a wicked scar behind his left ear I've never noticed before. "You don't have to do this alone. I've seen much worse—done much worse." His throat bobs in a swallow.

I've had to conceal the worst parts of myself from everyone who's been close to me—Kirdan, Anya—but Roje . . . sea-hardened and unaffiliated with either order in Aiyca, his biggest worry is how I'll see him.

"The doyenne and I didn't have the sort of relationship typical of mamas and daughters." *And then, of course, I can't have you witnessing me ask her for the whereabouts of the map.* "She might say things it's best you don't hear."

"Parents, mon," he says like he knows.

Roje's penultimate act is to cast bones into the circle. They're inscribed with more of the deep patwah and followed by a liberal splash of rum, completing the vow with blood and bone. It's hard to imagine the late doyenne responding to these taboo artifices. Nyába has always been my order's preferred means of communicating with the deceased, possession in exchange for knowledge. However bloody, I might prefer the Obeah way. At least I'll have the control Alumbrar hosts are without.

"Do you remember the words?" Roje asks as he helps me step over the burning candles.

"I do."

"I'll be right outside. If you need me, shout."

Once his footsteps fade and the doors are closed one by one in this labyrinthine suite, I step out of the circle to check Roje is truly gone before returning and beginning the ritual anew.

"Obújufra. Bone," I intone, not entirely able to squash my guilt at doing so. "Ta'k na mi, arik na mi. Priiz."

I'm startled as the ring of candles blazes brightly in the dark.

My heart hammers. That means someone has heard, Roje told me. But only the doyenne has permission to enter the circle, as her crown sits before me. All the same, dread snakes up the back of my neck. I reach for the Amplifier around my neck, remembering too late that I took it off before talking with Iraya, in case she saw it and commented. Which spirits, even now, could be drawn by the summons, the blood and bone?

Alumbrar are forbidden from reading Obeah books about these sorts of rituals; elders would say that the malevolence concealed in the words could jump from the pages to latch on to our goodness. They'd draw it away, until the fool who read the words was sucked dry, making it all the easier for dark entities to fill them up.

My bottom lip is already chewed raw at the risk, at the deliberate crossing of the line drawn between Alumbrar and Obeah; as my teeth sink into it, copper suffuses my tongue. I'd like to think the late doyenne won't do that to me, but . . . even now I cannot call her Mama.

The ring of fire extinguishes, momentarily plummeting the room into darkness and stealing me of my breath, before lighting once more. That's the second time.

Someone is here.

Surely even the dead can see the fast rise and fall of my chest, the way my fingers curl into fists and crush my kaftan. Is that her, the thick webbing of darkness in the alcove between this room and the next? Or is she the amorphous mass standing beside the bed?

"*Daughter*" is crooned right across from me.

Though I told myself I wouldn't, I scream. I can't help it.

"Quiet. We don't have much time." The late doyenne's duppy kneels beside the diadem; physically she looks as she did in her finery that fateful night she died, albeit more incorporeal. But her face is softer, her eye . . . it almost looks at me with fondness. "There are . . . entities in the place I have gone who do not wish for me to be here. But you summoned me, so I came, my dear daughter." She reaches across the circle like she means to take my hand. "However much seeing you warms my heart—"

"It does?"

"It does. But we must be quick."

"Right." Dazed, I shake my head. "I have questions."

"There is time only for one." She glances over her shoulder at something I cannot see. Something that makes me realize how tightly I am holding myself. Something that makes me want to surge to my feet and run. "Make it the most important, quick. They come closer."

"Who?"

"*What*," she corrects.

I swallow.

"Many of the dead have . . . turned on me. Decisions they made while they lived have become regrets, and they mean to hurt me." Her voice cracks. "I've been keeping my distance, secreting myself away. But then I heard you call, felt your need. And so I came, dear daughter. Speak fast, and speak true."

Do I ask about the Unlit, or—

"I need the map to the Conduit Falls," I blurt out.

"Behind the bed." The late doyenne angles her head across the room. "Concealed in a panel."

So close? I make to rise; her hand reaches farther across the circle, and I jerk back.

"Take me with you, daughter," she implores, eye wide. "It is hard to find."

Daughter . . .

"Lift the diadem, carry it out of the circle, and set it on the bed. I can instruct you better from there."

Roje said not to take it out.

"I don't think that's allowed."

"Who can decide that but you, my flesh and blood, Aiyca's champion." That earlier fondness blazes from her face with fierceness. "Look at you. I couldn't be prouder."

"Really?"

"All I wanted in life was for you to become the leader this island needed. My daughter, my second-born, my doyenne."

Disbelief, and something close to euphoria, replaces my fear.

"I just take the diadem up in my hands?"

She nods.

The conduit metal stings my fingers with a cold snap; I use the hem of my kaftan to hold it instead.

"Clever girl," the doyenne murmurs. "You've always been so clever, so beautiful."

Diadem in hand, I step out of the circle with my left foot.

"That's right," the doyenne's duppy encourages. "And now the second."

The room drops several additional degrees as my second foot touches the floor outside the Hearkening Circle.

"And now I just carry you?"

"And now I will reassume my position in the land of the living," the doyenne rasps, in a voice so different from the one she used before, I flinch, dropping the diadem. "And you, second-born, can take my place here, with the dead." Her expression, so open and docile, mutates into something hate-filled and spine-chilling in its depravity. "Did you truly think you could summon me here for aid?" Her duppy dims and flickers, but not like a waning candle, like a burgeoning flame. "Entrap me like an animal in a snare for you to poke and prod at? I am Judair Cariot, Doyenne of Aiyca. Viper and Stealth," she hisses.

A frame flies off the wall and shoots toward me like a launched cannon. I duck with a cry; behind me, it crashes into splinters against a wall.

"Consider this your duty, Jazmyne," the doyenne continues, that rasp nails against glass. "Alumbrar pickney are used to dying so that their parents, their island, may thrive."

Several vases take flight and swarm. I'm struck against the side of my head; dazed, I fall back into a shelving unit. It cracks like a giving bone.

"Now keep still." The doyenne advances. "And this will be over—"

"Jazmyne!" Roje rounds the bedroom corner.

The doyenne whips around in a movement that's unnatural in its speed, eye narrowing.

"The candles!" he bellows. "Extinguish the candles!"

The duppy, twisted and malevolent, exchanges its assault of me for Roje. He dives to avoid the attack with another shout for me to get to the Hearkening Circle. The doyenne advances, her silence worse than any maniacal laughter, a cold, focused rage. Gods help us.

No—Anya has *already* helped us.

Dual wrenches free her combs from my afro. My fingers settle into the grooves of the clips; I aim them at the doyenne's ghost and feel the awakening of the magic they contain, the bright glow of it warming away the death chill pervading this room. Two fizzing orbs of umber charge from either comb and barrel toward the doyenne, Roje.

"Not here!" he roars. "The—"

But a blast of will smacks him in the shoulder, and with an almighty crash into a sideboard, he goes down. The doyenne turns back to me with an abruptness that sends me back a step.

"*Mengkeh*," she snarls. "Idiot! Even with magic at your fingertips you make the wrong choice. You will *always* make the wrong choice." Her kaftan curls and eddies around her ankles as she glides toward me with that same warped malice, and I understand that these are the only words she means. Will *always* be the only words she means. "Aiyca will thrive better under me," she spits, and then charges.

Closing my eyes to her face, I will the candles to extinguish. For all their light to go out, knowing that I don't need to fear the dark. When I open my eyes, the doyenne is gone.

My knees buckle, and I drop to the floor, adrenaline thrumming through my body fast enough that the floor seems to vibrate with it. All those compliments she issued—lies, manipulation. She is as she always has been, and I can move on knowing that nothing has changed.

Wiping my face dry with the diaphanous sleeve of my kaftan, I crawl toward Roje's figure in the dark and hold shaking fingers beneath his nose. He breathes. Safe in that knowledge, I use the sideboard to stand, and then cling to walls, furnishings, until I'm wrapped around the bedpost. Sweat courses down my face, my body, by the time I've dragged it far enough away from the wall. It isn't as difficult to find the panel as the doyenne led me to believe. Another lie. Roje is still out cold when my blood fills the Glyph of Opening incised into the wall, and a door pops open.

Within, as promised, is the map.

Small, dirty, the scroll feels fragile, as if it's crafted from sand and one breath too many will blow it to pieces. Stumbling out to the hall, I find an attendant and send her to find aid for Roje; when I'm alone, I tear a covering off the closest lamp, unfurl the scroll in the circle of its light, and read.

I do laugh then; it's a hollow, brittle thing that echoes through the hall like the shattering of glass. For the sheet of breadfruit skin, the map to the Conduit Falls, is blank.

IRAYA

"Iraya." Shamar's mouth drops open when it's time to leave the following day. "You look— *Ow*." Delyse elbows him in the side. "Cha mon!"

"I think you should call her empress," she says, eyes roving from the gold fans Lucia clipped my braids back with to the supernal breastplate cinching in my waist.

"Actually," I deadpan, easing the moment from serious to more palatable for the sake of my turning stomach, "I think you should bow."

Amused, Esai shakes his head.

Delyse, resplendent herself in a beautiful eggshell-colored kaftan with her additional conduit gold concealed as a belt of circular disks slung low on her hips, bangles, and earrings, shakes her head at *me*. "Where did you find this, Lucia? It's as if it was made for Iraya."

I cut in before she can answer. "Oh, they're some old bits

and pieces you had lying around, isn't that right?"

The Tempera bears a smile as she shakes her head, but stays silent.

"Zander waits with the carriage, Empress Adair," Esai says. Disguised in a plain tunic and pants, he's without the uniform that would raise eyebrows where we're going. He keeps touching his hip, where, instead of his typical armory of weapons, a gold hunting knife sits.

One by one we line up to bid Lucia goodbye, touching our hands to our hearts and bowing our heads. When it's my turn, she sinks into a low bow.

Inexplicably feeling *things*, similarities between her and Nana Clarke, how they were both there when I needed them the most, I pull her up so that I can look upon her face. "Blessings for all you've done. I'll return to see you again."

"An audience with Xaymaca's empress." Humor twinkles in her eyes. "I shall have to tidy."

"Don't change a thing." I cast a look around at the clutter, knowing that I'm leaving something here too amongst the vestiges. "Vale, Lucia. Until we meet again."

Esai steers the kanoa along the delta, taking us from the Merchant's Paradise, where several passing sloops barely give us a second look. It's true that our braids, newly styled by Delyse last night, are worn differently in Zesia, but our finials, my chest-plate? Common fare. At the neck of the row, arched wooden gates are flung open to the Delta Province at large. Docking is a fast affair, seeing as Esai, with some doctored papers, manages to convince the witches standing guard—the Zesian doyenne's answer to Aiyca's Xanthippe, I assume—that we are traveling merchants from the Skylands.

"Did Kirdan supply you with those?" I ask, once we are safely through and ensconced in the activity of the wharf, where merchants travel by a neighboring public delta to land in this center of trade.

"His name, so yeh mon. Come, Zander's over here."

The carriage, smart and grand with a glistening exterior, has to be worth more than the gold I smuggled from the palace.

"Kirdan again?"

Esai nods with a sheepish grin. "That chest is for you." He angles his head at the vast wooden box strapped to the carriage roof. "More provisions, should you need them."

"Tell your general I can't be bought."

"You'll be able to tell him yourself, in several days."

"I look forward to it."

Behind closed curtains, for obvious reasons, I listen to the noises pealing throughout the province. It's a hum not dissimilar to Aiyca, though I know that Zesia's traders operate at a different pace to the lackadaisical calm of Aiyca. Even their travel is different. Our carriage is drawn by six ebony stallions. Jungle-prowlers are not as common in Zesia, where there's less territory for them to hunt in. And shadowcats like Kirdan's do not pull carriages here; their paws are better served for running across the dunes they hunt on.

"The heirs," I say. "Remind me of their ordering again?"

"Ghislaine was born first, yet she is the quietest of the three," Shamar says, reintroducing me to Kirdan's triplet sisters after our quick trivia session last night. "Avyanna is the second-born and speaks more than her sisters, mostly fluff to compensate for her lack of brains and beauty. Shaye is the washbelly, but don't let that fool you. What will sweet your belly—"

"Will also spoil it," I finish. "Yeh mon. What else?"

"They're heavily monitored by an uncle, Emissary Kaltoon Divsylar. One of the doyenne's brothers. The first two heirs won't like your arrival. The washbelly won't trust it. Beyond the prince's chest, we don't have any gifts to distract them with."

"I can be shiny enough while you and Shamar learn all you can about the Unlit and the presence they have in Zesia, so we can take it back to Aiyca, along with their army."

It's the plan we ironed out after my talk with Jazmyne last night, a conversation I haven't told them about. One I won't, considering how little I learned and how close to breaking she sounded. I thought that duplicitous Alumbrar had more fight in her, but her lack of common sense was a surprise. How can she justify underutilizing the shields when they're far more experienced than the Xanthippe? Especially given the Unlit stealing my identity to perpetuate more messages. They don't fight for me, but they're willing to use my name against me. Expediency is more important than ever before. To lose Aiyca . . . It doesn't matter that the title of empress lands like a stone in my belly each time it's used; I can't let that happen. I can't have succeeded in avenging Mama and Dada only to lose their legacy to one just as complicit in their deaths. I wish I knew this Unlit master. In that they have an advantage.

It must be the only one.

"Do you need both of us gathering intel?" Shamar queries.

"You had another idea?"

"I could stay with the Simbarabo." He shrugs. "They'll never betray Kirdan, but perhaps that loyalty can extend to an empress they know will protect them, as well as help them claw a modicum of respect back from the people they've served without thanks for so long."

"And I'll stay with you in the palace, Iraya," Delyse decides. "There's no better place to accrue gossip than amongst the bored and wealthy. You might need backup with the prince's sisters too. Something more diplomatic than gagging and shoving them in a closet."

I bark a laugh of surprise, and then we're all laughing. Though it soon dries up, splintering off into desperate gasps for air as if reality has taken us all by the throat. We are about to willingly walk into the home of the family who stood by while members of ours were killed in Aiyca. Who did nothing to prevent the conscription, and instead gained their independence from it. While I'm more concerned about my reaction, namely killing a lot of them, the Zesians' is something Delyse is considering too, by her next words.

"There's a possibility they'll try to imprison you," she says, solemn. "Not overtly. You are the last Adair. But because of who you are, they'll attempt to control you, suppress you. Maybe even kill you. And we have no leverage. What can we offer them that Doyenne Cariot didn't already give? Are you sure we can't—"

"We can't use the Grimoire as leverage, no," I tell her again, just as I did last night. Kirdan has it in his possession anyway. For now. "I told you, I will be enough."

Outside, one of the soldiers bangs on the roof.

"We're already in the Royal Horn, then." Shamar uses the informal name for the Sadirren Province, where the palace makes its home.

It's a slight I've heard before. It refers to the shape of the former parish to insult the trumpeting we're used to hearing from the royals here. Gods. I hate court.

The carriage slows to a halt. It's the only warning we have before the doors are flung open, late-afternoon light seeps into the carriage, and I behold Nimue Palace in all its glory. It's a mighty iridescent mollusk bordered by the Great Ocean to its front and left side, with the Singing Sands at its back. A snarling bastion whose lambent domed rooftops and soft, whitewashed curved walls only conceal the stinging venom it possesses.

A mighty staircase is hewn out of its stone base, not unlike the one I walked down in Carne Prison as I left, months ago now. Seems fitting, for what is this palace but another prison. At its base two J'Martinet stand in their gold and white. Though there's little to distinguish them from the Xanthippe, save their dark braids in place of silver—only two, rather than the two dozen Delyse and I sport—they are as different to one another as night is to day. They do not sit atop prowlers, like Cwenburg's guards, which tells me they have no need for aid. Immediately I am alert, mentally chasing the guzzu for attack I badgered out of Zander and Esai last night.

"Afternoon tea has started," one of the witches says as we approach the landing of rock. "We haven't been alerted to any late arrivals. I suggest you come back at a more respectable hour tomorrow."

Silent monoliths, Esai and Zander can only stand by, without half the gold these witches carry, despite the equal musculature, and none of their authority in uniform or out.

"How about this instead," I pose. "You can hop up those steps and notify whoever you need to that Iraya Adair, the Lost Empress, et cetera, is here to have a word with the royal family."

"Iraya Adair?" the second repeats. "But she is—"

Without warning, both witches collapse.

"Wasn't me," I say in response to Delyse's approving look.

"It was me," Shamar says. The thick golden bangle curled around his left bicep dulls after the expenditure of magic. He takes one of the witches' limp hands and holds it to the post at the foot of the stairs. With a chest-quaking groan, they begin to move, escalating upward toward the palace. "They were well guarded against combat guzzu, but Poisoners don't work with physical toxins alone."

I always thought he'd make an exceptional fighter.

"You should go," Zander says. "And so should we. Gods help anyone who tangles with one of the J'Martinet. To anger one is to anger them all."

"Blessings," I tell him, as a ruler would. "For all you've done."

"Take these." Zander hands me two favors, plain handkerchiefs. "One for Esai and one for me. If you need anything, if there's an emergency, given that the general is out of commission, toss one or both of those into the flames and we will come for you."

"Just like calling a hound. How useful."

Zander's scowl isn't as deep as I've seen it.

"The Cuartel is across the island too," Esai supplies.

Kirdan is across the island, he doesn't need to say.

"I'm sure Shamar will tell me all about it, since he'll be staying with you."

Both Simbarabo blink at me.

"Iraya," Shamar whispers. "I should come inside—"

"No. This isn't goodbye." We clasp one another's forearms, and though our journey has been rocky, I'm not entirely without concern ascending the staircase and leaving him to depart in the carriage with Esai and Zander. However surprising the gesture was, they are Kirdan's men, not mine.

The lone coven witch at the top of the stairs lets us into a courtyard without question, having no reason to doubt her sistren at the bottom. Behind the doors an attendant bows and beckons us after her. There is a steady breeze from the neighboring ocean tangling with the afternoon's sultry heat as it blusters beneath archways and winds around columns. Nimue, the Lady of the Waters, is clearly a palace built for the elements, and those who can withstand them. I draw myself taller as two monstrous doors are opened and Delyse gives our names to the herald. He does a double take, square jaw slackening. At our backs, there's the faint hum of commotion. The J'Martinet from the staircase?

"There's no time for this man to unstick his tongue," I tell Delyse.

"I can help with that, if you go."

Ready or not.

Heart slamming into my rib cage, I push the door open

and stride inside. Zesians sit atop beaded cushions behind low tables; their chatter falls away as my sandals slap across tile; my cape is kicked up with momentum and wind from the seven yawning archways open to the sky and sea behind the high table where a line of people in jewels and decadent clothing sit—the royals, and their bredren, sistren.

"Iraya Cordelia Boatema Adair" comes from behind.

A half smile lighting my features at the names of the women immortalized through me. Mama. My great-grandma several times over, who was the first Virago. The past, they stride alongside me, the present, while I work toward a better future. I thrust my chin higher as Delyse's magically magnified voice swells to replace the winds and chatter.

"Blessed of Aurore, First Face of the Supreme Being; Arrow of Clotille and Duilio, Battle Faces of the Supreme Being; Defender of Carne Sea; Heir of the Xaymaca Empire, her territories, and the Monster's Gulf; first of her name; and the only living heir of Empress Cordelia and Admiral Vincent Adair."

Like the tide relishing the rocks below, a sea of whispers laps at my heels, rising the closer I near the head table. Rich scents of spices and grilled meats reach me, though I don't make it too close before a small, scarred man rises and snaps his fingers. A coruscating shield springs up before the table. Magic. With the gold the J'Martinet are embellished with, more than the Xanthippe ever wore, this barrier carries heat. More impressed than afraid, I nod their way.

"Iraya Adair is dead," the man calls. "Nothing but a story."

"And yet," Delyse breathes, joining me, "here she stands."

A thin magi in sweeping robes rises to join the first. "What is your true name?"

"I suspect it's my temperament you wish to know more than my name," I reply, sure to make my voice strong, clear, carrying. "Something I'm happy to share with all who dine in the princesses' company this afternoon." They sit between the men; more handsome than pretty, they share strong noses with who I'm sure are their uncles, but the eyes that watch me with wariness carry Kirdan's bright curiosity.

"Is that a threat?" The first man clicks again; coven members move in from the edges, unleashing sizzling swords and hammers from their conduits.

My own magic strokes its finger down my spine, eager to respond, to test the chest-plate.

"As you can see," he continues, "we are equipped for threats of violence from imposters seeking to take advantage." He angles his chin upward in what I know very well is a fighter's acknowledgment.

I feel Delyse's question as surely as if she whispered the words in my ear. *Will we engage?* However much my body tightens in preparation to do just that, in this moment, it isn't about being seen for what I am, but *who*. An Adair. Someone worth more than a doyenne. More than the trinkets and gold Kirdan included in that chest I left behind.

"There's no need for violence." My hands spread before me, empty palms out in the very sign of supplication. "Not when—" I can't believe what I'm about to say. "Not when we are soon to be family."

Delyse shifts beside me; it's so slight, few would notice. Not when their focus is on me and my next words, fodder to the Divsylars who have only craved power, and a poison I must choke down to secure the checkmate I need to remain here.

"I *am* Iraya Adair. Not dead, but imprisoned in the Viper's Massacre your island should know well. We can discuss the details later, the princesses and I. Let's not fight now when there is much to celebrate." I steal a bracing breath, a prayer for the strength to do what must be done. For Aiyca. For Mama and Dada. "I'm here because Prince Kirdan Divsylar is my—" The word yields harder than I thought. Barbed, it digs in. "*Beloved.*"

Delyse's curse is swallowed in the flood of gasps.

"Yes. We are to be wed."

15

JAZMYNE

It is only a victory to Death if the living fail to fight.

This is what I tell myself once it's clear the palace Healer will have little difficulty treating Roje and me. What are a few broken ribs, bruises, compared to the certain death the late doyenne wished to dole out on us both?

And all for a scrap of paper I can't use to help me find the Conduit Falls.

I turned to those words again in the night when sleep is elusive, kept at bay by flashes of her malevolent face each time I'd drift off, hounded by the idea of her lying in wait elsewhere in the palace until her duppy is expelled on the Ninth Night. . . . When the first shards of noon light wake me from a sleep I'd only just found on the Eighth Day, I state the words again while my attendants sew wish-bags into the lining of my dress to keep any spirits far from me, under the watchful eye of the female contingent of my Stealths.

"Add two more, will you?" I instruct the girl knelt by the hem of my kaftan. "I want to make sure that—"

Twin screams echo through the palace eaves.

"That's close to here," Cleo comments.

In my dressing room mirrors, her reflection tucks a silver lock behind her left ear; concealed beneath a specially crafted tunic, her conduit's light is indiscernible, but I know she listens.

"What's happened?"

"Two attendants have fallen to their deaths."

Both girls tending to me gasp and immediately apologize.

"No need," I tell them, reaching for my neck, the locket. "Do we know what's happened?"

"They were turning mattresses," Cleo says. "On this floor. Opening doors, to ensure the doyenne's duppy doesn't linger. It—" She glances down at the attendants. I nod my ascent; they'll only find out from their bredren and sistren upon leaving my rooms. "It attempted to possess them. They ran and fell over the balustrade. Death was immediate against the tile below."

"I would advise we leave this floor, Regent." Emthera meets my wide-eyed reflection with a grim resolve. "I'll have one of the others speak with the Xanthippe."

The coven witches populate every corner in the palace by the time I reach the library; the order was spread far and wide. Until the doyenne's duppy is expelled tomorrow night, every precautionary measure against a second attempt to possess their regent is to be implemented without delay. Seven guards accompany me inside the library itself. A place I haven't had cause to visit in a while, it was once a citadel of knowledge frequented by the brightest minds across the defunct empire. Unlike the late doyenne, who only permitted visitation to Recondite Alumbrar, Healers, Empress Adair was liberal with who could study amidst such information. When training to earn my Healer color, my fellow scholars and I would make the pilgrimage here at least once a month. Then, I remember taking comfort in the endless stacks, knowing that if I was forgotten, another faceless Healer, my medical findings would always live on in the pages of a book. This morning it is the presence of the Xanthippe that aids in a similar calm settling around my shoulders—at least until I am spotted.

"Emissary—Regent! Forgive me." The Recondite startles. She's a librarian, her hair tells me. Buzzed low, the style frees their time for further study. "I wasn't expecting any visitors." She places the books she's holding on a cart and levers into a bow from her waist. "Doyenne Cariot burned brightly on this island."

"Our sky is darker without her." The common response is apt, for what do I have to look toward but the aforementioned?

"Do you— I suppose it's too early for you to have plans for the library?" The Recondite darts nervous looks at the formidable witches at my back, twisting her hands before her.

"It won't see many visitors for a while," I decide on the spot. "The doors will remain closed to all, bar the librarians and myself."

"Not even the council? I've seen the three remaining presiders in here this phase."

My brow tightens. "Not even to them, unless they have my written permission." Books can prove to be dangerous in the wrong hands. "What's your name?"

"Verena, my regent."

"Verena," I repeat, somehow managing to muster a smile. "Take me to a private room—your most secure. I mean to look over the Unlit records."

If my request surprises her, the librarian makes no sign of it. She takes up a witchlight to combat the windowless depths— the heatless and flameless candelabra prevents any likelihood of fire damage to the tomes—and she beckons me to follow with a returning smile of her own. Shadowed by my guard, we ascend the staircase that twists throughout the center of the library; to look down is to see the eye. *Omniscient, Never Myopic* is inscribed infinite times on the balustrade. The edict warns all who climb or descend these steps that while knowledge may be power, the latter will never last without the former.

Verena takes me to a beautiful room with three floor-to-ceiling walls of books cradling a vast wooden table in the center, which commands a view of the Strawberry Hills, rearing up to the north of the island, the rolling mounds verdant and lush.

"How is this, Regent?"

"Perfect."

"I'll retrieve the records for you."

In her absence, the Xanthippe garland the room with shimmering protective intent; I wander over to the windows. Beyond the estate's wall, death banners are just visible; they will shroud the many villas and establishments until the day after tomorrow's Ninth Night, when life returns to normal. . . . What a thought. I don't think I know what normal is. I was born an outcast, lost my sister to a sacrificial rite so our mama could keep the full extent of her power, became heir to a bloody throne, and now I must become Pirate Queen to secure the allies I need to face an army of primordial beasts from beyond the veil. Laughter comes sudden and fast enough to choke me.

Would it be a help or a hindrance to tell Aiyca's citizens what creeps through this island like a malignant growth, I wonder as I sweep tears away. The Master Healer I trained under always said to state bad news clearly, so that there was no doubt about a situation. To begin with I thought it cruel. Who would wish to hear that there was no hope, that they were dying? But it's giving *false* hope that's the true crime.

Verena returns, breathing heavily behind a trolley that, while full, contains fewer books than I thought there might be.

"Is that all?"

She hesitates.

"Wait outside," I tell the Xanthippe. When the door is closed, I encourage Verena with a nod. "Speak freely."

With a self-conscious tug of the conduit coin around her neck, her eyes turn glassy as she retreats to the stacks of mental knowledge those in her métier are feared and respected for. "Though the Adair empress was vigilant with recording all Obeah sentenced to Unlit status," she begins in a detached voice, "Doyenne Cariot was not as meticulous about tracking the Unlit's numbers. With the bloody beginning to her reign, and the introduction of conscription, she forced many more Obeah to flee for the island's periphery and join the castouts. I predict that while a decade ago their numbers were in the low thousands, they now run in the ten thousands."

My arms tighten around my middle, squeezing out a loud exhale. That vast number doesn't include their beasts from beyond the veil. I could be looking at double that, *hundreds* of thousands. And Anya is there, at Carling Hill.

Verena's conduit dulls, exchanging its light for the return to the life in her eyes. "I've worried you."

"No. No. You've helped me, more than you know. Should I have further need—do you still use the bells?"

She takes one off the cart; it's without a clapper, but the magic it holds will summon the librarian it belongs to. Then with a parting bow, Verena leaves.

Weak-legged, but determined enough not to be weak of spirit, I take a seat and open the first book. Breathing in the musty smell of the pages and tracing illustrations used to be my favorite part of library visits, but there's little enjoyment to be found in these records. Austere in a way I'm used to associating with my order, the pages only list family names and the crimes beside them. As day cedes to night, I grow sleep-deprived and hungry, and my sight begins to blur along with my focus, which is why when I come across a name I know well in the third book, I have to check it twice before I can believe what I'm seeing.

There, in a tidy script, is the name *Adair*.

I drag my finger across the page to the crime. *Treason*. The footnotes don't offer any further explanation, which is strange when I see that other crimes with just as little ambiguity, such as *Attempted Murder*, have been expounded on in great detail at the bottom of the page. Sitting back in the chair, I stare at a witchlight as it flickers on the wall. That's how my brain feels, flush with sense one moment and then lost of all the next. It shouldn't confuse me that Empress Adair would conceal one of her family members being involved in treason. I've never heard any tales about Adair turning on Adair. And Iraya . . . she might have known all this while and not told me. It wouldn't be beyond her scope of deceit.

"Reading about duppies?"

Jolting, I turn to the doorway where Roje leans.

"I thought you would have had enough."

Panting, Verena stops behind him. "Forgive me, Regent Cariot, but this pirate claims to know you, and your guard didn't stop him."

"I— Yes. Blessings, Verena. You may go."

Casting one last disparaging look at Roje, the librarian leaves us.

"Always so welcoming, your order." He eases himself onto the chair beside mine with a wince.

His stomach, bound in muslin, is visible through the low neck of his white shirt. So are several islands of bruises.

"What are you doing out of bed?"

"I should never have been in bed." He fingers a book, and I feel a rush of relief that I didn't request the cartography texts yet. "I missed something important this morning, and now we're all going to pay for it." Roje drags his gaze up to meet mine; the spark there is as diminutive as it was when I saw him after Vea's death. "I didn't handle matters as well as I thought I did before leaving the Iron Shore several days ago."

He exhales. "The doyenne wasn't a threat to my ilk, as I said that night in the drinking house. But the Unlit attacks have reached the Iron Shore. Namely the show they put on in St. Deirdre. After what happened at Black River two months or so back, they're concerned about another competitor infringing on their claim to the falls."

My mouth dries. "But . . . the Unlit have no magic."

"They're Obeah." Roje shrugs and then winces. "At least they were. Remember what I said before, that the pirates could rally the Obeah against the Alumbrar in exchange for their magical freedom? The Unlit can offer them the same. The Iron Shore doesn't want to take that chance."

Anya was right. I have been obsessing about the wrong things. Or the right things in the wrong order. Either way, the threat to Carling Hill has changed everything, and the faulty map is the least of my worries.

"They're bringing the race forward," I whisper. "Aren't they."

"I told them the new regent was ahead of the Unlit, that she was managing their attacks and had found a way to stop them momentarily, in the hopes that it wouldn't change things, but the Pirate Queens of Old overseeing the race, they, well—" He rubs the back of his head.

"How soon?"

"We have about a phase and a half, maybe less, until the race events begin," he admits. "There will be a Glide-By initially. A chance to meet the other ships, their crew. The Pirate Queens of Old have sent out the last calls across the Carne Sea and the oceans beyond. They want all ships entering to dock at the Iron Shore by the next phase end."

If I leave Aiyca now, what will I sail from? What will I return to?

"The crew and I will handle the logistics, but you'll need to start altering matters physically—your hair, for starters. Your clothes."

"Of course." My voice is light. "Dresses."

Roje leans forward. "It will be all right, mon. You have the map, so the clothing is the smallest part of what needs to be done. We'll get through this."

This is something I should have asked more questions about, before throwing myself at Roje in that Ol' Town taproom.

"How long have pirates searched for the Conduit Falls?"

Roje leans back and stretches his legs on either side of mine. "Months at the least, decades at most. It won't take us years, will it?" Roje checks.

"Oh no. But we should discuss terms."

"A fifty-fifty split of the falls sounds about right."

"It will be eighty-twenty." Of the gold Iraya directed me to. "With Aiyca keeping the majority."

"So this is how it feels to be pillaged." His tone flush with its typical humor, Roje shakes his head. "It's less enjoyable to receive than it is to give."

"The race doesn't entail more beyond the obvious, does it? Sailing for the falls?"

"More or less. The Pirate Queens of Old want the falls for the coins, but it's hard to believe it can be found when its location is guarded so closely. Pirates could sail for that horizon forever and fail to reach it, so the queens set parameters. You can be crowned victor if you return with something of equal enough value to the ultimate bounty. The last time the race happened and Vea won, close to fifteen years ago now, we sailed for the falls for a month or so, but that was a ruse. I didn't know it at the time, but all the while she was listening for intel about the Arrow of Clotille—do you know it?"

Wishing I did, I shake my head.

"It's a legendary cannon believed to be magically blessed by one of your war-faced gods."

"You pirates like your magi, considering—" I tap my chest; in the same place on his, Roje's dried slug hangs on a leather thong.

His golden eyes bright in the dark, Roje's mouth draws down into an expression that's almost somber. "That we do, and it keeps getting us into trouble. Decades ago, a crew aboard the *Squaller's Bane* stole the cannon and pillaged their way across the Carne Sea. With a never-failing aim and a sentient ability to determine where to strike, without movement, the Arrow of Clotille was a master which all ships and crews bowed before. Before the *Squaller's Bane* could make for the Great Sea, it was sunk, ironically, by a Squaller admiral. *The admiral, Adair.*"

"Iraya's pupa?"

"Yeh mon. His fleet was . . . *majestic.* The only vessels to cow the heavens, the earth, and the waters. He shot down the *Squaller's Bane* with magic, lightning, your Supreme Being's Fist itself, depending on the orator. Me?" Roje snorts. "I considered the cannon as lost as the falls, until Vea sailed us to the

site of the crash, long-lost, and dredged it up from the depths."
His tone lightens to one of wonder. "We returned, and it was
the most superior item. Vea was declared queen, and Clotille's
Arrow was mounted onto her vessel."

"That's impressive."

"That was Vea. She would love the fact that you have the
map. Only the falls can outdo her loot. The *Silver Arrow*'s
crew, our crew, will be pleased."

"But you remember that we will be the only ones to actually trek to the falls? I can't have vast numbers knowing the
location."

"I'm your first mate. The crew won't question it."

Good. That's one less worry. It will only be Roje I have to
convince that the perennial flow of golden coins from Anansi's
stories is more akin to a pond with a finite amount.

He continues talking about preparing me for the Iron
Shore, life on a ship, but he might as well have lifted me up
and thrown me over the balustrade in the heart of the library,
because for all the racing I've been doing already, I'm not
moving *toward* anything. I'm only going down—until Iraya
returns? Do I have to wait for her with her armies and her gall
and her blade aimed right at my heart?

"You're thinking about her," Roje murmurs; before I can
even consider denying the truth of his words, ask him how
he knows, he lands a look to stopper any lies. "You get this
pinched look on your face. What is it with the two of you?"

"I loathe her."

"Yeh mon, I get that impression."

"Regent—"

I turn from Roje; Verena stands in the doorway once again.

"Forgive me for interrupting once more, but they said it was urgent."

Filmore and Pasha enter the room.

"Thank the gods." I push away from the table. "What news of Anya?"

"The Unlit have triumphed in claiming Carling Hill," the latter announces without delay.

My entire head feels like it's been set on fire.

Aiyca's cradle of magic: treasured generations of family trees—power—taken. Lost.

"No, they haven't claimed it," Filmore says.

"What do you mean?" My voice is hoarse.

"The wording lacked specificity. Duppies of the glade aren't permitting Unlit *or* Alumbrar inside, but there was a battle for the land surrounding the family trees—" Filmore opens a fist to reveal an eyeball incised with a glyph; my stomach turns as he squeezes it until it bursts and a golden projection is cast from between his fingers.

On a bed of grass, my sistren lies between Xanthippe; Obeah are among their number too—Unlit, I suppose. All have creeping green veins on their bodies—hands, arms; Anya has them climbing across her left cheek like a plant grows beneath her skin.

"What's happened to her?" I demand. "Is she—" I can't bring myself to say *dead*.

"They're poisoned," Pasha says. "It was the Unlit's beasts. Teeth, claws, we don't yet know. The attack was . . . it was." He gags. "We took the injured to Sanar. Including Unlit we managed to capture. I can't say how many will survive. Questioning them sooner rather than later is recommended."

My eyes run across those sluglike veins beneath the skin of the injured. Something shatters in my chest. My heart. I think my heart might be breaking. For Anya and for Aiyca. The Unlit's attack means one thing—the worst thing. War isn't coming. It's here.

"Breathe, my queen."

That title from Roje's lips makes all those parts of me that loosened earlier draw tight again, embalmed in the responsibilities titles like queen, doyenne carry.

"Regent?"

That one too.

I thought I had time. I thought I could wait for Iraya to return before battle's song struck its first dissonant chord. What I wouldn't give to run to Anya, to ask her what I should do. But she already told me. I have to be present. I have to be Aiyca's leader.

"Yes, you were right to take them to Sanar." My voice filters in as though it's traversing a great distance. "Our people need the Healers." *What greater distance is there than time?* "The best." *Half a decade, to be exact.* "The Unlit too, since I will ensure they're questioned. So tell them—tell my *family*," I correct. Dada's side I haven't seen since I was a pickney. "I'll be on the way too."

As soon as I've told Aiyca's most influential the island is at war.

"Come." My legs hold beneath me when I stand; I wasn't sure if they would. "We need a room within the palace that can accommodate several hundred magi; I need Xanthippe, and several fireplaces to send messages and messengers." The Stealths and Roje accompany me through the library, listening intently and offering advice about how to quickly host a war council. "I'll need a carriage ready to transport us to Sanar the moment it's over, Filmore, Pasha."

"I'll come too," Roje says.

"Are you certain?"

"Of course, my queen."

Verena draws open the library doors and stands against the left to see our departure. "It was a pleasure, Regent Cariot." She bows, and something glints against her neck in the light of the wall sconces in the hall.

She does not rise; the librarian's head slides from her neck.

The volume of Roje's curse is second to the pitch of my scream as Verena's body slumps to the ground and her severed head rolls to look up at me, its eyes wide, its jaw slack.

A second scream rips through my throat; the sconce on the wall explodes, launching a battery of glass and metal toward me, the others. Turning my face in to my shoulder, eyes squeezed shut, I shout a request for answers.

The tone with which they're delivered sends a most bitter chill down my spine.

"A life for a life." Doyenne Cariot's duppy flickers down the hall adjacent to the library. "Your life for mine." She disappears, only to blip into focus closer.

"Mudda have mercy," Pasha utters, hoarse.

"It is what was promised." The sconce closest to the doyenne explodes. Her duppy gutters, like a flame in need of wood. "I have come to take what is owed, daughter."

"Run," I whisper. "For the gods' sakes. *Now.*"

The library doors thud closed; Verena's body is swept inside. The doyenne's duppy strengthens in potency. Her eyes narrow on me with a malice that stops my breath.

"Run!" I repeat; skirts in hand, I charge down the hall, Roje, Filmore, and Pasha close behind, the doyenne's duppy in pursuit.

16

IRAYA

Ushered into a chamber following the furor my announcement
incited, Delyse and I were supplied with food she tested for
poison with guzzu, and a promise from the click-happy man—
currently nameless, though I'd bet that chest Kirdan provided
he's a Divsylar—to return soon. Even as minutes seep into
hours, I am without worry. Delyse, on the other hand, may
pace a moat into the stone floor.

"I can smash that door to pieces, if you'd like."

"Preserve your magic," she cautions.

Her warning is clear. They might still come in here and
attempt to slay us.

Each stomp of her slippers is an admonition she cannot
give—won't, not when she doesn't trust using silencing guzzu
in here. There could be holes in the walls through which Doyenne Divsylar's council might spy on us and read our lips. If I
were confident in speaking, I'd tell Delyse that I've given the

doyenne the best reason not to kill me by speaking in a language she knows well: power. For a time, at least, since Kirdan and I will *not* be embarking on any journey to wedded bliss. Something I will clarify with him soon enough. But as long as his mama believes we are, I'll be untouchable in Zesia and should have more license to come and go as I please. Kirdan will find himself beloved by the same magi who have spat at his feet, and the Simbarabo will feel such gratitude toward me that they'll be willing to do anything I ask. If their general hears about our impending nuptials before I can explicate matters, he should reach this conclusion; a case of one hand washing the other. Hope won't spark in his heart that I've reconsidered his feelings.

Rocking onto my chair's back legs, I prop my feet on the table and congratulate myself on my ability to not only think well, but economically, under pressure. This is how the thin man finds me when he finally returns, hands clasped before him and robed sleeves billowing back in a way I imagine he thinks is intimidating but ultimately makes him look like a carrion crow in flight.

"Forgive us, Empress Adair," his companion, the scarred man, says, and in a manner that suggests he doesn't seek my forgiveness at all.

"For locking us in here, or for neglecting to introduce yourselves?"

The slightest muscle ticks in his jaw. "Both, it would seem. You may call me Krimpt. Others, Zesia's Minister of Defense."

Seems rather a mouthful, if you ask me.

"This is my brother, Kaltoon."

"Emissary Dívsylar," he corrects.

Then Kirdan lied about being an emissary too. Poor Jazmyne.

"I have business at the Cuartel," Krimpt continues. "The emissary will handle your stay." With a dangerous sort of look, the minister departs.

"And then there were three . . . dozen," I say, eyes skimming over the number of J'Martinet lurking in the doorway. Which I can't help but notice is wide open. If I didn't know better, I'd say Kaltoon is a little afraid to be alone with me. "Intimate."

"We needed to verify your existence," he drawls.

Contact whatever war dogs they have concealed in Aiyca to ask them what's happened.

"It took some time given that my nephew is in and out of consciousness," Kaltoon continues. "So the engagement has yet to be confirmed. But his lieutenant confirmed you are who you say you are. Though why the prince didn't say so months ago when you were first discovered in Carne Prison I don't know."

"There's something I don't know too."

"What?"

"Why you have yet to apologize."

His nostrils flare.

"Especially now," Delyse adds, to my surprise and pleasure. "When your brother already made his peace once he realized whom you are addressing."

Kaltoon levels a condescending glare down the length of his nose. "And who are *you*?"

Dropping my feet from the tabletop, I stand. "My Eye," I

say, pleased that Delyse keeps her shock in check. It's the position she would have vied for, if the empire still stood. Since we're pretending it wasn't dissolved a decade ago, we should fully commit. "And she isn't wrong. We have arrived, tired and dusty from the road, and you have locked us in this . . ." I cast a disparaging eye around what is actually a beautifully ornate chamber. "Cupboard." Indignance flares in the mossy depths of Kaltoon's eyes—for that is all he is, a weed. One entrenched in Kirdan's place beside his sisters. "Where are the princesses? Perhaps they know the meaning of hospitality and respect."

"Forgive me." Kaltoon's bow is not as deep as it should be, and for a moment I contemplate giving him a helping hand. "They have taken abed after the shock of your announcement," he says through gritted teeth. "I can take you to your rooms momentarily; there are but a few questions I need to ask about your departure from Aiyca—you killed Doyenne Cariot, I understand, but her daughter is the one who occupies the doyenne's seat as its regent."

Regent?

It takes every ounce of training I underwent before Carne, as well as in the prison, to keep my face clear. Beside me, Delyse doesn't flinch, but her thoughts must buzz with as much static as my own. That Alumbrar witch. She lied to me. Again. Or is it *already*? Gods.

"If you have come to ask for help stealing back your succession, then—"

"Your spies have neglected to inform you about the most important part of that story," I bluff. "Regent Cariot rules Aiyca with my blessings. I believe Doyenne Divsylar knows about working with Alumbrar." Kaltoon's smile slides off his mouth. Let him know that I've been spying too. "As for the rest of your questions," I all but hiss. "The impertinence of *you*, an *emissary*, interrogating me is something I'll be all too happy to discuss with the princesses, along with anything else they'd like to ask. In the morning. You understand?"

He chokes on what I suspect are arguments for the contrary, but eventually says, "Certainly, Empress. This way." Kaltoon billows out with his winglike sleeves.

Delyse and I follow him and the vanguard of J'Martinet through the palace. Great houses such as this tend to be nocturnal, with their many guests and attendants. But tonight it is unduly quiet. Even with the sprawling porticoes and patios, courtyards and balconies open to the sea and sky, it feels like a place of secrets. Delyse and I exchange a look.

"Why is it so quiet?" My question echoes, reinforcing it as fact before Kaltoon can think about lying.

His shadow looms like a specter on the wall beside him. "We do not permit many guests to wander in this palace."

Delyse clears her throat.

"*Empress*," he grinds out.

The torch to my right is blown out by one mighty gust.

Kaltoon flinches and instructs one of the vanguard to relight it.

"Afraid of the things that go bump in the dark?"

"Don't be ridiculous," he blusters. It isn't convincing.

Can he know then what stalks through this city? What might creep along the halls of this palace waiting to catch wanderers unawares at nightfall? He won't tell me, for fear of making Zesia look weak, of course. I suppose I'll have to go looking myself.

"Your rooms."

Twin doors are pushed open where they meet to reveal a sprawling living room with low stuffed couches, countless throw cushions, and a courtyard accessed through several archways, before which undulant alabaster curtains dance in the ever-present breeze from the surrounding waters. Several doors lead to unknown rooms. Delyse heads for one such set.

"Not those." Kaltoon glides over to bar her way. "This is the courting suite, for the happy couple." He grimaces at me; I return it in kind.

One bed?

"We didn't expect the prince to be the first to use these rooms, but so be it. Once he has been treated perhaps he'll honor the palace with a visit. Surely he won't bear to be parted from his love for long."

Perhaps Kirdan will remain injured and won't ever return.

"Tomorrow, the princesses will see you for a late breakfast. They'll send word with your staff—I can send them in now?"

"The morning will be fine."

"Doyenne Divsylar offers you her blessings and apologizes for not greeting you, but she isn't feeling like herself" are Kaltoon's parting words.

Delyse tracks him out of the door and then takes her time stringing guzzu like a net until the seating area has been shielded from unwanted ears. Even then, she sits close so our knees touch and casts a further guzzu around us in a protective sphere. For a moment we just sit; her darker eyes stare unflinchingly into my own. I brace for the undoing of all our work.

"That fact that you didn't tell me aside, that was . . . marvelous."

"Did I hear you correctly, mon?"

"They can't kill you, and, as the doyenne's future daughter-in-law, the most powerful witch in this empire, you have the leverage you need to convince her to send the Simbarabo to Aiyca. I think your brain is mightier than your sword arm."

"I can't tell if you're thinking too highly of me, or too highly of the Divsylars."

"What do you mean?"

"The plan is to extort the doyenne."

Mouth open, Delyse gapes at me.

"There's no time to convince her to offer aid. She will want to wait until Kirdan and I are married. And even then, she would likely find another way to delay my request. Not to mention the fact that I wouldn't give her the honor of being treated like an actual human." I scoff. "This witch stood by and let the Alumbrar, the Unlit, kill my family and overthrow our order. No. Once I have the Adair Grimoire, and I've learned how to stop the Unlit ushering in their beasts, I will request a percentage of the Simbarabo to accompany us back to Aiyca. As soon as the monsters are killed and the traitors apprehended, I will tell Zesia how to do the same here."

"Gods." Shaking her head, Delyse laughs. "You should have been a Stealth."

My grin feels so out of place, so foreign, and is short-lived after Delyse's next question.

"So you're not truly going to marry the prince?"

"No way."

"Then it isn't something the two of you discussed?"

"Again, no."

"Well, I'm pleased I don't have to share you with anyone yet. Aiyca's only just got you back. Zesia's prince doesn't get to muscle in—though he won't be pleased when he learns about his home's fate."

"You think that bothers me after all he did to get me here?"

She shifts in her seat. "It shouldn't surprise me, after your decade-long plan to exact revenge, that you can hold a grudge."

"Speaking of grudges, the sooner we return to Aiyca the better. Jazmyne is next on my hit list. Did you catch what he said? *Regent* Cariot."

"Yeh mon. The Jade Guild will keep an eye on matters. I'll send a missive tonight."

"Ask about the shields too."

Nodding, Delyse fights a yawn.

"You should rest."

"You won't?"

"Not yet."

She looks between me and the door to the bedroom I'm expected to share with Kirdan with a sympathetic twist to her mouth before leaving. She need not worry—a courting suite? I snort. After what I mean to do to Kirdan should he be foolish enough to show his face here, they might want to rename this room the *Killing* Suite.

Though he might not come. He seems so removed from this decadence, drawn in when everything else is so indulgent. And now I too must draw in, conceal the Warrior in me to lull my enemy into a false state of relaxation, because after announcing exactly where I am staying, word will travel via merchants; fire messages may even now smolder in hearths, read by disbelieving eyes and then shared by loose lips.

Iraya Adair lives.

The Unlit will hear and send their monsters, as planned. I will learn how to defeat them, and minimize further Aiycan bloodshed when we return home. *What about Zesian bloodshed?* a small voice whispers. The island at large I have no grievances with, but the royals, and whoever else decided not to offer Mama aid, they should sleep with both eyes open. So let *Them* come.

Let them all come.

17

JAZMYNE

The doyenne's duppy almost sent four more bodies to an early grave.

It's thanks to the mercy of the Mudda's Face of Fortune that we were all kept safe as we hid in the secret stairwell, behind the iron door leading down to the Adair trove.

"I can't stop shaking," Roje murmurs, after our rescue. Even so, his voice is carried by the high ceilings in the Witches Council Chamber. There's only the Stealths to hear him, stationed before doors fortified with iron, their magic reshaped from iron shields, decorative armor, door handles.

"Me too," I share.

If I thought my legs strong enough to hold me, I'd stand and pace rather than sit in this high-backed chair while the island's influential are collected and brought to me.

I expected to tell them I'm leaving for Sanar, to talk with

its Masters about a cure. I was confident in my ability to hold the line.

Now I can't stop thinking about Verena's head sliding off her neck.

Rolling across the floor.

I refuse to accept it as a sign, and yet . . . How can I hope to stave off this war with Iraya when I can't avoid my own mama's duppy?

"I can't believe none of your Alumbrar know how to expel the spirit," I say.

"We've never dealt with anything as malevolent as the doyenne's spirit. We haven't needed to."

"It might be worth speaking with the shields. Obeah gave me the ceremony to commune with her duppy. Why are the former guards still locked up?"

"Because of that knowledge," I tell him. "It makes them more dangerous than the doyenne's duppy. She will move on. We can escape the dead. The living are another matter."

An hour later, the Xanthippe have returned with everyone I requested: Ionie, Mariama, and Ormine; parish mayors; Cariot aunts, uncles, and cousins; as well as the Xanthippe and battalion commanders fill the palace's Witches Council Chamber wall to wall.

"What's the meaning of this, Regent?" Ivan asks. "Is this a late Eighth Night celebration? I volunteer myself to tell the first story." Elbows out, he fights his way to my left side at the head of the table. "There's a tale about your mama I bet you haven't heard before, Regent. I think you'll—"

"Storytime will have to wait."

Secrecy cost the late doyenne Aiyca. I can't fall victim to the same trap. Though, looking down the length of the table at the expectant faces gathered around it, I understand her taciturnity now more than ever. The truth is a weapon. This evening, I fall upon its tip.

"During my coronation, I spoke of dark skies. It's time to discuss who is behind them."

"What do you mean?" Ivan asks.

I exhale a slow breath, feel the tip of the truth burrow deeper in my chest. "The island is at war." And before they've drawn breath to ask questions, to exercise their umbrage, I launch into a condensed version of the entire sordid tale. The doyenne reneged on a deal with the Unlit, not the Obeah, and they have come to collect, with beasts from the other side of the veil. "The good news is that Carling Hill isn't allowing anyone inside. Alumbrar or Unlit. And the wounded are on their way to Sanar, as I will be too."

"You're leaving? What about the rest of us?" Ivan propels himself to his feet. "How will we be kept safe without you here? Monsters, I can't believe it."

Agreement comes from at least thirty additional mouths. The weight of their emotions, a complicated web I feel bound in, suspended and splayed before them for an easy devouring.

"I'm traveling to Sanar myself because I will be returning with Healers," I cut in. "I'll be gone for less than a day." With tomorrow's Ninth Night, I have no choice but to move with alacrity.

They don't listen.

"How are these monsters traveling across the island?" one Recondite Master demands. "I've seen no evidence of this army you speak of."

"How can you be sure?" comes from an Artisan of Cloth.

"And if there are monsters," Ivan booms, "I'd like to know why *you* get to escape this parish."

"I'm not escaping," I tell him, everyone. "I'm ensuring that if these monsters attack us as they are doing in Zesia, and no doubt the Skylands too, we can ward against them. This world will be saved by those who love, not destroy. Healers will be entrenched in every parish, mayors. The battalion soldiers and the Xanthippe will travel with at least one during every rotation. Additionally, battalion soldier patrols will increase, and the Xanthippe will have a heightened presence throughout major cities in each parish. Mayors for St. Ann, St. Catherine, and St. Bethann, you will see even more soldiers, as the parishes that surround St. Mary."

"That hardly seems fair," Ivan blusters.

"This parish is the island's Golden Seat," I tell him. "It cannot fall."

"You believe you can stand against the Lost Empress?" Ivan scoffs. "We've all seen her promises appearing around the island. Are we really meant to believe we'll be 'saved by those who love, not destroy'? Cha! She will crush us—not *you*, since you will be safe in Sanar."

"Ivan. Sit. *Down*." The voice that comes from my mouth is not mine, is not me. Not the me I was, safe from duppies, eager to assume my place on the living side of the veil. Not the me I was when I was training at Sanar with Dada. When I had a big sister. But it's me now. "I said *sit*."

Indignant, he makes a show of drawing his chair back.

"Roje."

Stepping out from my side, the pirate snatches the chair away from Ivan. Reddening, he scowls at Roje and looks for support. No one meets his eye but me.

"You believe you can do a better job?" I ask him, the room. "You'd like to stand here and make the decisions about which parishes receive more support, inevitably alienating and offending the others? Be. My. Guest." I make sure to meet every face, holding their focus until they cannot look at me any longer. "No? Then you can all listen. After Ivan has sat. *Down*."

"But my chair—"

Roje bodily moves him to the chair he dragged back from the table.

"Do you expect us all to listen without question," the Recondite from earlier says, "to tell our parishioners to do the same? Our families, when they see these alleged monsters? What about the Yielding, the shields? They're meant to protect us from acts of war such as this."

"We are not facing a known threat. We cannot continue as we were."

"Then what are you doing?" Ivan pipes up.

"I am working with the Lost Empress to recruit an army."

The questions start again. *She's alive? The messages aren't a Jade Guild stunt? Who is she?*

"Neither she— Listen! Please. Neither she nor I wishes for Aiyca to fall. She is an Adair. I am a Cariot. As first family heirs, it's our responsibility to take care of this island, its residents, and its problems."

"An Adair?" A Recondite picks up on, of course.

I suppose there's little harm in revealing Iraya's name now. "Iraya Adair."

Chatter sparks again, like a lit match.

"If our alliance doesn't show the danger of the situation we're in," I call, "then let this: I don't want you to lie about what's happening. Tell everyone. The Unlit have their sights set on Aiyca. They will do whatever it takes to possess it."

"The island will panic" comes from a Healer.

I turn to one of the Master Healers present. "Tell them what panic does to the mind."

"It sharpens focus and makes you more diligent about dangers—if you are measured. For those susceptible to anxiety, it will only exacerbate their suffering."

"Which is why the new council is days away from nomination. Until that comes to pass, the island will be protected by the last Yielding's success—" A lie. My first of the night. I cannot tell them about Javel. "They will also be protected by you all, by the Xanthippe, the battalion soldiers, and their own instincts won't fail them."

"You're serious about this?"

I don't know who asks the question. "As serious as the sure death that awaits us without Sanar's Healers, and without the

Lost Empress's army. We have to lean on one another, and we have faith in this plan. The Alumbrar way."

Which, from this meeting, isn't one I'm confident I can put my faith in—what do I have left? Who do I have left—that I'm not lying to? Including myself.

Hold back the Unlit, Supreme Being. Please.

Do not let Them come.

PART II

DO NOT
LET YOUR
LEFT HAND
KNOW
WHAT YOUR
RIGHT HAND
A DO

18

IRAYA

Delyse and I survive the majority of the night, at least.

But whether we survive the day relies on how I step next.

"My lady, can I help?"

Loudly, it seems.

Candles enkindle with my will; I turn to find an attendant standing across my room in a doorway I—*mengkeh*—didn't notice in the walls last night. A Stealth Nook. I know them well from my time as a pickney in Cwenburg. It doesn't matter how the placid face and clasped hands of the girl attempt to tell me she's a mere attendant; no one moves with her silence without training, whatever the absence of scarification beneath her right eye would have me believe. There are guzzu to conceal such things crafted for the very métier she no doubt belongs to.

"My lady?"

"Empress Adair."

"Pardon me?"

"My title is Empress, not *my lady*. And you, little mouse creeping between the walls—" At this, her fingers, knotted, tighten. "Who are you?"

"Fuma, Empress Adair." She bows; a thick braid slinks over an exposed, golden shoulder in a subtle sign of defiance. Multiple plaits woven through her waist-length hair would be too obvious, too great a sign that she serves the Zesian crown above all others. "Can I help you with anything?"

"What do you know about the appointment I'm to attend with the princesses this morning?"

"They'll expect you later than this." She turns amber eyes to the open balcony, where curtains as light as spider silk fail to entirely shield us from the brightening sky. "They won't be up for hours." Her mouth draws in on itself in silent admonishment. She said too much.

Or exactly what I'm meant to hear.

"Then I shall spend some time outside."

"Can I—"

"I'll be all right." I take up a robe draped across the velvet chaise longue at the foot of the bed. "As you said, it's early. You should rest. I know where to look when I need you now." I don't see it, but I feel her triumph crumble into doubt as she wonders if she revealed herself too early. Gods. Has the Adair name lost that much of its notoriety that our enemies sent a novice to watch me? Or is it another illusion . . . Perhaps a colony of mice creep through these walls, a handicap that will make covert operations difficult to be sure, but not insurmountable, I think, as the early rays of the morning gild my bare feet out on the balcony.

A thought summons the Mirror of Two Faces from beneath my pillow; when it appears in my hand, I curl my fingers around its handle and hug it close to my chest to keep it from being seen. I'll need a better place to stash it, given the extra bodies.

"Jazmyne Cariot," I whisper into its mottled surface.

Minutes pass.

What part of *keep the mirror at hand* did that throne warmer misunderstand?

"Jazmyne. Cariot." Teeth gritted, I give the jége a shake. What's more important than taking my summons?

Across the Singing Sands there's the faint mewl of the shadowcats who call its dunes home, and give them their name, but it's a much closer sound that snags my attention. For the eyes that watch as I approach the balustrade, head tilted as though the cats' screeching is mellifluous, when it's the steel-winged avians occupying potted olive trees that hold my real interest. At my approach, they seek higher purchase, but I'm sure they're similar to the guerra birds we kept at the Virago Cuartel for times when fires weren't available or possible and the Warriors needed to relay messages about threats to Aiyca. Resilient, strong, and possessing a humanlike intelligence, they are notorious symbols for battle.

An aimless meander takes me down the length of the balcony, where there are several woven nests ensconced in the eaves where roof meets wall—enough that I'm convinced Kirdan has something to do with their occupancy. This balcony might be a refuge for more than the birds, one that stretches past the Singing Sands and out across the undulating waves of the Great Ocean; its waves are dark beneath Nimue Palace's shadow. It's easy to picture him standing here, eyes turned out to the sea and the promise of liberty in distant lands. Though why he'd come here I don't know. Perhaps that's why he's so fond of a story; I imagine it's easier to accept the fictional when reality is already a nightmare. Absentminded, I touch the newest scar on my palm, not feeling its raised line so much as Kirdan's lips when we shared blood to use the Glyph of Connection. . . .

If Kaltoon didn't think his prince would have need for these rooms, why are there war messengers nesting on the balcony? Cautious, I enter the study. For its walls of books, dark rugs, and rich throws, it's sterile, a little stale. Nothing in here looks like him, so why is the balcony armed with war correspondents?

Why do I care?

I shouldn't.

I don't.

It takes seconds to shuck my robe, nightgown, and change into the innocuous kaftan I took from the stuffed closet and concealed beneath a sofa pillow last night. It's with equal ease that my conduit coin lights, and I will my hearing to stretch through the wood of the east door. As it was when I came to inspect last night, there are no guards, no rustle as they shift their weight to more comfortable positions. Before any watching eyes can send word, I draw the door open to embark out into the palace—and come face-to-face with Delyse.

Sitting down with a book in hand, her back leaning against the opposite wall, she tips her chin at me. "Wahan, Empress."

"Been there awhile, have you?"

"I knew what you would try." Abandoning her book, she hops onto her feet and follows me back into the study. "And I needed to speak to you without the listening ears. Though you're later than I suspected." Delyse lowers herself into a seated area before the fireplace. "How did you know none of their spy attendants watch this room?"

"I didn't."

"Iraya." She shakes her head. "The fact that this room is without guard, without Stealths, in its walls, makes it as easy to infiltrate as it would have been to exfiltrate. There'll be unhappy Zesians now you're back and their time unchecked is about to come to an end. And many who'll be even more offended that you're marrying the prince they haven't been grooming to take the doyenne's place."

I snort. "Kaltoon wishes he could kill me. That's why he's being so pleasant."

"You know what I mean, sistren." Her voice is light but enforced by our past.

Operating alone is a hard habit to break; sharing my intentions is even harder after so much time doing the opposite, after Kaleisha too, and the subsequent mess at Cwenburg, but . . . I promised I'd try.

"I thought I might start with recon, see what the Zesians here know about the monsters, given Kaltoon's reticence to discuss the palace's stillness last night. I didn't want to wait, not when—" Here goes. "Jazmyne reached out when we were at Lucia's. I don't think she's utilizing the shields."

Delyse curses.

"Have you heard anything from the Jade Guild? If they could

send Master Omnyra to speak with her, that would be perfect."

"Actually, yeh mon, I heard from them. That's another reason why I waited for you, and I'm glad I did. Our concerns are one and the same. There's been tension among our order."

"How so?"

Delyse twists her mouth. "You handled the Masters well, in Coral Garden. Ironically, they wish more Obeah saw you. Many of our order are denying that you exist, and the rest are convinced that the messages across the island are an invitation to rise against the Alumbrar."

Jazmyne truly is the gift that keeps on giving.

"It's—the Jade Guild are working on it, but I'll feel better when we return to Aiyca ourselves, and you're on the throne."

"Don't let Kaltoon or Krimpt hear you say that," I deflect.

Delyse rolls her eyes. "It's prudent that you comply with them if only to let them *think* you can be kept in line. We'll do recon and more to return to Aiyca, only it will need to be more covert than even you no doubt planned. Kaltoon sent across a list of appointments earlier." She plucks it out of thin air, with the aid of magic, and passes it over. "In addition to this morning's outing with the princesses, later tonight they're hosting your official welcome dinner."

Scanning the endless list of appointments, I make a noise of discontent.

"Oh, you wait. Today has nothing on tomorrow, when there's that fitting to ensure you have attire to wear at the litany of formal events coming your way. Including your engagement announcement, and the actual bacchanal to cement the union."

"They're hosting a bacchanal?"

"Of course they are. Think about the money."

Royal engagements have always spawned jump-ups. For a small few, it's not out of sentiment, but for what they signify: wealth for whichever island the intendeds are from, an increase in tourism, better relations between nations. Everyone wins when royals marry. So much so that everyone forgets what happens when royals fight.

"And that happens in *three phases*." I glance up at Delyse. "That's on top of the seven days I spent buried in sand. As much as I'd love to see how uncomfortable that all-but-orgy would make Kirdan, I can't be here for an entire lunar cycle." Jazmyne can't hold the Unlit off for that long, sure, but I can't pretend to enjoy this empress stuff for that long either. "Is there no way I can get out of it? Aiyca needs me home."

"It does, but the bacchanal coincides with Yule celebrations. If we want Zesia's support in fighting the Unlit, we need to play by their rules while we're here, and to be seen doing so." Delyse levels a wry look my way. "We'll be sure to order you some sandals with laces, when the big day rolls around, mon. Better for running."

"Bless the Cuartel and all those shield drills," I muse. Which reminds me of my plan . . . one there's just about enough time for, before meeting Kirdan's sisters. "Delyse, to fight these beasts—" Hell, to survive the wedding preparations, given the length of engagements. "I'll need training." My family Grimoire would be a great start, but books mean being stuck inside, away from all the monstrous action happening in Zesia's streets. "Here's a thought," I begin, my voice just shy of conspicuously carefree. "What about if I received instruction from a group of elite soldiers instead?"

"Are you ever not thinking?" Delyse shakes her head, not buying my act for a second. "I didn't realize, back at the Cuartel. Didn't see . . ." Her eyes tick between my own, something indiscernible in them. "While I admire it, there's a flaw in your logic. Empresses don't fight—I know, I know." She holds her hands up. "I'm following your lead, but we don't want Zesia to suspect you any more than they already do."

"You're right," I agree. "Empresses don't fight, but they do visit the sick."

Especially when one of them has my family Grimoire.

"*After* studying." Delyse's conduit coin illuminates, preceding the appearance of a stack of old tomes. "I paid a visit to the library."

"Guzzu?" I breathe, reaching for the topmost book. The pages inside are handwritten, just as I remember Aiyca's being; perhaps even by the same bright minds at the Recondite Institute located on a remote island within the empire. "This enchantment helps recall memories of place—this glyph is for turning walls incorporeal!" Granted, only the latter will help us, but still.

"Any complaints about a little tutelage first?"

"Not one."

Unlike our clandestine arrival onto the island, the second journey Delyse and I take through the Sadirren Province's capital after a couple hours of study is full of sights. Like Aiyca, Zesia's Order of Obeah members adorn themselves in bright fabrics, letting their scarification announce their trade for them; Alumbrar stick to their colors. Additional nonsecular, mostly affiliated with the Sodality of the Knife and Shadow, a monastery with a larger presence in the vast continent to the west of Xaymaca, cover their faces with velum-thin scarves, their own devoutness permitting only the parish's forgotten saints to see them unshrouded.

Either way, it's a covering I would appreciate, with all the focus centered on the small party of J'Martinet Delyse and I travel with. It was inevitable after announcing myself yesterday, but it's still a shock to the senses. *Ira* would have slunk through the city's streets, a denizen of their dark coves and alleys, but thanks to Kaltoon, an ever-present oil slick waiting to catch me unawares, *Iraya* must sit in a dress with a cowl so low, my belly button peeks out, looking like a rod has been thrust somewhere uncomfortable while pretending not to notice the pointing fingers, the whispering mouths, the literal halting of delta and regular traffic as the city comes to an all-but-complete halt to see the Lost Empress, hereby known as the Ornery Empress, the Leave-Me-Alone Empress.

"The basket is a nice touch." Delyse keeps her voice low so the punter navigating our way across the dark waterway cannot hear.

"Yes." In contrast I am loud. "I hope the provisions will aid in my . . . *his* recovery," I say for the ears that listen, adopting yet another role, this time of the loving wife-to-be.

The excitement in my voice isn't entirely fabricated. I requested peppers with the food I sent Fuma to prepare in the kitchens. Having laced every morsel with the Scotch bonnet, here's to each bite burning Kirdan from the inside out as they make their way out of every orifice—*after* I'm done with him.

We dock the kanoa at a point overlooking a beautiful oasis that gives Zesia's capital city its name, Green Island, where attendants already prepare for the breakfast Delyse and I are to have with the triplets, before the J'Martinet sift Delyse and me into the Changuu Province.

To the east of the island, the somber hill of buildings once housed the province's eponymous prison before Carne was built to accommodate the empire's criminals. This Delyse whispers to me as we're marched through gray streets. Unlike in the spotless, wealthy Horn, buguyaga are about in droves, clinging to shadowed pockets of pavement, cracked beneath the remorseless focus of a far-reaching sun. And all the while, the domineering prison structure looks on. Doyenne Divsylar hasn't allowed the soldiers who keep the island safe to forget its origins—to forget who they are, what they're believed to have done at birth. The bastions of metal gates that assault an otherwise clear sky deter them from breaking out, but also tell the Simbarabo that no one loves them enough to try to get *in*. I didn't think anyone could be worse than Doyenne Cariot, but perhaps this witch might be, gods. Stringency without reason is cruelty by another name.

Fists clenched, I lead the way inside the entry gate, instructing the J'Martinet to wait in a stark forecourt. Eclipsing Cwenburg's Cuartel, Zesia's is filled with an innumerable amount of soldiers. Thousands. Tens of thousands of Obeah, Alumbrar, and Aiycans. Running, or performing drills, they look like the unfeeling weapons this island has made them. And yet, Kirdan feels. Despite being sent here by his mama as a pickney, and enough that this is what he hopes to fix, if I allow him to become Zesia's doyen.

"Empress Adair," a familiar voice calls; Krimpt emerges from the sentry bohío with Zander not too far behind. "Wahan. We received word about your visit from the palace. This is Lieutenant Garaycía."

As he levers into a bow, Zander's face gives nothing away, but that's the point. We've never met—must not act like it, for the eyes that watch, even here. The Minister of Defense himself, and a bevy of forlorn soldiers so eager for praise, for consideration, that they would feed news to anyone with a kind word. Message received.

"You've been training?" I angle my head at Krimpt's and Zander's matching tunics, pants, and boots. "I thought your role more honorary here."

"With my nephew in recovery, I've stepped in to fulfill some of his duties" is his smooth reply. Indeed, there are few flies on this Divsylar. "I'm afraid I have business elsewhere, but the lieutenant is here to handle whatever your query may be. I'll see you at your welcome dinner this evening."

Delyse frowns after his retreating back. Kaltoon is an overgrown moth flapping in the sphere of my light, but the minister is harder to gain a read on. Is he happy, indifferent, or constipated? The mind wonders.

"As the minister said," Zander begins, "the general is still indisposed, but—"

"Even to me?" I ask.

Mouth twitching in his handsome face, those angles

highlighted by the sunlight trapped in the silver curtains of hair drawn back from his face in several braids, the lieutenant tips his head to the side. "Mmm, that's right. I believe congratulations are in order."

"Commiserations, you say?"

Putting up an even greater fight to conceal a smile, Zander bows his head. "I'm happy to handle your inquiry if you follow me." With quick, strong steps, he takes us away from the immediate traffic of the Cuartel into a building filled with doors—sleeping quarters, perhaps, with an office in the back.

Only when the door is closed does he speak again. "You have minutes to talk freely. Word will spread, Krimpt's spies will come."

"Silencing guzzu?" The disks on Delyse's belt spark and light, one by one, like lit candles.

"Will only affirm suspicion."

"Fine," I say. "Shamar?"

"A visiting cousin from family to the southeast of the Great Ocean."

"Good. Kirdan?"

Delyse turns to me, brows raised.

"You were serious about seeing him?"

"Serious as death."

Zander snorts. "I'll take you to him, if we're done here?"

"Almost. You know what he and I mean to do," I say. "Before that happens, I need training."

"*We* need training," Delyse cuts in.

Zander's focus settles on me; despite his Alumbrar features, his eyes are all Kirdan. "He said you would come, though you're later than he predicted. He swore you'd be up before the sun and over here making demands."

At my scowl, he smirks. Suddenly everyone is an expert on my movements and plans.

"We'll return tomorrow evening."

"I expected you to be back tonight, so tomorrow will do." Zander crosses to his office, opens the door. "The general doesn't know about your plans to wed. I thought I'd leave that honor to you."

"Magnanimous."

"Self-serving." He shrugs shoulders that strain against his tunic. "I'd much rather watch his reaction from the sidelines."

"Not today you won't." The sweetness in Delyse's voice is not without a sharp undertone. "I need an escort, and an excuse, to see Shamar."

Pleasantly surprised at the help, I nod her way.

From the offices, we three venture out into a yard that could have been Cwenburg's Cuartel, without the influence of the Masters. There are no trees or benches, no witchlight-jar garlands, no laughing shields egressing from classrooms or tossing weighted balls across courtyards. Austere in a way associated with Alumbrar, or the prison this structure once was, even the undulation of bohío-dotted hills seems rather . . . flat.

It's into one of these large, round huts, the clay of its structure long grayed, that Zander strides. As I blink away the harshness of the sun, cots materialize from the semidarkness; at the end of each sits a battered trunk—many of them.

"Please," I say as Simbarabo abandon books, missives, to shoot to their feet and slap a fist across their hearts. "At ease, soldiers."

Fourteen soldiers sleep in here, though at the moment there are only a handful. Including the prince. Not even exhaustion can humanize his bulk, his threat. It's like sneaking up on a sleeping prowler.

"If you'll excuse us, men, Empress Adair wishes to spend time with the general."

During their debouchment, I nod, smile, but my focus remains on Kirdan's still form. Why would he sleep in here with so many bodies? Irrespective of patrol shifts in the city, at one point during either the day or night, he would share this space, its air already thick, pillowy, with his sweaty compatriots' body heat when he doesn't have to.

"Your sistren and I will return in fifteen," Zander says, his voice already echoing as though he is at the other end of a tunnel. "I trust you won't harm him?"

"You and I both know you don't trust me."

He pauses. "Save the worst of what you'll do until I'm almost back, then."

My worst, the basket, I leave on the floor by the door once Zander and Delyse have gone. Kirdan is already in hell here, I think as I weave my way through the cots toward him, my sandals crunching against beads of sand underfoot—too much, considering the Simbarabo leave their boots by the door. . . . It dawns, then, why Kirdan sleeps in here. Vulnerable, he's never been more at risk of a successful assassination. The sand is a security measure, a subtle alarm to wake his men, who are his shields, voluntary walls between him and whoever would wish to do him harm. Krimpt? Kaltoon? His mama? Kirdan wants things to change. There is no greater threat to totalitarianism than individuality. Perhaps that's why, before I've cleared the final ring of beds between him and me, his eyes open.

"Are you here to kill me?"

"Not in this dress." I trail a hand across the headboard of the cot across from his. "While I'm not averse to playing the hand fate delivers, with you I'd want more of a fight. We could settle that age-old question, Virago or Simbarabo."

Kirdan eases himself up to sitting position without wincing. The muscles in his arms bulge beneath skin the same golden brown as the Singing Sands. It's been eight nights since we arrived in Zesia, and his body looks like it hasn't wasted a minute. The sheet slides down the hard ridges of his bare chest as he reaches for a cup of water by his bed.

"Should I begin groveling now?" Draining his cup, he returns it and drags a hand through his choppy hair, damp with sweat. "Or would you rather I apologize first?" Too fatigued to be anything other than earnest, Kirdan swings his feet onto the floor, leaving the sheet to bunch around his waist. "In that dress, I am at your mercy."

"Why don't we start with my family Grimoire and take it from there."

He grimaces. "I can't access it."

"Tell me where it is and I'll get it myself."

"It can't be taken from its secure place by anyone but me,

and since my uncle has divested me of my conduits, I can't get it."

"Use me, my magic."

It's hard to miss his mostly bare body brace against whatever he's about to say next. "I can't. The risk is too great."

"Convenient."

"For my uncle." Kirdan's face twists with bitterness. "You can't believe I want things to be this way? Me here, forced to have my men put themselves between me and every window or door, on the chance that the soldiers who would rather see my uncle in charge decide to expedite matters. Meanwhile, you're in the palace, which may as well be Aiyca given how difficult it is for me to reach you." He slams a fist into the cot; if it was wood, I wouldn't have been surprised to see it split. "I won't say I'm sorry that you're here, that, against the odds, you stayed. But I am sorry for the circumstances that brought you here. Lying to you. Again." He pins me to the spot with the weight of his focus. One that lays anchor in more than my body, my bones, but the very core of me. "Would you have come of your own accord if I asked you? Would you have stopped to listen to me tell you that I didn't only want you here, I *needed* you here? Iraya—" His jaws clench around whatever he might have said. For several seconds he merely breathes. "I tried to tell you why before, and you didn't listen."

On the peninsula.

"But you will listen now." Low, gravelly, his voice brokers no opportunity for rejection. "I wasn't trying to drown us when we arrived here. The guzzu in the black water didn't recognize me, my magic, after we activated the Rite of Warriors with the Glyphs of Connection. I don't want to chance being locked out of the liminal pocket I stashed the Grimoire in—the spaces we sift through? The same could happen if we use the rite, and the Grimoire could be lost forever." Breathing heavily, he props himself up against the cot frame. "Think what you will of me, Iraya, if it makes you feel better, but that recuses you from anger at my lies. Not when, in your mind, I'm already a villain." He watches me through hooded eyes, and I—given what's to come, the hurdles, the barriers—don't want to fight with him any more than I want to fight with Jazmyne at present.

But to trust him?

"I don't know what I would have said if you invited me to Zesia," I finally reply. "If you had been straight with me, presented the benefits, I might have come. But you didn't give me the chance. You robbed me of that decision, and now we'll never know. I get to be mad. I get to feel like I can't trust you. You've never given me the time to."

His blink is slow, resigned; he nods. "I don't want us to continue treating one another like enemies, Iraya. Things have to change. We have to."

Considering him, I run through my plan once again. Even if I don't betray him, there's still the matter of which island we help first, Zesia or Aiyca.

"How long until you're well?"

"I need several more days," he murmurs with a certain wariness. "At least. If Zander can continue managing my uncle."

"And you trust your Alumbrar second."

"With my life."

"Then I will find other ways to keep busy until you can bring me my family Grimoire."

His eyebrows lower.

"We want the same thing, Kirdan." Mind changed, I decide not to retrieve the basket. Even if he did survive the Scotch bonnets, I'm not sure our alliance would. "And as you pointed out in Cwenburg's gardens, I'm not a villain, which means you can't be either. But make no mistake, if you're not presenting me with the Grimoire in several days, I advise you make sure you're dressed. I suspect you'd like more dignity in death."

19

JAZMYNE

Xanthippe sift us in two carriages less than five miles outside Sanar. It reduces three days of travel down to a matter of hours, late morning on the Ninth Night. In theory, it was worth the motion sickness. Roje, who only stopped retching moments ago, disagrees.

As for me, one look at the alcázar and that calm, measured Healer I was meant to become, who the doyenne erased to instate as heir, floods my veins in a restorative infusion. Unusual, against the sharp angles of villas nestled into tumbling green hillsides overlooking the deep belly of valleys, the island's foremost Alumbrar Healing Center curves as though molded between the artful hands of the Seven-Faced Mudda, given how lovingly shaped and curated it is—something that, though resembling a building from a time far ahead of this one, is rumored by Anansi to be immediately palliative to all who gaze upon it. And I'm here to draw its best into the heart of chaos.

"That's the place, is it?" Rough with a lack of sleep, Roje's voice comes in from the almost-darkness across the carriage. "Looks like the form of a well-loved woman. Is it black?" He hinges forward to take a closer look out of the same window I lean toward.

"Maroon, like our color." The same colored dress I wear now, as loose and austere as my uniform would have been as a Healer. "It's meant to resemble a vial, a cure, hope."

And to me it was, for the longest while. The loss of that life strikes as sudden and fast as the news about Carling Hill's occupation, the late doyenne's attack on the attendants in the palace.

"Must be strange to return."

Perhaps it's the lack of sleep, the earliness of the hour, but I glance at Roje across the curtained depths of the carriage, in his soft leather jacket, the boots tucked into breeches that always seem one wrong move away from dropping to his knees, and don't fight the candor of my next words. "Doyenne wasn't the title I worked toward initially. I was in training to become a Healer, like Dada."

"I haven't seen him around."

"He was killed during the usurpation." Avoiding the sympathy I've come to expect with any mention of Dada's death, I look toward the window, seeking Sanar again. "Or by the late doyenne's ambition—" One Roje saw for himself during her attack. "If we were animals, Madisyn and me, she might have eaten us young." And then, so comfortable in the dark, too comfortable, I utter, "There are no monsters like the ones we live with."

"When I was born," Roje begins, "Mama threw herself to the waves and took me with her."

My inhale feels too loud, too brutal after all those soft syllables.

"Roje—"

"I don't know what I might have been." He doesn't catch my eye, as unwilling to accept sympathy as I am. "I was found by a pirate who nursed me back to health and raised me as his own. There's an honor among a crew that supersedes some families. You'll see when you board the *Silver Arrow*, when you bear the Coral Crown." He leans into the shaft of light bisecting the carriage intermittently from passing witchlight lamps to look at me then, to let me see him; a fierce pride is emblazoned in his face. "You are without a family, but you can view us as one."

On the ship Vea no doubt named, in part, for my sister . . . a vessel I might not see.

Leaving Aiyca when I thought I would be doyenne, Iraya would be elsewhere, and her order would be satisfied with the death of the witch who usurped their empress was one matter. Leaving Aiyca as regent, with Iraya set to return any day with an infamous army at her back, Carling Hill guarded by duppies, monsters on the prowl with poison in their veins, and a masked enemy set to fight me for this island?

I'm sickened by the hope that flares in my chest, knowing that, commensurate to what the Transmuter says, I could shorten the expedition for the Conduit Falls. Rather than sailing the empire for weeks, months, the *Silver Arrow*'s crew—with several of my Stealths, and Xanthippe—can drift along for a few days to a neighboring archipelago. For that I could send a proxy. Or perhaps it would be better to select another from Vea's crew. . . .

I won't tell Roje yet. First I have to show him, and by extension the crew, that they should still work with me even though it looks like I cannot be queen. All these secrets are becoming hard to keep track of. There is the war I hide from the island, the near loss of Carling Hill I have no idea how—if—I will break to Ira, and now the race I used to subvert yet another piece on the board in the battle for Aiyca.

The carriage slows; Roje draws the curtain away an inch. "Family or Anya first?"

For the longest while Anya has been my only close family. There are cousins on Mama's side, aunties and uncles, but it's always felt too competitive, like if I missed a step and reached for a steady arm they'd move out of reach. When I was a pickney, Dada's side of the family and I were close; I spent most of my time at Sanar. It's all I have to rely on, when I ask the Master Healer to give me her best and brightest to disperse across Aiyca.

That and more secrets and lies.

"Never mind, mon." Roje picks up his axe from the bench beside him and holsters it. "Your family is waiting. All of them, it looks like."

His warning is the sole one I have when, upon the carriage door being opened, and taking the hand offered to help me down the steps, a fan of unfamiliar Alumbrar are lined up in the shadow of the alcázar.

"Niece." An enrobed witch steps forward, her nose broad and her eyes small. Like Dada's, like mine.

"Aunty Galene." Her name comes to mind easily. "It's been too long."

"Welcome home." Arms wide, Dada's older sister envelops me in a tight embrace; turpentine is a third participant, potent as it is. The cleansing tang of it slinks around my body like a bandage, a form of comfort and support. "We've been anticipating your arrival since the missive." She draws me back to look at me with the keen stare of a Master Healer, and Sanar's head-witch-in-charge. Like a blade, quick and sharp, it penetrates to the bone. "You'll remember your pupa's side, of course."

Family members edge closer. There are few smiles, but mostly I'm met with a curiosity that devolves into something as cold as the stars when they glance over my shoulder. Filmore, Pasha, and the Xanthippe are there, of course. But their toll is paid in silver. Roje has dreads, but their dark color isn't the appropriate currency.

"There is much to discuss." Aunty Galene gives me one final pat before stepping back. "Your companion being one of them."

"Roje, meet Sanar's Master Healer."

He bends into a bow from the waist; the blade of his axe winks in the lights shining from Sanar's many windows. Aunty does not smile.

"No doubt you want to see your sistren." She waves a slender, lined hand and a girl clears the throng of family. She's about my age, my height, and her shaved head only draws the focus to eyes as large and enigmatic as the bush cradling the alcázar to its right and left. "My daughter—"

"Chaska," I finish. "I remember you, cousin. You look well."

She offers me a small nod in return.

"Chaska will take you to your sistren," Aunty continues. "I can escort your companions to the prisoners. The Xanthippe from Carling Hill managed to capture two of the Unlit. They've been healed and prepared for questioning."

Roje and I exchange a quick look.

"Why don't you go and see them with Pasha?" I offer Roje a smile, articulating that I'll be fine, likely better, without his presence.

"If it's all the same, I'll wait until we've seen Anya." Something in his tone, the stiffness in his body, makes me take another look at my family, Aunty.

With a calm serenity on her face, the latter nods. "Very well."

"Blessings," I feel the need to say to her, to those massed behind her. My family. "For all that you've done to heal the Xanthippe, the Stealths. You serve Aiyca with your benevolence, and she has never forgotten kindness. Nor has she ever needed it more."

"Blood follows vein," Aunty says. "To whatever end."

My cousin turns toward Sanar. "If you'll all come with me."

Inside is just as I remember, vast and clean, yet cave-like and intimate with the deep burgundy walls and soft warm lighting. A city in and of itself, Sanar might be the only building to make me feel small, yet strong. Capable.

"Regent," Chaska says, shifting to and fro like a river to

avoid running Healers, their robes and silver hair streaming like ribbons behind them. "Why not doyenne?"

In the noise and activity I pretend not to hear and instead I ask a question of my own.

"Do you work here?"

She nods; the movement is all grace. "I'll replace Mama when she's ready."

When we were pickney, it was a matter of teasing between our parents about which of us would step into the role of overseeing Sanar. Jealousy is a heavy weight in the pit of my stomach at the life I could have had if not for the course of destiny, the perils of fate.

"Much is different from when you were here," Chaska adds, glancing my way. "But then much is different with you too."

"We've both grown."

"Into better versions of ourselves?"

The oddness of her question makes me look sidelong at her. "What do you mean?"

"Fix your face," she mutters.

"What?"

"Fix your face. You look upset. Don't." Her shoulder brushes against mine as she's suddenly close. "Be measured, cousin. Be steady," she breathes. "Your mama, do you mourn for her?"

"Why?"

"Answer truthfully."

"*Why?*"

Her silence seems to speak, to tell me my life depends on the next words I say.

"I only mourned Madisyn and Dada."

Abruptly my cousin turns down a hall, leaving me reeling at the randomness of the conversation. "Your sistren is just through here."

The ward on the other side of a set of double doors is empty, still. Chaska, avoiding my gaze altogether, draws back a curtain, revealing a Healer crouched over a bed where a familiar profile greets me.

"Anya!"

"Wait." Roje thrusts out an arm, addresses my cousin. "Is it safe to touch her?"

"It is," the male Healer affirms. "The poison has been siphoned out." Framed by a soft halo of silver curls, his face is kind enough, soft enough, to indicate he hasn't yet become inured to patient care, which means he hasn't been working long enough. A student.

He moves aside at my approach; I take the seat close to the head of the bed, gather Anya's limp hands in my own. Sleeping, and in a soft brown robe rather than severe Stealth black, she looks at peace; the green veins beneath her skin are entirely gone.

"Who's been treating Anya and the Xanthippe?"

"I have."

My brows raise. "You've come across this poisoning before, then?"

He nods, his focus never wavering; if anything, it intensifies.

"We'll give you time with your sistren," Chaska says. "Nazeem."

With a bow, the Healer leaves with my cousin, closing the door behind them.

"Did you—"

"It's odd, without your sistren insulting me," Roje cuts in. "I might even miss it a little. I'm glad she'll be well." As he talks, he slips a writing tool and a pad from his pocket; he scrawls a quick note and passes it my way.

It reads, *I don't trust your family.*

"We'll be on the other side of the door" is what is spoken for whoever he believes listens. Paranoia, I'm half certain.

Chaska did act strangely, Nazeem too . . . but they are isolated out here where they have more reason to remain stuck in their ways, and to be stubborn about it. But my family doesn't matter right now; Anya does. Her chest has been rising and falling steadily enough that the knot in mine that grew when I first heard of the attack unwinds some.

"It's been a strange few days, sistren," I tell her. "I don't know what I would've done if you didn't survive this."

Her eyes open. "Is everyone gone?"

Emitting a sharp yelp, I jolt back; the chair grinds against the tile underfoot.

"Anya, my gods!"

She winces. "Easy on the ears, Jaz."

"Sorry, I'm sorry. I just— You're awake? Are you well?"

"Not quite, but we need to talk about the Healer before he returns." She clears her throat.

Coconut water sits on the side table. I start for it.

"No. I don't know if they're drugging it and I can't risk sleeping before I tell you—" She breaks off into a dry cough; each racking gasp for breath breaks part of me. "The Healer—" She coughs again.

"Can't you write it down? Let me get Roje; he has items we can use."

"He's unavailable."

I twist around as the Healer, Nazeem, slips back through the doors beyond the curtains; as the former close, I see Roje, Pasha, and Filmore are splayed across the floor in the hall.

"*Clips.*" Anya struggles to rise in the bed beside me.

I free the magically infused combs from my curls; my fingers sink between the teeth as I aim them at the Healer. His hands, held out before him in a supplicatory gesture, don't look nimble enough to set a bone or stitch a wound closed. They do look large enough to wrap around a throat, though—my throat.

"Don't come any closer."

"Your sistren should really drink some water."

"Did my pirate out there—" I jut my chin toward the door. "The guards, drink water?"

"I blocked their ability to eavesdrop with the same magic I used to heal your friend. Well, it's from the same place, at least. *My* home." Before I've adjusted to the thickening of his accent, the difference between our stresses and inflections, gold beams from the coin around his neck and silver hair melts into black, just as I saw on the Unlit in Coral Garden.

Mudda have mercy. He's Obeah.

Consuelo, help me. Sofea, show me a way out of here that won't take my life, Anya's, Roje's, the Stealths'. I raise the clips higher.

"Shoot, Jazmyne!" Anya chokes out.

"I'd rather you didn't." A shield springs from this imposter's

213

conduit coin; a lambent force of sparking magic that stands before him. "I am not your enemy. My birth name is Anan Opoku, and I am the fourth heir to the Skylands throne."

My forehead buckles beneath my confusion. "You're a Skylander?" And an heir at that. Allegedly. "What are you doing here? *How* are you here?" There's been a moratorium on sifting since the Unlit began rising against the late doyenne.

Anya's bare feet slap against the floor. "Get away from her," she snarls.

"I haven't moved a step. And I don't need to, technically. Magic, remember."

"How?" I demand.

"The magic?"

"All of it. If you are who you say you are and not one of the Unlit here to kill me, then how do you have magic? You're not a firstborn. Not to mention the fact that you're a boy."

"I have magic the same way that you have those clips. Someone with power gave me part of theirs to use. To use here, in fact."

"Why?"

"Because the monsters Iraya Adair seeks to kill are relations to the ones my island needs to save. I cannot expound on more than that, but, along with my siblings who seek to ascend to the Skylands throne, it's my duty to prevent you from damaging that world beyond the veil."

I long to look at Anya, to physically gauge her take on this, but her silence is confirmation enough. The Skylands have long been shrouded in secrecy. It's hard to determine if this magi is telling the truth or lying. I had no idea their succession

214

and inheritance procedures were different. Who would? No one in my generation, my parents', or my grandparents' generation has had any dealings with the reclusive largest island in the defunct empire.

"The Unlit sent us a message too," Anan continues. "Only to find that we are well versed in what dwells behind the veil, enough not to fear them, and enough to monitor the pathways through which they travel. It's how we know that if you continue as you are with Iraya Adair, the way of life on my island will be forever damaged."

"If I continue?"

Rolling his eyes, Anan lowers his hands. "You both seek to destroy the monsters, and the exit in our world through which those particular Oscuridad travel. The Skylands can't have that happen."

My hands around the combs tighten. "You want us to save the monsters determined to claw their way into Cwenburg Palace, into me? I don't think so."

"It's less about those monsters and more about their entire world. To destroy their method of travel will affect matters I cannot expound on."

"I believe I know all the same." There are stories about the Skylands' aerial fleet—the beasts with wings they take to the sky astride. I didn't know them to be monsters. I didn't know the Oscuridad, as he's called them, to be as varied in nature as the people living in Aiyca, Zesia, and indeed his home too. "You keep some of these beasts."

Anan presses his lips together. He says nothing, but it's almost a confirmation. "In exchange for your support with this thing I cannot discuss, I'll offer you my services. The Skylands' doyenne selects her heir regardless of numerical inheritance order or gender. Each birth cycle, the victor proves why they are fit to rule in various ways. This time around, I stand against several of my siblings tasked to save our home from being caught up in another Aiycan skirmish."

"So protecting the monsters, or rather their world," I amend, "will win you your title?"

Anan nods. "I will lend my skills to your plight. None of your allies will die of Oscuridad poisoning. Few Skylanders are trained to treat it. You're looking at one of the best."

That would be something. . . . Iraya could bring her army here, fight, and fall victim to the same veins that Anya did without hope of a cure. But the implications of trusting this Skylander, this stranger, crowd my thoughts, pound behind my temples. The biggest quandary is, why me? Why would he side with me and not Iraya?

"With such high stakes," Anya says, her voice hoarse from the coughing, "what you are offering in return isn't enough."

Eyes on Anan, I back up to put my sistren in my line of sight too. She wouldn't ask why her. Neither would the late doyenne. What *would* she ask? Nothing that would make her look weak, something that would only strengthen her. What do they have that—

"Army."

Anya's smile is beautiful in its triumph.

"You have an army," I state.

"Not me, technically." Anan glances between us. "One of my siblings handles those matters, and she's also in the race."

"If you want me to spare your beasts' world, you'll give me your army's fealty." We need numbers here—*I* need numbers to prevent Iraya waltzing in and sprawling across my throne with her insouciance and arrogance. Yes, Aiyca will be saved by those who heal, but it needs protection from those who destroy. "Speak with whomever you need to and be quick about it. As you said, when Iraya returns, she has plans to destroy all monsters on this island. If you have a hope of becoming the Skylander doyen, of securing my support, you will help me ensure she cannot dock at any of my ports."

Anan assesses me with a cool stare, one that's equal parts Healer and hubristic Obeah. "My siblings thought I was stakki to stand by you, but it takes a Healer to know just what we're made of inside." His nod is limned with respect. "I will see about getting you your army, Regent, since you are clearly the witch to beat. It may take some time."

"We don't have any. Iraya will return from Zesia soon."

"I have a way to track the Adair witch's movements, but as a sign of good faith, I will leave instructions for a poultice behind. It won't cure the poisoned, but it will put them in a healing sleep until they can be seen by a magi with the skill to cure them." He clicks, and a sheet with fine script appears in his hand. He passes it to me. "Partners?" After a moment's hesitation, I take the recipe. He glances at Anya, who wavers beside me. "And you should be in bed for at least a day longer; you can trust that, henceforth, there will be no drugs in your water." He turns to leave. "Little more."

As soon as he's drawn the curtain, Anya collapses onto the bed and reaches for the glass on the table. "I'm not staying here another day." With a wince, she makes to rise again; I hasten to her side, press a hand against her shoulder, and push her back down onto the bed.

"I need you to get better so you can join me—*when* you're fit to travel."

Her chest rises and falls with an alarming speed.

"The poison weakened you physically?"

"It was like dying over and over again," she wheezes. "And hoping the next inch of poison sludging through your veins would be it, the last, and you would—" She cuts herself off. "But I am already better than I was; recovery has been swift, thanks to Anan. I hate to say it. But perhaps it's better that we know? The Skylands. I couldn't believe it when I saw through his phony accent. What will you do?"

"Nothing rash." It isn't the truth, or a lie. It's just enough to stop her dressing and demanding to come home with me, because far from being lenitive, Sanar might prove to be the death of us all.

One Skylander of at least four sought me out, and it was the one who doesn't have any command of his island's army. What are the chances that sibling is sitting with Iraya right now, breaking bread as they discuss their plans to change a world they won't want me to be part of?

Unfortunately, given the questions I have about her involvement with Anan, it's Aunty, not Chaska, who arrives to escort me, Roje, Pasha, and Filmore to the Unlit prisoners.

Without holding cells or a dungeon, Sanar's closest detention location is the morgue tens of feet below the main Healing

Center. Dim and drawn with a cloistering intimacy, the rock is slick with water. Neighboring hot baths that bubble in a great healing pool naturally hewn by the hands of time are responsible. Roje's and the Stealths' boots, my sandals, slap through pools of moisture as we follow Galene to a door incised into the stone.

"I must ask what you plan on doing to the prisoners," she says, pausing outside.

"Filmore, can you soundproof that door, please."

At his command, a thin velum of gold slinks down the door and extends the length of the corridor.

"We'll question them," I tell Aunty. "It's imperative we understand their long-term plans."

"Am I to take it that you'll do whatever's necessary to extract a response?"

The diction in her words, their deliberate execution, makes me pause. Is it the Aiycan enunciation, the way some vowels are caressed by the mouth while consonants cut out, or is it that the question is more in line with how Chaska behaved earlier?

"That depends on what you mean by necessary."

"Then let me be clear." While small, Aunty draws herself taller with an imperious air. "Will you kill them if they refuse to talk? Will you violate their rights by exercising magic to make them do what you want?"

Will you be your mama? she is all but demanding to know.

The not-question, the understanding of Chaska's behavior, guts me.

I should have expected some fallout from the last time we

were all together. Galene, the matriarch since my grandparents passed, never supported Mama's claim for the throne, her hunger for it. Dada's death took away her last reason to interact with her, with us.

"This is a place of healing," Aunty goes on.

"Do you think I've forgotten that?"

"I think you were away long enough to, unless you can tell me any different."

"The regent doesn't need to explain herself to you," Roje murmurs; the lightness of his words is not to be mistaken for anything other than a threat.

The snort Aunty sends his way is somehow unimpressed, satisfied, and disappointed all at once. Let me put this in a way she'll understand: in the way I have always viewed Aiyca.

"Sanar is this island's heart, yes? That's the anatomy you focus on. I see the full body, all its damaged organs, the bruises on its skin, the splintered bones. Becoming doyenne, regent, has never been about adding to the island's pain. My only concern has been restoring this vessel. Healing it. I never forgot my tutelage, my duty, to excise disease and infection with *care*." There is more I could say, might say, to another. But Aunty is my elder, my matriarch, and as such, I cannot.

Water continues to *drip, drip, drip* around us as she surveys me with that keen eye.

"I prayed to Merce and Sofea that you hadn't lost your way," she at last says.

Her grip on the door handle eases; physically, the effect of my words works through her muscles, kneading away their tightness with skilled fingers. "If it's all the same for you, I'll

220

stay, watch your palliative touch at work."

Maybe she sees it in me, that while I am not Mama, nor am I the apprentice Healer who left Sanar years ago either. What I should have told Roje is that while there are no monsters like the ones you live with, it's the ones you carry inside that are the most dangerous.

"Actually, Aunty, I need you to work on gathering your most skilled Healers. Reassign cases, do whatever you need to. I'll be placing them across Aiyca in anticipation of war. I haven't forgotten that when an illness spreads, you prepare for the worst, even if you hope for the best. I'll wish to speak with them, to relay the dangers ahead, the treatment they'll need to learn for the wounds I'm expecting, and the scope of the attack that's likely coming."

"You haven't spoken about it with me."

"You'll be in the meeting also."

Aunty looks between Roje and me, her brow bearing the slightest frown, before she bows her head, touches my arm in farewell, and glides toward the stairs.

"Well handled," Roje murmurs. "Something isn't right with that one."

"She's concerned about me. That's all you saw—sooner than I did."

"Pays to be mistrustful."

"As a pirate?"

"As a person, Jaz."

"I don't trust the Unlit inside, for that reason—" I step back to include the Xanthippe and Stealths. "How will we handle the interrogation?"

221

"I have an idea," Filmore begins. "We know Obeah to be arrogant, and the Unlit have shown that they've retained that trait. I'm sure we'll find the answers we seek without too much trouble."

"What do I say?"

"Let them lead. Have a conversation. Their profile states that they'll be proud. Lean into the Unlit's accomplishments, and downplay your own abilities. They'll like it enough that they should give away what we need. If not, well—"

"I can have a word." Roje leans down and frees a butterfly dagger from his boot. "Bet I can slice out their secrets one by one."

With a guarded glance at Roje, Filmore opens the first door. "After you, Regent Cariot," he announces.

The room is full of boxes, and around its walls, witchlight sconces burn low; the absence of any windows and the dark stone mirror a cell far better than I expected.

"Regent, huh." The prisoner, sitting on a wooden chair in the center of the small room, snorts. "I hope you're here to say thank you, mon. Aiyca will be stronger without you."

"Then you mean to kill me?"

"Obviously." He's comfortable enough to lean back, and if I wasn't observing this insurgent with my own eyes I'd doubt reports that he was bound to his chair by his ankle; his arms have been drawn back enough that his shoulder bones protrude through the thin gray shirt he wears. "I'm surprised you're alive. But even plants snatched from the ground flower the following spring. They will have to make sure they take you out by the root next time."

My heart thuds in my chest at the smile he sends my way, more so than his words. Handsome, with smooth maple-colored skin, long braided hair that swirls in an intricate pattern, he looks like someone an Obeah parent would be pleased for their pickney to bring home.

"And when they cut me out, they expect to rule?"

"They will take Aiyca and govern it as it should be."

"I can admit that your ilk are talented, to have concealed themselves for so long. I can imagine what they have planned."

He snorts. "You can't. You have no idea what waits for you in Aiyca."

"I know about the Oscuridad."

"You know what we want you to know. What I'd like to know? When I'm being transported to Carne. I have no plans on telling you anything."

"We can see about sorting that transfer now," Filmore answers. "Regent?"

We all file out of the room. Once the door has been closed and the shield on silence erected, I ask Filmore why he pulled me out.

"That wasn't any time at all."

"Forgive me, Regent, but I think I know what he's talking about, or rather, what he refuses to say. He wasn't concerned that you know about the Oscuridad. That's not their surprise. It was intentional; I think to prevent us looking for anything else. Weapons."

"Weapons?" I repeat. "I thought the Oscuridad were their weapons."

"They seem more like soldiers," Roje says. "Numbers.

Against your Xanthippe and battalion soldiers the Unlit might face greater resistance, since they're without magic. But if they have magical beasts fighting on their side . . ." He trails off, the implications clear.

"Can you learn what the weapons are?" I ask Filmore. "There are more prisoners to interrogate."

"I'm not sure they'll break enough under questioning to provide the specifics we need." He looks sidelong at Roje.

The late doyenne would likely skin that Unlit herself if it meant learning the answers she needed. But I am not her, and Sanar is a place of healing. Aunty and Chaska need not have doubted me.

"No brute force," I tell them. "Knowing what they are would help, but at least we know they exist. And we can confirm that with the rest of the prisoners."

"Right," Pasha says. "And since they've concealed them across the island, they sound big. What do we know about the Unlit and weapons?"

Helpless, I shrug. "Iraya didn't say anything about this. The Unlit have always been too busy hiding, which we now know meant building their numbers and recruiting, but weapons beyond robbing magi for their own?"

"Conduit gold?" asks Emthera, one of my quieter Stealths, her voice deep, slow.

"Yes," I confirm, my belly turning. "They've stolen conduit gold for years."

Roje leans against the wall across from me, silent. Pirates have done the same with magi, robbing them of their conduits to sell for profit outside the empire.

"Have you done business with Unlit?" I ask him.

"We're not one for introductions, pirates." He shrugs. "Anyway, once a person travels to the Iron Shore, they're no longer Unlit, Obeah, or Aiycan. They're shiny and new."

"They would have worn gray."

He shrugs again. "Sorry, mon. Though, do they matter as much since you know about the conduit gold?"

"No," Filmore says. "Not when these shiny and new Unlit will have Transmuters in their number. And a dearth of magic doesn't nullify Obeah will. If they've made and concealed magical weapons across Aiyca—"

"Everyone who fights against them is in danger," I finish. "Filmore, Pasha. I need you to rally more Stealths. I don't care if they've only been schooled for a term; recruit as many as you can spare, and then divide them across all seven parishes to search for these weapons." Whatever they look like, however many there are. "Once you've found them, destroy them."

Before they're used to destroy us.

20

IRAYA

"It's beautiful here," Delyse sighs not an hour later, once we've supplanted the horrors of Changuu for the Horn and settled beneath the tented breakfast spot on Green Island. "Don't you think?"

Thoughts back at the Simbarabo Cuartel, with Kirdan, who doesn't want us to move as enemies passing in the night, weapons aimed at one another, my responding noise is non-committal. Yes, this province is a verdant paradise bobbing atop a broad intersection of the delta; a taste of what life is like in the uppermost echelon is visible to those in surrounding town houses, ones that crowd together like too many teeth on the shore to the left and right. But it's a morsel their jaws can never lock around, not entirely, and it's one the starving in the innermost ring haven't a hope of tasting. Will Kirdan change things here too, if he is doyen?

"Of course," Delyse says through a mouthful of star fruit,

"you'd have to pretend you can't feel all the eyes, or hear the whispering mouths."

"Then you haven't lost your mind."

"Or my sight, mon." Draped across a lavish rug beside me, she feigns a stretch, fingertips pointing out across the waters to a convoy of approaching kanoas.

Regret is as potent as the sweetness of the spoils attendants wait to serve. This is what I've looked forward to the least. Fighting monsters? Fine. Fighting Kirdan? Expected. But dining with three brats while my island is moments away from burning? They've made it so that no matter the dainty tents that have been strung up, the proud trunks of palm and ceiba swaying in the light breeze curling atop a delta that shimmers with dragonflies and the iridescent scales of its fish, rage simmers inside. No doubt they knew how I'd feel, the naevus my body contains. That's why our meeting is out here in the open.

They wish for me to know the island watches.

"Will we stand to greet them?" Delyse asks.

"Yeh mon." I sigh. "This should start civilly." I make no promises for how it ends.

"Wahan, Iraya," the first princess says upon setting foot on shore. "Excuse us for being so late, there's been more traffic than usual on the delta." Short haired and strong featured, she flaps a hand before her face. "It's already so warm. Are the tents chilled?"

I nod. She must be Avyanna. Shamar said she was loquacious.

"My sisters and I have been looking forward to this meeting ever since you wormed your way under Uncle Kaltoon's skin.

Where have you been hiding?"

"Let us greet her too, sister," the smallest of the three princesses says. Shaye, perhaps. She is delicate in ways they are not. "Wahan, Empress." She sinks from the knees in a curtsy; the silky fabric of her blue kaftan pools around her feet. "I must say, I too am curious to hear tales about where you have been."

Sweet, Shamar said. But sugar rots the teeth.

"And you must be Ghislaine," I say to the last to leave the kanoa. Olive-toned cheeks flush a mottled red; she nods but doesn't speak.

"You know us so soon?" Avyanna flings herself across several cushions.

"Beginner's luck," I drawl.

"I doubt that. What have you heard about us?" Shaye dips again to take up a buttery roll.

"That your uncle Kaltoon prepares you to inherit as your mama is unwell. Blessings."

"I suspect you know better than all of us how awful it is to lose," the youngest says. She tears off a piece of bread and drops it into her mouth. "Parents, that is."

And here it is, the rot.

For the first time I smile. Albeit at the thought of kicking her back into the delta and holding her head underwater until she—

"Take a turn with me, Empress?" Shaye asks. "Is it empress, given that you haven't been crowned?"

"Her family was crowned long before any of us came along," Delyse interjects.

"And you are?"

"Delyse is my Eye." Taking a subtle step between them, I brush against Delyse in a silent request to corner her mouth. "It would be my pleasure to accompany you on a walk." It seems we have much to discuss.

Shaye tosses pieces of her roll into the surrounding delta, sure to keep us close to its edge, where people watch from their windows and rooftops, and not farther inland, where she might trip and crack her head against a rock. Accidentally. The smartest of her sisters indeed.

"You survived Carne," she says. "That speaks of a sound mind."

"Or a stubborn one."

"Yeh mon, that too."

We pause by a lone shrine with great serpents coiling around its columns, but no clear sign of which Mudda's Face it worships. Like Aiyca, Zesia is a melting pot of smaller religions lost in the fight between Obeah and Alumbrar supremacy.

"And Aiyca?" she poses. I'm disarmed for a moment by the sight of Kirdan's kohl-lined eyes and sharp cheekbones in her face. "Much has changed since you've been away, but much, I understood last night, has changed upon your return too." She tosses another piece of the roll in the water. Something concealed in the green depths makes its surface ripple; the bread is devoured by a long pink tongue. "A slain doyenne, alliances with her daughter, who, I heard not so long ago, was unfit for rule."

"I have heard the same about you and your sisters, Princess."

"Then you should relieve your war dogs. It isn't me this island worries about." She drops more bread, amused, no doubt, by the fish who seeks it out. Pickney. "Tell me, do you know how magical succession is handled between twins and triplets?"

"It goes to the firstborn, as is the norm."

Something like triumph sparks in her face. "Unless the first has no interest in leading, like Ghislaine. She has already vowed to join the prioress, to apprentice in filling her position when she passes on."

"So it will be between yourself and Avyanna."

She gives me a look. One I interpret as meaning, *If you say so.*

Kirdan said his sisters were untried and foolish, yet there is something mighty in Shaye. I join her by the water. It shimmers here as it did by the tents, no doubt with the fish her bread has drawn.

"And what do you want from me?"

"From you?" She drops another piece of bread. "Why would you think I want anything from you?"

"Pulling me away to talk in private. You wish to be doyenne. You wish for me to help you claim the Golden Seat here."

"No."

"Don't play coy, not after—" My words stop, for as I watch the bread bob atop the delta, a single large eye opens and looks back at me from the water. "Get back, Princess."

"What?"

"There's a beast in the delta." One of the Unlit's? If they've progressed to breeding water monsters, gods help us. But they won't. So I have to. "Get back!" Magic mounts with my panic, coursing through my body in a rush of power. Kirdan's blade is in my hand in seconds. I aim it at the water, allowing a killing spark to shoot down at the shimmering beast. A primordial cry shakes Green Island.

The water worm emerges.

Rearing up in a shimmering explosion of color and fury, it writhes before the princess and me, its serpentine mouth open in a high-pitched shriek, exposing its soft, scale-free underside.

"Empress—"

"I have this." In fact, I'm disappointed by how easy this will be.

"Iraya!" Delyse shouts. "Don't!"

But she's too far away to help me, the J'Martinet too.

And so, calm with the focus combat eventually brings, I eye this serpent as it stares down at me and smile before a second death spark is launched from the tip of my dagger. It sparks clean through the beast's stomach; the creature goes down hard enough to raise a wave of water. My shield comes easily—and also before Delyse and the J'Martinet. When they arrive they are wet and wild-eyed.

"What have you done?" one of the J'Martinet gasps, eyes on the serpent as its lifeless body slinks back into the water.

"Saved the princess? And myself."

"You slayed one of the Delta Damsels," Avyanna whispers. "How could you?"

I look from her to Ghislaine, who holds a hand to her mouth; tears well in her eyes.

"It was attacking us."

"They are peaceful creatures," Shaye supplies, in a small, satisfied voice. "Until provoked. They have protected generations of Divsylar rulers. Hence the shrine."

The shrine.

I twist to look at it again, at the stone snakes that coil around it, the jewels in place of their eyes, and hear Nana Clarke's admonishments as clearly as if I'm eight years old once again.

"Offerings are made." Shaye glances down at the last piece of bread in her hand.

Bread she used to lure this creature here.

She set me up.

"We'll have to release a statement." She looks out at all the spectators around Green Island; appalled, horrified, maybe even afraid, they look down at the slain body of the creature retreating slowly back into the delta with the weight of death. "Zesians won't be pleased with your display and how you've attacked our customs, Empress. Disrespected them. Our poor brother." She holds out her hands; Avyanna and Ghislaine join her, closing in on either side in a unified front against me.

"Come, Iraya," Delyse murmurs. "We should go."

Staring at the triplets, I refuse to move.

"And after Carling Hill was sundered too." Shaye sighs.

Delyse whips toward her. "What?"

The jaws around the island, the many buildings, their inhabitants, are suddenly too close. So is the *sky*, gods above. The very world constricts like a noose around my neck.

"You were unaware your family trees have been overrun by enemies to the crown?" Shaye's sly gaze slides from Delyse to me; delight sparkles beneath her faux sympathy. "We heard news of it last night. This isn't your day at all, is it."

Did Jazmyne lose the wellspring of Aiyca's magic to the enemy?

Delyse's grip tightens around my forearm as I start for Shaye. "Everyone is staring," she hisses. "Stop. You can't be seen having disagreements with Zesia's future leaders after what transpired. *Come.*"

So as not to kill Shaye, I let her pull me along.

Leaving Carne all those months ago, I wanted destruction. I wanted to pull the meat of the world away from its bones. But during my time at Cwenburg's Cuartel, I moved on from that witch, grew. By tricking me into killing that Delta Damsel, the triplets just reminded the island that my ledger is steeped in red, that a Warrior is all I'll ever be.

21

JAZMYNE

"You're returning to Aiyca a victor," Roje tells me, exiting the carriage at Cwenburg and proffering his hand to help me out.

Indeed, Sanar's successes have stanched the wound Cwenburg's retreat created. My Stealth cabal's growing numbers means it will become a military unit of its own before too long; the Unlit's weapons are being hunted for as we speak; and thirty-five Healers will be traveling across the island in a matter of days, each of them carrying Anan's poultice recipe to treat Aiyca's poisoned—including Obeah. With Iraya in Zesia, this is the perfect moment to become a leader to them too.

"It feels good to hold the line," I admit. So good I don't mind that I'll have to go straight from the carriage to the Temple of the Supreme Being's Chosen on the grounds, to oversee the late doyenne's Ninth Night with the advisory panel and several additional influential families.

"You could go on the offensive." Roje pockets a hand.

"Start rounding up more Unlit. Maybe with the shields, if we can't trust Anan to rally his siblings in the Skylands to your cause. Are the Obeah still in the holding cells?"

Witchlight lanterns creak in the winds that inveigle their way in through cracks in the stables.

"I don't need the Obeah, Roje." He's not entirely wrong about Anan and his siblings. I'm half surprised Iraya didn't go to them. Their mythical winged steeds sound exactly like the sort of creatures that would fight well against the Unlit's beasts. "I'm fortified against the poison, thanks to Anan. Iraya will return soon, and the pirates will fall in line once the race has been won—" I avert my eyes. We need to talk about my participation in the race, but not now. I don't want to ruin what's been accomplished. "All that's left is to pray the late doyenne's duppy doesn't ruin matters."

Roje cocks an eyebrow. "You are confident. Pray for us too. We might be called to the Iron Shore for the Glide-By any day now." He looks out across the estate as if he can see those spears of rock that ensnare his home like the paw of a fabled sea beast. "It seems small in the grand scheme of things, but I have a girl coming to do your hair in the next couple of days. If anything changes before then, I'll find you. Walk good. Please."

Save for the occasional burst of fireworks from the island below, the sky provides little light to illuminate my path across the estate. Several Alumbrar startle at my presence beneath the portico in the Patio of Prowlers; dressed in a kaftan the color of soot, I could be a wraith—the duppy of the late doyenne many fear encountering.

"Forgive us, Regent Cariot." Clutching hands, the men edge away.

It's true that the palace seems the perfect setting for every eldritch creeper Iraya Adair warned me about, especially now the sigh of the wind has permanently replaced the griots who entertained beneath the sweeping embrace of the cotton tree and the festoon lights rarely have cause to be lit. But my order forgets—and Roje doesn't understand—we were made for the night. When my family lived in St. Catherine, I'd sit on the bluff outside our home to watch the light pinched between the sky and sea until the world became a stage for the stars Anansi said we descend from. Far from burning brightly when we start to collapse, I should have told Iraya that while Obeah made the mistake of looking down on us, Alumbrar are long used to educating the lost by telling them to look *up*.

"Evening, my queen."

Two pirates guard the palace entrance to the temple drive, twins I know.

"Koa, Kaius."

Indistinguishable from one another, both are fair skinned, with eyes the color of Lawson Bay. A sudden salvo of sparks fills the dark sky with bright beads of light. Both pirates reach for their weapons.

"It's fine," I breathe, though I am just as unsettled. My fingers seek the collar at my neck, and I scrabble to create space between the two. "The island is saying vale to the late doyenne."

"Did you need escorting anywhere?" Koa queries.

"No. I'm going inside."

Tension eases from my shoulders as I drop to my knees on the temple's seventh step and offer the Mudda's sign of seven to every shrouded effigy crowding the dais above. I need their strength since I must contact Iraya after this Ninth Night ceremony. Anan's army is not yet secured. She cannot be poisoned before returning with the Simbarabo.

A cry draws my attention to the temple's candlelit depths. Standing, I climb several more steps to see the primary altar. Enrobed ministers surround quivering bodies of Alumbrar where they lie before the golden rostrum. Their heads slam into the tile while the ministers dance around them. Nyába. Mouths gape open; with a crack that makes me recoil, jaws dislocate. The ancestors. They're filling their bodies. Unearthly cries echo down the steps, bales of pain, otherworldly triumph.

I flinch back, up, onto deadened legs. Mariama didn't tell me they'd be making their ancestral offerings tonight. Standing with Ionie and Ormine, she rocks to the Kumina drums. They're expecting me, but after my encounter with the doyenne, I don't want to stay and see how she intended to make home in my body. I'll give it a quarter of an hour, and then I'll return. Seeking out the back steps, I steal my way beneath ornate archways, shrink back into dark corners whenever a minister glides into view, until I arrive in Consuelo's Heart. There are seven chambers, one for each Face throughout the temple. Behind the towering doors, the wood fashioned after ribs, a clever ventilation system included by the Artisans who built the temple sends in tendrils of wind from outside, making the chamber feel like the goddess herself breathes in this room.

Long hallways are lit with soft witchlights, leaving

darkened coves where pilgrims can confess their woes to ministers, should they wish. After I leave the Ninth Night celebration on the porch, I don't encounter anyone as I weave through the Heart into its center; the multiple celebrations are elsewhere across the island. Consuelo's faceless golden idol is suspended from the center of the peaked ceiling. A slender arm reaches below as if to offer comfort. What must be thousands of witchlights hang with her, like stars in a night sky to guide the lost home. Sinking onto the cushioned dais beneath her, I offer up prayers that the late doyenne finds whatever is waiting for her in Coyaba, whether that be exaltation in its highest echelon, or torment at its nadir.

Heart open, my desires leak from the various cracks and fissures ruling has already created. I even offer up words for Anan, that he convinces his siblings to give me the fealty of their army. In fact, I'm so engrossed in muttering mercies, thanks, and pardons, I didn't notice anyone else entering the chamber; I might not have, had they not made a sighing noise from within the recesses untouched by witchlights or flame.

I scan for one of the temple ministers, or the addition of a pilgrim like me on their knees, but see none. A tinny noise echoes across the chamber. Closer than before, its pitch sets my teeth on edge. Whipping around, I peer between the billowing sheets. "Is anyone there?"

The height of the room throws my voice back mockingly. No one responds. Instead, the chamber wheezes around me, deep and lengthy as though parched, all moisture sucked away by a heightening chill.

"It's Regent Cariot—not the late doyenne," I'm fast to add,

not wanting to frighten anyone. "Jazmyne, former emissary to the crown. Whoever's there, and I know you are—" Another breath is drawn. It's heavy, laborious. "I command you come out."

They don't.

A prickling starts at the base of my spine, spider-walking a trail of gooseflesh up my neck. I rise to my feet. Someone *is* in here. It's an inexplicable knowing, when you're not alone. Perhaps a predatory inheritance from our very first ancestor; I feel it now, that tightness of skin, shallowness of breath, gathering of shadows in the corner of my vision. I was indifferent to being alone, before. That lack of foresight no longer seems as wise.

Not fearing the night doesn't mean I'm cavalier about what may hide in it.

The late doyenne's duppy.

"This is your final warning." Despite the chill in the air, the cloud of my breath materializing, I begin to sweat. "Show yourself, or risk punishment. Now."

It's a hollow threat made by a girl of paper, not might; one aware that if it were a minister, they would have made their presence known immediately, and any pilgrims too would have made their apologies once I gave my name. Still, I gather my kaftan in a shaking hand. Wait. Thunder is a distant rumble; lightning flashes too far away for its light to illuminate the many dark alcoves, curtained corners, in which anyone could hide.

Or, I think with a swallow, *anything.*

It could be nothing, I rationalize, patting at the wish-bags tucked into my undergarments—a fallen witchlight sconce rolling across the tile, a rodent that's squirreled its way inside. But I'm unable to expel the memory of the twisted wrongness of the late doyenne's face, the warped hatred, the memory of Verena's severed head. I have to wonder, what if it's *something*? Consuelo's Heart inflates again with a rattling draw of breath that no longer sounds like ventilation whispering through its shaft. I am alone. I have no magic. And I am the last of the Cariot heirs. If I fall—if I am snatched, who will stand between Aiyca and the growing dark?

With a calmness I don't feel, I turn and walk toward the archway that will take me out to the hall. A bead of sweat drips into my eye. The salt stings, momentarily blurs my vision. Something shifts in my periphery. My heart thumps its way up my throat. *Left at the T-junction, and then the first right around the therapy pit to the doors.* Everything can be explained, I'm sure. But in the morning, in the sunlight, when I am fresh and able to think.

If the doyenne lets you survive until morning.

The thought inveigles its way through a crack in my wall of sense. It is but one—until a metallic screech rings through the chamber and my entire resistance crumbles. Cutting through the therapy pit is faster. Quickening my pace makes the cushions beneath my feet deadly. I slide across one and almost lose my footing. My knee jars. A cry squeezes through gritted teeth, ringing within the temple's eaves.

Screech.

That makes two.

What *is* that? It has the hair-raising whine of a blade

dragged across a surface, or—

Screeeech.

Something stirs to my left. Close to my left. A shadow. Otherworldly fingers pulling back a curtain. I stumble the last ten yards, my sore knee twinging in protest, sure that something will grab me at any moment. Flying through the doors, I smack into something hard. A scream tears through me.

"Jazmyne!" Hands, hard and unyielding, shake me once. "Jazmyne, stop! It's me. It's Roje." He pulls me into his chest.

"Guzzu." A hand between us, I push back. "We need guzzu to stop it leaving."

"Stop what?" Roje pulls me back and peers into my face, looks overhead, to the riblike doors. "I can't see anything."

I twist around. Inside, the chamber looks the way it did when I first arrived—peaceful. As if nothing happened. But that creeping sense of unease doesn't dissipate.

"Guzzu. Now."

Roje's thumb meets the next tear that falls down my cheek. "I'll summon the Xanthippe."

Before he can do anything, the doors to the Heart bang open, smacking against the walls with a crack.

Wind surges out into the hall, extinguishing candle after candle, shattering witchlight after witchlight. Roje's hand finds mine as a solitary paw thuds down across the doorway. Larger than a jungle-prowler's, it could crush the chest of a fully grown man. My breath catches; Roje's stops. *Monster.* Neither of us says *Oscuridad.* Here. On Cwenburg's estate.

A second paw joins the first with a weighted muffled thump.

I don't know who moves first, me or Roje. One moment

we're still, the next running blindly in the dark, our hands clenched so tightly that pain rather than fear is the prevailing emotion.

"Don't look back!" Roje instructs.

But I do. A glance as we fly around a corner, my afro whipping across my face. A scream cuts through the reverence in the temple like a knife. Mine, as a colossal creature, something that could only have slithered up from the bowels of the earth, hurtles after us on six thick legs in near-silent pursuit.

Roje grapples at the wall, opens a door, shoves me inside, and launches himself in after. We exchange a brief look in the witchlight-lit room, a magicless pairing. At least, unlike outside, sconces burn softly on the walls as he frees his axe from its holster across his back. Braced for the Oscuridad to hit the door, I retreat deeper into the room, weaving past the chairs, the sofas, scanning our surroundings. There's another door, but no windows to smash and escape through into the gardens, where we can alert Xanthippe, the guests celebrating the doyenne's Ninth Night.

"Roje," I whisper, testing its handle. The door opens into another room next door, which has a second door. We can work our way through the connecting rooms.

"Run!" Barreling through the furniture, he waves his axe in warning.

Behind him, a monstrous muzzle dissolves through the wood; broad and fleshy, it's followed by not so much a nose, but two diagonal slashes beneath two narrowed eyes glowing an unnatural green. Not at Roje. At me.

"Run, Jazmyne!"

We tumble into the adjoining room, stumbling over legs and the train of my kaftan, limbs and the handle of his axe, across another windowless chamber and into the next.

"Is it a duppy?" I ask him.

"I don't think my axe will pass through it, no. Do these rooms go on forever, or will we eventually get out?"

I have no answers. I can't *think*.

"Xanthippe?" Overtaking me, Roje shunts a table away with a foot, rips the third door open, and bids me to hurry through.

"Maybe," I breathe. The last time I encountered a monster, I was with Iraya before a Rolling Calf. No. The last time was with Anya, in that underground treasure trove behind the secret door. The iron door.

"I know what to do!"

Roje glances over his shoulder and swears; the beast's head, shoulders, and front legs break through the stone wall like it's water.

"Whatever it is, make it fast!"

Pivoting from the connecting door, we run out into the temple halls. A sharp needle of pain works its way through my left side as I try to gather my bearings.

"This way!"

Roje's boots thud against the tile underfoot; the slap of my sandals is even more jarring as we twist through the temple, heading deeper and deeper inside until we alight before the Death Vault. Slowing to a wheezing stop, I unclasp the locks on the mighty iron door and heave. Roje's hands land atop mine; together we draw the door open. Must and the cloying scent of rot slither out. Javel's imposter lies within its dark depths, along with all those who fell during the attack at the Sole. Gods forgive me for what I'm about to lock inside with them.

"Stand aside," I tell Roje. "It's after me."

"That doesn't mean it has to get you!"

"No," I breathe, as the witchlights on the archway at the top of the hall extinguish and the vaulted ceiling is reduced to a net of shadows. "But it needs to think it can. And your scent will confuse it. Stand over there." I jerk my head toward the left of the vault. "And be ready to lock the door."

I want to close my eyes, gods know I want to squeeze them shut and pretend I'm not about to face down another of Aiyca's nightmares, but, positioning myself in the center of the open doorway, I make myself watch the Oscuridad prowl around the corner. Built like a distortion of a sand-prowler, of Joshial, it stands high on six thick legs; its flank is at once gray smoke and solid muscle.

"Jazmyne," Roje whispers.

My jaw is clenched around a scream. Lowering its broad head, the beast inhales once through its slitted nose; nodding as though in confirmation of some unheard order, it breaks into a sprint. Lights are extinguished by a frigid wind, one that rings in my ears along with the pounding of my heart, the tight gasps of breath as I stare certain death in the face and wait as it raises a mighty paw to duck and roll.

"Door!" I scream.

Roje slams it shut and hits the locks. Still on the ground, my legs numb, I stare up at him.

"Xanthippe."

They arrive in a murder of black and gold.

A third remain before the Death Vault door. The rest accompany Roje and me as we circle back to Consuelo's Heart, the crack of their cloaks, the tread of sandals against tile underfoot—the march of battle, the elegy of war attracts the ministers and presiders, Cariot relatives, along the way.

Arms locked around my middle, I stand in a knot of temple acolytes; Cleo and Emthera guard to my left and right in lieu of Filmore and Pasha, who inspect the prayer rooms with Roje. I answer the ministers' questions, Ionie's demands. All the while, my eyes remain fixed on the door, waiting for Roje or my Stealths to emerge and confirm that the beast I trapped in the Death Vault is the only one roaming the temple.

"Why didn't you bring more than a few Healers back from Sanar with you?" Ivan queries loudly. "We could have all been poisoned tonight."

I have no answer that will satisfy him. Tighter and tighter I hold myself while their many eyes land on me. It's with blessings to the Seven-Faced Mudda that Roje emerges from the Heart, instilling a hush over the ministers.

"What is it?" Ivan asks.

"I need to speak with the regent, alone." Roje takes me by my elbow.

"Wait a minute." Ionie's indignance echoes. "We deserve to know what's happening!"

Ignoring her, Roje leads me farther down the broad temple avenue to the privacy of a shaft of shadow thrown by a column. My family, the ministers, begin to shout. I glance over my shoulder; Cleo, Emthera, and a handful of Xanthippe stand, shields out, between them and us.

"Make it quick, Roje."

"There were no additional Oscuridad, but—" His voice heavy with dread, Roje glances over my head. "The Xanthippe were afraid in there."

My breathing shallows, stops a moment too long. If I didn't know about the cool room where the dead are stored, then going to my order's most lauded Warriors wouldn't have saved me. Roje's thumb finds my cheek again, strokes a rough course. In contrast to the chamber's chill, his hand against my skin is warm. When he folds me into his embrace, safe from spying eyes around our corner, and beyond the point of caring even if we weren't, this time I press against his chest where his heart thumps in an unwelcome reminder of how close I was to death and squeeze my eyes closed against the monsoon of tears waiting to fall.

"You're all right," he soothes.

But I might not have been—none of us might have been. The doyenne's duppy is a formidable threat, but monsters? It could have broken free and infiltrated the palace, cut through my throat while I slept, and feasted on me before sunrise. Roje's arms tighten around me as I begin to shake. My Xanthippe, the highest trained witches Alumbrar have, fear them.

Them. The missive writer.

They are not coming. The Unlit are here. In Cwenburg.

"Tell me what you need," Roje murmurs.

Anya.

Iraya.

To turn back time and refuse to accept my position as heir.
No.

"Lock the estate down. No one comes in or out without invitation. And—I need—I need—"

"Nothing is too shameful, remember?"

Swallowing, I nod. "The shields."

Roje draws me back to stare down at me, brow furrowed. "What?"

"I need the shields."

22

IRAYA

"Empress Iraya Adair!" the herald announces to the crowd milling before supper.

I sweep by him dressed both to mourn and warn.

Obeah wear white, on occasions such as this, celebrations, but tonight I am bound in darkness, and all the intent it carries. The dips of my waist are on display, the length of my legs sheathed in tight pants; low sleeves garland the tops of my arms, exposing the line of my neck, décolletage upon which a sole green gemstone sits entangled in conduit gold. It is the only color I sport. Many will see the jewel as an apology to the princesses, who I cut a deft path toward, for yesterday's unfortunate event. I stepped wrong, yeh mon. But this isn't a walk of penance.

Wraith-wrapped as I am, this is a promise.

"Wahan." I don't bow. Neither do they.

Instead, Ghislaine and Avyanna are drawn back; the shoulders of their Zesian companions barricade them from me. But Shaye, a familiar calculation tightening her features, raises a hand to halt the circling J'Martinet.

"Excuse my lateness." I project for all who listen, who gathered to welcome me. "I returned from temple a mere hour ago, where I have been spending my time in prayer."

Startling in the witchlights, the emerald fire in Shaye's eyes flares as though my lie is fuel.

Veritably, there is little truth to my words.

While Delyse and I have spent over twenty-four hours in an innocuous Temple of the Supreme Being's Chosen we found in the city, only returning to our rooms in the palace to sleep, it was not to pray. The chamber for Clotille's Face, her Heart, was the one place we could speak, scheme, without fear of being heard—at least, once Jazmyne didn't come to the mirror and it became clear we needed to move even faster than originally planned with Carling Hill, not lost, we had confirmed in a missive by the Obeah Witches Council member. Its surroundings are occupied by Unlit. Nevertheless, the ramifications are endless.

What if they decide to set their fires using family trees next?

I wouldn't. The late doyenne didn't dare to either. But whoever commands the Unlit is cut from a different cloth.

At least the dead are holding the line. In that regard, they are doing more than Jazmyne. But Carling Hill's duppies have no say in how long they linger before moving on. They will be called to Coyaba eventually, and they deserve to rest.

Something that could be expedited too. All it would take to rid them entirely, to smash the last resistance between fire and the inheritance of every magical family in Aiyca, is one word. Flint to the tinderbox. *Exorcism.* A mass expulsion of the dead could give the Unlit the access they need.

"You've spent the day in prayer?" Shaye repeats.

"As I said."

"Were you touched by the divine, or are you still determined to lay your hands on us?"

Whispers land like shouts. To the west of the room in the shadow of a pillar, where we decided she would be, Delyse gives me an encouraging nod. But while the first lie to the triplets was sweetly wrought, the second is bitter.

"Forgive me." I clear my throat; like my words, the choked sound rings for all to hear. "For today." What I mean is, *I know what you bitches did.* "I thought your lives were in danger, and I acted accordingly." *A mistake I won't make twice.* "In the future, I'll defer to the wisdom of the J'Martinet." *Even if they are miles away and have no chance of arriving in time to save you.* "In honor of the Delta Damsel I slayed, I will do my due diligence on this island's customs. I think now." The look I cast at the gathered faces flushed with rum and spirits, stomachs that strain against heavy belts, and gold-stemmed glasses clutched in the hand, is deliciously condemnatory. The sentiment doesn't leave when my focus returns to the triplets. "This celebration feels wrong after today's loss, and so I will leave. Little more."

Shaye's head shifts. Only an inch, but enough. She knows

what I truly meant. What I cannot say. Untried, Kirdan said. Clueless. He has no idea.

Anger burns across my cheeks, the back of my neck at the rising hum of conversation held behind angled hands as I navigate a way out. I hardly expected Zesia to fall at my feet, and yet I must have done, because I never considered that this disdain, this hatred, would be possible. The crowd tightens so that I must fight my way through; eyes cut or turn away from me—all but one canny pair belonging to a witch who stares with enough frankness to let me know that, unlike her ilk determined to make my departure as uncomfortable as possible, she bears no ill intent.

She takes a step toward me, and the crowd parts.

"Empress Adair, forgive me." Her words are muffled behind the scarf covering all but her eyes. Closer to black than the hazel and green common in Zesia, they're filled with intelligence. "I wondered if I might have a word." One look from her and her companions begin to converse with an unnatural loudness, one that will mask any conversation we have.

She's respected. Maybe even feared.

Just how I like my witches.

"And you are?"

"Melione, Empress." She bows her head slightly. "I am sorry for your loss."

"Judair is dead. No need."

The corners of Melione's eyes wrinkle. "Her daughter can't hold it against you if the two of you are working together." There's a question in her tone, however muffled the scarf makes her voice; I don't deign to answer. "I know you're on your way out," she continues. "But if you have the time during your tenure here, I'd love to have you over for tea."

To her credit, she doesn't flinch as I rake my eyes over every inch of her. "Why?"

"You of all witches, I'm sure, are familiar with the maxim 'the enemy of my enemy . . .'" The words come through with more clarity, for the first time. So does her accent. Mentally I startle at the shorter consonants, the abruptness of several inflections uncommon in Zesia, Aiyca too. "Only," Melione continues, lower once again, "I rather hope we can stand on the same side as something less begrimed than nemeses." She doesn't look at the triplets, but she may as well have. "The Stealth you have doing reconnaissance tonight will find out where I live. Should you choose to take me up on my offer, come by." She steps aside, revealing a clear path to the door.

"Blessings." I nod my thanks and step past her. Mentally I amend my initial impression.

Not only is she feared, respected—she's skilled too. Only a strong witch could conceal their presence in enemy territory enough to be invited into its center of mass. Surely Zesia can't know, wouldn't be foolish enough, to open their doors to a war dog from the Skylands. For that's what Melione is, what her subtle accent revealed her to be: a spy.

But then, I think, as I cross the grounds to meet Zander for our first training session, concealed from patrolling J'Martinet by one of the new glyphs I learned this morning, I don't know whether we have all underestimated the elusive third-largest island in the empire all this while, or miscounted the players already engaged in this game of possession for my war-weary home.

Delyse will make progress, in my absence. Contact with a Skylander in Zesia is more than I could have hoped for; if Melione is innocent or not, and ends up dying by some accident or other, I should write to the Skylands anyway. How grandiloquent would an attack launched from the sky and earth look? The Simbarabo on the ground, and the Skylands' winged steeds spearing down, like the supernal agents of destruction Nana Clarke used to tell me they were, when the empire joined forces to defeat the first wave of monsters that sought to conquer Aiyca. The mysterious Unlit leader might turn tail without the need for any bloodshed at all.

Not half an hour later, my back smacks against the cane mats in one of the Cuartel's smaller training rooms. Winded, and bruised in too many places to count, I scowl up at Zander. If Delyse had come, rather than lingering to keep an eye on Melione at the palace, he wouldn't be pushing me so hard.

"Again." He looms over me; his bare chest gleams under a fine sheen of sweat.

"In case it's unclear," I grind out, "it's been a damned long day—" *Eight* days, including the time I spent asleep in the sand. "And I need a moment."

"I heard about your earlier meeting with the princesses." He lunges at me with the wooden batons we're using in place of swords. Snatching a breath, I roll away. While I just miss his strike, his foot stomps down onto my train, tearing through the fabric.

"Hey!"

"You killed a Damsel today, Empress. And now your enemies are both living and dead," Zander says in his deep, condescending lilt, "not to mention the fact that they span across at least two islands in the empire. But you're upset that I ruined the ridiculous outfit you arrived to fight in?" He frowns down at me, as serious as I always thought Kirdan to be. But he's practically a jester compared to Zander, who I'm not sure would know a joke if it bit him on the end of the nose. Something I might try. If I can get close enough. "I don't know whether to pity you or laugh at you."

"I wasn't sure you knew what the latter is."

His biceps tense; sensing another lunge, I raise my own stick to deflect his hit when it does indeed come. Wood cracks against wood. The reverberations make my ears ring.

"Get. Up."

"I need a minute!"

The smoky kohl lining Zander's eyes is smudged with sweat, only adding to his dangerous mien. To think I was happy, smug even, when he suggested physical acuity before magical. In the hours we've been training, I've sweated out whatever combat Kaleisha taught me in prison and the confidence I built as Night Prowler at Cwenburg's cuartel. Before Zander, muscles rippling in places I didn't know they could exist, I am an amateur in the physical, and his indomitable will is making it harder and harder for me to abstain from magic. Knocking him on his back, just the once, would do wonders for us both.

Even if I have to cheat to make that happen.

"Minute's up. Move. Now."

I bite back a wince and stand. "Stop ordering me about. This is not role-play between you and Kirdan."

"You're right. This is preparation for battling monsters." Zander accents his last word with a vicious hit.

"Have you fought many of them?"

"Too many."

The cane stalks underfoot muffle our tread, but not the crack of the wood as I deflect the blows he rains down on me, teeth gritted.

"What are they like?"

"Better than you."

He is inexorable, but I'll be damned if I let him knock me down again. Zander stabs low. Stepping in rather than falling back, I take advantage of his low position and knock my elbow into the center of his upper back. Before he can twist around, my right leg hooks around the back of his left. The momentum takes us both to the floor. Shock forces his eyes open, revealing his surprise as I roll over him. My landing is shaky, but I rise in a crouch, the stick hanging loosely in my hand, satisfied with a victory at last.

"Nice move." He flips onto his feet. "How long did you train with the Virago?"

"Kirdan told you."

Zander shakes his head. "You move like you've had training. Albeit long ago. Muscle memory rarely forgets. You also disappeared for a time as a pickney, I recall from the stories."

"You pieced those very separate threads together and made a blanket?"

"I'm quicker than I look."

"A truth."

Zander's mouth twitches.

"Were you about to *smile again*? Careful, or I might think we're becoming bredren."

"I asked because Kirdan didn't say."

"Then how else were you convinced to help?"

"He told me about a girl who had to fight her way in the world, who would always have to fight her way in *this* world. A girl who could set it ablaze just to watch it burn, or use her flames to ensnare it in a purifying fire. He told me that I could help him support her, champion her in a fight for change. And I said yes, because the world, *this* world, needs to burn down so that it may start over."

My eyes sting with sweat, but I don't blink, can't. Even when Kirdan's not with me, he's always here.

"He makes me sound like some sort of—"

"Heroine?" Zander snorts. "When the war is won and they tell our stories, they will romanticize it as such, but only because they didn't see how raw you were in the beginning. So that's enough chatter, mon." His chin dips, along with his voice. "Come. Show me what they taught you in the Virago." He beckons me with both hands.

"You want me to attack now?"

"As you've barely been defending, why not." He does smile then, a vulpine flash of teeth and arrogance. "Show me, heroine. Let me see what those stories will say about you." He abandons his stick in favor of his hunting knife. The thick blade isn't meant for close combat, but in the hands of a skilled warrior, even a torn scrap from the bottom of a tunic is lethal.

While I'm still debating how long I might last with both the wooden baton and Kirdan's knife, drums echo through the walls, enlivening the mats beneath our feet with their reverberations.

"That mean something to you?"

"Yeh mon." In a shimmer of magic and gold, Zander's uniform—in black rather than umber and white, tonight—appears and covers his bare chest thread by thread, limb by limb.

I hate that I'm impressed but, damn, I want that guzzu.

He tosses the sticks when his Simbarabo regulation saber and hunting knife materialize on either hip. "I have to go. Just as well, I was about to send that little dagger flying."

"Easy to say now you're leaving."

He shakes his head. "Is that your conduit weapon?"

"No, it's a loan. I need to make a choice about getting one."

"It's not an easy decision." His words are issued with something close to understanding.

Conduit weapons aren't chosen on a whim, by happenstance. To Obeah, they are part of who we are. Mama bore a scepter, something small enough to be secreted up a sleeve or carried in hand and thought nothing of; delicate enough not to cut or slice. Dada's staff was understated, like him. Channeling would transform the wood into a golden rod, a shaft of living sunlight held in hand and wielded at his will. It towered over me as a pickney, and yet there was nothing else in the world I wanted to be my own conduit when the time came to choose one. . . . Loss twists itself into a knot in my belly at the thought of the staff rotting at the bottom of Carne Sea, or burned along with my parents' bodies on the funeral pyre the late Doyenne Cariot sent out to the horizon.

Choosing another staff would be easy but feels like a cheap imitation.

"A larger conductor will be the better option," Zander calls, his voice drawing me out of memory. "Given your naevus."

"Noted, mon."

"I can send an Artisan of Metal by. She's the only Master Kirdan trusts to forge his conduit weapons."

"Oh—blessings." Not entirely all bark, Zander, but his bite isn't a bother.

The drums thunder once more.

"What are they for?"

"Patrol" is his detailed reply. "With Esai—Esai!" At his shout, the soldier, who was polishing weapons in a small room off the seven-sided training space, emerges in the same Stealth-black ensemble Zander wears, along with one other who rouses an immediate smile on my face.

"Empress." Beaming, Shamar bends into a bow, a hand tucked at his back to keep his cloak from falling forward.

"I'm sorry, mon, do I know you?"

"Needed to look the part." He shrugs, his expression sheep-ish.

I think he likes this, being in the thick of an army not unlike the one he tried to form back in Aiyca with the conscripts.

"It's good to see you hale, Empress." Esai flushes at my wink and turns to Zander. "A word, if you don't mind, Lieu-tenant."

Edging closer to Sham, I nod after them as they pull away from our party. "Do you know what that's about?"

"Krimpt." His tone leaves no room for challenge. "He's been here every day, issuing orders, changing General Divsylar's strategies and training schedules. It's like he's preparing to step in permanently with the way he's been riding the soldiers, lambasting their poor form. I almost hate Kirdan for being out of commission, and I've only been training for a day."

"Krimpt is not only attempting to use the Simbarabo to rile Kirdan," I muse. "But against me too. He knows I want to bring them to Aiyca, knows my authority supersedes his own. But if he can make them hate me when we leave . . ." Gods. Wherever I turn there are knives. "He's having successes?"

"There will always be dissension, those who don't want to fight in wars and look for someone to blame, but mostly the Simbarabo are loyal to Kirdan. I only hope it will withstand."

"Have you seen him?"

Shamar shakes his head. "He's been undoing his uncle's damage."

Then he's up. Why hasn't he come looking for me? Not that I want him to. I just—there are things to do, and I need the Grimoire.

Zander and Esai rejoin us, their expressions as serious as I imagine mine and Shamar's are.

"You have plates to scrub, soldier," the former cuts out.

"You have him doing your grunt work?"

"It's fine, Iraya," Shamar mutters. "I'll see you around."

I wait until he's cleared the training space before turning on Zander and Esai. Beneath the weight of my stare, they both straighten their shoulders, draw themselves up taller; though my height might be rendered petite before these blocks of muscle and reams of obsidian fabric, as though the shadows of night themselves have been spun on a loom, I'm sure none of us is under any delusions about who is packing what.

"I want to see Kirdan."

"He's unavailable."

Raising a brow at Zander makes the soldier square his shoulders.

"I swear. As I have said before, he enjoys these moments with you. If he were available, I would gladly bring you to him. In fact, he would have been here himself."

He's not wrong, I realize with a stomach flip. Kirdan has made a habit of being where I am.

"Can we go now?" Zander demands. "I need to respond to the drums."

"Fine."

Rolling his eyes, Zander positions himself between Esai and me. "Let's go."

At his will, the training space is pinched into nonexistence, and somewhere new expands around us. A courtyard of stone surrounded by narrow stores all softly lit by lamplight.

"Where are we?"

"Near Green Island. I can't take you any farther. Gold allowance." Zander scans the dim streets. "A patrol of J'Martinet will be on duty several blocks to the north. Esai will escort you on foot."

"And you?" his companion queries.

Zander points to the battlements lining the wall where

Simbarabo, as tiny as ants from this distance, already stand, watchful. With a parting nod, he's swallowed by the night; a faint gold impression of him remains, shimmering in a dark that feels heavy in a starless sky. Perhaps Jazmyne's ancestors hide from their progeny's follies. Or maybe Krimpt's reach extends to the skies too.

Esai and I waste little time heading north at a brisk pace. He chews my ear off about fighting techniques, but his hand never leaves the pommel of his saber, and all the while he scans the street. They must think I was born back a cow to believe those drums, the urgency of their beat, could be anything other than a call for aid—a song for monsters. They hunt, tonight. Perhaps across the entire island given that in this neighborhood windows are shuttered over, and while the streets loom on, void of people, they are taut, like a drawn bowstring. In announcing my presence here, yesterday evening, I held open the door. But I won't cross the threshold, not yet.

Not until I secure myself a conduit weapon of my very own.

23

JAZMYNE

Light the color of a bruised plum spills outward across rug and tile; I trace it from the circle of salt and wish-bags around the chair Roje dragged before my bedroom door, up his body, to where his head is thrown back against the top of the love seat. He insisted on staying, after the Oscuridad encounter in the temple, hours ago.

In fact, he hasn't failed to remain by my side. Not as a mouthpiece; as a partner. I know Anya doesn't trust him, but if this relationship is even a fraction of what he and Vea had—something Kirdan and I never had, I see now—I'll be sorry to lose him as first mate. As a friend, in Anya's absence. Whatever passed between us in the drinking house was a shallow dip compared to the depths we've started to traverse. The ugly, the dire, the obscene. I hope telling him I'm not racing for queen won't ruin things between us. For I must, sooner rather than later. As it stands, this morning my dance card is already full.

Slipping from the bed so as not to wake Roje, I creep into my bathing chamber to retrieve the Mirror of Two Faces from beneath the sink.

"Finally!" Iraya cries from the surface. "I've been trying you for days!"

"You've been trying me?" I repeat, dumb with disbelief.

"Yeh mon. Can't you hear me?"

"I hear you, I'm just . . . surprised." She wouldn't have called to catch up, which means that either something has happened or—her focus sharpens with a speed that makes me draw back from those eyes like twin rings of fire in dark depths. Oh gods. She knows about Carling Hill.

"Yeh mon. I know." Incensed, her nostrils flare in warning before she explodes. "You lost Carling Hill, Jazmyne? Not only that, but you failed to tell me about it as soon as it happened. Mengkeh! How *could* you?"

"How did you know?" is all I can blurt out.

"How did you lose it?"

Sinking down onto the floor, I shake my head at her reflection, no excuses at the ready, despite telling myself I would have them by the time we spoke.

"I gave you two jobs. *Two.* Hold the line and don't allow the Unlit to establish a center of gravity. You have failed at both."

"Me?" I repeat, shock boiling to anger. "What about *you.* Where is the army you promised to return with?"

"Tread with care, Alumbrar," Iraya warns, in a voice as icy as her glare. "Turn the table and I will crush you with it. Did you free the shields?"

"Yes," I bite out. Practically.

"At least you did that right."

"That . . . right?"

"Stop repeating everything I say. It's annoying."

"I'm struggling to digest your *arrogance*." The words are hissed out. She doesn't even know that her Adair conceit is the reason why the entire empire is in trouble! Neither do I for certain, but if it's confirmed that Adairs are in the Unlit, the division her ancestors created, I can't wait to stop her venomous tongue with the information. "And what's more—"

"No. You can listen. Ford needs to get in touch with the Obeah Witches Council. He needs to convince them to work with you, to present a unified front to the island. Now the Unlit have surrounded Carling Hill—"

"Obeah duppies are guarding it from everyone."

"I know, but the dead won't be able to hold it forever. Then where will you be, Jazmyne? In this mirror's surface asking me for advice you don't listen to?"

"I didn't ask."

"You can hear it all the same. Now the Unlit have Cwenburg, they will begin campaigning, you understand?"

"They already have, thanks to you and your message in Coral Garden."

"Then what I'm saying is even more important. The Unlit will potentially have the ability to control magical ascension, if not now, soon. Obeah will turn against Obeah without a clear leader to follow in this event. They need the council."

They have me.

"Did you know the Oscuridad are poisonous?"

Not missing a beat, Iraya cocks a brow. "The beasts have a name?"

"I— Yes. They do."

"Am I to gather that was you telling me you learned their name, in addition to the fact that they're deadly, and not a slip of your deceitful tongue? Do you have a cure, at least?"

"At least? Not only am I idle, but I'm also a liar. Haven't you considered that I'm preoccupied? I have Sanar's best Healers traveling across the island today in preparation for monster attacks—yes, with a cure. *I* did that. Aiyca is being scoured for weapons the Unlit concealed based on intel I extracted from insurgents who attacked my soldiers at Carling Hill. I am no longer racing for queen, while maintaining my rapport with the pirates, who will protect this island too." I glance at the closed door. Hopefully I'm not too loud, and Roje is still sleeping. "I have not been idle, Iraya," I say, lowering my voice. "I am here and I am fighting. What do you have for me?"

"Concealed weapons?" Her brows draw in. "In addition to the Oscuridad?"

"What do you have for me?" I repeat.

She shakes her head.

"Can you at least tell me how they're moving across the island?"

"There've been no marching armies?"

"No. But they're planning an attack. I need more than you've given." Which is nothing. She has done *nothing* for Aiyca.

Iraya worries her bottom lip between her teeth, like she

knows it too. "Use the Obeah Witches Council, use the shields. Do you understand?"

"I've always understood."

"You can't lose any more territory, Jazmyne."

"I have safeguards in place. *I* am doing something."

"Good. Keep holding that line," she says. "Or all is lost. The Oscuridad . . . they are not strangers to Aiyca. They've been here a long while. I think even longer than we suspected."

"What do you mean?"

"I'm not sure yet, but when I am, you can trust that I know how to pass along information."

Her face disappears without forewarning. My head falls back against the wall. What did she mean about the monsters having been in Aiyca before? I summon an attendant with a call for aid; two appear. Both are Alumbrar, the only help permitted in the palace, with the exception of the shields in its grounds.

"What do either of you know about monsters and Aiyca? Are there any Anansi tales you heard, growing up?"

"I'm not sure what you mean, Regent." The older of the two glances down at the smaller girl. "There's the Rolling Calf and the sukuyan."

"Yes." I cut her and my memories of interacting with both Aiycan legends off at the quick. "I'm familiar with both. I meant beasts that might have had a name, and a role in our empire's history."

"I might know," the younger attendant says, with a softness that immediately raises the hairs on the back of my neck. "Before the empire dissolved, there was a story about the time all three major islands united to defeat a race of creatures that came from the sea to subjugate humans."

My shoulders lose some of their rigidity. There have been no rumors of aquatic Oscuridad—yet. What if Iraya was alluding to where the beasts are? Their scope could extend beyond the earth.

"What do you know about these creatures?" I press the attendant.

"Nothing beyond their defeat. They were banished to the Monster's Gulf. Allegedly, that's how the waters between Aiyca, Zesia, and the Skylands received its name."

"Which means we can't trust the story," the older attendant adds. "If I had a piece of silver for every name's origin story, I'd be a wealthy woman."

She's not wrong. Dada said my name came to him in a dream, along with me. He said I asked to join our family. Nonsense.

Whether the Oscuridad have been here before or not is something for Iraya to contend with. I don't have time for fiction when my reality is nightmare enough. Now the doyenne's threat has burned up with the sunrise on this tenth morning, it's time to prepare to meet with Ormine, Mariama, Ionie. The new names for my council and parish custos arrived after our return to the palace.

Still . . .

If the Oscuridad *have* been defeated once before, there is hope that they can be again.

This war will be won.

I simply have to ensure I am the victor.

24

IRAYA

Second only to the Unlit as an enemy in this war is time.

With Jazmyne proving herself to be a poor messenger as well as ruler, returning to Aiyca can't come soon enough. Tea with Melione is postponed for the morsels of guzzu tutelage Delyse can offer me in our suite, and that's only when Kaltoon isn't sending in seamstresses, chefs, decorators, to ask inane question upon question about jump-ups I couldn't care less about. What's more, Kirdan has yet to show. Two days have passed since Shamar told me the prince is active, and he hadn't made his way to me. I haven't felt so much as a whisper of his presence while walking the palace halls. He's fine to leave me the bed, but I want my family Grimoire. I need it to test a theory.

I think the Oscuridad are the monsters that sought to conquer Aiyca centuries in the past and found themselves banished to the Monster's Gulf. If that's true, we're facing off against legends, with a hierarchy of their own. Those imprisoned in the gulf fought independently. The current variations must be lesser than them, since they're being used as frontline soldiers, and therefore easier to defeat—if we can close the tears Kirdan spoke of.

With the princesses as dead to me as I am to them, my only remaining option to get aid to Aiyca—and to get home before Jazmyne loses any further territory—is the doyenne and her council. Studying Delyse's books hasn't proffered the right guzzu to banish the Unlit's beasts. While I was uncertain about extorting Zesia's doyenne to gain access to the Simbarabo after Kirdan and I formed that sort of truce, given his absence now, I feel less bad about meeting with his mama and fabricating how close I am to stopping the monsters, despite not seeing one up close since the attack on the Recondite in Aiyca. But Doyenne Divsylar is content to keep to her suite, where, it's alleged by court members I've been eavesdropping on, she brews potions and masters guzzu to use against *me*. If it would grant me an audience with her, I wouldn't mind an attempt on my life. As for the council, its members were rarely in the palace, leaving Kaltoon to preside over everyone and everything here. Forget Kirdan being the empire's first doyen, with Krimpt holding dominion at the Simbarabo Cuartel; his uncles took claim to that accolade long ago.

In Aiyca, I acted first and the repercussions came down like a mighty fist. Haste is the measure of a fool, but what is stasis? The death of a hero? Not that I consider myself a hero. They tend to have competent sidekicks, whereas all Jazmyne deserves is a kick.

The only progress to be found is in the conduit weapons Zander's Artisan crafted for Delyse and me. She arrived the morning after our first session, took a quick sketch of what I described, and then returned with the weapons, and a new conduit coin, for convenience, as I was leaving to attend yet another asinine meeting about the wedding. In addition to the knives in various sizes to line the Stealth bandolier from Aiyca, she crafted a long golden rod with a separation button. It's not Dada's staff, but even Zander is impressed when he introduces magic into our third training session and, raising the lambent batons aglow with will into a cross before me, I block the first fizzing amber spark of suppression he fires my way.

"Please don't tell me that's all you've got," I tell him, arms still raised.

"Tough couple of days?"

"You have no idea."

With a smile almost as dangerous as the weapons he's loaded down with, Zander launches spark after disk after blip after strobe. The intent behind the colors, the shapes, flashes through my thoughts—*suppress, cut, blind, shock.*

I could use my will to slow them, but there won't be time to do that in the haze, the rush, of battle. Instinct takes over. *Block with magic-infused batons, sever with own blip, shield against the glare, smack the strobes back toward Zander with left baton.* His eyes widen and he sifts in a blink, here and then elsewhere.

But I was prepared for that too.

My right baton hurtles through the air toward him; an inch from his beautifully surprised face, I summon my conduit back with a pulse of magical will and catch it in—if I do say so myself—a damn impressive show of dexterity.

"Quick study," Zander breathes.

"A compliment. Did I catch you in the head after all?"

"Yeh mon, don't think I didn't notice where you were aiming." His voice is wry. "You've decided on your weapon, then. I like the batons."

"I'm testing them. I used something similar in a small skirmish with a friend once."

Small skirmish, prison rebellion—semantics.

"The beauty of your naevus is that you can bear as much gold as you wish. So keep the batons, the dagger, and then add something bigger. How about—" Zander straightens as that same drumbeat from before thunders across the Cuartel.

"Want some help tonight?" I offer lightly. "I'm armed for it."

"Help with what?"

"Are we going to pretend I don't know that alarm is for the Unlit's beasts?"

After a beat in which he studies me, my stance, my more sensible apparel of plain pants, accessorized only with a thigh strap containing my new knives, the chest-plate, a train-free tunic, and the travel cape I cast around my shoulders, Zander stalks across the training space and offers his arm.

My laughter echoes along with the next chorus of drums. "We *are* going to pretend. Right."

"Three training sessions, a change of outfit, several weapons, a maybe-conduit, and you think you're ready to fight them?"

"You forgot my sparkling personality and can-do attitude."

Taking my arm when I refuse to take his, Zander sifts us back to the same square by Green Island. "Another patrol of J'Martinet will be on duty where you met them before. Can you make it by yourself?"

"No Kirdan, Esai, or Shamar?"

"Not tonight."

"Krimpt?"

"Krimpt."

Delyse wouldn't like *Iraya* to be alone here. Neither would Shamar nor Kirdan. But *Ira*, that denizen of the night and all things best planned for the shadows, purrs inside.

"Yeh mon. I'll be fine." I'll head right home.

After I've looked one of the Oscuridad in the eye and seen what it's made of.

The moment Zander disappears, I duck into a space between two shops and begin cutting away strips of my cape with Kirdan's blade. Breadcrumbs with my scent for the Unlit's nightmares to follow, I tuck them into bushes and drape them over benches as I make my way across the city. Unusual, for a hub such as this, there aren't even people of the night out, or faces illuminated only by the light of a roll-up as they step out to smoke. This city has to know about its monstrous interlopers, which will only work in my favor when it comes time to threaten the doyenne into relinquishing the Simbarabo.

Swinging up onto a low wall, I turn to the city battlements, where the soldiers wait with crossbows, spears, bows, and arrows. Nothing elaborate. A good sign. They can hold off the majority of the beasts. I need but one to slip through to test my batons, my naevus on.

An hour later, it comes.

I'm not quite back at the square when there's a rustle at my back; it's followed by a feeling of massiveness, solidity. *There you are*, I think, turning slowly. Something screeches to the left of the intersection. Before I can send a probe of magic to test what might lurk out of reach of the lanterns, my braids drift across my face, driven by a bitter wind from the east. The tang of rot makes my nostrils flare, drags my upper lip back from my teeth. That's not wind. It's *breath*. From many, many mouths.

With microscopic head movements, I rotate. The confines of the city streets will work in my favor against one or two, but . . . there are several more than that closing in on me. Clever beasts. Just as Esai reported. Though I've been baiting them for some time, I have no idea when they began following me.

Hunting me.

"Let's go, you otherworldly bastards," I breathe, before, with a turn of my heel, I sprint into the dark streets of Green Island.

It's hillier than it seemed from the delta, from my walk with Esai. Underfoot, the cobbled stones are uneven, treacherous, forcing me to raise my legs even higher. With the incline, the necessity for speed, my thighs begin to scream soon. Too soon. The only respite comes from the city's many plazas for temples. Bathed in witchlight, they offer momentary havens to slow, snatch in lungfuls of air, before I plunge back into the darkness of the city.

But the beasts, with their four legs to my two, catch up.

Mid-vault over a low wall, what's left of my cape is snatched back, the tie at my neck cuts into my throat, and my oxygen is guillotined long enough for panic to fill its space in my lungs. To swell and suffocate me of reason, of instinct. To dull the roar of the beast snapping at my neck, one I still haven't seen, and cannot see as my vision begins to spot. Death opens her arms in an embrace I feel scrabbling at the little consciousness I have remaining.

Are you witch or not? a small voice murmurs.

No magic yet. Need to save the gold I carry.

Then, Warrior, cut the tie.

The instruction comes from somewhere deep, somewhere warm I inexplicably know without hesitation to trust. Kirdan's blade is freed from my thigh; teeth gritted against the sharp sting of it against my skin, I cut. I'm freed. I'm gone. Every breath is weaponized into a jagged shard against my throat; stones vibrate underfoot with the intensity of the minarets' alarm. And just when I feel my mind slipping, energy slipping, moonlight is sudden and beautiful as I clear the province's labyrinth of streets and skid to a stop in Green Island's market square.

Keep moving, that voice commands.

But it's no longer time for running.

Right foot planted ahead of my left, I sink deep into my fighting stance and free the batons from their holster across my shoulder blades. Instead of their dual beams chasing the darkness away, their light bucks up against it like the meeting of equal forces.

A pair of angled yellow eyes comes in from the night.

Wicked with malice, they're second to the claws that rise like scythes from paws built to remove heads, to sever torso from legs. But it's the long muzzles—the *varied* muzzles, I note with quick assessment, as more beasts emerge around the first—that are most concerning. Sharing the tonality of shadows, in shades of black, brown, and gray, there are some as wide as the chests of grown men. Others have multiple rows of teeth, or jagged fangs that jut from the mottled skin above their lips like profanities, like they've been turned inside out. My bowels loosen when snarls rip through the heavens.

More creatures crouch atop rooftops. Their muscles ripple in the moonlight—dozens. Tens of dozens that look down on me like I am tonight's entertainment in an amphitheater. Shit. I thought the Simbarabo in the battlements would have the majority of them covered. I thought Zander would—

Realization knocks the remaining air from my belly.

My lack of escort.

He did this. I wouldn't have been able to lure these beasts out if Esai accompanied me, as he did for the past two nights— when all he could do was tell me about the creatures' speed, their intelligence. It was like an immersion in monster lore. And tonight, Zander asking me if I was ready to fight. Here I thought myself the clever one; those bag-o-wires set me up!

They want to know if I am Empress Adair by name or by nature.

"You wanted to see what I could do outside a training room, is that it," I murmur for them, since they no doubt lurk nearby. "You only had to ask if you wanted to watch."

I fire one fizzing spark into the knot of my monsters, and

then Green Island's plaza erupts into activity. The beasts charge, leaping down from rooftops, bounding across stone to reach me. Their nails clash and scream like weapons of steel, conduit gold; in the split second before I unleash my now ever-ready naevus, I'm almost sure I see some creatures with *wings*. But then there is only the alabaster flare of my will, unbridled and full throttle, aimed at the multitude before me. As I imagine it tearing through them like a tsunami of molten fire, so it happens, my magic almost delighting in the destruction of its first full attack. Without the Impediment Glyphs, exchanged for the breastplate, I'm like a solar flare with a universe to shine for—one I could make, if I want. I feel that deep-seated ancestral thrum, as though the living and dying are mine to command.

The beasts don't stand a chance.

With more gold, blinking away the bright light of magic happens with more ease than it did back in Coral Garden. My muscles throb, and fatigue is bone-deep, and yet I've never felt more in control.

"Come out, come out, Lieutenant Esai," I call. "You and I need to have a chat about the meaning of—"

A low growl reverberates through the smoky haze my magic left behind in the square, stopping my words clean dead.

Nothing could have survived that attack.

Get out of there, that internal voice demands.

A harsh snarl makes me jolt.

I concede a step.

Something exhales two puffs of the most piqued air I've ever heard.

Now.

Where did Zander say the Simbarabo patrol would be again?

Go!

Turning on my heel, I move so fast the city blurs around me; beneath the stars water shimmers. The delta. I pivot and run for a barrier between me and the monsters; running water is the hero in many of Anansi's stories, but Zesia has its own heroes. Snapping cuts through the night, sharp and furious. The dark creek stirs softly in the night air, and I utter an apology as I fling myself at them, using my magic to corkscrew across and over the broad water. My reflection's eyes are wide, bright, as I point a baton at the delta and launch a harmless gold strobe of magic into its dark depths, along with two commands.

Wake.

Protect.

My feet slam onto Green Island, close to the shrine for the Delta Damsels as the first serpent bursts from the surface of the delta. Frenzied and flailing, its jaws open wide in time to enclose around the first leaping Unlit beast—and promptly pass right through it.

"Incorporeal," I whisper, hoarse with shock.

Two more of the great worms rise with otherworldly shrieks, but it no longer matters. The Unlit's beasts cannot be beaten by their ilk, by blade, or by magic—not even mine.

A branch snaps at my back, I twist and raise my weapons, but it's no monster.

"Kirdan," I exhale.

Far from resembling one who looks close to death, his cheeks are flush with color, the delicate skin beneath his eyes without shadows.

"Were you part of this?" I ask.

He shakes his head. "I heard the alarms across the island, tried to help."

A snarl rips across the bank, where the first of the Unlit's monsters emerges from the water. It's as dry as it was in the square because, of course, it's barely more than a duppy—and yet, it can still touch. Still kill. I raise my batons; Kirdan angles himself before me.

With a scowl I step out from his shadow. "Don't do that. I don't need saving." *I need help*, I don't say, because he isn't looking at me, he's glaring at the magi who sifts into being across from us. The Warrior dressed in shadows, whose flare of silver hair streaking down his back like a shooting star comes second to the livid white-gold scarification emblazoned down a single cheek. Zander etches a glyph in the air and shunts it toward the beast, where it lands like a brand. He follows the magic with a golden spear; the monster's dying cries shake the entire island, my very core, before it disappears in a nebulous explosion of obsidian smoke.

Across the delta, soldiers tackle its ilk in a similar fashion, casting glyphs that render the monsters corporeal. My question—*how*—dies on my lips at the tone with which Kirdan next speaks.

"You used Iraya as bait?"

Zander straightens. "General." For that is who he is speaking to, in this moment, I realize with a shiver. Not Kirdan,

Jazmyne's lapdog. General Divsylar. Commander of this fabled military of bastards. "The empress was never in any danger, I wouldn't—"

"That was not your call to make, Lieutenant." Kirdan's diction is a weapon of its own. One Zander flinches from. "We who know what it means to be the thrown body stoppering destruction."

"Thrown body, ouch," I murmur, suddenly tired, heavy to my bones. "And here I thought you liked me, mon."

Zander remains at attention, but he lowers his eyes. "I wouldn't have been following you if I didn't."

"I don't recall giving you permission to speak, soldier."

I don't recall giving Kirdan permission to speak for me either. But . . . far be it from me to undermine the general of the army I so clearly need to take back to Aiyca. My focus drifts across the delta, to the square where the soldiers make short, efficient work of dispatching the beasts.

"How do you kill them?"

"They can't be killed on this side of the veil," Kirdan answers, short and sharp. "Zander, go and clean up your mess."

The lieutenant glances my way and then disappears.

"He thought I could defeat them."

"I will deal with him."

"But I couldn't," I continue. "And maybe it's better I know now."

"Iraya."

"Isn't it? Better that Zander was here, that you were here, when I thought I could take them all on and defeat them."

"Hey." Kirdan stands before me. "We can't have this talk here. Come, I'll show you how to etch the glyph with your baton, and then we can return to the palace."

As he helps me render the seven-point Glyph of Banishment, placing his hand over mine to guide my conduit through the air, all I can think of is my plan to use my knowledge against him.

Where would I be if he did the same? I know where. What I should consider is where can *we* be, Kirdan and me.

Together.

25

JAZMYNE

In my office, I trace my fingers across my new desk—one of the few survivors of whatever Kirdan and Iraya did in here after I left, during the Sole—and look out the window that sits at its back, the framed Strawberry Hills and Aiyca beyond them.

Be measured. Be steady.

I've sent several messages to my cousin in Sanar, but so far she's yet to reply with the information I requested from Anan. By all accounts, I'm the more favorable candidate for the Skylands to support. What has Iraya achieved but a new wardrobe and the fealty of bredren who once served by my side? The list of what she hasn't done is far greater. Even the advisors have little to badger me about. It is only the matter of the Unlit army's whereabouts we are all caught on, snagged on the hook of the unanswered question.

Perhaps Ford will be of more help than his empress.

There's a knock at the study door that pulls me out of my

thoughts; Roje strides in first, sends a wink my way; Filmore and Pasha follow; the Obeah, Ford, follows with two Xanthippe. Of medium build, the shackled magi moves as though boneless. Paired with the coven witches, stiff and unyielding beside him, they look an odd trio. His crop of curls spring in unruly angles; the sides have grown out, but I imagine he kept them meticulously shorn before. Altogether he looks like a buguyaga, not an Obeah capable of leading the shields. Is this another of Iraya's tricks?

"No crown?" he rasps my way.

"Let's not waste time with posturing. Iraya Adair told me to ask after you."

The indolence in his expression is gone in a blink.

"She lives, then."

"You doubted her?"

"Never. But to hear her name spoken by an Alumbrar . . ." He whistles long and low.

"You doubt *me*?"

He shrugs; those shoulders that were as loose as water moments ago are now straight, strong. I see what he means, and for a moment I'm almost emboldened by the thought that he thinks me capable of the same deception.

"I met with Iraya ten days ago, before she left Aiyca in the company of two Obeah and Prince Kirdan Divsylar, to recruit an army to fight enemies gathering in our shallows and our fringes. She told me to ask after you, said . . ." Not entirely comfortable repeating her prurient words, it takes a moment for them to come. "She said it's time to put those fingers to use."

A slow smile blooms on his face. "What do you need, Alumbrar?"

"Release him," I instruct the Xanthippe.

"Seriously?" Roje asks.

"If my empress sees something of value in this Alumbrar," Ford says, "I can try to."

"High praise indeed," I murmur. "Guard?"

Ford's wrist and ankle shackles fall away. He rubs the tender skin; it's then that I notice the scarification dancing across his fingers. He's a Grower. Relief is fast. *That's* what Iraya meant by that comment.

"A drink?" I offer. "Provisions?"

"Yes to both."

I nod at the guards; one strides to the door to pass along the message to their ilk outside.

"Please," I tell Ford. "Be seated."

With a marked difference to how he entered, he moves with the gait of one who fears very little about his company, and angles his seat so that he might watch the door as well as me. "You are running a different island to your mama, Alumbrar."

"Regent," Roje corrects.

"*Jazmyne*," I amend, with a silencing look at him. I need this Obeah's help, not his ire.

Ford merely sits back, at ease. "Do you wish for the same protection she had?"

"No. The protection I want includes the entire parish, not solely this mount."

A single thick eyebrow shoots up. "Obeah and Alumbrar?"

"Secular too."

He whistles again, and watches me as though I am a plant that suddenly started talking.

"What do you know of the Unlit?" I ask.

"They have their sights set on Aiyca. The two Obeah with Iraya are bredren and sistren of mine. We spoke with the Divsylar prince before the Sole. Pooled our resources, if you will."

In my lap my hands curl inward. The list of Kirdan's betrayals continues to grow.

"I wasn't aware Iraya left with him, though. She means to bring back his army?"

I nod.

He smiles again; it's almost rapturous, his admiration of her. "She's allied with you too?"

I hesitate. "I wouldn't put it like that."

He snorts. "I don't doubt it. Look, Jaz—"

Pasha makes a noise of indignation.

"There aren't enough shields in the cells to protect the parish," Ford continues, unperturbed. "For that, you'll need the Jade Guild."

"*You* need them, you mean," Roje says. "To snatch this palace from beneath the regent."

For the first time a shadow falls across Ford's face. One that makes me question how reliable his Grower scarification is, and what else his fingers might have held in the past.

"Unlike everyone in here," he says softly, "I am loyal to my ruler. If she has asked me to help, I mean to do so. As for what happens when she returns? I make no promises."

The food and drink arrive, thank the gods. Ford uses his

hands with difficulty; sympathy jars through me, enough to request a Healer from the departing attendant.

"No worries, mon. I'll have one of the shields do it."

My breath stills in my chest. They won't have magic without working for me. . . .

"Then you'll help?" I check.

"As flattered as I am that Iraya asked for me personally— you'll tell her, won't you, when you next speak? I was only handling matters here on the orders of someone else—the Masters. They're the ones you'll need to speak with about protecting the parish, but the shields can hold this mount, yeh mon."

"I only know about a council."

"They're one and the same."

Interesting. I thought the late doyenne took care of the Masters. Is anything she said true?

"How do I contact them?"

"I can, once my conduit is returned."

I hesitate again.

This feels redolent of the Shook Bargain with Iraya.

"Don't you need me for my magic?" Ford asks, that brow hiking up his forehead once more. "And there are several additional terms I seek. No silver hoods. No silver, period. We wear white, as Obeah always have done."

"What about white *and* silver?"

He tips his head.

"If we're to go to war it's important that the Unlit see us as a united front."

It's his turn to hesitate. "I'll run it by the team."

"Until I have my answer from the Masters, it's just you who'll have your conduit, and only while in my presence."

"Deal."

Ford and I make short work of drafting the missive; Filmore reads it twice before sending it into the fire at the Obeah's direction.

"I was willing to give my life for Iraya Adair," Ford says. "You I don't know, but I do know this—you are not your mama."

"Then help me with something else," I begin, but there comes a knock at the door.

Cleo enters and stops, glancing at Ford.

"Speak freely," I tell her. We might very well be working together soon enough. "Is it about the weapons?"

"Yes and no, Regent." The Stealth brushes her twists back from her face. "Two cities have fallen in St. Elizabeth."

I'm on my feet before I've thought to stand.

"Unlit?"

Cleo nods. St. Elizabeth is west of St. Ann, where Black River Port is—what's left of it, since the doyenne didn't deign to expedite repairs. Didn't have the time to.

Mudda have mercy.

"The message. 'The Lost Empress Remembers.' They wrote that first in St. Elizabeth. Which city fell?"

"Morant Bay," Cleo answers.

Her words eject all the energy from my body.

"They all but warned me when they wrote the message." I was a fool not to see it. "But their army hasn't been seen. Was it this time?"

"No, Regent. But their weapons were," Cleo continues. "That and the desiccated bodies of Xanthippe and battalion soldiers."

Mudda have mercy. "Desiccated?"

"The weapon is unlike anything we've heard about. Reports consist of an explosion; by the time the smoke cleared, the soldiers were dead. By all accounts, their weapon is extracting magic, and then using it to charge the weapon for another."

"It works like a grenade." Filmore frowns. "Which means there's a switch. The deaths are unfortunate, but we know more about their weapons now than we have before."

How did they manage to overwhelm two of our largest parishes without being seen?

"Sounds like they employed a pincer move," Ford says; we turn to look at him.

"I'm sorry?" I ask.

"Their move. You can predict where the weapons are located based on the Unlits' goal. They'll strike from the east next, to enclose you in this parish. Surrounded, you'll be trapped, with no way out when they come for the Golden Seat. . . . Shall we talk about those uniforms again?"

26

IRAYA

The Simbarabo never tire; the monsters are dispatched with militant efficacy Nana Clarke would have been proud to see implemented by the Virago. I, on the other hand, barely notice the magical leap from Green Island to the study in the suite, dazed as I am—stunned as I am to not be enough. Is this how Jazmyne feels most of the time? She almost lost Carling Hill. Will I actually lose this not-war?

"The beasts are not flesh and blood," Kirdan begins without prompt, leaning back against the door that leads out to the palace, arms folded across his chest. "It took us a while to learn that we can't harm them without momentarily altering their state of being with the Glyph of Banishment you saw. But they can kill us in either state, quickly or slowly. The claws and teeth bear poison."

Jazmyne said.

"Is there a cure?"

"She says yes, but I don't know it."

"Well, who provided the glyph?" I ask him.

"Lucia. A traveler brought her an item, a fossil, that carried a story of the monsters that sought to conquer Aiyca by sea thousands of years ago."

"The Hendern Cliffs."

Kirdan nods. "They were sent back to their side of the veil with the glyph."

"But you said they can't die."

"Once there, they can be freed again by the Unlit."

The good news is that if Kirdan doesn't know how to defeat the monsters, I can still extort the doyenne. The bad news? Can I still extort the doyenne with a promise to kill the beasts if they cannot die?

"There could be guzzu in the Grimoire. Have you looked?"

Kirdan shakes his head. "I've been waiting for you to look first. It was your mama's. I wouldn't take that right from you." He flicks his wrist, as though relieving himself of a cramp, and the battered book appears in his hand. "For the record, I always planned on giving it to you once I showed you why I needed you here."

With zero interest in feigning how desperate I've been for it, I snatch the Grimoire before he can change his mind. Small enough to carry in a bag, but not my pants pockets, I turn it over, drinking in the golden glyphs incised across its cracked leather cover. It's the closest thing I have to talking with Mama, Dada, Nana Clarke. Both sides of my family worked together to protect Aiyca since—since the history that inspired the Anansi story about the Witch of Bone and Briar.

"The Unlit have an infinite army courtesy of these tears."

"They will be larger now," Kirdan says. "More like gaps."

"Gaps then. These . . . Eldritch Gaps," I deliver with a faux lightness. "And we have no way of killing them at present."

"Eldritch Gaps," Kirdan muses. "Fitting. And yeh mon. But now I've dealt with Krimpt, my team can meet with yours tomorrow to talk strategy. It's too late, and, more importantly, too dark, to venture out now."

"Fine. First light. Goodnight." I take the balcony back to my room—where I almost launch my baton when I find Kirdan waiting in there, having sifted himself while I was walking. "What are you doing here?"

"I'm staying."

"I don't think so."

Kirdan shrugs off his baldric, unties the saber on his hip, and drops it onto the middle of the bed. "It's our first night together, *betrothed*."

Ah.

He's heard.

"No one expects me to stay in the Cuartel after your declaration now that I'm well." He loosens his laces with sharp, impatient tugs. "I would have been here sooner, but Krimpt took it upon himself to rile up my men about—" He cuts himself off.

"Me."

Straightening, Kirdan nods and drags a hand back through his hair. The ends are still choppy. "Here we are. I'm staying."

I cross my arms with a snort, hugging the Grimoire to my chest. "Don't consider me romanced."

"Your honor isn't in jeopardy—"

I choke.

"My sword can stay between us."

He's worried about *me*? "I don't think your men will take to me using it to cut at another of their precious snakes."

"What?"

"Oh—nothing!" *Cha mon.* I slam into the bathing room and grip the sink. The whites of my eyes are bright, my pupils like two dark moons. Full and swollen.

I am going to walk back out there and tell him where he can stick it—after I've looked at the Grimoire. A piece of my family history, as old as the first Adairs. A strange effervescence buzzes where it touches my skin, like the acknowledgment of something familiar, almost enough to forget what's waiting for me back in my bedroom.

Mama would have pored over the guzzu in this book, Nana Adair too—all of them, right back to the first Adair. Do they look on now, pleased that, after a decade, it's back where it belongs? Does it even belong to me, when I don't want to step into the role they occupied? The thought of giving it to another, Aiyca's ruler, whoever they may be, makes my head hot with jealousy. I don't want anyone else leaving their fingerprints on these pages.

Still unable to quite believe I'm holding it, I utter a quick prayer of thanks and open the book. It's been divided into sections based on métiers, by one diligent Adair or another, as well as additional categories—including one about monsters. At first glance, there's nothing specific about the Oscuridad. The Monster's Gulf crops up several times, which is a comfort.

Perhaps it's a sign of the ease with which we can defeat them—if the cure isn't isolated to a family secret. I'll have to study with more care when Kirdan isn't on the other side of the door. I use my magic to pry a tile from the wall and carve a book-sized hole in the stone behind it, before replacing the marble slab until even I can't tell which I removed without counting. Studying it in bed with Kirdan isn't an option until our two sides have met in the middle and I know which island we'll treat first, Aiyca or Zesia.

When I storm back out in my nightgown, he's sitting up, shirtless, in the bed, thumbing through one of the books Delyse and I were studying earlier. It's not the sight of his rippling pectoral muscles that kills all arguments on my tongue.

"Your scarification. Why is it visible when the other Simbarabo's only shows when they use their magic?"

Kirdan glances down at his chest, at the stark symbols and swirls dancing across the stretch of toasted-almond skin. "It's visible to show my soldiers I'm not ashamed of being Simbarabo. Under my governance, I want them to feel some semblance of family in our army. I want them to know that, when we die, they'll see familiar faces in Coyaba. Ones who understand their sacrifice and love them for it. Krimpt doesn't understand what true family is. Once forged, it's not a bond easily broken. But you know that." His words resonate within a deep part of me, one that still roams the mountains with my Warrior sistren, scents the richness of the coffee beans and freshly sharpened blades at our encampment. "No Grimoire?"

"Not tonight." Instead of turning him out of the bed, I approach to get in. I did spread my scent across the city tonight.

I won't be safe to cross the street, let alone anything else, come nightfall again. And then there are the monsters Kaltoon was reticent to tell me walk the palace. No after-dark forages for food for me. "Did you lock the door?"

"Of course."

Kirdan might not overtly watch me slip between the sheets, but I remember the chest-plate, the clothing he had made for me, and have no doubts that he knows how every part of my body moves across the bed where I settle on my side.

The coin around my neck flares as I will the lights to go out, his reading be damned.

"Count yourself lucky I'm not making you sleep on the floor." The ears that listen can be damned too.

"I do feel lucky tonight," he murmurs, and the candor in his voice makes me still against what might come next.

"Ears," I warn.

"I took care of them." The bed shifts beneath him; the sheets tighten across my body. "We may talk freely."

My lips dampen beneath my tongue. "Kirdan?"

"Iraya?"

I close my eyes against the sound of my name from his mouth.

"Just—shut up. Or I'll run you through with the dinner knife beneath my pillow."

His laughter—his laughter, I'll never get used to hearing it—shakes the bed.

It's difficult to tell how long I lie on my side, back to Kirdan and aware of nothing but him, before the first growl cuts through the silence in the suite.

Rocketing upward, I reach for the blade.

Lit by the glow of his saber, Kirdan creeps to the bedroom door, a finger to his lips.

"Delyse," I hiss, joining him.

"She knows to keep her door locked. I left a message. Do you think I let you keep that accidentally?" Kirdan knocks the dagger I hold with his saber; sparks clash between the metals. "Dinner knife." He shakes his head.

A low snarl reverberates through the wood of the door—wood, not iron.

"But the study door has been left unguarded since our arrival!"

Kirdan drags a hand through his chopped hair; it already looks longer. "I can't apologize for my family."

Puffs of air blow across our bare feet.

"You keep saying that, but you know what? I wouldn't mind if you tried."

"What do you want me to say? That they'd be happier with me dead? With you dead? I am the prince, but I am also Simbarabo. That should tell you enough."

A blast of air shunts me back onto the bed. Kirdan flings open the bedroom door. On the other side, unsightly, with at least a dozen tiny red eyes, the beast issues a triumphant howl. Sketching the glyph almost lazily in the air, Kirdan propels the golden symbol toward the beast. He follows the magic with a blade through the stomach. Crying out loud enough to rouse the entire palace, the creature dissipates into nothingness.

And yet, no J'Martinet come.

"Stay here," Kirdan orders, striding out into the dark lounge. To hell with him and his orders.

Jumping off the bed, I run for Delyse. She's holding similar batons to mine and peering out into the lounge through a sliver between her door and the frame.

"We knew it was a possibility they'd come for you," she says. "But in here?"

Now doesn't feel the best time to tell her about what I did in Green Island.

Delyse steps back, opens her door wider. "Sleep with me tonight."

"There are a few things the prince and I should discuss."

The study door slams.

"You're out here?" Kirdan snarls. "You know these beasts dwell in shadows, right, mon? There could have been more."

"I didn't know, actually," I half lie, starting after him. "Because you didn't tell me!" Glancing back at Delyse, I roll my eyes.

Kirdan's already back beneath the covers when I shut our door—*my* door. An intricate line of shimmering gold locks forged with magic appear; they are the sole light in the room.

"You could have started with those."

"I should have."

"Why didn't you?"

"Did you know the Simbarabo aren't allowed inside the palace? It's considered an omen of death and war because of our forbidden status. I might be a prince, but I still stay away from here as much as I can. There are only so many times magi hurrying to absolve themselves with the Mudda's sign of seven is amusing. It's why it took me so long to notice something was amiss here."

"Is that why you built the nests?"

"There are guerra birds roosting on every balcony in this palace, in case I needed to send a message. I couldn't trust my family to tell me anything before I was sent away to Aiyca. I wasn't sure what I'd return to, if I ever needed to come back here." He huffs a humorless laugh.

"They haven't been what I'd call welcoming."

"I heard about the Delta Damsel. I'm sorry I didn't warn you. I know them, and yet I hope they'll be better, do better."

"Then you think they left the door without guard deliberately?" I pad back to my side of the bed. "Your mama I expected to be despotic, but your sisters . . ."

"We've spent too much time apart. My uncles' influence."

"But they know about the monsters." They knew there was always a chance the beasts could infiltrate this suite, even before I left a trail for them to follow. Kirdan and I sifted back here tonight, but I traveled the delta, the city, on my way in from Lucia's, and again to meet with the triplets.

"Of course, though they won't call them monsters. No civilians have survived to recount anything about their appearances. I suspect either the beasts got them, or my uncle Krimpt did. Along with him, Kaltoon, the doyenne, and the council would sooner dismiss them as an unknown breed of shadow-cat and leave them to the Simbarabo to round up. The island knows something isn't right, but they refuse to face what." Kirdan sighs.

"We can figure everything out tomorrow."

We.

It should fill me with as much disgust as I feel for his brat sisters, his potentially murderous uncles, for who else would benefit from the removal of us both? But as I ease myself back under the covers, I know that the only reason I'll sleep through the night is the very fact that I am sharing a bed with Kirdan.

If any additional monsters break through his protections, he's closest to the door.

His dying screams should provide me with ample warning to run for my life.

"Goodnight, Iraya," Kirdan murmurs, his voice always soft in the dark.

That sharp zing through the base of my stomach is relief to have him as a shield.

Nothing more.

27

JAZMYNE

It takes two days for St. Elizabeth to fall in its entirety.

Once the capital cities were taken, Ford said it would only be a matter of time for the towns and villages to follow suit. He was right. What he didn't warn me about were the mass exoduses of people. Alumbrar and Aiycans have been flocking in droves to their neighboring parishes, seeking asylum from *the magi who move like smoke.* One of the few coherent responses we've been able to extract. They didn't take the parish with their monsters. Not the beast that chased Roje and me through the temple, anyway. A small mercy, given that everything has been like the falling of a monument, the loss of a limb, a violation.

Itinerant Obeah numbers have been fewer, which was to be expected, and only makes the absence of Iraya's council more infuriating. There has been no reply to the missive Ford sent. No word about their order potentially allying with the

Unlit—questions I am being asked by the Nameless now Aiyca has discovered it's at war, a confession I knew I'd have to make but wasn't ready for nevertheless.

At least Ford's prediction about St. Bethann hasn't come true. Xanthippe and battalion soldiers deal with small skirmishes between Obeah, but there has been no attack. Yet—a matter I've been in back-to-back meetings to ensure does not come to pass. The Blue Mountains are a key locale to attack from, given their scope and the elevated terrain. If the Unlit take them, the parish will be lost.

"Are we waiting for the Unlit to take that opportunity, or are you going to do something about it?" Ionie cuts out across the strategy table in the observatory. "Obeah have graduated from private meetings to public skirmishes as they recruit amongst themselves."

"I know. I have Xanthippe and battalion soldiers—"

"Watching? Standing by and doing nothing? Arrest the insurgents!"

"And give the Obeah another reason not to trust me?"

"If you care more about their trust than what they are assembling to do, you are a fool."

Standing by my left shoulder, Roje plants both palms on the map we moved and issues a guttural sigh that makes Mariama and Ormine exchange a frightened look. Ionie, breathing heavily, leans back in her chair.

"I am doing something about it," I defend myself, even if what I'm doing—all I can do—is wait to hear from the Obeah Masters. Soldiers have been dispatched to guard the roads between parishes, of course, but the Unlit's mystery weapon is more than capable of felling them like chaff. "You need to focus on the Swearing-In. Dismissed."

Two phases from now, I think, as they file out to the spiral staircase in this tower, I will ensure that I have nothing to do with those miserable old witches. The Unlit are actively seeking to occupy this island, and Ionie wants to issue barbed comments about exchanging decades of Squaller training to become an event planner. First the Nine Night for the doyenne, and now the Swearing-In of the new council presiders—whose names were waiting for me in a missive on the floor before the fire in my office, earlier today, right on schedule.

I still feel like I'm falling down that pit in the library. I don't know what's worse: this limbo, or how it will feel when I eventually hit the ground.

"That went better than before, I thought." Roje pulls out a chair beside me, drops onto it, and rocks back on two legs. "Do you trust them to handle the Swearing-In?"

"I trust that it will continue to keep them too busy to stew in their hatred of me breaking the traditions they hold dear. Pasha?"

The Stealth's magically enhanced hearing means I don't need to raise my voice to attract his attention where he stands watch in the stone hall outside.

"Regent?" He leans around the doorway.

"Any news on the weapon situation?"

The Stealth shakes his head.

There were further sightings of this Golden Explosion, we've taken to calling it, but we're no closer to determining what the Unlit are using to kill my soldiers, beyond an invisible grenade, or if they're already using Obeah across the island to help. They're getting gold and magic from somewhere.

"Come to me the minute you hear anything."

"Forgive me, my doyenne," Emthera says, popping her head around the doorway. "The Healer has arrived from Sanar."

"Oh," I groan, pulling a face at Roje. I'd forgotten that someone arrives today, and that I committed to showing them around St. Mary's Healing Centers—a double strike, since the tour will also alleviate the stresses of my parishioners when they see me hale in person. And then we're meant to dine with the Nameless Gennas as well as the mayor tomorrow evening. I'm not sure I can avoid it, given that whoever Aunty has sent will be the best of their métier. It might even be my cousin Chaska. "I'll meet them at the infirmary."

"Don't forget." Roje catches my arm as I rise from my seat. "The girl's coming by to do your hair soon. We leave for the shore in less than a day."

Something else to look forward to. My smile tightens.

"Walk good, my queen," he says.

"What will you do?"

"I'll find a distraction or two."

Envy becomes as oppressive as the surrounding air, warmer up here than it is in the cool stone halls of the observatory tower. Not at the thought of Roje with another, but the choice of the small, the simple, rather than losing oneself amidst all the great. This conflict, betrayal, reveal after reveal, is my reality, and I am sick of it. I'm sick of *holding the line* while Iraya enjoys her sojourn in Zesia.

Picking my way down the spiral staircase, a hand on the

wall, another holding my sky-blue kaftan aloft, tense for an attack against the palace, I'd give anything for a moment's peace rather than the whispering members of court who peer through my living wall of Xanthippe. The infirmary turns out to be just that. Dark walls, a chill in the air, and empty, it's the perfect sanctuary. One I should have remembered, as a Healer first.

"It's a relief that you still know how to find these rooms."

"Aunty!"

Folding me into an embrace, Galene cradles my head against her shoulder. "I thought I would be the best choice to ensure my niece and her subjects are kept safe from threat."

"I can't believe you came." This palace symbolizes everything she hated about the late doyenne. It will be lovely having family here, despite her feelings toward the place. "Send for more family, if you wish."

Drawing back, she smiles. "I might do that. In the meantime, I didn't travel alone. I thought you'd appreciate the return of your sistren."

Anya. Thank the gods.

"Where is she?"

"She's gone up to your rooms." Aunty glances behind me. "I half expected the pirate to be around, but I also thought you might be lonely."

"Thank you for taking such excellent care of her."

"Of course. Well, I know my way around the infirmary. All I require is an escort to my rooms. You should feel free to see your sistren."

"Emthera?" The Stealth stops pretending she's not listening

to our conversation. "Please show Master Galene to the Serenity Suite." To Aunty I explain, "It has the best bathing chamber. I hope it will aid in your relaxation, once matters worsen. For now—"

"Now I must train the Healers you have on staff, and there are always the sick in the parish below this mount to tend to. One day, you might accompany me."

"We have plans for tomorrow."

"Good." Aunty turns me to the door. "Now go. I know how eager you are to see her."

Once I'm clear of the palace's public spaces, I run the remainder of the way to my rooms. Anya has dropped items of clothing in the entryway of my chambers, draped her bandolier lined with various Stealth-related accoutrements on a lamp in the receiving room, and left her pants strewn across a chaise longue in the games room; coming across each item makes that knot of fear ever present throughout her absence unfurl—it dissipates entirely when the next item to be found is my sistren herself.

"That was fast," she remarks, drying her hair with a towel. "I didn't think—"

Not caring that she's wet when it's so much more important that she's *home*, I fling myself into her surprised arms.

"You shouldn't be out of bed," I say into her shoulder.

Her arms tighten around my back. "I couldn't leave you here alone with Roje for too much longer. Your aunty agreed."

"But how do you feel?" Drawing back, I inspect her face. She still looks wan, drawn.

"Eager to hear all that's happened now we're clear of

Sanar's listening walls." She tugs me over to the bench at the foot of my bed; we sit knee to knee as we have so many times before. "What's been happening with you and the pirate?"

To get the worst out of the way, I confess the truth about the Hearkening Circle, the late doyenne's attacks, the Oscuridad in the temple, Roje's news about the expedited race, my decision not to participate, and the blank map, worthy of nothing but fire kindling without whatever it needs to make it work.

I show her the latter too, removing it from beneath my pillow. I expect shouting, but Anya merely sits. Looks. Her face is unreadable save one pulsing vein close to her damp hairline that tells me all I need to know.

"Don't be angry with Roje. It was me who asked for the guzzu." My voice dips. "I wanted the map." It's the first time I've acknowledged it, even to myself. I had reasons, sure. But my desire outweighed them tenfold. I didn't want to be powerful in my knowledge. I wanted the knowledge for power. Even after all it did to the late doyenne, how the burden of want followed her to the grave.

"Jaz—" She bites her lip bloody. "I'm pleased you've come to your senses about the race, but you're no longer to scheme with the pirate behind my back."

I nod my acquiescence.

"And you're not allowed to die for Aiyca. One of those godsforsaken beasts *here*. I—" Her free hand clasps mine. "I can't lose you."

"I'll be more careful," I promise, opting not to share that Roje spent the night. "There is one more discovery I made, but I'm not sure if it means what I think it means. I was in the library after the attack, and I think that past Unlit have been related to the Adairs."

"No," she whispers. "You think they helped Judair?"

"I couldn't identify their crimes. Roje interrupted me."

"I bet he did."

"As you're sick, I won't hit you for that comment. You know Roje and I aren't like that."

"I'm glad to hear you haven't fallen for his flirtation. What did he say, when you told him about quitting the race?"

"I haven't told him yet. I want to meet the crew during the Glide-By to identify a replacement. I'll implore them to work with me myself. Leaving for the race became unwise after the Carling Hill attack."

"It was always unwise."

"You weren't saying that back at your place when we celebrated Light Keeper's Nine Night."

"I wasn't saying much, from what I can remember. My mouth was always consuming some alcoholic beverage or other."

My face feels strange as I laugh, and I realize it's due to doing it so little. "I've missed you, sistren."

"And I you." She knocks her knee against mine. "So, you suspect the Adairs are in the Unlit?" Anya whistles. "The problems never cease."

In the turning wheel of the Adair versus Cariot rivalry, only one family has found itself on top at any given time—and if there wasn't room for the two Adairs, then I doubt we three will get along.

"Of course, I don't have the time to sit in the library now

Aunty is here, and the Glide-By is approaching. . . ."

Anya rolls her eyes. "I suppose it's the least I could do to help. Even if I must spend that time in the *library*." She says the last like it's a filthy word.

"There's one more thing. After the Oscuridad almost-attack, I decided to talk with Iraya's shield bredren."

The harsh cluck of Anya's tongue against her teeth makes me jolt. "Counting on pirates was one thing, Jaz, but the shields? You think you can trust them to play by the rules?"

"I don't think our relationship will be like that." I chew the words out slowly, tasting the plan as it is formed. "It's more akin to trusting that they *will* break rules. We can't make them fit our ideal; that's how other Alumbrar have lost." Light Keeper spoke of the late doyenne's lack of malleability time and time again. "If I'm asking the shields to bend, so must I."

"I wish I were enough so that you didn't have to."

"You are enough." When she doesn't look at me, I take her chin between my fingers. "No one can be everything, Anya."

"But I am your first."

"And you will always be first in line to hear my thoughts, and I yours, but there are others who can help too. We cannot watch the palace, the island, the seas, and the future alone. But we can watch one another's backs. I need you here while I'm at sea, in a couple of days. Stay here and continue to *rest*. No, Anya," I insist when she attempts to interrupt me. "I'll bring Filmore and another of the cadre. If you feel up to it you can research those Unlit archives; check in on the Nameless, the new council members. There's also the Obeah Transmuter, Adriel. I need to see his progress for myself."

Admonishments are swallowed, choked down as she physically wrests for control. I am not the leader she left for Carling Hill. Perhaps she sees that.

"Fine. And the Obeah Masters?" she raises, entirely unable to help herself. "You said you might meet with them. What if it's a trap?"

"As I said, it's not for us to expect Ford and his order to play by the rules."

"And you?"

"I'm regent, Anya. I make the rules." I reach for her hand, give it a squeeze. "You should get back into bed."

Issuing a terse nod, Anya rises and heads toward the bathing room to dress. Taking up the map, I leave for the games room to seek out another place to stash it while giving her space too. We fight like sisters, love like sisters, but there are times when I think Anya might mistake me *for* my sister. She couldn't save Madisyn; neither of us could. . . .

Without the Masters, I'm not so sure we'll be able to curb that statistic when it comes to one another either.

28

IRAYA

I wake sheathed in a membrane of sweat.

Heady incense, spiced with cinnamon and something earthier, familiar, twines around my body like a silk nightgown, rather than the cotton one I went to bed in, rendering my limbs lethargic and cumbersome. The sigh that slips through my lips belongs to someone with far less responsibility; a returning exhale brushes across my cheek with a featherlight softness. I stiffen as, with the force of a boot to the throat, I remember last night's events.

It's not the encroaching sunrise percolating behind the curtains that scorches my body with its light. No, it's the tautly muscled male frame pressed against my back; the arm fortified with muscle draped over my hip with a proprietor's intent. Heat roils off our united frames in tangible waves.

Mine and Kirdan's.

Kirdan's and mine.

The sword that separated us is gone, and somehow we're skin to skin. My nightgown has slid up to bunch around my middle, and every breath Kirdan takes presses his chest all the more closely against my exposed back. . . . I shouldn't reciprocate. I should leap up and slug him. This I scream to myself across an internal chasm where sense and its antithesis are separated by miles of synapses ablaze with—with *something*. But all warnings fall on deaf ears when he issues a primal rumble, and it reverberates through each vertebra in my spine, my belly.

Lower.

Oh. Gods.

Almost as a third party, an observer, I feel myself lean back into the hard ridges of Kirdan's chest; his breath is hot against my neck, which means the curve of his lips can't be far behind. Chest just shy of bursting from the top of my nightgown, I press back a little harder.

"If you keep moving like that, there's going to be trouble," Kirdan murmurs.

Fueled with shame, humiliation, I fling his arm off my waist and roll across the wide expanse of bed in one maneuver. Rising to my knees, with the speed and precision of a black racer snake, I lean across the bed and jab at his stomach with a finger.

"Ow!" He crumples in on himself. "What are you doing?"

"What am I doing? What are *you* doing?"

"Sleeping, before you woke me." He stretches, a hand on his stomach. The sheet slinks down his body, revealing two deep grooves at the base of his stomach. . . .

"Where's the sword?"

"Not sure."

"That's convenient."

"Iraya, I wasn't the one who started—"

"Stop!" I fling out my hands. "*Stop.*"

With a different sigh than the ones he was emitting in sleep, Kirdan egresses from the bed, clothed only in loose sleeping bottoms. I don't mean to look, to watch, but I'm not surprised to see that his back, like my legs, is flayed with scars, a map of brutality that meanders and turns like Zesia's Sadirren Delta.

"I didn't dislike waking like that." Kirdan looks at me, those green eyes of his not as unreadable as they have been in the past. "For the record." That inexplicable heat zings between the two of us once more, coiling in the base of my stomach like some awakened creature of old. . . .

Anger. That's the creature. It's not desire.

He opens his mouth, but I'm faster.

"I'm going to bathe."

It's difficult to discern how I move from the bed to bathing chamber, but suddenly I'm before the sink, once again struggling to look myself in the eye. Back in Aiyca, two phases ago now, I was so sure of my decision, smart in fact, to focus on the greater danger at hand rather than playing house with this bag-o-wire. . . . And then we came here and I saw how highly he's esteemed by his soldiers; just now saw the scars he carries to bear the weight of this island on his back.

Kirdan's men see him as a hero for the same reason his island treats him like a villain, and it's frustrating to see him through their eyes. Every time I think I hate him, that I could gladly watch him be devoured by one of the Unlit's beasts, another masked layer is revealed and the face underneath isn't awful enough to abhor. In Aiyca, cast in Jazmyne's shadow, I didn't see him. Jazmyne. Her name sends my mind in a new direction. She needs to know about the monsters, the glyph to send them back to their side of the veil.

She answers almost immediately when I call her, which is unlike her.

"I see you are capable of learning," I tell her reflection.

"Actually, I was about to contact you." Scowling, she glances off at something I cannot see. Her Stealth sistren, I bet. "We've come face-to-face with the Unlit's weapons. They're using conduit gold to extract magic."

"Like a pirate's trapper?"

Jazmyne presses her lips together. "In theory, perhaps. We think it's more akin to a grenade. There's a trigger, an explosion, and the magic is withdrawn from the magi. Leaving them husk-like. We have no solution, as yet. Beyond the weapons, we have seen nothing of the Unlit. Not them, or their beasts. They haven't attacked the island at wide. They haven't done anything."

"Are you wishing they would? Let me tell you, unless you know how to handle them, pray to your gods for thanks that they're slumbering."

"But why are they?" she pushes.

Because Aiyca is clearly the island this mysterious Unlit leader wishes to rule, and not with fear, if the monsters don't hunt as they do in Zesia. The truth both surprises me and answers the questions I've been mentally asking myself for phases now.

"They won't be dormant forever," I tell Jazmyne. "Whoever commands them will send them for the palace, while avoiding island-wide bloodshed against Aiycans—you and I won't be so lucky. But I have a glyph I can show you. Do you have writing tools? Get some."

She looks off to her left again.

"Ensure this is distributed to the Xanthippe, battalion soldiers, and the shields." I describe the three concentric circles and the downward-pointing arrowhead atop them.

"When can I expect you?"

"I'm close to returning. Speak soon."

That was almost friendly. I don't know whether to be comforted by that fact, or suspicious. Although the lowered bath is deep and lengthy enough to swim several strokes from one side to the other, I'm in and out within minutes. I don't want to spend any more time in my rooms with Kirdan than I have to. The mirror is returned to the cubby in the wall; I remember too late that I haven't brought any clothes with me. My nightgown lies crumpled on the floor. I scowl at it, a witness, an accomplice, to the exchange of whatever took place in bed.

My thin robe it is.

"Can you tell Delyse where we're going today?" Kirdan asks as soon as I've opened the door. "Shamar is with Zander and Esai; the latter know more about my plight to banish the Unlit's beasts than the other Simbarabo, so they're fine to sit in our war council if you are." He turns. "Since you're—" Stopping at the sight of me in my robe, his lips utter, "Naked."

My stomach clenches.

"If we're sifting, I'll meet you outside as soon as I'm not naked."

Kirdan's eyes darken.

"As soon as I'm dressed, I meant." Inwardly, I curse my inarticulation. Bathing him in the encroaching dawn, the light gilds Kirdan's skin, shines through the dark strands of his hair until they're almost reflective. While without weapons, or clothing beyond the bottoms he slept in, he's never looked so dangerous, so capable of tearing something, someone, apart with his bare hands. His large hands. That were just holding me.

"You're thinking about it," he gutters out. "Us in bed."

My chin tips up, as though his words are a challenge, another battle between us. I should deny, deny, deny, and yet . . .

"So?"

"So, there's hope."

"For what?"

"For more nights when I fall asleep beside you, and wake to find you in my arms." He shrugs, utterly unfazed by the baldness of his words. Another new facet to him.

Even as my body turns boneless, I force bite into my next words. "I didn't put myself there."

"You didn't move away from me either, if memory serves, and you can trust that I won't forget a single detail." The step he takes toward me is indolent, but I'd be a fool to feel like anything less than prey. It's odd. I always thought I was the hunter of us two. "The places your body pressed against mine are still warm."

"Knock, knock."

I jerk around to find Delyse in the doorway. She takes one look between the two of us—Kirdan without his shirt, me in my robe, breathless—and her brow lowers.

"Iraya will catch you up," Kirdan says in passing. "I'll meet you both outside as soon as I'm dressed."

"How long have you been awake?" Delyse asks as soon as he's gone.

Still lost in Kirdan's fog, I blink at her, disoriented.

"Iraya?" Stealth-sharp, she glances over at the rumpled bed. "Did you—did he *sleep here*?"

"Something happened last night—not that," I add when her mouth opens. "Before the creature broke into the suite, I was attacked returning from training with Zander." My sensibilities come back the more I share about last night's events. "Kirdan stayed with me to be a second pair of eyes."

"*I* am meant to be your second pair of eyes. But here you are—" She stops herself.

"Go on."

"I just . . . I don't want Aiyca's place in your heart succeeded by the prince. Pleasure is all good and well, but in this case it isn't without its strings. He is tethered to this island by many of them, and you can guarantee that his uncle is eager to wed the two of you to ensure that, no matter what happens in the war, those ties will be so thick it won't matter if Kirdan is alive or dead. He will possess Aiyca."

"You think I haven't considered that?"

She lowers her eyes. "Forgive me, Empress."

"Titles?" When she doesn't look at me, I approach her.

"Delyse. I'm not putting Aiyca second. I will never put Aiyca second." She's polite enough not to mention our history, to say *again*. "I just spoke with Jazmyne and made sure she has the glyph I learned last night to banish the monsters back to their side of the veil."

Her eyebrows shoot upward, this time.

"Yeh mon. Kirdan's known about the beasts for longer than we have. Learning from him, specifically, discovering how to stop them, will only help Aiyca." The gaps, for instance. It's past time everything was on the table.

She exhales, and her shoulders lower from her ears.

"Any news on Melione?" The Skyland war dog who invited me over for tea sent another invitation this morning.

"I haven't found the time to watch her since the dinner, not while monitoring my fire for missives from the Jade Guild; forgive me. There's no news on that front, by the way. I can track the war dog down later, watch her, see who she interacts with."

"How about *we* watch her," I correct. "With Shamar in the Cuartel, we need all the eyes we can get to see the threats before they land."

"In the interest of seeing threats coming, be cautious around Kirdan. I don't need my Stealth training to notice that he looks at you like . . . like the moon must look at the sun when it gets its chance to shine."

"With envy?"

"With longing."

29

JAZMYNE

I join Aunty to travel into Queenstown to visit St. Mary's Healing Centers the day after her arrival. Sanar's Healers have revolutionized the city's two locations. When the Unlit deign to have the Oscuridad strike, we'll be prepared.

"I can't understand it," I mutter to Aunty. Arms linked, we walk streets that buzz with activity, with excitement to see me—us. Sanar's Master Healer and her niece, Aiyca's newly crowned regent. Xanthippe keep back the overzealous relieved to see something stable amidst the uncertainty of war. "Why haven't the insurgents set their beasts loose?"

"Don't seek out trouble, Jazmyne."

"It sought me out, and now it's hiding. It's not dormant, it's waiting; I can't see what for."

"You don't think like them, a matter that should bring you relief."

A scarred man thrusts his arm between two Xanthippe;

Aunty stops them wrestling back with a calm word and leaves my side to take his hand. The coin around her neck and the thick golden rings on each of her fingers glow; the man's scars, and likely internal pain, fade. Sobbing, he clutches at Aunty and repeats his blessings over and over. She moves on to another reaching hand, takes it between both her own. Awkward, without the magic to help, I smile—grimace—into the crowd. Anya told me to let them see me; it's better doing it with Aunty by my side. I wish we'd reconnected sooner. Talking with her since she arrived has been something I never had with the late doyenne.

Beyond the Alumbrar, nonsecular, a flash of gold catches my eye. An Obeah-woman pushes another; the latter's back hits a wall, and she shouts something at the aggressor. The crowd shifts, blocking my view. I step to the left, the right, pushing up onto my toes to see the outcome of the argument, to determine if I need to send the Xanthippe after them, but the passageway is empty. I make a mental note to discuss it with Filmore upon my return back to the palace.

"I know you want to heal this island," Aunty Galene says, joining me. "You know the steps to take. When you cannot see, you . . . ?"

"Feel. I know. I remember." During my training we'd feel for growths, shape where bones were broken so that we could set them once again. Once I inherited my magic, I would have felt for internal infections, the slowing of blood flow to the heart, stiff joints. My hands would have traversed flesh. Sighing, I let the crowd's roars fade to white noise as I try to visualize the Unlit as a failing body. But it is strong. So ours must be too.

With Aunty here, the world *will* be saved by those who love, not destroy.

Cwenburg's holding cells are far enough away from the palace that, by the time I reach the sinister facade of the gold-glyphed building, the squat block guarded by Xanthippe, I am slightly out of breath—though not due to physical strain alone.

The Obeah Masters' reply came moments after Aunty and I returned to the palace.

Its timing is one I can't ignore, and a sign of the power of their Bonemantises. Perhaps they were in town; perhaps they've finally accepted that we need to work together to curb their order before they align with the Unlit. I'm not sure; the missive spelled against anyone who isn't Ford opening it. Time is short. Roje will arrive soon to accompany me to the Glide-By, but I can't leave without ensuring the palace will be supported in my absence.

In the holding cell's shadowed cove, the coven members almost glow in their gold-and-black uniforms. They also shake at an incongruous chill seeping from inside the open door; a sultry fog, it coils and twists around their boots with a serpentine elegance—and threat.

"What is this?"

"With the number of magi inside, Regent," one says, "the suppression glyphs on the walls are working overtime to keep the shields docile."

With a nod, I venture through the doors. Rime crunches beneath my sandals; my breaths emerge in a parade of faceless phantoms—not unlike the Unlit. Shivering, and not entirely due to the frigid air, I draw my hands into my sleeves. The cells aren't just cold, they're desolate. The glyphs incised onto the walls eke not just the shields' physical energy, but their internal will. They peer out at me as I crunch past. Curiosity is the prevailing emotion. I suspect they've all heard from Ford by now. The Grower himself reclines in his cell, hands clasped behind his head, a jaunty whistle on his breath.

"They've replied, then."

Loath as I am to part with the missive, when he sits up and stretches a hand through the bars of his cell, I hand it over. The wax seal gives with little difficulty beneath one scarred finger.

"What does it say?"

"Has anything else happened since the attack in St. Elizabeth?" he counters.

My first, pressing instinct is to lie. But without Anya, without Roje, who better to discuss Obeah with than one of their own?

"Your order is fighting amongst themselves."

With a wince, Ford sits up properly atop his cot. "How bad is it?"

"I'm not sure. They're doing a good job of concealing themselves from my guard. I'd never heard of Obeah fighting internally."

"You haven't studied our history?" Ford huffs a laugh. "Someone who believes they can do better always slithers out eventually, baying for anyone who might listen to them, and the like-minded always do. So let me see if I have this right: the Unlit have started campaigning to win families around now they have possession of Carling Hill—"

My stomach bottoms out.

How does he know that?

"At this point, I wouldn't put it past them to take credit for killing the doyenne as a way to curry favor amongst the Obeah too, and you're learning about it too late." Ford glances beyond me, at the guards he shouldn't be able to see from where he is. "You should tell them that gossip and reporting are more or less the same thing, but the difference in intent is key." He looks back at me, his appraisal fast and frank. "They're terrible, Jaz."

"Alumbrar weren't made for this."

Merciless, Ford nods. "It shows."

"What does the missive say?"

He finally slides it my way; it's an effort not to look too eager as I bend to lift it, fingers scrambling against tile.

"'We *will* meet,'" I read aloud. "That's it? It doesn't say when, where."

"Whenever they want, I suppose. Wherever they choose too."

"And I'm supposed to what, wait?"

"Unless you plan on doing something else about it, Regent?"

My breathing is hard, loud. "Ordering your uniforms."

Ford inclines his head. If we weren't mortal enemies, I might think the look in his eyes is one of approval. I might think he pushed me to this place to see how I'd react.

"Gold and white, don't forget."

"You'll wear what you're given and like it."

Ford's belly laugh follows me deeper into the holding cells

as I approach the next set of doors. But it isn't mocking, far from it.

"Move the shields back to the Cuartel," I tell the nearest guarding Xanthippe.

"All of them?"

"All of them," I return over my shoulder. "And be quick about it." To Ford, I say, "I'll be away, for several days. You'd better guard this mount with your life."

"I will," he vows. "My empress needs a home to return to." He grins.

I almost return it.

The cells turn and twist away from the shields; the Xanthippe guarding the separating doors are eventually replaced with pirates. Not yet familiar with every crew member's name, I merely nod. Most smile back; several wink. When I pass the last set of iron doors, the air is warmer with only the one prisoner. Javel.

In the security of a blind spot, I watch him. Prone on the floor of his cell, his ceremonial tunic and pants that shone with the gold he had the audacity to infuse through the threading is now dirty, dull. Shoulders curled in, he looks . . . forlorn. Weak. It would be easier to kill him, but I can't. I also have no idea what to do with him.

"I thought you didn't want to gut the whiner?"

Startled, I flinch to a shadowed nook. Roje steps from its darkness, arms folded across his chest; the white shirt he wears beneath a vest of battered leather stretches against bunched muscles.

"He complains?"

"He's an Important Person, according to him. Though he soon shut up after one of the crew told him what they like to do to Important People." Roje shakes his head. "Are you ready?"

Tell him now. Tell him you can't race for queen.

"I'm ready."

At this point, lies are easier than the truth.

I am not afraid of leaving the palace to the shields while I'm at sea.

I am not worried that the Unlit will attack in the day I am gone.

I do not fear what is to come, when the Oscuridad are set loose across the island.

If I say them enough, I might start believing myself.

30

IRAYA

On the uppermost floor of a tall building block in the thick of the noise and people crowding the tightly cloistered streets not too far from the Cuartel, an intimate restaurant provides a view out across the province. In the far distance, the shimmer of sea could be sunlight dancing across coins. Both make me think of Jazmyne. She and I will need to speak after this meeting about the Unlit, whatever it spawns.

"Is this a safe space to meet?" Delyse queries.

"It's private here." Esai pours chilled coconut water from the jug at the center of the table we congregate at, and we have our pick. The eatery, rich with jewel-toned lamps and hanging scarves, is empty. "No one else will be allowed up. Our general is a handsome tipper."

"Before we begin," Zander says, "Empress, I should apologize for last night." He glances up at his commander in chief. "But I'm not going to."

My eyebrows raise, along with Shamar's; Esai buries his face in his glass. Seated on the other side of Delyse, a committed buffer, I can't see Kirdan's face. I wish I could.

"We needed to know if you could take on those beasts and win, and we needed the conditions to be raw. Respectfully, General, the empress was never in any danger. I did everything by the book—beyond it, given the preparation we underwent, the conduit weapon I ensured was present, and the number of Simbarabo available in Green Island last night."

"But you didn't tell me," Kirdan says, in the same voice he used last night. "And you didn't ask Iraya if she minded being sent into the streets like a sacrificial goat to prove your theory."

"I've found it's rare that the goat is asked."

After a protracted beat, Kirdan's fist curls around his tumbler. He should be recalling the Rolling Calf, and the way he set Jazmyne and me up. Or maybe it's the memory of bringing me here against my will that's stoppered his tongue. Either is a sufficient reminder of his hypocrisy.

"What happened last night is another example of the many times we have acted as individuals," he says, and though Delyse is between us, I feel the phantom touch of his hand on my shoulder to accompany the apology in his words. "It's time to discuss how matters will look should we form a partnership."

Shamar rests his elbows on the table. "And this is the official invitation to do that?"

Zander and Esai shift in their seats; it's hard to take the span of their shoulders beneath their capes, the various weapons gleaming like sharpened teeth on their bodies, as anything other than adversarial.

"I don't know about you all," I begin before Kirdan can answer. "But after that talk of goats, I could do with ordering some food."

It's the perfect way to get everyone communicating without the pressure of islands' worth of lives at stake. After a little caution, a little nosing, each side loosens up enough to do just that. Kirdan's eyes meet mine over Delyse's bowed head; even I can't deny the admiration visible in them, the gratitude. He thinks we're on the same side.

I'm running out of reasons why we shouldn't be.

After we've placed an order from the bowing proprietor for dishes of lemon-stuffed fish, spiced rice, dates wrapped with slices of ham, along with Aiycan favorites such as callaloo threaded with saltfish, fried plantain, and jerk chicken, the atmosphere has lost enough of its tension, so I move into the seat at the head of the table. One of us Gennas, Kirdan or me, had to. Outranking him, even as an ersatz empress, the move was mine to make.

Conversation keeps dancing around the edge of what we have to discuss while the food arrives and the candles burn low, but the weight of what we'll learn next, the anticipation of accruing knowledge to end this, means we don't wait for long once our bellies are full.

"I want each of you to speak freely. This won't work, *we* won't work, with barriers and shields up." Each face I meet, while far from relaxing, becomes more open.

"What's the Unlit's plan of attack been here thus far?" Delyse asks.

"Aside from the monsters, nothing."

"They've done nothing?" she checks. "No movement to block trade from your ports, no seizure of any significant land?"

Kirdan shakes his head.

"We don't know what they're waiting for," Esai supplies. "Over a month, and aside from catching people out on nightly walks—"

"As well as infiltrating the palace," Zander interrupts.

"Yeh mon. That. They haven't tried anything."

"They have."

Everyone turns to look at me.

"If they're in the palace, the next step is to take this island."

Xaymaca, that imposter Healer said back in Cwenburg. They mean to break the empire, defunct or no, fractured or no.

"I'd like to know what they're waiting for, the Unlit. They declared their intention for war in Aiyca with a missive to the late Doyenne Cariot. You said they've been here for almost four cycles?" I continue. "That aligns with the time I left Carne and the attacks began in Aiyca too. Have you managed to interrogate any of them?"

"We haven't managed to catch any." Esai leans in. "You'd think they have magic of their own, and they're sifting. But you can't, in Zesia, like Aiyca, without permission from our doyenne. We don't know how they're getting around."

"When the time is right, we'll draw out the Unlit," I decide. "We don't know why they're waiting, but we do know that we cannot afford to." Grim nods, the rolling of tight shoulders greet me from both sides of the table. "It's more than clos-ing the Eldritch Gaps here and in Aiyca—we need a way to destroy them. Whatever the permanent solution to this infestation, you'll need power. Lots of it. I have no army, but I can give you my magic in exchange for your aid in Aiyca. Do you accept, General?"

"We accept," Kirdan says.

"Just like that?"

"Just like that," he tells Shamar. "In the Simbarabo, we have an active military of over fifty thousand Warriors."

It would be a vast number against the Unlit alone, who can't hold figures greater than the low tens of thousands—but against their infinite monstrous army?

"They're yours to command in Aiyca," Kirdan continues. "*After* we've destroyed Zesia's Eldritch Gap."

Beneath the table, Delyse knocks her foot against my own. This wasn't the plan, I know.

"Zesia first?" Shamar asks with a frown. "That doesn't feel *just like that.*"

"And there is just the one?" I lean forward to better see Kirdan. "You told me multiple tears were created, on the peninsula. Gaps. Whatever."

"Multiple across the three islands," Kirdan clarifies. "And there are, but it's the gaps we have to worry about. And we know where ours is here—the primary source, as it were."

"You've seen it?"

"No. We haven't risked approaching without a way to plug it, so to speak. But it makes sense to try destroying it before returning to Aiyca, and locating yours. Then we can have a clear plan regarding how to close the gap in the veil there too. If you agree, Empress."

It is the trial run I wanted in Zesia, but it puts them in a better position—too great for me to blackmail the doyenne into giving me a portion of the Simbarabo to take back to Aiyca. Even if I'm not sure that's what I want anymore. Kirdan didn't have to tell me about that glyph last night. He might have done it in anticipation of this moment, but I don't think so. It isn't a move he'd make. Not with me. But he knows it's a move I'd make. At least before. Now? Who does Zesia have but Kirdan to fight for it? My home has too many people willing to fight for it, which will lead to another conflict to be solved, once the Unlit have been put down.

A conflict I could use the Simbarabo's help to win.

"The problem is," I chew out, as slowly as the tenuous situation demands, "none of us has a solution to closing the gaps." And we've been talking long enough for the sun to dip in a sky already striated with the first darkening strands of dusk. "Are we, any of us, in a position to make demands about which island is deserving of aid first?"

"And what's more," Delyse interjects, "jurisdiction states that your doyenne is the supreme entity in charge of Zesia's military. Forgive me for my bluntness, Prince, General, whichever you prefer, but as far as I know, you haven't the authority to swear the Simbarabo's allegiance to anyone bar your ruler."

Grateful for my tenacious Eye, I nudge her foot back in approval.

"The Simbarabo," Kirdan says quietly, "will fight who I tell them to."

"But will they fight Jazmyne?" Idly I free a dagger from my loaded bandolier and use it to pick beneath my nails. "She has a fleet of pirate ships behind her who I suspect won't make reentering Aiyca an easy task for us, given that we'll need vessels to carry your army across the Monster's Gulf. In fact, what's the point of recruiting anyone if she stands between us and the greater danger lurking in Aiyca?"

Zander frowns. "What are you suggesting?"

"I'm *asking* the general what he means to do about his tagalong now she's Doyenne of Aiyca. And soon to be Queen of Carne Sea."

Kirdan hinges forward and levels me with a look of disbelief. Did he really not think this question was coming? That after one night together, and an accidental one at that, I would roll over and show my neck? He wishes to rule Zesia, to whatever end, and as one of the Simbarabo he's used to martyring himself. Perhaps I'm the latest sword he's vowed to throw himself onto.

"If this is about choice—"

"Her or me, you mean?" My laughter is humorless. "Never. This is about your intent."

"I thought it clear enough."

"Not where it matters."

His nostrils flare. "As I said in Aiyca, there is trust to be earned on all sides, and since time is of the essence, as Miss Powell raised—"

"Miss Powell is my mama," Delyse cuts in. "Do you want her trust or mine?"

"What I want is for us all to agree on a plan to banish those monsters for good. Esai."

"The creatures arrived not too long after your prison

transfer, Empress Adair, as you said, which is why we suspect the beasts were invited here by Aiycans."

Delyse and Shamar look to me at the head of the table, their shock as apparent as my anger reflected back at me.

"The timing's too coincidental to be ignored."

"And your logic too convenient to be ignored," I grind out. "We can't travel back to Aiyca with the Simbarabo until we've fixed your problems, because we caused them?"

"Before Carne was built." Zander speaks before his general can. "Zesia had Changuu, the Skylands had The Drop, and Aiyca, with all its hubris, had isolation, believing that to be enough. Your outcasts were able to breed for long enough to entrench their progeny in society. So in a way, yeh mon, you caused this."

Kirdan glances down the length of the table at me and back at his lieutenant. "Stand down," he orders the former.

"No," I murmur. "Let us speak plainly about this. You blame us, but I'm not apologizing for the mistakes of my ancestors when they will win us this war."

Zander sits back in his seat, tips his head to the side in question.

"Kirdan, you said it yourself last night: Aiyca's Hendern Cliffs are meant to be the calcified remains of a creature who sought to conquer my home by sea. Its kin were banished to the Monster's Gulf. Have you all heard that tale?"

The others nod.

"Then you should know that without my ancestors' foresight, we wouldn't know that—" And I can hardly believe I'm saying these words, but with no time to keep debating in circles when we, none of us, have the answers to killing the beasts and closing the Eldritch Gaps, what else do I have? "We need to turn to stories to save our islands."

"Speak to a griot?" Zander scrubs a hand across his mouth. "How will we know which parts of their tale are embellished and which are true?"

"Lucia will know," I say, looking at Kirdan. "You've seen the miscellany of items in her home; magi have traveled from around the world to gift them to her so that she might tell them a story. I know she gave you the intel for the glyphs to send the beasts back to their side of the veil." I want to hear the story myself. "And if I can't extrapolate anything new, we can go to Aiyca. I know a griot there too." Should that tree fail to fruit, I'll wake the creature in the Hendern Cliffs and ask it how it came to be stuck there, if need be.

As for the Simbarabo . . . I don't know. Would Kirdan hold up his end of the deal—without any additional Shook Bargains? Would he sail for Aiyca with me after tending to their monstrous infestation here first? It is better to overestimate than the contrary, in battle. I can't say with any certainty that Aiyca's Obeah, the Xanthippe, the secular, will be enough. Not even after the Battle for Coral Garden, a retreat more than victory, since they could have summoned more monsters.

"Let's see what Lucia has to say. Then we decide."

Kirdan, Zander, and Esai have a silent conversation.

"We can go from here," the former says. "And then regroup, once we know more."

Zander sifts us to the edge of the city, where we commandeer a kanoa to sail down the Merchant's Paradise. It isn't until we pass beneath a fourth bridge, arching from bank to bank, garlanded with green leaves woven through with white poinsettia, that I realize they're Yule decorations. The year is at its end already. I've been out of Carne Prison for almost four full months, and look at where I am. Still paying for the late doyenne's greed.

Smoke climbs in the air as someone hosts a cookout, but the sky is otherwise unhampered by clouds. Ablaze with colors of crimson and magenta, it's so full of life, I don't anticipate anything but good news from Lucia. And then there's seeing her again, speaking with her. I find I'm looking forward to it.

"That cookout is strong, hmm?" Zander comments, steering the kanoa around a bend.

As we round onto a straight, we fast realize there's no cooking.

Lucia's villa is on fire, and it burns with jade flame.

Kirdan is on his feet in an instant, overboard and into the delta with a splash.

"General!" Zander shouts; with a curse, he abandons the oars.

I don't wait until we've moored either. Before I've thought too much about it, I've leapt over the side of the kanoa into the delta after Kirdan. The water undulates around my chin; its lapping, the roar of the flames, mutes Delyse's angry shouts. By the time I've waded across the delta, Kirdan has levered himself up onto Lucia's dock with one hand, and the other frees his saber; he charges into the smoke at the side of the villa at a sprint. I'm seconds behind him, quick enough to catch the gate, splintered from what looks like an entire body flying through it.

The merchants' province rises on stilts above the delta; connecting bridges, stone on the ground, and rope between the town houses create a disorienting map, like a tangled fishnet. Kirdan leaps onto a boathouse roof, stops. Crossing the first bridge, I hoist myself up beside him.

"They were there." He jerks his saber across the delta, to a ginnel opposite Lucia's villa front. One that provides a perfect vantage. "Watching her home burn. Watching her die."

Now it's us being watched by residents in kanoas, others sitting on the docks and banks outside their villas.

"It's more than that though," Kirdan continues, his focus darting from home to home, between the bridges and water. "They've been watching her this entire time, waiting for the moment to strike."

They've been watching us too, I don't tell him, don't grind salt deeper into what is sure to be a bone-deep wound. They must have known we met today, that we're working together.

They no longer feel the need to hide, and they want us to know it.

31

JAZMYNE

Carne Sea is choppy enough that Filmore leans over the side of the pullboat and empties his belly into the deep blue of its waters. My stomach turns too, but the sea holds no responsibility. It's the colossal spears of rock we're rowing toward, the Iron Shore entrapped between them like dangled bait—though I feel more like a thing to be devoured, dressed as I am. For what must be the umpteenth time, I tug my plunging blouse up to my neck.

"Stop fidgeting," Roje mutters out of the side of his mouth. Seated on the bench across from me, he moves with the to and fro of the tugboat, at ease in his skin and indifferent to Filmore's spewing. "I doubt any pirates will look below your face today. Or anywhere else, for that matter. You're practically a minister in those pants."

The pants—*pants*—are too tight; the blouse, though quite elegant with its fluted sleeves, dips too low in front. Factoring in the rocking of the boat, it's down to Roje that the other passengers don't stare at the way my chest echoes the boat's movement.

Self-conscious, I wind one of the waist-length twists between my fingers. I'll have to cover them once more beneath a gold hair tie for the Swearing-In, if their removal is anywhere near as time-consuming as their installation yesterday. Coupled with the string of beads around my neck Anya enchanted to alter my features, no pirate, Aiycan, Alumbrar, or Obeah will suspect me of being affiliated with the royal family, at least until the race is over, and the Iron Shore know who they will serve. Roje has promised the crew's loyalty, their fealty, about my true identity, to keep me from being targeted by pirates who won't want the Alumbrar regent winning the race—one I need to talk with him about today, after I've identified a replacement and convinced them to work with me. Iraya is making progress in Zesia, figuring out how to send the beasts back to their side of the veil and charming the Simbarabo. I can't fall behind.

"Stop fidgeting and *look*." Roje nudges the toe of my knee-high boots—*boots*. "Or you'll miss my favorite part about coming home."

For the most part, the northern reaches of the empire have been sky and sea with the sporadic monolith of archipelago rising like whale backs. But as mighty as they were, they're nothing in comparison with the floating city we sail toward. One even the waves of the Xaymaca trench and the Great Sea beyond concede to as, with a bone-shaking groan, two of the shafts of rock are drawn back with thick golden chains to permit our entry into the capital of the pirate archipelago.

"Remember," Roje whispers as we bob ever closer to shore, drawn into the riot of buildings and people, once the dock line has been tossed to a waiting pickney. "Don't put up with any rudeness. They'll smell fear and uncertainty, but they'll also know if you're popping style. Your act needs to be effortless, understand?" He waits for me to nod. "Clear your face. You look 'fraid. Try to look more like that Obeah—Iraya. Snarl less, though," Roje adds. "We're not looking for people to challenge you so soon."

And there are plenty of people watching the tugboat bob alongside a fleet of far greater vessels waiting to participate in the Glide-By. Roje warned me about what a spectacle the race is for islanders. An amalgam of runaways and tageregs, who ended up here when the rest of the world no longer fit, wait on the pier. Some stare with eyes the same steel as the shallows cutting rivulets along the hull, faces browned by the sun or flushed with rum. Others are half-wild, like the rolling green mountains to the east of the capital. The boat is moored, a ladder is lowered, and I have a fleeting desire to jump into the sea. I don't even know how to swim.

"Showtime." The word is an exhale against my neck as Roje helps me find purchase so I can climb up and onto the dock.

A body thuds before my feet seconds after I've scaled the ladder. I jump back in surprise, just as a honey-haired girl calls out, "Sorry about that." She inspects her knuckles with a tut of dismay. "I was trying to knock him into the water."

Her quarry, a spluttering man, swears in earnest at her feet.

Are you good is on the tip of my tongue when I recall Roje's warning. Iraya wouldn't check on this girl, tall with the confidence of one for whom the world has stepped aside to make way. A queen if ever I saw one. She'd congratulate her on a hit well delivered, and then step over the body without a second thought. While I can't speak to the deftness of the blow that felled this man, I can do the latter—at least, until he grabs my ankle and I go down like a bag of rocks. The wood of the dock splinters into my palms as my hands slam against them.

"A sucker punch?" the man growls. "Come here and fight me proper." He draws me in as though I am a net cast out to sea, hand over hand up my right leg.

Squirming on the deck, I kick out, hands flailing for someone—Filmore, Cleo, Roje—to save me, but of course they won't. The latter warned us about situations like this; he told them not to intervene unless the numbers weren't in my favor. Standing back now means Roje believes I can take this man.

He must not have figured that even against one, I am all but powerless.

"Is she a candidate?" is called from the watching crowd.

"She can't be. Look at her."

With a grunt, I twist onto my back. The bloated face of the man crests my pelvis, a wicked leer on his mouth. I roll my hands into fists, clench my jaw, and lever my left knee up and into his groin. His face contorts and he tilts. A cry of pleasure tears through the crowd.

"All right, wastrel." Roje hoists the groaning man away from me. "Up you get."

Another hand levels before my face. "Sorry," that honey-haired girl says once she's pulled me up, in the filthiest Aiycan accent I can't entirely associate with the peach hue of her skin. "If I *had* knocked him into the water, that wouldn't have happened. I'm Elodie, sailing master of the *Silver Arrow*. I'll get us where we need to be, during the race." She nods at the man being marched away by two others while Roje oversees. "You handled it well," she murmurs. "But next time react faster." A flask is passed my way. "It'll help with the shakes."

More like add to it.

"I'll go without, if it's all the same."

"Get on," Roje orders the crowd. "Now!" Instead of returning for me, he strides on, dispersing the crowd with his shoulders and his arrogance.

"Come." Elodie claps her hands. "To the ship."

On legs like jelly I follow her, my first candidate for replacement. The dock runs adjacent to the city proper. Sheathed between buildings are alleys and coves wherein soliciting women and men, pirates who range from staggering to swaggering, lurk on the streets that are barely paved. And if it's like this during the day, lawless and without filter, how much worse must it be at night? The vessels are far safer to focus on, the crew climbing rigging and polishing masts. There are some I'm familiar with, like the long and narrow sloop, or the broad galleons; there are square-rigged ships I've seen less in Aiyca, as well as the equally vast fleuts. The latter ships are built to transport large quantities of merchandise and often cross the waters to our empire. The *Silver Arrow* is a galleon; the dull cannons the late doyenne didn't prohibit in Aiyca's shores protrude from its polished mahogany side; masts and rigging stand tall and proud—along with its crew, who await on the deck when we board.

A wreath of nerves coil around my throat, my stomach, at the sight of so many people, the vast universe of this boat somehow bobbing atop the waters and not plunging to its depths.

One of the crew swaggers forward, thumbs hooked around his braces. "The size of my mast has left many a woman without words, Captain. No need to feel embarrassed."

Some of the crew snigger; several laugh outright; a sticky heat blazes up the back of my neck. What would Iraya do?

"Now, now," Roje begins. "Why don't we—"

"Perhaps it's you who should be embarrassed," I cut in. "As I'd noticed neither you, or whatever appendage you own that makes women so embarrassed, they can only stand in silence."

"No—that's not what I—"

"Wahan, crew of the *Silver Arrow*," I continue, above the soft laughter of a crowd won around. Roje inclines his head my way. "Blessings for entrusting me with your lives, your time, your fealty. I've been told there is no allegiance like the one found between a crew, and I am humbled to be welcomed aboard." I nod at Filmore, Cleo, and within seconds the crates of rum we transported here from Aiyca appear on the deck. The crew whistles. "Tonight you will wet your throats with the nectar of victory, but in the coming phases, you will line your pockets with it too." Someone cheers, and several whoops sound too. "Here's to finding the falls, and ushering in a golden age that sees pirates and Aiycans come together for the first time."

When the claps and cheers have ebbed, another of the former strikes up in a slow, mocking song. A girl steps from the bulk of the crew, pausing their attempts to crack open the crates of rum. Her face is concealed by the broad brim of a brown leather hat. She tips her chin, and I start at the chestnut complexion, her high cheekbones and narrow chin, the angled eyes, the springing mane of silver-tipped curls.

"A pretty speech, to be sure," she says. Not Madisyn. I blink. "But there's not much time for so many words when we're rocked by waves at sea." Several of the crew nudge one another. "I suppose the true test will be in whether or not you manage to remain afoot, or if you'll be thrown over and left to the mercy of the waves and the gods who churn them." She frees a dagger from up her left sleeve in a movement so fast, I feel the sharp edge of residual wind against my cheek. "Cheers, Jaz." The weapon is thrust into the side of a crate and released just as quick; a stream of sun-touched brown shoots out and across the deck; the pirates roar again, more eager for the alcohol than whatever this pirate sought to create between the two of us.

But in the rush of their bodies, she doesn't shift her eyes away from mine until she is swallowed by the crush.

"Who is that?"

"This one's all you, Roje." Elodie wades into the masses glutting themselves on the rum.

"Well?" I push.

"Synestra." A hand to the back of his head, where his dreads partially tumble down his back, Roje grimaces. "She's the pirate I promised our allegiance to before giving it to you."

*Syn*estra.

Mudda have mercy, she even shares a name with my sister.

"You kept her on the crew?"

"I had my reasons." He shrugs, avoiding looking directly at me. "One of them being that none other can scale the foremast like her in the midst of a gale. We need her. Speaking of—" He steps toward the crew. "That's enough liquor. We have a Glide-By to prepare for!" He joins the fray with an easy laugh, accepting a flagon of rum from a handsome olive-skinned man.

I hang back with Filmore and Cleo, that wreath of nerves around my throat tightening at the sight of them all so unmistakably a unit. Roje said no pirate would align with the Alumbrar. I have a day to change their minds.

32

IRAYA

It takes time before the Witchfire devouring Lucia's villa is quelled beneath the might of the Simbarabo's gold—more than we have in an already stacked countdown.

By then Kirdan and I have returned, unable to capture even one Unlit responsible for the blaze. Still dripping with delta water, Kirdan sprinted inside the villa before any of us could stop him, but he emerges again just as fast and blows a hole through the courtyard's boundary wall with his fist. Zander and Esai venture in next, transparent bubbles of magic around their faces to protect from smoke inhalation. When they finally egress, it's with their grayed cloaks wrapped around something long carried between them. *Lucia*, Esai confirms with a look.

Zesia's first responders flood the delta—Squallers replace the Simbarabo, choking the slow-to-shrink flames into submission with their magical dexterity; Bush Healers treat the neighbors who attempted to save Lucia—surrounded by so many people, so many potential victims, in this escalating war, I'm almost felled by the weight of their lives, the weight of Lucia's. I should have considered the Unlit would be watching those who interacted with me, that I'm still as much a danger here as I was to my order back at the Cuartel in Aiyca. Mama would have. Nana Adair too.

Kirdan's angular face is thrown into stark relief as he stares into the retroceding flames, his skin drawn so tight over the bone he looks half-dead. Blood follows vein, yeh mon, but it doesn't decide who is family, and for an unwanted son born into a world that would put a weapon in his hand rather than take it, hold it . . .

Delyse reaches for me as I start for Kirdan, but, dodging her, I take his bruised and bloody fist in hand, meet the gaze that gapes open with a familiar loss.

I know what it is to lose family you were close enough to save.

"Where are bodies taken here?"

Kneeling by Lucia, Zander looks up at me. "There are several mortuaries in the city."

"Take Lucia to the best," I instruct. "Tell them that it's by order of Empress Adair."

"Iraya," Delyse begins. "Perhaps we should return to the palace."

"No. You and Shamar go with Zander and Esai," I tell her. "Act in my place if there's any trouble." With my spare hand, I touch Kirdan's shoulder. "Let's go back to our suite."

I don't need to say it twice.

One moment we are standing before the smoldering ruins of Lucia's house, and the next we are in the palace, making our journey through the halls in silence. Kirdan's hand is still clasped in my own. I don't let go until we are in our suite. Wordlessly, he walks toward his study and I the bedroom. We pause in our respective doorways to look across the lounge at one another. No doubt he'd prefer the company of his men tonight, the muted surroundings of the Cuartel instead of this golden tomb—especially when he could offer Jákīsa for Lucia—and yet he's prepared to stay here to keep an eye on *me*.

Through and through he is a soldier who knows only the meaning of sacrifice. Being one and making them. Perhaps that's why I push the bedroom door open wider and turn inside without another word. He shuts it when he enters; his focus is a tangible thing as I toss throw pillows on the chaise longue at the foot of the bed and pull the covers back until, save changing into my night things, there's nothing to do but look at him.

"Sword?" I challenge, with a raised brow.

A web of magic pulses from his conduit; it shrouds the walls, the floor, the ceiling in a delicate coruscating membrane, twin to the silencing spheres I've seen Delyse cast.

"The doyenne has your dada's conduit."

His words echo, like I'm standing farther away; it takes a moment to hear, to process.

"What?"

"When Doyenne Cariot struck in the Viper's Massacre"— the words rush from Kirdan's lips, like they've been taking up space for days—"she sent the conduit weapon to Zesia as a sign of good faith, after she had already discussed our emancipation from the empire in exchange for not interfering."

"Your mama has Dada's conduit?" I repeat, dumb.

"Yes."

I shake my head. "Where?"

"I don't know anymore. When it first arrived, I took it to Lucia and she told me about the Witch of Bone and Briar. About you. Young, mengkeh, I told my sisters. They told the doyenne. I never found it again."

"Your mama," I repeat once more. "Has Dada's conduit weapon." My conduit weapon, really. The last item of my parents that must exist in the world. "And you knew about it. You knew about this . . . *too*."

"No," Kirdan says, and then he's striding around the bed. "Don't close off to me now, Iraya. This was the last thing I've been keeping from you. Lucia—" He chokes on her name. "I spoke with her when I knew. When I knew that what you meant to the world didn't compare with what you meant to me. She told me to be honest with you and I wasn't. I wasn't because—" His throat bobs. "After our initial meetings, the divide between us was too vast to traverse, and so I have *clawed* my way across it, inch by inch, to reach you. When I first felt like I might stand a chance of losing you to Jazmyne's schemes, I was *terrified*, and I couldn't understand why. I was raised in the shadow of Death's outstretched arm, reared to fear nothing and no one. I tried to fight what I felt for you, to run from it, but, Iraya . . ." Tenderness curls around my name. "Can't you see how badly I want you?" He takes a step toward me. "I stand before you as an honest man, freed from all secrets, because I don't want to be any less of myself when I am with you."

We're both breathing heavily again, like our fight involves weapons and fists, not words and feelings.

"Now," I murmur.

He shakes his head, confused.

My mouth is bitter as I swallow. "You don't want to be any less when you're with me *now*," I clarify, each word pointed and acute. "But not before, when you called me a liar and a coward. Not before, when you hid to steal from my family. And not before you stole me away to Zesia, like some summer bride. You were wrong about there being nothing between us." I seize his sword; equally as quick, his hand lands atop mine on the pommel. My magic rears, draws back in a wave of intent I could submerge him in. "This weapon signifies that there will *always* be something between us, Kirdan."

We two are separated by the outstretched hands of history. Its raised fists.

Maybe I didn't want it to be that way. Maybe tonight, before everything happened with Lucia, I might have—*we* might have crossed the line we've been edging toward. Gods.

"Leave," I order.

Expecting the fight in his face, the softness to turn to steel, I unleash a little of the witch I was back at Cwenburg. "*Now.*" I start forward, ready to bodily remove him.

"Not until we've sorted this out. I told you I didn't want us to be enemies."

"Then you should stop treating me like one!"

Kirdan recoils, as if I launched fists rather than words.

"Do *not* follow me."

He steps aside as I push past him, heading out into the suite, the study, and then the palace beyond the doors, furious with him, but even more so with myself. Why must I constantly be reminded? If friendship is the hangman's noose, then lust, infatuation, they are the act of being hanged, drawn, and quartered before the conflagration.

Since the late Doyenne Cariot used me to kill the Obeah in the palace, I've stymied the darkness that pulsates inside me like an organ when I should have embraced the parts of myself that lack light. War makes heroes out of few and villains out of most, Kirdan told me before spiriting me away to Zesia. From then I should have known, should have reminded him that I have no interest in being a hero. None in being a villain either.

I am Iraya Cordelia Boatema Adair.

Pausing in an alcove beyond the reach of witchlight or flame, I cut strips off the bottom of my silk traveling cape. Each flag I distribute—tied around a banister, tucked into the mouth of a bust, pushed through one of the priceless paintings lining the halls I slink down with intentions as dark as a wraith's—is set with purpose, a treasure hunt if you will. But I am not the prize.

Rendering myself near invisible with an Illusion Glyph, I will the winds forever whistling through this palace to carry me up until I am wedged in a ceiling corner like an arachnid. At the rush of magic, power my maneuver causes, the guarding J'Martinet flinch, but they do not look up at where I wait for the first monsters to come.

It does not take long for a rattling breath to plume down

the hall, for the temperature to plunge and a sentient fog to curl and writhe like a bed of serpents along the marble floor. Golden staffs illuminate like bolts of lightning in the J'Martinet's hands. Two of the coven members would find a small cohort of the beasts easy to kill; indeed, they stalk down the hall to meet the eldritch creature whose paws land with a screech of nails. But I laid many breadcrumbs tonight.

And the beasts are ravenous.

Several more enter the hall in a swirling formation of teeth, claws, and shadows. Glyphs are launched; the J'Martinet follow, spears in hand and silent war cries of determination in the lines of their bodies, the drawn focus on their faces. With the skilled witches distracted, I lower myself down from my corner, open the door to Doyenne Divsylar's suite, and slip inside. Springing into action at the noise from outside, this next set of guards sprint for the hall, conduit weapons at the ready.

And then there is only one more door between the doyenne and me.

Flooded with something cool, something frigid, a clarity Nana Clarke called the Killing Calm in the Virago, one we believed was a gift from Clotille's Face to keep our minds clear in battle, our strikes as deft as her own, as godly.

I feel her influence pervade my very essence as, with perfect clarity, I recall the guzzu I need to break past the shimmering barrier of wards on the doyenne's door; one I only glanced at that can recall memories imprinted to a place. It will be enough to create a ghostly projection of whatever magic the J'Martinet use to lock the doyenne in.

Forget being shackled to the beast called revenge and

dragged wherever it roams: I summon that beast. It rides where I will it.

Outside, the sounds of battle slow. The guards will return soon, and yet no memories materialize. The doyenne is sealed inside with guzzu, as I was in Carne. Escape from prison was easy enough. All I required was a helping hand.

Concealed from sight once more, I slip out. Each step is heavier than the last as that godly focus dissipates; it's a crushing blow to return without Dada's staff when I know it's here, but it's one I mitigate with reassurances that I will return now I have a better idea of the guard rotations and response times, as well as several more strips of my cloak in hand to draw the beasts to a couple more rooms. Kaltoon's and the triplets'.

I'm halfway across the palace when a high-pitched scream rends the night. Two more J'Martinet pass me, twin blades sprinting through the dark to— Twins.

Twins.

My gods. I can't believe I forgot. The staff is a nuisance, Kirdan's continuous lies an even greater one, but my path hasn't dead-ended quite yet. At least, not when it comes to aiding Aiyca. Lucia has a sister, and she's a Tempera too.

33

JAZMYNE

In any other circumstance, I might have enjoyed watching the ships sail past one another, elbow to elbow with Anya, the Stealths who refuse to leave my side, as sails proudly peacock down the procession created by two adjacent rows of ships. Their flags' use of color isn't unlike how Alumbrar identify; competitor crew members heckle one another; some fire cannons of confetti, or rotten fruit and vegetables. It's wild and riotous, but proud.

How I ever thought I belonged here is beyond me.

When it's time for the *Silver Arrow* to make her journey between the adjacent lines of ships, the crew group off, leaving me with my Stealths. And my decision.

Synestra is a clear frontrunner. The crew work and move like they're of one mind, which is artistry to watch. But if they are the dancers, she is their choreographer. Alone, she moves from group to group, as much of a first mate as Roje. He said she'd never work with me—the me I was then. Desperate, powerless, fooled by too many lies to count. What about the me I am now? I don't need to ask her to become queen; she already wanted it.

All I need to do is give it back to her.

Festoon lights are strung up in the *Silver Arrow*'s rigging by the time I've planned what I'm going to say and how I'll go about doing it. Docked for a night of debauchery during the one and only time we'll drink as bredren and sistren with the other ships, the crew line their stomachs with platters of fish and crustaceans the cooks brought up from the kitchens.

"Come and try this, Jaz!" Elodie beckons me over to where she sits with a small party of crew; at my responding shake of the head, another refusal, she glances over at Roje across the deck. He sits with an intimacy that suggests more than friends—family—beside the olive-skinned crew member from earlier.

His distraction makes it easier for me to rest along on the ledge of the ship, starboard side, my face turned toward a moon-drenched sky, to wait for when Synestra eventually comes sniffing at my heels to snap at me again.

"Regretting it, aren't you." She settles alongside me, back to the view. "That's the thing with stealing. Ofttimes the item isn't worth what follows. Vea learned this with your sister, and now the lesson is yours to experience with Roje."

My fists curl around the wooden lip. "It isn't like that with us."

"Because he takes Fabian to bed?" She huffs a laugh. "Bed isn't romance. It's a transaction. Sometimes one party will get more, the other less. Nothing. I was with Vea for years."

My eyes slide her way, but she looks out across the deck of the ship.

"The least she could have done was leave me this ship, but then you came." Her eyes cut my way. They are a peculiar color, like the flat metal of a weapon rarely used or taken care of. The dull surface of a body of water to which the depths remain unknown until you find yourself drowning in them. "You are not made for this life, and whether it is by accident or design, you won't last as captain of the *Silver Arrow*."

She pushes away from the deck.

"Am I to believe you're going to do something about it when you allowed yourself to be Vea's consolation prize, for all these years?"

Synestra stops; across the ship, the revelry stops too. In fact, everything stops but my tongue.

"You decided to allow yourself to be used to fill a void, and then to remain when you were set aside for another." Though my body already shakes at the attention, I hold firm beneath the growing fury in Synestra's face, the full lips that draw back in a snarl.

"All right, mon." Elodie claps her hands. "Let's all take a moment."

"I need only a second." Synestra exhales, freeing her cutlass.

"Ladies." Roje rises from his clinch. "Don't make me throw you overboard."

I tip my chin in his direction. "I don't need you to get involved." A lie. Even if I knew how to use the sword on my hip, I doubt I could draw it before Synestra would land her first blow. But let her see my stupidity and think it bravery.

"Be that as it may, we have an audience."

Ironites have taken up residence along the pier to watch the pirates and place bets for queen all day, but the adjacent ships watch now too, wait to see where we are weakest so they can strike. With a marked effort, Synestra holsters her blade.

"You had to get involved, didn't you?" comes another voice, one that sends my focus shooting upward to the rigging where a large shadow perches. "Just as it was about to get interesting, mon."

The figure drops down and lands with a muted thump from her soft leather boots; a long coat billows back in salt-scented winds tossed up from the sea. While her tone is musical with amusement, an overall drawn tightness to the dark planes of her face makes me wonder what happens to the people who demand happiness from her. Is it the dagger in her boot she uses, or the twin moon scythes like Vea's carried on her hip that she reaches for first? More shadows slip onto the deck, appearing with the same spectral silence, as though they crawled up and out of the sea, or ascended from the fog slinking across waters. Roje and my Stealths are by my side in an instant, Elodie too. Even Synestra places herself between me and this stranger.

"Fighting already?" She tuts. "That doesn't bode well. And here we heard you were the crew to beat."

"Then we are on uneven footing," Elodie says smoothly. "Since we haven't heard of you at all."

"This is Captain Shah, of the *Vanquisher*," one of her crew calls, a man with dark hair, a dark smile, and skin so pale it's almost bone colored. "You should know the name of the pirate who will defeat you."

"All I see is a pirate on a ship that doesn't belong to her, or her crew, for that matter, and without an invitation at that. Poor form, mon." Roje looks as he did that night with Kirdan on the Sole, like his hackles are raised and his legs are ready to spring.

"What about you?" Captain Shah leans around Roje to stare at me. "What do you see? Something so terrible it's scared you into silence." Her crew chuckles.

"Why should she speak to you," Synestra says, shocking me with her defense. "You crashed onto our ship. Clearly you're the one who wants to do all the talking."

Captain Shah doesn't even look her way. "And now I'm admiring the view."

My voice is steady. "Tell me what you see."

Weapons are unsheathed; their blades somehow find light in the dark, and glint in a sharp promise of what's to come. The captain smiles then, or at least her version of a smile, a quirked angle of her lips, like it's pierced with a fishhook someone just tugged.

"I see a crack, Captain," she croons. "And cracks let in water. Little more."

Just as soundlessly as she and her crew arrived, they slink off the boat, jumping over the side and landing without splashes. I remain still, but members of the crew run to look down.

"Rowboats," one calls to Roje, who stays by me.

"What was that?" Filmore mutters.

"Intent," Elodie says, with a look at Synestra, and then me.

"A target," Roje affirms. "On us."

Me.

"A *mistake*," Synestra spits. "She has seen our weakness in you and will no doubt tell the others. We've been marked."

"What does that mean?"

Roje drags a hand down his cheeks. "Every race there's a ship, a candidate, that becomes something of a unifying factor for the others. Everyone piles on top of them."

"Then let me make the issue simple," I say, seeing my opening. "I will stand down as your captain and potential queen."

The ship, having reclaimed some of its noise, its vim, quiets once again.

"You'll run scared?" Elodie frowns at me. "Leave us without a viable leader?"

"Jaz." Roje's eyes are wide with hurt, and a part of me twists inside.

"You have a viable captain." I turn to Synestra. "You. Our original bargain would stand. I will send a proxy to work with you to find the falls, you will swear your loyalty to me; Aiyca and the pirates will work together, but I won't be your queen. I'll be the doyenne who communicates with *you*, the de facto power of the Iron Shore territory."

Synestra's contemplative silence is all the encouragement I need to take Cleo's and Filmore's arms. Gold preservation be damned.

"Be marked or be victorious." I meet each face: Elodie stunned, Roje hurt, and their prospective captain thoughtfully suspicious. "I expect your answer before the Swearing-In of your nominated council presiders" are my parting words before the sift snatches me away.

34

IRAYA

Less than twelve hours after Lucia's death, Merchant's Paradise no longer stinks with the bitter tang of Witchfire, and the sky is cleared of all smoke, but nothing feels the same. The Unlit have tainted the reverence I came to associate this place with, the home in which my strength was restored, and my purpose launched with the speed and intent of a fired arrow. They have desecrated it, pissed all over it in a declaration of battle—and I'm not sure I have the Simbarabo to help me fight them, after Kirdan revealed the truth about Dada's staff.

"Are you awake?"

"Sleep would be a fine thing up here," I grumble back to Delyse.

The rooftop we've commandeered is one of few tall enough, and without a patio for entertaining, where we could sequester away to observe Melione's home before the visit I wrote to set up after returning to the suite last night. Unfortunately, it's lined with sharp stones that shift with every movement, grinding together like a discordant chorus of knuckle bones. So busy keeping still have I been, keeping alert, dawn has come and gone, giving room to a sun with no cloud to challenge for its rule. Its reach is indefatigable. Even the thoughts of guzzu from the Grimoire I've been mentally reciting evaporate.

"Whose idea was this again?" Delyse moans. "My sweat is sweating."

Since public buildings prohibit magic use, it made sense to assume private homes would enforce similar precautions. Even one tiny use of magic to summon a cool wind could set off alarms in the compound beneath us.

"I wouldn't mind so much if we could bathe before our visit."

"And I wouldn't mind so much if Melione actually had any visitors last night, or this morning," I return. "But hey, if it's water you want, mon, I can push you into the delta and make it look like an accident."

"I'll pretend I don't sense the move coming if you tell me why you're in such a foul mood." Delyse shifts beside me. "Did something happen with Kirdan last night?"

He wasn't in the room when I returned from my reconnaissance of the doyenne's rooms. After a fitful sleep with half the night spent jerking awake to demand he take me to see Lucia's twin, I gave up trying altogether when I found a note from him on the floor before the fire. He was preparing for Lucia's Nine Night, and he'd set an alarm inside the suite to prevent entry from anyone outside of our contentious circle. Staying out of my way after dropping the bomb about Dada's staff was the smartest move he's made since I've known him. But, of all the secrets he's kept, Dada's conduit weapon was one he could have taken to his grave. We could have been planning Lucia's funerary celebrations together, rather than him being wherever he is while I hide out on this rooftop to ensure the next alliance I make develops as poorly as the first.

"Enough of this," I evade, my already frayed patience wearing thinner. "I have a far better way to ascertain if this witch is from the Skylands."

Which is how, minutes after climbing down from the roof, we've crossed the delta via one of the bridges arching across it to knock on Melione's door. As she looks past out shrouded faces in recognition, I push my way inside, hook my left arm around her neck, and angle a blade beneath her chin.

"Let's skip ahead to the part where you confess that you are a Skylander living undercover in Zesia, and perhaps I won't ruin this beautiful home with your blood spatter."

"Empress," Melione wheezes, her hands curled around my forearm. "I'm not from the Skylands."

"You think it wise to deceive me when my knife is at your throat?"

"She's not" comes through a set of folding wooden doors leading into a connecting room, where a witch concealed in a heavy travel cape steps through. "She isn't from the Skylands." The hood is pushed back, revealing a long, thin face that gleams like polished mahogany. "I am."

"And who the hell are you?"

"You may call me Kihra, but my birth name is Nsõwaa Opoku."

"Seven," Delyse murmurs, in respect to her first name.

The stranger nods. "I am the seventh heir to the Skylands throne."

Well.

I can admit I didn't see that coming.

Just as firstborns are significant for the power promised upon inheritance, so are the seventh. They are believed to have the blessing of the Supreme Being's favor, and Kihra is a woman. She is even more blessed. Out of favor with most of the Seven-Faced Mudda's various identities, I might not even manage to strike this Skylander down before I find myself obliterated by any celestial hand.

If she speaks the truth.

"You have six siblings?"

Her nod is curt. "There's no more than two years between us."

"Why then are you an heir, if your eldest siblings turned eighteen so long before you?"

"Equity. My parents wished to wait until their youngest turned eighteen to raise the matter of succession. Now introductions are out of the way, I'd appreciate if you would lower your weapon from my sistren's neck."

"While we're on the subject of things we'd appreciate, I'd love to know why you both conspired to trick me into coming here."

Kihra huffs a humorless laugh. "You were invited to *tea*, yet you and your Eye arrived over twelve hours early to watch us from the rooftop. What would you have done if I revealed myself to you without Melione? Killed first and asked questions later, I bet."

"Why are you here?" Delyse remains between us. "Concealed as you have been, we have no reason to believe it's with good intentions."

"And how," I add, "did you arrive here without detection? That's what this clandestine behavior is really for, isn't it? Zesia doesn't know you're here." Neither Krimpt nor Kaltoon would permit a Skylander to roam their island without an escort, not when it's difficult to recall a single person who's ever seen a Skylander step from the safety of their treetops. "How have you done it?"

"To answer the first questions, I came to discuss the monsters from beyond the veil with you on behalf of myself and three additional siblings. But something else has come up that I will share first, something of great interest to you." Her eyes dart to Melione's. "However, I will have no further conversations until my sistren has been released."

"You are related?"

Kihra presses her lips together. Fine.

"If you're lying to me, Skylander," I murmur, "I won't need a blade, or this proximity, to take her head off her neck."

She tips her chin upward, nods.

Dropping my knife arm, I release Melione.

"I apologize that you thought I was deceiving you," she says, to my surprise. "I thought easing you into the idea with tea better, and, well. Forgive me."

Kihra sighs. "She just held a blade to your throat, why are you sorry?"

"Why aren't *you* talking?" I cut in.

"Yes, tell her." Rubbing her neck, Melione lowers herself

onto a stool. "Perhaps then we can have tea."

Kihra lowers her hood. Braids snake across her skull and fall down her back. She's a fighter. Maybe even a Warrior, though she bears no scarification—wouldn't, as heir.

"Are you related?"

"Melione was married to a sibling of mine."

"One Kihra helped me escape from."

The two women exchange a look that speaks of deep kinship.

"And the news?"

"Since you'll ask how I came about this information, some history: on my island, doyennes rule until such a time as when they decide not to. Yeh mon," she adds, nodding my way. "We believe magic is something to celebrate; why do you think we never get involved in your shit? Rather than the firstborn pickney receiving their inheritance, we are all blessed with conduits imbued with ancestral magic upon our eighteenth earthstrongs. When the doyenne is ready to retire, she picks the heir who embodies the most promising traits required to rule fairly and justly. This inheritance cycle, given the danger the Skylands' aerial fleet is in, as a result of the Unlit, Mama has added another clause: the pickney who can protect the monsters beyond the veil, the ones you fear—"

"I don't fear them."

"The Oscuridad," she continues. "Whoever protects the beasts will be crowned as the Skylands' new ruler."

Delyse and I exchange a look.

"What is it?" Kihra asks.

"I'm just not sure what your island's history of cowardice

and secrecy has to do with me," I deflect, rather than asking if she came to visit me second. After she spoke with Jazmyne, and gave her the correct name for the Unlit's monsters. This is where she must have heard it, from a Skylander.

"I spoke of ruling because myself and three of my siblings would like to throw our lot in with you." The look she gives me suggests she's regretting that decision. "Two others have sided with your opponent, the Cariot regent."

Meaning it was another who spoke with Jazmyne.

"You're one of seven," I say. "What of the last sibling, where do they stand?"

"In the ground," Melione answers. "My husband died of an internal sickness, and not a natural one."

Delyse eyes the tea set; I do too.

"Of my siblings who sided with Jazmyne, one is our most-skilled Bush Healer. He'll offer her aid in treating the poisonous wounds the Oscuridad wrought. The second is smart, Recondite smart; she will help the regent fortify the island against you once she finishes her studies at the conservatory."

Madness.

Our island is facing a real infestation, one I promised to bring an army to battle, and Jazmyne would rather plan to fight me for our home? Notwithstanding the fact that it *might not exist* with the way she's managing it. Gods above. If I knew how to sift, I'd send myself straight into her bedroom—my bedroom—that stakki, *irresponsible*—

"You take on métiers?" Delyse asks.

"Not as early on as civilians, nor is it a requirement, but some of us have, yeh mon."

"You are a Warrior."

"No. But I serve under one of my sisters who oversees the aerial army, and before you ask"—she looks to me—"she won't send them away from the Skylands to fight in your war."

"Then why are you here wasting my time?"

"The Skylands have always been the redheaded step-pickney between Zesia and Aiyca. We have been content to fly under the radar; my sister is a key example of that, but I—I have worked with the Oscuridad since I was a pickney, and—"

"What do you mean, worked with?"

She fights against her tongue. "I cannot go into further details, you understand?"

Her throat bulges. A gag order.

She lowers her tunic to reveal three white paw prints above her heart.

"You're a Wrangler," Delyse murmurs. I wonder if she's thinking of Nel back in Aiyca.

"It's for that reason I have to ask that you don't kill them, when you close their pathway."

"We call it an Eldritch Gap," I tell her. "Do you know how to close the gaps without killing them?"

"I cannot say."

Gods. "Then what *can* you say?" I'm already impatient, but now I'm growing bored.

"To close the Eldritch Gaps for good will flood my home with the types of Oscuridad who are being invited into your island, and many lives will be lost."

"Well, we need to destroy the gaps in order to prevent those beasts being summoned again."

Maybe it should be at the cost of the Skylands. What have they done to deserve mercy?

Nothing.

That means it's about what they *can* do.

Kihra places a hand over her scarification. "There's little I can offer you—"

"Fealty."

She blinks at me.

"Wrangler, despite being second to your sister, you have what all Gennas have, the loyalty of those in your care." If she's telling me their aerial army consists of a type of the very beasts set to destroy Aiyca, then I want her. Them. "And you have a choice to make about how deep your love runs for them. You have come with a message; let me send you home with another: after I have defeated Aiyca's and Zesia's enemies, if you do not help this empire to heal, I will come for the Skylands next."

"Wait, no. That's not—"

"Not what you hoped I'd say? Then we are both disappointed. I in your apathetic island, and you, because I am no doubt everything you have heard an Aiycan Obeah is meant to be: fond of war and unapologetic about waging it on their enemies. You tell your doyenne that Empress Adair cares not for whatever agreement she made with the viper Judair Cariot. I'll see her soon, and that can either be as enemies, or as allies. Come, Delyse."

"Now wait—" Melione stands. "Surely we can reach a better finish than that?"

I sweep past her and out to the hall.

"The Blue Mountains."

Hand on the door, I pause.

"There have been skirmishes in the Blue Mountains with the Oscuridad," Kihra continues; a crack of desperation permeates her otherwise steely veneer. "They're rarely reported due to the creatures that inhabit the hills, the prowlers and others, but it isn't monster versus monster out there."

I turn, look her dead in the face.

"That is the pressing message I wished to bring you. Not my siblings. Me."

"If you're lying to protect your island—"

"Take the message as a sign of *loyalty*, Iraya." Slicing a cut in her palm, she holds up her hand. A blood oath. "I will do what I can to offer you aid. I will tell my family your terms to keep us safe from the Unlit's Oscuridad. This is my promise."

Without the self-serving intent of a Shook Bargain, a blood oath is by far the most genuine of magical gestures, but it's second to the information Kihra shared, and what it could mean in the long run. If the Blue Mountains haven't been sundered by the Oscuridad, then she's just given me the one thing that might turn the table in this tug-of-war: answers to the questions that kept me awake in Carne. Answers I meant to seek for myself, before the Unlit stepped into my path and necessitated confrontation. The place I spent the happiest years of my life still stands, at the hands of, I can only hope, the best army Aiyca has ever known.

The Virago.

Bolstered by what Kihra confessed about the Virago, however little pragmatism lets me unequivocally trust the Skylander, or her promise to convince her siblings to fly for Aiyca, I inform Delyse about my time training with Aiyca's most lauded Warrior coven on the journey back to the palace. To her credit, she doesn't interrupt. Instead, once we're tucked away in my room, she sits with me at the desk between archways while I draft the missives I've been avoiding since leaving Carne.

> SISTREN,
>
> IF YOU LIVE BY CLOTILLE'S GRACE AND THIS REACHES YOU, KNOW FIRST HOW SORRY I AM THAT THIS HAS TAKEN SO LONG. TROUBLE HAS TURNED OUR SKIES STORMY, BUT THOSE OF THE EARTH HAVE NO FEAR OF RAIN, AND THE GROWTH ITS TEMPESTS FORCE.
>
> YOURS,
>
> I ALWAYS DARE

I trace my fingers above my old code name, drawing from the past that which I need now: the audacity of a Warrior who answers to none other than the goddess she serves and the weapon she carries; to become the Requiem of Steel I would have been in another world. For if the Virago live but haven't surfaced to tear any and all imposters from the throne, haven't ventured farther than the base of the Blue Mountains peak where we made home, something is wrong. *Please, Clotille, don't let me be too late. Please let Nana Clarke, my sistren, live.*

"Will they know that's you?" Delyse queries in a low voice.

"They'll know." But no one else will. If it's intercepted, the entire message is in code.

With Kirdan seeing to Lucia's Nine Night, there's no time like the present to lure seven guerra birds down from the high branches in their olive tree on the balcony outside the suite. It's easier than it was the first morning since I've been feeding them for a time such as this.

"How many of you are there?"

"Ten thousand active witches, when I was a pickney. There'll be more now, since my sistren will be grown."

"Then the Simbarabo wouldn't matter, if they're active."

I can't answer her. I'm still not sure. A decade is a long period of silence. It's hard to know what happened. What could have been significant enough to stand between my coven of Warrior witches and Aiyca's safety? They did not ride down from the mountains when the Alumbrar struck, nor did they make an appearance during the years I was in Carne, the years since. But if they live? The Simbarabo have nothing on them.

If they agree to fight behind me. They've never refused an Adair before, but they've never been silent for this long before. I'll soon see, one way or another.

"Fly fast and true," I tell each bird, breathing my intent across their feathers before I release them. Seven hopes, seven dreams, seven prayers. They soar through the pillars and over the Singing Sands, burnt copper beneath the blazing fingers of the setting sun.

"I hope your sistren answer." Following the birds' flight, Delyse looks to the sky, arms resting atop the stone balustrade. "But even if they don't, we still need to discuss Jazmyne. Carling Hill is under Unlit occupation, and thanks to my contact, we know at least two additional parishes have succumbed to the Unlit's influence in a bid to protect their family trees from burning, yet she's more interested in preparing to keep you from *your* throne."

"As if that's what matters."

"It matters above everything else." Delyse angles her head my way. "What are we fighting for if not for our order's return to supremacy? You didn't tell me you planned on asking Jazmyne to play island custos in our absence. But if you had, I could have told you we can't trust her to keep us informed about what's happening in Aiyca, nor can we trust her to keep the island safe from threats outside of you and us. We could . . . return. At present, we don't have the army we left to secure; nor do we have the guzzu that destroys the beasts entirely."

Hearing it like that is like taking a one-two blow to my stomach. She's right. What have I done here but acquire new clothes and weapons?

"If we go, you can reanimate the monster in the Hendern Cliffs, get our answers that way."

"I haven't ruled out the Simbarabo, or alternatives with the Oscuridad yet." And there's Dada's staff, and Lucia's twin. Something has to make leaving Aiyca for close to two phases now worth it. "I can't return until we have a clear path forward."

It takes Delyse a moment.

"No." She twists around to fully look at me at last. "I can't leave you here. I won't."

"You'd place me ahead of Aiyca's Obeah returning to supremacy?"

Arguments clash on the tongue she tripped herself up with.

"You won't," I'm happy to answer for her. "Because you can accept that it's the republic that has to thrive."

"But will it thrive without its empress?"

"I'll follow shortly." My shrug is casual, to put her at ease. Can she see how stiff my shoulders are, with her Stealth acuity? How I fight to sit here, make smart choices rather than rash ones like sifting to Aiyca and dragging Jazmyne out of Cwenburg? "But I can't leave yet, and I can't do what I need to here without you there, Delyse."

"And you can without me *here*? You are his sun, Iraya. He who has only known darkness. He won't let you go. He can't. And so *I* can't, because I don't trust—" Her teeth sink into her lower lip.

"Me?"

"Iraya—"

"I am not a sun." Indeed, there is a chill to my words as I meet her obstinacy head-on. "I am not a warm light for anyone to bask in, to chase from horizon to horizon. In this not-war, I am only something to run from. That is the only way the republic will survive. And so you will go to Aiyca, reconnect with the Jade Guild to ensure that when I return, I can enter my home; you will find the Virago, if they live, and guarantee I receive word of either outcome. You will begin searching for Aiyca's gap. And you will leave Zesia tonight."

Delyse's mouth opens.

"If that wasn't empress enough for you," I say, my voice lower, softer, buoyant with a false humor, "I'm sure I can find a scepter to wave around."

"I don't want to go."

"But you will."

Sighing in frustration, Delyse turns her back on the sky. "And what of Jazmyne?"

To kill her would leave Aiyca without a custos, and too many uncertainties. Even if she is defending the island against me, at least she's finally defending it. And then her removal raises the greater question, one neither Jazmyne nor I have voiced yet: Who will rule in the end?

"I will deal with Jazmyne upon my return."

"Then I suppose I'll go and pack." The mewling from the shadowcats on the dunes below doesn't mask the short staccato stab of Delyse's steps as she exchanges the sun for the shadows in the suite.

Let her be mad in Aiyca, where she can do more good than there is to be done here. Still, as I make my way across the balcony to the study, eyes on that line where the sky butts heads with the sea, I wonder if this will be the undoing of our relationship. Will she forgive me for trying to save Aiyca, or hate me for not saving it in a manner she deems fit?

If Aiyca was mine, if I was to sit on the throne at the end of this, that would be the first thing to go—the expectation that her voice, the council's voice, is more significant than mine in a bid to protect me, when in truth it's about control, their fear. One without it is a fool, but one with too much is a coward.

I am not without fear; in fact, it is one of my greatest strengths.

In the study, a fire lights in the hearth at my will. Retrieving Esai's favor from where I stashed it between two books, I toss it into the flames. But it isn't the puppy-eyed soldier who appears within a quarter of an hour, saber before him, and standard white-and-umber Simbarabo uniform as bright as a sunburst in the growing darkness.

"What's happened?" Zander demands.

"I didn't burn your favor."

"They were both mine." He strides around the room. "What do you need?"

"An escort off the island for Delyse?"

He twists around, both eyebrows low over his eyes. "Seriously?"

"In my defense, I didn't summon you."

With one of what I'm learning are his standard eye rolls, Zander returns his weapon to his hip.

"Why didn't you give me Esai's favor?"

"Why are you sending the Stealth away?"

I laugh softly. Never one for airs, this Warrior.

"Aiyca needs her."

"I gave you my favors because the general needs you." His hair settles on his shoulders, down his back; he's braided the front two sections off his face. Expression softening, Zander almost looks bashful. "Esai is capable, but he hasn't yet stepped into the shoes of Kirdan's third. If there was danger—"

"You like me too much to leave my fate in the hands of another, I understand."

Pausing, Zander cocks his head to the side as if he's never considered it before.

"There's no use in denying it. My death would bring you great distress. Admit it." I smirk.

"Whatever, mon." While he's dismissive, I note a faint

flush on his neck. "Look, I can't take your sistren to Aiyca until Zesia's Eldritch Gap, as you titled it, has been destroyed, closed, whatever. My place is by the general's side. But I can send a phalanx of our strongest soldiers to sift her as close as the restrictions allow."

"Blessings."

"I'll go and send the soldiers back here now."

"Zander?"

He raises a single thick brow.

"Your hair looks pretty."

With a beleaguered sigh, he sifts away—no eye roll, though. Knew he liked me.

My smile falls when I meet Delyse in the living area. Our parting isn't what I hoped it would be. She makes one final bid to stay, her voice low so the soldiers Zander sent to take his place don't overhear, asking me to send Shamar home instead.

"You will be what's best for Aiyca," I tell her. "I need you to go."

The look she gives me before the sift carries her away almost asks, *But are* you?

I'm trying to be, I might have answered.

"Vale, sistren," I murmur. "Until we meet again."

35

JAZMYNE

Dressed as I am, with twists instead of my usual afro, our arrival back to Queenstown's port is without fanfare, which means walking the wharf to where the carriage awaits brings new difficulties. A crowd of Obeah jostle one another by the coach stop; I take an elbow to the chest and fall back against Filmore with a loud cry.

"Forgive me, Regent." Encircling me with one lithe arm, he pushes our way through to the waiting carriage, where he pauses. "Someone's inside." He turns to me. "Family."

Oh no. Cleo opens the door; I hesitate. I might be better off with the crowd of arguing Obeah rather than the witch who waits inside.

"They've been fighting often." Sitting on the bench opposite mine, hands clasped in her lap, silver afro bound in a dark scarf, Aunty Galene scours me clean with a head-to-toe assessment. "Pirates?"

I sit, hard, and knock on the roof. The carriage rumbles its way from a walk to a canter.

"It's not what you think."

"I think you're so desperate to save this island, you're willing to lose yourself in the process." Head tilted to the side, Aunty sighs. "My sweet girl, I am so sorry for the life you've lived."

My throat thickens to the point that words are no longer possible.

"Crying isn't a weakness. In fact, I believe there's no greater show of strength than vulnerability." She opens her arms, and I fall into them. "You are becoming a pirate?"

Eyes closed, I shake my head.

"Then what?" She runs a hand down my head, one stroke, and I open up to her, confessing nearly everything about the race for queen, the gold the pirates want, and my deal with them—if it still exists after the Glide-By. "Judair caused this."

I nod against her lap. "And I have to cure it."

"You don't think you have? You spread Healers across the island in preparation for a war our order should have nothing to do with. Should those beasts attack, we have protection."

"I can't give up the throne. It's everything we fought for."

Running another hand down my head, Aunty doesn't respond.

"I've thought about it," I confess into the soft silk of her kaftan. "I've thought about leaving it all behind, but where will the Alumbrar be then?" Lost in the Adair and Unlit skirmish, victims in a war I let happen.

But maybe . . . maybe for this journey back to Cwenburg,

cradled like something dear, I can pretend this isn't my war.

Just this once.

Pretending is short-lived.

Aunty and I arrive back at the palace and separate. She to the infirmary, and me to the library, where, after updating Anya about my proposal to Synestra and the reactions from the crew I didn't linger to hear, she confirms what I suspected.

"Members of the Adair family *were* sentenced to join the Unlit."

I expected this and yet still hoped I'd be wrong. My teeth sink into my bottom lip hard enough to raise blood. How much more will be spilt by the time this island has been secured? This is why I cannot run. My order would be blind to their own deaths.

"The librarian—not the sweet Verena I was hoping to meet—" Anya pauses, so do I, in remembrance. "He helped me cross-reference the charges of treason. I didn't share who we were looking into, of course. According to him, treason is typically limited to state and crown, but there's also a personal stake to it—allegiance, like noncompete clauses and familial bonds."

My chest draws tight.

"The Adairs were the Mudda's chosen in the Order of Obeah, as your family is in ours—what if their family had qualms with which Adairs were chosen?" Anya poses, all but confirming my own initial thoughts. "Physical record keeping has never been a specialty in Xaymaca, but I don't doubt that if we spoke with a griot whose family lived when this island first came to be, they would confirm that throughout the years Adairs have fought amongst themselves for supremacy just as Adairs and Cariots have battled one another." At Anya's back, the Strawberry Hills flail under strong winds. Like them, I am left battered and bruised by the tempest of her words, their greater meaning. "I think the late doyenne worked with Unlit *Adairs* to reclaim the palace, and then betrayed them before they likely did so to her."

"I think so too," I whisper. Fighting a faceless, nameless Unlit was one thing, but going toe-to-toe with an Adair? "It's time to tell Iraya."

Weary in eyes and body, Anya nods.

We leave the library for my suite. Once the mirror has been retrieved, we sit side by side with it between us on the chair Iraya herself sprawled across after the last Yielding trial. If I didn't despise her, I'd feel sorry for her. I know all too well the perils of family members who wish to kill you.

"Iraya Adair," I murmur into the mirror's dull surface, every fiber of my being still.

"Try her full name?" Anya suggests when nothing happens.

I do, but it's heedless. She doesn't answer the first, the seventh, or the twenty-first call.

Falling back against the settee, Anya yawns and closes her eyes. "Does it matter if she doesn't know tonight?"

"I don't know. Yes? No." I need the Iraya from the Rolling Calf attack; I need that excitement at the challenge facing us from her own family. "I suppose I can wait."

"I don't want to do it here." Anya stands. "Let's go to Ol' Town."

"Is it . . . safe?"

"We'll wear disguises, and we won't talk about the empire, or pirates. You can tell me all there is to know about your cousin."

"Chaska?"

A deep pink gathers at Anya's jawline.

"Seriously?"

"She's nothing like your aunt, thank the gods. Nothing against her bedside manner, but Chaska's sponge baths were the best."

After a stop at the stables, we ride Joshial across the newly guarded temple drive and down the mount the palace sits atop into Ol' Town.

"There are so many people out." Anya verbalizes my thoughts as we take a table by the window in a café we used to frequent when life was slower and all we had to worry about was stalling the Yielding. "I can't tell if this town has always been so busy, or if I'm seeing enemies wherever I go now." The imprint of the attack at Carling Hill haunts her still.

My first instinct was to balk at the number of Aiycans out, hands swinging without a care in the world, but my shoulders lower, loosen at the reminder that pain is temporary, fear too. The greatest sign of strength is to persevere. To look that which frightens you in the eye and tell it, *not today*. And St. Mary is the safest parish, given it's home to the palace, me.

For a few hours at least Anya and I can pretend to relax while we wait to contact Iraya. But then a woman dressed like Synestra walks past—so similar to the pirate I do a double take to ensure it isn't her—and I'm thinking about the Iron Shore again.

"Is Roje annoyed that I quit? Is that why he hasn't come looking for me?"

"You didn't quit, you delegated."

"Maybe." A pile of crumbs is formed beneath my fingers on the table.

"How well do you know Roje, truly? And how well can you trust him? I know I tease you about him, but if I ever thought you were seriously entertaining romantic thoughts about him, I'd sift you away somewhere far."

"You don't have to worry there."

We're distracted by a crowd running past the window, followed closely by battalion soldiers, their silver hair like a beacon in the growing dark. Before I can ask, Anya's conduit flares around her neck as she stretches her hearing to determine what's happening.

The memory of Black River, the Unlit attack, smacks into me in a dazing reminder.

"I want to see what's happening," I say.

By the time we've paid our bill and retrieved Joshial from the designated prowler stop, shouting can be heard from the direction the soldiers ran toward, only now people hurry *away*. We risk a sift to the roof, with Joshial in tow, given the short distance. From our height, the market is bathed in the glow of a moon closer to red than yellow; the vibrancy enables us to see who is fighting, shoving one another in anger, conduit holders and the nonmagical alike. It isn't, as I thought, worried, the Unlit.

It's Order of Obeah members. Not a couple, like I saw in Queenstown. Not a crowd, like I saw on my way back from the race. A mob. A pushing, shoving, magic-shooting-from-conduits swarm—and they're attacking their own. Alumbrar and Aiycans begin elbowing themselves free of the crowd. Desperate for an Unlit sighting, I scan the growing number of dark braids, afros, that are indicative of the Obeah Order.

"Can you see anyone in gray?"

"Are you stakki?" Anya seizes my arm. "We need to get back to the palace before you're noticed and they come for you."

"Wait—"

"There's nothing you can do, Jaz!"

But there is. Weapons. I can arm my order, the shields, with more gold.

"Adriel," I breathe. "He needs to expedite the transmutation of the gold from the Adair trove. We're collecting it tomorrow."

36

IRAYA

Cross-legged on the floor in the bathing chamber, Grimoire open before me, I hold a mini tornado in the palm of my hand, a swirling vortex of gray and silver. One click and it grows large enough to cast my braids over my shoulders; a second click and it disappears.

"If you could see me now, Delyse," I murmur, triumphant, into the silence.

Hours into her return journey to Aiyca, with no word yet, I look forward to showing her the full-sized guzzu, and using it on the Unlit, along with a few additional magical tricks up my sleeve. What to try next . . . There's a shrinking guzzu that would come in handy. I could turn the enemy into the size of ants and then step on them. Or—

"Iraya Adair?"

Jazmyne's call comes from the Mirror of Two Faces, on the floor adjacent to the Grimoire.

"Iraya? It's urgent. Please be there. Please, please, please."

The good feelings instilled by magic practice sluice away as I pick up the mirror. Jazmyne's eyes, typically small, are unnaturally wide as she stares out at me.

"They've ousted you from the palace."

"No." She looks confused for a beat, then launches into it. "I suspected something that's since been confirmed. Anya and I checked the Unlit records to see if we could ascertain who might be behind—"

"What's the shortest version of this story?"

Her lack of scowl at my response makes my stomach cave inward.

"There are Adairs among the Unlit."

"Pardon me?"

"We checked the records recently; your family's name was there, and it was linked to the crime of treason. I think that the mastermind behind this entire skirmish, the faceless enemy who scared the doyenne so badly she instated you in the Cuartel, is one of your family members."

This could be another fabrication, a plan laid by her mama to ensure our order's enmity continued long after she was gone. It's the kind of spite I'd expect from her, and I pass that on to Jazmyne.

"It is something she would do," Jazmyne acknowledges, "but the librarian confirmed that record keeping fell by the wayside when the late doyenne usurped Aiyca. She wasn't noting down names as often as she should have; your family members' names were recorded long ago."

"You're certain?"

"As certain as I can be without a family record—do you know where I could find one here?"

"No."

Her next words are drowned out by the white noise in my head. That Griot-Bonemantis from Cwenburg's Cuartel spoke of a second family, but I never heard about Adairs attacking their own—and I wouldn't have, from the Blue Mountains, and later in Carne. In the case of the former, I was too young; in prison, I was too busy listening for all things Doyenne Cariot, with my parents dead and my aunties, uncles, and cousins assumed the same.

What if the Adairs weren't dead?

No Alumbrar could do all that has been done—even Judair didn't usurp Aiyca. Someone comfortable enough to commune with the other side aided her. . . .

"Iraya?"

"What?"

"If it is indeed a family member of yours, what can I do to guard Aiyca against them?"

Nothing.

"Adairs are tenacious, stubborn, possess iron wills. Whatever you do, they will only find a way around." I'm dazed, and my head feels heavy, my body like it's sliding through the tile I'm sitting atop. "You have the shields—"

"I spoke with the Obeah Masters too."

"Good," I breathe. "That will do until I return."

"And when do you?"

"I was meant to . . . do something here first. Finish it. Plug the gap the monsters are traveling through, once I find it."

"You've found a way to stop them?"

"Stop . . . more of them."

My mind is still reeling as I answer her questions. Adairs are fighting *me*?

"How?" she presses.

"I haven't—I don't know yet. Look, just work with the Masters and the shields. I'm moving as quickly as I can." Jazmyne's next remark is cut off when I turn over the mirror. Holy hell. I don't know what to do with my hands; my limbs feel like they're connected by barbed wire.

Adairs in the Unlit.

Adairs fighting me—they have to know it's me. But who can confirm it's them?

Doyenne Divsylar.

I'd planned on an invitation, but there's no time for formality. If Adairs are plotting to take Aiyca from Jazmyne, the only reason she's still in Cwenburg Palace is because they're allowing it, which means their plan is greater than we thought—more dire than I thought.

They want Aiyca, but they're waiting to take it, all of it, from me.

A gelid wind curls after me as I stalk through the palace halls to the late doyenne's suite, one that could be tossed up from the sea. Or breathed through the maw of something dead in the land of the living. Something is following me.

My hand seeks out the blade strapped to my thigh; caught between two corners—one at my back and one ahead—I take a step forward, and then, as quick as it takes my will to rekindle the witchlight, I twist and raise my blade to the throat of the stalker at my back.

Kirdan. Ablaze with my will, the weapon fills his eyes with golden light.

"I thought you were seeing to Lucia."

"That was yesterday."

"There are Nine Nights of mourning." I thought I'd have more time alone. Not entirely insensitive to the fact that I'm holding a weapon to his neck while discussing funerary preparations, I sheathe the dagger in my bandolier. "And it went . . . well?"

"The First Night went as expected. Tonight remains to be seen." He glances down the corridor; a muscle in his jaw beats his emotions into submission.

His deceit about the staff wasn't truly his.

That honor lies with his mama.

"I'm going to see the doyenne," I say. "For the staff." I brace for his disapproval, for the fight I didn't anticipate tonight, but one I'm ready for nonetheless.

"I'll show you the way."

Startled, I blink. "Why?"

"Contrary to how things have been between us, Iraya, I like to think that for all my foibles, I am not unjust. I am not unkind."

Not unjust, unkind, or stupid, I note, when we come upon the doyenne's heavily guarded suite. They've increased the numbers since my nighttime visit, and all are under strict orders not to permit anyone entry. Not even Empress Adair and Prince Divsylar, it becomes apparent as Kirdan introduces us.

I take a step forward, arms open. "Does it look like I'm here with a casserole and flowers? We have matters of great importance to discuss."

"No guests," the witch repeats, unyielding of mind and body, in the starched white and gold of her uniform. "Empress, prince, or otherwise."

Kirdan glances my way, a brow cocked in silent question. I could be diplomatic, but if Kaltoon, who no doubt spearheaded this order, wishes to treat me like an enemy and not the witch who will save his ass, I can act accordingly. My will to conceal the batons in my outstretched arms melts away, revealing the shafts of bright gold. I manage to fire two suppression sparks before the witches can shield, but these are not the inexperienced Alumbrar Xanthippe in Aiyca. Rather than walls of coruscating sparks, great beasts not dissimilar to the Unlit's pets slam down onto four legs before Kirdan and me. Saber aloft, he sets himself at my back as the creatures prowl on their wide paws to surround us. The ground beneath my feet rumbles with their magical reverberations. Impressive. If the Simbarabo have half this skill, I might stay and help Zesia first after all.

"Close your eyes" is a caution murmured solely for Kirdan as my naevus springs forward, a beast of its own awakened from slumber. Alabaster light flares and explodes outward in a flash of teeth and claws to tear through the J'Martinet's Self-Intent. A warm hand slides into my own, and, however unnecessary, that glorious feeling of amity, trust, is flooding through my veins, my fatigued muscles; blinking away the light reveals J'Martinet strewn across the floor, chests gently rising and falling.

Second only to the feeling of triumph is Kirdan's hand, strong and sure, in mine.

"You're not wearing your chest-plate," he says by way of explanation. "I'll watch your back."

I nod, slip out of his hold, and stride toward one of the fallen witches. "I need a hand."

"I believe you're familiar with cutting, but if you could refrain in this instance, I can help." Kirdan's expression is wry when I twist to look at him.

Zander's conduit light show on the delta was impressive, but it's nothing compared to the slow sluice of gold dripping down Kirdan's body—the fragments of it that bleed through his scarification like lambent veins, the threads in his cloak, his buttons, vambraces; it goes on. Even the golden hues in his skin look aglow with power and intent. How he kept this might concealed in Aiyca, I don't know. It takes more effort than it should to swallow. He doesn't have the show of alabaster light, like my tell, but that almost makes him more dangerous. To underestimate him simply because there is no sign seems like a waste of a final act.

Kirdan uses his will to lift one J'Martinet to her feet, and a phantom hand raises her arm until her palm is flat against the door; the magical protections retract, like an elasticated spider's web.

"The doyenne is difficult," he warns. "Be cautious."

Hand on the doorknob, I don't look back as I return, "She'll need more caution than I."

Inside, rather than the grandness of the suite, the vaulted ceiling and measure of conduit gold, the first thing that strikes is the smell: one of stale disregard, trapped heat, and a smoky haze through which I can just about see Doyenne Divsylar squatting in bed like a toad atop a lily pad, a pipe held between her teeth.

One pulse of will opens windows; another dissipates the gray film in the air.

"Who's there?"

"Your reckoning."

The great wooden bed creaks as Doyenne Saskia Divsylar, waist-length hair draped across one shoulder in a thick copper-and-charcoal plait, sits up. A goliath of wood, the bed contains gold that gleams in the gauzy clouds of smoke— but all the sharpness of the beast belongs to the mind of the witch squinting at me with eyes bright enough, perspicacious enough, to tell me that while her will to get her ass out of bed may have taken leave, along with any desire to change from her nightrobe, her danger hasn't left in its entirety. One I'm not familiar with. Hearing contrasting reports of this witch but never seeing her has made it difficult to build a complete profile. In my mind, she's been an amorphous thing. As shapeless and vague as the smoke from her pipe.

"Wahan, Doyenne. We have much to discuss."

"I heard you were here." She falls back against her pillows and exhales a serpentine plume through her nostrils.

My nose twitches. *Opiates.* Half a thought erects a clear shield around my head. It doesn't make sense for us both to lose our wits.

"You are the spitting image of your mama, Adair witch."

"That's where our similarities begin and end. Mama was

far better at diplomacy, but I find there's a time to talk, and a time to whet my blade."

It takes me a moment to realize the series of rasps are not the doyenne choking, but her laughter. Teeth gritted, I regret my decision to bring only the three knives. Though I could catch that smoke surrounding her with magically rendered fingers and choke her with it.

"Your tongue, I imagine, is far sharper than any blade."

"Because it speaks poniards?"

"Because it speaks too much." She draws in another lungful of smoke. "And I am in no mood for the verbal dances Judair Cariot lived for, you understand? So out with it. What do you want?" Annoyingly unperturbed, the doyenne reclines further in the bed. "To know why I refused to help your order in Aiyca? Why I remain here in my rooms with aches and illness for company? Or why I haven't ordered my guard to kill you where you stand for daring to enter this room and talk to me like you are somebody more than the orphaned pickney of a witch I used to know, and cared little about?"

Though slow to come, my smile stretches wide. "Entirely dead inside, are you, Saskia?"

For the first time, the smoke halts its somnolent dance.

"Doyenne," she corrects.

"*Empress*," I raise.

"Then you will be sworn in?" She hinges forward to squint at me through the smoke. "You will raise this empire and wrangle the pickney who have stepped out from beneath your island's shadow? Pray tell me, how will you do that if you don't survive the war you arrived here to beg my help with?"

This is what Kirdan meant by difficult. She's either stakki or high.

Easily tested.

I loosen a dagger after her voice has finished raising in the last impertinent question she will ever ask me again, and let it fly. It thuds through her braid, pinning it to the bed's headboard with a satisfying *thunk*. Her broad face, sickly complected, blanches. I run indolent eyes down the length of her braid to where it's coiled by her side. I suspect she's never cut it. I free a second and third blade. At my will, they illuminate to lambent bolts.

"What do I want, you asked. . . . I *do* want to know why you've been lying in here, mostly sound of mind if not of body, while your daughters are managed by crafty and duplicitous middlemen, and your son molders beneath the contempt of an island he works hard to protect every day. I want to know, *Saskia*, while I contemplate where my next blade will land, what you can offer me, as there will not be any begging on my part. You, however, should feel free to exercise that right."

Spluttering, she tosses her pipe down onto the sheets. "You dare—"

"I told you there was little similarity between Mama and me." I say this conversationally, hands splayed, a dagger in each. "She believed you would come when the Unlit attacked. She gave you the benefit of the doubt. She thought you would be Aiyca's salvation. I have no such beliefs. And neither should you." My voice dips to a midnight purr, one made for the witching hour and every dark artifice formed during it. "Because, Saskia, when you are happily sitting here puffing on your pipe while the empire prepares to face its greatest threat yet, *I* will come, and I won't offer you the benefit of the doubt. I am not your salvation. I am the spoiled fruit in the bowl that rots those surrounding it."

"What do you want?" she whispers, and it's almost disappointing how easily she gives in.

For all her sins, this witch is no Judair Cariot.

"Who leads the insurgents?"

Something flickers in her eyes. "You know already."

"Say it."

"Blood follows vein."

"They are no family of mine," I grind out.

"That doesn't lessen their claim to the throne. Or their hunger for it."

"They've been in touch?"

"You know what walks this island come nightfall."

Holy shit. "You are a coward."

Without the decency to look ashamed, the doyenne sniffs.

"Dada's conduit weapon."

She blinks at the change of conversation subject.

"Judair Cariot sent it here, to you," I expound. "A decade ago."

"Ah." She shifts. "It was chopped down."

Her words strike me like blows from the same axe.

"But I—I have many weapons you can take, if that's all you want," she continues.

As if they'd be commensurate. My gods. She took the last piece of my parents and desecrated it. I take one step, my first since arriving, toward her.

Not the last piece. That same sage voice I've been hearing of late enters my thoughts. It's right. Aiyca is the last piece of my parents' legacy; *I* am. It needs me—we need each other, and I won't save it standing here talking to this witch.

"There's nothing you have that I want."

Upon my exit the doors slam against the walls so hard, they splinter. Kirdan strides beside me the entire walk back to the suite. Attendants, court members, stumble over themselves to bow and preen, to simper; I ignore them. He does too. No words are exchanged until the door to the suite is closed, and his protections shimmer into being across the walls.

"Did you know?" I whirl on him. "Did you know who the Unlit are?"

Brows drawn tight in confusion, Kirdan shakes his head. "Who are they?"

I can't bring myself to say the words. Jazmyne and Doyenne Divsylar are likely lying to upset my focus, to distract me so that I don't make it back to Aiyca, or so that I fall victim to the Oscuridad.

"Nothing. No one," I lie. "Your mama hasn't led a coup against Aiyca, not from fear of my order there, the shields, but due to her own torpor, right?"

Kirdan shakes his head again, thrown.

"The Simbarabo's numbers surpass Aiyca's Xanthippe, as well as the first and second battalions, numerically and in deftness. If she wanted to take Aiyca, she would have faced a fight from Doyenne Cariot, but she would have defeated her. If she could have been bothered."

Leaning back, Kirdan takes his time looking me over.

"Is there something you want to say?"

"I want an answer."

"Right. . . . Well, why do you think the doyenne's never seen? The charade would be over."

"Then it was never your sisters you feared ruling, but your mama?"

"Not quite. Mama is waiting out the two years until they inherit, officially, but she does nothing in Zesia. My uncles run everything through my sisters, who have been taught little and shown worse about what it means to be leaders." He drifts across the living room, past tables and overstuffed chairs, removing his cloak, bandolier, as he goes. "You've been here for close to two phases, you've seen how matters operate. Mama is just as dangerous as Doyenne Cariot, but rather than greed, it will be her indifference that kills us. Unless I do something about it."

"Why?"

"Why?" he echoes.

"Why do you fight for this island?"

"Why do you fight for Aiyca?"

Mama. Dada.

"Maybe I don't get to say this, after last night. But because of Lucia—" His throat bobs. "I have to say this. You and I are not dissimilar. If there's something you need to say, you can."

"Lucia has a twin."

"That wasn't what I meant."

"I remembered last night. She can tell us the stories we sought from her sister."

Confusion tightens across Kirdan's features. "I thought the next step was to travel to Aiyca?"

"Not yet."

"Not until you've exhausted every avenue in Zesia," he finishes, with an unreadable look on his face. "I knew about Nyxia. I wasn't keeping her from you." *Not like whatever you're keeping from me*, his look suggests. "She's not her sister."

"I know that in cases of Tempera, they are like night and day. Do you think it a waste of a trip?"

That unreadable expression flashes across Kirdan's face once again. "We didn't decide which island would receive aid first. Part of me is grateful you wish to stay here, even if it's for another day, but I can't say with any certainty that Nyxia will have the answers we seek."

Honesty.

"And if she does, she won't make extraction easy—unless you're looking for a fight after talking with Mama? After talking with me, last night." Feet planted, Kirdan looks as though he anticipates round two, as if he wants it.

"I'd like to see Nyxia."

He stares me down like he's going to challenge me. "Fine," he relents. "But not tonight. We want as much daylight as possible. She is not her sister," he repeats. "We can leave tomorrow, after the meeting with Kaltoon."

"Until tomorrow, then."

I'm halfway to the bedroom door when he speaks again.

"I brought candles for the Second Night. Join me outside?"

I do. For Lucia.

Side by side with only the stars for company, we light the candles. Typically, Nine Nights are filled with the exchange of stories about the departed, but Kirdan and I stand in silence while the wax burns low. Until he breaks it.

"I understand your ire at the Unlit when you learned of their role in your family's deaths better now than I did in Cwenburg." His focus is on the horizon when I glance his way again. "If I learned who was leading their band of killers and cowards, I wouldn't sit idly, like my family. I wouldn't throw a dinner. I'd tear Lucia's killer apart with my bare hands until they were at the brink of death, but they wouldn't find release for a long, long while."

His hands curl into fists; my family might have played a role in Lucia's death, worked with Judair to kill Mama and Dada, and now to kill me.

"You said no more withholding," I say, in permission. Invitation.

As he exhales, his nod is slight, but one of conviction, of gratitude. "I hadn't been to the royal mortuary since Dada passed. And then it wasn't to sit with his body. It was to watch through a window." He shakes his head. "I wasn't permitted entry as I'd already been handed over to the Simbarabo. I learned then how gutting it is, to believe someone sleeping but to know they'll never wake. My own death I've stopped imagining, I've accepted. But to see Lucia—" His words choke off, lost to emotion and stubbornness as he fights tears.

Our hands are inches apart, but the distance feels closer to miles.

"I didn't see my parents," I tell him. In the night, where

sentiments seem less on display. "Doyenne Cariot sent their bodies out to sea in a quiet Nine Night in which the Obeah and secular were hardly permitted to mourn."

When it meets mine, his gaze is steady and deep, and the weight of his loss—two weights dragging him down into the depths of that living sea we almost drowned in.

"I know where the Unlit are."

My eyebrows shoot upward.

"We couldn't find them, before. They were careful. They drew no attention to themselves until they killed Lucia. The timing is too significant. I think they're readying for a greater attack."

"It makes sense."

"That area we chased them to after we found the villa aflame? I've had men watching ever since. They haven't seen the magi I seek, but they have seen various others visiting with packages. It's all very clandestine, the subtle exchange of goods done in a way that we wouldn't have looked twice at, ordinarily."

"You think they're holed up in there."

"I'll need another couple of days to be sure, but yeh mon."

"*We* will."

He looks at me then, his eyes as dark as the water beneath us. As bottomless.

"Lucia showed me kindness. I won't let her death go by without repercussions." And then there's the matter of confirming if Mama's side of the family are indeed members of the Unlit.

"What about keeping a low profile with the Unlit until it's time to leave?"

"What is left but to speak with Lucia's twin? I'll sail for Aiyca within a phase." After the bacchanal to keep everyone here fooled about the wedding. "Besides, are you planning on leaving any witnesses?"

"Iraya," Kirdan says, his voice soft. "You said it yourself, you sail for Aiyca within a phase. You. The Simbarabo's accompaniment is something we need to discuss, after Nyxia, I understand. I mean to keep my word and escort you home. But it will take longer than a day to discover where the Unlit are holed up considering they move all the time. I appreciate your commitment; you honor Lucia, you honor me." He swallows. "That being said, if you need to go, I won't hold it against you. I have an island. You have an empire."

I should say it. I should tell him who the Unlit might be.

But I can't.

"Besides, they'll have seen my men. We'll likely be walking into a trap."

I'm struck by a wave of emotion. But not of sadness. Of *purpose*.

When the dead speak, Obeah listen; when Obeah speak, the dead come.

"Indeed," I murmur. "But not theirs. Ours."

Mine.

It's time to learn, one way or another, if the enemy we seek, the enemy who killed Lucia and seeks to own Aiyca, is an Adair after all.

37

JAZMYNE

Beneath the zenith of Aiyca's sun, Golden Grove, the industrial heart of the island, seems as gilded as its namesake. Burnished in the wealth that passes through its streets in armored carriages drawn by merciless prowlers trained to consume thieves or anyone who looks a little too long and hard at the transported conduit coins. More Xanthippe, Obeah, and battalion soldiers stand guard here than they do anywhere else across the island; the only exception is the palace. Factories rise like great airships I've heard of from the west, where magic is rarer. It's into one of these hubs, where the atavistic meets something more chemical as it is transposed into fuel, that Anya and I walk—flanked by Filmore and Pasha, as well as a swarm of Xanthippe—for our appointment with Adriel, the closest connection I have to the Obeah Order. But it isn't the lone Obeah Transmuter we find waiting behind the doors of the meeting room when we enter. His absence throughout our tour should alone have prepared me for the fact that while I asked Anya to set this parley, it isn't under my control. It never was.

An elegant Obeah-witch rises at the head of a table of seven. "Welcome, Regent. My name is Master Omnyra." The brightness of her third-eye scarification bores into me all the way across the impressive room, gilded and filled with a warm, inviting light, as if this is anything other than a trap. A coup. "We've been expecting you."

Stunned into silence I can only stand, blink at the official gathering before us.

"What the hell is this?" Anya, without such restraints, snarls.

"The meeting you requested." An Obeah-man stands by the Bonemantis's left side. "There's no need for animosity, Anya."

She huffs a disbelieving breath. "Adriel. I should have expected this."

My eyes linger on the Transmuter, on the unrepentant shrug he offers Anya and the insolence in a face that, while still round with youth, bears that same insufferable knowing all Obeah seem to possess.

"Our order is beginning to tear itself apart from the inside out," Master Omnyra says, in a voice that, while light, carries the weight of authority. "And so my fellow Masters and I"—she gestures at her order seated at the table—"thought we might curtail the inevitable civil uprising, Regent. Please." Lowering back into her chair, she angles her head at the vacant seats closest to where we linger in the open doorway. "There is much to discuss about Aiyca's safety, and the matter of your race for Pirate Queen."

Weighted to the floor, I couldn't move to take a seat with them even if I wanted to. I raise a shaking hand to silence Anya's next question, though I know it's one we share.

How does this Bonemantis know about that?

Alumbrar Sibyls could only dream of half this accuracy. How else did the doyenne fail to find the jéges, including the one I wore around my neck, for over a year?

"You say there is much I wish to discuss with you." My throat constricts around the words. "But what is it you wish to discuss with me?" Me who only brought fourteen Xanthippe to stand against these seven Obeah—all of whom are experienced Masters who not only evaded the late doyenne's detection, but can kill us all without getting out of their seats. Their power is as certain as the air I breathe, the ground beneath my feet. "Iraya and I, we are—we are working together." The words sound small, pleading, as though I am hiding in their empress's skirts and begging them to spare me.

Pathetic comes from a voice in my head that sounds too much like the late doyenne's.

"We know of the alliance you have formed with the empress. We are interested in learning how you plan on keeping Aiyca safe while you are at sea." It isn't Master Omnyra who speaks. It's the Obeah-man to her left, a Master Artisan of Wood. "And, better still, how you plan on keeping it safe while you sit on the throne without any magic. The shields' numbers are depleted, and Aiyca is vast."

"I won't be sailing for queen. And I'm in no mood to measure argumentative acuity, Obeah. I don't have magic, but I do have armies."

"You have the hope of armies."

"Then let's move straight to your suggestions." I manage to say the words without entirely forfeiting my pride. But it is humiliating to stand before these Obeah like this. Like peering into a mirror and seeing everything I am not.

"Put the Masters on your council," Adriel says with another of those shrugs. "For the first time in centuries we work together for a common good—to right a situation your mama created. No Obeah within the Jade Guild wishes for Aiyca's sunder. We can put aside our pride, our . . . *dissatisfaction* with the Alumbrar rule and where it has positioned us—the island—in a bull's-eye."

"The late doyenne's sins are not mine."

"But Aiyca's salvation could be."

Only if I concede almost half the seats on my council to a lifelong enemy, and one presenting an evergreen reminder of their capacity for betrayal and railroading. I will not capitulate to intimidation, magically impotent or not.

"What of the gold?"

"We have the coins you requested, weapons too. But the issue of our alliance is time sensitive," Master Omnyra says, her eyes elsewhere.

"You can't expect me to make this decision now," I say. "Not when the Swearing-In is less than a moon phase away." How will my order, the island, react? How will the original, the relegated advisors react? There has already been a threat of mutiny. Has Omnyra seen that too?

"I think the sea cannot help but throw waves." The witch

shrugs the line of her shoulders. "Alumbrar have become used to betrayal when they cannot otherwise get their own way. It would be folly not to prepare for the worst. That is ruling, Regent," the prescient Master says, no doubt recalling the words the late doyenne used with me for no reason other than to unsettle me.

Be measured. Be steady.

"Tell me, Master, what else might the dead have whispered in your ears?"

"That they prepare space for you."

Bitterness claws its way up my throat at the complacent casting of her words, as though she threw something soft, not spiked, at my feet; beside me, Anya twitches, but even she wouldn't dare call out an Obeah Master Bonemantis.

"You don't have to go with them, Jazmyne. That day does not have to be today."

"If I give in to your requests, you mean?"

Anya edges forward. "Threatening Aiyca's leader is an act of treason, Obeah."

Filmore, Pasha, and the Xanthippe follow suit.

"So is coercion," I state. "Not to mention demanding that I give you places on my council in exchange for helping—"

"Oh no, we'll help." The Master Warrior cuts a look as acute as the conduit weapon strapped across her back. "We will continue to do all we can to keep Aiyca safe, but our enemies work from the shadows. How will this island see us as more, as something to believe in, if we do the same? It is for us to step forward into the sun. Or starlight." She snorts; her cohort do not laugh, but there is an air of humor, of mockery, that fills me until I am sick with it and there's only the need to purge.

"Show me why I should."

"Excuse me?"

Master Omnyra raises a hand; the Warrior stands down.

So do the Xanthippe, my two Stealths. One moment they're surrounding me, ready to charge at my word, and then they are crumpling to the ground like puppets cut from strings. Anya edges closer to me, and I swallow. Hard.

"We left Anya standing as a courtesy." The Bonemantis pushes up sleeves to reveal two forearms laden with a cache of gold bangles. "Our immediate fight is preventing the Unlit from darkening Aiyca's skies, as they have been trying to do since they were cast out. Work with us," she implores. "Let us work with you."

Surrounded as I am by my fallen guard, her request for permission feels fruitless; Anya, quivering beside me, seems to agree, but . . . After all I have done to acquire the might of Cwenburg, to let them reduce it to paper, the foundations to sand, is one thing. They shall not do the same to me. I am formed from stardust and divinity. I will not be felled in the same way.

"I'd offer you time, but—"

"There is none," I finish. "I know."

Our immediate fight is with the Unlit, that witch said. And it is, while I'm keeping Iraya's seat warm. But what about later? A decade of Alumbrar rule has been history making, and yet, when Iraya returns I might be another fallen star relegated to its annals as a dark wave rises to blot out all light in sight.

Obeah or Unlit.

Adair or Adair.

A glance at my sistren reveals her defeat at what she believes is inevitable, but someone must fight for the Alumbrar, and crown or no, official title or no, I swore that would be me.

"You denounce us as enemies and then follow your words with a display of unmistakable hostility contrary to that fact." My chest heaves with fear, with anger, with the weight of what I must say next. "But I stand by everything I have said." Their order has been floundering without a clear leader. That will only lead to Alumbrar vulnerability, Aiycan weakness. A victorious war is not fought on two fronts. "Show me why I should offer you seats on my council. Give me a reason to step into the light with you."

"And then?"

The question is a subtle transfer of power, from the Master to me.

"And then we win the war."

Iraya told me to hold the line.

After the Swearing-In, I'm going to destroy it.

38

IRAYA

"Emissary Divsylar has requested that you and Prince Divsylar join him in the conservatory for breakfast this morning," Fuma says, mere hours after Kirdan and I abandoned a map of the island, our hunt of the Unlit, to sleep. "Now the prince is hale once more, the emissary would like to begin planning in earnest."

Gods. The wedding. With the bacchanal and Yule approaching, that's the three phases I was already reticent to commit to, over. I am not staying for a fourth.

"It would be lovely to have a wedding while the palace is decorated for the holidays. Though . . . and I don't mean to step out of my place," Fuma says with care, "but I noticed the prince didn't sleep here, again, last night."

No. Kirdan left, after barely an hour of tossing and turning beside me, to jump-start the search for the Unlit.

"If you don't mean to try for pickney yet, you can tell me.

There's a tea I can prepare for you."

Denials rise on my tongue before I realize that we're meant to be stakki about one another. We would be trying for heirs. It's an exercise in restraint to ask for the tea and then enter the bathing chamber. The question isn't Fuma's fault. For that I can thank Kaltoon, and certainly might, this morning.

The thought of sitting to discuss a wedding feels frivolous when Lucia lost her life in an attack that, thus far, hasn't been acknowledged by the family who employed her. However long ago.

Following the lengthy process of being perfumed, buffed, and hydrated with a bitter contraceptive tea, I instruct one of the attendants to retrieve my golden bodice from the closet.

"But your ensemble, Empress." The girl fingers the long tunic, pleated and extending into a train that snakes down my back to trail along the ground, with something like dismay. "The beading around your midriff—"

"Won't protect me from attack." Something I need in this palace of prowlers, not to mention if word arrives that the Unlit have been found, and I need to leave. Then there's the danger of all the unchecked alabaster with this wedding context. It makes me look too similar to a bride.

"Retrieve the breastplate," Fuma instructs the girl; she hastens away. "Though I'm not sure what you think will attack you in the palace."

She fusses with the train; I watch her reflection and wonder if she's being glib. In her defense, in the day the palace doesn't look like it's haunted by incorporeal interlopers from the other side of the veil. Indeed, the conservatory—sparkling glass walls and an array of jewel-toned flora—is laid elegantly for breakfast when I arrive, after Kirdan. It's almost a shame to disrupt our surroundings with an argument. But given the seven Witches Council custos seated at the table—witches I haven't been able to secure an audience with—I'm all too happy to pull out my chair. Rather than throw it at Kaltoon for wasting my time with this.

Delyse was wrong when she thought Kirdan could replace Aiyca in my affections, but she *was* right about his uncle's hunger for our home, the empire. If this wedding was actually happening, I don't doubt I'd be dead the moment I said *I do*. Which is why I have to kill these monsters and move on from Zesia before he learns I mean to say *I don't think so*. The Council can help me with that, surely.

"My betrothed is away." I distantly hear Kirdan's voice. "No doubt imagining dresses."

Drawing out of my head, I find myself the point of the table's focus.

"I *was* away, but not thinking about anything as unpleasant as dresses."

"No?" Kaltoon cocks a single brow. "What could be more important than joining our two mighty nations?"

"Monsters," I state. "Ones that walk my island, this island, and the Skylands."

A glass shatters in the hands of the Warrior presider. She is the most visceral, this Obeah-witch with long, dark braids infused with copper, but her sistren also gape at me down the length of the table. Kirdan too stares as though he can't believe what I just said. Only Kaltoon bears an expression more irritated than fearful.

"Of course you know about the Unlit's beasts." I address only him. "Based on the cadence of your screams the other night, I wasn't sure you had the wherewithal to survive if they truly walked this palace."

He splutters a string of nonsensical outrage.

"You know what they are? I came to you," Kirdan grinds out at him from across the table. "And you dismissed me, them, said they were a feral breed of shadowcat."

"You don't get to speak to me like that, Simbarabo," Kaltoon spits. "You haven't the authority."

Kirdan, to my surprise—greater still after the past few days of witnessing him command his men without challenge or question—shrinks before his uncle.

The greater surprise, however, is what the sight of that does to me.

"I think you'll find it's you who has no voice here," I'm all too happy to purr. "Not now I can finally address the council you said was too busy to see me prior to this morning. No, no," I add as he scrambles to interrupt. "If you bear any fondness for your tongue you will cease using it or find yourself holding it. Understand?"

His cheeks near scarlet, Kaltoon's eyes bounce across the table.

He finds no support.

"We heard that *you* were too busy, Empress." Along with the Poisoner who spoke, the other six members of the Zesian Witches Council add their assertions.

"Well then, now seems as good a time as any to cut out the

middleman." I wink Kaltoon's way. "We, this empire, are on the brink of war. For the first time in decades, centuries, it isn't with one another. The Unlit, notorious for showing a complete lack of respect for the rules on which our islands were built, have outdone themselves. They're ushering in creatures from beyond the veil to aid in their attempt to wrest away Aiyca, Zesia, and the Skylands from the hands of those who rule over them. I have seen the damage in Aiyca, heard about the detrimental effects that will happen in the Skylands, and this phase they took the life of a friend here in Zesia. *Family*," I amend, glancing at Kirdan. "If you think your army means I will sit back in silence while you turn a blind eye to the fires being started across the empire, then you are as foolish as him." I angle my head at Kaltoon, whose own looks like a boil close to popping. "And if you think you are safe in this island, this palace, *my company*, while these beasts roam, you are already dead."

"We won't pretend to be foolish as to what hunts across our island." The Warrior glances across the table at Kirdan. "Not a feral breed of shadowcat. Something worse. Something other. But to dispatch J'Martinet to every province will only make the island aware that the problem is serious."

"And why shouldn't they know that it is?"

"Panic, Empress," the Healer says. "We are hoping to avoid it, something the engagement would help with. Morale has proven to help with war efforts. Even if the wedding must be postponed, the engagement would be beneficial in giving the island something to look forward to in an uncertain time. If we issue an increase of J'Martinet to the provinces simultaneously with the bacchanal, we might avoid incurring alarm. If not, well . . ."

"That choice is up to you, Empress Adair." The Transmuter clasps fingers riddled with scars before her.

In the face of their threat—for it isn't a choice—I can't help but think of my own scars. I've always been proud of these markers, this journal of the life I've lived and the choices I've made, for good and bad, incised on my skin. I am a living tale of everything I've done. But it's the marks to come that will define what I do next. For Aiyca, Xaymaca.

"Fine." I take the cut, internally wincing at the sting. "Now, I trust arrangements can be made without us. The prince and I have other plans."

In unison the table rises. All bar Kaltoon bow their heads as we leave; his wily eyes follow us the entire way across the conservatory until we are out of sight. At that moment, I stop and turn on Kirdan.

"You told me you want to become doyen of this island, and yet I've seen no evidence that you could command the authority necessary to rule your people."

He blinks at me but says nothing.

"Did someone take *your* tongue, and therefore your words?"

No. I'm just ashamed to speak them.

I start at the voice in my head. It's *the* voice. The one from the beast attack, the one that felt as though it was coming from that place of trust.

"It was you that night, at Green Island." Stunned, I gape at him. "Yours was the voice I heard issuing instructions." *Are you a witch or aren't you.* "How are you in my head?"

"The Glyph of Connection. Our blood exchange."

"Get out," I snarl.

"I can't always help it," he snarls back.

I edge forward. "How is it you can be so *nuff* with me, but when it came to standing up for yourself back there you were silent. Are you a Warrior or aren't you?"

He flinches back from his own words. "You would have preferred me to run my uncle through? Because I could have. I wanted to. I *always* want to." A muscle beats in his clenched jaw. "Killing is easy, Iraya. Killing is all I have known. To answer your question, I'm not sure if I can be more than I have been raised to be; I only know that this island needs me to be more, because under my uncles' control it doesn't stand a chance."

Stepping back, I look at him, *really* look at him, remember every name he's called me, every decision of mine he's lambasted, while, I can finally see, doing the same himself. He lied to Jazmyne, stole the Grimoire, stole me. *That's* why he couldn't talk back to Kaltoon. He's afraid to be seen, because doing so means standing out, taking ownership for who he has become, and he doesn't like it. He doesn't want to like who that is, and have his family see.

"You don't want them to see your darkness, do you?" I shake my head. "That's why you've sought to change *me*—"

"I don't want to change you, Iraya." Head-to-head, his focus is scouring in its intensity. "To fight my uncle is to admit to being every wrong thing this island has made me." His words are bleak. "A weapon first, and a man second. I don't want to give anyone that satisfaction. You are separate from that. Your darkness, as you want to call it, is liberating. It frees you from being blinded by the falsehoods in this world. I don't want to change that. I admire it."

"And you think your darkness is different from mine?"

"Isn't it?"

Realization bleeds through me with a painful slowness. Gods above.

"Are you saying it isn't?"

At the need in Kirdan's voice, I take great interest in a hideous painting of some family members hung on the wall at his back. "What I'm saying is that we cannot allow the council and Kaltoon to control the narrative. It's just another way to remain in charge while we fall in line, and I cannot, will not, play second to anyone again. Are you with me?"

"The island would panic. They weren't wrong about that."

"Not with the right leader." My throat tightens. "Kaltoon, Krimpt, this island, they didn't make you who you are today. It sounds like they broke whoever you were meant to be, and good riddance. This version is stronger, and someone who, if you allowed yourself, would find peace outside their spotlight."

"In the darkness?" Kirdan returns, his voice a slow stroke against my cheek.

"The wedding won't be happening." I make myself say the words fast, almost brusquely. "I said we were engaged to protect myself here. You understand?"

"Planning a wedding is a ludicrous power grab from my uncle. I also know"—his voice dips—"that Lucia wouldn't have died if I'd made him take me seriously. So yes, I understand. I have always understood."

"Have you made much progress with finding the Unlit?" I ask, softer.

"Not yet."

"Then let's change that."

So I can return home.

I wonder if he understands that too.

39

JAZMYNE

I thought a sky filled with stars would always be my favorite view—until Adriel's transmuted conduit gold arrives the morning after my sojourn to Golden Grove.

He did more than I could have hoped, more than I asked. Anya left to try on the new Stealth blacks woven through with conduit gold; there's even a cape for me, in addition to the new gold machetes for the Xanthippe, new gauntlets and epaulettes, as well as additional accessories I wouldn't know how to use. Ford can tell me what they are once he's returned from the Unnamed Isles.

We agreed, him, Anya, and me, that the peninsula east of the Blue Mountains was our best bet to establish the faux falls. Nel will go as my proxy, to direct Synestra and the *Silver Arrow*'s crew to a modest waterfall. The beauty of Anansi's stories is that they're easy to twist. I bet the map I found in the doyenne's room is simply a blank sheet. For all I know, Iraya's mama mined the conduit gold, and the map is an ancient lie, a disappointment—the last.

With the Swearing-In a day away, and the continuation of the "Lost Empress Remembers" messages appearing across the island, it feels good to have a tangible response to the Unlit. The Obeah Masters have outdone themselves. I'm almost willing to say yes. To give them a place on the council.

Almost.

Three knocks sound against my office door.

"Anya?"

"Not quite," Roje says, opening the door.

The new conduit gold–infused maroon cape in my hands slips to the floor. "I wondered if I'd hear from you before the Swearing-In." I wondered if I'd hear from him at all, given his surprise after my decision at the Iron Shore. As he leans against the open doorway, I scan the way his dreadlocks fall around his shoulders in a privacy screen. "How have you been?"

"Are we really going to do this?" Looking up, he gestures between the two of us. "Or shall we discuss the bomb you dropped before disappearing into the night, at the Glide-By?"

"You're annoyed."

"You walked away."

"I delegated."

Roje snorts.

"You've seen me fighting to remain regent, to stop civil unrest, to defend against monsters from beyond the veil. How could I be queen too?"

"With me," he says quietly. "With me, you could have been. I would have watched your back, as I have done on land. Now

I'll no longer be your first mate."

"You could stay."

The words swell in a looming silence.

"You can be Synestra's liaison, take one of the places on the council. Stay with me." *Be my family*, I don't add. Not yet. While the burn of Kirdan's betrayal has yet to heal. But maybe in the future, when all that's left is a scar and a memory.

"She hasn't agreed to run for queen."

I straighten. "What?"

"This is what happens when you don't communicate, Jazmyne." Roje's eyes flash with anger as they finally meet mine. "I'm left blindsided, something that was too glaringly obvious even for me to lie about; she sees, of course, and her only lasting impression of you is that you're slapdash, mon. Not of your word. Flighty."

Each insult lands like a stab in my belly.

"And you are none of those things," he finishes.

"What of Synestra? The council seats?"

"Don't hold those for us. We might not need them."

"Seriously? Will I end up fighting the Iron Shore too?"

Roje sighs. "I told Synestra about your alliance with the Obeah empress, but she goes by what she's seen. She's talking with the crew, but it could go either way. I'm sorry, Jaz."

"Don't be sorry. Be there, tomorrow."

"At the Swearing-In?"

I nod. "Bring the crew." If anything will convince Synestra, the presence of the Obeah Masters will. There will be no pirate-Obeah alliance. There can't be. "Please. Give me a chance to show her what we can be together. Please, Roje."

"Look—" He rubs his mouth, troubled. "I don't know if I can. If I can't convince her, the others, stay ready. For everything. I know what a fighter you are. It's a shame really, you would have made one hell of a queen." His hand falls away from a smile laden with sorrow, and something else, something guarded. "I was hoping we'd be allies but . . ."

He doesn't need to say it, and I won't—*can't* say it. I wish I could stop myself from thinking it, but the thought pervades. I might find myself fighting more wars than I have allies.

PART III

DON'T WAIT TILL TILL DRUMS BEAT TO GRIND YOUR AXE

40

IRAYA

Four days pass before we find the Unlit.

Our enemy is fast in comparison. It only takes them several hours to identify Zander and Shamar perched on the rooftop across the delta from their town home in the Merchant's Paradise.

But you know what they say about haste.

Had they stopped to consider that there might be more than two soldiers watching them, they would have been ready for Esai, and several more Simbarabo, to intercept them on all three rope bridges leading from their safe house. The struggle is loud enough to ring across the delta to where Kirdan and I watch alongside a unit of Simbarabo. The prisoners will be taken to a home we purchased together in the Horn. To his family and the rest of the island, it's our first as a soon-to-be-wed couple. We know it as something far more sinister. The house on a hill, with only olive groves for neighbors, will become a prison for interrogation.

Kirdan issues silent commands with his fingers. Some of his men take to higher rope bridges. More quiet, frightened residents leave their homes to ascertain the cause of the commotion.

"One down," Kirdan murmurs.

"You're welcome."

I had a theory: after considering what the Unlit have been doing in Aiyca, I determined that wherever the monsters hunt is a distraction to draw the Simbarabo across to the other side of the island. Then the Unlit take the opportunity to surface, do whatever it is that interloping wannabe usurpers do when they're squatting. Despite the doyenne's determination to conceal the Oscuridad, we'd narrowed it down to two settlements thanks to tips from Simbarabo, Zesians, and residents who whisper about monsters made of night. Tonight, when the Oscuridad emerged, we were ready.

It was merely a coincidence that I understood the method in their madness. Not entirely because when the Adairs find a routine that works for us, we keep at it until we can't. I'm not taking what we found as proof of my relation to the Unlit. But the logic is familiar. Worryingly so.

"If everyone knows about the Oscuridad, why hasn't the doyenne come out in the open with the Unlit's presence?" I'd asked Kirdan on the second night, when we ventured out into Changuu city come nightfall, Shamar, Zander, and Esai on our heels in the cramped streets. "I don't accept panic as an excuse." Not after the residents helped.

"Knowing the truth and accepting it are two separate things," was his response.

In the second target area, across the Sadirren Province atop a rope bridge gently swaying beneath my and Kirdan's combined weight, we turn to the next target.

Innocuous, the warehouse sits along a busy row of water-accessible storefronts. Kirdan stares into the night like he's daring it to do anything other than remain dark. It won't. He made sure of that: with the various Simbarabo Squallers hidden across the town, their combined will has summoned a wreath of clouds to block all light.

"Last chance to go and help the others round up the Unlit," he says.

Esai's and Zander's groups are merely catching the rats as they flee from the town house. We are about to infiltrate. From what we've observed over the past few days, the Unlit's numbers won't make this easy.

"Have you forgotten that this trap was my idea?"

"Simbarabo fight differently than Virago, Iraya. We are bastards bred for war, not heroes bred for glory."

I fight a shiver at the edge to his words. "You have my answer. Now, tell me again why you don't want to enter from the roof?" The height advantage is obvious. Not to mention, "We're forfeiting the element of surprise by entering on the ground."

"I don't want them surprised." Kirdan drops his hood. His hair is braided back from his face, highlighting cheekbones that have become even more pronounced with his grief; kohl encircles eyes that are bright with a dangerous sort of light. "I want them ready. I want them to fight." He hops down onto the slatted walkway, strides to the storage front, kicks the door open with a single power-laden blow, and enters.

The screams begin instantly.

Seconds behind him, I cross the threshold into a storefront. A shield balloons from the coin around my neck as I vault across the counter and land between a vast pair of ruined wooden doors. There's a flash of high ceiling, metal mezzanine, and stacked shipping crates before I find Kirdan beneath a swinging pendant light. Skirting several felled bodies, hogtied with golden restraints, I find him grasping another Unlit by a fistful of shirt, their face on the wrong side of his fist once, twice, three times. Save the magical ties, he uses no weapons beyond the brute weight and force of himself. Blood is splattered across his face, his fist—he swaps to the right and keeps going. Another Unlit runs at his back with a golden sword—conduit metal; I erect a shield between them; she hits it with a crunch and falls onto her back. Sparing a glance her way, Kirdan flings the subdued Unlit in hand aside, binds them both with the same restraints as the others without looking, his next target already in sight.

I'm not unimpressed.

Glass smashes above as the rest of the Simbarabo crash the party, swinging down on lambent tethers of magic launched from conduit weapons. What an entrance. By the time their boots hit the concrete, Kirdan has already moved on to another Unlit. He's like a tornado of righteous anger; his love for Lucia tears an ugly but efficient path. There are fewer Unlit to soldiers now. Rather than wading into the fray, I lean back against a crate and observe the enemies' formation. They're all Obeah, I think, and well organized, which tells me they expected to be found beyond hearing the first attack across the delta. Many shout, draw weapons, some magical, but they don't run—at least, not at first. A girl slips past Shamar, launches a blast of will that blows a hole through the wall, and sprints into the dust cloud it creates. Freeing my batons from my shoulder holster, I start after her.

Outside, I'm hit by Zesia's dry humidity. The Unlit girl shields herself against sparking orbs launched by Simbarabo positioned on the rope bridges.

"Stop!" Scanning their number, I spot Esai. "Stop attacking!" I yell, charging after the girl as she disappears around the corner at the top of the row.

"Wait!" he yells after me.

But, in pursuit of answers—why she alone is running— I can't stop.

Around the back of the stores, a lot is lit by a solitary witch-light lamp. The girl drags her feet through litter, old boxes, pieces of crate, like she's searching for something. She glances back; I plaster myself against a large trash can, count to five, and then look again. A wicked knife in hand, the girl drags it across her palm.

Shit.

Propelling myself away from the bin, I hurtle across the yard as a *crack* rings. Before the girl, jade fire erupts from a Summoning Circle. Different than the standard fires, it looks like a doorway. Freeing a knife from my thigh holster, I aim and throw; it nicks the hand the girl was stretching toward the flames. Glancing back at me, her eyes widen. I'm still too far away to stop her.

A hand emerges from within the flames, the dark brown skin unburnt. The girl smirks at me, takes it, and steps into the fire. I throw another knife after their hands; the flames enclose on themselves before I can ascertain if I hit a target, tucking and folding until nothing remains but the smoke trail dissipating into the night—and the Summoning Circle.

"Iraya!" Esai shouts behind me.

Toeing the etchings in the ground, I wait for him to make it to me. "You shouldn't have run alone," he castigates.

"If I'd waited, we wouldn't know how the Unlit have been traveling incognito." I nod down at the circle; rather than being delineated with candles, it's been formed of glyphs— Summoning Glyphs, Communication Glyphs, and others I can't name. "Have someone you trust copy this down," I tell Esai. "I suspect it will be the first of many that will need to be removed from across the island. Is Kirdan done?"

He shakes his head. "He started interrogations. He's in the warehouse. Simbarabo are taking the majority to the house, but one of the Unlit asked for you by name, said he's an uncle— don't run again!" The soldier grabs my arm and immediately drops it like it burned him. "Forgive me, Empress. I'll sift you there. You shouldn't be out in the open if they were expecting you to be here."

"And we suspect they were."

Though it's not a question, Esai nods.

"Permission to touch you—to hold your arm." Flushing, the young soldier looks everywhere but my face.

"Permission granted."

We appear behind a solitary Unlit on his knees before

Kirdan. The general scans me from head to toe before tipping his head to the side in question. As to which, I don't know. Am I hurt? No. Did I get the answers I sought? One of them. Now I'm left with more.

"Tell your general about the Summoning Circle," I mutter to Esai, prowling around the prisoner; Kirdan concedes his position so that I take point.

The man is unremarkable. Older, with copper hairs in his beard, lines in the corners of his eyes, his mouth. There is no immediate sense of kin, but would there be? It's been over a decade since I saw most of Mama's side of the family.

"You asked for me," I say.

"And who are you?" His voice is deep, slightly breathless.

"Iraya Adair."

The man huffs a humorless laugh. "She said you'd come."

"Who?"

"Aiyca's true leader."

She, not They, as we were first told.

"And I'm not Aiyca's true leader?"

"You are an imposter," he spits. "*The* imposter, who fooled Cwenburg's shields, several Masters calling themselves a council in Aiyca, and the Alumbrar regent. But you have not fooled those of us who knew Iraya Adair."

Delyse said my order didn't see me enough. A third of the shields were killed, the rest remanded in Cwenburg's holding cells. She was right. Anyone could have claimed responsibility for the sign I left before leaving for Zesia. Shit.

I glance at Kirdan, Zander, Shamar, and Esai, my only company. If a show of my naevus is what it will take, that's what it will take. Let Oscuridad, more Unlit, come at the lighting of my beacon. We can take care of them too.

Summoning my naevus is different to calling my magic; where the latter comes at a sprint, my naevus is less of a creature under my control and more of the most intrinsic, ancestral parts of me. It's always alert, awake; it only needs me to look its way.

"My gods." The Unlit's mouth drops open at the corona of white-gold light engulfing my body. Following the breathing patterns I've read about in the Grimoire, I isolate that light to my scarification and let it dim elsewhere across my body.

"Do you believe me now?"

"B-but—" The Unlit swallows. "She told us she was unable to secure her magic. She said you would use tricks, but that feeling . . ."

"What feeling?"

"Your naevus." He blinks up at me in wonder. "That's how your mama's would make us feel whenever she would use it. Like—like home. Like every Adair who ever lived was in the room, reminding us that while they may have died, they weren't gone. Iraya Adair." He dips his head. "Forgive me, Empress."

"Isn't it niece?"

A sheepish expression on his face, the man glances over his shoulders at the Simbarabo. "I might have fabricated our relation to spare my life. But I do know Adairs! The Lost Empress—that is to say, the witch telling everyone that she is the Lost Empress—she is an Adair. She's rallying many of your kin, who have been in hiding mostly while the Alumbrar have ruled."

"Adairs are in the Unlit?" Kirdan asks, moving to stand by me.

"Dear boy," the Unlit says. "Since the outcasts' inception have Adairs been in the Unlit."

I don't look at Kirdan to gauge his reaction.

"It was one of the Adair empresses herself who stripped the first of her relations of their magic. She sent them to the island's fringes after a dispute about which of them deserved to rule more. Of course," this chatty prisoner goes on to say, "all seems to be forgiven now the Lost Empress—er, the pretender, is in power."

"Iraya?" Kirdan turns to me. "Did you know about this?"

"Jazmyne said something to the effect," I admit. "I wanted it confirmed, and it hasn't been."

"But—"

I silence the prisoner with a look. "I want to hear from someone who has a stake in the fight for Aiyca, not a man fooled by a witch who gave my name and several shitty excuses as to why she couldn't prove it magically."

"She was convincing enough without the magic," the Unlit mutters. "No offense."

"What else can you share?" I demand. "Do you know their next plan of attack? Do you know what they plan to do with Aiyca? Do you know what the glyphs on the Summoning Circles you've been using to travel across the islands mean?"

Shifting, the Unlit looks between Kirdan and me. "I don't know the answers to most of those questions. But I know what the pretender wants." His dark gaze settles on me. "You. They plan to kill you before their army, before your army, to prove that you are the one who is pretending."

That's not news.

"What of Zesia, why were you here?"

"To prevent the island offering Aiyca aid. She expects to take most parishes within the next two phases. By the time you arrive back home, she will have turned everyone against you—even the Alumbrar regent."

"Oh?"

"She will spare her life, and those of her order, if she concedes the throne."

Then my likelihood of traveling back into Aiyca, after all that's gone, and all that remains to pass, is reliant upon Jazmyne keeping her word and holding the line.

Shit.

41

JAZMYNE

I thought I knew the worst of what was coming.

Even before my talk with Roje, hours ago now. War. Many deaths—including the possibility of my own. But it isn't until Iraya requested this summit with her side, mine, and the shields who feel more like ours now, that it hits me. We're here. It's happened. We're at the point of no return. All things considered, our meeting feels both timely and too late, the morning of the Swearing-In.

"The Imposter Empress knows you're coming home?" I repeat Iraya's words back to her reflection in the Mirror of Two Faces. "*She* knows. I don't understand the significance."

Not of Iraya's words, or how they precipitated this summit she demanded at the break of dawn, when her shouting from the mirror in the bathroom roused me out of a tense sleep. Uncertain if I'm alone and desperate not to be, I look first to Anya, and then to Ford and Nel, almost brushing noses with each given how closely we're all crammed onto the chaise in my study, with me holding the mirror between us.

"When you announced yourself in Zesia," Anya begins, "it was clear—"

"Empress."

Anya frowns down at Ford from her seat on the back of the settee. "Pardon me?"

"It's *when you announced yourself in Zesia*, Empress."

Iraya's reflection raises two amused eyebrows.

One of Anya's knees digs into my back. "I wasn't aware a decision had been made regarding your succession, *Empress*."

"That's quite all right," Iraya says, magnaminously. The cheek of her.

"We should have started further back," Kirdan says, before Anya or I can bite back at Iraya. He still has that measured consideration from the mirror's surface, in that measured way of his that used to put me at ease. Now I can only wonder what his angle is. "This is the first time we've all spoken together, rather than relying on pieces of information here or there." He exchanges a look with Iraya. She nods.

Nonverbal cues. Interesting.

"Here's what we know: the Imposter plans to oust Iraya as the pretender, and she'll attempt to use you to help her do it, Jazmyne. Whether you comply or not."

Our eyes meet. His shift away first.

"Last night, we discovered that the Unlit have been traveling beyond the veil. It's why we've been unable to track them with much success in Zesia."

"Wait—" Anya grabs my wrist and turns it toward where

she's perched on the back of the settee, so that she can see Kirdan. "You mean to say they're doing the same in Aiyca?"

"That would explain why no armies have been seen," Nel adds. "It's the sort of cleverness we should expect, if the Imposter is an Adair."

Rather than address the subtle question, Iraya says, "The Unlit are using Summoning Circles to call the beasts, who then help them cross the veil. I've only seen creatures on six legs or more, and a few with wings, but the hand I saw last night looked like it belonged to something standing, like you and me. We have to factor in that there will be kinds of Oscuridad we've yet to encounter, and that the Imposter likely won't let you see them all until I've returned home. It's not a trap, since she'll know I know, but she does have an advantage we can't ignore."

"Is she your relative?" I demand.

"It's looking like she might be." Those rings of golden fire around Iraya's otherwise dark eyes seems to flare. "Waiting for me to return home means she'll want Aiyca firmly in hand. She's working on the Obeah, but so am I through the council of Masters."

"And if she shows herself before you come home?"

"You contact me, and I'll find someone to sift me to Aiyca."

Not Kirdan? They sit together, but they don't look any closer than they did the last time I saw them together. Unless they're pretending. . . . It shouldn't matter, but he threw me away for her, and I can't see why.

"Your advice is hubristic, even for you." I scoff. "You can't stave off the war alone."

"Jazmyne's right," Kirdan says.

I hate that my heart still responds to praise from him.

"We need real solutions. Now."

No one responds. How *can* we guard against an invisible moving army, with its monsters and magic and might? In the palace beyond my study, low-level noise thrums as attendants shepherd food and floral arrangements outside to the Courtyard of Moons. The council's Swearing-In is hours away, and I haven't heard from the Obeah Masters since our meeting, but—the *Masters*. I might have a way for them to prove their merit to me.

"The Summoning Circles," I begin. "We could station Obeah by them, to watch, not to engage, and develop an index of their beasts. Once we have that, we can work on strategy to defeat them. Some métiers will be better than others, and we have Obeah Masters adept in strategy who can lead their respective fields in battle."

"Right." Ford draws the letters out, slowly. "And we could assign métiers to then guard those specific circles."

"That divides our army." Nel stands to pace away from the sofa. "And doesn't help fortify wherever the final stand will be."

"No. But it tracks the monsters," Iraya says. "If each métier knows which beast they're responsible for, location doesn't matter. They will assemble wherever the battle demands. It's a good plan. You can see to that, Regent?"

"I can."

"And what will you do when the Imposter propositions you?"

"You think she will?"

"It would be easier for her if you were alive," Anya answers. "You speak for the Alumbrar, and you can help her control whatever narrative she wishes to push across the island. Two voices condemning Iraya will be more believable than hers alone."

For all her faults, and regardless of what will pass between Iraya and me after the Unlit have been defeated—we will defeat them, we have to. They with monsters on call cannot be allowed free rein of my island.

"I won't capitulate to the Imposter."

"I hope you mean that," Iraya says. "The Unlit here will be reporting my every move to her, and we're close to finding answers about how to nullify the Oscuridad. My return is imminent. More so than it ever has been. That means the moment you leave the palace, Regent, she will come for you. As an Adair—" I think we all watch Iraya swallow—"she'll kill anyone who gets between the two of you."

It's what I would do, she doesn't need to add.

"I'll do my part," I tell her, surprising myself when my voice doesn't shake. "You'll come home when?"

"We have a meeting with a witch who knows her monsters. Depending on what she has to say, I'll return in less than a phase."

"With the Simbarabo." Anya doesn't ask.

"Yes," Kirdan answers.

Allies to enemies in a matter of words.

"How will you arrive here, and where?"

"Let me come back to you with that information," Iraya

says. "It won't be a port, though; likely a bay. Will you ensure we have entry?"

"I will let the Sea Defense Captain know today."

Iraya nods. "Before we go, do you have writing tools at hand?"

She describes the Summoning Circle, the strange glyphs it consisted of. Ford sketches, intermittently raising his facsimile up for her approval.

"That's it," she says, the final time he holds his rendering aloft. "You should concentrate on the cities, of course, but don't forget the country. We don't want to be—"

"Ringed," Nel calls across the study. "We know."

"Until you return," I tell Iraya, Kirdan.

"Hold that line" are her parting words before the reflection turns blank.

Ford falls back against the settee with a long exhale. "She looked good. You saw, didn't you? I didn't want to tell her, you know, but I thought she looked good. Strong."

"Don't you have somewhere to be?" Anya swings her legs onto the floor.

"Wait—Ford, I need you to get a message to Master Omnyra. I'd like to speak with her before tonight's festivities." There's a fair being held at the foot of the palace mount following the Swearing-In later this morning, with vendors and food stalls. I was meant to attend with the new council.

He stands and stretches. "I'll see what I can do."

"No, you have to just *do*!"

Nel straightens; Ford lowers his arms; Anya rounds the settee.

"Whaap'm?" my sistren asks.

"Iraya said the Imposter would remove all obstacles to get to me."

"If you *left*." Anya takes my hands.

"Would Iraya wait for me to leave?" Inside my chest, my heart thumps hard enough to hurt. "Did she wait for the doyenne to leave? She made sure she was brought here, inside this palace. She didn't let anything stand between her and what she wanted." The Imposter is an Adair too, lest we forget. "Has Adriel's shipment of gold arrived yet?"

"I'm not sure— What is it? What's wrong?"

The room spins. I don't think I'm taking in enough air. "I think her relative might attempt to take me today."

If Iraya is as close to returning as she says she is, I am the key to her reaccessing Aiyca.

She cannot open the door, win the conflict, if I am dead.

42

IRAYA

How do you fight the worst parts of yourself when you've always relied on them to survive?

I look askance at Kirdan, to check if he heard my thought. He walks beside me in silence, as he has since the summit ended. Somehow, I know it's not so much that he doesn't have anything to say. He's waiting for me. I think he's taking the longest route possible down to the stables, where Niusha waits for our journey to Nyxia.

You can't stave off the war alone, Jazmyne said earlier. The sentiment isn't new. Delyse has been drumming it into me—or she was, when she was here. Our correspondence has been less personal, with her back in Aiyca. I sent across a sketch of the Summoning Circle we discovered in the Merchant's Paradise yesterday, but she's yet to reply. On the one hand it's a comfort that nothing of merit needs reporting, but anything she says will be a ripple in the greater ocean of trouble Aiyca is in; just as I couldn't tell Kirdan Adairs might have been in the Unlit, initially, I can't say what I'm thinking out loud now either.

There is a witch in Aiyca telling everyone she's me, with success. She's rallying Aiycans with the Adair name. How many will I have to hurt before I can convince them who I am? We were lucky in the Merchant's Paradise. Several light shows later, and where there were once Unlit, I have a handful of loyal magi willing to do anything I ask. But the few are always more amenable than the many. Another part of this relative's plan, I bet. Judair was formidable, but she was Alumbrar. Fighting this Imposter will be like fighting my looking-glass self. Not quite the same, but still difficult.

Obeah do not kill Obeah.

"Are you listening in?"

Kirdan doesn't miss a beat. "You're not broadcasting, and I wouldn't probe."

"I don't understand."

"I can explain."

"Later." Our weird mental connection is the least of my worries in this moment. "Right now, I need to know if the words I say out loud can also be overheard." I nod at a passing guest, who gapes at Kirdan and I. Twin storm clouds in our dark tunics, pants, we travel with speed through the marble halls.

"Consider whatever we say private." Kirdan's conduit coin flares in the pommel on his hip, and a membrane-like golden film encloses around us.

"Before we left Aiyca the first time, you told me war makes killers out of most, and heroes out of few. You said you wouldn't let me become the former. How?"

He turns to look down at me.

"Believe me, if there was anyone else I could ask—"

"Don't do that." His voice is soft. "Don't reduce this."

I look away first. He's right. Things have been different between us for a while.

"Fine. Tell me. Please."

"You're asking about it. You're thinking, feeling. In Aiyca you moved alone, you consulted no one. Anything you felt was suffocated into submission by your rage."

"That was easy."

"For me to summarize, yeh mon. For you to live, no. I know that it's a struggle to make the right choices when the wrong ones are easier. You with Aiyca, and me with my uncles. Being a killer comes down to flesh and metal. Being something more?" Kirdan releases a humorless laugh. "It's the same thing. Only, instead of cutting someone else, you take the hits. And you stand to take many of them, Iraya."

Our eyes meet. The palace around us is reduced to insignificance.

"If you weren't questioning yourself, something would be wrong."

"I don't know if I can kill her, the Imposter," I admit.

Pressing his lips together, Kirdan nods. "Then you're already better than she is."

"I didn't say I wouldn't."

"You didn't say you would." Kirdan places a hand on my lower back and steers me down a set of stone steps. His touch is both light and heavy against the straps of the breastplate he had made for me. "Sometimes you have to go into the darkness to find the light."

When we reach the bottom, he doesn't remove his hand.

I don't tell him to.

In the stables, Niusha, pewter eyes brightening in recognition, almost bowls me over in her excitement. The shadowcat is as large as most of the steeds housed, but wider, built for endurance and sleek speed in ways they are not.

Hands stroking through the fur that looks aubergine the longer I focus, as I remember it did the first time I met her, I follow Kirdan around the stable as he retrieves a saddle, bags. "We're riding the entire way?"

"Once we've sifted there. The actual city is glyphed from sight until you pass through its wards." He summons two scarves and passes one my way before tying the second across his mouth.

"To stop others entering, or the twin getting out?"

He glances at me across Niusha's back. "Both."

The concern and a little excitement about what we'll find is a great enough distraction against the feel of Kirdan at my back when we mount Niusha, and the reminder of the last time we were this close. His chest to my back. His breath against my neck.

"Hold on," he murmurs.

"To what?"

One strong arm slides around my waist, draws me back against an indomitable chest; the other takes the reins in hand.

"To me."

My stomach tightens.

"The landing will be rough."

Somewhere . . . lower . . . tightens.

The ride too, I suspect.

Moments later, the sift spits us out in an ocean of wavelike dunes.

We barely hit the sand before Niusha bounds into a leap, another, and breaks into a canter, wide paws distributing her weight on the shifting beads. A shimmering shield of magic is all that protects my eyes from the sand that surges around us; combined with his weight against my back, Kirdan's arm, a vise around my waist, keeps me atop the shadowcat.

There is little to see, and little opportunity, with Niusha's speed, but I feel the power of the coruscating shield around the city before I see the iridescent shimmer of its wall. Blown back with the force of its might, my head knocks against Kirdan's chin as Niusha breaks through it, and we skid to a stop before an undulating ruin entrenched in a valley of sand.

For the vastness of the dunes, this locale seems stifling. Claustrophobic. While the sky seems to press down in a smothering weight, there is less sun. Less . . . life.

"Can you feel why I didn't want to come here in the night?" Kirdan dismounts; I follow, something atavistic about my urge to mirror his movements. He has been here before and survived to talk about it.

I don't get the impression everyone who's been here can say the same.

"What is this place?"

"The Oasis of the Singing Sands." His kohl-lined eyes, all

that's visible of his face thanks to his scarf, look toward the rising dunes, and the dead civilization between them. Stone-blasted facades have been decimated; roofs have been torn from their height, whether by wind or by hand I don't know. None of the latter lingers here now. Only the soft moans of a susurrus as it billows through gaping doorways.

It's hard to imagine living in a place like this out of choice.

"It's a prison, isn't it?"

"In a different way than Changuu once was, yeh mon."

Lucia's twin must be in need of everything . . . *gods-dam-nit*. We didn't bring anything in exchange for the story.

"Kirdan, we forgot—" My words die at the sight of his hair. It doesn't move, not so much as twitch, in the winds that ulu-late through the crumbling archway to the city in the sands. My own braids lie still on my shoulders too. It would be eas-ier to explain away their weight, but my diaphanous train is limp also. When I speak again, it's something quieter than a whisper as my hand creeps to the baton over my left shoulder. "What happened here?"

"This was once a thriving oasis in Zesia," Kirdan returns; like mine, his voice is low; his hand rests atop his conduit weapon too. "You know how respected water is here. There was a great lake, an invention of magic. A settlement of Obeah who disagreed with the doyenne's edict to keep Alumbrar sweet retreated here. They lived for many years without contention." He shifts his body, chest to me, left shoulder to the open west; right to the still, quiet ruin. "Travelers would come to the Oasis of the Singing Sands and tell their tales before venturing into the island's cities for trade," Kirdan continues. "They'd leave items behind, so they could forever be remembered. I think that's what attracted her here. Lucia was certain of it."

"Her sister?"

Kirdan nods. "Lucia's ability to discern emotions, to extract them from items, tired her twin, Nyxia, and so she sought to claim the strength of stories herself."

The oasis is void of people, yet thick with atmosphere, with tension. Any fool could see what Nyxia took from the oasis. Might its inhabitants' bones remain, or did she consume those too?

"It took travelers too long to stop coming. Lucia did all she could to warn them, even went as far as collecting items in the hope that she could sate her twin's appetite, but . . . it was too late. Nyxia became as dark as her namesake, as unforgiving. Doyenne Divsylar trapped her here herself, in the tomb she turned this oasis into, with guzzu from the Adair Grimoire."

"Mama?"

"Oversaw everything."

"Don't suppose you could have told me that before we came here, mon."

"Would it have stopped you?"

"No. But I might have brought more weapons."

Kirdan runs eyes as hard as stone over me. "You are the only weapon you need. Come. Niusha will wait here for us."

The moment we enter the city, the winds stop. Air turns stale and dense. It's the sort of day that fills your spirit as well as your bones, a thing with fingers that twist through your insides and drag you down from your very core until, senses dulled, your body grows increasingly heavy while your head seems to lighten. It's harder than it has been since losing the Impediment Glyphs to muster my will. Channeling through the breastplate is as difficult as crossing this sand. It's risen in this city without feet, brooms, running pickney, to scatter it. When my batons light, it's without their typical lambency.

Go back, their dull glow seems to say. *Leave this place.*

"Where does Nyxia live?" I pant, my lungs as heavy as my limbs.

"I don't know." Kirdan's words are thick. He too is affected by this strange place, the lull of it, the lack of ebb and flow. "But it doesn't matter. She'll find us."

And so she does; creeping close enough that I hear her only when she is a breath away. Stepping out of her reach, I turn, smile.

"Wahan. Nyxia, I presume?"

The day is thick with heat. You wouldn't know it by the cape this witch sports, the oversized hood in which no features are discernible. There is only a stench of things best left unconsidered.

"Have you come for a story?" is rasped from the depths of the hood.

"Yes," Kirdan answers.

"There will need to be payment."

"I have that covered."

"Then come this way," the witch croons.

I'm not too lethargic of mind that I don't notice how nimble she is across the sand. If she doesn't remove that hood when we arrive at her home, I might have to tug it off myself to see what she hides beneath.

Her villa is less desolate than others we pass. Several walls are missing, but those that remain hold up a woven rooftop. Inside is another matter. It's filthy with dirt and detritus. Rugs emit clouds of dust beneath our feet; every surface is cluttered with furniture, some upturned, others righted. It's like a home that was half destroyed, and left a mess. Not a liveable one, I would have thought.

"Drink?" At home in her chaotic surroundings, Nyxiz fumbles with wide, squat bowls the color of ivory and mud.

My stomach turns.

"Blessings, but I'm fasting. Prince?"

Before Kirdan can refuse, Nyxia reaches for a jug amidst a mound of stained sheets and pours into one of the cups before offering it to Kirdan. Rust-colored dirt is caked beneath her long, yellowed nails.

"You think us unlearned of your ways, griot," he says, folding his arms. "We will take only one thing from you, a story we request. And you will have only the one item from us in exchange."

A hoarse sputtering gutters from beneath the hood. "Very well." She tosses both cups onto the pile of sheets by the jug. "Which story do you wish to hear, Prince Divsylar? Oh yes," she adds, before he can ask how she knows who he is. "My sister spoke of you often. Why didn't she come? I haven't seen her in these long years."

"She's dead," I answer. "And we're looking for a story to bring her killers to justice."

Though she's shrouded in fabric, I notice Nyxia stiffen.

"Dead?"

Her long-fingered hands raise to the hood. "Someone killed Lucia?" is rasped from pink lips that bloom like petals in a face that could summon spring, it's so delicate, so fine and pretty. A surprise, after her nails, her voice.

A trap.

Her youth comes from digesting people, their stories, and while she might not have made it out of this oasis for a time, that's not to say others from across the waters beyond the Great Ocean haven't stumbled across this place, their homes too far away to hear what happened to the loose-lipped before them. Which begs the question, why didn't Mama prevent people coming *inside*? Why didn't Doyenne Divsylar?

They couldn't. The unwelcome thought slithers into my mind. Not all magic is understood yet.

"When did she die?" Nyxia bats long lashes at Kirdan, and then me.

"Too soon."

"Then her Nine Night still happens." Her eyes are a soft, youthful brown; they make her anguish all the more pitiable.

Still, Kirdan does not drop his hand from the snarling shadowcat atop his saber, and I reach deep inside for my own toothed predator.

"We wish to know—"

"About the Hendern Cliffs," I interrupt. We have but the one story. I know this to be a success; there's little point wasting our chance asking generally about the Unlit's pets. "Tell us the story of the monsters that attempted to conquer Aiyca by sea."

Kirdan shifts beside me. "Iraya—"

"Adair?" My surname shoots from between Nyxia's lips arrow-fast, and just as sharp.

"Yeh mon. Heard of me?"

"Travelers still seek out this pocket of Zesia."

As I suspected.

The witch eases herself into a patchwork chair. "I knew your mama, girl."

"Empress."

Nyxia cocks her head. The move dislodges her mournful mask and reveals a glimpse of the true creature she is underneath. Lucia I didn't think old but . . . there is an agelessness, an arrogance born of immortality, in Nyxia's expression.

I tip my head in recognition. One apex predator greeting another.

"However entertaining I'm sure the tale would be, we won't waste this time hearing a story from your past." I shrug one shoulder. "So, the Hendern Cliffs?"

"As you wish." Her blink is slow, deliberate. Skin shutters down over brown and rises to reveal milky white—not standard fare for griots who are not Bonemantises. But Nyxia isn't a standard Obeah-witch. I'd challenge that she isn't human enough to be a witch at all. "The monsters came from the water," she intones, her voice reinforced with the voices of many, her ancestors. Might Lucia join her once her Nine Nights have come to pass? "They crawled from a great chasm at the bottom of the seabed where they watched witch rulers come and go, and decided that they were far cleverer, far more deserving of homes on land. And so they battled the empress and her people. A folly. These witches sent the creatures back from whence they came, locking them in together with guzzu and repellents to those not of this earth."

"The stone," Kirdan says. "How did they manage to turn the creature to stone?"

Nyxia smiles slow. "Will, Prince. Will. The war was bound and broken by three."

"Three, not seven?" I ask.

"You know the significance of numbers, Empress."

Three rulers within the empire, once.

Three islands engaged in conflict with one another, once.

Three ruling families, again. Soon.

"I'm not sure we know anything," Kirdan points out. "You haven't given us any details."

"You should have specified, I'm afraid." She blinks; the white clears from her eyes. "And now there's the matter of my payment."

Kirdan starts forward. "Now wait—"

"I'll take the Adair witch."

I cock my head. "You can try."

"Your mention of three intimates that I'll need her," Kirdan says. "The empire will."

Then he knows what *bound and broken by three* means too. Or thinks he knows.

"Come, Nyxia," I coax. "Let's not fight. If you help us, I can reconsider this prison you're in."

Nyxia laughs. "What care I for an empire that imprisoned me here? Or a sister who leeched my magic from me until everything I was—beloved, beautiful—withered and twisted into this creature who relies on the stories of others to remain even half as beautiful as I was in my youth?" She runs an idle finger along her chair's patchwork arm; it rustles in a manner that draws the eye closer to what looks like . . . *hair*. It isn't fabric, as I first thought. It's pieces of *skin*. "I've wanted my sister dead for many decades, Prince. And now she is gone, I can have both. Beauty, and the blood and bones I've come to rely on to sustain me." In the time it takes to blink, she pushes herself up and out of the chair. "You can get in my way and die too, if you wish. There's something between the two of you." A dark red tongue darts out to drag across her bottom lip. "A story of suppressed feelings. I don't doubt you'd taste delicious as a pair, but I need only the one of you, the Adair witch."

"Stand aside, Kirdan. I'll take care of this."

"Actually . . ."

I glance at him, note the hesitation in his face, the hand that's fallen from his weapon.

The floor falls away at my feet, because even *now* I'm still surprised by this bag-o-wire.

"That's right, Prince," Nyxia croons. "Go."

He doesn't look at her. That unrelenting focus is, as always, on me. "What will you do, Iraya, when you have no further reason to hate me? She's not staying, witch." Kirdan takes my hand; I'm so stunned, I let him. "And neither am I."

On his final word, our magic awakens with a roar.

"Remember," Kirdan instructs as a golden sphere expands around the two of us. "For the bond to work you need to want this. You need to want life. You need to want me." He swallows. "As I want you."

Nyxia collides against the shield; spit foams at her mouth

corners, and her clawed hands beat against the magical protection. Dust rains down from the ceiling, the earth beneath our feet trembles, and yet the shield does not fall. It does not waver. And not because of me.

I take Kirdan in, the scope and gall of him, his quiet confidence as Nyxia's screams ring on and larger debris bounces off the shield.

"You could let me die," I breathe. "Leave the story eater to do to me what she has done to so many others. Delyse and Shamar would question your actions, yeh mon, but you needn't have worried about them until the Unlit threat passed. Why, Kirdan?" His fingers tighten at his name. "Why are you helping me?"

He huffs a disbelieving laugh and then, with a sudden mercurial shift, grips my forearms, drawing our bodies closer together so that I feel his words against my mouth as well as hear their whispered hoarseness.

"Because, you *idiot*, I—" Steady with a silencing fury, his eyes say what his lips cannot; just as suddenly as he held me near, he pushes me back. "Why do you ask when you *know*." His thumb drags across my hand. "Into the darkness."

To find the light.

We are the same. The same. The same.

My naevus raises its head and bares its teeth at Nyxia.

With a tumultuous roar of magic, she's repelled backward from the shield as though kicked and sent through a wall. A phantom touch brushes against my cheek, and then Kirdan spirits us away, back to Niusha, before the house turns entirely to rubble.

43

JAZMYNE

Atop the royal balcony overlooking the Courtyard of Moons, there is little to remind me of the last time I stood here with the late doyenne. Then, prior to the premature announcement of the Yielding's cancellation, my order seemed indomitable, perennial. As stalwart as the north star. I decided we couldn't risk a night of stars for this late afternoon's Swearing-In. Maybe darkness would have helped. The setting sun's rich hues burnish the staff, the court, Dada's family—all I would allow—in a weak light the color of a dulled weapon. Indeed, they seem fragile.

Laughter travels up the mount, from the fair below I won't partake in later. Can't. If I survive. Oh gods. Please let me survive this.

Don't let the Unlit come.

It would be the perfect opportunity to make a stand. Seer's Eyes sold out, purchased by all unable to enter the palace to witness the first new council in ten years. The glyphed clear orb produces an internal smoke, inside which, with corresponding glyphs incised into my platform, my address will appear in miniature. Everything that happens here is visible and audible. All that cannot be seen is the sheer number of Xanthippe present, armed with their new conduit gold accessories.

At my left elbow, Anya leans in. "There's still no sign of Roje and the crew."

"And what of the Obeah Masters?"

"I can't see them either. I'm sorry, Jazmyne."

Disappointment is an old friend of mine, and yet it never loses its bitterness. First I'd hoped this address would be before the secular and nonsecular alike; then I planned on utilizing the night to win Synestra around. At least the council will be in place after this. For whatever comes next.

"Niece?"

Adorned in maroon and gold, Galene drifts across to where I sit on the throne.

"Are you not feeling well?" She lays a soft hand against my brow. "You look fevered. Didn't you take the tincture I left for you earlier?"

Drinking a bath-sized portion wouldn't have helped. I cast another look around the balcony, at Ivan and Demar with Ionie, Ormine, and Mariama, the council witches and parish custos, my Stealth cadre standing guard with their trainee couplets. Wise.

"Jazmyne?" Aunty moves into my line of sight. Lines of concern undulate across her forehead. "You're worrying me.

Perhaps we can reschedule this for a time when you are feeling better. You and I might take a walk away from here."

No walks. No leaving the palace grounds.

"All is well, Aunty," I lie.

"Sorry to interrupt," Anya says. "But are you ready? If you want the court to spend time at the fair before curfew, we need to begin the Swearing-In now."

With the tightness in my throat second only to the grip of terror in my stomach, I nod.

"Did you still plan to swear me in as your second?"

My stomach plummets. "Oh, Anya. Forgive me, I forgot."

"That's fine. Good actually."

"You don't want to?"

"I do, but . . . I think the evening will already run long with the number of presiders and war council members to be sworn in. I can wait."

"No. No, we can do it tonight."

"I can wait. The sooner this event is over with the better." Leaning in, she presses a quick kiss to my left cheek. "We can celebrate once the war is won."

Perhaps it's guilt at my lack of forethought that makes my body feel heavier than usual as I push up using the arms of the throne, and make the short walk to the balustrade. For a moment it tips forward; the world tips, and I with it. We hang, suspended, on the edge of something both terrible and great. War and peace. Defeat and victory. Anya's conduit beams on her chest, casting a shaft of light out into the crowd of less than six hundred; they quiet and shift to me.

"Wahan, Alumbrar," I call down to the gathering, and beyond. "From light we are born."

"And to light we cleave" is returned.

My words stick in my throat, turn at odd angles in protest. "By now, many of you will know that war is knocking, and if we must, we will answer. But I am doing my best, alongside our allies, to fortify our doors. To take a stand against those who would see us beneath them." I draw a breath, another. "These are strange times, in which relying on tradition could prove to be the weak joint we put our weight atop only to fall down. To do so would mean being trampled by our enemies—our enemy. For a long while that has been the Obeah. But not any longer. We have a new enemy—" Whisperings spark in the gathering below, forcing me to raise my voice. "One that is both known and unknown to us all, Alumbrar, Obeah, Aiycan. The Unlit. I confirm what my envoys have recently relayed, not to frighten you, though I understand that fear during this time will be unavoidable. I tell you because this island has been under threat for far longer than we have known, and will be for a while longer yet." I look to the new council members waiting to be sworn in. "But we gather tonight for a joyful cause. Please join me in welcoming Aiyca's newest Witches Council, as well as the parish presiders who will be on hand for all maladies." I clap hard enough to dislodge the shake in my hands as the group of fourteen Alumbrar fan out to my right. With the island watching, I wish there were Obeah and pirates in the mix, but none of them wanted these roles. No one else wanted to step forward for this island. "The oath to put Aiyca ahead of oneself is a

452

promise," I begin, reading from a script the late doyenne used. "One that—"

"You cannot keep."

Stiffening, I turn to the voice traveling across the balcony. Ionie. Flanked by Ormine and Mariama, her face is tight with a wicked fury.

"Tonight," she continues, turning from me to the gathering below, "we stand against this witch, who is not the best advocate to usher us through these trying times. Magicless. Inexperienced. Idealistic. You heard her, Alumbrar—" Magically amplified, her voice carries far and wide. "She dismisses the traditions that have permitted us to rule without defeat this past decade. Where is the Yielding? Where is the ceremony that has kept us safe this past decade? War has come to our threshold, and yet there is no mention of selecting the next Yielders. It is clear that with Regent Cariot in charge, the gods will forsake us. And so—" As one, all three witches jerk forward. "We invoke the Rite of Challenge to oust this pickney from the throne before the Unlit bring war to our doors."

Everything falls away but the ring of their words. Rite of Challenge.

I've never heard of such a thing.

"What say you, Regent?" Ormine asks with relish, when she has barely been able to function since believing her eldest son dead. And yet here she stands wielding my title with a pointed malice that strikes me in the center of my back.

"What do I say?" Though my voice is not as loud as theirs, as magically consuming, it carries in the silence. "My power isn't one that can be worn around the neck or carried in hand.

But it is one I can wield. It's one I *will* wield toward the enemy—toward all enemies who mean to stand between Aiyca and safety. Whether that is because they mean to sunder it, or wrest it from the rightful hands of its leader—one who inherits her title from the Supreme Being Themselves." I stood before seven Obeah Masters and challenged them. I stood before Iraya Adair and challenged her. Let them see firsthand that I do not cow in the face of an impossible threat. "To invoke an archaic rite I have never once heard of is to damn *yourselves* in the eyes of the gods."

"But what about in the eyes of your fellow women?" The words are spoken in unison by all three presiders from the pits of their stomachs, their voices deep enough to incite an army of gooseflesh across my body.

The presiders go up in golden flames.

Screams rend the night below; Anya grabs my arm, draws me back. Even as we stumble back, the crowd begins to shriek, to call out with unfettered horror, terror. The flames shrink, reducing in size until each presider carries a fist-sized ember around her neck where her conduit hangs.

"In the eyes of your fellow woman," they continue with their unsettling bass. "Your time is over."

Anya and I mirror one another's expression of stunned terror. I have never seen Alumbrar use magic like that before, never seen them act this way before.

"Seize them," I order, my voice hoarse.

Ford and three additional shields materialize from the dark in a slow build of gold, silver, and white—they are more than the missing stars in the heavens, they are a spectacle in their own right. One that fills the night in a way I wouldn't have thought I'd be grateful for.

"Blasphemer!" Ionie hisses. "You work with Obeah?"

Below, the audience begins to murmur, to stir. I can't lose them to this coup.

"I have learned more lessons than I can count since the late doyenne's assassination. The most pressing is that war cannot be won without allies."

"In that, Regent Cariot, we agree."

Master Omnyra crosses the balcony; she is accompanied by two additional Masters from Golden Grove, the Warrior and the Artisan of Metal. My legs weaken with gratitude, with relief. Of course she knew what I needed. Her. Them.

"No other leader has ascended to the throne with war on the horizon," the Obeah Master Bonemantis says, stopping by my side. "I think that, even if we don't yet know how to get along together, we can accept that we will not survive apart."

Taking advantage of the interruption, Ford takes Ionie by the arm; the other two shields with him attach themselves to Ormine and Mariama too, and then all six retreat backward across the balcony, inside the suite, and out of sight.

"Know this"—Master Omnyra looks to me, her third-eye scarification almost winking in the late afternoon light, and takes my left hand—"Aiyca's Obeah can accept that it will be Regent Cariot's holding of the line that will enable us to see tomorrow, and all the days beyond it."

Here it is, my sign of trust.

Squeezing her hand, I raise our arms. "The late doyenne's remaining presiders will not cost us this island; they do not know my reach. Behold, it is great enough to unite two orders who, while neighbors, have always been worlds apart. Know this, Alumbrar: we are of one many people, and it will take all the peoples of this island to stand against the Unlit and the rising dark. I ask you to put aside your misapprehension for the greater good, for the only good. We say our skies are darker when we lose a loved one. Look above you, Alumbrar. The dark is kept back only with light. My new council will be a perennial dawn. A star-laden night. Behold," I repeat.

There is no applause, but there is no protest either. I haven't the time to linger on the island's reaction, not as I continue reading from my script. Three Alumbrar are swapped out for the three Obeah Masters. Unlike Ionie, Ormine, and Mariama, they do not cause a scene. With understanding nods, they join me in standing witness to fourteen witches' Swearing-In. Their right hands atop their hearts, their left bound to mine one by one, as the island's leader, and voice.

I said I would not capitulate; I promised to destroy the line Iraya asked to hold. The threat I thought would come wasn't meant to be from within my own walls, but let my enemies, my naysayers, know the light I spoke of that will keep back the darkness—none will be brighter than mine. Blinding, dazzling, as cold as the celestial dust I descend from. If need be.

For Aiyca? Without question.

44

IRAYA

Kirdan and I forgo the Cuartel for our suite at the palace. Our bedroom.

It takes a moment for my eyes to adjust to Kirdan's shape in the premature dark created by drawn curtains, the rise and fall of his chest, our fingers still intertwined. Night spills through the pillars; the air is sharp with salt from the waters below. The freshness only heightens the hum in my body, a residual high from the energy that coursed through it. That mighty tumult of our conjoined will.

"I'll send a message to the Cuartel," he murmurs. "Let Zander tell the others we're not coming." Our fingers part; his boots eat up distance between us and the desk; a small witchlight lamp is enkindled.

Meanwhile a quick war is fought between my head and heart.

I've congratulated myself on knowing the baser things

people want, in seeing it in their faces long before their actions out who they truly are. But Kirdan . . . What if it isn't Xaymaca he wants, or Aiyca. What if it *is* me?

What if it's been me this entire time?

"I told them not to come here tonight either." Kirdan rounds the desk; the conduit in his saber blinks, and a fire sparks in the hearth. Its light casts shadows that make these rooms, palatial, shrink with intimacy. "It will raise alarm."

"And Nyxia?"

"She can't leave, and anyone who visits her will be devoured like all the others before they can make it out to tell anyone what happened today." He casts the missive into the flames and then turns back toward me.

Always toward me. No matter how many times I have pushed him away. And what about me? I haven't consistently been repelled by this Warrior. This soldier. This fugitive with the heart of a king. Though not to prove the naysayers wrong, but to fight for what he believed in. And he believed in me. Not, as Delyse said, because he is the moon. Far from cold, I feel it, the touch of his flame.

"We should go to bed," he murmurs.

His words are both a challenge and a question.

I was wrong before. That lone thread tying us together has never existed. It's always been a vast web of them, a chaotic knot that's made it impossible to fully draw back no matter how I've tried.

"I've hated you for so long I didn't think I could feel anything more."

Disappointment is a crushing blow on Kirdan's face—at

least until I draw my tunic overhead. Then uncertainty takes over. Though that's soon eclipsed when I shimmy out of my pants, my intent clear as the ink spill of his irises overwhelms the surrounding green.

"I think," I say, sliding one arm from the sleeve of my cotton undershirt. "I think I've actually wanted you so much, I convinced myself that all you could want from me is my title, my name. But . . . that's not it, is it? You who have spurned the riches of this palace to live with nothing—to embrace a life where richness is measured in the company you keep and the lives you save." Nodding like a man in a dream, he drinks my words like they're water and he's been wandering the Oasis of the Singing Sands without any. "Of course, it's a lesson I've had to learn the hard way. Typical of you, not to make something easy for me."

"How much simpler could I have been?"

"At times, fewer words, Prince. At others, more." I take another step; we're an arm's length away from one another.

"And now?"

The atmosphere, already tight, becomes as delicate as cracked glass.

"Now," I utter. "Well."

Undone by him a while ago, he has long laid me bare, stripped me of idea and station. What are clothes? Inconsequential as the final item, the final barrier I have against him, slinks to the floor. And yet, there is still caution in the face that doesn't dip, one that asks if this is another deception in the game we have played for so long. Too long.

"You look afraid. Worried you won't enjoy this?" I can't help teasing, perhaps because I am not entirely in my element either.

Kirdan reaches for my hand and twists our fingers together. Callus against callus, scar against scar, for we are the same, he and I. *The same, the same, the same.* "We're trying to prevent a war," he murmurs, head lowering as I raise mine. "I remember you commenting on what a folly it would be to ignore that." His hand slides around my bare back, lower . . .

"Then kiss me like it's our last," I breathe against his mouth. "Not first."

And he does.

It isn't the sweet kiss of new lovers; there is no indolent dance of tongues and fingers, the coy teasing of two people who know they have all the time in the world. His is the touch of a dying man. Mine can equally be considered ephemeral.

So I push harder, demand more.

His shirt I tear away from his shoulders with the aid of magic; he breaks us apart, eyes glazed with sin while his mouth utters something so filthy, so unexpected, I laugh with delight.

"I didn't think good soldiers spoke like that."

"I was damned before I was born, Iraya. There is no redemption for me."

Raking my nails across the scars on his back, I've never felt more alive, more distanced from death against all the places his body is hard, unyielding. Drawing back incites protests, until I retreat to the bed, lower myself onto it. My eyes never leave his as I slide backward across the sheets.

"I've never done this before," I confess, here on the brink of no going back.

Clearly blessed with more self-restraint than I possess, Kirdan's focus remains on my face. "Are you sure it's what you want?"

"Yes." I think I might die if I don't feel him in deeper places.

Heady with lust and wild with want, I'm almost panting as Kirdan unbuckles his belt and unbuttons his pants until he is as naked as me, as proud of his body. He strides to the bed, takes an ankle in either hand and tugs me toward him. If that's not thrilling enough, he abandons propriety and takes a long, slow look that's so ravenous, so unexpected, my legs turn to water.

"Are you going to keep standing there," I breathe, chest heaving, "or do something about what you see?"

When our bodies come together, connecting in a way that makes my spine arc, and we are eye to eye, chest to chest, it's both tender and rough, patient and urgent, before the mighty lungs of war can snuff the blaze out.

JAZMYNE

Most of my emotions at Ionie, Ormine, and Mariama, I can bite down to the quick, except curiosity. Why did they choose the Swearing-In of all nights to make a stand? They've never diverted from their belief that I wasn't entitled to rule Aiyca, but if they wanted an audience, why not during my sham of a coronation?

The longer I plaster a smile on my face for the Seer's Eyes and those who watch from home, the greater my curiosity grows.

"Something is bothering me about the presiders," I tell Anya. "Did you think their behavior strange?"

"I thought they did what I've been expecting them to do. You too."

"Something perturbed me about the advisors' demeanor." Master Omnyra's approach was unheard; both Anya and I are startled.

"Have you seen anything?" my sistren asks her.

"I see a great many things, some that come to pass, many that don't. I'll accompany you to the holding cells."

"I didn't say anything about the holding cells."

Master Omnyra angles a knowing smile at the dissipating crowd below. "You would have."

"Actually." Aunty threads her arm through mine. "I planned to accompany my niece to see the presiders. I was worried about their state of being."

Master Omnyra turns her entire body toward Galene. "You think their ailment physical?"

"Or mental."

"Wait," I interrupt. "You think someone did this to them?"

"I thought so," the Obeah-witch says. "It seems as though you agree, Master Galene."

"I can't determine cause without assessing the witches."

"We can all go," I decide.

"No, no." Master Omnyra inclines her head. "I'll make my own way across. You three go on ahead."

Anya, Aunty, and I leave the council members, presiders, and guests to themselves. We exchange the diminishing buzz on the balcony, as people leave to attend the fair, for the heavily guarded palace grounds and holding cells where Ford waits with a shield witch.

"Evening." The former nods at us before taking off down the stretch of dark hall. Nel is beside him; their respective cloak and cape stream behind them in alabaster cataracts. "That was quite a show back there, wasn't it? I'll be honest, after the advisors, we don't know how many more magi have been compromised."

By what? I don't ask, can't afford to when I didn't notice anything was amiss. Torn between feeling foolish and concerned, I take long enough dallying over whether I should be transparent and ask, or find some sly way of determining what's happened, that we come upon my answer standing behind bars like . . . like they're asleep with their eyes open.

"What's wrong with them?"

I've never known Ionie to avoid launching a barbed insult my way, and yet there she stands, frozen, as though the air in here hasn't returned to normal since the shields' exodus.

"Their minds are gone," Ford states.

"I see that." The words are barely a whisper as I assess Ormine, Ionie, and Mariama, as stiff and still as they were on the balcony, only their shoulders curl in, their heads hang, as though they were held up on strings and now— "Possession," I murmur, understanding at last what their odd behavior outside was the result of. A shiver tears its way down my spine. "Did they go willingly to the Unlit or were they captured?"

"That's something I'd have to ask you." Arms folded across his chest, Ford stares down at me in the dimness of our surroundings. There is no sympathy in his face, only the expectation of a soldier in need of facts. It calms me. This is business.

Even though it feels personal.

"Alumbrar have always accepted the ancestors willingly during nyába." Ford looks between me, Aunty, and Anya. "But your order don't need willingness to possess, do they?"

"No," the latter answers. "What we saw out there was more than nyába. In fact, it was the complete opposite. They were being controlled, not filled. We let the dead remember how it feels to live, not to walk in our bodies."

"Then it stands to reason that the Alumbrar willingly left the magical protections of the palace to seek an audience with Unlit," Nel says. "They were then possessed and sent back in here stuffed full of ill wishes to oust you." She nods my way, like she can't stand to say *regent*.

"How would the Unlit cast an enchantment of this strength without magic?"

"Remember the fighting you came to me about?" Ford scratches the side of his fresh trim.

My stomach jolts. "They've started ransoming family trees?"

"They haven't had to. We went down into the parish, hung around a few Obeah haunts, and the common tale is that the Unlit claim to have a legitimate heir to the throne, someone they're calling the Lost Empress." His face grows pained at the treasonous claiming. "And the Obeah contingent of the island is listening."

"What about Iraya?"

"The shields and the Jade Guild are the only ones who know about her, and we're having a hard time separating ourselves from the Unlit. They've taken almost a third of our numbers; many are magic wielders, to answer your earlier question. They have bredren and sistren they're convincing to defect too, only they don't know they're defecting. It's a problem."

Mudda have mercy.

"Iraya doesn't know the extent." She didn't mention it when we spoke earlier this morning. "I thought she was communicating with you?"

"The Masters speak with Iraya via a proxy." Ford shrugs.

Master Omnyra might know more, when she comes. "If Iraya knows how strong the Unlit's hold is becoming, she might return sooner. I'll contact her."

"Until then, what do we do with the advisors?" Anya queries.

The witches haven't moved since we arrived. I'm not sure if they're blinking.

"Aunty?" I turn to where she stands at our backs. She's been quiet; likely she isn't used to the setting. "Is it safe to return them to their families?"

"Only if you'd like to terrify them," Nel states before Aunty can answer. "The fact that the Unlit haven't ransomed Obeah trees doesn't mean they'll stave off the Alumbrar. Your order won't trust in you if they believe themselves susceptible to attack. If you can't protect them, they might turn to someone who says they can. Though, maybe the Imposter has their limits."

"And if they don't?" Anya asks.

Nel turns away from the cells. "Pray to your gods and hope you still have their favor."

There's Obeah turning on Obeah who will soon turn on Alumbrar, who will cry for help—cry for me, and I have no idea how anything bar the war we have been trying to stave off will save them.

"That's your advice?" I call after her.

"Can you suggest anything better?" Ford frowns at the presiders, lifeless in their cell. "Because I sure as hell can't."

"I might have a solution," Aunty says. "Anya, if you could go to the infirmary and gather my medical bag, there are several remedies I can try. Jazmyne, you and I can write to their families."

"And me?" Ford asks.

"As you were, Obeah."

"Jazmyne?" Anya checks.

"It's a plan." The only plan. "Meet us in my study— Oh, would you tell Master Omnyra where we are, if you see her? She was meant to be here." Ford nods.

"Come, niece. We should make haste." Aunty all but drags me from the cells and through the grounds.

"Wait—my dress!" The fabric doesn't tear, but the same can't be said for my Achilles if we keep walking this fast over stones that were laid hundreds of years ago. "Aunty! What's the rush?"

"Forgive me, niece, but I have tried things the simpler way."

"Come, let's cut through the fruit grove and walk on even ground."

Not slowing, Aunty doesn't answer.

Unease steals into my chest, draws it tight. "Did you see something?" I cast a worried look over my shoulder. "Oscuridad?"

"Would that make you leave?"

"Leave?" Jerking my arm free, I stop.

"Jazmyne, please."

I step back to avoid her reach. "What's going on?"

Aunty glances around the grounds; we're in a Xanthippe blind spot, on this path. If I'd realized how isolated it is, with nothing but topiary for company, I would have assigned more guards here, shields, but I never walk this part of the palace.

"Will you listen to me when I tell you that I'm doing this for your own good?"

The distance between my hands by my sides and the clips recharged with Anya's magic feels yards in length.

"That everything tonight has been for your own good?"

"The advisors?" I whisper.

"It took the smallest suggestion for them to say those things about you. They harbored that hatred already; I simply brought it out to show you that you owe this island *nothing*."

My hands make it to my chest, where I clasp them.

"Ruling was never in your family; your mama set you on this course. I am merely righting it." Aunty takes a step closer to me. "Righting you. Helping you return to a life that won't cause you death, but will help you stop it in others. We're leaving the palace tonight. I'd hoped to keep you conscious, but it will be easier to leave with you asleep." With her last word, a yellow spark of suppression zips from the coin around her neck.

With a cry, I twist away; my cape flies up in a shield of literal protection.

"Master Artisan of Cloth," I explain to Aunty's look of confusion. "I'm sorry."

"You don't have to be, if you come with me."

"Not about that." Having freed my hair combs, I aim both fists her way and fire at her chest. Anya's will is magnified by the Amplifier around my neck, and Iraya's blood that still exists in my veins.

At the impact of my suppression sparks, Aunty releases a startled *oof* and falls back onto the ground.

Panting, I stand over her body and scream.

46

IRAYA

"I've been thinking about the Eldritch Gaps," Kirdan murmurs a while later, his body coiled around mine.

"I must have erred somewhere, then."

He shifts; I feel him look down at me. "You need to fish after all we exchanged?"

"You're the one who wishes to discuss work."

"Can you think of a better place?" He draws even closer, like he's trying to imprint this night on his skin, immortalize it. Stiff beneath him, I don't give. "Fine. How do you feel?" The question is almost bashful.

Remaining in character, I fight a smile, not quite at ease with the rush of fondness for this lionized Warrior who in this moment doubts how well he handles his sword.

My mirth gutters.

In killing Lucia, seizing Carling Hill, the Unlit have reminded me that it's no longer Just-Ira. Kirdan tips my chin upward; questioning, his eyes are twin jewels gleaming in the witchlights beside the bed.

"I feel—I feel like I have a lot more to lose." While I whisper the worry, it falls between us like a living, writhing thing; my stomach turns at the act of dispensing something so vulnerable.

"Or," he murmurs, "we have a lot more to fight for." He kisses me, his lips soft and unyielding, patient and demanding, and for an innumerable length of time I lose myself in the taste of him, the feel of his hands, his hair, the smell of his body, *him*.

It's dangerous, this thing between us that pales time into insignificance.

We *should* be discussing the gaps.

I should also get up and check for messages from Delyse. She would condemn me for this, for lying in the arms of this soldier.

"Did you agree that Nyxia's tale suggested we need all the heirs to close the gaps?" I ask when, chests heaving, we surface for air.

Kirdan blinks, eyes unfocused enough with lust that I want to throw myself on him again. Seriously, this much want might make me sick. Shoving against his chest, I roll back and out of reach.

"You'd deny a dying man his final wish to hold you?"

Dread hits me like a sucker punch.

"Don't jest about that."

A frown undulates across Kirdan's forehead; he levers himself up with his arms. "Iraya." It might be the softness of his voice, second only to the care, the affection with which those hands built for destruction held me. But at the sorrow in his eyes, one tied to his existence as a magical fugitive, I suddenly want to hit something—many things.

"'Bound and broken by three,'" I force out. "What did you think of it?"

Frown deepening, his hand twitches like he means to reach for me, for the conversation I want no part in right now. "It does sound like we'll need all the heirs, yeh mon."

"Were you aware there's a Skylands' heir in Zesia?"

"No."

The sorrow in his eyes steels into a cool focus as I tell him about my interaction with Kihra, and the competition between the heirs.

"I'm not sure if we can rely on them to close the gaps here," he muses. "All Zesia and the Skylands have in common is our emancipation from the empire. So, when do we return to Aiyca?"

"You'd leave without securing the gaps here?" I can't conceal the shock in my voice, though I wish I did when Kirdan reaches for my hand, entwines our fingers, and I find myself wondering how many more moments we'll have like this before Death joins the party and makes this a fatalistic threesome.

"I think we might have a better hope of convincing Kihra from the Golden Seat, in Aiyca."

"Well, I don't think we should leave Zesia until we have the means to control the gaps. The Skylands are just as invested as us. Their reasons differ, because—" I tug my hand free, the circles Kirdan was making with his thumb too distracting. "Their reasons differ because Kihra said to destroy the gaps would endanger their population control." She was only too happy to share that, but dodged several other questions she wasn't magically gagged against, like how she entered this island to begin with. "We shouldn't alienate them. Diplomacy, it's far harder than running someone through with a sword."

"You can say that again." Kirdan rolls his eyes.

"You know where the biggest tear is in Zesia. Wait, you didn't know about the Summoning Circles, did you? How did you find the tear?"

"It's always been visible. We didn't notice any Summoning Circles. I don't know how they're keeping it open—maybe prolonged use? Like when you keep opening a wound you don't let heal." Kirdan shudders. "I have men keeping watch, but the Unlit haven't visited it in phases. I'm not sure if it's what they intended to do, make the gap stay open."

"Well, thanks to the Summoning Circle found tonight, we know how to identify the gaps that aren't yet powerful enough to remain open. It got me thinking. The Unlit can always etch more into the ground, onto walls behind trash cans, and wherever else the Simbarabo will find them concealed. What we need is a midpoint between destroying the gap and—and caulking it, like you would a wound, but with what?"

"Iron?" Kirdan shrugs. "Like your mama used for the door to her trove. Nyxia mentioned 'not of this earth' in her ramblings. It's a known repellent for the other, and I know an Artisan of Metal who'll see us at first light."

"Iron is fallible to humans. There'd always be a risk someone could remove whatever we string across the gap . . . unless we use a locking glyph from the Adair Grimoire. It's all but impenetrable." My lips are sore from kissing, and worrying them between my teeth only highlights the pain. "If we blocked the gaps and then used the glyph to seal it, no more beasts could get through. They'd always be there, waiting, but better that than our plan relying on the Skylands sharing their secrets. What do you think?"

"I think we should test the iron and the glyph before we use it on the gaps. The Simbarabo will need a demonstration, at the very least. I'm thinking a net and the locking combination Rete."

"Rete as in a net?"

Kirdan nods.

"Okay," I muse. "Well, the rete isn't solid, but the interlocking squares will enable us to see the circles beneath. How many soldiers will we have?"

"I'll get away, and I can bring Esai, Zander, and a handful more I'm close with."

"Shamar will come."

"But more than that?" Kirdan winces. "I couldn't say."

"What of your female soldiers? Do you have any covens who aren't in the J'Martinet?"

"I have a cousin we can ask."

"Tomorrow?"

"Tomorrow." He falls back against the pillows once more and draws me across the bed until I am back in his orbit. "Not to ruin the mood, but we said no further withholding, remember."

I'm unable to stop my body seizing up.

"To go back to what I said earlier, though I've always

accepted that I will die before a time most would consider themselves to have lived—" He pauses. "Reaching this place with you means I've never feared death more than I do now."

My eyes close, shuttering against his words, the almost imperceptible tremor in his words. How much time have we wasted—have *I* wasted? There's so much I don't know, the good memories, the times he has walked in the sun and left that cold shadow of death behind.

I could stop it.

I could stop everything, remake Aiyca, the empire, as I want it. Make a world where pickney don't grow up fated to die, where Kirdan could live to a ripe old age, and we could have *time*.

"But I believe you said last, not first." Soft kisses land on my forehead, my cheeks; Kirdan shifts to bracket me between his powerful arms; more kisses dust across the flat of my nose, my neck, and I shift from *not in the mood* to *cannot get enough*. And I hate that I want him so much I feel it in the prickling of my skin, how sensitive, how responsive it grows. But the thing I hate most? I might need to get enough. He could die.

Me too.

47

JAZMYNE

I had to leave Aunty to find help, and then I found that I couldn't go back. I couldn't look at her lying there, knowing she was trying to help me by hurting me, and that I injured her too in the process.

The Xanthippe I send to retrieve her, I also instruct to escort her back to Sanar. She wasn't wrong in what she said, or her sentiments. But I'm not the trainee Healer I was when she knew me best. And I'm not the late doyenne either. I am someone who knows the burden of power and won't crumble beneath its weight, or fall walking the knife edge of its road.

This I implore Chaska to understand in the letter I write. I add it to Aunty's things I pack for her trip home. By the time I return to my rooms and retrieve the Mirror of Two Faces, the day is done, and I haven't spoken with a soul outside my guard, since leaving Aunty. It feels odd, but satisfying to know

I have a council to see to the running of Aiyca's day-to-day, which frees me to contact Iraya.

"Your timing could do with some work, Cariot."

Bare shouldered, she's bound in a sheet or something. I don't look too closely.

"We spoke not even a full day ago. A problem has arisen already?"

"The Imposter is succeeding in winning your order around. You have to come home. She is turning Obeah against Obeah and creating the perfect storm for a civil war."

"That's why you contacted me?"

"This is about Aiyca. That was one of your stipulations."

She pulls a face. "This feels like it's about you. I can't be there to hold your hand, Jazmyne. You know what you have to do. Every decision should keep that in mind."

"But—"

"I'm in the middle of something. Hold the line. I'll be home soon."

Her reflection disappears from the mirror.

Unbelievable.

She thought I would cost us this island, when in truth her order may be responsible without her guidance.

A knock thuds against the wood of my door down the hall. Anya? Word from the Xanthippe about Aunty, perhaps? Stashing the mirror, I shut the bathroom door and move through to my receiving room.

"You may enter," I call.

"Another second and I don't think I would have waited."

"Roje."

He fills the doorway; his white shirt looks as though it was hurriedly tucked in. Beneath it, his chest rises and falls as though he ran here from Black River. Eyes that look dark, from this distance, scour every inch of me.

"You're a little late for the Swearing-In."

"I know you're pissed, but don't give me the cold shoulder right now. I encountered your sistren outside; she said you were attacked?"

"I'm well. The shields were there, the Obeah Masters too, I was safe."

He nods at the chair beside mine.

"Of course."

Collapsing into it, he watches me through heavy-lidded eyes and exhales one long, tormented breath.

"You're here alone. Did Synestra refuse my offer to be queen? Because if that's the case, Roje, I don't need you to spoon-feed me bad news. You can give it to me straight, no chaser."

"She said yes."

All my bluster takes flight.

"She said yes?"

Roje moves close enough to me that I have to tip my head up to look into the soft, sad planes of his face.

"Then why do you look so . . . defeated?"

"I know things were different in that drinking house, phases ago."

My head erupts into flame.

"But I prefer how things are now. Do you feel our kinship?

That despite me being from the sea, and you the land, that we are bredren and sistren. We're close."

"I do. But I don't understand—what's wrong?"

"I worked hard to convince the crew, Synestra, to trust you. But given what happened the last time they saw you, they all agreed that they need insurance. Synestra will work with you and will be your queen, if you navigate our way during the race."

"Leave the palace?"

"You would have, before."

"The entire point of not racing is because I *need* to be here."

"For what? You have fortified your home, this parish, better than any witch without her magic should be able to. Do you doubt your preparedness?"

"No, but—"

"And, as you said, with the map we won't sail for long."

"Yes, but—"

"That's the proviso, Jaz." Roje winces. "And by all things considered, it's small."

Not after what Iraya told me, and what I heard from Ford. Obeah are rising against Obeah. The Imposter Empress wants this seat, without me in it.

"I'll keep you safe."

"That's not— I can take care of myself." From this palace.

But the only way to be truly safe, from Iraya's rule, an Obeah civil war, might be to leave and work with the pirates. Secure the army Anan didn't come back to me about.

"What am I telling the crew?"

Iraya said to trust my judgment. Roje is right; I have made Aiyca safe. And this parish is one of the most secure parts. I can egress without notice. No one need know I'm not here. And we'll only be gone for two days.

"Tell them—" I wet my lips with my tongue. "To raise anchor."

IRAYA

Jazmyne's harried demeanor during our conversation was enough to chase Kirdan and me out of bed early, the morning after seeing Nyxia. There are rete to order, in the Sadirren's Metal Quarter.

In a small market of tents, the air is thick with heat, despite the delta curling through its streets just as it does in the Horn. Artisans of Metal thrust hot blades straight into the rivulets bisecting pathways. Ordinarily, I imagine the hissing and spitting, the clang of hammer against metal would overwhelm the chattering of visitors, but Zesians gather to watch in the double figures, growing in number as Kirdan and I meander our way through the tents.

He slings an arm around my shoulders, draws me close. "Just smile and wave." He nuzzles my neck; the crowd giggle and whisper. I refuse to wave, but I don't scowl at anyone. A success.

The witch we commission, the same who crafted my batons and knives, Raelar, tells us to return at the end of the day.

"Don't you have other commissions?" I ask her, concerned. We've asked for five nets, with all but nonexistent gaps in the lattice.

"When the empress, who I imagine is going to reunite the empire, and her future husband ask me to make them instruments I'm almost certain they're using to do the former, and word gets out that I'm a royal smithy, you can bet that I have other commissions." Raelar laughs, then sobers quickly. "Not that I've been bragging. Or telling people what I'm creating for you. The shop is for show, during high season. Yule gifts and such. I've done all your work in my private workspace out back."

"Rest easy," I calm her. "You are this royal's smithy whenever I'm in Zesia. Blessings."

Her olive cheeks turn a mottled red, and she dips into a bow.

Kirdan and I take our leave into the tents.

"If I didn't know any better," he says, waving at a giggling group of pickney who point our way, "I might think you enjoyed that."

"Knowing me as well as you do, though," I murmur, drawing him down to listen. "Means you know I'm *this* close to kicking you in front of all these people if you don't get us out of here."

Kirdan's still laughing when we sift away, exchanging the Sadirren Province for Changuu and our meeting restaurant where Shamar, Zander, and Esai wait.

"Is that coffee?" I reach for a jug; it skirts backward.

"Magic," Shamar orders.

Rolling my eyes, I move the jug the magical way; when coffee splashes over its rim, I pull a face at Shamar.

"Good night's sleep?" Zander looks between his general and me as we sit side by side across from them at the table. "Thank the gods for that."

"I'll pretend I didn't hear that, soldier." Kirdan's left hand slides down my right thigh.

"Well, I won't," I say.

Zander's smug expression tightens.

"What did you mean?" I ask.

"I—well. I only meant that you both look rested."

Esai snorts into his lap; Shamar openly laughs and claps Zander on his back.

"I didn't think that was what you meant at all. Perhaps we can circle back to it later," I can't help teasing. "For now, I need a favor."

Zander lights a fire and waits while I write a message to Delyse about the rete. We don't know if they will work, but she might be able to test one before us, if the Jade Guild member she's living with passes on my message in time. It's been a few days since I've heard from her; she might be out on assignment.

"We need to talk about closing the gaps before Kirdan and I have to walk through the ballroom before the bacchanal," I begin, once the message has been sent.

Over a breakfast of eggs, sausages, sweet fresh fruit, juice, and enough coffee to wake the dead, I tell the three soldiers about my meeting with the Skylander, and all she said about

482

destroying the gaps. "Since we don't know how to do that anyway, Kirdan and I have planned to block the Summoning Circles with rete. We don't know if they'll work, so tomorrow will be the test before the plan is implemented across the island."

"Before or after we leave for Aiyca?" Shamar asks.

I look to Kirdan.

"Leave that to me," he says.

49

JAZMYNE

The expediency of the race wouldn't be a problem, Roje said before leaving last night, if I were staying at the Iron Shore, as I was expected to when I would have been queen—to which I told him, it would be less of a problem if Synestra had given me an earlier response. He stopped complaining after that.

My exodus from the palace happens in a flurry of meetings: with the Xanthippe and shields first, to discuss security; then it's with the new councils to leave instructions about what is to be done with the comatose advisors if, in two further days, there's no change. We're leaving the holding cells, parting ways beneath a sun so blinding, I don't see or hear that carriage rumbling up the drive until I'm almost flattened by it. The Xanthippe are under strict orders not to allow anyone onto the palace grounds, with the exception of—

"Chaska."

My cousin steps down from the carriage in her maroon

Healer uniform and an expression of great discomfort. My body tightens in warning.

"Why are you here?"

She hesitates. "Is there somewhere we can talk? Something has happened."

Something terrible, I learn, when we recess in my study—with Anya, Ford, Pasha, and fourteen Xanthippe on the other side of the door—and Chaska informs me that Aunty is dead. My hand is hot against the bare skin of my décolletage.

"And you're sure it's the Unlit?" I ask my cousin.

Stoic about death as only a Healer can be, she nods. "Without a shadow of a doubt. You see, they wanted her to hand you over to them."

My fingers curl around my desk. "That's why she tried to steal me away?"

Chaska purses her lips as she contemplates her next words. "We were concerned that you were living here without your dada's influence, without Madisyn's. Mama worried you would turn into Aunty Judair. When the Unlit approached her, she told them she would remove you from the throne in her own way. She thought she was helping you. We all did.".

"The family knew?"

"Only a few of us. We thought it was for the best, when you came to Sanar. At least, they did." My cousin flashes a look up at me, one measured, sage. "You're different than they thought, stronger, still concerned with the care of the island. I see many diseases at Sanar, of the body and of the mind. If you were similar to your mama, I would have helped Mama remove you from here, when she asked. But we never would

485

have handed you over to the Unlit."

My head is heavy beneath the weight of all Chaska said as I shake it. "And so they killed Aunty?"

"That's what we suspect. I was traveling in to collect her, to try and soothe any residual tension between the two of you, after her failure to, as you said, steal you away. They caught her during a routine visit among the proletariat in Queenstown." Chaska's voice does not waver; she could be discussing the weather rather than the murder of her mama. "At least she died doing what she loved most."

Treating the sick, or defending me?

Melancholy strikes me in my chest, my heart.

"She burned brightly in this world."

"Our skies are darker without her," my cousin returns, as mechanically as she has delivered everything else in this conversation. "I do not blame you, Regent. Nor do I fear death, the Unlit, or anything else they represent. Ones such as us have pulled back many a life from the other side of the veil with enough success to not balk at the impending challenge, for which you have Sanar's full support."

"Master Healer."

"There are exams I must take, but that's the goal. To step into Mama's shoes. To continue the work, and to start work anew, with Anan. Yes," she says, in that matter-of-fact manner. "I know who he is and what he seeks. I also know some of his tricks." Her mouth twitches in the first display of true emotion. "You have family, Jazmyne. More than you have ever known or felt. Aiyca will not be lost with such a cure." Chaska's hand twitches, like she means to take mine; ultimately she

486

doesn't, but the intent was there.

"Will you linger here, in your mama's absence?"

"Yes. If you'll have me."

"Sanar won't miss you?"

Chaska rises. "Anan is teaching every Healer there how to cure the Oscuridad poison."

"Is that why he's been too busy to reach out about the army he promised me?"

My cousin hesitates. "He has no say in his sister's affairs, from what I know of him. But he will do what I cannot there, and I will do what he wouldn't be able to for you here."

"I'd like that. I have to be away for a couple of days, but when I return, we can spend the Third Night talking about Aunty and Dada?"

"I'd like that."

Me too.

"And if you're not back?" Ford questions from across my study, once Chaska has been taken to the infirmary and I've summoned him inside. "If the ship capsizes or you're devoured by a sea beast?"

"I expect you to keep this palace, this parish, safe and to stop touching items on that shelf."

Withdrawing his hands, Ford retreats. "We're still weeding the Unlit from the Jade Guild, but we're being vigilant. Don't worry about us, Jaz—" At my scowl, he grins. "You should keep an eye on your pirates. They play dirty."

Anya, Pasha, and Filmore wait for Ford and me in the vestibule as they have so many times before. We have several more matters to close before I depart tomorrow. Framed in a shaft of light streaming through the lunar window above the door, they look fated to be sang about; immortalized in moments around fireplaces and before bedtimes.

I offer up a prayer to all seven of the Mudda's Faces that this won't be the final time that I stand in this place, with these people.

I hope the songs sing of our survival, not that we were cut down too young.

50

IRAYA

Less than an hour before our meeting with Lena, Kirdan's cousin, two witches meander through Zesia's bazaar.

The first, an elegant arm looped through one of her betrothed's, who stands handsome and imposing beside her in his uniform of umber and white, stares with wide eyes at the city of tents stretching into the glare of the late-afternoon sun; she marvels at the quality of the trade on offer, laughs at pickney who chase one another through the legs of shoppers, or dance to the chiming of bells ringing mellifluously through an air rich with saffron and cumin. The witch is unbothered by the buzz of Zesians who have flocked in droves to see her, the famed empress and her prince lover. He too is at ease, smiling fondly down at her as she beams at stall owners sweating in the shade beneath their tents, paying exorbitantly for produce and textiles, paintings and sculptures; all the while she sends a cooling wind to calm their fevered brows until only their hearts are warm toward her.

The second witch, me, would trip her up if we passed one another in the street.

"Zander looks as though he's enjoying himself." Resting in the shadow of a chimney, Kirdan stares down at our duplicates in the bazaar. "I don't think I've ever seen him smile this much since the last time it rained."

"That might be due to my skirts he's wearing. It is warm today."

Bearing a Glyph of Transformation, as well as a vial of my blood around his neck, Zander has been physically transfigured into a facsimile of the empress we need to win over the people of Zesia, while Kirdan and I meet with the extra bodies we require to help secure the Eldritch Gaps.

We should have left for the drinking house the moment the sun dipped, but I cannot tear my eyes away from Zander and Shamar. The former might be a better Iraya Adair than I could ever be. Nana Clarke spoke of torture when I was a pickney. Hot nails driven beneath fingernails; water poured into your mouth in a perennial deluge until you drowned, and kept drowning. But this, the simpering and walking, the smiling until, surely, one's brain feels as though it's ready to ooze out of the nearest orifice, she didn't warn me about.

Mama made it look so easy.

"Perhaps I should be less hard on him," Kirdan muses.

"Zander?"

He nods. "After the time he had as a pickney, and later as a Simbarabo, being looked at with admiration rather than fear, hatred, is a welcome change of pace."

Whenever one of the shields would look at me as the shoppers look at Zander, Shamar, I didn't realize how necessary a reminder it was that, while I might not be inherently good, it didn't mean I'm the opposite either.

"I'm glad you know that."

"I thought I told you to stay out of my head."

At my tone, caution enters Kirdan's expression. "You seriously don't like it?"

"It's creepy."

"Not romantic?"

"In the right circumstances there's a certain pleasure that comes with being invaded, yeh mon."

He chokes.

"But mentally? I'm not sure that does it for me."

"Then keep me out."

"How do I do that?"

"Shield your thoughts." He shrugs. "Only let me in when you want me. Like now." Kirdan steps in closer. "Is this considered an invasion?" His breath brushes across my forehead.

"Had your breath been foul, I'd say so, mon."

He blinks at me, and then laughter booms out of him like thunder; before we're spotted, I drag him around the side of the chimney.

"Try and control yourself." Our bodies connect, mine slotting into all the right places against his. "We're in the middle of an important task."

Already closer to black than green, his eyes shadow. "You'll pay for that later."

"In the worst ways, I hope."

Managing not to devolve into senseless animals, we leave the rooftop for the alley running alongside it. Cloak and cape hoods up, respectively, we veer toward an establishment where anonymity is currency, and to stare too long at anyone will guarantee bruises. At the very least. As for the very worst, mouth curled against the stink of unwashed bodies, blood, and the gods only know what else I'm stepping in inside this dim drinking house, I'm not fooled into believing the visually unarmed patrons propped against the bar are without weapons, ones still stained with the blood of whoever they encountered last. Any tested Warrior knows to treat their instruments better.

Kirdan said little about his cousin we're meant to be meeting this evening; still breathless from our time in the bathing room, from the full scope of his body—even better wet—I let him get away with it. Idiot. No one who frequents an establishment like this will hold their own against the Oscuridad. My hopes of a skilled cabal of witches is ground into the sticky floor underfoot.

A ruckus rings with the clarity of chaos ahead. Smashing glass, the upheaval of furniture.

"There's a fighting pit here, isn't there?"

"Not at this hour." Kirdan begins shunting patrons aside with his shoulders. Close behind him, I will my hearing to discern the difference between typical jostling in establishments like this, and whatever it is that's sending Kirdan careening ahead like a pushed boulder.

We clear an archway; standing behind an upturned table, a witch in draped silk levels a braided leather bullwhip. Pure conduit metal, it beams like a shaft of sunlight in her rich brown grip, though it's second to the glint in her eyes, the flash of teeth bared in a smile that doesn't welcome challenge but will face it all the same. She's flanked by two more witches; both Zesian, they're also in similar draped silk and armed with golden weapons, though theirs remain holstered.

"Lena?"

The witch with the whip tips her chin at Kirdan. "Cousin. This gallin asked me how much."

A scrawny slip of a man quivers before Lena and the upturned table; he practically dissipates into sweat as he beholds Kirdan, all shoulders and cheekbones and a cutting glare.

"I told him to fight me for it."

"P-please," the stranger whimpers. "I don't want to—I didn't mean—"

One hand on a generous hip, Lena cuts her bullwhip through the air with a sky-splitting crack; the man falls silent, save for his whimpering, and I wonder if I picked the correct Divsylar to take to bed.

"As entertaining as it is to watch you spar, cousin, it seems unfair to stand by while you unleash yourself on this man." Hand engulfing the shoulder of the gallin, Kirdan indicates that I'm to move aside before he tosses the man into the crowd piled at our backs, knocking them over. Before the same hand, the walls stretch across and seal, preventing any outside entry.

"All this time away, and you still know how to ruin my fun." Lena belts her weapon; the table rights itself as though lifted by invisible hands; her companions sit on the chairs as they're righted. The clear leader of their party, Kirdan's cousin, rocks back on two legs of her chair; she makes a cursory inspection of her cousin, before eyes a startling gray land on me. "You are the empress." A chair slides away from the table in a magical invitation to sit.

I don't.

"And you the knife for hire."

"I'm very expensive."

"I don't doubt it."

"And yet you've come all the same" is said by one of her companions. The witch sports a bob of thick braids; they're spliced with feathers and golden beads. "Rumor has it, you haven't the wealth to commission fighters."

"If we're listening to rumor I can go, and leave you to your gossip and tea."

A smile flickers its way to the forefront on the second companion's slender face.

"Or we can discuss facts." Taking the chair back, I twist it around so that I am straddling the dark wood of its seat. "I mean to destroy the monsters plaguing this island."

"We do," Kirdan says; and though he keeps his hands to himself, the phantom weight of his palm lands on my right shoulder. It isn't an admonishment, but a reminder. I'm not doing this alone; I don't have to. "But Krimpt is blocking the Simbarabo. This is where you come in, cousin."

That light in Lena's eyes turns cold. "You know I won't speak to him, so don't talk blood."

"You don't need to speak to your uncle—"

"Uncle?" She glances at Kirdan; something softens in her

face. "Krimpt is not my uncle. He's my pupa." With a sigh, she rocks forward in the chair; its front legs land with dull thuds. "My cousin wouldn't tell you that about me, because he's noble like that. The opposite of Dada. The opposite of me." She looks to her companions with a crooked grin. "So if you've come to appeal to my better side, let me say now that I don't have one. If you want my help, what will you give me in exchange?"

Kirdan and I didn't discuss this, but I don't think we needed to. Something he no doubt knew. It's both terrifying and a relief to be seen. He knew I would understand what Lena wanted.

"Before I was empress, I was Virago."

All three witches before me sit up.

"Or maybe I was Virago after, technically. But my time training with my sistren in arms was the best period of my life. There is no greater honor I could earn than that name. And it takes one to know one, Lena." There is something hard in her face as she looks at me, but something hopeful too, though it's faint. "Fight with me, and I will commission you here in Zesia to lead a legitimate coven to undertake those duties Virago did in Aiyca."

Kirdan's hand once again brushes against my shoulder in a phantom touch of approval.

Lena's companions fidget beside her. They will need to work on hiding their emotions better, in the future. It's too easy to read them, as easy as Kirdan finds seeing into my darkness, and knowing that for all the shadows and obsidian, there is light there too. Enough to offer a witch who has only ever known a world without it, judging by how she reacted to mention of her pupa.

"You have magic of your own, rather than an imbued weapon?" I ask.

"We all do, but I told you, I'm not noble."

"The people we protect believe we are noble; to them we are. But it's also fine to enjoy stabbing things with pretty weapons." I shrug one shoulder. "Someone has to. Covens are about walking into the fire. Not because we don't fear getting burned, but rather due to understanding that wounds are easier to heal than worlds. I'm not speaking about islands," I add, before Lena can interrupt. "These witches—" I nod at her companions, her second and third. "Are your world. They will have worlds of their own, who will have worlds, and so on. It isn't about saving Zesia, or Aiyca, Lena. It's about saving your world." Something I'm only just understanding myself.

Lena drags a hand through her sleek, dark hair and huffs a humorless laugh. "The stories haven't detailed how pretty a speech you Virago can make."

"Will you help us?" Kirdan asks.

She glances first to her right, and then her left; all three witches' shoulders straighten for a fight. "I won't answer to *him*."

Krimpt, I don't need her to clarify.

"Or the doyenne."

"You will work with me." I look up at Kirdan. "Us."

"We'll need to discuss."

"Less impetuous than when we were pickney." Kirdan snorts.

496

Lena almost smiles, but her eyes shift back my way.

"You have until nightfall."

She raises a single brow in question.

"Not afraid of the dark, are you?" I ask.

"In this city, I am the dark."

Rising, I cut a grin her way. "Come and find me, once you have your answer."

"How will I know where you'll be?"

"I plan on making that easy for you."

51

JAZMYNE

To tell Iraya about the race for queen, or not to tell Iraya.

The question haunts me throughout the night before it's time to travel to the Iron Shore; indeed, unfazed by daylight, it lingers like a specter while I dress in the same too-tight pants and tunic for my journey back to the Iron Shore.

"Do you feel unwell?" Anya asks from the vestibule, where, along with Filmore and Pasha, she waits for my attendants to bring the last of my bags down from my suite. "You've been quiet. We don't have to—"

"We do." Turning beneath a ceiling I have looked up at for almost half my life, I exhale. "I am well, sistren," I say, turning back to a concerned Anya. "Merely looking forward to returning home once this is all over."

And *this* is a spectacle from the minute we sift into the Iron Shore.

It's a strange juxtaposition. We left Aiyca on the brink of

war, however well prepared I made sure the island was; while the Iron Shore, a place I always heard was dangerous, is full of light, of excitement. Much like the Glide-By, the island's residents flock to the docked ships; pickney wave flags bearing the insignia of what I assume is their favorite ship to win. Majestically erect against the clear skies above the Xaymaca trench, the *Silver Arrow* sits seventh in line atop waters clear and flush with schools of vibrant fish—the luck of the number feels like a sign of the Mudda's favor. Cordoned back from the ships, a gaggle of teenage girls call for Filmore and Pasha. My Stealths, lithe and dangerous in the black clothing they would not be parted with, wave back.

My shoulders relax at the hum in the air. The race for queen, for the Coral Crown, reminds me of the Obeah magical inheritance ceremonies of old—and soon to come again, I hope. This day makes me hopeful for life after the war.

"Welcome!" Roje calls, as the crew races up and down a narrow gangplank without concern. "It's a beautiful day for it."

Elodie waits at the top of the narrow strip of wood up onto the deck. "Jaz, you could look less like vomiting. Everything from here on will be easy. We sail with the permission of the cannon, we win, and then we return home with a legendary bounty."

A heavy arm slings across my shoulders. "I'm sorry I couldn't travel with you," Roje says, once his sailing master turns to help Anya, Filmore, and Pasha with the luggage they carry. "There's usually trickery the night before the race, ripped sails, holes in the hull of the ship. I slept here with some of the crew, Synestra, to ensure we were kept safe."

"Right. And there are no holes?"

Roje laughs; it is as musical as the cry from the gulls overhead. "There are no holes that shouldn't be on this ship."

"Is there anything I can do?"

"Stay out of the way," Synestra comments in passing.

"She's not wrong." A hand above his brow to block the sun, Roje shakes his head at his captain. A witch *I* made captain. "Though she could flower up her language."

With an apologetic grimace my way, Elodie strides after the captain.

"I'll need to stay close to them both, no?"

"Unless you'd like to hand over the map."

I squint up at Roje. "Not a chance."

He laughs once again. "I didn't think so." Lowering his arm from across my shoulders, he places a hand in the small of my back and leads me across the deck. It is a hive of activity, much like the ships to the left and right of us. Captain Shah is nowhere to be found. A small mercy. "You can remain here, at the wheel with Synestra and Elodie, for as long as you can stomach it," Roje says.

"Where are we heading first?" the latter asks, gathering her blond hair into a messy bun atop her head.

"We head toward the Blue Mountains," I share. "I'll issue the next instructions once we are close."

"That is close," Synestra muses, her focus on a large map splayed on the stand beside her helm. "To think, the falls have been there this entire time."

I will myself not to fidget. As she turns her scrutiny my way.

"If not for Jazmyne's map," Anya intervenes. "we might have gone on never knowing where to find them."

Synestra shifts her dark eyes, so similar in shape to Madisyn's, to my sistren. To her credit—or perhaps down to her training—Anya shows no sign of being affected.

"When does this race start anyway?" she asks, light, conversational.

"Your guess is as good as mine." Elodie sidles up to Anya, a pastel dream in her pale yellow shirt and off-white pants, compared to the deep blues my sistren wears—a necessity, to prevent her and the boys from looking too much like a unit. "These celebrations have been happening since sunrise. The shore will be happy to have a new queen." She glances at Synestra, who, cheeks coloring, does not look up from her map.

Her focus is rewarded when, not even an hour after boarding, the cannon blasts, and the race begins.

My Stealths and I are redundant as sails are opened, oars are manned, and Synestra, donning a brown hat with a broad brim, begins shouting orders.

Encouraged with cheers and screams from the crowds gathered to witness the ships' departures, the Silver Arrow pulls abreast with the ships to the left and right of us. Excitement takes over when the magical hand I asked Anya, Filmore, and Pasha to provide us with nudges our bow into first place. I've never won anything before, not truly. I thought I'd won doyenne, only to be crowned regent, but today, in the next two days, I will win the Iron Shore.

"We have company," Anya says, nodding across the waters

Down the line—far enough away to be a blip against the vast sea and sky, another vessel edges forward with alacrity.

"Can you read its name?" I ask, not dear about which Stealth finds out.

"The *Vanquisher*," Pasha murmurs. "That belongs to that pirate from the Glide-By, no?"

Captain Shah. My stomach twists. "That it does. Perhaps we can knock them off course?" I suggest—and as though being punished by the Seven-Faced Mudda for such a thought, the *Silver Arrow* is hit starboard side. The ship rocks. Crew shout. Anya grips my wrist as our footing seesaws beneath us.

"What was that?" I breathe.

Roje strides toward us, a bucket with fruit in hand. "Are you hurt?"

"No—I—I'm well. We are," I confirm, with a quick examination of Filmore, Pasha, and Anya, whose lighter skin now bears a sickly pallor. "What happened?"

He grins. "See for yourself." Divesting the bucket with one of the passing crew, he beckons us after him, to peer over the side of the ship—which I cannot.

Filmore does; straightening, he frowns. "Paint?"

Roje points across the waters, where three more ships have drawn a lead against the line of vessels. Two possess cannons that are aimed our way. There's a bang, and a plume of smoke, before the *Silver Arrow* rocks with another blow.

"What are they doing?" I ask, waiting for the cry of water on board, the announcement that we are sinking.

"Delaying our journey. It's twofold. Come with me." Roje

strides across the ship, where several crew draw the *Silver Arrow*'s cannons into position. "We can't sail with blemishes on our ship, it's against the rules—"

"You didn't tell me about any rules," I point out, hopping over a rogue onion. A pirate races down the deck after it seconds later.

"They're not too important for you. Our vessels must be presentable; if we see any sea beasts we're not to sail back for the Iron Shore—"

"Sea beasts?" Anya squeaks.

"Nothing to worry about. So, the splotches on our ship," Roje continues. "Means we'll have to find a spot to stop and clean it, preferably before it dries beneath this infernal sun, which of course will force us to delay following that map of yours."

"I think I understand," Pasha says. "The others, they're cheating? They mean to delay us by staining the ship."

"You expected outlaws to fight fair?"

Ford's warning rings through my thoughts with the clarity of a death knell.

"It's all right, mon. We got a few tricks too." Roje nods at cannons being loaded with rotting fruit—including the rogue onion that passed us moments ago.

Elodie calls down from the rigging on the central mast. "How's your aim, Anya? We've some paint grenades we could do with a little extra help tossing."

Anya looks my way for permission, before using the rope net to pull herself up.

"It's like a game," I say, my tone of wonder.

"Did you expect bloodshed in the beginning?" Roje smiles down at me. "Watch. You might learn something."

Watching is all I want to do—witnessing the explosions of color, the unadulterated joy on Anya's face when she lands a grenade on a passing ship. Even Pasha and Filmore take turns joining Elodie on the rigging. While I pass, my trepidation about today clears with a cleansing gust of salt-imbued air. One that smells faintly of rot when our own cannons begin to fire. How terrifying can the race be when weapons made for destruction become weapons used for joy? I can do this for two days—three, if we must stop to clean the ship.

"Will you have a go?" Roje asks, tipping a basket of the most putrid vegetables yet into the mouth of the cannon he operates.

I worry my bottom lip between my lip in contemplation. Aiyca is safe. Iraya is on her way back. And though the latter presents its own challenges, I am in pursuit of meeting them with this race, and the fleet sailing behind us to be won in my victory. "I think I will."

For a moment, I can enjoy this experience.

At least, I can pretend to.

For though my trepidation has faded, it was but a temporary instance. Playfulness will not let me forget that, far from the crew, the outlaws that surround me, I am not fighting fair. If they discover my deception, if anything goes wrong in pursuit of the falls, these cannons of fruit will be turned my way—and I'm confident they will be armed with real weapons.

52

IRAYA

The sharp ring of my hammer striking a nail fills the dead end.

Splayed in a quiet junction where wall meets wall, in the tightly cloistered streets of the Delta Province, like the spiderweb I need to catch a host of monstrous flies, the rete rattles like discordant steel pans.

"This next part is the most significant of the process," I tell the two Simbarabo with me in the alley, Venrier and Roran. Slotting the hammer into my bandolier, I scan the Glyph of Prohibition, copied onto a piece of cloth from my family Grimoire, which Venrier holds aloft. "The magic of the glyph lies in the complexity of the interlocking circles." Larger and smaller, some concentric and some only partially overlapping, it's complicated enough that I keep pausing to check the facsimile. I should have been tracing the glyphs as I hammered each slip of conduit gold into the wall. And yet, my mind has been turning to Kirdan and me in bed, the bathing room, on the balcony this morning with only the sun for company. We split up to avoid being distracted, yet here I am, being distracted. Wanting is a dangerous thing, but it's second to having, knowing. A shiver tears down my spine at the memory of his hands. His left holding my chin in place so he can watch me, while his right—

"Empress!"

In addition to the shout, my senses flare a belated warning. I flinch away from the wall; an otherworldly paw slams against the stone in the place my head was a split second ago.

Shit.

A sweep of a thick tail sends Venrier flying down the alley. His hair and cloak undulate like banners behind him. Sketching glyphs to render the beasts corporeal, Roran can't block the Oscuridad that dissolves into smoke, slips past him, and solidifies before me with neck-snapping speed. I duck again as a second paw punches into the stone; dust flies in a blinding cloud. Spluttering, I am even slower to move when a third attack gutters into the earth at my feet, and the force of it launches me into the air. My heart plummets into my stomach. All guzzu jumble in my thoughts; my ears ring with the attack, but I will myself higher and slam one of my batons into the wall. The action sends an excruciating echo of pain up my arm and into my shoulder. Teeth gritted against the scream in my throat, I look down. Through the haze I take a quick assessment of the scene from the safety of my vantage point: Venrier blocked by a hulking creature on six legs; from its *back*, many monsters pull themselves free in a flurry of bony arms and legs, gnashing teeth and guttural cries. Its back is like a doorway, or a birth canal. My mouth, open, dries at the sight of what I'm seeing. There have to be at least a dozen of them down there. Their nebulous forms make it difficult to discern creature from smoke. Bleeding, Roran can't draw his glyphs fast enough to fight back. He'll be torn to pieces, all so the creatures can get to me—it's my scent Shamar and Zander have been spreading across the city. In the alley below, a mass of amorphous bodies climb atop one another to reach me; they push against one another and the rete. One I haven't secured properly.

Still, it holds as I pant from above. Switching arms, I rock to and fro and then swing my body in an arc over to the other side of the net. The beasts snap and claw at the metal; their flesh sizzles against the conduit gold. Head cocked to the side, I approach, inspect, saved by chain links too small to permit even their incorporeal forms. We didn't anticipate that the metal would hurt, only hold them back, which it does. It's working—which is why it's a shame to holster my batons for the hunting knife on my hip.

The wicked curve of metal slices through the center of the net as if it's made from nothing more than air. As for how quickly the monsters notice the opening, I cannot say.

I'm already running.

Arms pumping, I blaze the path Kirdan and I planned with the others. Left at the bend, hurdle over the planters on a public green; left again at the apothecary, slowing only to launch strobes of magic at each Glyph of Protection and Alarm the Simbarabo have been sketching as they've accompanied Zander and Shamar through town, unnoticed by the crowds enamoured with our ersatz selves. In my wake, the high pitch of an alarm encourages those in the market on the adjacent street, now aglow beneath the soft flicker of witchlight lanterns, to evacuate toward the coruscating shields of gold birthed from the ground in shimmering walls that will keep them safe from the beasts huffing and grunting at my back.

That's one hundred yards down; the market is four hundred in length. I need the center.

One hundred more to go.

"We'll need theater," Zander said to me while we schemed.

The sandstorm roused by the many feet of the Oscuridad is certainly that, along with the wall of protection that crests the market, but I prefer to think of what comes next as flair: the purposeful removal of my cape, which is a perfect copy of the one Zander has been wearing. He sports an organza kaftan beneath his. I wear tight white pants with golden piping along the outer legs, a tunic in the same fashion with billowing sleeves to conceal armored gauntlets; bound like tucked wings around my center, the golden bodice from Kirdan takes flight with one pulse of will. Lambent light flares in a corona around my body, bright in the denseness of the surrounding night as I hit the two hundredth yard, my chest heaving with the speed of my sprint. The gasps sound in the gathering crowd before I have freed my batons from their holster across my shoulders in a single deft maneuver.

I don't bother hiding the smile that cuts across my face as I combine the metal to form a single long staff. Over the euphoric click of two halves becoming one, the world slows down. I pivot in the sand, turning to the herd of cantering monsters. Peace settles across my shoulders like a physical mantle. A single prayer to Clotille is all I utter before, as I saw Dada do in the face of a rising storm at sea, I plunge my staff down into the ground with both hands and unleash everything I have with the white fist of my naevus—splayed across its magical knuckles, a duster by way of the Glyph of Transposition required to render the beasts corporeal.

It is an undoing.

Power roars down the street in an explosion of force. It's a struggle to keep my eyes open in the storm of wind and magic, but I fight to all the same, not wanting to miss a second of my missile firing into the heart of darkness. The world seems to rock, but, clutching my anchor, both the physical and spiritual, I am steadfast and unmoved. I am Witch, Warrior, Weapon. *Empress*, a voice whispers inside. Internal ceilings are shattered as my magic keeps coming, keeps charging, with no end in sight. But I will have a limit, and I cannot reach it when there are still gaps to close. It is a painful reining-in. Rather than drawing my hand from the fire, calming down is more akin to keeping it there. Clenching my jaw, I pant against the pain to draw back, to be a girl again rather than a final solar flare against the surrounding dark. Blinking away the light, I come to in time to avoid the paw emerging through the smoke.

Dodging back to frightened screams in the crowd, I wrench my staff from the earth, split it in two, and plunge the left baton into the beast's neck. A flash of umber and alabaster streaks past me in a mighty wave of sheer force. The Simbarabo. A ululating war cry peals like a death knell as the soldiers launch themselves on Oscuridad stragglers. I wasn't about to let tonight's glory be mine alone, Krimpt be damned. There was no way he could keep the soldiers away, lock them into training, before an audience this vast.

In their number, I spot Roran. His waist-length hair is drawn back with a scarlet ribbon—my concession so I could spot my Simbarabo amidst their bredren. The two who volunteered to accompany me into the alley knew what could happen to them, what they would need to face while I inspected the chain mail and set the Oscuridad up for this moment. *The* moment. I cannot see Venrier.

"He died in the alley." Accompanying Kirdan's words, three spears sink into the haunches of advancing beasts. "It was a good death. He would think it worth it, for this." He turns kohl-rimmed eyes to the crowd behind the barrier, who, upon seeing us take hands, wave, burst into deafening applause, cheers that have an air of the past to them, like it isn't me standing here, but Mama.

Above the crowd, three silhouettes stand on a rooftop. Against the evening sky, they are cast in shadow, but one of them nods our way. Lena. She witnessed what the rest of the city saw: Iraya Adair saved the Royal Horn. The Lost Empress.

A hero, to them.

And it doesn't feel half bad.

The head skitters across the floor, sliding in its own blood to rest before the triplets and their table. Magi recoil, jumping up from their seats to retreat from it. The steel pans come to an immediate halt; they're exchanged for my deliberate jostling of all the weapons I sport in my bandolier, on my hips, and across my back. Kirdan too, who I know is capable of moving like a silent storm, rattles like a bag woman beside me.

"Apologies for the inevitable stains," I call, striding after the rolling head.

It lands before the table, as I will it, mouth askew and agape, its eyes open and foggy—with the help of a little magic. A real Oscuridad head wouldn't have survived being separated from its body, but this boulder Kirdan and I took from the palace gardens, enchanted, and coated in blood from a wound on his forearm has worked so well.

Shaye rises from the low cushioned seats. "What is the meaning of this?"

With less elegance, Kaltoon scrambles to join her. "Your grace, leave it to me." Aiming his anger my way, he puffs up like the poisonous toads that dwell in Aiyca's wetlands.

Not breaking stride, I exhale a burst of magically powered air his way, and he falls back into his seat with a surprised cry. "I suggest you stay down."

Krimpt, still seated, looks on with a slight downward turn to his mouth.

"The meaning of this, Princess"—I address Shaye as Kirdan and I stop before the head table—"I would have thought that clear. You all doubted the existence of the monsters your loyal Simbarabo have defended you from, and yet here lies the evidence." I plant a booted foot on the head. Though I fight the urge to kick it into Shaye's calculating face, she flinches like it met its target. "While you have been here, dining, the beasts grew brazen enough to enter your market. They would have killed, had we not been present. Had the Simbarabo you forbid to dwell in the Horn been present."

Turning my back on the nobility at the head table, quelled and castigated, I address those who came running at the offer of free food and drink. "I know we are no strangers to monsters, across Xaymaca. Both the eldritch and the human. But the creatures dwelling here, the Oscuridad, do not disappear with salt or a wish-bag. They cannot be thwarted at crossroads. These creatures are being ushered in from the other side of the veil by one with the sole intent to subjugate this empire to her will. She who killed its last empress and does not fear paving her way to the throne with the blood of those she deems unnecessary. The army of soldiers loyal enough to protect you, even when you have treated them like stains, like sin, is joining me in the fight for the empire. I want to know who among you has their bravery? Who among you will fight to keep this island safe from the war that slinks, even now, up to the windows of your sleeping pickney, your elders?" My voice swells without the aid of magic, with something atavistic, as if Mama knew I needed her tonight. As if all the Adair witches who bore the weight of the empire across their shoulders knew I needed them too. "It's time to decide whether you will be part of the solution, or if you will add to the problem." At this Kirdan and I readjust, in sync and connected. Facing down his sisters, his uncles, once again, I feel my eyes narrow. "And choose wisely, or there'll be much more blood in this island's future."

Kirdan and I take our leave, stride matching stride, heads held high. There is no applause, no cheering here.

There is nothing like a demand for courage to root out the

cowards. But fear can be a more powerful motivator; I need the residents of this palace terrified.

The Simbarabo, unwelcome here, wait in the forecourt at the base of the palace stairs, bloody and euphoric after a successful evening. After this skirmish is over, and Aiyca is safe, the first sunrise will light a world made anew. A world where the gluttonous and indolent will no longer thrive, not so long as they are within the reach of justice's fist—my fist. Witch, Warrior, Weapon, yeh mon, but now, I accept, something more. Aiyca's redemption.

An empress. *The* empress. Let that unnamed bitch in Aiyca contest my existence now. I dare her.

Fighting the Oscuridad in the Royal Horn, traveling to the Singing Sands to face off with a story eater, all beneath the Adair banner, was something I didn't know I could have. Wresting Aiyca back from this Unlit is about more than preserving my family's legacy, I've realized. It's about continuing it.

The Golden Seat isn't mine. It's *me*.

Empress Adair.

53

JAZMYNE

We sail until it grows dark, docking for the night at Port Royale.

"Will there be further tricks?" I ask from the shore, eyes on Roje's handsome bredren from the Glide-by as he makes short work of crossing the shallows back to the *Silver Arrow*.

"Perhaps," the former says. "The crew remaining on the ship will keep an eye on matters." Elodie secures Anya's arm on her right and mine on the left. "Come, my favorite drinking house is several streets away."

Whenever I've visited St. Jayne Parish in the past, it's never been to this side of the port, where the streets run so tightly together a carriage could never fit between them, and gasps of pleasure ring from the shadowed depths of alleys. Too debauched for Alumbrar, it's notorious for smugglers, pirates, and women who deliver their babies to overflowing orphanages. Scandalized to the point where I am reduced to a pickney,

I glance at Anya and find my sistren distracted by Elodie. Amused, and unsurprised, I glance back at Roje, who, earlier, asked if I'd like to bet how long it would take for his sailing master and my first to slink off. His focus, serious, shifts to me as though we are back on the galleon, he starboard, me port, fated to meet in the middle beneath turbulent waters.

Twisting back around, I don't look his way again. Not over a dinner of oxtail stew, hot and rich and hearty. Or later, when candles burn low, their wax oozing down slender masts, and various griots entertain patrons. But it's futile, for as Anya and Elodie become more wrapped up in one another, and the crew disappear in dark corners, high on the thrill of the race, the victory I promised them, the world rocks and Roje and I meet in the middle.

Perhaps then, when we four egress to the upper floors in the drinking house, where a steady night's sleep is promised, I should have been ready to say no when Roje invites me up to the rooftop.

"I'll come too," Anya says, turning from Elodie's crestfallen expression.

"No, sistren." A hand on her arm, I shake my head. "Stay." *Be happy*, I don't add.

Roje and I alight to the rooftop, which is lit by stars and garlands of witchlight lanterns. I allow myself one unguarded moment to appreciate the beauty of the heavens, of Port Royale debauched, perhaps a result of the Xanthippe patrols I had to reduce. Elbows on the chest-high wall alongside Roje, I stare out into the city. Xanthippe glitter in the night like a shoal of golden fish, cutting through lanes, passing battalion soldiers.

Success is made all the sweeter knowing that, in a matter of days, I'll have secured the last bastion to stand against the Unlit. Roje seems to be thinking the same, given his next words.

"You've done well, Regent."

"Is that what you brought me up here to say?"

"I need to have a reason to bring you up here?"

"No." It's not quite the truth from me. He and I have become friends, and he's not without romantic options, but each of our encounters are dogged by that one moment in the drinking house, when I was ready to do anything if it meant securing him as an ally. Now we're here, what if he expects something? "But if you're done, I'd rather not be ravaged any more by blood eaters after a day of being subjugated to their swarms beneath the sun." I'm halfway to the door when he speaks.

"Would you leave it behind?" His back still to me, he doesn't move.

"Aiyca?"

"Yeh mon. Would anything make you leave it behind?"

At his next word, the joviality of the din ringing in the city fades to insignificance.

"Anyone?"

Awkward in these pants I had to oil my legs to wriggle into, I fidget. Does he ask for himself? Feeling as illuminated by the stars as I did all day beneath the blue sky, I am too cowardly to ask for clarification.

"I have a duty to this island," I settle for.

Roje's hands curl into fists where he stands; his back seems to quiver. I feel a fool for wondering if my rejection affects him physically when I spot the dark mass moving through the city. Nothing and now something in, what seems, the blink of an eye, amorphous, it seeps down from the sky itself as though tugged by a mighty hand. It undulates up and down. Wings. It moves like a swarm of creatures with wings. My breath catches. My gods . . . are those *winged* Oscuridad? Screams rend the night for but a second as Aiycans are swallowed by the obsidian wave. Fear sprouts claws that cut me deep to my white meat, dig in.

While I don't fear the night, I'm not cavalier about what hides in it.

And here it is.

This isn't the beast from the temple. This is a horde. An avian swarm.

"We need to get back to the ship." My boots slap across the roof; I wrench at the door. It doesn't open. "Roje, help me! Roje—" He still stands by the wall.

"Have you noticed," he says, "that things have a habit of turning to shit around you?"

Something as insidious as the wave of darkness roiling through the city spreads within my body.

I am split into three. The person who yanks more forcefully at the door, the novice who lays a hand on the hunting knife at her hip, and the girl who befriended the outlaw who turns slowly to face her. *Pirates play dirty*, Ford said. How dirty might Roje be willing to play for a map to an endless cataract of golden coins? Everything plays as though the axis the world turns on is stilled by the same great hand orchestrating matters across the empire. Roje lifts a powerful arm to free the axe strapped across his shoulders. Long legs stride toward me as he draws it back. Abandoning the handle, I fumble for the sword at my side with both hands, ducking as the axe whistles through the air and thuds into the door.

Felling the wood in three deft strikes, Roje kicks the remainder of it away.

"You must terrify them." Axe lowered to his side, he reaches back for me. "You're right, Genna. We need to return to the ship."

Hand in hand, we thunder down the stairs to the landing where Anya and Elodie await. A golden shield stands between them and the stairs below, where fire, jade and obscene and nightmarish, burns with all the light being eked away outside.

"Jazmyne!" Anya reaches for me. "Thank the gods!"

Our fingers almost touch when a smoldering beam plummets down from the ceiling; with a scream I shrink back against Roje.

"Anya? ANYA!" I scream.

"Come on." Roje drags me back across the landing. "She'll be fine. She's tough as a foot bottom, with her magic. And Elodie I know can handle herself. We need to move. The floor is unstable." He scans the landing and then boots open the door closest to us. "Turn away," he orders, picking up a chair.

I twist around, burying my face in my arms.

"Could do with magic now," Roje comments.

I turn to find him standing by the window.

"It's too high to jump."

"Help me with the bedsheets."

My hands, surprisingly, don't shake as we knot the bed-sheets into a ladder we waste no time tossing from the window. I go first, at Roje's insistence. Hand over hand, knot over knot, I don't shake, I don't even think of the ground. My mind is on Anya, Elodie too, and the fire that they were shielding against. The one they fell into. Anya and Elodie will be safe. They won't die. I refuse to entertain it.

But Roje and I might. I can't ignore it while it's facing me right now.

Between the fire and a four-legged Oscuridad eating the bowels from a magi split from their neck to trouser-line, I would have taken the former. That's three different types of Oscuridad I have seen now. Six legs, four, and winged. Mudda have mercy.

"Come on, Jaz. You know the drill." Roje tugs me into a run.

It's a pattern I know all too well, though I've never experienced it this close before.

Port Royale will fall tonight.

My sistren, allies, are in danger.

I'm not entirely able to shake the feeling that I'm not safe. That I was wrong to leave the palace. Something is amiss. We shielded my presence in the race, and yet when I am in Port Royale, it's attacked. Or not *something*, I think, as Roje and I clear the eatery and find Elodie and Anya blackened with soot out front, alive: *someone*.

The Imposter. They might know I'm here, which begs the question: Might I know them too?

54

IRAYA

"Does it ever go?" I ask Kirdan, our limbs entangled in the bed in our suite.

"What?"

"The need." It's like no matter how close we are, it's never enough. In the time we've had since the spectacle in the Horn it's felt like I'm pressing our interactions between the pages of my memory, preserving them like flowers betwixt the pages of a book.

"I hope never." Kirdan's hand strokes indolent circles on my back. "Do you—" He hesitates. "Do you ever think about after? When the battles have been fought and won, and you and I have nothing but time?"

"I didn't before." I always wanted to live to see the Virago, Nana Clarke, again. I didn't imagine this. Us. I didn't imagine that I'd be in a position to make plans to step out of the darkness and spend time in the light. I still won't. Not until my blade is pressed against the neck of whoever leads the Unlit, commands the Oscuridad. Tipping my head up, I watch the way dappled dusk light dances across the beautiful planes of Kirdan's face, the angles of his cheekbones, the sooty lashes. "Do you?"

"I didn't either," Kirdan murmurs. *Before you*, he doesn't need to elaborate.

If I don't make it . . . I should say, but my throat clenches around the words, against their sentimental fatality. That has never been us. This wasn't a beginning.

We both knew it was always an end.

"Come." I plant a kiss on one solid shoulder. "We should dress for the bacchanal." Prepare for our pilgrimage to the gap, in the morning.

"Wait." Kirdan's arm closes around my body, keeping me molded against his side. "I want to remember this for a moment longer."

Using my right hand as leverage, I push myself up and swing my right leg over his middle. Straddling the width of his hips, I look down at Kirdan with the same intensity he looks up at me with.

"I can give you a better memory."

The celebration vibrates through the dressing room floor when I leave my bath, trailing slivers of citrus fruit and mint leaves I was soaking in. Given all that's to come, closing the gaps, traveling to Aiyca, their steady beat echoes the sonorous boom of war drums.

This doesn't feel like an engagement for marriage; it feels like the prelude for battle.

Fuma beams at me in one of the mirrors as I'm clothed—if what I'm wearing even passes for clothing. The top is two slips of fabric that cling to my breasts, with straps wrapping around my shoulders; my entire stomach is exposed. She clips a golden chain around my neck; it drapes around my stomach to connect at the base of my spine, where the skirt sits. Though *skirt* is as generous a name as my top, given the slinky bolt of silk that just about preserves what little modesty I have left, so long as I don't make any sudden turns.

"Are you coming tonight?" I ask Fuma; she draws half my braids up into an artful tumble atop my head.

"Of course. The entire island has been trying to receive an invitation. It's been a long while since the last palace bacchanal." She flushes.

"Anyone you're hoping to meet on the dance floor?"

She flashes a coy look at me.

There's no room for secrets during a bacchanal. If Zesians are anything like Aiycans—which, from the bed frames stationed beyond gauzy curtains in the ballroom, I believe they might be—after this evening I might see more of Fuma than I ever intended to. There's a reason the celebrations are reserved for royal weddings. If everyone were allowed to host a bacchanal, islands would be overrun with pickney, leading to greater risk between siblings when the time comes for magical inheritance.

Finished with my hair, Fuma asks one of the attendants to retrieve the box. "The prince sent a gift," she explains as the green velvet box is deposited in my hands.

Surprised, I turn, expecting him to be behind me, but he left to ensure Zander, Esai, and Shamar are ready to visit the gap. I wish he were here when I open the box and behold the ornate spokes of the crown inside—not a tiara, a delicate circlet. This crown is a weapon, with sharp shards of gold thrusting skyward and emerald jewels peppered across the band that sits behind my ears. There will be no mistaking who I am tonight. No running. Not unless I want to take out several eyes on my way.

"Do you like it?"

That isn't the question Kirdan is asking me with this crown. He's asking if I'm ready. For tonight, and all that comes after. If I am ready to do it with him, as opposed to alone.

"I think I should give the prince my answer."

In lieu of Delyse or any additional members of my court from Aiyca, Fuma and several attendants who work the suite accompany me through the palace to the ballroom.

From the staircase, we can see through the glass tops of the doors. Out in the forecourt, carriages line up; guests cross the yard to enter through the ballroom doors. Most are dressed in as little as me, their skin spilling over waistbands and out of dainty twists of fabric. Bacchanal is permission to shuck the niceties of society, to strip down until your darkest desires are laid bare for whoever wishes to watch, to indulge. Deciding to take charge of Aiyca is one thing; feeling comfortable about all it entails another.

"Empress Adair!" Kaltoon swoops up to accompany me down the stairs.

Fuma waves her departure and disappears through the servants' doors to take a different route into the celebration. I nod my thanks; Kaltoon steps into our path, frowning.

"But where is the prince?"

"You know how he enjoys making an entrance."

The emissary tips his head to the side in confusion. "We need to announce you both for the evening to begin. My nephew was given specific instructions. Don't—"

"Be late," Kirdan finishes, slipping through the west ball-room doors. "I'm here."

In a collarless jacket with golden embroidery curling down its lapels, the rest of his ensemble is all black to my white. Kirdan looks good enough that I can't decide if I want him in those clothes, with his hair drawn back in a sleek bun that highlights all of my favorite features on his face, or if I want him out of them, his hair unbound and between my fingers.

"Same," he gutters out, teeth sinking into his full bottom lip.

"Yes, well," Kaltoon flusters. "Let's announce you."

Kirdan moves to my side, takes my hand in his, callus against callus. "You look beautiful in that crown, Empress Adair."

Focused on him, I barely register the doors being opened. A thin haze of smoke slinks between draped gazebos of diaphanous fabric. Edging the room, four-poster beds, with privacy hangings drawn back, alternate with alcoves created by additional bolts of white silk. Bodies already writhe and twist in the dark, bucking and rolling to the beat of the drums, the pans. Hands and limbs, teeth and tongues, it's as scandalous as I thought it would be—enough that little mind is paid as the herald announces Kirdan and me.

"This won't do." Kaltoon's head swivels on his stalklike neck. "We have to stop the music."

524

"Leave it," I tell him. "They know tonight is for us. Let them show honor the way the celebration is intended. The prince and I plan on doing the same." I don't check Kaltoon's face as I draw Kirdan across the dance floor. The first few beds we approach are already occupied. Magi worship one another with tongues and toys, several without drawing their privacy curtains. At the first free bed, Kirdan takes me by my waist and lifts me onto its soft platform. Eyes on me, he shucks his jacket with a tantalizing slowness as he ascends the steps to reach me. A pulse of will—his or mine, I don't know—makes the white and scarlet silk hangings fall around us.

"What can I do?" he murmurs.

"You can help me with these glyphs."

Kirdan gets to work securing the privacy curtains with magic, ensuring no curious hands can pry them open; I recall the glyph from the Adair Grimoire to replicate our shadows. Unlike most of the other symbols, its shape is without angles and acute lines. It's a pattern of curving half circles, and it takes me several attempts to render them perfectly.

"I'm ready for you."

Nestled between the pillows on the bed, I stare up at Kirdan as he brackets me between both powerful arms. We shift positions, allowing the glyph to record us and re-create shadowed facsimiles against the silk hangings.

He raises one hand to cup my cheek. "This ensemble is something else. Remind me to ensure Fuma receives a large Yule gift."

With our alibi secured inside the bacchanal for the Unlit watching us, Kirdan and I sift from the palace to a quiet bystreet in the Horn where Zander, Shamar, and Esai wait beside two carriages. The three soldiers startle at the sight of us—of me. Embarrassment burns through me. It's like being caught in my undergarments by my brothers.

"Did the glyph work?" Shamar asks, his eyes fixed on a spot above my head.

"Yeh mon."

"Good. Right."

Glancing at Kirdan, he nods and climbs the driver's ladder to sit atop the second carriage. Esai follows without a word, his cheeks red.

"What about Lena?" I ask Zander.

"She's already on her way to the gap with six of her closest sistren." He too won't look me in the eye. "We can leave, if you're ready."

"Almost." I clear my throat; Zander finally looks at me.

As I saw him do, I will my clothing to dissolve its way into my white pants, sleeved tunic, and golden breastplate. Shamar explained it's a flashier show of Summoning, to swap what is here for what is elsewhere—like the crown Kirdan gifted me. I send that back to our suite, along with the clothes I swapped out.

"I can never make myself glow, as you did that day in the Cuartel. Is it something extra you add?"

Esai sniggers inside the carriage; a faint red, Zander climbs atop the cab of the first carriage without another word. Kirdan joins him, as we discussed, so I can rest. He doesn't stay up there the entire ride. At one point I wake, and he's asleep at my side, on the modified interior we turned into a single giant bed in both carriages, so by the time the sky is alight with dawn, a brilliant blaze of mango and blood orange, all five of us have spent the journey across the island asleep at some point.

Over breakfast in the cab, modified once more to have benches and a table, Zander and I discuss the soldiers who will be laying the rete across the Unlit's Summoning Circles. The several thousand soldiers Krimpt didn't dare challenge me in taking should manage to close them with little difficulty over the next few days—by which time, we five and a few thousand more Simbarabo Fighters will sail for Aiyca to clear the way for the tens of thousands I will negotiate for with Doyenne Divsylar once we've blocked Zesia's source.

Outside, driving the horses, Kirdan stamps his foot twice.

We're here.

The source is located in the Eolian Caves to the west of the island, on the edge of land that was once sand, until the Supreme Being breathed the sandstone cliffs and caverns into being. Seeing them in person when we stop the carriages in their mighty shadow is another matter altogether.

"Wow," Shamar murmurs, hopping down from beside Esai.

There's a sense of otherworldliness to the deep red of the formations. Like the colossal mountains of stone, the tunnels connecting them could swallow you whole and history would forget about you.

"Legend has it," Esai begins, "that the Seven-Faced Mudda still blows through the notch between Roamu and Reim, brother cliffs, to temper their ire of one another. She wanted to show them that separately they are nothing, but together

527

the sum of their parts can create something beautiful."

"A home for monsters?" Zander snorts. "Surely Anansi didn't mean the Oscuridad when he spun that tale, mon."

"He might have." Lena crests the slope of dune before us. "Some say the spider god is the original Oscuridad." Her companion witches appear next, the lower halves of their faces shrouded against the sand; two caravans are parked at the base of the hill.

Shrouded in the same muted red as the beads of sand underfoot, as the caves before us, they are so redolent of the Virago I shake my head to ward off any mirages.

"Have you made progress?" I ask.

Lena looks me over. "Wahan to you too, Empress. We arrived several hours ahead of you, waited for the first light of dawn, and ventured inside via that north fissure." She points down at a sliver in the rock face. "Unfortunately, there are parts of the caves that are as dark as if it were night still. I bet Oscuridad roam there. Are you certain you can fight in all that gold?"

I return her smile. "With more skill than you on your best day."

"Really, mon? I heard the time away from your Virago sistren made you soft."

"Only in the places I'm meant to be. Want to find out?"

"All right." Kirdan steps between us. "We have the day to work through the tunnels. Can you two put your egos aside until we're done? Good." He answers his own questions and re-creates a rendering of the Eolian Caves before us in a shimmering gold projection he weaves, not from his conduit, but from the air around us. He summons beads of sand themselves to replicate our mighty surroundings. "The source is here." Kirdan points in the center of the structure. "About three miles in, though it will feel longer with the climbing. Lena, three of your cadre can enter from the north, and four from the west. Any additional tears, signified by the Summoning Circles, need to be bound with the rete."

Esai removes one of the crates from his carriage and levitates its wooden frame across the sands. Three miles, with the crates—notwithstanding any passages too narrow for them— won't be easy, but it isn't about locating every tear so much as it is about securing a perimeter of safety for us while we block the largest gap.

"Iraya and I will enter from here; Zander, Shamar, and Esai, you'll take the south." The map dismantles, reduced back to beads of sand that fall to our feet. "It's likely that we'll encounter Unlit too. Try telling them that the Lost Empress is with us. Word will have spread about Iraya's appearance in the Horn. They should have doubts about the witch they serve in Aiyca. But if they fight—" Kirdan looks at me.

"If they fight, don't lose," I finish. "But don't kill them."

"Well, I feel inspired to succeed," Lena deadpans. "Meet you in the middle. Bet we get there first."

"You're on." We shake hands.

She and her sistren take to their caravans and fly across the desert, leaving an arc of sand in their wake.

"Death is not fear," Zander says, clasping Kirdan's hand in farewell. "It's freedom." They hug, clapping each other on the back; Esai steps in to repeat the same gesture.

"Go home. Don't you die," I order him.

"Yes, Empress." He won't hug me, which makes me roll my eyes. Instead he dips into a bow and looks up at me. "Don't you die either."

"You know me to be stubborn." I shrug. "I plan on beating Lena to the center."

Forcing a laugh—for my sake or his, I don't know—Shamar moves to talk with Kirdan, which places me before Esai and Zander.

"Take care of him," I tell them, my voice unraveling with each word. "And each other."

Blinking furiously, Esai nods, dips into a low bow, jerks up again, and turns for his carriage.

"We don't say goodbyes, as Simbarabo," Zander explains in his deep, arch tone. "They are episodes of sorrow, and for us, departure from life has always been more of a cause for celebration. But I will be sorry if this is our end, Empress Adair. Iraya." He clears his throat. "The world has yet to burn, and I imagine it will be a beautiful sight."

"Don't imagine. Be there. With me."

The soldier angles his head and offers me a soft smile. "Take care of him."

"With my life."

"As he will you with his. As I will too." He turns for the carriage. "See you in the center."

I thought sitting in a palace, atop a throne, and sending my soldiers to die for me the worst part of ruling. Now I know why Mama did it. There is safety in distance. This . . . this hurts.

Kirdan and I leave our carriage, given the half-a-mile distance to our entrance and the necessity of retaining an escape vehicle. Battered beneath the sun as we cross the dunes, crate with the rete held aloft with magic, neither of us discuss what will happen if the net doesn't work across the gap we believe to be Zesia's source. The Adair Grimoire hasn't provided any alternatives, and Nyxia's not-explanation hasn't become any clearer in the time since she tried to eat me. One thing *is* clear, however: if I will it, so it happens. If the nets fail, then I have to be enough. Somehow I'll have to close the source.

I'm drenched in sweat when we reach the caves hollowed into the mountain by time and nature; it takes my head and eyes a moment to adjust to the shadows, the cooler air between the rocks that block the sun.

"It's a great honor to fight beside you once more," Kirdan says as we check vambraces and weapons and hydrate with skins of water. "Should anything happen—"

I cut him off with a hard kiss against his mouth. He returns my embrace with just as much force, as much defiance. This is not passion; it is a middle finger to death and dying.

Henceforth, it's a near-silent prowl through the red stone; our surroundings are still, but Kirdan and I temper even the echo of our breathing, so as not to alert the Oscuridad, the Unlit, that we are in place. It works. The creatures we come upon are dispatched before they realize they have company. Mentally, I've been cataloging the different types of beast. Thus far, all stand on at least four legs and amble like prowlers—a mercy that they lack basic intelligence. Several yards in, a slick patch makes me grip the wall—which gives, a wedge of rock swinging down from above. Kirdan tugs me back as I flinch, and, instinctively, will the rock to explode. The clamor of its destruction echoes on and on in an advertisement—an alarm: *here we are.*

The conduit in Kirdan's saber glows bright, and the chest with the rete disappears, is no doubt tucked away in a liminal space. "Forget the Summoning Circles."

"But we need to—"

"Run," he finishes, pointing down at the earth.

It trembles.

They're coming.

My heart thumps in my throat; we have to flee in single file due to the varying widths of the tunnels. Better at controlling his will, at focusing it on specific elements, Kirdan is faster than me, but he stays at my back, urging me on, shouting advice about how to make myself move like the wind.

It doesn't help.

"I'd rather fight!" I shout over my shoulder.

"We need to preserve energy!"

And the rumbling underfoot, the growing volume of thudding feet behind us, is more than the Oscuridad I fought in the Horn; then, I had the Simbarabo to help me defeat them.

"What do we do?"

"I've been doing it!" Kirdan returns. "Just keep going!"

It takes us miles, and my entire lung capacity, to break out of the dark and into the sun.

"We can break here," Kirdan says, not even winded.

Panting, I double over; he passes me the skin.

"I was throwing up glyphs as we ran, similar to those along the Cuartel boundary in Cwenburg Palace."

Ones to shock, I remember, to make you forget where you are, to send you to sleep.

"I'm sorry," I wheeze. It was careless of me to make so much noise."

"At least we know where they are." He rubs my back. "We'll avoid the east route on our way back."

The remainder of our climb is without excitement, thank the gods; and somehow, we make it to the center before most of the others.

"We used all our rete," Zander boasts, the first to arrive.

If I had the energy, I'd laugh. But the run has near wiped me out.

"We'll prepare the meal." Kirdan kisses the top of my forehead. "Rest."

My stamina is humiliating, but it could be worse. I doubt Jazmyne could have run for as long as I did. We wait for a fraught half hour as the others filter in—with the exception of three of Lena's witches.

"They'll be here," she says, brushing off Shamar's query into the fresh scratch along her cheek—stone, not a poisonous claw, she says. "Those Oscuridad are something else, but no match for my sistren."

None of us challenge her.

But while we can stall to prepare a meal, that doesn't take more than a couple of hours. Once it's been consumed, we've all checked our weapons over twice, and the sun has dipped even lower along the horizon, there's no ignoring the fact that Lena's witches still haven't appeared. Uttering a slew of curse words, Kirdan's cousin stalks off and out of sight.

"What happened?" Zander demands from the three witches still sitting with us.

"The beasts had two legs," one of them responds. "They stood like men, even if they no longer looked like them, and they were smart. I don't know if the others encountered them too, but—we barely escaped."

Oscuridad that looked like former men? Kirdan and I exchange a concerned look.

"Did the glyph work?"

"When we managed to hit them. I swear"—Lena's sistren looks haunted—"it was like they knew what we were doing. We had to run. The others—they were slow."

"We should get started, then." Zander frowns up at the sky. "I don't want to encounter the two-legged ones at nightfall."

Lena is coaxed around. But while she rejoins us, her lost witches do not resurface.

It's with a more subdued manner that we reconvene our mission. We are all more careful, more cautious. Zander silences footsteps; Esai our breath. Shamar stretches his hearing onward; I cast a shield around what remains of our party; Lena and her witches keep their weapons aloft at the fore and the rear—despite this, when we come upon the gap, I can't help feeling grossly underprepared.

The atmosphere should have been our first indicator. Unlike the proximity to the Summoning Circles across Zesia, here the air bears a chill—one that causes each of us to shiver. It is as if we have left the arid desert for ice caves to the north of the Great Sea. Though, I do not think there is any likeness to Zesia's main Eldritch Gap.

The source is a vast split in the rock face from which wrong-ness oozes and pulsates like a wound in the world. Malaise settles in my chest, as heavy and pressing as if one of the Oscuridad paws is pressed there. As a group, we edge back outside to crouch on the roof of a cave where we can watch for things that may egress.

"When was the last time you were here?" I ask the Simbarabo, Kirdan.

"A while ago. It's grown." The latter frowns. "But it's still as unguarded as it was then."

"There were guards." Lena frees a hemp pouch from her pocket and upturns it into her palm; an eye rolls out, one that's squeezed in her palm until it oozes between her fingers to congeal on the baking stone at our feet. An image is projected, a memory. Magi in gray usher beasts through the gap. It's a sickening birth, an inversion of what is meant to be beautiful as these pockmarked creatures drag themselves into our world. "We managed to capture this earlier." She sits back on her haunches as the births continue to play for us.

Shamar crosses himself in the Mudda's sign of seven.

"Let's seal that gap before those guards return," I say, meeting the faces of my companions. "Lena, you and your coven can stay ready to strike anything that attempts to come through. Zander, Shamar, and Esai, you can nail the rete to the wall—at least three I think—and Kirdan and I can sketch the glyphs to secure the binding. We move fast, and we move efficiently to avoid a bottleneck in the mouth of the cave, you understand?"

The responding nods are grim but determined.

I'm not sure if it's my mind, but the cave seems darker when we enter a second time, as if the sun knows there's something offensive about its incongruous presence and wills its light to bend away from it, repelled by the undeniable affront of existence.

The first nails go into the stone with ease.

The second do not even touch the rock.

It happens fast: Kirdan propels magic my way to shunt me out of the reach of an insidious arm extending through the gap. His saber follows through in a downward swipe as another arm, claws bared like a fistful of knives, shoots out.

"Quick, the nails! The hammer!" Scrambling back onto my feet, I sketch the glyph to render the beasts corporeal as Lena and her witches strike and strike again.

The Simbarabo, Shamar, take over hammering the nails in the wall. It's a sweaty, bloody free-for-all, and when the net is secured, it isn't our finest work, but the beasts on the other side of the veil are kept at bay.

"I'm not rehanging that." Stepping back to criticize our work further, Lena trips over something.

Kirdan.

Prone on the floor, his right gauntlet has been shredded by four claws.

No.

No.

Zander drops to the floor where Kirdan begins to convulse.

The time it takes me to react, to join him with a force that leaves my knees singing, feels too long. A creeping trail of green veins encircles his forearm where the sleeve hangs.

"Poisoned." The words are choked out.

Esai looks at me across his general's bucking body. "Do you know the cure?"

Green gives way to white as Kirdan's eyes roll back in his head and he stills. I think my heart stills too. Something stops in my chest. Maybe my lungs. I'm not sure if I'm breathing.

"Iraya!" Zander yells. "Do you know the cure?"

"No." I snap out of my reverie. "But I know who does. We need to get him to the Horn. *Now*. Lena—"

"We have this under control." Pale complected, the witch stands back with her sistren. "None of us were injured. Go. Take care of him."

"I won't forget this."

She flashes a smile dulled of its typical irreverence. "I'm counting on it."

55

JAZMYNE

The shadow that swallowed Port Royale seems to accompany us to the Unnamed Isles Anya and I chose as the base for the faux falls. The crew keeps looking my way, as though I brought the pall with us. Perhaps I did.

"We'll dock soon," Synestra says.

The shields Ford deemed trustworthy enough will have planted the gold by now. Once moored, the crew and I will wander for a day or two, left to the mercy of the map. Another fabrication. My sistren and I argued about the length of time we should spend wandering. I wished for a longer trek, something I'm glad she talked me out of now only one port city stands: Queenstown.

"I can't believe it's been this close all this while, and we've never found it before." Synestra's voice is light, careful. "I swear every body of water affiliated with Aiyca has been searched by pirates throughout the centuries."

"Had they brought an heir with them," I return, my voice similarly at ease, "one who knew the deep patwah to reveal the falls, it would have been found." The lie is one Iraya Adair gave me the inspiration to spin.

"How fortunate then for us," Synestra says.

Within the Blue Mountains national park, but on its edge enough to be out of the way, quiet, the Unnamed Isles are verdant in a way that's untouched by human hands. Tightly cloistered together, they're best navigated by foot. The sandy shore of the largest isle abuts the the rear of the mountain range. Anya turns down Roje's request to sift us there on behalf of my Stealths. Her defiance has been subtle, the shoring of magic, the sideways glances at the crew, the dark circles beneath her eyes, which were always open whenever I would jerk awake throughout our overnight journey here.

So we are rowed by two of the *Silver Arrow*'s crew, including the handsome man Roje was drinking with, during the Glide-by. We meet eyes for the first time. I offer a tight almost-smile, my mouth stiffened by nerves. There is something in the returned twist of his lips, something mocking, before he looks away.

Filmore and Pasha forge ahead to clear our path. The mangrove thrives in damp, porous lands. Every step taken feels like five. Beneath the canopy of twisting branches dense with leaves, it doesn't take long for our party to drip with sweat, to gripe about the journey.

We stop at the first water we come to.

"But is it safe to drink?" Anya asks, grimacing down at the black water.

"Yeh mon. Its darkness is due to the fact that it contains the same peat that gives Black River its name." Roje bends to unearth a handful. "Did you know it's incendiary?" He squints up at me. "Fight fire with fire, I believe you said. Perhaps your sistren can dry this for you."

Anya snorts. "Do I look like the company fool?"

"Is that a question you want answering?" Almost impatient, Roje thrusts the hand forward. "It's for Jazmyne."

Frowning slightly, Anya's coin sparks and, by her will, the clump of wet earth in Roje's hand dries. Freeing a small sack, he pours it inside and passes it my way.

"Remember, it only needs fire."

"Come." My sistren straightens. "We should join the others."

Like the preservation of her gold, it is another precaution, as though she doesn't want them to think we are conspiring. Or she doesn't want to miss what they may be saying. If we are suspected . . . I cannot come this far to *only* come this far.

"We should think about setting up camp for the night," Anya says a while later.

"Are we close?" Synestra asks.

I nod, scan the map. "Roje and I can make the rest of the way alone at first light."

"Forgive me," he exhales.

And as though they are the words everyone was waiting to hear, Anya, Filmore, and Pasha form a barrier around me. But we four are nothing compared to the shapes that drift in from the trees; at their head is a pirate I recognize.

"You."

"Me." Captain Shah, the pirate from the Glide-By, and from yesterday, takes position by Roje's side.

"You followed us?" I look between the two of them. "What's going on here?"

The captain tips her head to the side in pity. "I was told you were no wit, but I assumed you'd be smarter than this, mon."

"She didn't follow us," Anya supplies, while I blink, confused. "She colluded with *them*."

No.

I expect Roje and Synestra to refute Anya's words, but solemn, they merely stand and look on.

"I imagine you're disappointed," the captain says. "You should have known better than anyone after your family betrayed mine."

Realization arrives far slower than it should.

"You wrote the missive."

I am coming.

"Well done."

Beside me, Anya bridles at the condescension in the voice of this interloper.

"You are not a pirate."

"My tale is woefully unoriginal, I'm afraid. You feature in much of it, though. Your mama sought the help of my own to wrest Aiyca from the Adairs, and then betrayed her. My kin and I were rounded up and sent to Carne for too long, until once again I found myself standing before your mama in Carling Hill."

The last Ascension, when Iraya revealed herself?

"I see your confusion. Let me help you. I am Aiyca's Lost

Empress. I am here to take back that which you stole from my family. And I don't care if I have to tug it from your corpse. One way or another, I will receive that map." She clicks, and too fast to scream a warning, two of her company thrust weapons into Filmore's and Pasha's backs.

"No!" I yell anyway.

Anya grips me, holds me back from running to the Stealths as their bodies drop. The pirates in Captain Shah's company fall upon them, using blood from their wounds to paint glyphs on the ground. My stomach twists at the anguish in Filmore's face—he's still alive. They both are!

"Stop," I beg. "Please."

"You have seen firsthand what my army can do," this pretender says. "Now give up the map or watch your sistren meet the same fate." Bindings snap around Anya's body; they suspend her in the air like she's being held by invisible hands. "I will feed her, limb by limb, to the beasts beyond the veil. And then, if you are still unwilling, I will feed them parts of you."

Jade fire erupts where the bloody glyphs were rendered, born from some kind of circle similar to the one of hearkening Roje and I used—I look at him now. He does not meet my stare. Cannot meet my stare. Is this the Obeah-witch who provided the enchantment for this very moment? Has he been working me this entire time?

"Hand over the map," the pretender repeats. "And I will spare you the pain of me cutting off just enough of you to make you talk."

This time there is no mistaking the eyes in the depths of the flame.

Synestra looks on coldly. Roje, arms folded, raises two fingers with a deliberate slowness and pats his chest once, twice. He does it again before I feel the weight against my heart.

The peat.

It only needs fire.

"I need to retrieve the map from my pocket," I say. "It's warded to all hands bar my own." It takes everything in me not to glance at Anya, to fall victim to the shake in my hands as I retrieve the bag of incendiary peat and toss it into the flames.

"No matter," the witch says. "There are guzzu to pick the falls' location from your skull."

The world explodes.

An obsidian cloud balloons out of the fire with a deafening bang. A hand, familiar, tugs me forward. A voice, urgent, hot against my neck, turns my body and tells me to run.

"Jazmyne!" I twist to the desperate cry of Anya's voice.

"You can't." Roje's refusal is rough. "You need to go." He struggles to formulate his words as he has done before. Then I thought it sentiment, feeling. But he was unsurprised by the pirate, the Obeah claiming to be the true Lost Empress. Has he been bound? "Come back for us." He pushes me again.

I stumble through the smoke; Captain Shah barks orders; Anya continues to call my name. The tears that stream have nothing to do with the acrid burn of the peat. Once I clear the bilious cloud, I run.

Again.

I run and don't look back.

56

IRAYA

I issue directions for Melione's home to Zander with as much detail as I can. The sift is still out, though, and with Kirdan a dead weight magically held aloft between the two Simbarabo, the time it takes to order magi on the bank aside, to bang on her door—before I give up and will it off its hinges—takes too long.

To her credit, Melione and Kihra react fast. The doors to the former's dining room are opened, the table cleared, and Kirdan is placed with a care that throws me back to one of the first times he touched me with the same consideration. When he told me, after we finally connected, how terrified he is to die knowing we wouldn't have had enough time.

"I can't cure him," the Skylander says as she crushes herbs in a bowl. "I wasn't trained to. But I can put him in a restorative sleep to slow the spread of the poison. It will have to do until he can be taken to my brother in Aiyca. There is no one else close enough, or with more incentive to help, than Anan. If you want this soldier to live—"

"General," I correct. "Prince." *Mine.*

"And we do," Zander says.

"Then," Kihra emphasizes, "you need to take him back to Aiyca."

Beside me, Shamar touches my shoulder. "We have done what we were meant to do here, Empress. Perhaps this is a sign from the gods. We return to your home to end this once and for all."

The bacchanal would have ended in the early hours of this morning; my absence, along with Kirdan's, would be dismissed; given the proclivities on display, it would make sense that we retreated up to our suite at some point during the engagement celebration; royal pickney don't birth themselves; the largest tear has been closed, and I have information to seal the Summoning Circles I can sell the doyenne in exchange for the Simbarabo. It doesn't matter if the soldiers told Krimpt which glyph I used. She doesn't know how the Unlit are moving across the island; with that freedom, they can continue carving Summoning Circles and inviting the Oscuridad into Zesia, at the Imposter's behest.

"Okay." I look to each Simbarabo, Shamar. "We'll go to the palace and speak with the doyenne."

"Later," Melione says. "The prince will rest, and I'm sure you need to also, judging by your appearances. I can put on tea?"

Kihra issues a curt nod.

"We need to think of a container to transport Kirdan in too," Melione says, bustling out of the room.

My muscles pulse with pain; it's a reminder of all we've done today, the success of closing the gap, before dusk. All that remains is to hear from Lena—and indeed to figure out how I'll transport Kirdan to Aiyca, safely. Easing into a seat at the table, I lean back and watch Kihra tend to Kirdan's wounds; my blinks turn sluggish, my breathing eases; something soft is laid over my legs, then—a shrill alarm cuts through the tranquility of the Merchant's Paradise, and I've jerked onto my feet.

"What is that?"

"I'm not sure." Shamar bends for the blanket that slid off my legs.

"It doesn't sound good," Melione murmurs, eyes on the Simbarabo, tense and alert around the table.

"It's not. It's specific to the palace and hasn't sounded throughout my lifetime," Zander explains, looking my way. "It's a call to arms. Nimue is under attack." He looks down at Kirdan; I do too.

And at the sight of him, still and wan on the table, I don't care about the alarm, the people within the palace. What happens here isn't my problem—has never been my problem. But the man before me, the man I haven't had enough tomorrows with, he is.

"We need a ship," I say to no one in particular. "It doesn't have to be large. We can return for the Simbarabo another time."

"Empress." Esai shakes his head. "You hear the alarm; we cannot leave."

"Your general is dying. And if the choice is between Kirdan

and the family who never cared for him, well, that's not much of a choice."

Zander presses his lips together but doesn't challenge my words. Neither does Shamar.

"I don't know if I'll make it to the end of my point before you kill me, but we said we would preserve Zesia." Esai bites his bottom lip. "I have siblings here. Sisters I see when I can. My grandmother tried to smuggle me out of Zesia. These are the people Kirdan always told Simbarabo we were fighting for. The good people who don't deserve to suffer. If you won't save them for them, what about him?" The soldier nods down at his general. "What about his legacy? Do you think he'd stand by and do nothing?"

"I'm not doing nothing. I'm saving him!"

"He wouldn't want to live knowing it was so others could die. The residents of Changuu especially. If the palace falls, if *Zesia* falls—" Esai shakes his head. "I don't like staying any more than you do. But you said you wanted to protect Aiyca. Fight. Protect it. Secure it a powerful ally. A debt to be repaid."

After, Kirdan said.

Before I would have left without looking back, but that would be an insult to who I have become—who I have been with him, yeh mon, but who I have made myself. *I* ride the beast.

I am not shackled to it.

A tight breath is drawn through my nose, another. "Shamar, stay here with Kirdan. Esai, I need ships. Find me enough to make staying here worth it and then meet us at the palace. Zander—" The soldier's jaw is set as if he means to refuse me.

"You told me the world deserved to burn. Help me make that happen, so it can be made anew. Help me make a world he would want to wake in."

I hold out my hand for the sift; the alarm rings on.

"Zander?"

He meets my eyes at last. "He cannot die."

"No," I agree. "But those responsible for his state can."

Nimue grounds are ablaze with jade flame. Zander and I take down a horde of Oscuridad before we've set foot inside the palace.

It's like the Simbarabo dispatched today didn't block any gaps.

Either Krimpt interfered, or the Unlit among the monsters, robed in gray and many of them, too many, armed with gold conduit weapons, prevented the soldiers from doing what needed to be done.

"Do you think they closed any?" I ask Zander, thrusting my baton through the flank of a two-headed beast on the escalating stairs, unmanned, their witch covered in green veins and still on the ground. "Or are we about to face more monsters than you and I can take care of?" In an evening, which will feel like a lifetime considering it's only become dark in the last several hours.

Zander wipes blood from his forehead. "Both? I don't know. Talk less, kill more!"

Battling our way to the top of the entryway staircase, Zander and I exchange a look at the J'Martinet bodies that have already fallen, their blood splattered across finials, and launch ourselves into the fray. I can't quite sink into that place where the world narrows down to me, my weapons, and my instincts. Not when half of myself is back in Melione's villa. But I do my best to beat back the monsters. Dodging the swipe of a mighty paw, I sketch a glyph and launch it toward another herd of creatures attacking guests in a courtyard. If the Unlit attacked during the bacchanal, they would have had more success. Why move now, an entire day after?

Shit.

"Zander!" Rolling across the back of a corporeal beast, I shunt it toward one of the J'Martinet's waiting weapons. "The triplets. The doyenne. We need to get to them!"

Zander and I sprint through the palace halls. The court screams beneath the paws of beasts, but we do not stop. We cannot stop. If Zesia is left without Doyenne Divsylar—the motivation behind this attack after we closed the largest gap— the country will lock down, protect the heirs, and I won't get the army I need in time.

We round the corner to the doyenne's suite, screams at our heels. The J'Martinet tremble when they see us, their staffs, sabers, drawn. Zander and I call out our identities before they can fire.

"We are not at liberty to—" one begins, but at my raised hand, her words peter away.

"I don't want to hurt you for working the position you've been charged to, mon," I say, mustering calm and manners. "I'm not here to harm your doyenne, or her heirs, but someone is. Some*thing* is. I mean to stop them, and all agents under their employ. Are you under their employ?"

The witch shakes her head.

"What about the rest of you?" I ask, raising my voice. "Will you stand in the way of safety, or against danger?"

Though they exchange no looks, the witches stand aside in unison. When I am close enough to the doors, the witches there lay their hands on the wood so that they open for me.

I take a quick measure of the room. The triplets rising to stand from a couch adjacent to the bed, where the doyenne squats as I saw her last. Krimpt ceases his pacing before the balcony; a hand reaches for the saber on his hip as he looks between Zander and me.

"What is the meaning of this?" Kaltoon demands, storming toward me. "They were told not to let anyone in. Did you kill them? Of course you did, you—"

Magic would suffice, as it has before, but tonight I level a punch at his nose that takes him clean off his feet; the triplets scream; the great frame of the bed creaks; and Krimpt unsheathes the dull steel of his blade.

I connect my batons; a pulse of will makes the gold shine.

"Now," I begin, looking first to Krimpt, and then to his brother sliding backward across the tile using his hands and butt. "I want ten thousand soldiers to sail back to Aiyca with me. Grant them, and I'll protect you from the Oscuridad."

"And if I refuse?" With more dignity than one wiping at their bleeding face with the sleeve of their robe should have, Kaltoon peers down his nose at me. "You'll kill us?"

The doors heave as though pushed from the outside by a large hand.

"I won't, no. I'll leave the beasts outside to do the dirty

work. There's enough blood on my hands." Turning on my heel, I head back toward the doors.

"Bedpost."

Stopping, I turn back to look at the doyenne where she lies in the bed, swollen and sickly.

"You asked me where your pupa's staff was." She flinches as the doors buckle. "Western bedpost. Take it, help us, and you can have the soldiers."

The brothers are silent; only the battle outside the doors rages on.

I look closely—wood splices through the vast frame of twin posts wrapped with wooden vines, leaves. "You . . . chopped it up?" And then sat in bed day in and day out before it, to celebrate a victory. My body turns cold. Stiff. Whatever is present in my face makes her focus drop to her hands, open in supplication.

"Please, Empress."

The doors crack at my back; Zander nods, ready to fight. Kaltoon and Krimpt stand back, either by their doyenne's design or in fear at what I will do next.

Oh the things I could do. I could drag that witch from her bed and use both hands until they broke. I could—I could take dada's staff. My staff.

I could be more, better, than this family sniveling before me. Even if I really want to be less. Base. Monstrous.

I take a breath, another. The chill in my bones ebbs.

"You good?" Zander murmurs.

"Getting there." Hand out, I will the staff to come to me, to pull from the bed and into my hand.

The doors to the suite crash open as the bed fractures, the canopy falls, and the doyenne screams. Dada's staff in my left hand, the golden batons forming their own in my right, I cross them and unleash the tumult of centuries of Adair magic into the heart of writhing beasts. There is something different about the staff. I feel it even before I see that the beasts are gone without the explicit use of the glyph. Visualizing it was enough for this great conduit. Mine. Dada's.

Unlit spool into the bedroom.

Half a thought erects a shield behind me, protecting the Divsylars. Another sends the group of Unlit back through the door, as though swept by a single great hand—bar one. Launching Dada's staff, it catches him on his shoulder; he flies back against the wall with a pained cry, pinioned there. I stalk forward, freeing a dagger from my bandolier.

"Who is your master?"

Struggling, he quivers against the knotted staff of wood spearing through his shoulder. Any lower and he'd be dead.

"The Lost Empress!" he yelps.

"Let's try that again, since I am in fact the Lost Empress."

"No. There is another! She dwells in Aiyca. She—she commands the runaways from Carling Hill, the Unlit from the island's peripheries, and the Obeah across the island. She fights for *us*."

"I need a name. Or I'm going to tire of your lies."

"It's true," Ghislaine says.

I turn, look across at Kirdan's sisters; Shaye and Avyanna gape at their older sister, at Ghislaine.

"When you arrived," the girl goes on to say, "I thought you

were here to kill Mama. I thought—I thought I'd be free."
She looks down at her feet. "That's what the Lost Empress
promised. Help her infiltrate the palace, seize control, and she
would spare my sisters and me. Then you arrived, and you
didn't do anything your missive said."

"Because I didn't send it."

"I know that now."

"You betrayed us?" Shaye's hands curl into fists. "Seize
her," she instructs Zander.

"That's the first sensible decision you've made since I met
you, and it's just as well." Hand out, I summon the staff. It
jolts from the shoulder of the Unlit with a wet squelch. He
collapses with a pained groan. "Because once I am through
killing the Imposter who has infiltrated my home, I plan to
return to Zesia and expunge any similar threats to my plans of
reinstating the Adair rule across the empire." I look at each sister, the doyenne in the ruin of her bed, and her brothers. That
chill edges in once again. I breathe, shrug it off, and smile.
"Now, shall we discuss my ships?"

57

JAZMYNE

I never thought I'd be in a position to potentially pray for a quick death.

Indeed, while running for my life, breathless and ragged from the many reaching fingers of mangrove in this isle, I have nothing to do but castigate myself for the many great things I didn't consider:

Being tricked into losing Cwenburg.

Scramble over the fallen bark. Keep your footing. Ignore the needles of pain lancing through your side.

Opening my arms, my heart, to another man who, when faced with honor or betrayal, once again chose the latter. His aid, the confusing things he said, don't matter.

Is that howling, and is it getting closer?

And now I face a future as murky as the shallow valleys of water I splash through, aware that I should be quiet but unable to slow, to stop, because who knows—if I do, I might very well dash myself into one. And I cannot. Because while I am without Anya, who I hope is running too, and without country or crown, I remain Jazmyne Amancia Cariot.

To be afraid isn't to be without hope.

Slowing before a tree, chest heaving, I glance around the swamp, wishing so fervently for a glimpse of silver hair, I almost convince myself that I spot someone out there in the denseness of the trees. Blinking back the burn of sweat, I grab a branch on the nearest tree and hoist myself up. The experience of hand over hand, the quivering in my arms is redolent of Iraya. She would recommend seeking higher ground, to better survey the land.

As high up the tree as I can be without it shaking, I realize my mistakes too late. On the ground, the knots make it difficult to see the undulating terrain, but not as impossible as it is from up here. Blinded by the canopies of all trees except those in my immediate vicinity, to climb back down would be a folly I might not walk away from—because I am not Iraya. I shouldn't have thought I could be.

"Consuelo," I murmur, slapping a blood eater dead on my arm. "Protect me." For it will be dark soon, and I won't even have starlight for company. I imagine Iraya's cruel taunt back when we were attacked by the Rolling Calf, and fight tears.

No one at Cwenburg will know where to look for me, except my Stealths. But without Ford and Pasha, how will they know I need them to find me? If I do not return, the palace risks being breached. Javel was not sacrificed. The new councils don't know he still lives in the Holding Cells. Why did I leave? Better still, how am I to return?

With more care than I have done anything in my life, I lower myself onto a branch thick enough to sit on with some measure of comfort. The Mirror of Two Faces is bright amidst the dull green of surrounding leaves, my own muddied apparel.

"Iraya Adair," I call into its face.

She doesn't come.

I begin to shake. "Iraya. Adair. I need help!"

A blade presses against my neck with a quiet suddenness; I almost take my own head off jolting against it.

"What name did you say?"

My gods. I didn't even feel the branch move.

"Pirate, what name did you say?"

As though duppies, girls, women, emerge in the surrounding trees, glimmering gold like fireflies in the waning light. Obeah. Unlit. The ersatz Lost Empress has found me after all. I reach for the combs in my afro.

A golden spark zips through the trees to catch me in my fingers.

"Don't move," I'm warned.

"But do feel free to answer my question," the witch opposite me says. "Which name did you say?"

"Why ask what you know," resignation makes me tell her. "Or are you claiming Iraya doesn't exist now, in addition to stealing her identity as the Lost Empress?"

Nimble as a dancer, the girl at my back shifts to stand before me. "Whoy! Have we met before? Did I do something to catch the wrong side of your tongue?"

Her sistren in the trees heckle her. But, speechless, I can only shake my head, for between two large eyes are two vertical scars stained white-gold. In fact, incised into the brows of all the witches are the same scars. I didn't notice before, given how filthy they are, but . . . the uniform of pants, a slip-fronted tunic adorned in copious golden finials, is white.

"You're not runaways," I whisper.

The Warrior, one eyebrow raised in amusement, shakes her head. "While we are clarifying matters, mon, you are saying that Iraya Adair, the Lost Empress, lives? Not only that, but you know her?"

Her coven, for what else can they be, lean in as though what I say next is of the utmost importance.

"Yes."

"Roje was telling the truth then." The witch before me smiles; broad and beautiful, it chases some of the darkness beneath the canopy away. "I hoped you'd confirm that."

Then something cracks against my skull, and the world goes dark.

58

IRAYA

The Divsylars wanted to discuss far more than the ships.

There was talk of a parade, from Shaye of all people. Just as quickly as it was raised, the idea was extinguished beneath the fire in my glare. While she might have been ready to play happy families, her uncles too, only so they might wield me before monstrous enemies, I am going home.

They can clean up their own damn mess.

Delyse has been notified of our timeline; with Shaye's help, Zander, Shamar, Esai, Melione, Kihra, ten thousand Simbarabo, and I board a fleet of ships to sail to Aiyca in the eve, following the victory at Nimue.

Kirdan would have beseeched me to wave to the Zesians gathered at the water's edge, along the pier at the busy port, to see off the Lost Empress and her general, especially since it's due to their good fortune that we were able to sail with so many soldiers—and many of their trade ships—but Kirdan sleeps in a glass coffin beside me. If I can't find a way to convince Anan to spare him, he won't say anything ever again.

With a significant shift, the galleon pulls away from the pier close to the Delta Province. I cross the cabin on unsteady legs to secure the door before taking out the Mirror of Two Faces.

"Jazmyne Cariot," I try, as I have been since stumbling up to the suite I shared with Kirdan, covered in blood and wounded, hours earlier.

She still doesn't answer, and I need her ready to welcome us into Aiyca in five days' time. The heavy weight of Niusha's head on my thighs stops me hurtling the mirror at the wall. Forlorn, the shadowcat mewls beneath the hand I raise to run through her fur; we both watch Kirdan, stiff and silent, before us.

A knock sounds on the door. I cross the room in two steps to open it.

"Aiyca has been lost," Shamar breathes, as though he ran here.

A glance back at Kirdan reveals Niusha has curled herself around the frame in which he resides. Good. Shamar leads the way out onto the deck where Melione, Kihra, Zander, and Esai stand in a huddle away from the sailors. I spare a nod the captain's way as we join them.

"Tell me everything."

It's too short for a song, but long enough for an inscription on Jazmyne's tomb—the Fool Regent, they'll call her, who bargained with pirates already aligned with the Unlit.

"They waited until she was at sea in the race for queen—"

"I *told* her to stay put."

"—before they took the island, under the leadership of the Lost Empress."

"Don't call her that," Shamar castigates Kihra, the harbinger of the news.

"Whatever. The Cariot regent hasn't been seen since the warning missive arrived at Cwenburg," Kihra expounds. "They are to vacate, or the Lo—the Imposter," she amends, "will take it by force with her army of Oscuridad."

"Your information is credible?"

"My brother sent a message. You know how."

"He pierced the veil?"

She nods.

"Then he can pierce it again and take me across."

"It doesn't work like that." She shakes her head. "You need a sponsor to move through without being torn apart by anything looking to return to this side of the line. I cannot expound any more than that. I have already said too much."

"On the contrary." My voice is low. "You could have said a great deal more, sooner."

Melione looks out to the line where sea meets sky. "Do you think Jazmyne is dead?"

"She's not." My hand loops my wrist, the Shook Bargain there. "But who knows how long that will remain so, and we are some distance from Aiyca, with a tenth of the soldiers we need to fight for it—against a witch telling everyone she is me."

"And people are listening," Kihra adds.

"Thanks, mon, that makes everything better."

Boiling with a steady rage that makes formulating a plan

nigh impossible, I stride away from the others to the starboard side; Zesia is already a stroke against the horizon, a part of my past as we sail toward an uncertain future—one I hoped to secure by winning the battle.

I didn't consider that might mean losing the war.

"The route," I begin, turning back to my party. "The captain said it doesn't have to take us across the gulf, is that right?"

Zander nods. "There's a trade stream; it works like a sift. The coordinates at sea will transport the ships to a checkpoint guarded by Aiyca's Sea Defense."

"And if I wanted us to cross the gulf instead?"

"Suicide," the lieutenant answers. "Over half these ships aren't equipped with cannons. We'd need weapons to sail there."

"Actually," Esai adds, "we'd need death wishes. No one survives the crossing."

"Well, we have to."

With Aiyca lost and Jazmyne unavailable once again, our only hope of winning this war is to fight fire with fire.

"Do you trust me?" This question I aim at Shamar, Zander, and Esai.

Eyes flick between my own. "Yeh mon," the first answers.

"But that doesn't mean we always think you're sane," Zander deadpans, with Esai's nodded agreement.

"You might be right there." And then I tell them about my plan. How I read the Grimoire, my ancestors' notes about the Monster's Gulf, assimilated what the Skylanders do with their own Oscuridad—not taming them, working with them. *Fighting* with them.

Kihra purses her lips, but doesn't contest my assertions.

"Aiyca is lost." I shrug, like I can't feel the weight of those implications across my shoulders. "The Imposter won't make entry an easy feat. I need a battering ram to smash those doors in."

Collective realization dawns.

"You mean to leash one of these things—my gods." Shamar gapes at me.

"I mean to try. I have to appeal to the prison guards first."

As rich as Shamar's mahogany skin is, it seems to pale. "And if you fail?"

"That's not an option."

Not for Aiyca. Not for the thousands of soldiers aboard the ships I bullied the Divsylars into giving me. Not for Kirdan and Niusha below deck. And not for me.

Not today.

59

JAZMYNE

Virago.

I wake with the name on my tongue, in a dank dark that feels both endless and intimate. There is no better eraser than time, but having woken on the ground somewhere cold, somewhere dark, my eyes covered by a strip of fabric, hands and feet bound, the memories return piece by piece. Skilled beyond measure, I remember from the stories. The coven of Warriors served the Adair line faithfully. Until the late doyenne's usurpation, when, save for Empress Adair's vanguard who died like the Masters, the bulk of their number were nowhere to be found. I suppose Mama presumed them dead.

We didn't know then nothing in Aiyca that dies remains that way.

The rock beneath me is smooth; no scents save for the wild, and something earthier, rich, permeate wherever I'm being kept. Aside from my own breathing, loud in my ears without

my sight, there is nothing to suggest I'm with company . . .
except those stories I heard about the Virago: duppies raised
from Coyaba itself to do Adair bidding. Devil tings.

My breath grows louder. If they've lived here all this while,
without detection, how have they survived? I don't want to
know. Don't want to consider what they might have done to—

"She thinks we're going to eat her."

The scream that rips out of my chest, my core, echoes long
after the laughter of whoever is in here with me sputters to a
raspy stop.

"Alumbrar are too tough, unyielding, to be enjoyable,
Regent," a second voice croons. "We prefer swine or poultry."

The cover is snatched off my head without warning; a thin
face materializes as my eyes adjust to the bright light filtering
into the stone cavern of my surroundings.

"Do they truly say we ate people, in Aiyca?" the witch asks,
not the one from the tree, the one with laughter in her eyes and
something of Iraya Adair in the arrogance of her expression.

"Iraya," I blurt out, taking in the four witches positioned
before me. "I know the daughter of your empress."

A tall witch steps from the light at the cavern's mouth into
the shadow where I'm sitting atop a pallet. "You said as much
yesterday, mon." It's her, the puckish-faced jester from yesterday. "We have heard all about your relationship with Iraya.
From Roje."

"What do you know of Roje?"

"More than you." She leans on a solid wooden staff. "Tell
me, how was your chat with your dear mama that Seventh
Night?"

"You're the witch who gave him the guzzu?"

"Taal." She nods at the first witch I spoke with. "That's Rhonda. Zeplin has the half shaved head, and Faehn is the one who looks like she'd rather skin you alive than have this talk."

I look around at them all—my inspection of Faehn is cursory—dressed in tones of green that camouflaged them in the park, hale, *alive*. A decade's absence is no small feat, for an ordinary person; perhaps Virago are used to such avoidance of capture.

But not discovery.

"Unlit did not triumph in St. Bethann," I begin slowly. "All reports I received detailed that they've been kept at bay here. I thought it was my measures, but it's you, isn't it? You've been fighting."

"That's enough questions from you."

In the time it takes me to blink, the puckish-faced witch, Taal, becomes as serious, as threatening, as Alumbrar pickney were told Virago are.

"Roje says you're good people." She straightens, and the entire move is limned with a predatory elegance. "But he isn't a particularly good person himself, and you're Alumbrar. Enough said, mon. He's told us everything happening in Aiyca. Iraya Adair has traveled to Zesia to return with their army, and you were holding the line until her return."

"But what you didn't account for," Zeplin says, sweeping the the long braided half of her hair over her shoulder, "is that the Imposter Empress has been waiting for you to leave the palace so that she may sink her claws into what she believes hers."

"Why?" I demand, pretending I don't know Iraya warned me of the same outcome.

The witch tuts and wags her pointer finger from side to side. "As I was saying. We managed to thwart your capture, but Aiyca won't be safe while she is still at large. Iraya will return, and when she does, she will need a clear path onto the island. With you here, and a few shields standing between the Imposter, the palace, and full control of Aiyca, that responsibility falls on us. And you."

"We have an offer for you." Taal shrugs. "We need a liaison to travel down into St. Bethann to relay a message."

"A Shook Bargain?"

"That is not a currency we use here. Either you keep your word, or we hunt and kill you." Faehn carries no visible conduit gold I can see, but her teeth flashed when she spoke. The thought of a mouthful of metal and their earlier jesting about diet makes me a little queasy.

"I—I need time to think. Since you don't want me asking questions."

"Oh, you can ask now," Zeplin says, rising from her crouch. "It's just so annoying when you're trying to explain something and someone keeps interrupting."

"It's enough to make you want to kill them." Faehn hasn't blinked once, I don't think, since my cover was taken off.

"Thinking time," I press.

"You can have three days." Taal turns toward the mouth of the cavern; my restraints fall away. "We'll send food and provisions."

"Am I a prisoner?" I call, rubbing the raw spots on my wrists.

"That decision is up to you, Regent."

The three others join her in the mouth of the cavern, step out into the sun, and drop.

Scrambling to my feet, I run to the entryway and utter a prayer that I haven't yet eaten. Below there is nothing but a canopy of verdant trees stretching to a blue horizon; their tops are dusted with snow rarely seen south of this elevation. I'm trapped, chilled, and they—they must be insane or immortal. There are no other explanations.

Edging back to my pallet, I find a fruit platter and jug of water alongside some strips of saltfish, bammy, and items to wash with. The cavern is raw, but clean. Glyphs incised on the walls are warm to the touch. Either there is a spring within these walls, or an enchantment to abate the cruelty of the mountain's winter outside. A small mercy given the drop— one I might be thrown down if I don't agree to help usher Iraya onto the island.

It's better than being up that tree, alone, waiting for the Imposter to catch me as she no doubt has Anya. I offer a prayer for my sistren. Is she with Roje too? He told me to return for him. He worked with these witches to ensure I'd be safe from the Imposter. One who he has been working with. I don't—I'm not sure how I feel about that yet. I don't understand it. I don't understand him. Could I work with the Virago, become their liaison, and find a way to meet with the Nameless? If so, they could locate the *Silver Arrow* for me. Anya. And then? The Imposter, Captain Shah or whatever her real name is, she has the faux falls, the Oscuridad, the Iron Shore—wait. She is not their queen.

I am.

Kicking off my boot—glyphed to be kept impervious to water by Anya—I lift the sole to reveal the hidden compartment in the heel, from which I pull the blank map to the Conduit Falls. It still doesn't work, but it might not have worked with the late doyenne either. I thought the rationing of the conduit gold a means to prevent the Obeah rising against her, but what if she didn't have the location of the perennial source of coins? Either way, I have both the locket around my neck, the Mirror of Two Faces the Virago must have dismissed as a simple looking glass, and I hold what the Iron Shore wants, in the map. Not only am I the victor of the race for queen—if I can find the *Silver Arrow*, Anya—I hold the majority of Aiyca's magical artifacts.

Iraya will have the Simbarabo, but I'm not out of the fight for our home just yet.

PART IV

BUT
A
LITTLE
AXE

60

IRAYA

For the first two days at sea, when I'm not sparring with Zander or talking strategy about the Oscuridad we're to catch with Shamar and Esai, Kihra and Melione, I study the Grimoire from the hammock beside Kirdan's pyxis.

Compared to the grunts the Unlit have summoned from beyond the veil, what waits in the Monster's Gulf are gods. The highest echelon of beasts, who, had they attacked anywhere else, would have been successful in their coup to subjugate Aiyca to their will. If they'd managed to possess my home, its gold, the world would likely have fallen before them.

I'm not sure freeing one of them is the best idea I've had.

The surrounding waters are flat, but our journey feels precariously inclined. If I'm successful, we stand to gain a powerful ally. If I fail . . . I cannot.

The only respite to be found is playing with Niusha, whenever I can draw the shadowcat away from Kirdan. Mostly because the sailors are terrified to see her up close, and their jolts whenever she prowls by have been the closest Kihra, Melione, Zander, Esai, Shamar, and I have come to laughing.

The shadowcat refused to leave her rider's side the third day. The crew weren't grateful.

Not when the fog came instead.

Cloistered in a corner of the main deck, Melione, Kihra, Shamar, and I rise from the map of Aiyca we've been discussing. A series of shouts ring from the sailors as, without warning, the ship is engulfed by a colossal floating island of the vapor. We are swallowed by its nebulous maw; the gray mist pulsates like something sentient. It could have whispered, *I've been expecting you.* My forearms, bare, pucker into gooseflesh. Now isn't the time to quiver like a novice facing her first opponent. *Warrior. Witch. Weapon.*

"Ho!" the captain bellows, instructing his crew to bind sails, to ready oars instead.

"Why would they do that?" Melione asks, reaching for Kihra's arm.

Knowing the answer from my time at sea with Dada as a pickney brings zero comfort. "To prevent shredding. To control our speed." I raise my chin, roll my shoulders back. "We're here. We've arrived at the Monster's Gulf."

There are stories you hear as a pickney, thinly veiled warnings, in truth, you dismiss. The Monster's Gulf is one of them. Tucked up in bed, wide-eyed as an older sibling, cousin, coven witch, relayed tales about the dark pit in the Great Sea preventing Aiyca, Zesia, and the Skylands from attacking one another, you'd be forgiven for dismissing it as another Anansi tale—but the Adair Grimoire, however sparse, was very clear. The beasts are real, and my ancestors sent them to this prison as a warning. Not only to additional monsters that might think of attempting to dominate Aiyca, but also to our neighbors. *We defeated these beasts; can you?*

"Zander and Esai picked a hell of a day to visit the other ships." Shamar peers ahead, where the three galleons ahead of us disappeared, folded into the fog like it flung its arms wide in a choke hold masquerading as an embrace. "We should have arranged a signal, a flare or something."

"We didn't know about the fog." Kihra's look is condemning.

It wasn't mentioned in the Adair Grimoire.

"Excuse me—" I stop one of the crew rushing past. "Is the fog to be expected?"

"We've never heard reports," she answers, adjusting her eye strap. "But there hasn't been a successful crossing since—"

"I know, since before my family turned the gulf into a deterrent."

"Are you thinking the fog could be a safety feature to stop ships crossing?" Shamar asks.

"Something like that."

How many explorers who hadn't heard of the gulf would turn around? They might forge ahead in the hopes it cleared. Which it could. But what if it doesn't? We could find ourselves turned around, bows aimed at one another, without knowing until the fatal crash. And then there's the chance that one of the beasts is doing this. The Grimoire said the gulf is guarded to stop the monsters escaping. It didn't say anything about their magic. Given the time they've been down there, they may have learned a trick or two.

If I had nothing to do but watch over an army of failed monsters, and I was of their ilk myself, I might cause a shipwreck or two, to stave off an eternity of boredom.

"Melione, you should go below deck."

"I'll accompany her," Kihra says.

"We'll look in on Prince Divsylar." The first squeezes my hand in passing.

"Don't suppose you'd like to join them?" Shamar tries.

"Not a chance, mon. We're here because I made it so."

The soft glow of lanterns sparks in the rigging above, where, with a burst of will, I make myself see—just about—crew and Simbarabo armed and waiting. Good. Though, with my vision not what it was before we entered the fog, we might be just as at risk of being shot as whatever is causing the fog. Accidentally, or by design, if the fog turns us against one another. We cannot linger. It's time to do what I came here for—why I risked ten thousand soldiers.

"Draw your weapon, Shamar."

Startling, as though unaware his broadsword wasn't already in hand, he unsheathes his blade. Golden light fills the weapon from the pommel to its tip.

Equally ready, my magic is a spiraling force I picture tunneling down, down. It penetrates the ship floor, breaches the hull, and continues whirling through the waters. Deeper and deeper still I send it until, eyes closed, the current is a weight I can reach out and hold, tug. I extend a lambent hand of pure will and knock once, twice, against the deep wall of water.

I'm here.

Come for me.

The ship, propelling through the waters, rocks softly. Several people swear.

Below the surface, I keep knocking until I reach seven.

A pulse brushes against my magic, like the head of an animal seeking a comforting stroke. My magic cups it—and then I know nothing but pain.

A scream bursts through my lips.

"Iraya!" Shamar takes my arm.

The sharp edge of what feels like teeth enclose around my will; I shake, drag. They don't relinquish. I withdraw, pulling back, drawing my magic up and out and—

"Iraya!"

The connection breaks; I open my eyes, stop the scream dead in my throat.

"What happened?" Panting, Shamar grips both my arms, like while I was fighting off whatever latched on to my magic below the surface, he was fighting me.

We're surrounded by Simbarabo; the soldiers hold swords, staffs, bows and arrows. Each weapon is pointed outward; underfoot, the ship's soft rocking has turned into a veritable seesaw.

"Tell me," Shamar demands.

"I let the guards know I'm here. They didn't seem pleased."

I can't see down into the depths the creature unsettling the boat must be swimming through. Maybe creatures. Ones shaking away the stupor of staying dormant for tens of years. However sleepy, whatever latched on to me left its impression in my magic. Its hunger, and thereby its recognition of my ancestors who sentenced it to its watery grave. Rage will make stiff limbs strong, and it will come. They might. For me.

"Keep alert," I call down the length of the ship. "I think we should expect at least one visitor."

The captain issues a sharp curse and orders the crew to ready the cannons.

With Dada's staff below deck anchoring an enchantment I cast around Kirdan and Niusha, I have only my bandolier of conduit blades and the batons. The latter two I free and connect until they are one long staff, leaving a hand free for additional weapons, should I need them.

But the time doesn't come.

The third day eases into night, and no creature breaches the surface of the gulf.

"Zander and Esai won't return now," Shamar says, while we shovel down a quick dinner on the top deck, our weapons in reaching distance. "It's too hard to pinpoint the location of the ships when we're moving, and they can't see us this deep in formation."

We both whip around at a muffled shout from the captain, but no tentacles wrap around the mast, no giant eyes blink through the fog.

"They could answer our messages, though," I say, lowering my hand from the batons now strapped across my shoulders. Several missives have been taken by Simbarabo to the fireplace in the captain's quarters. "I don't understand where the guards are."

But then we all do.

"Ho!" the captain calls again, and a net is lowered, hauled back on board; wooden pieces drop onto the ship's lower deck.

The bite of dinner still in my mouth suddenly tastes like dirt.

"Why didn't we hear anything?" I ask, unholstering my weapons to form a staff once again.

"The fog," one of the Simbarabo says as fourteen arrive to encircle Shamar and me. "It's likely suppressing sound, blinding us in a way."

Oh gods. Zander. Esai.

"They would have sifted away," Shamar says, echoing my thoughts.

"Then why didn't they send us a missive in warning?"

"Because the fighting isn't over," another of the Simbarabo soldiers intones, moon blades held aloft in steady hands.

Outside the glow of lanterns and conduit coins, the fog ahead of us has become as impenetrable and thick as a cloak over our heads. Dark. Too dark.

"There are monsters imprisoned with mouths big enough to swallow ships whole," Shamar whispers, furious. "And you might have set one of them loose instead of a guard. Maybe more."

My own guilt is present in every tight muscle in his face.

I cost those soldiers their lives.

"What about flares?" I ask the Simbarabo closest to me.

"Why do you think they didn't send flares—the beast will come for us!"

It will come for *me*, if I light the way.

"Cover your eyes."

"I'd rather see my death coming," Shamar says beside me.

"No more of us are dying today. Move with me," I instruct the soldiers. Together, we edge across the lower deck until I am in its center; a pulse of will illuminates my batons as I thrust their length downward. A hole cracks through the wood. "Now," I call for all on the ship to hear, "cover your eyes, and hold on to something."

There's probably guzzu to generate the light I need; if I were a trained Squaller, I'd know how to crack a hole in the heavens and let it rain. Instead, I reign. My breastplate, batons, gauntlets, even the thread in the clothing Kirdan had made for me. I am a human bolt of power and intent. The fog holds stubborn for a while; I give more. Pushing upward and out, I imagine myself growing bigger than the Monster's Gulf. As the cover lifts, thins, a faint din rings, like it's sounding from the bottom of a well.

"There! Hold, Empress!"

Quivering, I squint against the brightness of my own magic, which reveals the horror of a beast half draped over a capsizing ship. Without discernible shape, it seems to summon more tentacles at will, until the vessel it occupies crunches like a bone in its hold. My gods. Nodules run the length of its hide, like scarification. Battle wounds. The Grimoire didn't say if the prison guards fought too—if that's what this thing is.

"What do we do, Empress?" Simbarabo stand ready to attack, to fight for their bredren.

Ready to die for me.

But I said no more would fall.

I free my staff from the deck with a tug, split it back into two, and holster the respective halves across my shoulders. My breastplate I undo with a thought; it crashes down onto the deck behind me.

"What are you doing?" Shamar asks, turning.

"What we came here for. Do me a favor? Cut the Oscuridad open if it swallows me."

Shamar makes a grab for me a split second after I've already turned, slipped between two soldiers, and made a run for the starboard side. Rather than skidding to a stop and giving myself time to think about how grave an error I might be making, I place both hands on the side, swing my legs over, and plummet into the dark waters of the gulf below.

61

JAZMYNE

"I have several conditions of my own" is my opening gambit to Taal and her sistren on the third day—at least, I assume it's the third day; the sky outside the cavern opening has been lit with stars since I—from a safe distance—draped a sheet from my cot over the edge in summons.

The Obeah-witch raises sparse eyebrows. "Can't wait to hear them."

To tear them apart, she likely means. But I used the entirety of my thinking time to ensure my plan is without fault.

"I will meet with your Obeah outside the park, but I get to see my allies first. They need to know I'm alive." Lying about this, I decided, wouldn't be wise. These witches will expect it of me, if Roje told them everything.

"The Nameless."

The fact that Rhonda didn't phrase that as a question is all the confirmation I need.

"Yes."

"Next?" Zeplin bites into a plum, like this meeting is an inconvenience.

"Once I have left here twice, and returned twice, my role as liaison is over."

Faehn's upper lip curls back, revealing the gold grill I glimpsed when we first spoke, days ago. "Listen, if you're not with us, you're—"

"Not against you," I interrupt. "Fighting for the same cause."

"In our way." Taal crosses arms, limned with muscle, over her chest. "Your Nameless aren't an army."

"No. But they can help those who aren't fighters either. It's not soldiers alone who bleed in battle. Aiycans need warning. They need leading."

Taal shrugs. "Sit back and wait Iraya out."

"I have every intention of waiting for Iraya to return." If I'm by her side now, she can't surprise me later. "But I won't sit back, no. Do you agree to my terms?"

"Two trips." Taal nods. "The second will be to usher in Iraya's return. The first happens today."

Rhonda clicks, the gold beads in her braids spark to life, and a pack appears at my feet.

"We need to finalize preparations for Iraya's arrival," Taal continues. "You'll travel down the mountain and meet with one of the Jade Guild who will accompany you to see your Nameless. Then you will go to our meeting as our proxy, listen, and report back to us tomorrow morning."

"Tomorrow?"

Zeplin tosses her plum seed out of the cavern. "Get dressed.

I have the honor of accompanying you for your first descent."

"You expect me to dress before you?"

Taal snorts. "Zeplin, she's all yours. See you both tomorrow morning."

They egress the same way they did three days ago, plunging into the open sky like they're concealing wings on their backs.

"Tell me that's not how we're traveling down the mountain?" The Blue Mountains or Dry Harbor, I'm not sure. I hope the latter. It's smaller in scope.

Zeplin's response is to turn her back. "Get a move on, mon. There's a weakness in your patrol we'll exploit in an hour or so."

"Weakness?" I ask, shimmying out of the smock I changed into three nights ago.

"Your rotation. The battalion soldiers and the Xanthippe don't communicate well with one another. You should have integrated them better."

Biting back a petulant response, I draw the tie on the waist of the pants, slide my feet into the boots, and tug the tunic over my afro.

"Don't forget the cape. If your hair is spotted by Unlit in Exmoor, you're dead."

That town is in the foothills of the Blue Mountains park; the closest Nameless outpost is hours away in Four Paths. I should have argued for a carriage—I should have argued for a great many more practical things, I realize, when Zeplin beckons me over to the mouth of the cave. Before I can ask if she means for me to scale its sheer face, she pushes me over the edge. My shock feels like it lasts an eternity, before a scream tears through my lips; it launches flocks of birds from trees across the park.

"Corner your mouth and flail less!" Zeplin shouts. Arms flattened at her sides, she shoots past me. "Or you'll miss the opening."

Which opening? I try to ask. But I can't do anything other than strip the lining from inside my throat. Then I'm falling through it, a break in the canopy, beneath which is a net. Impact is abrupt enough to knock the air out of my stomach, silencing me as I roll legs over head, side over side, to the edge, where I immediately empty my belly of the meal I ate last night.

"That better be it," Zeplin says, somewhere at my back. "Come on, the next part of the descent is more your speed."

She calls it a sky pod, the diamond-glass orb attached to conduit gold thread that propels it through the trees and down from the snow-covered peak of the mountain. I had no idea it existed. That something like this was even possible.

"And you Alumbrar believe yourselves superior." Zeplin snorts, watching me. "You couldn't even design a pod light enough to be suspended on thread this thin."

"Please don't discuss the thinness of the thread."

Between being pushed from the cavern, and the sky pod, when we dock at a platform in the mountain, I'm so relieved to see the mossy steps we have to take the remainder of the way, I don't care that there are likely a hundred logs beaten into the soft earth, at least, down into the sprawling park, a manicured jungle, below us.

"I wondered if you knew what the descent was like, and that's why you negotiated for two trips."

"If I knew, I would have argued for one."

"Not a fan of the sky pod, hey?" A man steps from the shadow of a wooden gazebo, like a checkpoint, at the foot of the steps.

My heart thuds in my chest. "Or strangers lurking in the dark."

"Guy." The Obeah-man, about my age, maybe a few years older, doesn't offer me his hand. "Zeplin, we'll return as soon as all safety measures have been ascertained."

"We're expecting you early."

With another nod, Guy starts walking.

"Wait!" I look between him and Zeplin. "The closest Nameless outpost is in Four Paths. It'll take us all day to walk there."

"You should have negotiated for a carriage." Zeplin shrugs, echoing my earlier thought. "Guy doesn't have one. Do you?"

"No."

"I need the carriage."

"Maybe trip two. Go on."

"You're not coming with us?"

"Consider this a test, Jazmyne. Faehn is hoping you fail. I'm— Get down!"

Ducking into a squat, I twist around. A shield formed entirely of golden magic balloons from an unknown conduit on Guy's person. The vast rectangular force field stands between us and—nothing. So close to the mountain range, the canopy of trees is thicker here than it is as the park unfolds. It's so dim I can't discern anything but the many trunks of trees and frames of pergolas.

"Philo," Guy calls. "I didn't expect this of you." As an aside to Zeplin and me, he explains, "He was Jade Guild. Recently defected. He knew of this meeting point."

At last, three figures draw away from the dark and step into the glow of Guy's shield; dressed in gray tunics and pants, the boy and two girls stand before something else. Something that remains in the shadows of the park at their backs. Its bulky mass sets my nerves on high alert; darker than its surroundings, what I can see is . . . not human.

"You picked a duppy empress," the man calls. Philo, perhaps. "I'm fighting for the Adair legacy."

"You're fighting for a liar," Guy states. "And you will die a traitor."

"Only one of us will die in this park."

The Unlit step apart, permitting what's at their backs to step into the light. My insides clench with fear. An Oscuridad sits atop *another* Oscuridad. The beast on six legs prowls forward on paws the size of a man's head, like the one Roje and I evaded in the temple. The rider . . . I retreat a step before him. It. Something that might have been a man once. Before. On the other side of the veil, before his time there distorted him into this spindly skeletal nightmare of what a human should be. There is a sunken pit where his mouth once was; folds of skin hang where cheekbones should be; only his eyes seem to hold any life. A warm green, they observe Guy, Zeplin, and me with an unmistakable hunger. I didn't receive reports about beasts like this.

Like *him*.

"Excuse me," Philo says. "I should have said three of us will die, and by us I mean you and your companions."

The Unlit beast and its rider charge at the shield; my heart leaps into my throat as I expect it to smash, but it holds. Guy charges with it before him, like a solid wall. The Oscuridad dissolves, turning to shadow. The Unlit girls brandish sparkling silver swords, their partner a wickedly curved scimitar, like Kirdan's. Three of us will die, their man said. I reach for the clips beneath my hood.

"Don't you dare," Zeplin snaps. "If they know you're Alumbrar, they'll put two and two together. Come to me. Just—shit. Shit!"

The Oscuridad rematerializes before us—close, before us.

Zeplin smacks her fists into the air, shouting warnings at Guy to turn around and help me. It's curious, her body. The skin on her hands flattens, like she can't pass something invisible.

"What is that?"

"Just come to me!" She waves, frantic, her eyes on the Oscuridad as he dismounts and sends his irreverent steed to charge into battle against Guy. "You'll be safe over here, Jazmyne!"

The beast on two legs cocks its head to the side at my name; the pit where its mouth would be shapes out the word, like it's committing it to memory. One long leg steps back. Like it means to flee, to run away to someone with my name—to Captain Shah? No.

I don't let myself think about an alternative. My afro tumbles free as I lower the cape and reach for Anya's clips.

"Ready something sharp!" I shout at Zeplin.

"No! Come to me and you'll be safe, mengkeh." She smacks

her fists against whatever is keeping her from me again. "You can't fight that thing!"

She's right. My bowels loosen. Gods, she's right.

The Oscuridad looks between Zeplin and me. Roje and I were chased by one I wouldn't have expected to talk, but this creature . . . if it had a proper mouth, I wouldn't be surprised if it could hold an entire conversation with me. My hands quiver. Sketching the Banishment Glyph Iraya showed me to render the beast corporeal, I shunt the fizzing gold symbol toward it—miss. The locket against my upper chest warms—but of course. I have to think bigger. I have to believe in bigger. In me.

"What is that?" Zeplin shifts back and forth in my peripherals. "What are you doing?"

"Ready your weapon!" I shout, tracing the glyph again. Its second birth is singular. A sparking manifestation that fills the darkness beneath the canopy. The Adair Amplifier is a kernel of sunlight against my chest. Aiming, I push the glyph forward with both hands; the Oscuridad watches it travel and dissolve into its stomach. "Quick, Zeplin!"

I daren't look away from the Oscuridad. Not a second later a golden weapon spins through the air with a faint whistle and hits the Oscuridad dead center of its forehead. With a baleful moan, it disintegrates into smoke. I did that. Me.

"My gods, what was that glyph?"

"Do you have a second knife? Guy needs it— Guy, move!" The Obeah-man dispatches the last of the Unlit, ducks and rolls across the earth; I fire another glyph. It puts the last to shame. With the Amplifier's might, it is a vast force against the night. Both a shield and a sword. It slams into the beasts on its flank as it rears around to strike. "Hit it!"

Zeplin's blade lands a split second after the sword Guy shoves into the beast's side; as it dissolves like the first, my legs give; my knees slam onto the ground. That was . . . something I never want to do again. My stomach twists; if it was empty from earlier, there'd be trouble.

"Regent," the Virago exclaims. "I didn't know you could fight. Guy, are you good?"

"Yeh mon." On his back, the Obeah-man stares up at the sky. "I'll send some of the others to clean up these bodies."

"I'll take care of it. Go now," Zeplin orders. "We don't know if more will return, and I need to tell my sistren about that glyph. Regent—"

Not yet able to stand, I look over my shoulder at where she was stuck throughout the duration of the battle.

"Enjoy your carriage ride. I'll see you in the morning."

Guy, it turns out, is quite chatty once he's "borrowed" us a cart to transfer us from Exmoor to Four Paths. I understand that to appear normal we should talk, but, after we've exhausted my surprising victory against the Oscuridad, I can't stop looking around, scanning the secular and nonsecular going about their lives. Do they know that I'm missing? Do they think me dead?

These are two of the questions I ask the Nameless when Guy drops me off and leaves to ditch the cart. I have thirty minutes before he returns. The updates are brief. No word has been issued about my death or disappearance.

"What might that mean?" I think out loud, at ease here. It isn't so much that I'm surrounded by my people, but that I'm away from the weapons and the monsters.

"That the Imposter intends to find you," one of the Nameless says.

Either that, or she'll lie and tell the island she already has me leashed and lying by her feet when she makes her move on the palace—the palace!

"What news of Cwenburg?"

"No official word. It's guarded from the base of the mount right up to the gates."

Then Ford is keeping his word. Blessings to all seven of the Supreme Being's Faces.

"The Unlit are showing themselves more in St. Mary now. Businesses in Ol' Town are packing up and moving in anticipation of a battle between yourself and the Lost Empress. The Imposter," the witch amends.

"What do you need us to do?" an older Aiycan woman asks; the ratio is almost equally split between the nonsecular and my order. It's everything I wanted, and I don't even have the time to stop and appreciate it.

"I need you to find a pirate ship." Unperturbed by the exchange of curious looks, the shock, I raise my hood to leave once more. "It was last seen around the Unnamed Isles."

"But why—"

"That doesn't matter. Once you've found it, track it wherever it moves, and wait for me before all exits of the Blue Mountains national park in two days." Not only will I find Anya, but Roje and the *Silver Arrow*'s crew. "Don't show yourselves unless I give word."

"For what?"

I meet every face in the cramped room. "My rescue."

"What about our order, Aiycans, what do we tell them about you, where you are?"

"Don't tell them where I am. But you can say I'm still fighting for this island, that I'm doing all I can to win."

Even going so far as to walk into a Jade Guild safe house, to take notes on their plan to meet Iraya at St. Bethann's Bay. Apparently she's been in communication with the Virago for phases, yet she would be mad at me whenever we spoke for withholding information. Well, she can't know that her sistren are unable to travel beyond whatever invisible barrier was keeping Zeplin in place, otherwise she wouldn't be relying on them to provide her safe passage along the bay and up the spine of the Blue Mountains. And why couldn't Zeplin move? It might have something to do with why the Virago haven't been seen since Iraya's mama ruled the empire. Someone didn't want them to interfere, this past decade.

And if they cannot help Iraya, regardless of the Simbarabo she sails here with, Alumbrar success might come down to stepping back while she and the Imposter destroy one another.

Adair versus Adair won't be the beginning of the Obeah's return to rule.

It will be their end.

IRAYA

I wake to stars visible outside my porthole, which means we survived the Monster's Gulf.

With a groan, I attempt to sit up; my elbows push against something hard for leverage, rather than the coarse fabric of my hammock.

"She's awake."

A hand pushes into my shoulder, keeping me on my back.

"Take it easy, Iraya." Zander's commanding drawl is tight. "You've been out for a while."

He edges into my vision, along with Esai, Shamar, Kihra, and Melione.

"Kirdan?"

"Fine," his lieutenant answers. "Now tell us what happened."

"What happened?" I repeat.

They exchange looks of concern above me.

"Was I hit?"

"You don't remember diving overboard?" Shamar reaches for the weapon on his hip.

"If you're going to attack me, I'd like to use a chewstick first."

"Why don't you remember what happened?"

"Give me a moment and I will." Knocking aside the hand that tries to keep me on my back, I sit up and lean against the wall in this tiny cabin.

The others move back in a defensive semicircle, like they're expecting greater resistance.

"We sailed into the fog, and the ships at the head of the fleet were attacked by something. I—" Images, unclear and scattered, come to mind. The cold shock of hitting water, the guzzu to help me breathe. There was a flurry of limbs as I tried to propel myself toward a surprise I wasn't expecting. Something ancient and conniving that opened a single eye, as large and consuming as the surrounding gulf, and then . . . a plan.

"I had a plan," I tell the others. "A plan you knew about. To appeal to the guards of the prison within the Monster's Gulf—" Zander swears, as he did the first time I told them, I remember. "To bargain for their help in releasing one of the creatures to use against the Oscuridad in exchange for . . ."

"In exchange for what?" the lieutenant snaps.

"I—I can't remember."

Striding forward, he snatches up my arm and brandishes the damning suction marks that curl around my wrist like a bracelet. "For this? You bargained with monsters banished feet below water level, and you can't remember what you promised them?"

"Hey now." Shamar steps in. "She's been out for days, give her time to—"

"Days?" I interrupt. "What do you mean?"

"We arrived in Aiyca hours ago, Iraya. You—you dove into the water," Shamar explains, looking around at the others. "I jumped in after you but couldn't see anything."

"We fished him out," Kihra resumes, crossing her arms. "A little while later, the attacks on the ships ceased, and you bobbed up to the surface. We didn't know if you were dead or alive." She looks at where Zander stands with his arms folded, his shoulders raised. "There was . . . concern. Blame."

"Your waking was a fraught time." Melione sits on the edge of the bed beside me. "If you can't remember—perhaps it's a mercy. Not many people can associate with monsters and emerge entirely whole. But at least you're you."

"You thought whatever I spoke with sent a changeling," I say, realizing their defensiveness. "How can you be sure it hasn't?" The war against the monsters that sought to conquer Aiyca is legendary. Changelings walked my island's streets with the faces of those they'd killed; bredren and sistren were none the wiser, until their bloody ends. And I knocked for those monsters.

"You bear a beast's mark." Zander's tone is like ice.

For the first time I look down and note the suction marks curled around my left wrist.

"No changeling would carry a bargain, for fear of being unable to remove it when they turned themselves back. Idiot."

"Grouch."

Zander visibly swells. "Reckless. Fool."

"Overbearing—"

Shamar takes a step forward; Esai responds in kind. No. No.

We weren't meant to return to Aiyca divided.

"Enough." I sigh. "I—I apologize for worrying you all." For starting this facetious argument. For potentially causing more trouble, rather than the solution I'd hoped to secure. The brand around my wrist is a giant question mark. Not just what I might have promised the creature in the deep, a prisoner or a guard, I know not, but what it will give me in return.

"You may have caused more harm than good," Zander says. "You understand now, don't you?"

Rather than restarting our argument, I take a breath. "Tell me what happened when I was recovering."

I'm updated about casualties and losses during the sea Oscuridad's attack, how Yule passed with everyone either watching me or the horizon, but the Sea Defense didn't object to the fleet's ingress into Aiyca's waters. Jazmyne must have spoken with them before she went missing.

"Delyse sent word from the inn she mentioned in her last missive," Shamar says. "She'll already be waiting for us. But I can go ahead alone to tell her that we need more time."

"No. If she's sent word and it's safe, this is our window." Especially since, without the sea creature I'd hoped to leash, we will effectively be trapped on these ships if the Unlit launch an attack from inland. "What of Kirdan?"

"My brother is here, with Kirdan," Kihra says. "We didn't think putting you in his quarters was wise after, you know." She raises her eyebrows at the mark on my arm.

Lowering my tunic sleeve, I swing my legs off the bed with a wince. "Take me to him."

Anan resembles his sister in the way siblings do only when you know they're related. With good humor, and a healthy dose of fear, I'm pleased to see, he tells me we brought Kirdan to Aiyca in time. He administered the first dose of the cure and, once I pinned him against a wall and leveled one of my knives beneath his chin, assured me he wouldn't attempt to harm Kirdan further. Between me and Niusha, who watches the Skylander through one sleepy eye from the bed Kirdan's been moved to, he will be quite fine.

"Protect him," I tell her. Her tail curls around my hand, as though in promise.

"I doubt anyone will dare get close, with her there," Melione says.

Anan edges around the shadowcat, who makes no move to give him space, like picking his way through a field of upturned knives.

"Kihra." I turn to the Skylander, who watches her brother. "What of your promise to have your sister fly her army here?"

Anan glances over at me. I nod Kirdan's way, indicating that he mind his business.

"There has been no reply as of yet."

The Skylanders might be hoping I'm killed in the war.

"Death won't stop me collecting what's owed, if your family doesn't help."

"What do you call my brother's presence here?"

"A start."

"We'll send another message," Melione says, always the

peacekeeper. Or bullshitter.

"Then I suppose you'll be staying here, with the lieutenant."

Zander, to his credit, doesn't react.

"I would like that, Empress," Melione says.

She's not a fighter, I understand. "I'll send a signal when it's safe for you to set foot on land. With my reply from the Skylands."

Lips pursed, Kihra nods; the two witches step out into the hall. Anan accompanies them, with a promise to return and look in on Kirdan later.

"Niusha will tell me if you don't."

"She speaks?" He sends a frightened look her way, before hurrying through the door.

"I should be accompanying you," Zander argues the moment we are alone on land.

Though fatigue hits me then, the reminder that I was just lying down, I stand tall before him. "To shout at me some more?"

"To stop you making those reckless choices you're so fond of." He looks at Kirdan, unconscious on the cot. "The general would expect me to stay by your side in his absence."

"The general has no say in Aiyca. And neither do you. I outrank you both." I mean to smile, to soften the sting of a truth, but everything hurts. "Comb your hair, think fondly of me."

Zander rolls his eyes.

"I'm not sure we can trust the Skylanders," I confide.

"In that we agree."

"Then it's settled. You'll stay and keep Kirdan, yourself, safe."

"I'll send a sign once we're united with Delyse."

I'm in the passageway when I hear Zander's uttered thanks. It wasn't a decision he should have made, me or the general he's served his entire life. Besides, I'll be as safe as safe can be, once I've reunited with the best witches across the Great Sea.

St. Bethann's Bay has no official dock for ships, which we wanted. The rocky inlet isn't ideal for much, with the stones too sharp to make sitting comfortable, and the coral reef knifing from its side dangerous to boats. All we need to cover against is the palatial cliffside restaurant overlooking the waters. Simbarabo Squallers aid with that from the ships concealed in Admiral's Cove, a place Dada frequented when I was a pickney. The bulk of the fleet remains docked by the peninsula Kirdan spirited me away to after All Souls' Night, for now.

Under a cover of thick fog, our ascent up St. Bethann's Bay is unnoticed. Like most of Aiyca's coastal towns, the narrow streets and sandy inclines are ideal for a small cadre's covert entry. Tonight, myself, Shamar, Esai, and fourteen Simbarabo slip past homes and closed storefronts like ghosts; the town seems untouched by Unlit. Delyse said she'd work with the Jade Guild to keep the streets clear and quiet for us a phase ago. I knew sending her ahead was the right call.

Vigilant for Summoning Circles, Unlit, or Oscuridad, our party slinks through the streets I remember from my childhood whenever my sistren and I would venture down the mountains. Exmoor's verdant park, Bluefields farming settlements, and St. Bethann's Bay were as far as we could travel.

"The inn is just there." I point out its location to the others where we wait in the recess between a butcher's and a town house. "Let me send the signal for Zander now."

"No—" Esai stops my hand reaching for the batons holstered across my shoulders. "Let's wait until we're before the inn. We might still encounter the Oscuridad or Unlit."

"It's only a matter of—"

The night splits apart with a deafening shattering of glass.

I'm thrown out onto the street before the inn. My ears, my head, ring with the explosion. Logic can't permeate, nothing is clear but pain, and the sensation of something wet trickling down the side of my forehead. Coughing, I roll onto my side and lever myself up. Bodies. Everywhere. Long-haired and dressed in their furtive uniforms for hunting. Simbarabo. My gods. Esai. Shamar. Clenching my teeth against calling their names, I force myself to stand, to free my batons from their holster. Something isn't right. Something—

"For Aiyca."

A shard of cold metal sinks into my left shoulder with a quick bite, and then burning. My baton falls from my left hand, clatters against the ground as weakness spreads down my limb from the knife embedded in my shoulder. But that pain is secondary to the one that threatens to floor me when the knife thrower steps through the hanging smoke from the explosion.

"For Aiyca," Delyse calls. "You must die, Imposter Empress."

The Imposter is here too? I glance over my shoulder, to the left and right amidst the rubble of the inn's front yard.

"*How* can you look for another?"

The blood pooling beneath the golden weapon jutting from my arm is hot.

"*You* sent me here to do what's best for Aiyca," Delyse continues. "This is what's best. You, out of the way."

The ringing in my head intensifies.

My gods.

"You've defected?" My ears feel stuffed.

"I am on the course I have always walked." She tips her chin up. "For Aiyca."

"But—"

She throws another knife; I shield against it, my right arm and baton jerking forward to parry her hit with a golden force field.

"You fought for me to be this—to do this. I'm home. I'm here!"

"You are here too late, Iraya. I tried to tell you not to put us second."

"I didn't."

"You did! You chose him over us!" Delyse's lips peel back from her teeth. "You didn't take an army, you fell in love with their general. Amidst a war, you were more concerned with flirtation and romance. How *could* you?"

"How could *you*?"

At my question, her face tightens.

It's my only warning before I'm hit from both sides, behind, ahead, by a ringing assault on my ears. The noise has a pitch so high, I drop back down onto my knees and slam both hands over my ears to avoid it. My left arm barks in pain at the movement; shredded muscle tightens around the knife, and I cry out.

Delyse stands across from me, panting but otherwise unaf-
fected.

A second knife flies from her bandolier.

It lands below the first.

My vision swims, my ears remain stuffed as though full of
blood. My head—with the noise, the excruciating burn of my
senses, it's hard to breathe, to stop myself combusting into a
mess of flesh and bone fragments. Even so, I know what's happening. I know and I can't believe it.

Delyse has decided I am not worthy, and she's going to kill
me for it.

63

JAZMYNE

"Don't let the Jade Guild hog Iraya, okay, mon?" Taal, my companion for the second descent down to the park, sits with her feet up across the bench opposite me. "They'll want to talk her ear off, but it's important she comes here as soon as she arrives."

"Why don't you come and bring her back yourself?" I probe, drawing my cape tighter around my shoulders. Fur-lined, the Yule gift was waiting for me two mornings prior. Despite telling myself I wouldn't wear it. I'd forgotten about the holiday. About innocuous things like opening presents and eating eleven courses with family, bredren and sistren. Of course, I didn't do the latter. The Virago left me alone. "I'm sure Iraya would be happier to see you than me." When they've visited with food, or to magically clear my chamber pot, none of her sistren have answered my queries about their inability to leave the park.

"It's obvious you knew her. Don't you want to welcome her home?"

"Did you miss what I said?" Rolling her eyes, Taal crosses one ankle over the other—only to slam her feet onto the floor as a mighty impact rocks the sky pod.

My hands brace against the bench as we swing on the rope of conduit gold I always thought was too thin to correctly support the pod's weight. "What was that?"

"Either Iraya is still as fond of an entrance as she was when we were pickney—" Taal stands, unperturbed by the unsteady pod, and cranes her neck, trying to see above the dense tree line. "Or trouble."

"She's fond of that too."

When the sky pod docks, Guy alone waits to greet us.

"What happened?" Taal demands.

"Trouble," the Obeah-man confirms. "The others went ahead to the inn. Can you ride?" he asks me, indicating the jungle-prowlers pawing at the earth behind him.

I nod.

"Then what are you waiting for!" Taal shouts. "Go and bring her home. Bring her back to me, you hear?"

Guy helps me straddle the auburn creature and then mounts the obsidian beast with the single horn protruding from its forehead. "Keep up" is all he says before digging his heels in.

The distance between the park and St. Bethann's Bay is shorter than that to Exmoor. In less than an hour, my cape is stored in a saddlebag, and we bound from the bush and skid out into the stone streets of the coastal town. Bent low against my prowler's neck, I keep Guy in sight. Up and up we climb; people fall back from us with angry shouts, but we don't slow, not until the fray of battle rings clearer than the clatter of prowler nails against stone. Guy's beast leaps atop a low garage and then onto a rooftop. My heart shoots to my throat as my creature follows, scrambling to stop across the gravel atop the flat landing where several others stand and look.

"Stay with the Master," Guy shouts. Dismounting, he brandishes his spear and launches it down into the crush of bodies in the streets below. There are no monsters, only Obeah fighting Obeah, some in gray, and then—long-haired soldiers who move like marionettes controlled by Duilio, the Mudda's Face of War and Blood and Metal. My breath catches. Simbarabo. She actually did it.

"I thought I'd see you here."

I startle at Master Omnyra beside me.

"You're not in the palace?"

"I'm several places in this moment, and soon to be elsewhere." She turns back to the battle, to two witches in a clearing unhindered by fighters. One soldier is banging against something invisible around them, just as I saw Zeplin do yesterday. Flinging himself at the barrier again and again, he shouts at the witch who is on her knees, encased in a coruscating corona of white-gold energy.

The witch in a chest-plate of gold.

"Iraya—" A gasp sticks in my chest. "What is she doing?"

"Do you recognize the weapon from St. Elizabeth?"

It is a terrible way to die, to literally be siphoned of something as intrinsic as your ancestral magic. But . . . Iraya's army will be mine. There is no way to rescue a magic wielder from that weapon. She might be standing against it for now, but her gold will burn up eventually. Or her body will, without sustenance. The Xanthippe's skin turned supple, in St. Catherine, when they found themselves in the same trap. It began to draw downward as though hooked and pulled, before sluicing away from bone. Their caskets, I was informed, were kept closed during their First Nights.

"She won't last much longer. Which means it's time." Master Omnyra takes my hand and holds it against her chest. "You'll know what to do."

With that ambiguous statement, she climbs astride Guy's prowler and digs her heels in. It canters toward the edge of the roof; my scream is drowned out by the battle, and unnecessary as, in an elegant arc, beast and witch fly above the crowd to land in their midst, unharmed. Before Master Omnyra has dismounted, she's killed three Unlit with a short sword she disarmed from the first.

Death is turned into a performance of beauty as, weapon in hand, she twists and rolls past magi, leaving bodies in her wake with an ease that belies her age. The path she clears, it is toward Iraya.

The soldier outside the Unlit's trap keeps shouting at her in between strikes against the Unlit, but he too is lagging. The second witch with Iraya in the trap merely looks on, like she knows the end is near.

I could leave.

The thought is a silent scream above the noise, but nothing has felt so calming since Iraya's Imposter chased me from Roje, my crew. A crew I could find now, if I left. Is that what Master Omnyra alluded to with her comment that I know what to do? She's breached the last guard before the weapon's chamber; all have been felled with one deft strike from her sword. The Master lunges for the closest weapon panel with her hand and looks right up at me as it explodes in a storm of golden light and stone. The prowler beneath me rears onto its his hind legs. I slide off and hit the roof with a cry.

Smoke has already reached my height. Coughing, I roll onto my front and, hand before hand, knee after knee, crawl to the edge of the roof where the prowler paws and whines. The Unlit fighters are gone—or dead. Only Simbarabo remain, along with Guy, his Jade Guild compatriots, Iraya, and—gagging, I turn away, wishing I hadn't seen her talking with the witch she was knelt before, who now lies in her lap. Something red and fleshy oozes out from where they should be. Mudda have mercy.

"You're still here?" Guy calls up at me. "Good. The more people who saw Omnyra's sacrifice, including Alumbrar, the better. I don't want her forgotten, you hear?" Tears fall freely down his face. Down many of the Obeah's faces.

"She's gone?" I whisper, my eyes filling.

"She took out everyone bar those she shielded against the explosion." His voice breaks. "She saved us."

In more ways than he knows.

Her dying act was to neutralize the Unlit's weapons. They can be beaten, with death. Sacrifice. Valor. Aiyca's sky will be darker without such a witch. Obeah or no.

I'm helped down from the roof by Guy, who uses his magic

to lower the jungle-prowler; reuniting with his beast, it nuzzles its horn-free head into the obsidian beast's neck.

Shadows are all that's left of the dead.

Master Omnyra has her own shadow too.

Iraya glances up as we approach; she dips her head, brushes her face across her shoulder, and lays the body of the witch in her lap down. Closing the eyelids, she mutters something inscrutable before standing.

"Empress Adair." Guy dips into a bow beside me; the dozen other surviving Obeah follow suit.

Doing my best to keep my face neutral, I remain upright; the soldiers Iraya arrived with stand at her back, except the one who was throwing himself at the weapon to get to her, and one other. Both are Obeah. Both stand by her side. Where is Kirdan?

"We were sent by your sistren in the Virago to meet you," Guy continues. "Please, if you are willing, we can take you to see your sistren."

"You'll forgive me for lingering a moment." Iraya's voice is . . . different. Less of a drawl, it's more clipped, command-ing. "The only Obeah among you I knew has died touching something that made me feel like my organs were liquefying, and you are in the presence of the witch who lost this island." Her eyes shift to me. The rings of fire in their depths burns me to the white meat. "You'll understand why, despite your valiant fight, I'm not going anywhere until I get more than a little line about *my sistren in the mountains*." She doesn't look like she was just on her knees, unable to stand and fight; her jaw sets at an angle I know well, the insolence, but it's her eyes that worry me. Remiss of their usual humor, they look . . . haunted, like she's traveled with duppies and doesn't fear creating a few more.

"You need to follow us," I say.

In one unified move, the nine Simbarabo behind her edge an inch of their sabers from their pommels. My bowels loosen, but I force myself to look only at her.

"I did just help save you."

"Must have missed you in the fight," the Obeah Warrior to the left of her mutters. He might be a shield. He looks familiar. My cheeks flush. "Taal."

There's a brief flash of shock on Iraya's face, there and then gone, lost amidst the blood splatter on her face, the exhaustion.

"Where." Less of a question, it's more of a demand.

"You know where."

"We'd better leave," she says to the magi at her side.

"You trust this Alumbrar?" one of them queries, not bothering to lower his voice.

"I trust that her story is long," Iraya answers. "About the time it will take to go where my sistren wait for us." She turns to issue orders to the soldiers in her company. "Find the remainder of those weapons in this city. I want to know how to stop them without—" She breaks off. We all look at the stain, all that's left of Master Omnyra. "Without sacrifice." Her focus snaps back to me like a catapult. "Walk and talk, Alumbrar. Let's start with how you lost Aiyca."

I try to ignore the snort from one of her men. "I'd rather start with how I saved you."

64

IRAYA

The strangest part of Jazmyne's tale is that I listen to it while we scale the Blue Mountains in three different vehicles, all of which she calls a sky pod.

Vying for worst part? Delyse's betrayal, and the fact that Master Omnyra isn't with us.

When Jazmyne's tale ends—one that didn't include as many details as I would have liked about the palace, and how she lost it; a conversation still to be had, later—I replay the Master's final words to me, as well as those from our first meeting. Did she know then that my return would lead to her death? What strength to know and not run. To stand and fight. To arrive and look Death in the eye as a friend.

And Delyse, my gods.

Across from me, Shamar looks like he might never speak again. If my shock paralyzed me, his reaction, once he regained consciousness after the initial explosion, was like she was already dead. Like she had left this mortal coil, and something else slid back into the world wearing her face. But it was her. My Eye. An extension I sent here ahead of myself—someone who made me want to trust, be open—and she blinded me.

The republic must thrive. Her last words when she lay dying in my lap.

They might have been an apology, if she were anyone other than herself. I think they were an excuse, a reason. She still wanted things to happen her way, to the bitter end.

How many more of my order will be willing to do the same?

"Wow," Esai utters across from me. "Is that snow?"

It is.

The Blue Mountains' otherwise gray peaks are dusted with a thin coating of it; during my first end-of-year season here, I couldn't believe I'd lived eight years without experiencing anything so cold in Aiyca. Rain is typically welcomed; tropical storms are dangerous. But snow was entirely of its own. My heart, racing, slows, calms. Home. I've finally returned—the island landing we made hours ago doesn't count. This mountainous range, the thin air, the chill that pervades my tight pants, the thin material of my tunic—this is where my heart has been, these ten years.

The sky pod alights to the left of the central peak, between two mighty brackets caped witches shove into position, locking the vehicle in place. Below our vantage, to the right of the peak, bohíos and tiny gardens hewn into the mountain mainly face the sea lapping at the rear of the range, rather than the bush we traveled up and through. People peer up at the pod;

those on the platform step back. Suddenly conscious of the state of my braids, the dirty clothing we've traveled in, I'm both anxious to egress from this too-delicate pod and uncertain if it would be better to travel back to the foot of this gods-touched range. Will Clotille welcome or punish me for leaving? For taking so long to return to the place that shaped who I am, and who I should have been?

I sit in place long enough that Esai touches my knee. "Is this where we are meant to be?"

"It is," I tell him, and myself.

The caped figures wait for us on a narrow path bracketed by mountain walls. They lack the influx of gold they'll carry in war, but their surety, their unflinching confidence, suggests they can't simply be residents of the mountain.

"As I live and breathe." One pulls away from the others; we share the same height, the same lithe build. She lowers her hood; her hair is shorn in a low frohawk, one with a complex pattern of geometric lines on the left and right sides of her head. "Do you recognize me, cousin? Or—" She takes a slow inspection of my breastplate, the bandolier, and chuckles. "Have you become too nuff to recall how many times I used to beat you during drills."

My gods.

"That was a nice trick with the guerra birds, though. It seems you've remembered a thing or two from our time together."

"Taal?"

Pleasure lights eyes with the same rings of gold as mine before we crash into one another.

I breathe her in. She smells like home. Like metal and earth, and the icy clarity of an atmosphere that bred the fittest covens of Warrior witches. Her companions lower snow-dusted hoods. Most bear two scars on their foreheads, though they look old enough to carry the third for magical inheritance.

"Taal Clarke, my gods. *You've* been here all this time?" I draw back. She bears more scars than she did when we were pickney—through her lip, an eyebrow—there's a jagged one alongside her left ear. But it doesn't feel as though a decade has passed; I could be a pickney again, running wild with her across this compound as we prepared to follow in our family's footsteps. Dada's family.

"It's you who has taken long to return, sistren." She matches my inspection, her eyes lingering on my single scarification. "You grew up, on the outside. Inside you're still as stubborn as you were at eight."

"Cha. Two minutes and you might be more annoying now than you were back then." Older than me by two years, she did often beat me. "I have some people I want you to meet, sistren." I introduce her to Esai and Shamar. The rest of the surviving Simbarabo look warily on. Typically, if our two sects were meeting, it would be in battle. "We're all feeling the effects of our travel," is my excuse for the dip in temperature. "We lost people."

Taal nods. "We're likely to lose a lot more before the year is over."

"Who else has survived from our family?"

"All of us. Clarkes and Adairs."

Mama's family are here too?

She nods. "When you left the mountain for the palace, they

flocked. They were under orders to run. To find safety. I can bring you to everyone now or—"

"Nana?"

Taal's expression falls. "She lives, but . . . there was a cost for our secrecy all these years." She glances at Esai, Shamar, the Simbarabo, and jerks her head toward a path bracketed with large stones. "You know where to find her. She wants to tell you herself."

I turn back. "Esai, I—"

"Go." He glances at Shamar, who stares at the floor beside him. "We'll wait here until you return."

"Actually, would you return to Admiral's Cove? Take as many Simbarabo as you need, and alert Zander about what happened. Check on the general too."

He nods. "I'll return with haste."

"Be safe."

"And you, Empress Adair."

He takes his leave with a bow, half the remaining Simbarabo, and Shamar, at my insistence. I want Anan to look him over for shock, and there's no need for me to have a shadow here. Not among the Clarkes. It's the Adairs I have beef with.

"Zeplin," Taal calls. "See that those who remain are fed, watered, and comfortable."

A witch with the left side of her head shaved, and the right braided, nods.

I don't need an escort to Nana Clarke's home, but I'm glad for Taal's silent company through the mountainous tunnels not unlike Carne's network. Like the Simbarabo in Zesia, and the Skylands' aviatrixes and aviators, training at the Virago

Cuartel has always been secretive. To conceal our drills from visitors in the park below, the compound training facilities are hewn into several of the peaks and connected by internal passages. The air thins the farther we climb, but when we reach the final landing, I take the stairs at a run to Nana's cave-like suite. Carved by magic, the glittering rock interior oversees the entire junior pavilion—where I trained at eight. Pausing in the doorway, I look out of the curved glass window, at a place that seems preserved by time. Witches a lot older than I was spar on platforms within the heart of the mountain peak; some use magic; the gold winks in and out of sight as they weave and dance in a way that turns battle into poetry. No sound travels, thanks to the magically imbued glass.

"A decade has passed, and yet you are still reluctant to enter my rooms."

I start, and then turn to the bed I thought empty. It's not. Nana Clarke is just terribly thin beneath a white sheet. My tears come fast and are reluctant to go. I run to her side and drop to my knees beside her bed, too fearful to take a hand that's skin and bones.

"You're a woman now," she breathes. "Let me look at you."

Opening my eyes sends a spear of fright through my chest. I don't want to remember her like this, a slip of her former self. Her eyes, once so fierce, sunken and cloudy. Her lips dry, despite the oil glistening on them. But I must honor her, so I look. I look and begin to cry as though I've sprung a leak, and a decade of tears seek exodus.

"What happened?" I choke out.

Her hand shifts under the cover, like she means to touch my

cheek; either her arm is too weak, or the sheet too heavy. I do reach for her then, and it is like touching something between worlds. Something ephemeral.

"I used my magic to protect the pavilion." Her words come with a slowness that makes my head hot, my body restless. I've seen this before, with prisoners in Carne. She's not long for this earth. "When your pupa fell, it was returned to me, as is custom when one's pickney dies. Your mama, she suspected what was coming and prepared for it. Were the Unlit to attack, family would sift across the island to us. They would be kept safe under my protection, until you returned to assume your rightful place leading Aiyca."

She sacrificed herself. They did.

Mama and Nana.

My chest gives.

"You waited for me." My voice is thick with tears. "You held this compound, for a decade, for me. I should never have left." The words are spat out, to myself, in an audible castigation. "I don't know why I didn't listen. Why I had to go and ruin everything."

"Stop that," Nana snaps, and as though it took all her energy to raise her voice, her next words are softer. "All pickney return home, Iraya." She sounds exhausted. "There will be time to cry when I am gone. Before that comes to pass, tell me of your life, my child. Tell me how you have lived, and I will tell you the same."

My tale is short and punctuated with hiccups. If I needed another sign that she's weakened, it's that she doesn't draw me to her chest to silence me—or clip me around my ear. I'm halfway through the good parts, like killing the doyenne, when I realize that most happy memories are to do with Kirdan. Either the new moments we've shared, or the old when I would amuse myself by irritating him.

"You know love?" Nana closes her eyes; her wrinkled face softens into a smile of complete bliss. "Nothing makes me happier, my child. Love is the anchor that keeps us living."

And yet she is dying for love. For me. As did Mama when she—when she held a line she knew she would never cross as a victor. What greater sign of commitment, of faith, is there than that? I have to be worthy of it. Of them both.

"Nana. Mama knew about the Unlit? Why wasn't I told?"

"You hated the idea of ruling. You believed it would trap you. Here in the mountains, you found freedom, but you always had purpose: to protect, to serve. What attributes are those if not a leader's? A different leader. The best of the Clarkes, who fought from the shadows as the Adairs led. And better than the Adairs, who could never see past the end of their own noses. You are the light meeting the dark, a daughter of the sun and the moon, two incomparable powers no man or beast stands a chance of defeating, my child."

"But if I'd stayed—"

"You are exactly where you were always meant to be, Iraya. One of my greatest joys has been serving Aiyca's empress, continuing the line as a Clarke envoy." She breaks off, coughing and choking.

Starting forward, I hover over her, uncertain of how to help. "We don't have to talk anymore, Nana. I'll sit here with you. Let me just sit here with you. *Please.*"

Stubborn, she doesn't stop talking. Recounting old advice, warning me about which Virago I should avoid traveling with. Taal, I'm happy to hear, is one of the best, even without her magic. Only when Nana's voice turns so hoarse she has to stop talking do I start. I tell her about my plans, how I am going to *live*. The After I will have.

I don't know when her bedroom begins to fill, with Warriors, and the Adair and Clarke aunts and uncles I wondered about; I only look up to find them there, just in time for Nana to slip away.

65

JAZMYNE

Cross-legged on my pallet, my knees hugged to my chest for warmth, I don't dare fall asleep. Iraya and I both know there was much I didn't say in the sky pod—couldn't, before the Simbarabo. Regardless of their alliance with her. She will come, and I want to be ready.

She arrives with the night.

Swinging in like she's made the jump her entire life, she lands in a crouch and stands slowly, unraveling like some supernal Warrior of the Seven-Faced Mudda in her white and gold. I hate how my heart begins to thud, that my skin pimples into goose-flesh before her. I am a far cry from who I was in the palace, dressed in these muted rags. I hate that our power imbalance is evident in our physicality. Even my hair. Her braids are fresh, neat; my afro will lock if I don't find a comb soon.

"I didn't lose Aiyca." It takes every muscle I possess to

rise like I am not afraid of being thrown farther than the net beneath the canopy; of being ripped into tiny pieces with the magic she must have in full now. "The war has started, but it has not been won. Cwenburg is safe under the shields' protection, along with the Xanthippe. As for the Unlit's weapons—I couldn't have foreseen what they'd make, that they'd craft a device capable of drawing magic from its wielder using the Glyph of Communication. You didn't."

Iraya, still in shadow in the mouth of the cavern, doesn't move. The warmth in the magically tampered walls seems to dissipate, along with the fire that started of its own accord, when my dinner appeared in a pot atop it. Beyond Iraya, wind and a light snowfall bluster.

"Taal told me what you've done since being here," she at last says. "And of course you were there to help in the Bay, but you know what's coming."

A scolding.

"You had one job—"

"One? You left to recruit an army, Iraya. You left!" My breath clouds between us. "*I* had to fend off the Unlit from Carling Hill, from the ports, from islanders who have been traveling across borders to remain safe. There's been insurgence from Obeah. I had to balance all the plates, and you arrive back here with the *single* task you had to do accomplished. Well done, you. *You* did one thing."

"And you did the one thing I told you not to do."

"I saved *you*!" I pant. "I *saved* you. Do you think you could have done a better job as Aiyca's magicless leader? I held the line up until five days ago." Desperation wheedles into my voice, and I hate that I'm once again showing weakness before her. "I did beyond what you asked. I united Obeah, Alumbrar, and Aiycans. I held the Unlit at bay. I kept morale high."

"For a time." Vowels have never felt sharper. "No one talks about who almost won, Jazmyne. To almost win is to still lose." She takes another step; witchlight from my lantern cuts across her face, highlighting angles that have become sharper, while she's been away. Her beauty is crueler for it. "Notwithstanding all that you did, for which I can give you recognition, the pirate gambit is making you look quite the fool. Who do you think the Unlit purchased the gold from to make those weapons? Where do you think they received the idea to siphon magic away from magi?"

"Roje wouldn't have done that to me if not for the Imposter."

She sighs. "I didn't know what I would do when I saw you. Before, I might have pushed you from this height, or dragged you across the island to warn everyone against your stupidity, but what is the point if you yourself cannot see where you've erred? You let a pirate into the palace, and the gods know where else—" I flinch. "A pirate who sold you out to the Imposter. I'm having to say vale to one woman who just sacrificed herself for me, you, and a platoon of soldiers she would have considered an enemy, if they hadn't arrived with me. In addition to Master Omnyra, I have only reunited with another woman who held the line for ten years, *ten years*, Jazmyne, who is also dead. And you could not manage ten phases." She issues a humorless laugh. "We have danced around Aiyca's leadership for long enough, you and I. Before I left, you might have been closer to doyenne, but you were running unopposed. Now, so long as I live and breathe, you have no business ruling Aiyca."

"Because you want it now?"

She tips her head my way. "I have never hungered for power, Jazmyne. Never sought out leadership. Not once."

"But you—you tried to take Aiyca from me."

"I don't try to do anything. Mengkeh. You still think this? That when we worked together the first time that was my goal? It was not. When I set my mind to a task, it is done; let me show you—" Her voice dips, along with my witchlight; her breastplate illuminates, softly, as gradually as a rising sun. "As empress of Xaymaca, and her territories, I hereby strip you of the title regent—"

Startled, I cry out as something severs inside, as though parted by a hot blade.

"And any claim to Aiyca's throne you believe yourself to possess. Jazmyne Amancia Cariot, for your service to the crown, you are hereby spared prison or isolation, but under my authority, you will never rule Aiyca."

Warmth pools through my body, like a gush of blood. It's the oath. Her words have prompted a physical separation of the promise I made when I was crowned; I feel it as surely as if an axe was taken to one of my limbs. Clutching my chest, I drop down onto my knees before her.

"But without my crown," I manage to say, "I am nothing."

She looms over me, majestic and so far from being human,

she might be a god. "You never had a crown. And you no longer have Aiyca."

A ragged sob tears out from between my lips, and then another. I don't know when Iraya leaves, only that this is worse than isolation, worse than prison, this emptiness.

I'd rather be dead.

66

IRAYA

Taal is waiting for me when I swing down from the net after my talk with Jazmyne. The surrounding bush is aglow with jars containing sparks of magic. It was a ceremony undertaken by the newly inherited; magic would be expelled, along with a promise to forever keep the empire's darkness at bay. The jars double as weapons, should the compound come under attack. I flick one that's low enough to reach, and almost smile. To think of them existing for the decade I was in Carne should expel my darkness, knowing Nana lives on through the traditions she's left behind, but war doesn't only kill the dead.

"Not feeling sorry for yourself, are you?" My cousin re-moves a knife from the leather bandolier strapped across her chest and throws it at the tree I'm leaning against; it thuds into the bark by my arm. "Not a flinch. I wasn't sure you'd have it in you, given this moping." She walks toward me; the second aerial begins to whir its way down the conduit gold rope from the next stop. "Look, you're not the cause of Master Clarke's death, or any other self-pitying thing you're thinking." Taal yanks her knife from the tree and spins it between her fingers. "The Master had her orders from your mama, who received hers from Master Omnyra. Lock up the compound to keep you safe."

Aghast, I look at a face so similar to my own. "What?"

"The Master didn't tell you? Shit."

"Taal, that was why Nana locked this place down? I wasn't even here. I *ran*."

"Who's to say this wasn't how matters were always meant to be? You survived, and returned here, where you were always meant to—"

"Be, Taal. I *was* meant to be here. Not return."

"Gods. You've spent too much time with that Alumbrar." She drags a hand across her face. "Is she alive?"

"Yeh mon."

"And you truly killed her mama?"

I nod.

"Could you have done that if you stayed here?"

"With you all, yeh mon."

Taal's expression turns triumphant. "You would have been stuck here, with us! You wouldn't have been able to kill the doyenne. From what I heard of the prediction, you were always meant to reach this moment. You were meant to win us this war."

But will I? I don't voice.

"I know Nana's death isn't my fault, I know it, but I still feel like—like—I *feel*. That's the problem." That's why I couldn't leave Delyse to die alone after Master Omnyra's sacrifice. "You don't know what I've done." Risked everyone's lives with a bargain I can't remember making with a sea monster; witnessed the death of the witch who was meant to be on my team; sailed home with my—Kirdan, poisoned, with me.

Taal knocks her shoulder into mine. "Master Clarke will forever be with us, her lessons, the way her voice would do that thing when she was disappointed with your performance—do you remember, mon? She's here, but so is the witch responsible for all this. A decade ago, you didn't want any part in ruling, and who knows if it would have changed here as it so obviously has for you out there." She scans me with an acute intelligence. "Never forget, Virago have always served Adairs. You are not alone in feeling, or in wanting justice for what has been lost."

I take her hand, rough and calloused, and know she means every word. "I don't want you to serve me. Fight with me, sistren. By my side, as we were made to."

"And here I thought you would never ask, officially." Grinning, Taal pulls me into a crushing hug.

"You doubted I would?"

"I doubted the strength of my words in the face of your self-pity."

Laughter barks from between my lips. I tighten my hold on her. "I didn't allow myself to miss you. But I did, sistren."

"Not to ruin the mood," Taal says, drawing back. "But will you let Jazmyne leave? We agreed to, after you arrived."

"You might have, but I didn't. She has a way of causing trouble when left unchecked."

The sky pod hums to a stop; we enter, and Taal tugs the string that signals to the witch on the other end that we're ready to begin our ascent.

"Well, we have enough of that coming our way," she continues, a thoughtful twist to her mouth. "Master Clarke's death means that the pavilion's protections have fallen. Witches are in the battlements, the trees, walking the perimeter she cast, but if you have a plan, we should talk about it before the monsters begin climbing this mountain—after the First Night."

I turn to her in the dark. "Do we have time to stop?"

"Think about it as more of a pause. The dead give us much. We should honor them."

In agreement, I nod. "Whatever the decisions we make about the battle, tonight will be the last we spend here for a while."

"Then let's go out in the style Master Clarke and Master Omnyra deserve."

Once I've checked in with the Simbarabo, who Zeplin escorted into an empty bohío, Nana's First Night is everything I wanted for my parents. It's everything I would have wanted for Delyse. Though I should think of her, I should guarantee she moves on to whatever awaits her in the afterlife, but I can't acknowledge her tonight. Not when she caused Master Omnyra's death and robbed me of more time with Nana. Delyse was complicated; I'm glad I knew her, but I don't yet know if I'm sorry she's gone.

And tonight is for Nana Clarke, Master Warrior and Bastion of the Blue Mountains. Guardian, and all-around queen. Not to mention Omnyra, Bonemantis extraordinaire and Excellent

Secret Keeper. My relatives tell hours of stories about both by candlelight; more food than I can consume is distributed. Growers have kept my family sustained for the past decade, and the Jade Guild have left salted meats for them.

Transient, I don't linger with one group for too long. There are aunties and uncles who seem so much older to me now. They tell me how they fled when the Unlit struck, how they've been anticipating my return. Eventually Taal steps into my path, as well as several additional cousins who have since become Virago. All bear more scars than me; they fill me in on their exams, and how they entertained themselves for the decade I was in Carne. Only the eldest Virago have their magic. All those around my age and younger haven't been able to go to Carling Hill, given the protections on the mountain. Something I mean to solve, before the year is out. Ideas buzz along with the blood caters, present even in the chill we ward with fires and glyphs. So much so that I cannot relax, or forget about the talk to be had with everyone, the address I've yet to make. When the candles burn low and the food is stored for the night, there's a silent shift of expectation. My relatives, it seems, are of the same mind.

"You'll do fine, mon," Taal murmurs beside me, where she has all but stayed since my arrival. "And the coven has your back, always. Did you want to use the Loquacious Lectern?"

"You still call it that?"

Nana would castigate us from the pulpit about messy bohíos, lapsed chores. She took to the stone stand the day Mama and Dada came under attack. The memory strikes with venom. She'd looked at me, that day, found me in the crowd of

Warriors, and told us we wouldn't all be traveling to the palace. I didn't know then that it was to keep me safe, that Mama had worked with her to ensure that I wouldn't die beside her. I'd heard that my parents were in danger, and I'd fled, down the mountain using the pulley system we had, where I found a kind witch from the market I visited to sift me into Ol' Town, at the base of Cwenburg's mount.

"Yes," I tell Taal. "I want to use the Loquacious Lectern. And I need a favor: Can you send Zeplin, or one of your other charges, to retrieve and then keep an eye on Jazmyne? I want her to sit in on the talk with the coven's lieutenants afterward."

"The majority of them are standing guard, but you can speak with their seconds."

I nod. "See to it for me."

"My pleasure, Empress."

The Loquacious Lectern is more weathered than it was when I was a pickney; I trace the knots and chips with my fingers, imagining Nana standing here—no. I don't have to imagine it. She is here. Her power is mine; it's in me. The dead live on through those who love them.

"Wahan." My family, the Virago, fall silent with alacrity. I have nothing prepared, but, fingers gripping the stone platform, I find I don't need more time to consider what I'm going to say. "I used to dream of returning here when I was in Carne. Then, it was always to become who I had been at eight, when I left to fight for Mama and Dada during the Viper's Massacre. Returning today has made me realize that's impossible. I can no more be the person I thought I would than I can bring Nana Clarke back from the dead." I pause to swallow, my throat thickening. "That would be ignoring all the lessons I've been taught on the journey that has led me here, to become a new kind of empress for Aiyca. With your help, I'm going to take this island back from the last witch who will ever come between me and my legacy, our legacy as Adairs and Clarkes."

"But," a witch calls from the crowd, "the late Empress Adair sent you here to protect you from the Unlit. Surely you should—"

"I haven't the time to listen to anyone else telling me what I should be doing," I interrupt. We reached this point sooner than I hoped. Well. There's no time like the present to clarify a few matters. "Respectfully, I don't want to pull the rank card, since it seems to give you license to dictate how I spend my days, so hear this: I escaped from Carne." Practically. "Infiltrated Cwenburg Palace, and killed the late doyenne without the full extent of my magic. From there, I traveled to Zesia, where I stopped their infestation of Oscuridad, and sailed here with a tenth of their army. Expel all thoughts of controlling me, of instating me in place like a monument, of anything else you are considering to keep me pinned here. I am an Adair, yeh mon, but I am also a fighter, a liar, a witch, a weapon, and most of all I am pissed that, instead of mourning the witch who gave her life to keep you safe, to keep a home for me, as well as those who have died to ensure I made it here, today, I cannot strategize to avenge her. I have to stand here and tell you all that you have no control over what I do."

"Empress." An aunty I vaguely recognize looks helplessly around at my relatives. "We cannot allow you to—"

"Virago," Taal calls. "Defensive measure one." The small portion of the witches not guarding the compound, the park, move before the platform base in a position I practiced with many of them as a pickney.

"You will strike us?" the aunty asks, aghast. "Iraya, these traditions are in place to *help* you."

"And they are respected," I tell them all. "But archaic. Mama wouldn't expect me to sit on a throne knowing I can do more." I believe this now, after my talk with Nana. "She would recognize the need to protect me, but you're not doing that. You're fighting me when there is another battle to be endured across the island. And if you are fighting me, you are in my way. You are in Aiyca's way. You are standing in *the* way of the traditions you uphold."

The Adairs and Clarkes, our family bredren and sistren, mutter amongst themselves. I didn't expect them to give in, but it's disappointing all the same.

"The protections have fallen; this haven is now discoverable. It will be protected, of course, but come morning, the majority of the Virago, myself, and my Simbarabo allies are leaving. If you wish to fight with us, meet here at first light. Otherwise, vale. If I survive the war against the Unlit, I hope to see you at my coronation." I didn't expect applause. It does not come. "Blessings. Virago platoon second lieutenants, meet me in the war room."

The Virago who serve under the lieutenants keep my family at bay; I don't look at the open mouths or furrowed brows as I take the stone steps down from the platform and keep walking into the stone hall and up toward the war room.

Unlike Nana's rooms, the heptagonal chamber is lit only by witchlights, making it dark, truncated.

"No respect for the Loquacious Lectern, those Adairs and Clarkes," Taal says, sweeping in, along with several dozen witches in a range of ages.

"Yes, well, you had ten years to warm them up for me. What happened, sistren?" I half jest, in a bid to lighten the pall that accompanied us from outside.

Taal snorts. "I doubt fifty years would have softened those tough backs."

"The future is bright."

"We might not live to see it."

"Thank the gods for small mercies."

There is some laughter, but it feels too soon.

"How many witches do your lieutenants each command?" I ask the seconds.

The Virago numbers are vast. Greater than the thousands of Simbarabo who survived the attack at the Monster's Gulf, but less than their army overall. And even fewer are in possession of their magic. Any number would be reduced to insignificance in the face of the Unlit's, but I am beginning to worry about the lives I have called up to fight alongside me.

"A question." One of my cousins steps forward. "Do we call you Empress, or Genna?"

"Call me anything *but* General." Not because I'll think of Kirdan, fighting the poison from the Oscuridad. I'm doing that anyway. "Who was Master Clarke favoring for that position?" I turn to Taal, who looks everywhere but at me. "The room isn't that big, sistren."

"Fine, mon; yes, Master Clarke tapped me to be general, and one of your cousins to replace her as trainer. We would have undergone the Rite of Challenge and fought her, before she gave her life to protecting this pavilion, but I didn't want that. Not alone."

"Why not?"

"You know, other plans. Maybe." Taal shrugs. "That depends on you. I don't want to ask and ruin a moment if you planned on writing a message in the clouds, or having someone sing me a certain request."

I don't know what she means until I do.

"I thought our talk earlier clear enough, but I see that I must say it. Not sing it, mind. Be my second, Taal, and the Virago general."

She exhales. "Thank the gods you said it, mon. I didn't want to seem greedy."

The other witches laugh once again.

"You'll forgive me for not throwing you a Swearing-In, given the war and all."

"One we will end quickly." Taal looks to me for permission to speak. "I thought we should bring the fight to the Unlit at first light. We don't allow them to use their beastly assets. We don't give them the time to rally the troops. They will know you're here, that there has already been an attempt on your life. We strike hard and sudden."

"I don't know if they'll allow that," I muse. "And if we should rely on that plan without more concessions. They're likelier to strike while it's dark. We might not see dawn once we leave this mountain. As soon as they know we're mobile, it's only a case of where the fight will take place. On our turf, or theirs."

"Permission to speak, Empress?" one of my older Clarke cousins asks. "I'm Cedella Clarke. Master Clarke was considering me as her replacement." She nods at Taal, maybe for allowing her to be the one to tell me. "We didn't interact much when you were here. I'm pleased to see you return so hale."

"Blessings. Let's not stand on ceremony. Speak."

"What about Squallers?" she suggests. "We can use them to control when dawn arrives. To strike in the dead of night will be a move the Unlit are not anticipating. We could then flood them with sunlight and vanquish their beasts without use of the Glyph of Banishment."

"Jazmyne told you?"

"She showed us, actually," Zeplin says.

"I like the idea, but the gold—"

"Excessive," Cedella concedes. "So, perhaps a last resort."

"I agree. I think the Squallers should go to Carling Hill." I lean down onto the table and search for their figures amongst all the métier renderings. The wave, with a sun and cloud carved into the wood pieces, slides across the table. "Blessings. If you stand before Carling Hill, whatever reinforcements they summon won't be able to permeate the glade—if it's still keeping the Oscuridad out?"

"The dead are doing the work of the living," another cousin confirms.

"Then, Taal?"

"I'll assign numbers. Simbarabo?"

"You'll have several platoons. Carling Hill is the center of the Unlit's gravity. It was their first acquisition in this war. Mostly." The particulars don't matter all that much. What does is that they are there, and they are waiting. "It's important to them, and us; to win it back will be a turning point in this battle."

Cedella nods. "Is that where you'll be?"

"Not at first."

I fill them in about the gaps, the need to locate and close the smaller ones as well as the source—the large visible pathway they'll have created through excessive use. "I need to distract this Imposter while the Simbarabo close the gaps in St. Mary, and its neighbors, St. Bethann and St. Elizabeth. Though I understand that the latter has fallen."

"We can send Virago there also. Two witches to every two Simbarabo."

"Can we spare that many?"

"Two is like sending six of us." Taal shrugs. "And if it's only to win the city back from occupation, it'll be a training exercise to our witches. If you want to take it back? At present, it's more of a symbol of their reach than Carling Hill, since monsters can walk there. Everyone will wonder which parish will be next. But if we take it back, we'll send the Unlit scrambling and give some hope to our islanders. Shouldn't take more than a subunit of Virago; that leaves you with around four units to accompany you wherever you're planning to be. Which is?"

"Hang on." I shift the pieces around on the map. "If we make the Unlit think I'm going to the palace; you'll be clear to get into St. Bethann; Kirdan's lieutenant can locate the source—"

"I should go with him," a small voice says.

We all turn to Jazmyne, standing at the back of the gathering. I'd forgotten about her.

"I sent my Stealths to find the Summoning Circles you warned me about, but I also had them searching for the Unlit's source from the moment you left. I should have realized when the enemy moved in on Carling Hill that it would be close." Jazmyne swallows and tips her chin up. "I think this source you spoke of is along the coast, by the Hendern Cliffs. No prisoner ships have sailed since your arrival from Carne. It's private, hard to access by anything other than a boat, and the family trees prevent unauthorized entry into the parish at large."

Taal whistles. "I didn't know you knew that many words that weren't questions, Alumbrar."

Jazmyne scowls at her.

"That's good intel, but you're not going with Kirdan's lieutenant general," I decide. "You're just as much a target as I am, which means we can't send you anywhere without adequate defense, and they need to focus on the gaps, not protecting you." Kirdan showed me this the hard way.

Jazmyne sets her jaw. "Are you sure that's the reason?"

"I'm not saying any of this for fun, believe me. You will go with a unit of Virago to the palace to deliver Ford a message. Remind him about the tunnels I found a couple months back. The white flags will take him down the mount. He can lead you inside from the entrance I'll provide you with. Stay there, hold the palace." I look around the room, at my Warriors in arms. "If we're going to discuss symbols, we can't forget one of the most important to Aiyca. After St. Elizabeth has been won back, the Unlit won't make any further small plays. They'll go for the Golden Seat, not knowing it's already under a stronger guard. With the Virago's help, perhaps some Simbarabo too, if we can spare the ships. The shields can hold Cwenburg until the battle is over."

"And where specifically will you be?" Cedella fingers the crown figurine.

I take it from her with a smile. "Everywhere."

We continue planning, discussing logistics, numbers, and the weapons they've been storing for when the protections would fall. It's more than I could have hoped for.

"Rest up, sistren," I eventually breathe, my body aching almost as much as my head. Esai will return soon from the Simbarabo ship, and I can relay the plans to him. Then I need to sleep before the first units leave in the morning. There are weapons to distribute, and fortifications to put in place for the old and young who will remain here.

The Virago leave—dare I say it—excited about tomorrow, about seeing the world that carried on while they were preserved in magic up here. About kicking some serious Unlit ass.

"Are you limping?" Taal teases me as I use the wall for support in the tunnels. "I hope I didn't make the wrong choice, choosing to accompany you everywhere."

"I'm not too tired to kick you, sistren."

Laughing, Taal leaps out of the rocky hall and onto the platform outside. "Er, Empress Adair, you might want to see this."

Gods. What now?

634

I pad over to the entrance, wincing at increasing from a shuffle, and see—my family.

A sea of faces illuminated by conduit weapons—spears with pointed tips, staffs, swords, bows and arrows, wicked blades that have no names I've heard of. Singular, the hundreds of Adairs and Clarkes render the sky, unhindered by clouds and filled with stars, ordinary.

"We will go where you tell us to, Empress Adair," the aunty who challenged me earlier says. "We thought about it, and to win Aiyca back we cannot fight among ourselves."

"My words did this?" I mutter in an aside to Taal.

"Your words and the Virago," she returns. "I told you we have your back. Our family needed to know they were the only ones standing against you."

I reach for Taal's nearest hand, squeeze it.

"We must support our leader," Aunty continues. "As Master Clarke did and would have, in you. Of this earth," she says; my entire body breaks out in gooseflesh. "We rise."

She takes the knee, and then those behind her do, and those behind them.

"*Of this earth,*" they call, the Obeah dictum one I haven't heard in years. "*We rise.*"

And behind my kneeling family, Melione, Kihra, Anan, Zander, and Esai stand looking on; between the Simbarabo, upright and conscious, *alive*, is Kirdan.

JAZMYNE

Iraya and Kirdan have accomplished what he and I were meant to, and I cannot stand it.

Not the breadth of feeling exchanged in the looks they give one another. It's what comes after, when she commands her family to rise and introduces them to Kirdan en masse.

"Prince Divsylar of Zesia, General of the Simbarabo, has saved my life on multiple occasions; without his dedication to restoring this empire to the greatness it knew under the Adair rule, well, I'd still be here now—" Taal, Zeplin, and more Virago laugh quietly amongst themselves. "The journey simply wouldn't have been as smooth. I know our islands have a fraught history, but just as you are accepting me as I am now, I ask that you accept the general, and his men. They are here to fight with us, for Aiyca, for Xaymaca under my rule."

It is another knife between my ribs, watching her introduce family to Kirdan, the Simbarabo close by his side. I'm startled by Anan's presence; he stays back with a witch who looks like him, and another woman with the silken long hair of Zesia. Iraya has the Skylands on her side too? Mudda have mercy. Enemy shaking hands with enemy; hostility exchanged for curiosity. This was meant to be my story. Instead, I am relegated to the shadows of the mountain tunnels, forgotten on the edge of change.

Taal breaks away to join me; in the tunnel's darkness, I hope she can't see me wipe my tears on my shoulder.

"I thought you knew him." She nods at Kirdan.

"So did I."

"Give me a moment to gather some supplies, and I'll take you back to your cavern."

I don't argue. Why would I? No one out there is looking for me. My plans to join up with the Nameless have been scuppered, and according to Iraya, I will fight this war how she chooses. A sky pod down the mountain later, my hollowness has been filled with anger.

"Why didn't you tell Iraya about the pirates?"

My anger is such that I don't turn back to look at Taal—I can't. If I do anything beyond pace the five steps across my cavern and the five steps back, I might scream. It wasn't enough to humiliate me in private, she had to announce to her armies that I am worth nothing more than being watched over like a problematic pickney.

"Regent?"

"Not regent."

"I'm going to need you to use those conversational skills you exhibited back in the war room, mon."

"She didn't tell you." My laugh is an odd, twisted thing. "Your dear empress stripped me of my titles."

"And?"

Shock stops me midstride. I turn to Taal; she leans against the left side of the cavern, at ease and as insolent as her cousin. They only had to stand beside one another to confirm the similarity in their features, mannerisms.

The desire to run at her, to push her into the darkness at her back, is a pulsating need.

"Did Iraya send you here to torture me? Is that what this is?"

"Not her style."

"Is it yours?"

Taal's smile is small and slow; it might as well be Iraya smirking at me. "I see what you want to do. I wouldn't, unless you'd like to experience how it feels to land without the safety of a net."

"You look like her."

"Answer my question."

"About what?"

"Roje. Why didn't you tell Iraya about him?"

Suddenly exhausted, I lean against a wall, slide, and just keep going down until I'm on the ground. "She knew he betrayed me already."

"That's not what I meant." Taal straightens. "You planned to return to him, as well as your sistren the Imposter is keeping. As for that Imposter, she likely imprisoned your Stealth in the hopes that you'll go after her, and she can take you. Though you wouldn't have considered that."

Taal is right. Gods.

"Why didn't you tell Iraya you have a plan for the pirates?"

Even shrugging requires too much effort. "She seemed busy ignoring me and making plans to keep me out of the way."

"And you decided to play dead and make it easier for her?" Taal laughs. "You Alumbrar. You're either betraying us, or yourselves. Look, we march for war at dawn. Aren't you the daughter of a family of Healers?"

"I am, yes."

"You heard which parishes Iraya plans to station soldiers in, and then there's Carling Hill. They'll all need Healers stationed there. Not just Bush, but Alumbrar too. And Iraya needs more ships at the Hendern Cliffs. You could have the command of the Iron Shore's entire fleet, if you still want it."

"Wanting leads to disappointment."

"At least you'll be feeling. I'm sure it's hard to be disappointed when you're dead."

I turn to her. "And you think I could make a difference in living or dying?"

"Don't you?"

"Are you asking for my help?"

"No." Taal slings a pack at me; I fumble to catch it. "What's this?"

"*My* help." She turns to the open night, bright with the glow of a half-moon. "Just because you hit rock bottom, *Regent*, doesn't mean you have to remain there."

68

IRAYA

As much as I want to inspect every inch of Kirdan, having him by my side upon our return to the war room, with his men, my coven, Kihra, and Melione is enough. His fingers brush against mine where our hands swing at our sides. My urge to smile is sickening.

"Do you have an answer for me?" I ask the Skylanders, across the war table.

Kihra sighs. "My family do not understand how serious you are about the army. If I can speak with my sister and mama in person, show her what you have here, and what you did in Zesia—"

"How?"

"Doyenne Opoku is a Bonemantis," Melione explains. "She knows guzzu to extract memories. We can show her what she refuses to face."

To the left of Kirdan, Zander twists one of the daggers in his bandolier. "You would return home?" he asks. "What of your husband's death? We understood that you hid in Zesia to be protected from Doyenne Opoku."

"She will be protected." Kihra tilts her chin upward; Melione looks at her in a manner that suggests she's with the right sibling, at last.

"Is your return home an attempt to avoid this war?" Kirdan asks; his voice is like gravel from misuse.

"No," Anan answers. "I will stay. If you introduce me to the Master Healers here, I can work with them to create a poultice to extract Oscuridad poison; they might even know how to neutralize it."

Cedella steps forward. "I can take you."

"No, you stay," Zeplin says. "It's more important that you hear. My Genna can report to me later."

Taal nods in confirmation; after touching his forehead against his sister's, Melione's, Anan is taken away.

"What if your sister still says no?" I ask Kihra. It's more than reminding her of my threat to travel to her home, once this war is over. There are Oscuridad with wings. Carling Hill will put my armies' backs to the cliff and the sea; we need their support. "Or the doyenne?"

"I plan on doing my best to ensure that doesn't happen."

"How will you return home in time?"

"We will travel the Eldritch Gaps."

Kirdan glances down at me, perturbed. "Won't that weaken the veil here?"

"It will be but once," Melione says, "so no."

"'Should be'" isn't a risk I'm willing to take after Nana Clarke worked herself to death fortifying this mountain." Rhonda and Faehn, from Taal's unit, escort the Skylanders down into the national park, with my parting words still ringing in the war room: *Xaymaca is fractured only in name, at present. I consider all refusal to offer aid an act of war. Even if I do not live on, my allies will ensure I'm avenged.*

"Have you planned a contingency?" Kirdan asks when they are gone. His face is wan and drawn, but his eyes filled with a Killing Calm not unlike my own.

"The battle has been all but planned without them, yeh mon. But victory will be a hell of a lot easier with their aerial Oscuridad."

"Where am I, with you?"

Zander clears his throat; Taal's eyebrows shoot upward. I must say what propriety is stopping them from saying.

He'll be a liability if he accompanies me; I will too, if I am watching him the entire time rather than executing my plan. "I thought you could stay with Zander and close Aiyca's source" is about as polite a way as I can convey that. "It's likely to be bigger than the one in Zesia, and I need your experience so I can focus on moving across the island."

Palms resting on the table while he surveys the pieces, Shamar looks up at me. "You'll be making yourself difficult to track, to predict?" They are the first words he's spoken; I wasn't sure he was following the conversation, given how lost he looks without Delyse.

I nod. "And showing the island who I am. The Imposter has

been saying she hasn't been able to inherit her magic. I'll start by debunking that. And I have an idea about where she'll want to fight me."

"Carling Hill," Shamar states.

"Yeh mon. I could draw her away, maybe, but I think it's kind of perfect. Everyone can inherit, and then use their magic to join the fight."

"If we're tending to the source—" Kirdan eases himself into a chair. "That means recon, strategy, likely fighting Oscuridad."

"Oscuridad are the monsters, right?" Taal asks.

"Yes. Sorry."

"I guessed." She waves a hand.

"So, with your travel, we're looking at about a phase, at least?" Zander queries.

"Sounds about right," Taal answers. "We don't want to give the Imposter too much longer to call her army to battle."

"How will we cover so much ground?" Esai asks.

"Magic and regular travel to cover Aiyca. Now Iraya has accepted her title, she's lifted the moratorium on sifting. An empress ranks above a doyenne. Everyone can now, so be vigilant."

"And if we need you?" Esai turns to me. "A neutral retreat would be wise."

"Cwenburg," I suggest. "I'm sending Jazmyne and some Virago there; it's under shield protection and has yet to fall."

"I don't think you should go there." Kirdan's tone is absolute. "It will be expected."

"The palace mount is a solid advantage to fight from," I rationalize. "And I have ways of getting inside that the Unlit do not." If the Imposter were a true Adair, she would know about the tunnels, and the palace would already be breached. "Like I said, I'll be everywhere, difficult to track, and even harder to predict."

"Then let's add some certainty." Even slumped in a chair while the rest of us stand, Kirdan commands the authority of his position; even the Virago listen intently, with respect. "On the fourth day, head to the palace, Iraya. If we've encountered any trouble, we'll send a fire message to the hearth in the late doyenne's study."

Dada's study.

"I'll provide a description of where we are for your reply."

"And if you don't send anything?"

"We'll likely be too busy killing those beasts," Esai answers.

"You will remain with the empress," Zander tells him.

"No, Esai will be with me," his general grinds out. "And you will accompany the empress."

The three soldiers scowl at one another.

"I think," Taal whispers to me, "we should let them fight it out. Shirtless. Maybe no pants too."

"Mengkeh."

"Me?" she asks, mock-outraged at being labeled a fool.

"All of you! Kirdan, you need your second right now."

"Since I agreed," Zander begins, "how does that make *me* a fool?"

"No offense intended, Esai," I continue, shooting a censoring look his lieutenant's way. "I need you to command the unit of Simbarabo I'm bringing with me across the island. Anan is accompanying us, as you know, and he'll need protection the

Virago working with me cannot give."

"No," Kirdan objects. "I want you to have the most experienced team traveling with you."

"What are you calling us?" Taal's eyes narrow. "Chicken scratch?"

"He respects your position and ability to protect me, just as much as he respects my ability to protect myself, not to mention himself and his men." My tone leaves no room for further negotiation. "Since we are done here, and dawn grows closer by the hour, you are all dismissed to replenish your weapons, to visit the Master Growers providing the nourishment packs, and then to try to rest before we win this war tomorrow." Breathing hard, I meet every scowling face until their eyes drop. "Dismissed. I'll speak with you all in the morning. Taal?"

"I'll sort your man dem out with beds, don't worry. You take mine. My unit and I will bunk with another."

Zander pulls me aside before he's escorted out of the mountain. "Anan advised the general engage in as little physical activity as possible," he tells me, with a knowing look.

"I'll make sure he stays on his back," I say.

Zander's mouth pops open.

"You know, as opposed to sitting up in a chair." I give him a wink.

It's easier to adhere to the rules while I escort Kirdan around the compound. Family try to stop us, to pull me down to engage Jákīsa for Nana Clarke. Not quite able to mask his stumbling beside me, how his conduit weapon on his hip flares in and out as he no doubt uses magic to ensure he won't have to lean on me, I make my excuses.

It becomes harder to adhere to after Kirdan and I close the door to Taal's bohío, which she must have beaten us to, since rather than the four beds for her and the three closest witches in her unit, there is but one. It is large and covered in furs of animals that do not roam Aiyca. She must have had another witch summon them here. A tub sits across from it, filled with steaming water. In any other circumstance, this would be romantic. I make myself think of the Oscuridad, of their salivating mouths and many eyes and legs. Kneeling, methodically I untie Kirdan's laces, removing his boots and socks.

"You don't have to do that."

I make the mistake of looking up at him from on my knees. "And you don't have to fight every attempt to offer you aid." Instead of the pithy critique, my words come out low.

Kirdan's throat bobs as he swallows. "If I wasn't so exhausted, I'd make a comment about your hypocrisy right now."

"A blessing from the gods. Now drop your pants, lose the shirt, and get in."

It's hard to do anything other than savor the way he peels off his tunic, that focus less exhausted than it was and pinned on me as he draws his pants down powerful legs corded with muscles. I haven't forgotten my warning from Zander; it would be easier to keep my hands to myself if we weren't going to battle tomorrow, Kirdan didn't look the way he does without clothing on, and the chance of never seeing him again wasn't so high.

Turning away as he straightens is an effort.

A bowl of herbs sits on a small table at the end of the bath. After two splashes indicate he's in the water, I tip them in. The water clouds, and he groans.

"What?" I ask, turning.

Cheeks reddening, Kirdan leans his head back against the lip of the metal tub. "It feels good. Restorative. I'd say join me, but I think Niusha groomed me at some point. I'm covered in slobber."

"You didn't bring her?"

"I wasn't sure how she'd fare on this terrain. It's also cold. I'll bring her with me tomorrow though. Sifting to the ship and back will be easy enough."

I nod. "Call out when you're done. I'll wait outside."

"Don't go." Kirdan surges forward to reach for me; water sloshes over the rim and onto the wooden floor. "I lost a phase. Zander caught me up, but I want you to tell me what I've missed."

Water glistens on his broad chest, where the new scar from the Oscuridad puckers in a dark blemish diagonally across his left pectoral.

"Okay." Acquiescing, I sit on the small table. Out of reach, but not out of sight.

Kirdan eases back against the bath. "Are you ready for tomorrow?"

Yes, I almost lie. But we made promises to one another.

"The plans feel solid. I'm confident in them, in you all. But I'm not sure if I'm ready."

"What about?"

"The Imposter. We will face off, and only one of us can win. I don't know if I can kill her." I trace a bead of water running down the musculature delineated in the center of Kirdan's chest. "It's justice to take her life. Or it would be, if she were anything other than Obeah. Other than family." It's a question I've avoided asking myself since I learned her identity. When she was nameless and faceless, her end would have been that of the late doyenne's. Now? "If I kill her, how am I any better than she is, her relatives? But if I don't, what makes prison the better choice now than it was when Mama had the same choice to make, and sentenced the Unlit to banishment?"

"No one would blame you for killing her."

Kirdan's face is somber when I look up at him.

"No one. As for sparing her, the fact that it's a consideration after all her family did to yours, this island, the empire, and all she still has planned, well . . . you are a better leader than I. It is a strength to consider mercy when revenge would be more satisfying."

"I was hoping for more of a yes-or-no answer."

A soft laugh escapes Kirdan's mouth. "Now you wish to be told what to do? Watch me answer and find myself held under water by your hand, Empress."

"This hand?" I lower my right into the bath and splash him.

He doesn't flinch; instead a wicked smile curls across his mouth. A second after I'm on my feet, poised to run for a safer distance, Kirdan stands, launching dual waves of water over the sides of the tub, grasps me around my waist, and pulls me down into the bath with him.

"My *clothes*!" I gasp, my eyes squinting against the medicinal burn of the water. "Don't!" I laugh. "You'll hurt yourself."

His arms hold me hard and fast, but his grip softens.

"I'll be gentle. I haven't held you enough, Iraya."

At the sincerity in his tone, I stop struggling against his lap, look at him. We're close enough that I could count the water droplets clinging to his inky lashes, his eyebrows.

"You're not strong enough for this."

"You don't know by now?" he whispers. "I'm always stronger with you."

There's no time to be slow when we will separate at dawn. Kirdan tears at my clothes with an urgency I reciprocate, using my magic to loosen the ties of my breastplate, to launch it across the bohío onto the bed. Kirdan uses his to sever a line down the center of my tunic and both pant legs so they can be pulled back. Then there is nothing between us, between the hot pulse of my body and his.

Not time. Not death. Nothing.

Later, while I am lying on the bed, in a clean pair of pants and a tunic, Kirdan, having finished his stew at the table across the room, joins me.

"I have something to give you." The bed dips beneath his weight as he lowers himself beside me with a wince. "It's something I've been thinking about since I woke, and Zander caught me up on all I missed while you were saving my life." A package materializes in Kirdan's hands.

"Liminal spaces?"

He nods and holds it out. "It's heavy."

"That's an understatement," I grunt, lowering it onto the bed to tug the paper away from—"A block of conduit gold?"

"One I thought you could weld atop the piece of your dada's staff you salvaged from Doyenne Divsylar's bed." I thought I knew every look Kirdan gave me, every stomach flutter, quickening pace of my heart, but this look I haven't seen. It near leaves me breathless. "The hammer is your perfect conduit weapon, Iraya. Who knows more about swinging the gavel of justice upon those who have needed it most." He slides his fingers between mine. "When I first saw you in the prison, I knew you'd change my life. It has been better, full, for knowing you."

With my words trapped in a throat that suddenly feels too thick, I kiss him; I want to keep kissing him until I am sick of it. But that moment might never come, for us.

"Thank you," I breathe against his mouth, our chests rising and falling against one another's.

"I wish I could see you use it against the Imposter."

I knew he wouldn't go down without a fight.

"You cannot come. Even if you are strong, and more intelligent than anyone with hair like yours deserves to be."

Kirdan blinks at me and then throws his head back. He laughs hard enough that tears gather in the corners of his eyes, and I know why. I know he has to laugh to stop the alternative. To stop considering the cruelness of time when you find something to cherish. I don't get to do that with him, us. With Nana Clarke. With my family and sistren here. I barely have time to look at who I was, who I thought I would be, and who I am. I slide down and wrap myself around him until I can't tell where I start and he ends.

"Me too." He places a kiss on my forehead. "Me too."

Wrapped in his arms, I wait for sleep to take me.

It doesn't.

JAZMYNE

You've made the jump before, I rationalize, a yard away from the edge of the cavern mouth.

Taal was right, though only the Mudda knows why she'd issue such advice. I thought to get rid of me, judging by the provisions she packed into the bag. But they included a change of clothing, with a cape that, while lighter than the fur-lined gift I wear, is heavy enough that it has to be sewn with conduit gold. I'm not sure why she's helping me. Or why I feel like I can trust her. Regardless, I've spent enough time looking up. It's time to reassume the position I was always meant to have—*if* I can jump down onto the net I know exists.

Then I can make my way down the mountain to the Nameless, but—*cha mon*. I cannot. Turning from the mouth with a scream of frustration, I run toward my cot, turn around, and—

"Kirdan."

He stands in the mouth, close to where I was trying to

build my courage to jump from.

"Thought it was time to enter when I heard you running."

This close, he's larger than I remember him; he looks both familiar and like someone I've never met, in his umber-and-alabaster uniform spliced through with gold, and shorter hair. The hair I had Roje chop.

I take a step back. "She sent you."

His head tilts slightly; I never noticed, how his every move is a sign of his skill, his acuity. Like Iraya. "Is that what you think things between her and I are like? What you think I'm like?"

"I don't think about things between you and her," I bite back, hating how petulant I sound but unable to stop myself. "And I stopped thinking about you when you betrayed me for her."

"If you're still mad, we have nothing to talk about."

"Of course I'm mad." The pack slips down my arm. "You don't want to apologize?"

Crossing his arms over his chest, Kirdan shakes his head. "Jazmyne. The only reason I know time has passed since we last interacted with one another is due to my hair's growth. Yours? I don't see it. How can you act so entitled after everything? You were family to me!" His shout echoes throughout the cavern. "You saved me, when I found you crying, when I saw that you were not your mama. And yet here you stand, and I see nothing of that girl!"

"You expect me to believe you cared about me?" I laugh. "You've heard about what happened with the pirates." It isn't a question. "I bet you're thinking, how could I be so foolish. First I thought you cared about me—"

"Roje." Kirdan shakes his head. "From what the Virago said, he didn't have a choice. He had to think about the Iron Shore, respecting Vea's legacy. Just as I had to think of my home."

"There's no need for lies now, Kirdan." He wanted Iraya.

"I'm not lying. You are, to yourself, which is why you see deception in everyone else. If you will take anything away from this talk, take that." A muscle beats against the skin stretched taut over his jaw. "I came here tonight because I cared for you, Jazmyne. In many ways you were more of a sister to me than my own have been. But you weren't what's best for Aiyca, and I see now that you still aren't."

"And I suppose Iraya is?"

"Rather than deflecting, why don't you consider what you have given, not done, *given*, or even offered, that makes you the better choice."

He turns to leave.

"What *I've* given?"

"I offered to kill the late doyenne for you," he says over his shoulder. "I might be damned as Simbarabo, but I didn't have to volunteer. Who have you cared for enough to offer up part of your soul to save?" Not waiting for an answer, he drops down into the dark.

How could he ask me that? I permitted the death of the late doyenne, giving up almost my *entire* soul for Aiyca—and then there's Anya. Could he think I'd leave her with the Imposter Empress? I might not be the leader he wanted, but I won't let Kirdan define me based on my worst choices. Or Iraya.

Before I can think about it, I swing Taal's pack over my shoulder, run toward the mouth of the cavern, and leap.

70

IRAYA

We don't have the next Eight Nights to honor Nana Clarke, but I can't think of a greater honor than the Blue Mountains descent. Staggered, we wait for dusk by the first sky pod.

The silence is reverent in the bush, sparkling with dew and ice. In a low murmur, Cedella informs me that it's the first time in a decade that the Virago have donned their service uniforms. And that the witches did it for me. When I was a pickney, there was nothing I wanted more than the emerald cloak with gold piping, the matching pants, white tunic, and gold vest; even their sandals were exciting to me, with the laces climbing their legs like golden vines of stability—not even the silver version I wore as a shield can dim their shine.

"It's for you, Empress," my cousin whispers with a smile. "And so is this." She presents me with a Virago cloak.

Before the coven I would have dedicated my life to serving, Taal helps me fasten the golden fibula to my shoulder plates.

They're shaped like the Aeng horn of Virago legend she, as general, carries at her hip.

"Sistren, are those tears?" she asks, her own eyes filling with water.

Nana Clarke must be loving this.

"Of earth and ash, we rise," I call out into the damp morning, the Virago dictum—a play on the Obeah turn of phrase—just as special as the weight of the fabric around my shoulders in an embrace that feels predesigned.

"*Of earth and ash, we rise*" is returned by my sistren.

Kirdan looks on with the Simbarabo, Shamar, his pride unmistakable.

Platoons of Virago begin to egress down into the park, from which they'll travel east and north across the island. Simbarabo will join them along the way—but not the three I've come to think of as family. Esai will accompany me, and Zander and Kirdan will travel on with Shamar to the Hendern Cliffs.

The lieutenant, dressed for stealth in black boots and pants, a long-sleeved tunic beneath a leather vest, and a cloak to conceal the wealth of conduit gold he's armed with, surprises me by taking my hand and lowering his lips onto the back of it. "It has been an honor to serve a leader as wily, creative, and fearless as you, Empress Adair. My only regret so far is that I wasn't there to witness your dive into the Monster's Gulf. I hope I live to see you conquer this world."

I find I have to blink quite rapidly, all of a sudden. And Zander, truly trying to ruin me, breaks into a smile that rivals the burgeoning dawn.

Shamar steps up next. "I wish I went first now."

Taal snorts quietly behind me.

"You can listen instead, Sham." I take both his hands in mine and stare up into his eyes, so my meaning won't be misunderstood. "You do not have my permission to die. You will live, and you will grieve her. I won't begrudge you that. Do you hear me? I expect to see you, living, when I arrive at the Hendern Cliffs."

Shamar's throat bobs. The scars across his chin undulate as his mouth twists.

"That is an order from your empress, soldier. One who owes you a great debt for helping me reach this place. Do you understand?"

With something like gratitude in his face, he nods.

And then I am facing Kirdan.

He left me for a short while, yesterday eve, to speak with Jazmyne. He didn't tell me what was said; I didn't ask. It didn't matter. The flashback to this morning in bed, when, face-to-face, we broke every rule Zander and Anan outlined for us, is visceral. So is the kiss he plants against my mouth, the first hand he fists in my braids, and the second, which presses against the base of my spine, welding me to him in a breathless, desperate farewell.

With just as much speed as the embrace, Kirdan wrenches his face away from mine. "Don't die," he orders, his voice rough and throaty.

"That was going to be my line," I whisper. Along with the thought *I—I wanted more time.*

"Me too." His eyes shift to the new weapon strapped across

my shoulder. We made an early trip to one of the compound's Master Artisans of Metal. The witch welded his gift to me atop Dada's staff, with additional fortifications of conduit gold. "Fight for more, every time you swing that weapon. Fight for Aiyca, and fight for us too." He turns away before he lets my hands go.

Zander and Shamar join him; the three of them, silhouetted against the sky before the former's sift takes them back to Admiral's Cove, will stay with me forever. If Jazmyne is right, and the source is located within the Hendern Cliffs, their time won't be any easier than mine. I'm not sure if Kirdan will survive a second poisoning. Not when Anan will be accompanying me across the island. But I won't think of that. I'll fight. For more.

"That was both the hottest thing I've ever seen, and the saddest."

"Why hasn't one of your unit brought Jazmyne down yet?" I ask Taal, ignoring her comment. Hers is next to leave. "Don't tell me she's refusing to move."

"Ah, poor timing on my part, mon. I should have told you before the emotional farewells. Jazmyne left, late yesterday eve."

"She did what?" I turn to her. "Did Kirdan—"

"No. Though perhaps I should say yes." Taal does not step back, but she swallows in the face of my growing glower. "You made me your second, and your general. I'd also like to point out that I have two years on you, and a lot more training, mon. Your naevus or no."

"But no magic," I grind out.

We pause to see the penultimate unit off in the aerial.

"I won't apologize for acting in your best interests, Iraya," Taal continues, as the witches, instead of waiting for the sky pod, sift away. "Aiyca needs all the help it can get to succeed in this war. Jazmyne and I had a chat about her connections with Healers and sea reinforcements for the Hendern Cliffs."

"And you think you can trust her to do that? Taal! She has betrayed me at every opportunity."

"She saved Zeplin."

"What?" I turn to Taal. She nods.

Taal sobers. "And a Jade Guild ally of ours who helped with food deliveries and medicine for a decade. Jazmyne shared the Glyph of Banishment all Virago now know. If she betrays us, which I don't think she will, I'll take care of her."

"*When*," I correct. "When she betrays us. So be ready."

As I must be.

For a witch without magic, Jazmyne has proven herself to be formidable. It would be a folly not to consider her a threat during my tour of the island.

Having only just returned to my mountain home, leaving has come about too soon. But I'll be back. And it feels right, traveling down the mountain in the company of my Virago sistren via sky pod, since we have a lot of ground to cover magically, and preservation is more important than ever. Though I didn't foresee Esai and the fourteen Simbarabo Kirdan insisted on leaving behind at eight, when I dreamed about becoming a legendary Warrior. What follows, though, is closer to what I did.

The murmur began in Four Paths city. A sighting of a witch

calling herself Empress Adair, joined by two bands of fabled Warriors. The first, a coven unheard of for a decade, resurrected from the past; the second a small phalanx of silken-haired soldiers from an enemy island who hadn't set foot in Aiyca for about the same length of time. Neighbors challenged neighbors, family members argued—until they saw the cavalcade for themselves. One in the morning, another in the afternoon, one during a sleepless night sitting at a window—more than the cloaks of alabaster, emerald, and gold, the deftness of the sparring when faced with the magi who told them *they* were fighting for the Lost Empress, a bright flash of white-gold light. One so distinctive, it couldn't be anything other than the first family naevus. A pickney was among the earliest to catch a glimpse of her. He said she was beautiful, tall, with a head of braids down to her waist, and scarification glowing in a promise on her forehead. He told his mama she winked at him before disappearing into the night. By the time the residents of Four Paths were ready to believe, and actively waited to see her, to touch her, to fall down at her feet in apology for believing in another, rumor began that she was in Bluefields, another town hours away. But she left a message in a shimmering gold script across the tallest buildings in the city.

THE ADAIRS REMEMBER

Two days after the true Lost Empress was spotted along the border between St. Bethann and St. Mary, St. Elizabeth fell under siege from the witches who served the Adair throne. Virago. Witch. Warrior. Weapon. Every town, village, city, wrested back from the monstrous influence, rumored to have chased Alumbrar, Aiycans, and Obeah from their homes, carried the same message.

THE ADAIRS REMEMBER

The Lost Empress was everywhere. She was a wraith to exact justice; a duppy stirred from sleep to save her order; an ill wish, a threat, a savior, beloved.

My favorite story is reported by Zeplin when she returns from her watch and updates us with the latest news she heard: that I became Death, during my time in Carne, and the world will bow before me to avoid being sent to the nadirs of Coyaba.

Taal snorts. "Don't let this get to your head."

Pointing at a rat large enough for a small child to ride climbing the wall in the abandoned store we've been squatting in all night, I tell her it's unlikely. The first couple of days, fueled by adrenaline and the act of doing something to unsettle the confidence the Unlit must have felt when they ousted Jazmyne, were enjoyable. After three more days on the road, sleeping in abandoned buildings, wild cane fields—if we slept at all—during the day so we could travel at night, I'm ready to stop at the palace, regardless of what Kirdan thought about it.

"Any word from the palace unit?"

Cedella shakes her head. "Nothing. They're either behind us, or they were caught."

We've been exchanging reports with the Virago traveling across the island. Enough to build an index of the beasts in the Unlit's arsenal, but as yet we haven't seen any creatures on six legs, never mind the winged beasts they also have—worse, from the reports of my Warriors who fought them while wresting back cities and towns from occupation. But there are none worse than the Oscuridad on two legs. These beasts think and talk like women and men, yet are reported to be scarce in number. We've debated if they are some kind of general.

"I don't like this." Taal checks Main Street in Ol' Town once more. "It's too quiet, and it's getting dark."

"Already?" I join her at the window and peel back the paper covering the glass. It's late afternoon, but the sky is already mottling with indigo.

"Iraya." Esai indicates that I join him with the Simbarabo across the store. "Look," he whispers. "The general didn't think going to the palace was a great idea, and I agreed, but if we don't move soon we might end up trapped in the labyrinth of stores with an entire horde of monsters for company. I think they've been tracking us, and waiting for the perfect place to lay ambush."

In agreement, I repeat his warning to our company at large. "We have to move, now. Before it's too dark." I'm not certain I know the exact location of the tunnel entrance at the base of the mount, but no one else needs to worry about that now.

We leave the store the same way we entered, via the back. Ground coverage is slow, given the darkening sky and stretching shadows. At every corner, I expect Oscuridad, Unlit, waiting.

Our party is almost clear of the market town at the base of Cwenburg's mount when I hear it—the soundtrack from my time in Zesia. The rumbling snarl of too many mouths, the thud of paws against earth, and the sinister click of teeth and nails.

"Where is the entrance?" Esai demands.

"A mile from here, to the west of the drive up the mount. But I—"

"Go," the Simbarabo orders. "We'll stall for you."

"Esai."

Steeling his face, the soldier, older than me but somehow younger, turns to Taal. "Make sure the empress gets in the tunnel. If we're not there, leave without us."

"You'd better make it there," I tell him. "That's an order."

He swallows. "Go."

The Simbarabo step out of our cover and into the street; I hear nothing of their skirmish over Taal's shouted orders to run. Arms pumping, I lead the way through the last of the market. In a flat-out sprint, I haven't the breath to tell Taal I don't know exactly where the tunnel is, and that I'm the only one who can open it. And then I hear it again, only this time it's the thump of pursuit, the screech of something above.

"Shit!" Taal screams. "Cover us overhead."

I don't look. Can't, as we breach the market and the palace mount rears up.

"Where's the door?" Cedella asks.

"Just—shield me! I need to find it."

"Find it?" She looks at me, aghast. "You don't know where it is?!"

"Shut up and do what she said," Taal snarls. "Respectfully, Master Clarke."

662

I run my fingers down one of the knives in my bandolier and begin shoving my hand against the mossy rock of the mount, muttering the Adair name over and over.

"Any luck?"

"When I have it, you'll know!"

This is the tunnel I used whenever I snuck away from the palace, including the night I ran to the Blue Mountains. Then I was smaller, and I remember climbing for what felt like half a day before I reached the roof. Wait—climbing! *The entrance is on the ground.*

"I see Simbarabo and a shit ton of Oscuridad! Do we need another plan?"

My fingers sink into the groove of the tunnel door, at last.

"I've got it. Help—" I turn to the sky; it is like heaven and hell have been painted in reverse. Choked with clouds in obsidian and gray, the color to be found is in the deep red of the winged beasts—as though born in reverse, with their soft flesh on the outside. Eyes an unearthly—unholy—green glow in long muzzled faces that screech at a pitch that makes my blood run cold. "Help me!" I shout out.

Taal sheathes her blade to lend me her weight to shift the cover.

"Why not use your magic?"

"My mind is a little preoccupied!" I shout back, glancing up at the sky once more.

"Fair enough." Taal laughs weakly.

The cover finally lifts with a creak. "Get inside," she tells me. Rising from my crouch, I turn toward Ol' Town to look for Esai, his men; pinioned against the sky, the Oscuridad's great membranous wings have closed the distance with alacrity. Gnarled hands, arms, swing low as they swoop down on the sprinting Simbarabo. The soldiers' swords swipe up to sever limbs from bodies. Mostly. Some receive wicked scratches from the Oscuridad's claws and even teeth before they manage to bat the flying mutts away. I call for Anan to ready cures. Leading their number, Esai waves frantically; he's close enough that I can see the word he's shouting—*Go*.

"Iraya!" Taal screeches. "He's going to make it. Now get inside before I push you!" She starts forward like she means to.

I scale the ladder belowground quickly, will the sconces on the walls in the tunnel to illuminate in a brilliant flash of warm light, and then shout for the Virago to join me. Taal enters last; feet and hands gripping the side of the ladder, she zips down and keeps her focus on the open cover.

"The moment you see a monster, slam it," she tells one of the lieutenants.

Come on, Esai, I will, my heart thumping. *Come on, come on, come on.*

And then he's there, falling.

"Catch him!"

A split second before he hits the ground, he's stopped, suspended by the magic of all who can wield, I suspect. Including me. Taal runs and pulls him away from the opening as Simbarabo jump down after him.

Esai groans.

"Oh gods." I peel back his collar, revealing a livid scratch oozing green. "He's been scratched, poisoned. Anan!"

The Skylander runs over, and skids to his knees, vials in hand.

"I'm fine." Brushing everyone's hands away, Esai stands, stumbles.

"You aren't! I'll carry you up to the palace and we can treat you there."

"I'll carry him." Taal elbows me aside.

Suddenly, we're both shunted back as, with wide eyes, Esai turns up to the eye of the tunnel. The lid is slammed down, and above us, something, or someone, begins to scream. I'm still struggling onto my feet, detangling myself from Taal, when the darkness on the other side of the ladder shifts, and two green eyes blink at me from the darkness.

The torches go out.

"Run!" Esai orders. "Leave me."

"To hell with that." Lights spark, cutting through the inky surroundings; Zeplin bends and hoists Esai across her shoulders. "After you, Empress."

"See through the dark, Iraya," Cedella advises. "Don't worry about the sconces. I have them. Go!"

Freeing a baton, I hold it before me like a lit torch and let the light guide me through the dark, my eyes on the ground for the stakes I laid during the wet season, when I spent time in the tunnels, desperately trying to ignore the sudden changes from light to dark as my cousin battles with the Oscuridad for power over the latter. Spotting a stake, I pivot sharply. There's a thump behind me.

"Don't stop!" Taal orders as I slow to check.

But Zeplin and Esai are on the floor, and the tunnel sconces are flickering out row by row behind us.

Esai's eyes slide to mine. "It's been . . . the greatest honor of my life," he wheezes.

Realization is a knife in my heart.

"Don't you dare."

"Fighting beside you and the general."

"Don't!"

Taal grabs my arms, keeping me in place. Zeplin looks up at her and nods.

"No!" The echo of my shout is stopped dead by the tunnel caving in, as a bolt of red light brings down the roof and the penultimate row of sconces turns dark. "Esai! Zeplin!"

"Come *on*." Taal tugs at me.

"We can get them out."

"We cannot," Cedella says. "And unless we want to hear what the Oscuridad does to them, we have to leave, and we can't get out of here without you, Iraya. So rally and lead."

My cheeks wet beneath a steady stream of tears. It's like I've been cut open, and my blood is running clear.

"We mourn once this is over," Cedella says, fierce. "Now move."

Furious, helpless, I scrub my face against my sleeve and do as the Virago's next Master Warrior said. If I didn't come here, Esai, Zeplin . . . We had so much time, I made sure of it. And yet, the sky darkened faster than it should have. Almost like—like—my plan.

"They used Squallers." I keep our momentum, but I look

at Taal, Cedella, what remains of the Virago and Simbarabo. "They had to. Why else did the sky darken?"

"You think we have a mole?" Cedella asks. "Virago are loyal, Iraya."

I don't doubt it, but I know what misguided loyalty looks like up close. Delyse, in my lap, telling me all she did was for Aiyca. "I'm not sure. The Imposter claims to be an Adair," I say in the silence of my companions. "We could think similarly. We might share training. Or, she could be the preferred Adair." She has sat back, avoided wading into the fray as many Obeah believe their leader should, and here I am knee-deep in trouble with a trail of dead in my wake. Not all my family could have believed in the knee they took, yesterday eve.

It is the fight I thought I was winning, with my appearances across St. Bethann, the Virago and Simbarabo victory in St. Elizabeth. Not me and Them, me and the Unlit leader.

Me and Aiyca's Obeah.

But if this witch and I are so similar and we think the same, Carling Hill won't be my next stand. It will be the final stand, after I'm forced to make the choice I have not yet—mercy, or death.

71

JAZMYNE

The jump from the cavern is the worst part of finding Anya.

At first.

The Nameless, though not Warriors like the Virago, are waiting when I stumble out of one of the national park gateways at the foot of the Blue Mountains. Taal must have ensured my journey down the mountain would be undisturbed, for I didn't encounter a soul. The Nameless might not have taken the knee as Iraya's family did for her, but the fifty I recruited demonstrated their loyalty in a manner that I readily accepted: they reached out to the four remaining Stealths in Anya's cadre at the palace; collectively, they located the *Silver Arrow*—In the short time we have to assemble, before Iraya sends a sect of one of her many armies after me. Emthera takes the lead position, with Filmore and Pasha dead. A blow we have time to mourn during our three-day trip along the coast to the pirate ship, docked in the town of Alligator Pond's shallows.

Concealed in the belly of one of several Alumbrar Squallers' sloops, there would be no room for Filmore or Pasha, but their presence is missed all the same.

They won't have their Nine Nights, in the ceremonial sense, but the steel in the brows of my Stealths, mine, is enough of a sign that they won't be forgotten.

"The entire fleet from the Iron Shore do not wait at Alligator Pond," Cleo says, while Emthera looks on. "I sifted in and out. There are but a handful of ships at sea. The pirates row in to the shore."

"And Anya?"

Cleo glances at Emthera. The look is guarded, even in the solitary candle's light burning before us. "She is there. She won't be easy to retrieve."

My new commanding Stealth shifts beside me. In any other space, I might have missed the sign of discomfort, but we five sit, packed together with little room to breathe, amidst our sailor's accoutrements—the partner of one of the quieter Stealths. He leans back against a barrel, as though seeking some kind of personal space. Or resigning himself to a difficult retrieval mission.

"Captain Shah?" The Imposter.

"She didn't appear to be there when I checked in, Regent."

I bite back that I am not regent. Titles don't matter at present.

"We'll need a distraction to get her," Cleo informs us. "Something to draw those watching Anya away."

"I have the distractions we need." Several jars of them, courtesy of Taal. I'd thought them lights, until Emthera near fell off her perch when I took one receptacle out to use in place of a candle. The jar's contents are, effectively, explosives. "Perhaps we split up. One of us per group of Nameless. We each trigger our magical explosion, and when the pirates are distracted, we run for Anya."

"I like it," Cleo says. The others nod. "What comes after, with the pirates?"

I wish I knew.

"Leave it with me," I bluff.

Indeed, pretending to be fearless is the order of the evening, once we dock at Alligator Pond, and the Squaller on deck of the Sloop above signals that all is safe with a boom of thunder. We converge on a private dock of a home belonging to one of the Nameless. My party of Stealths and I splits into three, each with a jar of magic. The boys take a group of Nameless each; both Emthera and Cleo insisted on accompanying me. We command a larger group of my followers. Staggered, we sift the shoreline where Anya is being kept. Great sand dunes stand against the night in the coastal town. To our right, a strip of drinking houses and eateries glow beneath the soft lights of witchlight orbs garlanded on strings in palm trees. Music and laughter ring into the night, along with the sweet smell of barbecued meat. My stomach rumbles. Save the roti on the ship, I haven't eaten well since I was imprisoned by the Virago. Or saved by them.

Emthera, Cleo, me, and our nervous Nameless wait at the first dune—the last to set off our explosive. Our vantage provides the clearest line of sight toward Anya. My heart leaps at the sight of her. Alive. Even if her rescue will be as difficult as the Stealths didn't want to tell me it would be. She sits on a small island adrift in the large inlet of fresh water surrounded by the beach, with her back against a coconut tree. Connected to civilization by a long dock, it's equidistant to the shore where we wait; every now and then a tail will crest the surface of the waters, and Anya will draw her legs in further. I'd always thought Alligator Pond a misnomer, that none dwelled in this watery inlet, and yet I've seen the spikes along their backs, the glow of their eyes in the dark.

Beyond Anya, lapping against the black sands of her island, the Xaymaca trench stretches toward a full moon, at large in the night like an all-seeing eye. Bobbing atop its waters is the *Silver Arrow*, alongside three ships I don't recognize.

"Can you read those names?" I ask Cleo, crouched behind the sand dune beside me. "We need to know if there's a ship out there by the name of the *Vanquisher*."

"It's not there, Regent."

"And you were certain you didn't see Captain Shah along the beach?" I ask Floyd, one of the Nameless; as a Recondite, he was one of three Nameless who actually volunteered to venture across the sands when we arrived; posing as a family alongside Emthera while she scouted the number of pirates present for the Imposter—spirit shunting to communicate with those hidden behind neighboring dunes, my Stealth is unable to provide answers.

"While she wasn't present earlier," Floyd says, "it doesn't make sense to discount her now."

Emthera's eyes roll back down as her spirit returns to her body, and the shunt ends.

"All is well. Are you ready to signal, Regent?" Cleo asks.

"Yes."

She whispers the order for the magically sensitive ears of the Stealths stationed across the beach. In *five, four, three, two, one*—a blast of lambent magic erupts upward into the night. A stream of pirates emerges from the eateries, the bars, along the beach. They question the origin of the sparks, the shower of sand that took flight as though kicked by a mighty foot in the dark.

"Send the signal for the second explosion," I command Emthera.

It discharges even farther up the beach, to draw the pirates away from Anya. For a second time, sand and fire plume outward. The shower of falling beads rustles sinisterly, in the night. Outraged, more of the race participants surge onto the beach and run toward the chaos—where they won't find my allies. The Stealths will have them concealed from the magicless pirates. I can't believe this is going as well as it is.

Of the same feeling, Cleo's eyes shine with excitement in the dark. "Are we ready for the third?"

"There's still too many inside the bar," an older Nameless, without magic, points out from our magically secured hideout. "There could be casualties."

"Send the fourth signal then," I decide. That jar of magic was rigged in a tree even farther down the beach. It was meant to act as a blocker, trapping the pirates between the burning bars and the beach fires, but the Nameless is right. There could be casualties, and I don't want to spill any pirates' blood. Not when I need them.

Emthera shakes her head. "They're not acknowledging me."

"What does that mean?"

"It means something is wrong. The explosions may have frightened the Nameless at the previous post."

I believe it.

"We have to go and expose that jar, otherwise we won't get Anya." The pirates will spread across the beach without the blockers in place. "Cleo, you're with me." Emthera I leave behind with the Nameless, in case something goes wrong.

Our vantage was meant to be the closest on ground level, so I could reach Anya. Now we need height to survey the beach. Cleo and I, cloaked from sight with magic, scale the rocky verge rearing above the sand dunes. We should be able to see the others from this angle—through their own cloak, thanks to the Stealths' trickery.

Unless they've been caught.

"Do you see them?" I ask Cleo.

"No."

"I'm going down there."

"Wait—you won't have cover from my magic. Just—wait."

With more than enough cover from the night, I slip down, landing on the sand with a muffled thump.

"It's fine," I call up to Cleo.

"I think you'll find it's far from fine, Regent Cariot."

They come in from the night like wraiths, the pirates. Their leader, the man striding straight for me, is the only one I recognize. He stood with Captain Shah when she first climbed aboard the *Silver Arrow*, at the Iron Shore.

"She said you would come for your sistren." Hair as obsidian as the surrounding night flutters against his pale forehead. "She didn't say that you would come alone." This man, whose name I still don't know, runs a disdainful look over me.

I shake my hand in a way I hope Cleo interprets to stay put.

"She doesn't know me." I make my voice strong, even as my mouth dries at the number of pirates before me. My Stealths, the Nameless, cannot stand against them in combat.

Neither can I.

"She knew enough. You might have died with more dignity, if you came with numbers. As it stands, I'm willing to hear you beg."

"You will never."

"Then your death will be slow."

"And yours long overdue, I bet," a familiar voice says.

Before the Imposter's companion turns his head, a golden disk is launched from over my shoulder. Blood gushes from a red smile across his neck. Someone screams. Virago shoot past me, their golden swords and staffs aimed at the pirates.

"You followed me?" I ask, turning around to find Guy using his staff as a prop to lean against. My Stealths appear, rounding the dunes to run for me.

"Taal said to keep an eye on you."

"And you were happy to help?"

He straightens. "You saved my life, Regent Cariot."

Cleo stands beside me, silent, but there nonetheless to bear witness.

"In this war, that means we're on the same side. Now, I heard you're looking to save your sistren and win us a fleet of pirates to sail around the coast to the Hendern Cliffs. What can we do to help?"

"Help?" Emthera asks, arriving with one additional Stealth to catch the end of the conversation.

"Yes," I tell her. "Help. Where are the others?"

She eyes Guy. "Moving the Nameless to safety."

"Good." I turn back to Guy. "I need to get my sistren, and then address the pirates here."

"We should stop killing them, then?"

I nod. "We're about to be on the same side."

Ten years of being trapped atop the Blue Mountains weren't spent idly. The blood of Captain Shah's watchdogs already stains this rocky overlook black beneath the starless sky when Guy calls the Virago off.

"Let's get Anya, the *Silver Arrow*'s crew, and go from there."

Guy traveled with seven Virago. They feel like an army of ten times the size, given the lambency of their weapons against the night. The shield they cast around themselves, me, and Guy keeps the pirates from attacking as we cross the beach to the bridge to reach Anya. Scowling, they keep close, ready to launch themselves at us once again when the protections fall.

The rope and wooden planks shift with our weight but otherwise feel sturdy.

A Virago with a shock of red hair turns to me. "She should be able to hear you, if you want to shout for her."

The shield strobes around us.

"She'll hear me through this protection?"

"She'll hear."

The shield blips again. There and gone, in a split second like a witchlight in need of charge.

"Okay." Oddly self-conscious, I walk farther up the bridge until I'm at the tip of the rectangle we're traveling in. "Anya? Anya! Can you hear me?" Pausing reveals how loudly I'm breathing. "Anya! It's Jazmyne! I'm crossing the bridge."

The effervescence of the shield ebbs.

"Anya!"

"Jazmyne?" She shifts to the sound of my voice.

"Anya! It's me."

"Get off the bridge, Jazmyne!" Anya surges onto her feet but keeps back from the waters. "Go back!"

Guy takes me by my arm, stopping me mid-step. "Why would she say that?"

As if in answer, the shield flickers for several more seconds before night resumes its dominion. The waters, rippling all night, go still.

"Get off the bridge! They're in the water—can you hear me, Jazmyne? They're in the water!" Anya's voice gives way to a scream as something bursts from the water's edge. Something that drags its sleek body across the shore using thickly muscled arms; a tail, like that of a great fish, trails behind it, ridged like a gator's. That's where the similarities end. In the dark, it looks the color of an oil spill. A living shadow. And it's dragging itself toward my sistren, who doesn't bear any conduit gold I can see.

Guy swears. "The Unlit have beasts that live in the water?"

"Oh gods." I told Iraya to go for the source at the Hendern

Cliffs. They abut Carne Sea. And there are Oscuridad who swim.

"The bridge is glyphed against magic. We need to get back to where we can use it before we are hemmed in by beasts and pirates." Guy tugs at my arm.

"What about Anya?"

Guy looks at her, and then back at me. "The risk is too great for one, Regent. I am sorry."

"But you would risk it for Iraya?"

"She is my empress."

"And Anya is my family." The decision isn't easy, but it is necessary. "Get back." I wish my voice shook less. "To where your magic still worked. I'm going to help her."

"You don't have the training," one of the witches needlessly points out. "You could die."

Between my fight for Aiyca and Anya, there is no choice.

"I hope your aim is better than your optimism."

Guy presses a golden dagger into my hand. "If the beach is without the glyph prohibitors, the magic in this will work. Seven blessings."

Anya screams; I start running. The thuds of my sandals dull in my ears. Sixty yards become forty, which become fifteen; wooden planks underfoot are exchanged for sand. Anya is close enough that the terror on her face sends a jolt of pain through my chest. Sitting atop a boulder, she stabs a useless branch down at the Oscuridad.

"An—"

Something closes around my left ankle, tugs; the chill of its skin, the clammy wrongness, makes me scream; I whirl and stab blindly, not hitting anything solid. Iraya's Banishment Glyph is sketched with shaking fingers. It hits the beast right in its eyeless and noseless face; screaming, I kick at it until I am free.

"Jazmyne! Throw the knife to me." Anya sketches the glyph; I launch the knife; leaning to catch it, she falls off the rocks. The creature is gone before she hits the ground.

"Are you okay? Did it scratch you?"

"No. I—I'm well." The knife slips through her fingers. Clambering back onto her feet, Anya limps over and encloses me in a breath-stealing hug. "I can't believe you came for me. Roje said you would."

"He did?"

Nodding, Anya draws back; tears have tracked paths through the dirt on her face.

"Come," I tell her. "He's next."

Hand in hand, Anya and I sprint back across the bridge; the aquatic Oscuridad pull themselves up onto the dock, but the Virago are ready for them. Golden glyphs spark through the night; weapons follow. And when Anya and I reach them, someone else is ready for us—Elodie, Synestra, and Roje stand before the calmer crowd of pirates on the beach.

"All hail Jazmyne Cariot," Roje calls, his eyes blazing in the dark. "The True Queen of Carne Sea, in possession of the map for the Conduit Falls."

Synestra doesn't challenge him.

I leave Anya to stand before the pirate. "It's still yours, if you want it."

Surprise flares across her features. "But—after what we did?"

"Do you want to answer to Captain Shah," I begin. "Or oversee the Iron Shore and work with Aiyca's leader to avoid being decimated by legendary armies you don't stand a chance against otherwise." All she has to do is look at the Virago, how they stand, how they wield their weapons, to understand that they are several classes above the Xanthippe. "Command the fleet to join the skirmish against Captain Shah at the Hendern Cliffs, and Vea's captaincy is yours. I won't contest. But stand against me, and you stand against Aiyca's Obeah too."

Synestra does look over my shoulder then; she swallows. "Join your fight?"

"Captain Shah has ushered monsters from the other side of the veil into our skies, onto our streets, and into these waters. You knew about it. You helped her."

"The fight is our burden too," Roje mutters.

I make myself look at him.

"And if I agree?" Synestra asks. "What do you want? Our heads for what we did?"

"Why did you?"

She looks at the pirates, still gathered around us. "Captain Shah promised us free rein of whatever was left. Like we're no better than scavengers. She didn't understand what we want, what we deserve."

The crowd nods, murmurs its agreement.

"And what do you want?" Guy queries. "In the past it hasn't seemed to be much different than what the Imposter is offering you."

"We never wanted to struggle to belong in the empire,"

Elodie answers. "We did what we had to. But what we want? Peace."

"Then fight for that *with* us," I tell her, everyone on the beach. "Because Captain Shah is bringing one thing." I point at the bridge over Alligator Pond, where the creatures are once again swimming beneath the surface. "And it isn't peace."

Synestra laughs. "You deliver a mediocre speech, Alumbrar. But you're not promising peace either. Why should we help you?"

"If you want peace, I have learned, you must prepare for war."

72

IRAYA

The rest of our journey unfolds in silence. We have, all of us, lost fighters. Taal told me she served with Zeplin since she was in her early teens. And Esai—gods, his sisters and grandmother will mourn for him. As will Kirdan and Zander. Me. I will ensure he is honored for his sacrifice. This Imposter will be put down for me, him. For all we have lost and will lose.

The tunnel's incline eventually levels out; I have an easier time locating the hatch to egress. Slowly, so as not to startle anyone on the other side, I push it upward with Taal's help and call my identity out into the night.

"Come out" is returned by a voice that lowers my shoulders from my neck.

The hatch is thrown back against the earth in the gardens adjacent to the forecourt. It is teeming with Xanthippe—a group of witches I never thought I'd be so pleased to see; and in their number are shield faces I remember.

"I'm impressed," I say, emerging with my hands up. "Your response time was fast enough that I could be convinced you knew I was here."

Ford, grinning so widely his back teeth are visible, sheathes his sword. "Someone started a fight with some monsters in Ol' Town. I was hoping it was you." He rocks on his feet, like he wants to sweep me up in his arms, but he casts an awed look at the witches and Simbarabo who emerge behind me. "Empress Adair."

"Formalities? From the same magi who once asked what did the earth say to the Grower?"

Taal snorts beside me.

My arms lower, opening in an embrace Ford wastes no time crashing into.

"Forget the finger," he says into the top of my head. "Take both my hands, my heart, my lungs. I am entirely yours, Just-Ira."

The nickname makes me flinch; Ford draws back and looks at me with concern. Rather than address everything that happened with Delyse, I greet the other shields whose names I remember and introduce everyone to both cadres of Warriors with me.

"Is there somewhere we can talk?"

Ford laughs at me. "This is your house."

"Won't you be talking with all of us?" Nel steps out of the crowd. I hadn't noticed her.

Nodding her way, I glance at Taal, ask a wordless question.

"You can keep to your watch," my second tells the shield. "Especially this area. We were followed, and I'm not sure a cave-in will stop the Oscuridad. Do you have conduit gold large enough to cover this opening?"

Nel inclines her head. "Who are you?"

Taal grins at what is an unmistakable challenge. "Would you like to find out?"

"Do as the Virago says," Ford cuts in, with an apologetic look my way. "They're the *Virago*. My gods. Iraya, let me update you as to what's been happening."

"I *will* talk with you all," I tell the shields. "After. What I will say now is, blessings for protecting this mount. The palace is one of Aiyca's greatest symbols. The fact that it still stands lends hope to all suffering beneath the shadow of war. Thank you." I'm sure to address the Alumbrar as well as my Obeah ilk. "Taal, if you stay here with the Virago and Simbarabo, you can help to fortify that entrance."

"As you wish, Empress."

Inside, the palace is bright with what seems like every sconce, candle, and witchlight lit. It feels bizarre to be back. Like it suddenly isn't as large as I remember it being.

"Have the monsters breached?"

"Not since the initial attack on Jazmyne a month ago." At my raised eyebrows, Ford whistles. "You didn't know. Jeez. She told me she was communicating with you."

"Talking," I correct. "She doesn't know the meaning of communication. Who remains here?"

"Alumbrar spongers seeking protection mostly; the new council was here until recently. They left to be of use across the island. Jaz had a cousin here who left to ensure Healing is available to any who encounter monsters. Last but not least, we have Xanthippe here too."

"I'm amazed none of you have killed one another."

Ford gives me a look, as if to say, there have been moments.

"What about the prisoners in the holding cells?"

"There were only a few Unlit, and one Alumbrar who kept insisting he was meant to be sacrificed." Ford shrugs. "I didn't think Jaz wanted to continue the Yielding. Seemed safer to send the magi to Carne than to set him free and risk him hurting himself."

"I agree."

"I had some of the coven witches sift them to Carne, and then stay to guard."

"Smart. Smarter than me bringing monsters to your door."

"It's your door. You could have brought them elsewhere, since I've taken such great care of this place, but I won't hold it against you. Not when you arrived with Virago. That one with the frohawk, you'll have to put in a good word for me. Do you know how rare it is to meet a girl, *woman*, who laughs at my jokes? Hey, where's Delyse? I thought she'd be with you."

There has been no time to stop and acknowledge the many knives I carry in my back as a result of Delyse's actions. I do now, as I consider my next words.

"Ford. I'm so sorry," I settle on. "She—she died, a phase ago now."

His face crumples.

I clasp his forearm; he grips mine back.

"That will kill Nel." He half laughs, half sobs. "It's killing me."

She almost killed me.

"She died fighting for Aiyca, if it's any consolation," I whisper. One day I'll have to tell them the truth, when we honor the dead, and Delyse's name isn't mentioned with the same acclaim. Maybe. I don't know. But we won't hash matters out now. "We'll mourn the dead after the war is won."

Straightening, he wipes the moisture away from his eyes, his cheeks. "The tunnel."

"The tunnel. If you're up for it?"

"Let's get those bastards. For Delyse."

"For Aiyca."

Updating Ford covers the distance to the Xanthippe armory, where I fill my bandoliers and various holsters with the gold I didn't want to leave the Blue Mountains compound without.

"We need to install some security measures. And I need a fire to send a message to Kirdan and the Simbarabo, a bath, a change of clothing, and a vat of coffee."

"Is that before or after we've fortified the palace?"

"The missive needs to be now. The rest after. The fortifications I have in mind won't take long."

My message to Kirdan is short. I have reached the retreat location, and I'll be moving on forthwith. Kirdan's reply doesn't come before Ford and I have rounded up the others. I don't allow myself to worry—can't—not when mentally I'm deep in the plan I made after the tunnel collapse. No, earlier. When the Oscuridad I didn't see enter came in from the dark and the lights went out. That was the moment I knew we lost Cwenburg.

While I tell myself I've accepted it, the shields and Xanthippe have a harder twime agreeing with me when I tell them the palace won't survive the war. Part of it, at least.

"But this is the Golden Seat," Ford says, dismayed. "We can't blow it up!"

"And we're not," I tell him, all of them. "We're blowing *part* of it up."

The Imposter outmaneuvered me with whoever relayed where we were in Aiyca. It isn't difficult to imagine Carling Hill as my next stop—unless I give them a reason to think me wounded, or, better still, dead in a fight for this palace. My home, once. I told Jazmyne, the Warriors, and Alumbrar before me, that it's a symbol for Aiyca; it's both more and less than that. It's been a tug-of-war between Obeah and Alumbrar, an item coveted by the Unlit, and a point of hope for Aiycans. I wouldn't render it firewood without taking the time to consider what that will mean, and what Aiycans will think when they look up and see part of it burning. But—

"There is no other way," I tell the four factions before me. "It has stood long enough to keep hope alive, but right now it must burn."

I repeat it to myself when Kirdan's reply still doesn't come, and we set the explosive jars taken from the Blue Mountains as far away from the gardens, my family's wing—blocked off by the doyenne when she moved in, a quick inspection reveals. I linger for longer than the minutes I spend sketching Glyphs of Protection on the doors and walls of the suite Mama and Dada slept in. My nursery is as it was before I moved into the bedroom Jazmyne claimed this past decade. The time I spent in the palace as a shield almost feels wasted. I killed the doyenne, yeh mon, but I killed Iraya Adair too, in a lot of ways. She didn't return to her childhood home. But she's here now. I'm here. And I'll be back to rebuild. If I survive what comes next.

"Are you sure about this?" Taal asks, as the forecourt begins to rumble, and the Xanthippe remaining behind, the witches who said they received orders from their regent to hold the line—the same witch who could be dead right now, for all I've heard of her—level their weapons at the manhole we opted to leave clear of gold, of the locking glyph, to avoid the creatures appearing all over the palace grounds. "We didn't receive any word from General Divsylar's unit. We could have waited longer."

An end. Not a beginning.

Another problem if they're dead and the tear in the Hendern Cliffs remains open.

"I'm sure," I tell my second.

But later, watching the east wing of the palace go up in flames from the incline of the Strawberry Hills, where several Xanthippe sifted our party of close to one hundred before returning to the palace, I don't feel sure. I feel sick.

Not even our location, the memories tied to my time with Dada, can abate the roiling in my stomach, the tenseness in my muscles, the urge to lie down and give myself to the leaves and the moss. But, at the fore of the hundred-strong party of soldiers, I have to keep moving.

"We're still a couple of days out from Carling Hill," Taal breathes beside me. "I advise against sifting, given our close proximity. We don't know how far the Unlit will be spread."

"I agree" is my response.

"How do you want to play this?"

"For now, we keep going as we are."

"Are you good to keep going?"

So long as I don't turn back to watch my home burning . . . maybe?

"Don't ask questions you don't want answered truthfully."

"Fair enough."

And so we march uphill, through the verdant leaves of a hill with no fruit to get us through its climb. Taal didn't ask how we'll breach Carling Hill. Perhaps she's waiting for that one. I am too. The duppies should allow me entry, but I don't know how close we'll get with the Unlit's occupation.

It is said first wars are the worst—all the more so for the loser.

Right now, I have no idea what victory will look like. I can't even picture it.

"Do you hear that?" I ask Taal a while later. Night is thick around us, but it will be better to sleep during the day out here. "I think someone's running."

It's Ford who answers. "Who has the energy to run?"

Willing my hearing to extend outward, like a net, I sift through those behind us; each footstep is more or less the same. Heavy and tired. But—as I reach even farther back, the tread changes, lightens, as it would if someone was running uphill on their tiptoes.

"You can't hear?"

"Are you rubbing in the fact that you have magic and I do not?" Taal grumbles.

"I imbued your weapons. Use one, will you? I think—I

think we might be in trouble."

Ford pauses; Taal's left sickle blade glows on her hip.

"I'm right, aren't I?"

Grim-faced, they nod.

"Sounds like two-legged Oscuridad," Taal says.

"Two-legged?" Ford repeats. "Like they're human?"

"They're like distortions of humans. We've encountered them in the Blue Mountains national park before."

"The others are light work compared with what's hunting us."

"I agree," Anan says.

A single eyebrow raised, I twist to look at him over my shoulder.

"Permission to speak, Empress?"

"Get up here."

Slightly shorter than Taal, Ford, and me, he jogs to catch up. "There are things I cannot tell you about the Oscuridad, but given what pursues us I must. Their race functions much like an army. You have the generals, like the prison guard we encountered in the Monster's Gulf."

"Vast," I explain to Taal. "And this is what we suspected when we accumulated the index—one you did not contribute to."

"I shouldn't be doing it now either." Anan breathes heavily. "But these monsters—I didn't think the Unlit would be foolish enough to attempt to leash them. They are like lieutenants. The creatures on four legs or more are frontline soldiers. They go in and use brute force, ferocity, to cripple armies. The lieutenants are capable of thought. A rare echelon can even communicate verbally. If that's who hunts us, then I agree, Empress, we are in trouble."

"What would your recommended course be?"

"To reach this hill's summit at once. We don't want them to circle around us and pen us in."

Anan's message is sent backward, through the Virago, Simbarabo, and shields. As exhausted as most of us are, there is nothing like the immediate threat of death to put a fire in the belly. My thighs and lungs burn with the exertion. Cooler than others, the night's chill offers no relief; it heightens the sense of dread during our silent sprint up the Strawberry Hills. Where Taal or I stumble, we are brutal in dragging one another up. Ford has never been silent for so long. It's unnerving. Joints grind, and bones ache, but we must push.

"Do you hear that?" Taal wheezes beside me, Anan, too slow on foot, clinging to her back. "Sheets."

"What?"

"She means *sails*," Rhonda corrects; what's left of Taal's unit have formed a barricade around us. "She can hear sails, and so do I."

Sails propel ships, which can mean several things, but I hope for only one.

The Cariot traitor's triumph.

JAZMYNE

On the *Silver Arrow*'s upper deck, Anya and I stare out at the fleet sailing around us, ready to go to war against Captain Shah, the Imposter, their jailer, together. Word spread quickly; the ships making their way home after Captain Shah announced herself victor of the race turned around when they learned about Synestra's possession of the map. If they're not in our nearing-thousand-strong number, they're on their way.

Roje, who has hovered since my arrival at the Iron Shore but has yet to attempt to speak with me, fusses with the sandbags along the starboard side, close enough to overhear Anya and me, if we were doing anything other than leaning against the bow. We said everything we needed to while the crews were busy preparing the ships for the voyage across the Great Sea.

She was taken from me; I returned for her. That's what you do for family. You show up.

"Want me to get rid of him?" Anya murmurs. "He could accidentally fall overboard."

"I thought he reassured you that I'd come?"

"Doesn't mean he's not a lying liar, mon."

We're about half an hour out from the Hendern Cliffs, the fight that waits. I'd rather my talk with Roje be now so I'm not distracted later.

I call his name, indicate that he join me; Anya slips away with a whisper of luck.

Sheepish, Roje joins me but makes no attempt to look me in the eye.

"I was under the impression that you wanted to have this conversation. If you don't—"

"I do," he says quickly. "I thought you'd want to speak first, to ask your questions, but since I'm talking, rambling, let me apologize now. Jazmyne." He looks up for the first time, and the depth of sorrow in his face feels as deep as the waters the ship speeds across. "I didn't want to embroil you in this—no. That's a lie. In the beginning, I didn't care about what happened to you."

I suspected as much, but it hurts to hear all the same.

"Vea was dying. Captain Shah, Lei, caught me in a weak moment. If we could find the falls and reclaim power from the magic wielders, for the first time in our history, pirates could be an equal player in the empire. Synestra was on board; she hated that your sister still had a hold on Vea, even in death. We told Lei when you asked me to back you. She suggested we use you to find the falls, and I agreed." Shame-faced, he shakes his head. "Then I saw you in action, and it was like Vea had returned. Not in all ways, but the ways my anger had allowed me to forget."

He's said as much before. But words have never meant less.

"Lei was using us to achieve everything she wanted. Yet you were in the thick of matters, making decisions, traveling, delegating, feeling. You showed me that I was continuing the problem, that Lei was adding to the animosity, extending it. I changed my mind. But after your trouble with the Zesian, I knew words would mean nothing—if I could speak them, and I wasn't bound by a Vow of Silence."

"You are not any longer?"

He shakes his head.

"Then look at me."

As though weighed down, Roje struggles to lift his eyes. When he does, I'm not sure how sincere the anguish there is. How can I be?

"Lei wanted me to get you out of the palace," he continues. "So she could proposition you. I held her off, made sure you were in a position of safety. I brought one of the Unlit onto the palace grounds to carve the Summoning Circle that welcomed the Oscuridad into the temple. They thought it was to kill you, but I did it because you needed the shields, and I could see no other way to convince you."

"In Port Royale," I state, my voice cold even to my own ears. "On the roof. You locked the door."

He nods. "I was going to try and tell you about Lei's plan; then I saw how afraid you were of me, and I couldn't. So I did the next best thing."

"The peat." How didn't I realize it before?

"The peat and the plea to come back for me, for us. We needed you."

"I needed you too." The ship's side is damp beneath my arms as I rest them against it. "After Kirdan, the late doyenne's death, I needed you, Roje. I wish you'd told me about all this sooner."

"So do I. But I didn't give up on you. You know I know how it feels to be tossed into the waves and forgotten. Please—" His voice lowers. "I know I'm in no position to ask, but please don't do the same to me, Jazmyne."

I turn into the wind to dry my tears before they can fall, and I grip the bow's railing. "I don't know if I can forgive you."

"You forgave him." Roje's voice is low.

Kirdan.

"He betrayed me, yes. For the greater good. One I was obstructing. One I couldn't see above my own wants." Something I recognized, sooner than he thought. "But you, Roje, you betrayed me because to you I was nothing. You used me, and I recognize that now you're sorry, but I stand by what I said. I don't know if I can forgive you. I don't know if you deserve my forgiveness any more than I deserved Kirdan's."

He expels a soft laugh. "Five hundred ships aren't enough?"

Lit by lanterns and starlight, the fleet gliding across Carne Sea is majestic. But they have yet to stand before the Oscuridad and not turn tail.

"We'll have to see" is my answer.

After a moment's hesitation, Roje rests alongside me on the ship's side. The *Silver Arrow* glides alongside Aiyca's southern green belt of bush. In less than a day we'll reach Carling Hill, and beyond having the numbers to offer assistance, I'm not sure how much the fleet can do. We have no magic; to teach the pirates the Banishment Glyph would be moot. Perhaps we can fight the Unlit. They're mortal and fallible to blades crafted by man, rather than magic. The heavens wink, as though in approval. They wink again, a golden flare against the dark sky. A shooting star?

"You saw that, right?" Beside me, Roje straightens.

"Anya?" I call, squinting where the light was generated, above the escarpment. No, in it. "Anya!"

"What is it? What did you do, Roje?"

"Not him." I level a finger upward, at the shadowed bush. "Up there. What do you see?"

It takes her a moment; she curses. "Obeah-witches."

"Unlit?"

"I can't recognize their uniforms."

"If they're in uniform, they're Obeah," I confirm. Not quite able to say that they're Virago. That Iraya has not one army, but two. One she sailed here, and a second she practically raised from the dead.

"Captain!" Roje calls.

The entire ship lines the starboard side; some crew climb the masts, spyglasses aimed up at the tens-of-feet-high summit. In a matter of seconds, I stop envying their tools. I don't need them when a witch in white and gold bursts from the tree line and sends a golden shower of magic up in an unmistakable call. To us.

"Iraya," I breathe.

"Who?" Synestra asks.

"Adair. The Lost Empress," Roje supplies. "I think she's asking for aid."

"They're all running out of those trees!" one of the spyglass users from above calls down. "I think they're being pursued."

Elodie backs away from where we watch. "Should we help them?"

"I thought that was why we came." Synestra turns to me when I don't proffer agreement. "Jazmyne?"

As much as I'd enjoy leaving Iraya up there for a while longer, so she knows how it is to be without hope, that only gives whatever is chasing her time to catch up.

"What do you have to help?"

"Uncover the ballista," Synestra orders. "See that the message is passed back."

The *Silver Arrow*'s black flag is lowered and exchanged for an amber banner of cloth with the number thirty scrawled on it in dark woad.

"Thirty ships will copy what we do. Anya, tell Iraya to send no more than five of her ilk to each ship, when the time comes," Synestra orders. "And stay out of the way."

My sistren relays a whispered message to Iraya, nodding to convey its delivery.

"Drop anchor," Roje bellows, striding across the deck.

A hatch in the center deck is opened, and a platform is raised into sight. Atop the wooden stage sits a contraption of metal and wood. One I've never seen in such a size before. The crossbow is large enough that I couldn't operate it. Elodie, tall and powerfully framed, climbs into the seat. Roje and several others turn the ballista's metal frame so it's facing the escarpment, where Iraya unleashes another shower of sparks. Rope is knotted around a colossal arrow, which three crew lift onto the loading arm of the weapon. Its handle, to Elodie's left, is drawn back with difficulty, extending the thick cords from which the arrow will spring to their capacity.

"Tell her to move from the edge," Synestra commands.

The arrow is released with a deafening snap. Faster than I've seen anything move, it tears through the sky with a piercing whistle and embeds into the rock, creating a connection between the rock cliff and the *Silver Arrow*. The next twenty-nine ships fire their arrows in quick succession. Witches hook their emerald cloaks over the rope and propel themselves down onto the ships. All bar the *Silver Arrow*'s. Our rope remains undisturbed.

Iraya launches another battery of golden sparks above. Like the crystallization of ice against the stone in my cavern, they spread into a shimmering wall, almost as great as the escarpment she stands atop.

"What is she doing?" I murmur.

"She's waiting for her crew to get to safety first," Elodie answers. "Protecting them from whatever is chasing them."

"It's what Vea would have done," Synestra says, in a tone very close to awe.

The wall holds as ropes begin to be severed from the arrows in the cliffside. One of the crew in the rigging with a spyglass calls down that they've changed their flags. Everyone is ready to go. Except us.

"Tell her to get a move on." This comes from Roje, where

he paces before the ballista. "Otherwise we'll have more than five visitors on board."

A crack splinters through Iraya's wall.

The crew, Anya, and I take a collective step back. I don't want to know what type of Oscuridad could do that to magic as strong as that possessed by Aiyca's first family's heir.

"The rope has gone taut. Raise anchor!" Synestra calls.

Landing lightly, the first witch nods her thanks at Synestra, standing at the wheel on the upper deck. Obeah, she's dressed in a manner I've not seen since I was a pickney.

"Was it on two legs?" Roje asks her.

She brushes away the tight curls that have escaped from her single braid. "Yeh mon. And they breached the Strawberry Hills. Empress Adair is holding them off."

"Alone?" Roje whistles.

Three more witches board; the *Silver Arrow* begins to edge forward, even at half-mast, as we still wait for Iraya. A second crack zigzags a tangential line across her shield; the rope jerks twice, with two bodies. Taal and Faehn. Neither of them speaks. Both witches look up, at the wall, at their empress.

"Get ready to cut that rope," Synestra tells Roje.

My heart beats in my throat, my stomach further south, as we wait for the penultimate witch flying down from the cliff, her arms aloft as her cape provides a barrier between her hands against rope burn. The thick cord jerks again, as Iraya leaps for it. And then again.

"She has company!" Roje palms his axe, like he wants to cut the rope *now*.

Iraya flies down the rope, with what has to be magical

help, since she is faster than her coven members were before her. Several yards from the deck, she swings her body forward, leaping. Airborne, she twists, and severs the rope with a sparking purple disk of magic. As its length falls, she grabs the shorter end attached to the ballista, and, using the momentum and weight of her fall, swings herself onto the deck. She lands on her feet.

"Thanks for the ride."

She's met with a stunned silence.

Iraya doesn't speak until the ships are far from the summit of the Strawberry Hills. Enough that the tall, skeletal shadows atop it, just visible behind her cracked shield, have faded from sight. Then, and only then, does she permit Taal to help her below deck. In the captain's quarters, myself, Anya, Roje, Synestra, and Elodie request an update as to what is going on.

"We were last at the palace," she explains, rolling her shoulders beneath her emerald cape. "The shields held the line, and the Xanthippe remained to ensure our fortifications don't fall. But none of that will matter if we don't close the Eldritch Gap welcoming the Oscuridad from beyond the veil."

"We know our role," I say. "And we're here to offer aid."

As visibly exhausted as she is, Iraya's eyes are not without their intensity.

"The crew know all about the Unlit's pets. Until recently, they were working with the Imposter Empress." Better to tell her than have her find out.

Taal, the three other Virago—Rhonda in addition to Faehn I recognize—straighten.

"But we're not any longer," Elodie clarifies. "As you witnessed, we did just save you from certain death."

"Yes." Iraya flickers those eyes over to her. "Nice shot." Her tone is light, but the delivery feels more like a threat than a compliment.

"We're sailing for the Hendern Cliffs," I tell her, drawing back her attention. "And we're half a day out. So whatever you need to do before we arrive has a tight time limit."

"My coven and I require only food and rest."

"You stay here." Synestra heads for the door; Elodie follows. "We'll send food down."

"We'll come up," Taal says with a quick look at Iraya. "I'd love to take a look at your ballista, and whatever additional weapons you have on board. The Oscuridad can't be killed without a certain glyph. Which you no doubt know about. We can help your fleet by incising as many glyphs as we can on your weapons, and imbuing them with magic. And you have magic in your trappers, right?" She continues talking as the door closes, leaving me with Iraya, Anya. Roje, after looking my way, leaves too.

"I stripped you of your titles," Iraya begins, unperturbed by Anya. "Am I to assume you've resumed your position as Queen of Carne Sea, yet another illegitimate accolade?"

"So long as you're comfortable with—what was it you said? Making an ass of you and me."

Iraya laughs.

"Irrespective of what power you think you have over me," I tell her, refusing to feel embarrassed. "I'm here for Aiyca."

"*Kirdan* has far fewer letters than what came out of your

mouth." She sits up, suddenly not looking tired at all. "You're here for him."

"You didn't ask a question, which means you know that yes, I'm here to help him *too*."

"Do you love him?"

That gives me pause.

"Come, Jazmyne. Let us, for once, be honest with one another. Would you like your sistren to leave to make it easier for you?"

"Do *you* love him?" I put to her, before Anya can chime in. She doesn't hesitate. "I'd like the time to find out."

Honest. Fine.

"I think I must care for him still," I begin. "Otherwise I wouldn't be working so hard to return to who I was when he was in my life."

She nods. "When we arrive at the Hendern Cliffs, I can't go to him. Not right away. I have to establish our stronghold. The Imposter needs to be found. My armies need a Genna at the fore. Will you?"

"Will I?"

"Go to him," she states, without obscurity. "Ensure that he knows a life with love."

If anything happens to her. Exhaling, I sit in Elodie's vacated chair across from Iraya. She rummages in a pack left behind by her coven members and produces a familiar vial.

"This will provide seven doses of Oscuridad poison antidote. He's going after Aiyca's source, and we almost lost him in Zesia, when we blocked theirs."

We almost lost him.

"Will you?" She slides the vial across to me; the tiny glass bottle an antidote to more than the Oscuridad's poison, it feels a cure to that which has festered between Iraya and me even before we were born. Our positions in life didn't give us a chance, but Kirdan might as he unites us in something similar in passion to hate, but more.

"I will."

We sail through to first light, when the *Silver Arrow* noses around Hendern Bay, and a slew of arrows pierce our foresail.

Iraya throws a shield with alacrity and runs to the bow. Her coven and I join her.

"I don't think our forces are winning," Taal needlessly points out.

They're not.

Synestra, Roje, and Elodie join us. Atop the Hendern Cliffs, a line of archers several rows deep angle weapons onto the sliver of shore curling along the base of the rock face. Magi—Simbarabo and Virago—attempt to deboard from their line of vessels grounded in the shoal. For every two that make it down the gangway onto the shore, two more are struck down by arrows like bolts of sunlight. And where the arrows fail, leaping Oscuridad breach the water to snatch at runners.

"You undersold their skill, Cariot." Iraya's tone is accusatory.

"They couldn't jump that high at Alligator Pond."

"Those Unlit are using conduit gold in their arrowheads," Rhonda cuts in.

"Where is the Zesian general?" Iraya asks. "Do you see

him on board the Zesian vessels?"

Rhonda shakes her head.

"Then he's inside." Iraya says it like a certainty.

I repeat her words as a prayer. I don't want Kirdan dying with the belief that I'm a selfish person.

"How are we going to breach the cliff?" Taal asks.

Iraya stiffens beside her.

"The rope trick was cool, but I don't feel like pulling myself up. My arms won't be strong enough after to fight and win. Sifting feels stupid with arrows flying. And it's for that reason we can't sail any closer. For one, the Zesian ships are in the way, and another, we'll be shot at too."

"Fire me," Iraya says.

Synestra takes one look at her and strides away, across the ship.

"I'm serious, Jazmyne." The Obeah-witch is emphatic. "Fire me into the cliffside."

"That's stakki," Roje says. "The impact could kill you."

I agree. "Why do you want that?"

"Because I remember," she says, as if it's an explanation. "You weren't with us in the Monster's Gulf, but you need to trust me."

"You remember?" Taal asks.

"I didn't make a promise without getting something in return."

"Then forget them," Taal says. "I'll shoot you into the cliff."

"Jazmyne?" Roje turns to me.

"I don't know why you're asking her." Taal steps past Roje to inspect the ballista. "She has no authority in Aiyca any longer now its true empress has returned."

"She has authority on this ship," he insists.

"Wait." I stop Roje and turn to Iraya. "Is this for Aiyca?"

She blinks at me. "It's for everything."

For Kirdan.

"Do as she says."

"Like we needed your permission," Taal mutters.

The entire crew watches as Iraya straddles the arrow in the ballista, Elodie draws the lever back, and the arrow takes to the sky with a force second only to Iraya's will.

IRAYA

At the sight of the Hendern Cliffs, rearing up from the shoal-colored waters of Carne Sea, the memory of my plunge into the Monster's Gulf stretches before me like a tunnel. I'm catapulted through what happened, what I could not remember: the water was glass against my skin, cold and sharp as I willed a shield to bubble around my head. Only then could I breathe.

So I could face the tentacled Oscuridad attacking my fleet.

Framed by seaweed shoots floating like strands of hair, and vast enough to make the endless waters around us feel intimate, the beast looked the god the Grimoire warned me it would be. As amorphous as the surrounding waters, its silvered form was indeterminate, save the many tentacles; most undulated to keep it afloat, the others torpedoed upward, to tear holes through the ships' hulls. I swam for it, willing my legs to move with the swiftness of the current. I remember its voice, the rumbling cadence of it, though I could see no mouth, no eyes. It asked me if I'd arrived to slay the creatures of the gulf. *Many have come to kill what has never died* was its warning. It who was as bound to the waters as the prisoners it served.

I told it I didn't want to kill them. As an Adair witch, as Empress of Xaymaca, and all its terriotories, including the gulf, I wanted to free one.

And as the arrow launched from Jazmyne's ship sinks into the white stone of the Hendern Cliffs, and I'm rocked hard enough to rattle my teeth, my bones, I slap my palm against the stone and utter the words the Oscuridad rumbled for this very moment, before it ceased its attacks and wished me luck in freeing one of its wards—with a warning to be careful, I remember now. It might have been a guard. I hope it was. But that's a problem for another hour.

With a shudder, the stone awakens beneath my hand with a stiff creak, another, until the entire cliff is falling, pulling away from its rocky purchase. Teeth gritted, I wrap my arms around the arrow; at my back, screams and cursing ring across the sea; the discordant clash of battle ceases; and an eye opens to the right of where I cling; a cold yellow, its lid is mottled, creased, like its stone surroundings.

It blinks in question.

The answer comes to mind with the same ease as everything else. "Rise, and fight. With me, empress of Xaymaca and its territories. Win me this battle, and then you are free."

That ancient eye narrows in understanding.

"That is my promise to you," I breathe; reaching for the

pointed side of the arrowhead, I slice my palm across it and hold it aloft so the beast can see my blood oath fall. "Defeat the Oscuridad in the water, and then leave. Spare my ships and the people aboard them. Spare my people on the shore. Do this, and you are free. Do this, and don't come back, or everything I agreed to with your kin in the Monster's Gulf will be nullified."

With a shuddering backward trajectory, the entire cliffside comes alive.

Swinging up onto the Oscuridad's frame—maybe its head; I can't see it clearly from my position—I hoist myself up its rocky exterior, hand over hand, as it pushes farther and farther away from the cliff. Heaving myself up onto the flat top, I encase my body in a golden shield of will and look for the Simbarabo. Protected behind shields of their own, they scale the cliff from the beach, but they're too far away.

I have to go on alone.

Breaking into a run toward the cliffside, growing in distance as the Oscuridad beneath me softens after centuries of calcification, I take a quick assessment of what awaits. The stadium I stood before months ago, when I revealed myself to the doyenne, is filled with archers, who shoot down at the shore below and across the clifftop to where the Simbarabo climb to meet me. Many are hit. They fall. I free my hammer midstride. The nexus of the hill, its clearing before it declines into the valley of family trees, has few Unlit—Squallers. My Squallers. My magic users they've managed to persuade to defect. Their hands are raised to the sky, palm side up; clouds are summoned to blot the sun of the morning. The air smells like soil and rain, like darkness and an incoming squall. This Imposter thinks just as I do, which means she is here, watching me in this very moment. If I let the sky darken, her beasts will come.

One of the Unlit shouts. Our eyes meet. I'm close enough to see her shock, her fear.

The lowest row of archers in the stadium turn my way. Golden arrows are notched; bowstrings are drawn back. Magic imbued or otherwise, it looks like they're using conduit gold. My shield won't stand against them all.

"Aim!" is bellowed by the Unlit.

Beneath me, the Hendern Cliffs' monster jerks downward; the earth shakes with two weighted tremors. I think it's standing. Its body and the cliffside have officially separated, leaving a chasm between me and Carling Hill.

I'll have to jump.

"Fire!"

Magic helps me to launch myself up and over the gaping space between me and certain death. My naevus guarantees my survival. It billows out, a storm of its own, a nebulous explosion of might to burn those arrows up before they can land. To knock the archers off their feet. To warn the Unlit that insurgence is futile. To show the Imposter who the hell *I* am. Who she is not and will never be.

Witch. Warrior. Weapon.

Iraya Cordelia Boatema Adair.

Lost Empress Now Returned.

I land in a crouch—one knee against the earth, along with a hand to brace my landing; the hammer I clutch across my chest, where the breastplate shines with a lambent force of power. With the groan of something mighty dying, the stadium collapses. Old wood bows, and the Unlit cry as they are swallowed in its rubble.

At my back, something mighty crashes into the sea. Rising, I turn to the edge I cleared; Jazmyne's fleet works with the Virago and the Hendern Cliffs' Oscuridad to fight the Unlit's aquatic force. The ancient being, a god, is smaller than whatever I encountered in the gulf, but hard where that prison guard was soft. Fists of stone crash down and rise with monsters in hand; they're squeezed until green blood courses down the beasts' hands. Though rocked by the momentum of the Oscuridad's hierarchical struggle, Jazmyne's fleet holds its own; farther out from the cliffside, cannons and ballista arrows are fired into the water. I can't see the fissure through which the Simbarabo and Shamar—Kirdan—disappeared. But, beneath me, somewhere, I hope they're all right.

I hope freeing the Oscuridad from the cliff won't impede their mission.

It's time I finish my own.

The Unlit have been helping one another onto their feet; those harmed in the cirque collapse have dropped their weapons to aid in rescue efforts; overhead, the sky is poised between blue and gray, light and dark, with the Squallers standing uncertain.

"Do not pick up your weapons," I call, "and you will be spared. I know you've been told you're serving the Lost Empress, but I haven't asked anyone to serve me, only to fight alongside me." I holster my hammer but keep my shield raised.

"My name is Iraya Cordelia Boatema Adair, and I am sorry I wasn't here for you, and you felt you had no choice but to turn to an imposter." I take several steps forward, addressing the Squallers, the magi with visible scarification on their faces, bodies, the Obeah rather than the Unlit. "I don't blame you for wanting to fight for Aiyca. But this isn't the way. Obeah do not kill Obeah."

"What do you call your performance just now?"

The voice comes from a pit of the insurgents, standing off to the left of the hill; I can't determine who spoke, but their familiarity is staggering. I've heard their voice before.

"An unnecessary end. If I died, the Imposter's path to my family's legacy would be clear." Scanning the crowd, I add, "I cannot let that happen. But I don't want to hurt my order."

"And the Unlit? What about us?"

"I'd be open to listening to what you have to say, but what else does your presence in this holy glade, across not only Aiyca but Zesia too, signify if not an attempt to challenge me for my parents' legacy? Am I wrong?"

"In that you are right," that familiar voice says. "We are here to right a wrong your parents caused. And I am also here to correct a mistake I made."

The knot of Unlit opens, and out glides a witch who makes my heart stop.

"If I knew the witch I was training in Carne was the daughter of Mama's cousin, who stole the position of first family," Kaleisha says, "and then banished mine when they notified others in our order about it, I would have killed you the first day we met."

"You?"

"You're several months late on the uptake, Ira." The two syllables of my moniker are spat out, cut from her tongue with an acuteness that makes me flinch. "I said the same in this very location when you named yourself before Judair. You. Surely not." She wears only gray, like a washed-out version of my pants, tunic, and cape, yet she holds herself like a leader. "Not my sistren who I guided through Carne. Who I spent countless years with discussing my plans to join the insurgents, to fight for Aiyca. Not that witch who didn't bother telling any of us who she truly was."

"You're my cousin?"

"Not by choice."

"Is that what you've told yourself to justify killing me?"

A vein beats in her forehead. She doesn't smile or laugh. It's like she is the stranger I believed the Imposter to be. "It isn't personal, Ira." She pauses. "Actually, I suppose it is. You knew who you were, what you would mean to Carne's prisoners, but you didn't say a word about it. You don't deserve the Golden Seat. You're not deserving of a quick death." She unsheathes two short swords from either hip. "Aiyca deserves more than a 'fraid empress. A witch who arrives at the end of the fight, rather than its beginning."

"Don't do this," I beg her. "I don't want to hurt you."

"I do this for Aiyca, the island you forsook."

"I never forsook my home."

"You are delusional. There is no greater enemy to progress than apathy. I won't let you ruin Aiyca any more than you have." Her eyes don't leave mine as she turns to address her companions. "No beast or person is to interfere. This kill is mine, for all of us."

The Unlit roar their approval.

There is no one up here to shout for me—but then, I've always preferred the whistle of my blades swinging toward the neck of my opponent. Even if this time it is Kaleisha.

If it must be her.

The witch who kept me alive in Carne. Who nurtured me, educated me. Gods . . . why? Why does it have to be Kaleisha?

"Your family worked with Judair to kill mine?"

"They did."

With a nod, I remove my hammer from its holster. "I vowed to kill those responsible, but I will give you the same opportunity I gave the Unlit and Obeah you have misled. Stand down and I will spare your life."

"I don't want your mercy, *Iraya*." My full name is said with mocking; Kaleisha spins her weapons with a dexterity that reminds me she is the better fighter of us two. "I want you dead."

She runs at me; my shield pulses out to block her, putting me in an unfavorable defensive position.

"You're going to fight me with magic; that hardly seems fair." Circling me, Kaleisha, Captain Shah, looks as sleek and predatory as a shadowcat.

"Stand down, then." *Please.*

"I meant for you." Quick as a finger snap, she rotates her fist to the side and fires a strobe of magic at my shield; a crack shoots a line through the gold.

I stagger back.

"I've been collecting magic for a long while, Iraya." She rotates the left blade once more. "It will do until I have mine."

"You have no family tree," I say, as realization arrives too slowly.

"They are *our* ancestors." Kaleisha darts in; her hands blur before me; I block the first lunge, my hammer rising up to trap her moon blades. A second swipe stings against the top of my thigh; blood splashes against my white pants. "You'll tell them I said *Blessings*." Her booted foot swings up and sinks into my chest-plate; the momentum forces me back, legs overhead. "Finish the darkening, and welcome the first wave," Kaleisha orders the Unlit. "This won't take long."

Winded, I clutch at my stomach.

A line of green flames erupts upward through the ground behind the witch I can't believe has been leading this crusade. An angry maw, it gapes from the cirque to the edge of the family trees on my left in a straight line. As vast as it is, it can't be a single Summoning Circle in play. This fire is from the source in the mountain. The source Kirdan, Zander, and Shamar were unable to stopper. Oh gods. Kaleisha prowls toward me; at her back, winged Oscuridad burst from the flames and into the sky. Tens of shriveled fleshy beasts with veiny, membranous wings splayed appear beneath a rapidly darkening sky as the Squallers undo the light. Undo me.

Kaleisha was right. I did stand by. I put my wants before those of my people, and not just after Carne, before too. I didn't seek a way to make the title fit me. I discarded it.

Tens of winged Oscuridad turn into hundreds.

Nana Clarke is dead because of my choice. The Virago I've

only just reunited with will go the same way. There will be no time for Kirdan. For anybody.

If I keep sitting here.

"Oh, you've decided to stand." Kaleisha stands back to watch me use my hammer to propel myself onto my feet. "Much better than being slain in the dirt."

Breath stabs through my lungs. Her kick might have broken a few ribs.

"It doesn't have to be this way, Kaleisha," I wheeze. "I have more magic than you. You won't survive my naevus, and I don't want to kill you."

"Yes, you do. You want justice for your parents' deaths, for every death my Oscuridad will cause here today."

The swarm of hundreds is growing enough to blot out the sky.

"In that we are similar, cousin. I want this ground to run red with those who hurt my family too." Shucking her cape, Kaleisha breaks into a slow run toward me, moon weapons brandished to her left and right.

Ribs grinding in protest, I shrug off my cape and swing my hammer to meet her.

At our weapons' collision, magic echoes outward; shielding against it, I remain on my feet. Just a fist swings through the swirling detritus; its knuckles are encased in gold; my shield shatters. Instinctively, after my training in Zesia, my hands go up to block Kaleisha's hit. She follows it with another, from the left. My forearm sings beneath the blow. Rallying, I shunt my hammer upward. It's blocked with a golden shield. Kaleisha smiles at me through our crossed arms.

I knew I'd be outmatched in combat, but magic I wasn't anticipating.

Arching backward through the air like a gymnast, Kaleisha whips her moon blade at my feet mid-leap. I dodge, only to take a hit to my shoulder. I tumble, too close to the cliffside. Stones cut into my hands as I fight for purchase.

"This was fun, but I'm growing bored, Ira."

One blast from my naevus and I could finish this. Finish her. The Oscuridad rocket down to attack Simbarabo, and the Virago who have now joined me up here. But I can't be sure the soldiers and Warriors would survive. Yet, the beasts keep coming.

I plant my hammer's handle into the dirt and push myself onto my feet. "We both know I can end this at any time," I feign.

"Then do it." Running toward me once again, she shouts, "Welcome the second wave!"

With a resonate tremble, the flames reach higher; from their depths canter the Oscuridad on four and six legs. The beasts with teeth where there should be none. The distortions of mutts. Fresh and plenty, they crash into the Simbarabo defending the threat from the sky—the Virago only just cresting the destroyed cliffside.

Dropping my hammer, I reach for the batons. One in each hand, I match Kaleisha parry for parry. Her smile reaches full capacity, exposing the gap between her front teeth I was always so fond of. Distracted, she doesn't notice me drop a baton to free my right fist, which I swing right into her mouth. She doesn't fall, but she stumbles. I launch myself at her. Magic and weapons, fury and disappointment. Frustration could boil me from the inside out. I could scream at how this has manifested.

Between blows, Kaleisha gives me a strange look. Perhaps I did scream.

No.

Flipping back, she looks to the sky; I do too. The Oscuridad circle on their bat-like wings. But it isn't from them that the noise heralds—it's from the swarm undulating up and down across the sky, one growing ever larger as it draws close. The cry rings again, a throaty ululation that makes the hairs on the back of my neck stand erect.

I know those beasts on wings of obsidian feathers. Their singular front legs hang down beneath their necks, as powerful as the two drawn in to slim flanks—upon which riders with white ribbon braided into their hair rise on the backs of their aerial steeds, and, drawing bowstrings loaded with golden arrows, spears tipped with golden blades, launch themselves at the Oscuridad with another throaty ululation.

The Skylands.

Kihra and Melione. My gods. They brought the Skylanders' army.

The steeds, long muzzles atop thick necks, kick and bite at the Oscuridad. Where their riders fall, they do not crash down onto the ground; as if they have trained as Squallers in addition to Warriors, they remain airborne and continue attacking the Oscuridad. It's a hideous entanglement of death and wrongness, and I've never seen anything more beautiful. With the respite they provide, the Simbarabo issue a returning war cry, and attack the six-legged Oscuridad anew.

"Concede," I call to Kaleisha.

Her eyes lower from the sky to survey the battle taking place around us: her monsters aren't coming with the same alacrity from the flames, and I have aerial and aquatic reinforcements— the allies I coaxed and bullied to get here for this moment. Awareness enters her face. She cannot win here.

To my surprise, she turns tail and runs.

Unperturbed by the Witchfire, she runs straight for it. With limbs like stone, I start after her. A rogue spark from the aerial battle blasts a hole at my feet. Propelled upward and back, I shield against the landing. By the time I'm righted, crouched, batons aloft, Kaleisha is gone, and the flames continue to burn. There'll be no stopping this war without closing the gap. Battles are fought on all fronts, the land, sea, and sky—but it's what is happening beneath me, in the stone caverns of this mountain, that will dictate victory.

Sweeping up my hammer, I survey the line of flame, the destroyed cliff edge where the beast pulled loose. The stairs I climbed months ago are gone. How bad will the jump be?

"Iraya!"

The clear call of my name makes me look back up; one of the riders banks over the ruined stadium, its archers defeated by Simbarabo.

"Iraya!"

Kihra is unrecognizable. Adorned in armor of gold, white, and a rich brown, she waves.

"Kirdan needs me below!"

She nods ahead; already at the edge of the cliff, I time the beat of her beast's wings, the way she urges it on, not with reins, murmured encouragements perhaps, guzzu. The creature lowers and banks toward me, swooping beneath the cliff.

Leaping over the edge, I reach for Kihra's outstretched hand. Catch it. She hoists me onto the saddle behind her.

"You came!"

As I wrap my arms around her waist, she huffs a humorless laugh. "Like you gave me a choice. Where is the general?"

"Down."

She digs her heels into her Oscuridad's side and urges the beast down to the beach, where the battle continues.

"They could do with help too."

"You can't see, but I just rolled my eyes." She turns to shout. "Look behind you."

It's more than the lightening heavens, clearing of winged Oscuridad, it's the supernal agents of destruction—the Skylands' army—standing upright on their winged steeds, snaking through the sky at our backs. They branch off, arching over the Carne Sea, to dive down into the fray below.

75

JAZMYNE

Soldiers are bled from the sea and the sky.

Clasping Anya with one hand and the ship's ties with another, I utter a slew of prayers to whichever gods can guarantee us safe passage, calm stomachs, and the strength to withstand the thrashing of the Hendern Cliffs' Oscuridad.

For a time it seemed as though we would win.

The slinky creatures below the surface sated the appetite of Iraya's beast. And those that evaded its ancient grip fell prey to Virago or pirate. Then, like ooze from a wound, the winged Oscuridad darkened the sky. They came for Iraya's beast, scratching at its skin. Not the stone I thought, it bled green until the waters turned. It's been below the surface for a long while. Too long. The pirates and Virago continue to use the ballista, and in some cases their hands and teeth, to banish the beasts back to their side of the veil. But they keep coming.

"Ho!" Anan shouts from beside me, having sifted from

ship to ship to find Iraya, only to find me instead.. "She did it. *Look*."

At first I don't know what he's talking about. The sky is still dark with the weight of membranous wings—and then I see it. Them. The three-legged steeds kicking and headbutting their way through the fray. Atop their backs are riders in bronze and gold. Ululating like this assault is something enjoyable, they dive-bomb down and clash with the winged nightmares attacking my fleet.

The Skylanders' colors are just as distinctive as the Simbarabo's uniforms of umber and gold, where they battle on the clifftop, and the Virago in green, white, and gold spearing magic and weapons down at the Oscuridad in Carne Sea. For a moment, I'm foolish enough to think they're here for me— until a familiar witch in white and gold swan dives from the back of one of the Skylander steeds, hits the shore across the waters with a roll, and runs for the fissure in the cliff face.

The Skylands came for Iraya.

The Simbarabo came for Iraya.

The Virago came for Iraya.

She raised a monster from the Hendern Cliffs.

"She is something else," Anya breathes beside me.

"Not you too."

Awed by the Skylanders striking from the sky like bolts of golden lightning, she doesn't even hear me. No one has, since Iraya shot through the air on the arrow, survived, and then reanimated a calcified monster large enough to swallow an entire ship.

And now she's running toward Kirdan, even though the

Oscuridad are still coming. There is a time and a place, which she knows, which means that—Something is wrong.

Rising from his crouch, Anan waves his arms, whistles.

"What are you doing?" I ask.

"Getting a ride out of this death trap."

"Take me with you."

That catches Anya's attention. "Why?"

"I need to get ashore."

"But why?" she presses as Anan shouts for a rider by name.

"Because I've been cowering here behind these crates when I should be in the thick of this war."

Anya gapes at me. "You're stakki. There is no safer place for us. Unless this ship capsizes."

"Get ready, Regent," Anan warns.

Two riders break away from their formation to swoop down and land on the deck. From afar, their steeds seemed the size of horses, of Joshial, who I hope is safe at Cwenburg. Close up, the ship's deck couldn't hold more than three of the winged creatures. In contrast to their elegantly lithe bodies, the bones protruding through skin the color of charcoal, their wing feathers are a silky obsidian.

Anan greets the riders by name as I approach the not-horse closest to me. Eyes a foggy green blink down; lashless, they look as though they shouldn't be able to close. Its muzzle is long, and leathery to the touch, but beneath my hand, the creature turns into the affection.

"Beautiful," I murmur.

"Definitely stakki" is Anya's hushed reply.

"Are you coming up?" The rider's silver hair is bound back

from her face in four thick braids laced through with white yarn. She's Alumbrar. My eyes widen. "Today?"

I take her hand.

Anya draws closer. "Can it carry three?"

"He's strong enough to carry five. Come up."

Roje provides Anya with a boost. She slips onto the beast's bare back, behind me. Anan rides with the other aviatrix.

"I'll be seeing you then," Roje says, apologies still brimming in his gaze.

"If you live, we can talk about forgiveness."

He nods, and pats the aviatrix's steed.

"Hold on," she warns over her shoulder.

We take to the sky with a single sweep of the steed's mighty wings.

My stomach rushes to my throat at the speed, the trajectory; for a moment there is weightlessness, and then we plummet. Anya's arms become a vise around my middle as with a powerful sweep of its wings, the Oscuridad propels us onward with stomach lurching force for a second time.

"I can't land on the shore," the Skylander shouts. "So you're going to have to jump."

Anya's arms tighten again, way past the point of discomfort around my waist; I think I echo the maneuver, because the rider laughs.

"Where I am from, Alumbrar are braver than this." Her steed bears no reins, yet turns without any prompt; sunlight glistens in its feathers, bouncing off the richness of the black as we undulate to avoid rogue Oscuridad, weapons that fail to meet their target. We keep turning, leaning. Anya's grip is preventing me from drawing a full breath.

"Going down!" the witch shouts; her steed turns a hundred eighty degrees.

Anya slips off first. I go with her.

The shock of the water isn't anything I could have prepared for. Coughing and spluttering, I surface, my eyes squinting against the salt in the shallows. Grateful for the Virago's pants I was given, I wade to the shore with less difficulty than my skirts would have provided and wait for Anya, who, after pausing to heave violently into the sea, joins me in running for the fissure.

Rogue sparks and strobes from conduits volley back and forth across the shore; Simbarabo, recognizing us somehow—likely due to the fact that we're the only fighters not trying to kill them—wield their weapons with expertise, clearing a path for us to sprint down.

One blink inside the fissure, and sunlight is replaced with shadows. Anya steps ahead in the passageway that will only permit one at a time; her conduit coin has never seemed smaller, weaker than it does now. She does not talk. Neither do I. Her question is asked with a head tilt. My answer is a nod.

We go on.

After the cavern, the Blue Mountains, my steps are more certain than hers. But—as we round a corner, air shoots past my ears as I duck and fall back into Anya with a shout.

Iraya edges around the corner. "My gods, Cariot. Why didn't you announce yourself?"

"Us?" Anya helps me stand. "Why didn't *you*?"

"I've fought about a dozen Oscuridad since entering. I'm not announcing anything. Why are you here?"

"You have to ask."

She surveys me, and then takes us both in. "You're unarmed. Brilliant." Rolling her eyes, she separates her golden staff with a muffled click and hands us a half each. "Glyph and strike. Jazmyne, you know how to use imbued weapons?" I nod, almost reaching for the hair clips I lost somewhere along the way during this journey.

"Keep your conduit dark, Stealth. Both of you follow me."

Sticking close behind her as we navigate the mountain without any light, I barely use the weapon. Quick, even faster than she was at Cwenburg, Iraya cuts down the six-legged Oscuridad with a clinical focus. There is no enjoyment in her face, as there was when the Rolling Calf attacked us, only a sense of impatience. She wants to reach Kirdan.

The mountain hallway opens up to a cavern with three dark mouths; a low rumbling echoes down all three.

"Look alive, witches" is all Iraya says for the half hour she cuts down Oscuridad. Anya manages to send several back too.

I'm on my second when a third hits me from the side. The ground is damp against my back as it snaps wide jaws above. Golden bar held aloft, I scream for help as my arms are lowered by its weight.

"Hold on!" Anya calls.

Aggression turns to anguish on the creature's face; it looks back too slowly at my sistren, who sends it to the other side of the veil with a strike against its flank.

"That was too close," she says, helping me to my feet.

Iraya doesn't say anything at all. Pausing by each tunnel opening, she tilts her head as though listening, chooses the one farthest on the left, and keeps going. Her fast walk turns into a run, down a declivity, and then back up slick stone steps. Crouched beneath a low ceiling, she pulls herself up onto a ledge with little trouble. She doesn't wait for Anya and me to help one another climb. But she does wait, we see, when we reach the top. A finger to her lips, she turns to another thin opening in the stone. This one would be just about wide enough for Kirdan's shoulders. Metal strikes stone beyond it; someone curses. And then I hear it.

"Leave!"

Kirdan's command—whether to the beasts or his men I don't know.

Iraya's face draws tight with a stubborness I know well. I can tell what a struggle it is for her to step as slowly as she does through the crack in the stone walls. She pads along in her sandals, silent as the surprise of vengeance. Light flickers across the floor. Firelight.

I smell it before I see it.

It's enough to make me gag. Iraya whips around, furious.

I can't help it. Rancid, the odor is like hot death. Like the stink of rot when it stops being too sweet and becomes putrid.

Witchfire fills the cavern beyond the end of the walkway. It licks the walls, stretches up to a ceiling whose end is indiscernible. My gods. And it burns through something that cannot be a gap, given the sheer scope of it, the pustulous ooze of it.

"That isn't a gap," Anya murmurs, echoing my thoughts. "It's a *doorway*."

There's a temporary pause beyond where we hide.

"Run!" Kirdan bellows.

Whether or not the warning is for us, Iraya springs into action. Not away from the fire, toward it. Hammer in hand, she charges to meet the creatures to the left of the hewn cathedral, hesitating only for a split second before she swings her hammer at one's legs. The two-legged Oscuridad turns itself to smoke and passes through her weapon with a laugh.

It's the creature I fought in the national park. The ones on the clifftop when I rescued Iraya, only *more*. This one's mouth is more human, albeit exaggerated upward in the corners, like someone took a knife to it. Intelligent green eyes narrow with a sadistic pleasure. Long-limbed, if it gets itself around a person, I imagine they'd never know freedom again. I take a step back. Several.

"Treat the sick!" Iraya orders. Darting back, she frees a dagger from her bandolier and begins sketching; without warning, it flies from her hand. The two-legged Oscuridad, like a giant spider, lumbers toward her with its spindly limbs. "Jazmyne!" Iraya reaches for a second blade. "Get the fallen the antidote!"

A second two-legged Oscuridad raises a hand aloft to Kirdan; though they are yards apart, he shoots backward, narrowly avoiding the flames that have engulfed every wall in here. Part of the floor too—close to where several soldiers lie, fallen.

"Shit. *Shit.*"

The curse is all the more terrifying given I've never heard Anya use it before. But it is nothing compared to the head spinning on the neck of a third Oscuridad. My stomach gives a frightened jolt, and the urge to run is so strong, I am almost sick with it, as we are spotted.

"We need a hand!" Anya shouts.

"Kind of busy!" Iraya returns. Something cracks behind us. I hope that was her hammer against one of the Oscuridad.

I need to know they can be defeated.

Like it's on a rotating platform, the Oscuridad's shrouded body before us turns to match the angle of its head; its green eyes pin me and Anya in place, and something stirs at its bare feet. Another soldier. His hand curls around the creature's ankle, pulls, and sends it flying backward.

Move. Move.

My legs are as unsteady as a newborn's beneath me, but I manage to stumble to Kirdan.

"Jazmyne?" Disoriented, he looks up at me.

"Have you been poisoned?"

"Just dazed. You came?"

"I came."

Iraya skids into view before us; her lip has been bloodied, and she holds her left wrist like it's badly injured. All the same, she uses both hands to raise a dome of gold around us—and the fallen across the cavern; in their number is a beast, some kind of large cat.

"I can't kill these things," she breathes, frustrated.

"Not alone." With a wince, Kirdan pushes himself up onto his knees; Iraya helps him stand.

"Poison?" Her hands cradle his face.

His hands curl around hers; he shakes his head. I feel like I should turn away, and like I can't stop watching.

"You didn't die," he murmurs.

Iraya's laugh sounds sob-like. "Not yet. And I'd rather it happened in the sun than down here."

"Perfect," Kirdan rasps. "I was thinking we could do with some light." He lowers their hands.

"There's thinking and then there's doing," Anya points out as the two-legged Oscuridad lumber ever closer. Though there are but three, compared to us all, the bodies of the injured don't fill me with any hope. "I'm thinking we start doing. Now!"

Iraya and Kirdan ignore us.

"We took one look at the gap," he continues, "and knew the rete wouldn't work. This one can't be blocked. Not with the gold we have. It has to be destroyed, broken, before any more of those sentient Oscuridad cross over."

"We could force them back and then close it," she muses. "We didn't think we'd get the heir. Kirdan, the Skylands *are* here, they showed, but there's still no clear frontrunner, no clear voice for their island. But—" Iraya, to my eternal surprise, looks to me. "Maybe there is *a* voice. You believed yourself to be Aiyca's heir, to be from a first Alumbrar family. There is no magic more powerful than self-belief." She says it like she knows personally. "You said you deserved to rule. Do you still believe that?"

Kirdan looks down at me, not with contempt, but . . . hope. "I want to."

"You need to." Iraya is emphatic. "Or this won't work."

"What?" Anya says, her baton leveled before her as the Oscuridad close in. "I'll do it!"

"No. It must be Jazmyne."

"I don't have magic."

"That doesn't matter. Are you a leader? Are you Aiyca's rightful leader?"

I can't believe Iraya is asking me this when she brought three armies, and I just the one. Of course she also looks the part, even cut and bruised, exhausted. In my borrowed clothing, my hair in a state I don't want to consider, I've never felt less worthy of walking into Cwenburg and claiming the Golden Seat.

"I'm not sure."

Iraya's face falls.

"But . . . I want to fight for it. For Aiyca. For this side of the veil."

She frees a hand from Kirdan and holds it out to me. "Then let's do this."

"Do what?"

"Send those otherworldly bastards back where they belong, and stop any more from crossing over through this *thing*."

Kirdan takes my left hand, closing our circle. I'm hit with a visceral memory of our Shook Bargain. The single hands we piled on top of one another, while our seconds crossed fingers behind our backs. How far we have traversed from that night, how far yet we have to go.

"Do we say anything?" I whisper. "Is it guzzu?"

Iraya's focus settles on the Oscuridad in the fore, and behind them the wall of fire climbing up through the roof; her eyes narrow. "We don't need to talk, we only need to feel."

"What?" Kirdan asks her.

"Its undoing. Its destruction. Its *end*. Bound and broken

by three. Us. We've done it to each other, and now we do it to them. For Aiyca, its past, present, and future."

Her lashes flutter down to her cheeks; her face tightens with intensity; adorned in gold, she begins, as she has done without magic, to glow. To be a light from within outward, a pulsating audacity in blood-splattered clothing.

The two-legged Oscuridad pause.

Spreading outward, Iraya's warmth touches their bare feet. The first recoils, backs away. The second and third follow. Back and back farther still, her magic pushes them toward the otherworldly gate. His face softened with awe, and maybe something else too, Kirdan closes his eyes slowly, like he can't bear to look away from her. Like he wants to savor the phenomenon that is Iraya Adair. For better and worse.

The flames begin to shrink.

Startled, I'm even more surprised when a tear glides down my cheek. This is what I wanted Aiyca to be, what I wanted the future to be. Alumbrar and Obeah. Zesia and Aiyca.

Anya, standing off to the side, cries too.

I have no magic, but I am eligible to inherit. Three days prior, my earthstrong came and went without recognition. Let the veil recognize it now. Let it feel the Cariot ancestors who fortify me, who inform where I am from and why I work so hard to get to where I want to go, strengthen me now. This veil will close. No more monsters shall pass.

An undoing, Iraya called it.

It is a remaking.

Of the mountain's wall itself, which knits closed, suppressing the flame that, minutes ago, seemed to be from the nadir of

Coyaba itself. The roaring, devilish crack of it becomes muffled, muted. The beasts she banished beyond its line shriek and curse, their fingers scrambling for purchase. It is otherwordly, the cries they emit. But Iraya does not flinch. Neither does Kirdan. I too remain in place. Steadfast. When they reach the light, they recoil. Again and again. Iraya and Kirdan do not see as I do, do not open their eyes to see that I too am engulfed in a supernal golden light. That we three shine against a darkness that will not consume our home.

So it is promised.

So things do.

"Look," I command the others.

Kirdan is first to comply; he tips his head back to survey the now-open ceiling above us, through which a shaft of daylight filters. "It's . . . over?"

"This part is." Iraya's laughter is exhausted joy as the gateway, that infernal mouth through which the Oscuridad slithered, closes in its entirety. "You believed," she says to me, with a small smile that is just as smug as ever but somehow less insufferable.

Still aglow with that heavenly gods light, I utter a thanks to the Faces of Benito and Sofea, for the former's fortune, the latter's guidance.

"What now?"

Iraya's hand tightens around my own. "I plan on winning this war. What about you?"

76

IRAYA

The Antidote is administered to Shamar and Zander, who both took strikes from the two-legged Oscuridad so Kirdan wouldn't have to. Niusha also receives treatment, and reacts positively to it, thank the gods.

"You're sure you're hale?" I ask Kirdan, for what must be the tenth time as we levitate the sick out of the mountain, his shadowcat included. I stroke Niusha's fluffy head; she turns into my touch with a throaty purr.

"Tired, but alive," he says from behind me. "With you. I didn't know if I'd see you again."

"It's a blessing the Skylanders came when they did."

"Where is Esai?"

"Kirdan . . ." My face crumples. His does, for but a second.

"Was it an honorable death?"

"The most. He—he stood between us all and the Unlit, with one of the Virago, other soldiers."

Lips pressed together, Kirdan nods. "Then my next kill will be in honor of him."

Between us, we transport the entire platoon who entered the mountain with him. Those who survived the Unlit's attack and the two-legged Oscuridad. The dead have to wait. Jazmyne and Anya are many Simbarabo ahead of us; far out of hearing distance. Well, the former is. I could cast a silencing guzzu, but I need every drop of energy I have to defeat Kaleisha.

"I know the Imposter."

Kirdan looks back at me, his face drawn with grief, concern.

"We were in Carne together. She's stronger than me, Kirdan." I hate admitting it out loud. "Faster. She even has magic-imbued weapons, so my ace has been outplayed. She trained me, in prison. I can't see a way past her."

He's silent a moment. "You didn't use your naevus." It isn't a question. We both know I could end her with one well-placed strike.

"At this point, maybe I should try it. I've tried appealing to her. She wants Aiyca. I think she might take it from me."

A phantom hand brushes against the back of my neck. "When it comes to an opponent who is stronger, smarter, bigger, whatever, you use that against them," Kirdan coaches. "You know this. Level the mat. Use what you know about her against her. We'll do it together, if you want."

He must think I'm deaf to his wheezing; if I concentrate harder, there's a slight grinding in his chest when he draws breath. Something is cracked in there. As it might be in me, but I'm able to soothe my pain with will. If he cannot, he won't have the endurance to join me against Kaleisha. I don't want to risk invoking the rite against her either. We can't both die.

"Iraya?"

Helpless, I look at Kirdan, unable to tell him yes or no. I don't want our last conversation to be an argument.

It's strange to leave the silence of the mountain for the chaos outside. Oscuridad still battle above us, their wings and feet, claws and muzzles locked in their skirmishes. At sea, the Hendern Cliffs monster bats at the Unlit's pets whenever they veer low enough; Virago and pirates fire at the sea, down at the shore, and up on the clifftop, where the Witchfire no longer rages.

"Where are you going?" I ask Jazmyne, lowering Shamar to the shoal. Anan begins work on him and Zander first. They both took hits, I'm sure, so Kirdan wouldn't. Several Virago help the Skylander treat the others behind a shield of gold protection.

"Up there." Swallowing, she rolls her shoulders.

"I can help with that," Kirdan says.

He takes each of our hands; Jazmyne's Stealth sistren takes her spare. The sift is another sign that Kirdan is not at full strength. Both Jazmyne and I steady him as he stumbles.

"I have this," the Alumbrar tells me. "Go."

But I can't knowing he might not be able to defend himself. "Give me a moment and he won't need either of us." My hand tightens around his; want floods my veins, tunnels through my body, to him, to the blood we shared, to the glyphs incised on both of our arms. It feels as good as the first time, like we were always meant to meet, to rely on one another. Kirdan stands straighter; his hand tightens around mine, and the mouth that has traced the most intimate parts of me softens as he breaks our connection.

"Iraya, I—"

"Don't die," I tell him. Committing his face, his size, his scars, to memory. "I expect this clifftop to be empty by the time I return, General. That's an order."

"Iraya, I have something to say to you."

If he's trying to say what I think he is, I don't want to hear it like this. I want it to be in bed, or a bath. Somewhere the ground isn't saturated with blood and the cries of the dying don't ring.

"Tell me when I'm back."

Unwilling to watch his face for any change, any sign of concern about what I have to do, I run for the glade of family trees—the only place Kaleisha could have gone. They part for me, as they would have done for her. An Adair. It's a weird marriage of the present and past, the journey. The fatigue in my body is so similar to that deadweight post-Carne. Kaleisha's presence is the same too. I vault across fallen trees and duck beneath low-hanging branches, pushing and pushing. The air I breathe is bitter with smoke, and—smoke?

She did not.

Freeing my hammer from its holster, I beat my way straight through, instead of around the concentric glade to reach the One That Came First.

What's left of the Adair family tree.

Kaleisha stands before it; she is reduced to insignificance before the mighty blaze—the angry red and orange of it. The hot core that splinters bow from trunk and turns leaves black.

She didn't use Witchfire. She wanted the acrid smoke. Breathless, my legs buckle beneath me; twigs and stones cut into my knees as they hit the ground. Oh, Mama, Dada. Forgive me.

Forgive me for what I'm about to do.

"Took you long enough to make it to me." Triumphant before her destruction, Kaleisha turns and unsheathes two daggers from her gauntlets. "Let's see your skill when you fight me one-on-one, without magic."

"I thought my magic was what you wanted?"

"I don't need this tree. I can use a trapper to extract magic from cast guzzu and then have an Obeah Transmuter repurpose it for me. This way, I can give magic to everyone who wants it. Everyone your family kept it from. Then you will know how it feels to have nothing."

"And you're doing all this to avenge your parents?"

Kaleisha tilts her head to the side. "I took Aiyca for my parents. Killing you will be for me, Iraya. You could have so much, been so much; instead you're standing with Aiyca's enemies against me. Against change. You deserve to die. And for this island I am willing to make that happen."

Her magic makes her fast. Almost sifting fast. One moment she is within burning distance; the next she is before me, and her daggers are aimed. The first at my heart. The second at my throat. Defending, I block both hits with the long handle of my hammer. With a sleight of hand, I remove two golden bangles from her wrist.

Use her strength against her, Kirdan said. Level the mat.

Kaleisha has always been an attacker. She loves to charge in and strike, forcing her opponent to defend themselves into a corner. But Carling Hill's glade is circular, and I have no problems with going around and around while I strip her of each item of conduit gold on her body. Too busy darting in to head-butt me, she doesn't notice that gripping her head is a front to unclasp the chains draped over her braids. She drops. A foot sweeps out; cartwheeling away, I tear an anklet from her. Each time she attacks, I defend and strip, block and unclasp, until there is nothing left but the gray pants and tunic she sports, the gold chain mail, both ears' worth of hoops. She wouldn't notice, because she rarely needs to defend. It's not something she thinks about, when she's raining down blows. Her weakness. My strength.

"Don't tell me your magic is gone already?" she goads, retreating some. "As dead as your ancestors."

"I wouldn't speak about them like that."

"Like the avaricious traitors they were?" Arms spread before the burning tree, she laughs. "They can't harm me now. *You* can't harm me. I will become life itself. Perennial."

"Haven't you heard that the dead are always with us?"

"Not yours. Ours. Not any longer."

"The Adair family tree lives on." I hold my hammer aloft. "You didn't burn every piece of it."

Kaleisha's eyes shift between me and the pieces of Dada's staff that form the handle of my conduit weapon; does she feel, as I do, the drop in temperature, that chilled otherness, and sudden crowded discomfort, like someone is standing close to you—many someones—though you can't see them?

"Being Obeah has never been about living, Kaleisha. It has always been our deference, our reliance, on the departed. If you cannot see that, you are not Obeah. And are undeserving of my mercy—both in this life, and the next." I raise Dada's staff before the burning tree; wind whips through the trees; my braids circle around my head; the golden block of conduit metal brightens—not like a sun, like several. "Take her," I issue to the dead.

With a choked cry, Kaleisha is snatched upward into the air, as though pinched between two mighty fingers, and dangled before the Adair family tree. Struggling, she kicks her legs, fights. It's only when her limbs begin to jerk with exaggerated movements that it dawns. She isn't struggling; she's being shaken, rattled in the hands of the dead. Aloft, her limbs turn supple, her head bows, but she's still shaken. Jerked from left to right until her legs look close to snapping away from her torso.

I turn away before it happens and do not turn back to inspect the muffled thumps that hit the glade floor at my back.

77

JAZMYNE

During the time we were under the mountain, Roje and the majority of the *Silver Arrow*'s crew made it to Carling Hill.

Surrounded by Virago on the clifftop, Roje uses a different sort of axe, conduit gold, to lop off the heads of beasts the Virago render corporeal. Elodie fights at his back. Synestra, still in the waters on the *Silver Arrow,* fights with the majority of the fleet—their ballista arrows are aimed at the cliff face, where Oscuridad emerge from the bush. Should Warrior witches, Obeah, or Simbarabo fail, glyphed arrows strike.

It is everything I wanted for Aiyca—not the war, but the unity. The drawing together, not apart, in times of trouble.

"Small up yourself!" Kirdan bellows.

Anya tugs me back; the bulbous tail of a six-legged Oscuridad slams into the earth where I was. Iraya's baton in hand, I sketch the Glyph of Banishment. Kirdan skids in, saber drawn, and slices the beast's head off its neck.

"You should return to the ship," he breathes; turning toward a cluster of his men, he launches several golden blades into the shoulders of Unlit soldiers advancing at their backs. "Before you are hurt beyond remedies." His shadowcat leaps above the fray, an obsidian force of beauty and ferocity; her jaws close around a winged Oscuridad rendered corporeal by a rogue glyph. Tearing its head off takes a second. In the next, she has bounded onto an Unlit; their companion she fells with a swipe of her paws. "Jazmyne—" Kirdan spins his hunting knife in his left hand. The Unlit soldier before him turns and flees. "You have proved yourself. You have represented your order well—this island well. Now you need to take cover. I need you to take cover, so that we might—so that you and I can have an after."

"You mean it?"

He nods. "We should talk. Which means you need to survive."

"He's right," Anya says beside me. All she has done is guard—all we have done, save for striking down the few Oscuridad who approached Kirdan when his back was turned, is watch over our allies, and shout warnings.

The problem is, I don't merely want to watch.

"Go now!" Kirdan shouts. He braces as a mammoth Oscuridad, the distortion of a jungle-prowler, with multiple horns arching from its forehead, ambles his way.

"Come on." Anya tugs at my hand.

I tug her back, the opposite way. "No, *you* come!"

We run for Carling Hill's glade of family trees, skirting around the fray. A winged Oscuridad swoops low. Anya and

I drop with twin cries. Our arms fly upward. A golden lasso snaps around the beast's ankle. Faehn draws it in, gold-plated teeth gritted. With a grateful nod her way, I pull Anya after me once more. Passing the dead, with soldiers having fallen on both sides, we plunge into the family trees. Anya's shield flickers in and out as we catch our breath in the safety of its tight formation. Exhaustion is a weight we both carry—hers all the more so from having to protect us both. But I can pull my own weight. It's time—beyond time—to inherit my magic.

"Perhaps we can stay here," she breathes. "The spirits might still keep those beasts at bay."

"Or we can locate my family tree."

Anya blinks at me. "I missed it!" she shouts, catching on as only she can. Bottom and bench, we two. "I can't believe I missed your earthstrong!"

"But you will witness my inheritance."

We turn our backs on the chaos atop the cliff, and run deeper into the glade.

My family tree isn't as deep in the grove as Iraya's; close enough that I can still hear the battle raging, I slow before the Cariot family tree. Neem, its broad reach is flush with rich green leaves and soft white flowers. Used for various medicinal remedies, it's a popular tree among Healers, and grows with a plethora of them for neighbors. I wish I could take the time to pick flowers for a crown, as Madisyn planned to do when she inherited, but there is only the time to savor this occasion for just a moment before reaching for one of the lower boughs.

Power sparks through my body.

Beginning in my right arm, it burns a searing trail through

my limbs in a cleansing fire, like the tea Dada would make when I fell ill as a pickney; it stings my nostrils, just as the faint medicinal tang that clung to him did even on the days he didn't work. Madisyn bore the same scent, though hers was slightly sweeter; my eyes fill with tears as I identify the floral notes of the perfume she would use to mask her work. The late doyenne I do not feel at all, do not sense, as, with a sense of completion, the burn in my body softens to an effervescent zing.

Tears gather in my eyes, blurring the surrounding trees. Weight falls on either shoulder—a phantom touch, but there all the same. *Fight*, Dada seems to whisper. *Cure*, Madisyn too says. There is no burst of white light as there was when Iraya inherited, only an internal change. My body feels stronger, more certain of itself. I am the late doyenne's daughter, but I'm also a descendant of more than her. Better than her.

"How do you feel?" Anya asks, when I turn to her.

Iraya's baton I clutch in both hands. *There is no magic more powerful than self-belief,* Iraya said inside the cliff.

I can still heal this world.

I too can be a small axe.

In my grip, the baton begins to glow. At first it is an impression of light, as though reflecting a greater source. But it builds, magnifies; the winds in the glade churn at my feet; the trees around Anya and me seem to inhale in wonder as my will flares in a golden burst.

Anya looks on, tears in her eyes.

"I feel ready," I tell her. "I feel ready to fight."

And I will, for Aiyca, regardless of my stripped status.

Together, Anya and I make our way out of the glade. An Oscuridad prowls toward a fallen pirate. I wish I could manifest a golden lasso, like Faehn, but there is no time for flashy magic. Instead, I hit it with the glyph. The pirate thrusts a blade upward. The beast turns to smoke, and fades away. It's no more than I have done before, but the magic is mine. It came entirely from me.

"I wish I could use a knife to help," Anya says, sketching a glyph herself with Iraya's second baton. "But I don't have the stomach for it."

"We don't need to," I tell her, sketching another glyph. This time the fatal strike is landed by a Simbarabo with silver hair. An Alumbrar. He nods at me, and runs to help a Virago formation. "We just need to help where we can." Together, we fight our way back to Roje, Kirdan.

The former doesn't lose his grin as he swings whatever conduit gold he can get his hands on, removing head after head and sending the Oscuridad back where they belong.

"That's thirty, Prince!" He tosses one over his shoulder at Kirdan. "How many have you?"

"Enough to lose count," Kirdan returns. Catching sight of me, my baton of gold, both eyebrows raise on his forehead spattered with green blood. "Your earthstrong."

In confirmation, I will a spark of suppression to hit an advancing Unlit. While it comes, it doesn't travel any great distance, and fizzles out. My cheeks burn.

With a snarl, Kirdan's shadowcat tackles the castout. Woman and cat roll. Only the latter stands, sniffs my way, and runs back into the fray.

"You have your magic," Kirdan says, with a softness that feels redolent of who we used to be.

"Hardly."

"You will have time to perfect it. You—you make it match your intentions." He nods my way.

Something has healed between us, on this day. Something I hope we can talk about, again.

His attention is drawn beyond me; before I can turn to see what it is, I hear her.

"The Imposter is dead." The words are not shouted, but they ring with the clarity of a death knell. One that ceases all activity on the clifftop. Above, Oscuridad bank. Aiycans, Skylanders, and Zesians pause to turn to the Obeah-witch in white and gold. "She was slain, not by my hand, but by the dead whose spirits roam this holy land. I don't mean Carling Hill. I speak of Aiyca. Its valleys and mountains. Its beaches and bush. This is your final warning," Iraya calls; across the clifftop. "Enemies of the crown, put your hands up, and you will be spared. Keep fighting for the Imposter, against me and mine, and you will meet your ends one way or another. Like the traitor you served, for I command armies of the living and the dead."

I almost want to toss my weapon to the ground as the Unlit do. One after the other concedes, puts their hands up. The Virago and Simbarabo bind them in golden cuffs—magic I can't even begin to attempt myself. Taal joins Anya and me.

"You've survived then."

"Long enough to inherit."

She whistles. "We are to inherit also, the eligible Virago, just as soon as our empress is done."

With what, I find out, is uniting with Kirdan. And his shadowcat. Suddenly by Iraya, either having sifted or ran, he stands before her, close enough to share breath, and look for all the world as if they are alone—as if they are Empress and General Adair, celebrating a successful victory. She runs an absentminded hand across the shadowcat's back as she slinks around the two of them, ringing them against anyone attempting to interrupt.

"Oh, Jaz." Anya takes my hand. "There's still the pirates."

As if he heard her murmur, Roje turns my way. The Iron Shore contingent make their way over to me. They are cut and bruised; fewer in number, and exhausted. I could make them fight again. We could turn on Iraya, on her aerial legion who continue to send the winged Oscuridad back on their side of the veil above us, and her Warriors and Zesian soldiers who do the same with the terrestrial creatures around us but—I do not want to be the cause of Aiycan blood staining these shores. We are, all of us, of one many people. Today's victory has proven that. I can't be the infection killing that goodwill.

"No more," I tell Anya, the pirates joining us. "No more."

Not destruction, not scheming, not going toe-to-toe with Iraya and losing.

"Taal?"

"I know," the Virago says. She whistles for several Virago. They sift us back to the *Silver Arrow*, where Synestra waits with the crew who did not vacate the ship.

"Please don't tell me we have to do that again," the captain wheezes. Slumped on the deck before the ballista, somehow she still has the energy to scowl at me.

"All we have to do is return home—you to the Iron Shore, with the gold from the falls?"

Roje nods, guiltily.

"And me—" After I've checked on Joshial, perhaps I'll take him and egress to a Healing Center in St. Mary, or Sanar. Chaska won't mind. She'll need help treating all the victims of this war. As for Anya, there is always work for a talented Stealth. She will be fine. "I will figure that out."

"There will always be a home for you at the Iron Shore," Roje says.

Nodding, I head down the deck and wait for the ship to draw back from the Hendern Cliffs. Only when we are turned around do I take a final look at the scene atop the cliff, un-surprised when no one calls out to stop us, but somehow disappointed all the same.

78

IRAYA

The palace is salvageable.

It was my greatest relief, upon returning with Kirdan, along with Shamar and Ford. The latter duo, my new general and lieutenant general, will oversee the shields. Much will require rebuilding, but then so will the island. The empire. Two phases have passed since the stand at Carling Hill, since my ancestors' spirits took Kaleisha's life—since I commanded them to—but her mark has lingered. Oscuridad still roam certain streets in Zesia and Aiyca, come nightfall. Respectively, Simbarabo and Virago have been out on patrols sealing Summoning Circles and banishing the beasts back to their side of the veil, until Jazmyne, Kirdan, and I can close each gap permanently.

Plans. I have so many of them. Ideas I wish I'd been able to discuss with Mama. Beyond repairing a lifetime's worth of damage in Aiyca, there is the empire to think about, a legacy to reestablish. Shamar and Ford are but one step to reworking matters. Taal has returned to the mountains, to train her newly inherited magic under Cedella's guidance as Master. The latter promised she'd have my Genna, my second, in fighting shape before the end of the year. Kirdan left me this morning to return to Zesia, with Zander. Esai's family have waited long enough to learn of his fate. And then there is the Divsylar family to contend with. Lena, and the Zesian Virago we've yet to name, will keep them in check. I'll join them soon, and together Kirdan and I will travel to the Skylands. Not as husband and wife, much to the disappointment of his uncles, I'm sure. Nor as intendeds. He and I know what we are to each other: submersion into the darkness, and the light after. After Aiyca has a leader it can respect, I need to put an end to the little boys being labeled as thieves, as forbidden in Zesia; likewise, the first family in the Skylands cannot pit their pickney against one another for succession either. None of those changes can happen if I remain here, which is why I have my candidate for Aiyca's Golden Seat brought up to the Empress's Eye.

"Before you even consider the likelihood of coming close enough to push me from this height," I say, turning to Jazmyne, "I didn't bring you here to argue."

"We never meet with that goal in mind, and yet it happens." Hands clasped before a plain kaftan in maroon, she shrugs.

"I heard you were working to treat the wounded in Queenstown."

"With my cousin. You made it clear I wasn't welcome here."

"You didn't fight me on that. Why?"

A flash of the witch I knew before the war makes her spine

straighter, her jaw clench. "If you brought me here to stroke your ego, I would sooner *you* pushed *me* over the edge."

"I'm being serious, Jazmyne. Don't waste this time. Why haven't you fought me for the palace, for Aiyca?" There was a moment when she returned to collect her belongings. I thought she would attempt to move in. Instead, after ascertaining all prisoners in the Holding Cells had been transported to Carne, before the Stand at Carling Hill, she left.

She stares at me; seemingly deciding I'm not lying to her, she sighs. "If it wasn't the manner in which you humiliated me, when I arrived to collect my items after Carling Hill, to look in on the prisoners, my sand-prowler, and the Xanthippe, then perhaps you can recall stripping me of my titles and all but threatening me with exile if I attempted to challenge you." She purses her lips. "And there was also the fact that you rode an arrow into the side of a cliff. One that was the calcified body of a monster one of your ancestors defeated, and used it to help you defeat more monsters. Who could stand against that?"

She's not wrong, but I would rephrase—who else would have done that, for Aiyca?

"Of all the times to invoke Alumbrar abnegation, you chose now. Jazmyne, you convinced the Iron Shore to fight with you, arriving in time to defend Kirdan, the Virago, and Simbarabo while they were trying to staunch the flow of monsters. I watched you fight, albeit poorly, atop the Hendern Cliffs. Newly minted with your ancestral magic, and you sent Oscuridad back to their side of the veil. Hell, even without magic you did that."

Sniffing, she tips her chin up at me.

"When will you admit it?"

"Admit what?"

"Escaping the Blue Mountains, taking the pirates back from Kaleisha, and bringing them to the stand at Carling Hill was your Rite of Challenge to the throne. That was you showing the island, me, Kirdan, everyone who doubted you, that you deserved to be Aiyca's doyenne."

"Because I lost."

"Did you?" A soft wind gusts through the observatory. My braids shift. I raise a hand to the sharp spokes of the gold crown Kirdan gifted me, so that it doesn't fall. Jazmyne's eyes lift to it, trace the emeralds that match Kirdan's eyes, and I'm certain the light inside her own dims. "You weren't competing by empress standards, it's true, but I saw none other racing alongside you."

A variety of emotions play across her face: shock, suspicion, pride, disbelief, hope.

"I am not skilled at holding any kind of line." Hands clasped behind my back, I twist the ties hanging down from my breastplate. "The thought of staying in one place for too long brings me as much discomfort as I suspect you standing here, in this palace, in maroon rather than gold, is bringing you."

Jazmyne sighs again. "If you're playing with me—"

"What will you do about it?"

She opens her mouth, closes it, only to open it again. "Leave." She looks up at my crown again. "I don't need you to validate my abilities. Or to bring me here to talk in circles. If you want something, ask."

"I don't want something. I need it." Our eyes meet. Obeah

and Alumbrar. Enemies and allies. "You."

The hope in Jazmyne's face becomes the prevailing emotion, after suspicion.

"Aiyca needs a leader in place who will continue to fight for it, even when they don't have a reason to. Even when monsters crawl out of tears in the world, and they don't have a drop of magic to fight with. I might not like you, Jazmyne, but I've respected you. At times."

"I'm not sure this is one of them."

"We have a history that cannot be ignored. I don't trust you."

"Nor I you. But—" She hesitates. "From the way you fought the Unlit, the allies you recruited, the enemy you vanquished, I trust that you will make this empire better than it has been."

"And I trust that you will keep Aiyca safe when I'm not here to do it myself." I cross the observatory to stand across the table from her. "I will be sworn in as empress once the dead have been put to rest. I need you to be Aiyca's doyenne."

"How would that work?"

"You will handle policy and council matters—I liked your idea of blending orders, but there will be an even number of Obeah, Aiycans, and Alumbrar, with one council member from Zesia, as an impartial vote. We will have a seat on the Skylands council, and they will sit on Zesia's. Essentially, you will rule Aiyca, and I will oversee the empire from the best place to ensure parity between islands."

"From here?"

"From everywhere. You'll have to ensure this palace is utilized."

"I will live here?"

"You can. You can even keep my old bedroom."

"This all sounds too good to be true."

"In theory, everything does. The only way to know for sure is to jump." I shrug. "To sit astride the arrow and fly. To slay the monsters, their masters, and emerge better for it. The only way is forward. What do you say, Jazmyne?" I offer her my hand across the table. "Truce?"

ACKNOWLEDGMENTS

My final tale in the Witches Steeped in Gold world will be in four parts. I'm a sucker for symmetry. But I promise, Dear Reader, that this last tale will be a short one.

To my family, immediate and extended, thank you as always for your support. Mum, you're still the bee's knees. Chris and Calvin, you're welcome. Friends, I am grateful for you all. Sorry I haven't texted back all year. If you've opened this book to find your name and broke several toes when it slipped off your laps, you'll know why I didn't add you. Hopefully you're also grateful it's just several toes and not an entire foot. Silver linings.

Suzie Townsend, I am blessed to have you in my corner. Thank you for adopting these witches and treating them like your own. Thank you to the amazing New Leaf Team for welcoming me into the family from the jump. Sophia and Kendra—what would we do without you? Dani—thank you for being there in the beginning. To Taylor Haggerty and the team at Root Literary, thank you for taking on this debut back in 2018.

Harper and Hot Key, it's been a pleasure. Thank you to the

br.illiant teams working behind the scenes to help me wrangle this monstrous book into shape. In the US, my wonderful editor Alice Jerman, who didn't bat an eyelid when I told her this book might be large enough to use as a stop to prevent a car rolling downhill. Kirdan and Iraya's best bits are for you. Thank you to Clare Vaughn, and the team at Frenzy and Epic Reads; the talented team in Design, Chris Kwon, Jenna Stempel-Lobell, Alison Donalty, Nick Oelschlägel. Ashley Straker, who has given me the gift of my characters visualized on multiple covers. Bethany Reis, Jessica Berg, Gwen Morton, Veronica Ambrose, and Dan Janeck—Round Two. Thank you for soldiering through this book. I also feel like I should apologize for increasing your screen time. . . .

My UK family has grown—to those who have left, Carla Hutchinson and Amy Llambias, thank you for being early champions of this book. To those who are still with us, Emma Matthewson for overseeing the start and end of this duology. Molly Holt, thank you for being a PR and person wrangler extraordinaire. Isobel Taylor, Sophie McDonnell, Kate Griffiths, and Marina Stavropoulou, thank you for working your magic behind the scenes. To those who have joined us along the way, Tia Albert and Ella Whiddet, welcome! Feels like you've been here since the beginning, thank you for supporting me and my main witches.

Part Four, Dear Reader, is for you. Whether you've been here from the start, or joined the coven along the way, thank you for choosing this book.

My skies have been made brighter with you all.

⌐⫶⊱ MÉTIERS ⫶⫶

Familial vocations undertaken by firstborn daughters at birth

OBEAH

~

Artisans of Cloth
Scarification: A diagonal white line
on the left or right bicep, three for Masters

Artisans of Metal
Scarification: A pair of crossed white hammers
on the upper arm, two for Masters

Artisans of Wood
Scarification: Crossed white clubs
on the upper arm, two for Masters

Bonemantises—Seers
Scarification: A white eye between their brows,
three lines within the iris for Masters

Bush Healers
Scarification: A white bowl on both palms, with a cloud of
smoke above it for Masters

Growers

Scarification: White vines crossing the fingers on the dominant hand, multiple leaves for Masters

Poisoners

Scarification: White dots horizontally set across the chin, three for Masters

Squallers

Scarification: A circle on the back of the dominant hand, three interlinked circles for Masters

Stealths

Scarification: A white line horizontally set beneath the right eye, three lines for Masters

Transmuters

Scarification: A white alchemical symbol of transmutation on the back of the neck, a triangle within two circles for Masters

Warriors

Scarification: A vertical white line between the eyebrows, three for Masters

Wranglers

Scarification: White paw prints above the heart, three for Masters

ALUMBRAR

Artisans of Cloth
Color: Peach

Artisans of Gems
Color: Pewter

Artisans of Wood ·
Color: Steel

Erudites
Color: Sapphire

Growers
Color: Emerald

Healers
Color: Maroon

Sibyls
Color: Scarlet

Squallers
Color: Arctic blue

Stealths
Color: Black

Transmuters
Color: Umber

Wranglers
Color: Sand

SUPREME BEING
The Seven-Faced Mudda

FACE OF AURORE	Goddess of Creation
FACE OF BENITO	God of Fortune
FACE OF CLOTILLE	Goddess of Warriors and Might
FACE OF CONSUELO	Goddess of Consolation
FACE OF DUILIO	God of War and Blood and Metal
FACE OF MERCE	Goddess of Compassion
FACE OF SOFEA	God of Pathways